PRAISE FOR
THE BORN IN TRILOGY

BORN IN FIRE

"Refreshingly realistic [and] compelling." —*Publishers Weekly*

BORN IN ICE

"Captures the charisma and earthy charm of Ireland." —*Publishers Weekly*

BORN IN SHAME

"Lively and compelling." —*Publishers Weekly*

PRAISE FOR THE NOVELS OF
NORA ROBERTS

"Roberts, a huge name in the romance genre, delivers . . . luscious prose." —*The Boston Globe*

"Roberts has a warm feel for her characters and an eye for the evocative detail." —*Chicago Tribune*

"A page-turner." —*The Washington Post Book World*

"[An] amazingly talented and prolific author." —*The Romance Reader*

"Roberts has created another page-turning novel." —*USA Today*

"Roberts is indeed a word artist, painting her story and her characters with vitality and verve." —*Los Angeles Daily News*

"Thank you, thank you, thank you, Ms. Roberts." —*The Columbia State*

Turn the page for a complete list of titles by Nora Roberts and J. D. Robb from The Berkley Publishing Group . . .

Titles by Nora Roberts

HOT ICE
SACRED SINS
BRAZEN VIRTUE
SWEET REVENGE
PUBLIC SECRETS
GENUINE LIES
CARNAL INNOCENCE
DIVINE EVIL
HONEST ILLUSIONS
PRIVATE SCANDALS
HIDDEN RICHES
TRUE BETRAYALS
MONTANA SKY
SANCTUARY
HOMEPORT
THE REEF
RIVER'S END
CAROLINA MOON
THE VILLA
MIDNIGHT BAYOU
THREE FATES
BIRTHRIGHT
KEY OF LIGHT

Anthologies

FROM THE HEART
A LITTLE MAGIC

The Once Upon Series
(with Jill Gregory, Ruth Ryan Langan, and Marianne Willman)

ONCE UPON A CASTLE
ONCE UPON A STAR
ONCE UPON A DREAM
ONCE UPON A ROSE
ONCE UPON A KISS
ONCE UPON A MIDNIGHT

Series

Three Sisters Island Trilogy

DANCE UPON THE AIR
HEAVEN AND EARTH
FACE THE FIRE

The Gallaghers of Ardmore Trilogy

JEWELS OF THE SUN
TEARS OF THE MOON
HEART OF THE SEA

The Chesapeake Bay Saga

SEA SWEPT
RISING TIDES
INNER HARBOR
CHESAPEAKE BLUE

The Born In Trilogy

BORN IN FIRE
BORN IN ICE
BORN IN SHAME

The Dream Trilogy

DARING TO DREAM
HOLDING THE DREAM
FINDING THE DREAM

Titles written as J. D. Robb

NAKED IN DEATH
GLORY IN DEATH
IMMORTAL IN DEATH
RAPTURE IN DEATH
CEREMONY IN DEATH
VENGEANCE IN DEATH
HOLIDAY IN DEATH
CONSPIRACY IN DEATH
LOYALTY IN DEATH
WITNESS IN DEATH
JUDGMENT IN DEATH
BETRAYAL IN DEATH
SEDUCTION IN DEATH
REUNION IN DEATH
PURITY IN DEATH
PORTRAIT IN DEATH
IMITATION IN DEATH

SILENT NIGHT
(with Susan Plunkett, Dee Holmes, and Claire Cross)

OUT OF THIS WORLD
(with Laurell K. Hamilton, Susan Krinard, and Maggie Shayne)

NORA ROBERTS

IRISH BORN

BERKLEY BOOKS, NEW YORK

A Berkley Book
Published by The Berkley Publishing Group
A division of Penguin Group (USA) Inc.
375 Hudson Street
New York, New York 10014

IRISH BORN

Book design by Patrice Sheridan

First edition: November 2003

Library of Congress Cataloging-in-Publication Data
Roberts, Nora.
Irish born / Nora Roberts.—1st ed.
p. cm.
Contents: Born in fire—Born in ice—Born in shame.
ISBN 0-425-19589-9
1. Ireland—Fiction. 2. Women—Ireland—Fiction. 3. Americans—Ireland—Fiction. 4. Love stories, American. I. Title.
PS3568.O243A6 2003
813′.54—dc21

2003056083

Printed in the United States of America

10 9 8 7 6 5 4 3 2 1

CONTENTS

BORN IN FIRE

Dear Reader,

All of my life I've wanted to visit Ireland. My ancestors came from Ireland and Scotland, and the pull has always been there to see for myself the green hills and to sit in a smoky pub while listening to traditional music being played. When I was able to make the trip with my family, I knew I was home the moment I landed at Shannon Airport.

Setting a story in Ireland was a natural decision. Both the land and its people inspire, as well as thrive on, stories. The idea, for me, was to write of Ireland, and of family, as they intertwined in my heart. In each book in this new trilogy I chose to feature one of three sisters, different in type but bound by blood. Their lives have each taken a different course, yet it is Ireland that inspires them, as it inspires me.

Born in Fire *highlights Margaret Mary Concannon, the eldest sister, a glass artist with an independent streak as fierce as her volatile temper. She is a woman who is both comforted and torn apart by family, and whose ambitions will lead her to discover herself and her talents. Hand blowing glass is a difficult and exacting art, and while she may produce the delicate and the fragile, Maggie is a strong and opinionated woman, a Clare woman, with all the turbulence of that fascinating west county. Her relationship with the sophisticated Dublin gallery owner, Rogan Sweeney, won't be peaceful, but I hope you'll find it entertaining.*

And I hope you'll enjoy, in this first book of my Born In trilogy, the trip to County Clare, a land of green hills, wild cliffs, and enduring beauty.

Nora Roberts

To Amy Berkower,
for a decade of
taking care of business

I never will marry, I'll be no man's wife.
I intend to stay single for the rest of my life.

NINETEENTH-CENTURY IRISH BALLAD

ONE

He would be in the pub, of course. Where else would a smart man warm himself on a frigid, windblown afternoon? Certainly not at home, by his own fire.

No, Tom Concannon was a smart man, Maggie thought, and wouldn't be at home.

Her father would be at the pub, among friends and laughter. He was a man who loved to laugh, and to cry and to spin improbable dreams. A foolish man some might call him. But not Maggie, never Maggie.

As she steered her racketing lorry around the last curve that led into the village of Kilmihil, she saw not a soul on the street. No wonder, as it was well past time for lunch and not a day for strolling with winter racing in from the Atlantic like a hound from icy Hades. The west coast of Ireland shivered under it and dreamed of spring.

She saw her father's battered Fiat, among other vehicles she recognized. Tim O'Malley's had a good crowd this day. She parked as close as she could to the front entrance of the pub, which was nestled in a line of several shops.

As she walked down the street the wind knocked her back, made her huddle inside the fleece-lined jacket and pull the black wool cap down lower on her head. Color whipped into her cheeks like a blush. There was a smell of damp under the cold, like a nasty threat. There would be ice, thought the farmer's daughter, before nightfall.

She couldn't remember a more bitter January, or one that seemed so hell-bent on blowing its frosty breath over County Clare. The little garden in front of the shop she hurried by had paid dearly. What was left of it was blackened by the wind and frost and lay pitifully on the soggy ground.

She was sorry for it, but the news she held inside her was so fearfully bright, she wondered the flowers didn't rise up and bloom away into spring.

There was plenty of warmth in O'Malley's. She felt it nuzzle her the moment she opened the door. She could smell the peat burning in the fire, its red-hot heart smoldering cheerfully, and the stew O'Malley's wife, Deirdre, had served at lunch. And tobacco, beer, the filmy layer that frying chips left in the air.

She spotted Murphy first, sitting at one of the tiny tables, his boots stretched out as he eased a tune out of an Irish accordion that matched the sweetness of his voice. The other patrons of the pub were listening, dreaming a bit over their beer and porter. The tune was sad, as the best of Ireland was, melancholy and lovely as a lover's tears. It was a song that bore her name, and spoke of growing old.

Murphy saw her, smiled a little. His black hair fell untidily over his brow, so that he tossed his head to clear it away. Tim O'Malley stood behind the bar, a barrel of a man whose apron barely stretched across the girth of him. He had a wide, creased face and eyes that disappeared into folds of flesh when he laughed.

He was polishing glasses. When he saw Maggie, he continued his task, knowing she would do what was polite and wait to order until the song was finished.

She saw David Ryan, puffing on one of the American cigarettes his brother sent him every month from Boston, and tidy Mrs. Logan, knitting with pink wool while her foot tapped to the tune. There was old Johnny Conroy, grinning toothlessly, his gnarled hand holding the equally twisted one of his wife of fifty years. They sat together like newlyweds, lost in Murphy's song.

The television over the bar was silent, but its picture was bright and glossy with a British soap opera. People in gorgeous clothes and shining hair argued around a massive table lit with silver-based candles and elegant crystal.

Its glittery story was more, much more than a country away from the little pub with its scarred bar and smoke-dark walls.

Maggie's scorn for the shining characters squabbling in their wealthy room was quick and automatic as a knee jerk. So was the swift tug of envy.

If *she* ever had such wealth, she thought—though, of course, she didn't care one way or the other—she would certainly know what to do with it.

Then she saw him, sitting in the corner by himself. Not separate, not at all. He was as much a part of the room as the chair he sat on. He had an arm slung over the back of that chair, while the other hand held a cup she knew would hold strong tea laced with Irish.

An unpredictable man he might be, full of starts and stops and quick turns, but she knew him. Of all the men she had known, she had loved no one with the full thrust of her heart as she loved Tom Concannon.

She said nothing, crossed to him, sat and rested her head on his shoulder.

Love for him rose up in her, a fire that warmed down to the bone but never burned. His arm came from around the chair and wrapped her closer. His lips brushed across her temple.

When the song was done, she took his hand in hers and kissed it. "I knew you'd be here."

"How did you know I was thinking of you, Maggie, my love?"

"Must be I was thinking of you." She sat back to smile at him. He was a small man, but toughly built. Like a runt bull, he often said of himself with one of his rolling laughs. There were lines around his eyes that deepened and fanned out when he grinned. They made him, in Maggie's eyes, all the more handsome. His hair had once been gloriously red and full. It had thinned a bit with time, and the gray streaked through the fire like smoke. He was, to Maggie, the most dashing man in the world.

He was her father.

"Da," she said. "I have news."

"Sure, I can see it all over your face."

Winking, he pulled off her cap so that her hair fell wildly red to her shoulders. He'd always liked to look at it, to watch it flash and sizzle. He could still remember when he'd held her the first time, her face screwed up with the rage of life, her tiny fists bunched and flailing. And her hair shining like a new coin.

He hadn't been disappointed not to have a son, had been humbled to have been given the gift of a daughter.

"Bring me girl a drink, Tim."

"I'll have tea," she called out. "It's wicked cold." Now that she was here, she wanted the pleasure of drawing the news out, savoring it. "Is that why you're in here singing tunes and drinking, Murphy? Who's keeping your cows warm?"

"Each other," he shot back. "And if this weather keeps up, I'll have more calves come spring than I can handle, as cattle do what the rest of the world does on a long winter night."

"Oh, sit by the fire with a good book, do they?" Maggie said, and had the room echoing with laughter. It was no secret, and only a slight embarrassment to Murphy, that his love of reading was well-known.

"Now, I've tried to interest them in the joys of literature, but those cows, they'd rather watch the television." He tapped his empty glass. "And I'm here for the quiet, what with your furnace roaring like thunder day and night. Why aren't you home, playing with your glass?"

"Da." When Murphy walked to the bar, Maggie took her father's hand again. "I needed to tell you first. You know I took some pieces to McGuinness's shop in Ennis this morning?"

"Did you now?" He took out his pipe, tapped it. "You should have told me you were going. I'd have kept you company on the way."

"I wanted to do it alone."

"My little hermit," he said, and flicked a finger down her nose.

"Da, he bought them." Her eyes, as green as her father's, sparkled. "He bought four of them, and that's all I took in. Paid me for them then and there."

"You don't say, Maggie, you don't say!" He leaped up, dragging her with him, and spun her around the room. "Listen to this, ladies and gentlemen. My daughter, my own Margaret Mary, has sold her glass in Ennis."

There was quick, spontaneous applause and a barrage of questions.

"At McGuinness's," she said, firing answers back. "Four pieces, and he'll look at more. Two vases, a bowl, and a . . . I supposed you could call the last a paperweight." She laughed when Tim set whiskeys on the counter for her and her father.

"All right then." She lifted her glass and toasted. "To Tom Concannon, who believed in me."

"Oh, no, Maggie." Her father shook his head and there were tears in his eyes. "To you. All to you." He clicked glasses and sent the whiskey streaming down his throat. "Fire up that squeeze box, Murphy. I want to dance with my daughter."

Murphy obliged with a jig. With the sounds of shouts and clapping hands, Tom led his daughter around the floor. Deirdre came out from the kitchen, wiping her hands on her apron. Her face was flushed from cooking as she pulled her husband into the dance. From jig to reel and reel to hornpipe, Maggie whirled from partner to partner until her legs ached.

As others came into the pub, drawn either by the music or the prospect of company, the news was spread. By nightfall, she knew, everyone within twenty kilometers would have heard of it.

It was the kind of fame she had hoped for. It was her secret that she wished for more.

"Oh, enough." She sank into her chair and drained her cold tea. "My heart's about to burst."

"So is mine. With pride for you." Tom's smile remained bright, but his eyes dimmed a little. "We should go tell your mother, Maggie. And your sister, too."

"I'll tell Brianna this evening." Her own mood shifted at the mention of her mother.

"All right, then." He reached down, brushed his hand over her cheek. "It's your day, Maggie Mae, nothing will spoil it for you."

"No, 'tis our day. For I never would have blown the first bubble of glass without you."

"Then we'll share it, just us two for a little while." He felt smothered for a minute, dizzy and hot. He thought he felt a little click behind his eyes before it cleared. Air, he thought. He needed a bit of air. "I'm in the mood for a drive. I want to smell the sea, Maggie. Will you come with me?"

"Of course I will." She rose immediately. "But it's freezing out, and the wind's the devil. Are you sure you want to go to the cliffs today?"

"I've a need to." He reached for his coat, then tossing a muffler around his throat, turned to the pub. All the dark, smoky colors seemed to whirl in his eyes. He thought, ruefully, that he was a little drunk. Then again, it was the day for it. "We're having us a party. Tomorrow night it'll be. With fine food, fine drink and fine music, to celebrate my daughter's success. I'll expect every one of me friends there."

Maggie waited until they were out in the cold. "A party? Da, you know she'll not have it."

"I'm still the master of my own house." His chin, very like his daughter's, jutted out. "A party there will be, Maggie. I'll deal with your mother. Would you drive now?"

"All right." There was no arguing, she knew, once Tom Concannon had made up his mid. She was grateful for that, or she would never have been able to travel to Venice and apprentice herself in a glass house. Never have been able to take what she'd learned, and what she'd dreamed, and build her own studio. She knew her mother had made Tom pay miserably for the money it had cost. But he had stood firm.

"Tell me what you're working on now."

"Well, it's a kind of a bottle. And I want it to be very tall, very slim. Tapered you see, from bottom to top, then it should flare out. A bit like a lily. And the color should be very delicate, like the inside of a peach."

She could see it, clear as the hand she used to describe it.

"It's lovely things you see in your head."

"It's easy to see them there." She shot him a smile. "The hard work is making them real."

"You'll make them real." He patted her hand and fell into silence.

Maggie took the twisting, narrow road toward the sea. Away toward the west, the clouds were flying in, their sails whipped by the wind and darkened with storm. Clearer patches were swallowed up, then fought their way free to glow gem bright amid the pewter.

She saw a bowl, wide and deep, swirled with those warring colors, and began to fashion it in her head.

The road twisted, then straightened, as she threaded the rattling lorry through hedgerows yellowd with winter and taller than a man. A roadside shrine to Mary stood at the outskirts of a village. The Virgin's face was serene in the cold, her arms spread in generous welcome, foolishly bright plastic flowers at her feet.

A sigh from her father had Maggie glancing over. He seemed a bit pale to her, a little drawn around the eyes. "You look tired, Da. Are you sure you don't want me to take you back home?"

"No, no." He took out his pipe, tapped it absently against his palm. "I want to watch the sea. There's a storm brewing, Maggie Mae. We'll have a show from the cliffs at Loop Head."

"We will at that."

Past the village the road narrowed alarmingly again until she was threading the lorry along like cotton through the eye of a needle. A man, bundled tight against the cold, trudged toward them, his faithful dog following stoically at his heels. Both man and dog stepped off the road into the hedges as the lorry eased by, inches from the toe of the man's boots. He nodded to Maggie and Tom in greeting.

"You know what I've been thinking, Da?"

"What's that?"

"If I could sell a few more pieces—just a few more, mind—I could have another furnace. I want to work with more color, you see. If I could build another furnace, I could have more melts going. The firebrick's not so costly, really. But I'll need more than two hundred."

"I've a bit put by."

"No, not again." On this she was firm. "I love you for it, but this I'll do on my own."

He took immediate umbrage and scowled at his pipe. "What's a father for, I'd like to know, if not to give to his children? You'll not have fancy clothes or pretty baubles, so if it's firebrick you want, then that's what you'll have."

"So I will," she shot back. "But I'll buy it myself. I've a need to do this myself. It's not the money I want. It's the faith."

"You've paid me back tenfold already." He sat back, drawing the window down a crack so that the wind whistled through as he lit his pipe. "I'm a rich man, Maggie. I have two lovely daughters, each of them a jewel. And though a man could ask for no more than that, I've a good solid house and friends to count on."

Maggie noticed he didn't include her mother in his treasures. "And always the pot at the end of the rainbow."

"Always that." He fell silent again, brooding. They passed old stone cabins, roofless and deserted on the verge of gray-green fields that stretched on, endless and impossibly beautiful in the gloomy light. And here a church, standing against the wind that was unbroken now, was blocked only by a few twisted and leafless trees.

It should have been a sad and lonely sight, but Tom found it beautiful. He didn't share Maggie's love of solitude, but when he looked out on a sight like this, with lowered sky and empty land meeting with barely a sight of man between, he understood it.

Through the whistling crack of the window, he could smell the sea. Once he'd dreamed of crossing it.

Once he'd dreamed of many things.

He had always searched for that pot of gold, and knew the failure to find it was his. He'd been a farmer by birth, but never by inclination. Now he'd lost all but a few acres of land, enough only for the flowers and vegetables his daughter Brianna grew so skillfully. Enough only to remind him that he had failed.

Too many schemes, he thought now as another sigh fetched up in his chest. His wife, Maeve, was right about that. He'd always been full of schemes, but never had the sense or the luck to make them work.

They chugged past another huddle of houses and a building whose owner boasted it was the last pub until New York. Tom's spirits lifted at the sight, as they always did.

"Shall we sail over to New York, Maggie, and have a pint?" he said, as he always did.

"I'll buy the first round."

He chuckled. A feeling of urgency came over him as she pulled the lorry to the end of the road, where it gave way to grass and rock, and at last to the windswept sea that spanned to America.

They stepped into a roar of sound that was wind and water lashing furiously against the teeth and fists of black rock. With their arms linked, they staggered like drunks, then laughing, began to walk.

"It's madness to come here on such a day."

"Aye, a fine madness. Feel the air, Maggie! Feel it. It wants to blow us from here to Dublin Town. Do you remember when we went to Dublin?"

"We saw a juggler tossing colored balls. I loved it so much you learned how yourself."

His laugh boomed out like the sea itself. "Oh, the apples I bruised."

"We had pies and cobblers for weeks."

"And I thought I could make a pound or two with my new skill and took me up to Galway to the fair."

"And spent every penny you made on presents for me and Brianna."

His color was back, she noted, and his eyes were shining. She went willingly with him across the uneven grass into the gnashing teeth of the wind. There they stood on the edge of the powerful Atlantic with its warrior waves striking at the merciless rock. Water crashed, then whipped away again, leaving dozens of waterfalls tumbling through crevices. Overhead, gulls cried and wheeled, cried and wheeled, the sound echoing on and on against the thunder of the waves.

The spray plumed high, white as snow at the base, clear as crystal in the beads that scattered in the icy air. No boat bobbed on the rugged surface of the sea today. The fierce whitecaps rode the sea alone.

She wondered if her father came here so often because the merging of sea and stone symbolized marriage as much as war to his eyes. And his marriage had been forever a battle, the constant bitterness and anger of his wife's lashing forever at his heart, and gradually, oh so gradually, wearing it away.

"Why do you stay with her, Da?"

"What?" He pulled his attention back from the sea and the sky.

"Why do you stay with her?" Maggie repeated. "Brie and I are grown now. Why do you stay where you're not happy?"

"She's my wife," he said simply.

"Why should that be an answer?" she demanded. "Why should it be an end? There's no love between you, no liking, if it comes to that. She's made your life hell as long as I can remember."

"You're too hard on her." This, too, was on his head, he thought. For loving the child so much that he'd been helpless not to accept her unconditional love for him. A love, he knew, that had left no room for understanding the disappointments of the woman who had borne her. "What's between your mother and me is as much my doing as hers. A marriage is a delicate thing, Maggie, a balance of two hearts and two hopes. Sometimes the weight's just too heavy on the one side, and the other can't lift to it. You'll understand when you've a marriage of your own."

"I'll never marry." She said it fiercely, like a vow before God. "I'll never give anyone the right to make me so unhappy."

"Don't say that. Don't." He squeezed her hard, worried. "There's nothing more precious than marriage and family. Nothing in the world."

"If that's so, how can it be such a prison?"

"It isn't meant to be." The weakness came over him again, and all at once he felt the cold deep in his bones. "We haven't given you a good example, your mother and I, and I'm sorry for it. More than I can tell you. But I know this, Maggie, my girl. When you love with all you are, it isn't unhappiness alone you risk. It's heaven, too."

She pressed her face into his coat, drew comfort from the scent of him. She couldn't tell him that she knew, had known for years, that it hadn't been heaven for him. And that he would never have bolted the door to that marital prison behind him if it hadn't been for her.

"Did you love her, ever?"

"I did. And it was as hot as one of your furnaces. You came from that, Maggie Mae. Born in fire you were, like one of your finest and boldest statues. However much that fire cooled, it burned once. Maybe if it hadn't flared so bright, so hard, we could have made it last."

Something in his tone made her look up again, study his face. "There was someone else."

Like a honeyed blade, the memory was painful and sweet. Tom looked to sea again, as if he could gaze across it and find the woman he'd let go. "Aye, there was once. But it wasn't to be. Had no right to be. I'll tell you this, when love comes, when the arrow strikes the heart, there's no stopping it. And even bleeding is a pleasure. So don't say never to me, Maggie. I want for you what I couldn't have."

She didn't say it to him, but she thought it. "I'm twenty-three, Da, and Brie's but a year behind me. I know what the church says, but I'm damned if I believe there's a God in heaven who finds joy in punishing a man for the whole of his life for a mistake."

"Mistake." His brows lowered, Tom stuck his pipe in his teeth. "My marriage has not been a mistake, Margaret Mary, and you'll not say so now, nor ever again. You and Brie came from it. A mistake—no, a miracle. I was past forty when you were born, without a thought in my head to starting a family. I think of what my life would have been like without the two of you. Where would I be now? A man near seventy, alone. Alone." He cupped her face in his hands and his eyes were fierce on hers. "I thank God every day I found your mother, and that between us we made something I can leave behind. Of all the things I've done, and not done, you and Brianna are my first and truest joys. Now there'll be no more talk of mistakes or unhappiness, do you hear?"

"I love you, Da."

His face softened. "I know it. Too much, I think, but I can't regret it." The sense of urgency came on him again, like a wind whispering to hurry. "There's something I'd ask of you, Maggie."

"What is it?"

He studied her face, his fingers molding it as if he suddenly had a need to memorize every feature—the sharp stubborn chin, the soft curve of cheek, the eyes as green and restless as the sea that clashed beneath them.

"You're a strong one, Maggie. Tough and strong, with a true heart beneath the steel. God knows you're smart. I can't begin to understand the things you know, or how you know them. You're my bright star, Maggie, the way Brie's my cool rose. I want you, the both of you, to follow where your dreams lead you. I want that more than I can say. And when you chase them down, you'll chase them as much for me as for yourself."

The roar of the sea dimmed in his ears, as did the light in his eyes. For a moment Maggie's face blurred and faded.

"What is it?" Alarmed, she clutched at him. He'd gone gray as the sky, and suddenly looked horribly old. "Are you ill, Da? Let me get you back into the lorry."

"No." It was vital, for reasons he didn't know, that he stand here, just here at the farthest tip of his country, and finish what he'd begun. "I'm fine. Just a twinge is all."

"You're freezing." Indeed, his wiry body felt like little more than a bag of icy bones in her hands.

"Listen to me." His voice was sharp. "Don't let anything stop you from going where you need to go, from doing what you need to do. Make your mark on the world, and make it deep so it lasts. But don't—"

"Da!" Panic bubbled inside her as he staggered, fell to his knees. "Oh God, Da, what is it? Your heart?"

No, not his heart, he thought through a haze of bleary pain. For he could hear that beating hard and fast in his own ears. But he felt something inside him breaking, bursting and slipping away. "Don't harden yourself, Maggie. Promise me. You'll never lose what's inside you. You'll take care of your sister. And your mother. You'll promise me that."

"You've got to get up." She dragged at him, fighting off fear. The thrash of the sea sounded now like a storm breaking, a nightmare storm that would sweep them both off the cliff and onto the spearing rocks. "Do you hear me, Da? You've got to get up now."

"Promise me."

"Aye, I promise. I swear it before God, I'll see to both of them, always." Her teeth were chattering; stinging tears already ran down her cheeks.

"I need a priest," he gasped out.

"No, no, you need only to get out of this cold." But she knew it was a lie as she said it. He was slipping away from her; no matter how tightly she held his body, what was inside him was slipping away. "Don't leave me like this. Not like this." Desperate, she scanned the fields, the beaten paths where people walked year after year to stand as they had stood. But there was nothing, no one, so she bit back a scream for help. "Try, Da, come and try now to get up. We'll get you to a doctor."

He rested his head on her shoulder and sighed. There was no pain now, only numbness. "Maggie," he said. Then he whispered another name, a stranger's name, and that was all.

"No." As if to protect him from the wind he no longer felt, she wrapped her arms tight around him, rocking, rocking, rocking as she sobbed.

And the wind trumpeted down to the sea and brought with it the first needles of icy rain.

TWO

Thomas Concannon's wake would be talked about for years. There was fine food and fine music, as he'd planned for his daughter's celebration party. The house where he'd lived out his last years was crowded with people.

Tom hadn't been a rich man, some would say, but he was a man who'd been wealthy in friends.

They came from the village, and the village beyond that. From the farms and shops and cottages. They brought food, as neighbors do for such occasions, and the kitchen was quickly stocked with breads and meats and cakes. They drank to his life and serenaded his passing.

The fires burned warm to stave off the gale that rattled the windows and the chill of mourning.

But Maggie was sure she'd never be warm again. She sat near the fire in the tidy parlor while the company filled the house around her. In the flames she saw the cliffs, the boiling sea—and herself, alone, holding her dying father.

"Maggie."

Startled, she turned and saw Murphy crouched in front of her. He pressed a steaming mug into her hands.

"What is it?"

"Mostly whiskey, with a bit of tea to warm it up." His eyes were kind and grieving. "Drink it down now. There's a girl. Won't you eat a little? It would do you good."

"I can't," she said, but did as he asked and drank. She'd have sworn she felt each fiery drop slide down her throat. "I shouldn't have taken him out there, Murphy. I should have seen he was sick."

"That's nonsense, and you know it. He looked fine and fit when he left the pub. Why, he'd been dancing, hadn't he?"

Dancing, she thought. She'd danced with her father on the day he died. Would she, someday, find comfort in that? "But if we hadn't been so far away. So alone . . ."

"The doctor told you plain, Maggie. It would have made no difference. The aneurysm killed him, and it was mercifully quick."

"Aye, it was quick." Her hand trembled, so she drank again. It was the time afterward that had been slow. The dreadful time when she had driven his body away from the sea, with her breath wheezing in her throat and her hands frozen on the wheel.

"I've never seen a man so proud as he was of you." Murphy hesitated, looked down at his hands. "He was like a second father to me, Maggie."

"I know that." She reached out, brushed Murphy's hair off his brow. "So did he."

So now he'd lost a father twice, Murphy thought. And for the second time felt the weight of grief and responsibility.

"I want to tell you, to make sure you know, that if there's anything, anything a'tall you're needing, or your family needs, you've only to tell me."

"It's good of you to say so, and to mean it."

He looked up again; his eyes, that wild Celtic blue, met hers. "I know it was hard when he had to sell the land. And hard that I was the one to buy it."

"No." Maggie set the mug aside and laid her hands over his. "The land wasn't important to him."

"Your mother . . ."

"She would have blamed a saint for buying it," Maggie said briskly. "Even though the money it brought put food in her mouth. I tell you it was easier that it was you. Brie and I don't begrudge you a blade of grass, that's the truth, Murphy." She made herself smile at him, because they both needed it. "You've done what he couldn't, and what he simply didn't want to do. You've made the land grow. Let's not hear any more talk like that."

She looked around then, as if she'd just walked out of an empty room into a full one. Someone was playing the flute, and O'Malley's daughter, heavy with her first child, was singing a light, dreamy air. There was a trill of laughter from across the room, lively and free. A baby was crying. Men were huddled here and there, talking of Tom, and of the weather, of Jack Marley's sick roan mare and the Donovans' leaking cottage roof.

The women talked of Tom as well, and of the weather, of children and of weddings and wakes.

She saw an old woman, an elderly and distant cousin, in worn shoes and mended stockings, spinning a story for a group of wide-eyed youngsters while she knitted a sweater.

"He loved having people around, you know." The pain was there, throbbing like a wound in her voice. "He would have filled the house with them daily if he could. It was always a wonder to him that I preferred to be on my own." She drew in a breath and hoped her voice was casual. "Did you ever hear him speak of someone named Amanda?"

"Amanda?" Murphy frowned and considered. "No. Why do you ask?"

"It's nothing. I probably mistook it." She shrugged it away. Surely her father's dying words hadn't been a strange woman's name. "I should go help Brie in the kitchen. Thanks for the drink, Murphy. And for the rest." She kissed him and rose.

There was no easy way to get through the room, of course. She had to stop again and again, to hear words of comfort, or a quick story about her father, or in the case of Tim O'Malley, to offer comfort herself.

"Jesus, I'll miss him," Tim said, unabashedly wiping his eyes. "Never had a friend as dear to me, and never will again. He joked about opening a pub of his own, you know. Giving me a bit of competition."

"I know." She also knew it hadn't been a joke, but another dream.

"He wanted to be a poet," someone else put in while Maggie hugged Tim and patted his back. "Said he'd only lacked the words to be one."

"He had the heart of a poet," Tim said brokenly. "The heart and soul of one, to be sure. A finer man never walked this earth than Tom Concannon."

Maggie had words with the priest about funeral services set for the next morning, and finally slipped into the kitchen.

It was as crowded as the rest of the house, with women busily serving food or making it. The sounds and smells were of life here—kettles singing, soups simmering, a ham baking. Children wandered underfoot, so that women—with that uncanny maternal grace they seemed to be born with—dodged around them or scooped them up as needs demanded.

The wolfhound puppy that Tom had given Brianna on her last birthday snored contentedly under the kitchen table. Brianna herself was at the stove, her face composed, her hands competent. Maggie could see the subtle signs of grief in the quiet eyes and the soft, unsmiling mouth.

"You'll have a plate." One of the neighbor women spotted Maggie and began to heap food together. "And you'll eat or answer to me."

"I only came in to help."

"You'll help by eating some of this food. Enough for an army it is. You know your father once sold me a rooster. Claimed it was the finest cock in the county and would keep me hens happy for years to come. He had a way with him, Tom did, that made you believe what he was saying even though you knew it for nonsense." She piled great portions of food on the plate as she spoke, taking time out to pat a child out of the way without breaking rhythm. "Well, a terrible, mean bird he turned out to be, and never crew once in his miserable life."

Maggie smiled a bit and said what was expected of her, though she knew the tale well. "And what did you do with the rooster Da sold you, Mrs. Mayo?"

"I wrung the cursed cock's neck and boiled him into stew. Gave your father a bowl of it, too, I did. Said he'd never tasted better in his whole life." She laughed heartily and pressed the plate on Maggie.

"And was it?"

"The meat was stringy and tough as old leather. But Tom ate every drop. Bless him."

So Maggie ate, because there was nothing she could do but live and go on. She listened to the stories and told some of her own. When the sun went down and the kitchen slowly emptied, she sat down and held the puppy in her lap.

"He was loved," Maggie said.

"He was." Brianna stood beside the stove, a cloth in her hand and a dazed look in her eyes. There was no one left to feed or tend to, nothing to keep her mind and her hands busy. Grief swarmed into her heart like angry bees. To hold it off awhile longer, she began to put away the dishes.

She was slim, almost willowy, with a cool, controlled way of moving. If there had been money and means, she might have been a dancer. Her hair, rosy gold and thick, was neatly coiled at the nape of her neck. A white apron covered her plain black dress.

In contrast, Maggie's hair was a fiery tangle around her face. She wore a skirt she'd forgotten to press and a sweater that needed mending.

"It won't clear for tomorrow." Brianna had forgotten the dishes in her hands and stared out the window at the blustery night.

"No, it won't. But people will come, just the same, as they did today."

"We'll have them back here after. There's so much food. I don't know what we'll do with all of it. . . ." Brianna's voice trailed off.

"Did she ever come out of her room?"

Brianna stood still for a moment, then began slowly to stack plates. "She's not well."

"Oh God, don't. Her husband's dead and everyone who knew him came here today. She can't even stir herself to pretend it matters."

"Of course it matters to her." Brianna's voice tightened. She didn't think she could bear an argument now, not when her heart was swelling up like a tumor in her chest. "She lived with him more than twenty years."

"And little else she did with him. Why do you defend her? Even now."

Brianna's hand pressed a plate so hard she wondered it didn't snap in two. Her voice remained perfectly calm, perfectly reasonable. "I'm defending no one, only saying what's true. Can't we keep peace? At least until we've buried him, can't we keep peace in this house?"

"There's never been peace in this house." Maeve spoke from the doorway. Her face wasn't ravaged by tears, but it was cold and hard and unforgiving. "He saw to that. He saw to it just as he's seeing to it now. Even dead, he's making my life a hardship."

"Don't speak of him." The fury Maggie had held back all day broke through, a jagged rock through fragile glass. She shoved away from the table, sending the dog racing for cover. "Don't you dare to speak ill of him."

"I'll speak how I choose." Maeve's hand clutched at the shawl she wore, drew it tight to her throat. It was wool, and she'd always wanted silk. "He gave me nothing but grief while he lived. Now he's dead and has given me more."

"I see no tears in your eyes, Mother."

"And you won't. I'll neither live nor die a hypocrite, but speak God's own truth. He'll go to the devil for what's he's done to me this day." Her eyes, bitter and blue, shifted from Maggie to Brianna. "And as God won't forgive him, neither will I."

"Do you know God's mind now?" Maggie demanded. "Has all your prayerbook reading and rosary clacking given you a line straight to the Lord?"

"You'll not blaspheme." Maeve's cheeks reddened with temper. "You'll not blaspheme in this house."

"I'll speak how I choose." Maggie echoed her mother's words with a tight smile. "I'll tell you Tom Concannon needed none of your stingy forgiveness."

"Enough." Though her insides were trembling, Brianna laid a steadying hand on Maggie's shoulder. She took a long, careful breath to be certain her voice was calm. "I've told you, Mother, I'll give the house to you. You've nothing to worry about."

"What's this?" Maggie turned to her sister. "What about the house?"

"You heard what it said at the will reading," Brianna began, but Maggie shook her head.

"I didn't take any of it in. Lawyer's talk. I wasn't paying attention."

"He left it to her." Still trembling, Maeve lifted a finger and jabbed it out as an accusation. "He left the house to her. All the years I suffered and sacrificed, and he takes even that from me."

"She'll settle down right enough when she knows she has a sturdy roof over her head and no need to do anything to keep it," Maggie said once her mother left the room.

It was true enough. And Brianna thought she could maintain the peace. She'd had a lifetime of practice. "I'll keep the house, and she'll stay here. I can tend them both."

"Saint Brianna," Maggie murmured, but there was no malice in it. "We'll manage it between us." The new furnace would have to wait, she decided. But as long as McGuinness kept buying, there would be enough to hold the two houses together.

"I've thought about . . . Da and I talked about it a little while ago, and I've been thinking. . . ." Brianna hesitated.

Maggie pushed aside her own thoughts. "Just say it."

"It needs some fixing up, I know, and I've only a bit left of what Gran left me—and there's the lien."

"I'll be paying off the lien."

"No, that's not right."

"It's perfectly right." Maggie got up to fetch the teapot. "He took it to send me to Venice, didn't he? Mortgaged the house and weathered the gale Mother brought down on his head for doing it. I had three years of training thanks to him. And I'll pay it back."

"The house is mine." Brianna's voice firmed. "And so's the lien."

Her sister had a soft look about her, but Maggie knew Brianna could be mule stubborn when it suited her. "Well, we can argue that to death. We'll both pay it off. If you won't let me do it for you, Brie, let me do it for him. I've a need to."

"We'll work it out." Brianna took the cup of tea Maggie poured her.

"Tell me what you've been thinking."

"All right." It felt foolish. She could only hope it didn't sound so. "I want to turn the house into a B-and-B."

"A hotel!" Stunned, Maggie could only stare. "You want to have paying guests nosing about the place? You'll have no privacy at all, Brianna, and you'll be working from morning till night."

"I like having people around," Brianna said coolly. "Not everyone wants to be a hermit like you. And I've a knack for it, I think, for making people comfortable. It's in the blood." She stuck out her chin. "Granda ran a hotel, didn't he, and Gran ran it after he died. I could do it."

"I never said you couldn't. I just for the life of me can't see why you'd want to. Strangers in and out every day." Why, it gave her the shudders just to imagine it.

"I can only hope they'll come. The bedrooms upstairs will need freshening, of course." Brianna's eyes blurred as she thought through the details. "Some paint, some paper. A new rug or two. And the plumbing needs work, God knows. The fact is, we'd need another bath altogether, but I think the closet down at the end of the hall upstairs would serve. I might have a little apartment added off the kitchen here, for Mother—so she won't be disturbed. And I'd add a bit to the gardens, put up a little sign. Nothing on a grand scale, you see. Just small and tasteful and comfortable."

"You want this," Maggie murmured, seeing the light in her sister's eyes. "You truly do."

"I do, yes. I want it."

"Then do it." Maggie grabbed her hands. "Just do it, Brie. Freshen your rooms and fix your plumbing. Put up a fine sign. He wanted it for you."

"I think he did. He laughed when I talked to him about it, in that big way he had."

"Aye, he had a grand laugh."

"And he kissed me and joked about me being an innkeeper's granddaughter, and following tradition. If I started small enough, I could open for summer this year. The tourists, they come to the west counties in the summer especially, and they look for a nice, comfortable place to spend the night. I could—" Brianna shut her eyes. "Oh, listen to this talk, and we're burying our father tomorrow."

"It's just what he'd want to hear." Maggie was able to smile again. "A grand scheme like that, he'd have cheered you on!"

"We Concannons." Brianna shook her head. "We're great ones for scheming."

"Brianna, that day on the cliff, he talked of you. He called you his rose. He'd want you to bloom."

And she'd been his star, Maggie thought. She was going to do whatever she could to shine.

THREE

She was alone—as she liked best. From the doorway of her cottage she watched the rain lashing Murphy Muldoon's fields, slashing wildly over the grass and stone while the sun beamed hopefully, stubbornly, behind her. There was the possibility of a dozen different weathers in the layered sky, all brief and fickle.

That was Ireland.

But for Margaret Mary Concannon, the rain was a fine thing. She often preferred it to the warm slant of sun and the clear brilliance of cloudless blue skies. The rain was a soft gray curtain, tucking her away from the world. Or more important, cutting out the world, beyond her view of hill and field and sleek spotted cows.

For while the farm, the stone fences and green grasses beyond the tangle of fuchsia no longer belonged to Maggie or her family, this spot with its small wild garden and damp spring air was her own.

She was a farmer's daughter, true enough. But no farmer was she. In the five years since her father's death, she'd set about making her own place—and the mark he'd asked her to make. Perhaps it wasn't so deep as yet, but she continued to sell what she made, in Galway now and Cork, as well as Ennis.

She needed nothing more than what she had. Wanted more, perhaps, but she knew that desires, no matter how deep and dragging, didn't pay the bills. She also knew that some ambitions, when realized, carried a heavy price.

If from time to time she grew frustrated or restless, she had only to remind herself that she was where she needed to be, and doing what she chose to do.

But on mornings like this, with the rain and the sun at war, she thought of her father, and of the dreams he'd never seen come true.

He'd died without wealth, without success and without the farm that had been plowed and harvested by Concannon hands for generations.

She didn't resent the fact that so much of her birthright had been sold off for taxes and debts and the high-blown fantasies of her father's. Perhaps there was a tug of sentiment and regret for the hillocks and fields she had once raced over with all the arrogance and innocence of youth. But that was past. Indeed, she wanted no part of the working of it, the worrying over it. She had little of the love of growing things that stirred her sister, Brianna. True, she enjoyed her garden, the big defiant blooms and the scents that wafted from them. But the flowers grew despite her periods of neglect.

She had her place, and anything beyond it was out of her realm, and therefore, most usually, out of her mind. Maggie preferred needing no one, and certainly needing nothing she could not provide herself.

Dependence, she knew, and the longing for more than what you had, led to unhappiness and discontent. She had her parents' example before her.

Pausing there, just past the open door into the chilling rain, she breathed in the air, the damp sweetness of it tinged with spring from the blackthorn blossoms that formed a hedgerow to the east and the early roses struggling into bloom to the west. She was a small woman, shapely beneath the baggy jeans and flannel shirt. Over her shoulder-length, fiery hair she wore a slouch hat, as gray as the rain. Beneath its bill her eyes were the moody, mystical green of the sea.

The rain dampened her face, the soft curve of cheek and chin, the wide, melancholy mouth. It dewed the creamy redhead's complexion and joined the gold freckles scattered over the bridge of her nose.

She drank the strong sweet breakfast tea from a glass mug of her own design and ignored the phone that had begun to shrill from the kitchen. Ignoring the summons was as much policy as habit, particularly when her mind was drifting toward her work. There was a sculpture forming in her head, as clear as a raindrop, she thought. Pure and smooth, with glass flowing into glass in the heart of it.

The pull of the vision beckoned. Dismissing the ringing phone, she walked through the rain toward her workshop and the soothing roar of the glass furnace.

From his offices in Dublin, Rogan Sweeney listened to the ring of the phone through the receiver and swore. He was a busy man, too busy to waste his time on a rude and temperamental artist who refused to answer the sharp knock of opportunity.

He had businesses to see to, calls to answer, files to read, figures to tally. He should, while the day was young, go down to the gallery and oversee the latest shipment. The Native American pottery was, after all, his baby, and he'd spent months selecting the best of the best.

But that, of course, was a challenge already met. That particular show would once again ensure that Worldwide was a top international gallery. Meanwhile the woman, the damn, stubborn Clarewoman, was crowding his mind. Though he'd yet to meet her face-to-face, she and her genius occupied too much of his mind.

The new shipment would, of course, receive as much of his skill, energy and time as it required. But a new artist, particularly one whose work had so completely captured his imagination, excited on a different level. The thrill of discovery was as vital to Rogan as the careful development, marketing and sale of an artist's works.

He wanted Concannon, exclusively, for Worldwide Galleries. As with most of his desires, all of which Rogan deemed quite reasonable, he wouldn't rest until it was accomplished.

He'd been raised to succeed—the third generation of prosperous merchants who found clever ways to turn pence into pounds. The business his grandfather had founded sixty years before flourished under his leadership—because Rogan Sweeney refused to take no for an answer. He would achieve his goals by sweat, by charm, by tenacity or any other means he deemed suitable.

Margaret Mary Concannon and her unbridled talent was his newest and most frustrating goal.

He wasn't an unreasonable man in his own mind, and would have been shocked and insulted to discover that he was described as just that by many of his acquaintances. If he expected long hours and hard work from his employees, he expected no less of himself. Drive and dedication weren't merely virtues to Rogan, they were necessities that had been bred in his bones.

He could have handed the reins of Worldwide over to a manager and lived quite comfortably on the proceeds. Then he could travel, not for business but for pleasure, enjoying the fruits of his inheritance without sweating over the harvesting.

He could have, but his responsibility and thirsty ambition were his birthrights.

And M. M. Concannon, glass artist, hermit and eccentric, was his obsession.

He was going to make changes in Worldwide Galleries, changes that would reflect his own vision, that would celebrate his own country. M. M. Concannon was his first step, and he'd be damned if her stubbornness would make him stumble.

She was unaware—because she refused to listen, Rogan thought grimly—that he intended to make her Worldwide's first native Irish star. In the past, with his father and grandfather at the helm, the galleries had specialized in international art. Rogan didn't intend to narrow the scope, but he did intend to shift the focus and give the world the best of the land of his birth.

He would risk both his money and his reputation to do it.

If his first artist was a success, as he fully intended her to be, his investment would have paid off, his instincts would have been justified and his dream, a new gallery that showcased works exclusively by Irish artists, would become reality.

To begin, he wanted Margaret Mary Concannon.

Annoyed with himself, he rose from his antique oak desk to stand by the window. The city stretched out before him, its broad streets and green squares, the silver glint that was the river and the bridges that spanned it.

Below, traffic moved in a steady stream, laborers and tourists merging on the street in a colorful stream in the sunlight. They seemed very distant to him now as they strolled in packs or twosomes. He watched a young couple embrace, a casual linking of arms, meeting of lips. Both wore backpacks and expressions of giddy delight.

He turned away, stung by an odd little arrow of envy.

He was unused to feeling restless, as he was now. There was work on his desk, appointments in his book, yet he turned to neither. Since childhood he'd moved with purpose from education to profession, from success to success. As had been expected of him. As he had expected of himself.

He'd lost both of his parents seven years before when his father had suffered a heart attack behind the wheel of his car and had smashed into a utility pole. He could still remember the grim panic, and the almost dreamy disbelief, that had cloaked him during the flight from Dublin to London, where his mother and father had traveled for business and the horrible, sterile scent of hospital.

His father had died on impact. His mother had lived barely an hour longer. So they had both been gone before he'd arrived, long before he'd been able to accept it. But they'd taught him a great deal before he'd lost them—about family and pride of heritage, the love of art, the love of business and how to combine them.

At twenty-six he'd found himself the head of Worldwide and its subsidiaries, responsible for staff, for decisions, for the art placed in his hands. For seven years he'd worked not only to make the business grow, but to make it shine. It had been more than enough for him.

This unsettled sensation, the dilemma of it, he knew had its roots in the breezy winter afternoon when he had first seen Maggie Concannon's work.

That first piece, spied during an obligatory tea with his grandmother, had started him on this odyssey to possess—no, he thought, uncomfortable with the word. To control, he corrected, he wanted to control the fate of the artistry, and the career of the artist. Since that afternoon, he'd been able to buy only two pieces of her work. One was as delicate as a daydream, a slim almost weightless column riddled with shimmering rainbows and hardly larger than the span of his hand from wrist to fingertip.

The second, and the one he could admit privately haunted and enticed him, was a violent nightmare, fired from a passionate mind into a turbulent tangle of glass. It should have been unbalanced, he thought now as he studied the piece on his desk. It should have been ugly with its wild war of colors and shapes, the grasping tendrils curling and clawing out of the squat base.

Instead, it was fascinating and uncomfortably sexual. And it made him wonder what kind of woman could create both pieces with equal skill and power.

Since he had purchased it a little more than two months before, he had tried with no success to contact the artist and interest her in patronage.

He had twice reached her by phone, but the conversation on her part had been brief to the point of rudeness. She didn't require a patron, particularly a Dublin businessman with too much education and too little taste.

Oh, that had stung.

She was, she had told him in her musical west county brogue, content to create at her own pace and sell her work when and where it suited her. She had no need for his contracts, or for someone to tell her what must be sold. It was her work, was it not, so why didn't he go back to his ledgers, of which she was certain he had plenty, and leave her to it?

Insolent little twit, he thought, firing up again. Here he was offering a helping hand, a hand that countless other artists would have begged for, and she snarled at it.

He should leave her to it, Rogan mused. Leave her to create in obscurity. It was certain that neither he nor Worldwide needed her.

But, damn it all, he *wanted* her.

On impulse, he picked up his phone and buzzed his secretary. "Eileen, cancel my appointments for the next couple of days. I'm going on a trip."

It was a rare thing for Rogan to have business in the west counties. He remembered a family holiday from childhood. Most usually his parents had preferred trips to Paris or Milan, or an occasional break in the villa they kept on the French Mediterranean. There had been trips that had combined business and pleasure. New York, London, Bonn, Venice, Boston. But once, when he had been nine or ten, they had driven to the Shannon area to take in the wild, glorious scenery of the west. He remembered it in patches, the dizzying views from the Cliffs of Mohr, the dazzling panoramas and gem-bright waters of the Lake District, the quiet villages and the endless green of farmlands.

Beautiful it was. But it was also inconvenient. He was already regretting his impulsive decision to make the drive, particularly since the directions he'd been given in the nearby village had taken him onto a pitted excuse for a road. His Aston Martin handled it well, even as the dirt turned to mud under the ceaseless driving rain. His mood didn't negotiate the potholes as smoothly as did his car.

Only stubbornness kept him from turning back. The woman would listen to reason, by God. He would see to it. If she wanted to bury herself behind hedges of furze and hawthorn, it was her business. But her art was his. Or would be.

Following the directions he'd been given at the local post office, he passed the bed-and-breakfast called Blackthorn Cottage with its glorious gardens and trim blue shutters. Farther on there were stone cabins, sheds for animals, a hay barn, a slate-roofed shed where a man worked on a tractor.

The man lifted a hand in salute, then went back to work as Rogan maneuvered the car around the narrow curve. The farmer was the first sign of life, other than livestock, he had seen since leaving the village.

How anyone survived in this godforsaken place was beyond him. He'd take Dublin's crowded streets and conveniences over the incessant rain and endless fields every day of the week. Scenery be damned.

She'd hidden herself well, he thought. He'd barely caught sight of the garden gate and the whitewashed cottage beyond it through the tumbling bushes of privet and fuchsia.

Rogan slowed, though he'd nearly been at a crawl in any case. There was a short drive occupied by a faded blue lorry going to rust. He pulled his dashing white Aston behind it and got out.

He circled around to the gate, moved down the short walk that cut between heavy-headed, brilliant flowers that bobbed in the rain. He gave the door, which was painted a bold magenta, three sharp raps, then three again before impatience had him stalking to a window to peer inside.

There was a fire burning low in the grate, and a sugan chair pulled up close. A sagging sofa covered in some wild floral print that mated reds and blues and purples teetered in a corner. He would have thought he'd mistaken the house but for the pieces of her work set throughout the small room. Statues and bottles, vases and bowls stood, sat or reclined on every available surface.

Rogan wiped the wet from the window and spied the many-branch candelabra positioned dead center of the mantel. It was fashioned of glass so clear, so pure, it might have been water frozen in place. The arms curved fluidly up, the base a waterfall. He felt the quick surge, the inner click that presaged acquisition.

Oh yes, he'd found her.

Now if she'd just answer the damn door.

He gave up on the front and walked through the wet grass around to the back of the cabin. More flowers, growing wild as weeds. Or, he corrected, growing wild *with* weeds. Miss Concannon obviously didn't spend much time tidying her beds.

There was a lean-to beside the door under which bricks of turf were piled. An ancient bike with one flat tire was propped beside them along with a pair of Wellingtons that were muddy to the ankles.

He started to knock again when the sound coming from behind him had him turning toward the sheds. The roar, constant and low, was almost like the sea. He could see the smoke pluming out of the chimney into the leaden sky.

The building had several windows, and despite the chilly damp of the day, some were propped open. Her workshop, no doubt, Rogan thought, and crossed to it, pleased that he had tracked her down and confident of the outcome of their meeting.

He knocked and, though he received no answer, shoved the door open. He had a moment to register the blast of heat, the sharp smells and the small woman seated in a big wooden chair, a long pipe in her hands.

He thought of fairies and magic spells.

"Close the door, damn you, there's a draft."

He obeyed automatically, bristling under the sharp fury of the order. "Your windows are open."

"Ventilation. Draft. Idiot." She said nothing more, nor did she spare him so much as a glance. She set her mouth to the pipe and blew.

He watched the bubble form, fascinated despite himself. Such a simple procedure, he thought, only breath and molten glass. Her fingers worked on the pipe, turning it and turning it, fighting gravity, using it, until she was satisfied with the shape.

She thought nothing of him at all as she went about her work. She necked the bubble, using jacks to indent a shallow grove just beyond the head of the pipe. There were steps, dozens of them yet to take, but she could already see the finished work as clearly as if she held it cool and solid in her hand.

At the furnace, she pushed the bubble under the surface of the molten glass heated there to make the second gather. Back at the bench she rolled the gather in a wooden block to chill the glass and form the "skin." All the while the pipe was moving, moving, steady and controlled by her hands, just as the initial stages of the work had been controlled by her breath.

She repeated the same procedure over and over again, endlessly patient, completely focused while Rogan stood by the door and watched. She used larger blocks for forming as the shape grew. And as time passed and she spoke not a word, he took off his wet coat and waited.

The room was filled with heat from the furnace. It felt as though his clothes were steaming on his body. She seemed sublimely unaffected, centered on her work, reaching for a new tool now and then while one hand constantly revolved the pipe.

The chair on which she sat was obviously homemade, with a deep seat and long arms, hooks set here and there where tools hung. There were buckets nearby filled with water or sand or hot wax.

She took a tool, one that looked to Rogan to be a pair of sharp-pointed tongs, and placed them at the edge of the vessel she was creating. It seemed they would flow straight through, the glass so resembled water, but she drew the shape of it out, lengthening it, slimming it.

When she rose again, he started to speak, but a sound from her, something like a snarl, had him lifting a brow and keeping his silence.

Fine then, he thought. He could be patient. An hour, two hours, as long as it took. If she could stand this vicious heat, so, by Christ, could he.

She didn't even feel it, so intent was she. She dipped a punt, another gather of molten glass, onto the side of the vessel she was creating. When the hot glass had softened the wall, she pushed a pointed file, coated with wax, into the glass.

Gently, gently.

Flames sparked under her hand as the wax burned. She had to work quickly now to keep the tool from sticking to the glass. The pressure had to be exactly right for the effect she wanted. The inner wall made contact with the outer wall, merging, creating the inner form, the angel swing.

Glass within glass, transparent and fluid.

She nearly smiled.

Carefully, she reblew the form before flattening the bottom with a paddle. She attached the vessel to a hot pontil. She plunged a file into a bucket of water, dripping it onto the neck groove of her vessel. Then, with a stroke that made Rogan jolt, she struck the file against the blowpipe. With the vessel now attached to the pontil, she thrust it into the furnace to heat the lip. Taking the vessel to the annealing oven, she rapped the pontil sharply with a file to break the seal.

She set the time and the temperature, then walked directly to a small refrigerator.

It was low to the floor, so she was forced to bend down. Rogan tilted his head at the view. The baggy jeans were beginning to wear quite thin in several interesting places. She straightened, turned and tossed in his direction one of the two soft-drink cans she had taken out.

Rogan caught the missile by blind instinct before it connected with his nose.

"Still here?" She popped the top of her can and drank deeply. "You must be roasting in that suit." Now that her work was out of her mind and her eyes clear of the visions of it, she studied him.

Tall, learn, dark. She drank again. Well styled hair as black as a raven's wing and eyes as blue as a Kerry lake. Not hard to look at, she mused, tapping a finger against the can as they stared at each other. He had a good mouth, nicely sculpted and generous. But she didn't think he used it often for smiling. Not with those eyes. As blue as they were, and as appealing, they were cool, calculating and confident.

A sharply featured face with good bones. Good bones, good breeding, her granny used to say. And this one, unless she was very mistaken, had blue blood beneath the bone.

The suit was tailored, probably English. The tie discreet. There was a wink of gold at his cuffs. And he stood like a soldier—the sort that had earned plenty of brass and braid.

She smiled at him, content to be friendly now that her work had gone well. "Are you lost then?"

"No." The smile made her look like a pixie, one capable of all sorts of magic and mischief. He preferred the scowl she'd worn while she'd worked. "I've come a long way to speak with you, Miss Concannon. I'm Rogan Sweeney."

Her smile tilted a few degrees into something closer to a sneer. Sweeney, she thought. The man who wanted to take over her work. "The jackeen." She used the term, not terribly flattering, for a Dubliner. "Well, you're a stubborn one, Mr. Sweeney, that's the truth. I hope you had a pleasant drive so your trip won't be wasted."

"It was a miserable drive."

"Pity."

"But I don't consider the trip wasted." Though he would have preferred a strong cup of tea, he opened the soft-drink can. "You have an interesting setup here."

He scanned the room with its roaring furnace, its ovens and benches, the jumble of metal and wooden tools, the rods, the pipes and the shelves and cupboards he imagined held her chemicals.

"I do well enough, as I believe I told you over the phone."

"That piece you were working on when I came in. It was lovely." He stepped over to a table cluttered with sketch pads, pencils, charcoal and chalk. He picked up a sketch of the glass sculpture now annealing. It was delicate, fluid.

"Do you sell your sketches?"

"I'm a glass artist, Mr. Sweeney, not a painter."

He shot her a look, set the sketch down again. "If you were to sign that, I could get a hundred pounds for it."

She let out a snort of disbelief and tossed her empty can into a waste bin.

"And the piece you've just finished? How much will you ask for it."

"And why would that be your business?"

"Perhaps I'd like to buy it."

She considered, scooting up on the edge of a bench and swinging her feet. No one could tell her the worth of her work, not even herself. But a price—a price had to be set. She knew that well. For, artist or not, she had to eat.

Her formula for figuring price was loose and flexible. Unlike her formulas for making glass and mixing colors it had very little to do with science. She would calculate the time spent on producing the piece, her own feelings toward it, then factor in her opinion of the purchaser.

Her opinion of Rogan Sweeney was going to cost him dear.

"Two hundred and fifty pounds," she decided. A hundred of that was due to his gold cuff links.

"I'll write you a check." Then he smiled, and Maggie realized she was grateful he didn't seem to use that particular weapon often. Lethal, she thought, watching the way his lips curved, his eyes darkened. Charm floated down on him, light and effortless as a cloud. "And though I'll add it to my personal collection—for sentiment, shall we say?—I could easily get double that for it at my gallery."

" 'Tis a wonder you stay in business, Mr. Sweeney, soaking your clients that way."

"You underestimate yourself, Miss Concannon." He crossed to her then, as if he knew he'd suddenly gained the upper hand. He waited until she'd tipped her head back to keep her eyes level with his. "That's why you need me."

"I know exactly what I'm doing."

"In here." He lifted an arm to encompass the room. "I've seen that quite dramatically for myself. But the business world is a different matter."

"I'm not interested in business."

"Precisely," he told her, smiling again as if she'd answered a particularly thorny question. "I, on the other hand, am fascinated by it."

She was at a disadvantage, sitting on the bench with him hovering over her. And she didn't care for it. "I don't want anyone messing in my work, Mr. Sweeney. I do what I choose, when I choose, and I get along very well."

"You do what you choose, when you choose." He picked up a wooden form from the bench as if to admire the grain. "And you do it very well. What a loss it would be for someone with your talent to merely get along. As to . . . messing about with your work, I have no intention of doing so. Though watching you work was certainly interesting." His eyes cut from the mold back to her with a speed that made her jolt. "Very interesting."

She pushed off the bench, the better to stand on her own feet. To gain the room required, she shoved him aside. "I don't want a manager."

"Ah, but you need one, Margaret Mary. You need one badly."

"A lot you know about what I'd be needing," she mumbled, and began to pace. "Some Dublin sharpie with fancy shoes."

Twice as much, he'd said; her mind replayed his earlier words. Twice what she'd asked. And there was Mother to care for, and the bills to pay, and Sweet Jesus, the price of chemicals was murderous.

"What I need's peace and quiet. And room." She whirled back at him. His very presense in the studio was crowding her. "Room. I don't need someone like you coming along and telling me we need three vases for next week, or twenty paperweights, or a half dozen goblets with pink stems. I'm not an assembly line, Sweeney, I'm an artist."

Very calmly, he took a pad and a gold pen out of his pocket and began to write.

"What are you doing there?"

"I'm noting down that you're not to be given orders for vases, paperweights or goblets with pink stems."

Her mouth twitched once before she controlled it. "I won't take orders, at all."

His eyes flicked to hers. "I believe that's understood. I own a factory or two, Miss Concannon, and know the difference between an assembly line and art. I happen to make my living through both."

"That's fine for you then." She waved both arms before setting her fists on her hips. "Congratulations. Why would you be needing me?"

"I don't." He replaced the pen and pad. "But I want you."

Her chin angled up. "But I don't want you."

"No, but you need me. And there is where we'll complement each other. I'll make you a rich woman, Miss Concannon. And more than that, a famous one."

He saw something flicker in her eyes at that. Ah, he thought, ambition. And he turned the key easily in the lock. "Do you create just to hide your gift on your own shelves and cupboards? To sell a few pieces here and there to keep the wolf from the door, and hoard the rest? Or do you want your work appreciated, admired, even applauded?" His voice changed, subtly, into a tone of sarcasm so light it stabbed bloodlessly. "Or . . . are you afraid it won't be?"

Her eyes went molten as the blade struck true. "I'm not afraid. My work stands. I spent three years apprenticing in a Venice glass house, sweating as a pontil boy. I learned the craft there, but not the art. Because the art is in me." She thumped a hand on her chest. "It's in me, and I breathe in and out into the glass. Any who don't like my work can jump straight into hell."

"Fair enough. I'll give you a show at my gallery, and we'll see how many take the jump."

A dare, damn him. She hadn't been prepared for it. "So a bunch of art snobs can sniff around my work while they slurp champagne."

"You are afraid."

She hissed through her teeth and stomped to the door. "Go away. Go away so I can think. You're crowding my head."

"We'll talk again in the morning." He picked up his coat. "Perhaps you can recommend a place I could stay the night. Close by."

"Blackthorn Cottage, at the end of the road."

"Yes, I saw it." He slipped into his coat. "Lovely garden, very trim."

"Neat and tidy as a pin. You'll find the beds soft and the food good. My sister owns it, and she has a practical, homemaking soul."

He lifted a brow at the tone, but said nothing. "Then I trust I'll be comfortable enough until morning."

"Just get out." She pulled open the door to the rain. "I'll call the cottage in the morning if I want to talk to you again."

"A pleasure meeting you, Miss Concannon." Though it wasn't offered, he took her hand, held it while he looked into her eyes. "A greater one watching you work." On an impulse that surprised both of them, he lifted her hand to his lips, lingered just a moment over the taste of her skin. "I'll be back tomorrow."

"Wait for an invitation," she said, and closed the door smartly behind him.

FOUR

At Blackthorn Cottage, the scones were always warm, the flowers always fresh and the kettle always on the boil. Though it was early in the season for guests, Brianna Concannon made Rogan comfortable in her serenely efficient manner, as she had all the other guests she'd welcomed since that first summer after her father's death.

She served him tea in the tidy, polished parlor where a fire burned cheerfully and a vase full of freesia scented the air.

"I'll be serving dinner at seven, if that suits you, Mr. Sweeney." She was already thinking of ways to stretch the chicken she'd planned to cook so it would feed one more.

"That will be fine, Miss Concannon." He sipped the tea and found it perfect, a far cry from the chilly, sugar-laden soft drink Maggie had tossed at him. "You have a lovely place here."

"Thank you." It was, if not her only pride, perhaps her only joy. "If you need anything, anything at all, you've only to ask."

"If I could make use of the phone?"

"Of course." She started to step away to give him privacy, when he held up a hand, a signal of command to anyone who has served.

"The vase there on the table—your sister's work?"

Brianna's surprise at the question showed only in the quick widening of her eyes. "It is, yes. You know of Maggie's work?"

"I do. I have two pieces myself. And I've just purchased another even as it was made." He sipped his tea again, measuring Brianna. As different from Maggie as one piece of her work was from another. Which meant, he assumed, that they were the same somewhere beneath what the eye could see. "I've just come from her workshop."

"You were in Maggie's workshop?" Only true shock would have driven Brianna to ask a question of a guest with such a tone of disbelief. "Inside?"

"Is it so dangerous, then?"

A hint of a smile crossed Brianna's face, lightening her features. "You seem to be alive and well."

"Well enough. Your sister is an immensely talented woman."

"That she is."

Rogan recognized the same undercurrent of pride and annoyance in the statement as he had when Maggie had spoken of her sister. "Do you have other pieces of hers?"

"A few. She brings them by when the mood strikes her. If you'll not be needing anything else at the moment, Mr. Sweeney, I'll see about dinner."

Alone, Rogan settled back with his excellent tea. An interesting pair, he thought, the Concannon sisters. Brianna was taller, slimmer and certainly more lovely than Maggie. Her hair was rose gold rather than flame and fell in soft curls to her shoulders. Her eyes were a wide, pale green, almost translucent. Quiet, he thought, even a trifle aloof, like her manner. Her features were finer, her limbs softer, and she'd smelled of wildflowers rather than smoke and sweat.

All in all she was much more the type of woman he found appealing.

Yet he found his thoughts trailing back to Maggie with her compact body, her moody eyes and her uncertain temper. Artists, he mused, with their egos and insecurities, needed guidance, a firm hand. He let his gaze roam over the rose-colored vase with its swirls of glass from base to lip. He was very much looking forward to guiding Maggie Concannon.

"So, is he here?" Maggie slipped out of the rain into the warm, fragrant kitchen.

Brianna continued to peel potatoes. She'd been expecting the visit. "Who is he?"

"Sweeney." Crossing to the counter, Maggie snatched a peeled carrot and bit in. "Tall, dark, handsome and rich as sin. You can't miss him."

"In the parlor. You can take in a cup and join him for tea."

"I don't want to talk to him." Maggie hitched herself up on the counter, crossed her ankles. "What I wanted, Brie, love, is your opinion of him."

"He's polite and well-spoken."

Maggie rolled her eyes. "So's an altar boy in church."

"He's a guest in my home—"

"A paying one."

"And I've no intention," Brianna went on without pause, "of gossiping about him behind his back."

"Saint Brianna." Maggie crunched down on the carrot, gestured with the stub of it. "What if I were to tell you that he's after managing my career?"

"Managing?" Brianna's hands faltered before they picked on the rhythm again. Peelings fell steadily on the newspaper she'd laid on the counter. "In what way?"

"Financially, to start. Displaying my work in his galleries and talking rich patrons into buying it for great sums of money." She waved the remains of the carrot before finishing it off. "All the man can think about is making money."

"Galleries," Brianna repeated. "He owns art galleries?"

"In Dublin and Cork. He has interests in others in London and New York. Paris, too, I think. Probably Rome. Everybody in the art world knows Rogan Sweeney."

The art world was as removed from Brianna's life as the moon. But she felt a quick, warm pride that her sister could claim it. "And he's taken an interest in your work."

"Stuck his aristocrat's nose in is what he's done." Maggie snorted. "Calling me on the phone, sending letters, all but demanding rights to everything I make. Now today, he pops up on my doorstep, telling me that I need him. Hah."

"And, of course, you don't."

"I don't need anyone."

"You don't, no." Brianna carried the vegetables to the sink to rinse. "Not you, Margaret Mary."

"Oh, I hate that tone, all cold and superior. You sound just like Mother." She slid off the counter to stalk to the refrigerator. And because of it, she was swamped with guilt. "We're getting along well enough," she added as she pulled out a beer. "The bills are paid, there's food on the table and a roof over all our heads." She stared at her sister's stiff back and let out a sound of impatience. "It can't be what it once was, Brie."

"You think I don't know that?" Brianna's lilting voice turned edgy. "Do you think I have to have more? That I can't be content with what is?" Suddenly unbearably sad, she stared out the window toward the fields beyond. "It's not me, Maggie. 'Tisn't me."

Maggie scowled down at her beer. It was Brianna who suffered, Maggie knew. Brianna who had always been in the middle. Now, Maggie thought, she had the chance to change that. All she had to do was sell part of her soul.

"She's been complaining again."

"No." Brianna tucked a stray hair away in the knot at the nape of her neck. "Not really."

"I can tell by the look on your face she's been in one of her moods—and taking it out on you." Before Brianna could speak, Maggie waved a hand. "She'll never be happy, Brianna. You can't make her happy. The good Lord knows I can't. She'll never forgive him for being what he was."

"And what was he?" Brianna demanded as she turned around. "Just what was our father, Maggie?"

"Human. Flawed." She set her beer down and walked to her sister. "Wonderful. Do you remember, Brie, the time he bought the mule, and was going to make a fortune having tourists snap pictures of it in a peaked cap with our old dog sitting on its back?"

"I remember." Brie would have turned away, but Maggie grabbed her hands. "And I remember he lost more money feeding that cursed, bad-tempered mule than he ever did with his scheming."

"Oh, but it was fun. We went to the Cliffs of Mohr, and it was such a bright summer day. The tourists swarming about and the music playing. And there was Da holding that stupid mule, and that poor old dog, Joe, as terrified of that mule as he would have been of a roaring lion."

Brianna softened. She couldn't help it. "Poor Joe, sitting and shivering with fear on that mule's back. Then that German came along, wanting a picture of himself with Joe and the mule."

"And the mule kicked." Maggie grinned and picked up her beer again for a toast. "And the German screamed in three different languages while he hopped about on one foot. And Joe, terrified, leaped off and landed right on a display of lace collars, and the mule ran, scattering tourists. Oh, what a sight. People shouting and running, ladies screaming. There was a fiddler there, remember? And he just kept playing a reel as if we'd all start dancing any moment."

"And that nice boy from Killarney caught the mule's lead and dragged him back. Da tried to sell him the mule there and then."

"And nearly did. It's a good memory, Brie."

"He made many memories worth laughing over. But you can't live on laughter alone."

"And you can't live without it, as she would. He was alive. Now it seems this family's more dead than he is."

"She's ill," Brianna said shortly.

"As she has been for more than twenty years. And ill she'll stay as long as she has you to tend to her hand and foot."

It was true, but knowing the truth didn't change Brianna's heart. "She's our mother."

"That she is." Maggie drained the beer and set it aside. The yeasty taste warred with the bitterness on her tongue. "I've sold another piece. I'll have money for you by the end of the month."

"I'm grateful for it. So is she."

"The hell she is." Maggie looked into her sister's eyes with all the passion and anger and hurt boiling beneath. "I don't do it for her. When there's enough you'll hire a nurse and you'll move her into her own place."

"That isn't necessary—"

"It is," Maggie interrupted. "That was the agreement, Brie. I'll not stand by and watch you dance to her tune for the rest of her life. A nurse and a place in the village."

"If that's what she wants."

"That's what she'll have." Maggie inclined her head. "She kept you up last night."

"She was restless." Embarrassed, Brianna turned back to prepare the chicken. "One of her headaches."

"Ah, yes." Maggie remembered her mother's headaches well, and how well timed they could be. An argument Maeve was losing: instant headache. A family outing she didn't approve of: the throbbing began.

"I know what she is, Maggie." Brianna's own head began to ache. "That doesn't make her less of my mother."

Saint Brianna, Maggie thought again, but with affection. Her sister might be younger than her own twenty-eight by a year, but it had always been Brianna who took responsibility. "And you can't change what you are, Brie." Maggie gave her sister a fierce hug. "Da always said you'd be the good angel and I the bad. He was finally right about something." She closed her eyes a moment. "Tell Mr. Sweeney to come by the cottage in the morning. I'll speak with him."

"You'll let him manage you, then?"

The phrase had Maggie wincing. "I'll speak with him," she repeated, and headed back into the rain.

If Maggie had a weakness, it was family. That weakness had kept her up late into the night and had awakened her early in the chill, murky dawn. To the outside world she preferred to pretend she had responsibilities only to herself and her art, but beneath the facade was a constant love of family, and the dragging, often bitter obligations that went with it.

She wanted to refuse Rogan Sweeney, first on principle. Art and business, to her mind, could not and should not mix. She wanted to refuse him secondly because his type—wealthy, confident and blue-blooded—irritated her. Thirdly, and most telling, she wanted to refuse him because to do otherwise was an admission that she lacked the skill to handle her affairs alone.

Oh, that was a pill that stuck bitterly in her throat.

She would not refuse him. She'd made the decision sometime during the long and restless night to allow Rogan Sweeney to make her rich.

It wasn't as though she couldn't support herself, and well, too. She'd been doing just that for more than five years. Brianna's bed-and-breakfast was successful enough that keeping two homes was no heavy burden. But they could not between them afford a third.

Maggie's goal, indeed her Holy Grail, was to establish their mother in a separate residence. If Rogan could help clear the path to her quest, she'd deal with him. She'd deal with the very devil.

But the devil might come to regret the bargain.

In her kitchen with the rain falling soft and steady outside, Maggie brewed tea. And plotted.

Rogan Sweeney had to be cleverly handled, she mused. With just the right amount of artistic disdain and feminine flattery. The disdain would be no problem at all, but the other ingredient would be hard coming.

She let herself picture Brianna baking, gardening, curled up with a book by the fire—without the whining, demanding voice of their mother to spoil the peace. Brianna would marry, have children. Which Maggie knew was a dream her sister kept locked in her heart. And locked it would stay as long as Brianna had the responsibility of a chronic hypochondriac.

While Maggie couldn't understand her sister's need to strap herself down with a man and a half a dozen children, she would do whatever it took to help Brianna realize the dream.

It was possible, just possible, that Rogan Sweeney could play fairy godfather.

The knock on the front door of the cottage was brisk and impatient. This fairy godfather, Maggie thought as she went to answer, wouldn't make his entrance with angel dust and colored lights.

After opening the door, she smiled a little. He was wet, as he'd been the day before, and just as elegantly dressed. She wondered if he slept in a suit and tie.

"Good morning to you, Mr. Sweeney."

"And to you, Miss Concannon." He stepped inside, out of the rain and the swirl of mist.

"Shall I take your coat? It'll dry out some by the fire."

"Thank you." He slipped out of his overcoat, watched her spread it over a chair by the fire. She was different today, he thought. Pleasant. The change put him on guard. "Tell me, does it do anything but rain in Clare?"

"We enjoy good soft weather in the spring. Don't worry, Mr. Sweeney. Even a Dubliner shouldn't melt in a west-county rain." She sent him a quick, charming smile, but her eyes were wickedly amused. "I'm brewing tea, if you'd like some."

"I would." Before she could turn to the kitchen, he stopped her—a hand on her arm. His attention wasn't on her, but on the sculpture on the table beside them. It was a long, sinuous curve in a deep icy blue. The color of an arctic lake. Glass clung to glass in waves at the tip then flowed down, liquid ice.

"An interesting piece," he commented.

"Do you think so?" Maggie blocked the urge to shake off his hand. It held her lightly, with an understated possession that made her ridiculously uncomfortable. She could smell him, the subtle woodsy cologne he'd probably dashed on after shaving, with undertones of soap from his shower. When he ran a fingertip along the length of the curved glass, she suppressed a shudder. For a moment, a foolish one, it had felt as though he'd trailed a touch from her throat to her center.

"Obviously feminine," he murmured. Though his eyes stayed on the glass, he was very aware of her. The coiled tension in her arm, the quick tremble she'd tried to mask, the dark, wild scent of her hair. "Powerful. A woman about to surrender sexually to a man."

It flustered her because he was exactly right. "How do you find power in surrender?"

He looked at her then, those depthless blue eyes locked on her face. His hand remained light on her arm. "Nothing's more powerful than a woman at that instant before she gives herself." He stroked the glass again. "Obviously you're aware of that."

"And the man?"

He smiled then, just the faintest curve of lips. His grip on her arm seemed more of a caress now. A request. And his eyes, amused, interested, skimmed over her face. "That, Margaret Mary, would depend on the woman."

She didn't move, absorbed the sexual punch, acknowledged it with a slight nod. "Well, we agree on something. Sex and power generally depend on the woman."

"That's not at all what I said, or meant. What draws you to create something like this?"

"It's difficult to explain art to a man of business."

When she would have stepped back, he curled his fingers around her arm, tightened his grip. "Try."

Annoyance pricked through her. "What comes to me comes. There's no plot, no plan. It has to do with emotions, with passions and not with practicality or profit. Otherwise I'd be making little glass swans for gift shops. Jesus, what a thought."

His smile widened. "Horrifying. Fortunately I'm not interested in little glass swans. But I would like that tea."

"We'll have it in the kitchen." She started to step away again, and again his grip stopped her. Temper flashed into her eyes like lightning. "You're blocking my way, Sweeney."

"I don't think so. I'm about to clear it for you." He released her and followed her silently into the kitchen.

Her cottage was a far cry from the country comfort of Blackthorn. There were no rich smells of baking wafting in the air, no plumped pillows or gleaming woodwork. It was spartan, utilitarian and untidy. Which was why, he supposed, the art carelessly set here and there was that much more effective and striking.

He wondered where she slept, and if her bed was as soft and inviting as the one he'd spent the night in. And he wondered if he would share it with her. No, not if, he corrected himself. *When.*

Maggie set the teapot on the table along with two thick pottery mugs. "Did you enjoy your stay at Blackthorn Cottage?" she asked as she poured.

"I did. Your sister's charming. And her cooking memorable."

Maggie softened, added three generous spoons of sugar to her tea. "Brie's a homemaker in the best sense of the word. Did she make her currant buns this morning?"

"I had two of them."

Relaxed again, Maggie laughed and propped one booted foot on her knee. "Our father used to say Brie got all the gold and I the brass. I'm afraid you won't get any home-baked buns here, Sweeney, but I could probably dig out a tin of biscuits."

"No need."

"You'd probably rather get straight to business." Cupping the mug in both hands, Maggie leaned forward. "What if I were to tell you plain I'm not interested in your offer?"

Rogan considered, sipping his tea black and strong. "I'd have to call you a liar, Maggie." He grinned at the fire that erupted in her eyes. "Because if you weren't interested, you wouldn't have agreed to see me this morning. And I certainly wouldn't be drinking tea in your kitchen." He held up a hand before she could speak. "We'll agree, however, that you don't want to be interested."

A clever man, she mused, only slightly mollified. Clever men were dangerous ones. "I've no wish to be produced, or managed, or guided."

"We rarely wish for what we need." He watched her over the rim of his cup, calculating even as he enjoyed the way the faint flush seemed to silken her skin, deepen the green of her eyes. "Why don't I explain myself more clearly? Your art is your domain. I have no intention of interfering in any way with what you do in your studio. You create what you're inspired to create, when you're inspired to create it."

"And what if what I create isn't to your taste?"

"I've shown and sold a great number of pieces I wouldn't care to have in my home. That's the business, Maggie. And as I won't interfere with your art, you won't interfere with my business."

"I'll have no say in who buys my work?"

"None," he said simply. "If you have an emotional attachment to a piece, you'll have to get over it, or keep the piece for yourself. Once it's in my hands, it's mine."

Her jaw clenched. "And anyone with the money can own it."

"Exactly."

Maggie slapped the mug down and sprang up to pace. She used her whole body, a habit Rogan admired. Legs, arms, shoulders all in rhythmically angry movements. He topped off his tea and sat back to enjoy the show.

"I pull something out of myself, and I create it, make it solid, tangible, real, and some idiot from Kerry or Dublin or, God help me, London, comes in and buys it for his wife's birthday without having the least understanding of what it is, what it means?"

"Do you develop personal relationships with everyone who buys your work?"

"At least I know where it's going, who's buying it." Usually, she added to herself.

"I'll have to remind you that I bought two of your pieces before we met."

"Aye. And look where that's got me."

Temperament, he thought with a sigh. As long as he'd worked with artists he'd never understood it. "Maggie," he began, trying for the most reasonable of tones. "The reason you need a manager is to eliminate these difficulties. You won't have to worry about the sales, only the creation. And yes, if someone from Kerry or Dublin, or God help you London comes into one of my galleries and takes an interest in one of your pieces, it's his—as long as he meets the price. No résumé, no character references required. And by the end of a year, with my help, you'll be a rich woman."

"Is that what you think I want?" Insulted, infuriated, she whirled on him. "Do you think, Rogan Sweeney, that I pick up my pipe every day calculating how much profit there might be at the end of it?"

"No, I don't. That's precisely where I come in. You're an exceptional artist, Maggie. And at the risk of inflating what appears to be an already titanic ego, I'll admit that I was captivated the first time I saw your work."

"Perhaps you have decent taste," she said with a cranky shrug.

"So I've been told. My point is that your work deserves more than you're giving it. You deserve more than you're giving yourself."

She leaned back on the counter, eyeing him narrowly. "And you're going to help me get more out of the goodness of your heart."

"My heart has nothing to do with it. I'm going to help you because your work will add to the prestige of my galleries."

"And to your pocketbook."

"One day you'll have to explain to me the root of your disdain for money. In the meantime, your tea's getting cold."

Maggie let out a long breath. She wasn't doing a good job of flattering him, she reminded herself, and returned to the table. "Rogan." She let herself smile. "I'm sure you're very good at what you do. Your galleries have a reputation for quality and integrity, which I'm sure is a reflection of yourself."

She was good, he mused, and ran his tongue over his teeth. Very good. "I like to think so."

"Doubtless any artist would be thrilled to be considered by you. But I'm accustomed to dealing for myself, for handling all the aspects of my work from making the glass to selling the finished piece—or at least placing it into the hands of someone I know and trust to sell it. I don't know you."

"Or trust me?"

She lifted a hand, let it fall. "I would be a fool not to trust Worldwide Galleries. But it's difficult for me to imagine a business of that size. I'm a simple woman."

He laughed so quickly, so richly, that she blinked. Before she could recover, he was leaning forward, taking one of her hands in his. "Oh, no, Margaret Mary, simple is exactly what you are not. Canny, obstinate, brilliant, bad-tempered and beautiful you are. But simple, never."

"I say I am." She yanked her hand free and struggled not to be charmed. "And I know myself better than you do or ever will."

"Every time you finish a sculpture you're shouting out this is who I am. At least for today. That's what makes art true."

She couldn't argue with him. It was an observation she hadn't expected from a man of his background. Making money from art didn't mean you understood it. Apparently, he did.

"I'm a simple woman," she said again, daring him to contradict her a second time. "And I prefer to stay that way. If I agree to your management, there will be rules. Mine."

He had her, and he knew it. But a wise negotiator was never a smug one. "What are they?" he asked.

"I'll do no publicity, unless it suits me. And I can promise you it won't."

"It'll add to the mystery, won't it?"

She very nearly grinned before she recovered. "I'll not be after dressing up like some fashion plate for showings—if I come at all."

This time he tucked his tongue firmly in his cheek. "I'm sure your sense of style will reflect your artistic nature."

It might have been an insult, but she couldn't be sure. "And I won't be nice to people if I don't want to be."

"Temperament, again artistic." He toasted her with his tea. "Should add to sales."

Though she was amused, she sat back and crossed her arms over her chest. "I will never, never duplicate a piece or create something out of someone else's fancy."

He frowned, shook his head. "That may be a deal breaker. I had this idea for a unicorn, with a touch of gold leaf on the horn and hooves. Very tasteful."

She snickered, then gave up and laughed out loud. "All right, Rogan. Maybe by some miracle we'll be able to work together. How do we do it?"

"I'll have contracts drawn up. Worldwide will want exclusive rights to your work."

She winced at that. It felt as though she were surrendering a part of herself. Perhaps the best part. "Exclusive rights to the pieces I choose to sell."

"Of course."

She looked past him, out the window toward the fields beyond. Once, long ago, they, like her art, had felt like part of her. Now they were just part of a lovely view. "What else?"

He hesitated. She looked almost unbearably sad. "It won't change what you do. It won't change who you are."

"You're wrong," she murmured. With an effort, she shook off the mood and faced him again. "Go on. What else?"

"I'll want a show, within two months, at the Dublin gallery. Naturally, I'll need to see what you have finished, and I'll arrange for shipping. I'll also need you to keep me apprised of what you've completed over the next few weeks. We'll price the pieces, and whatever inventory is left after the show will be displayed in Dublin and our other galleries."

She took a long, calming breath. "I'd appreciate it, if you'd not refer to my work as inventory. At least in my presence."

"Done." He steepled his fingers. "You will, of course, be sent a complete itemization of pieces sold. You may, if you choose, have some input as to which ones we photograph for our catalog. Or you can leave it up to us."

"And how and when am I paid?" she wanted to know.

"I can buy the pieces outright. I have no objection to that since I have confidence in your work."

She remembered what he'd said before, about getting twice as much as what he'd paid her for the sculpture she'd just finished. She might not have been a businesswoman, but she wasn't a fool.

"How else do you handle it?"

"By commission. We take the piece, and when and if we sell it, we deduct a percentage."

More of a gamble, she mused. And she preferred a gamble. "What percentage do you take?"

Hoping for a reaction, he kept his eyes level with hers. "Thirty-five percent."

She made a strangled sound in her throat. "Thirty-five? Thirty-five? You thief. You robber." She shoved back from the table and stood. "You're a vulture, Rogan Sweeney. Thirty-five percent be damned and you with it."

"I take all the risks, I have all the expenses." He spread his hands, steepled them again. "You have merely to create."

"Oh, as if all it takes is sitting on me ass and waiting for the inspiration to come fluttering down like raindrops. You know nothing, nothing about it." She began to pace again, swirling the air with temper and energy. "I'll remind you, you'd have nothing to sell without me. And it's my work, my sweat and blood that they'll spend good money for. You'll get fifteen percent."

"I'll get thirty."

"Plague take you, Rogan, for a horse thief. Twenty."

"Twenty-five." He rose then to stand toe to toe with her. "Worldwide will earn a quarter of your sweat and blood, Maggie, I promise you."

"A quarter." She hissed through her teeth. "That's a businessman for you, preying on art."

"And making the artist financially secure. Think of it, Maggie. Your work will be seen in New York, in Rome and Paris. And no one who sees it will forget it."

"Oh, it's clever you are, Rogan, taking a quick turn from money into fame." She scowled at him, then stuck out her hand. "The hell with it and you. You'll have your twenty-five percent."

Which was exactly what he'd planned on. He took her hand, held it. "We're going to do well together, Maggie."

Well enough, she hoped, to settle her mother in the village and away from Blackthorn Cottage. "If we don't, Rogan, I'll see that you pay for it."

Because he'd enjoyed the taste of her, he lifted her hand to his lips. "I'll risk it."

His lips lingered there long enough to make her pulse stutter. "If you were going to try to seduce me, you'd have been smarter to start before we had a deal."

The statement both surprised and annoyed him. "I prefer to keep personal and professional matters separate."

"Another difference between us." It pleased her to see she'd scratched the seamlessly polite exterior. "My personal and professional lives are always fusing. And I indulge both when the whim strikes." Smiling, she slipped her hand from his. "It hasn't as yet—personally speaking. I'll let you know if and when it does."

"Are you baiting me, Maggie?"

She stopped as if thinking it through. "No, I'm explaining to you. Now I'll take you to the glass house so you can choose what you want shipped to Dublin." She turned to pull a jacket from a peg by the back door. "You might want your coat. It'd be a shame to get that fancy suit wet."

He stared at her a moment, wondering why he should feel so completely insulted. Without a word he turned on his heel and strode back into the living room for his coat.

Maggie took the opportunity to step outside and cool her blood in the chilly rain. Ridiculous, she told herself, to get so sexually tied up over having her hand kissed. Rogan Sweeney was smooth, too smooth. It was a fortunate thing he lived on the other side of the country. More fortunate yet, he wasn't her type.

Not at all.

FIVE

The high grass beside the ruined abbey made a lovely resting place for the dead. Maggie had fought to have her father buried there, rather than in the tidy and cold ground near the village church. She had wanted the peace, and the touch of royalty for her father. For once, Brianna had argued with her until their mother had sullenly closed her mouth and washed her hands of the arrangements.

Maggie visited there only twice a year, once on her father's birthday and once on her own. To thank him for the gift of her life. She never came on the anniversary of his death, nor did she allow herself to mourn in private.

Nor did she mourn him now, but sat down on the grass beside him, tucking her knees up and wrapping her arms around them. The sun fought through layers of clouds to gild the graves and the wind was fresh, smelling of wildflowers.

She hadn't brought flowers with her, never did. Brianna had planted a bed right over him, so that as spring warmed the earth, his grave sprang with color and beauty.

Tender buds were just forming on the primroses. The fairy heads of columbine nodded gently among the tender shoots of larkspur and betony. She watched a magpie dart over headstones and sway toward a field. One for sorrow, she thought, and searched the sky fruitlessly for the second that would stand for joy.

Butterflies fluttered nearby, flashing thin, silent wings. She watched them for a time, taking comfort in the color and the movement. There had been no place to bury him near the sea, but this, she thought, this place would have pleased him.

Maggie leaned back comfortably on the side of her father's headstone and closed her eyes.

I wish you were still here, she thought, so I could tell you what I'm doing. Not that I'd listen to any of your advice, mind. But it would be good to hear it.

If Rogan Sweeney's a man of his word—and I can't see how he'd be anything else—I'll be a rich woman. How you'd enjoy that. There'd be enough for you to open your own pub like you always wanted. Oh, what a poor farmer you were, darling. But the best of fathers. The very best.

She was doing her best to keep her promise to him, she thought. To take care of her mother and her sister, and to follow her dream.

"Maggie."

She opened her eyes and looked up at Brianna. Tidy as a pin, she thought, studying her sister. Her lovely hair all scooped up, her clothes neatly pressed. "You look like a schoolteacher," Maggie said, and laughed at Brianna's expression. "A lovely one."

"You look like a ragpicker," Brianna retorted, scowling at Maggie's choice of ripped jeans and a tattered sweater. "A lovely one."

Brianna knelt beside her sister and folded her hands. Not to pray, just for neatness' sake.

They sat in silence for a moment while the wind breathed through the grass and floated through the tumbled stones.

"A lovely day for grave sitting," Maggie commented. He'd have been seventy-one today, she thought. "His flowers are blooming nicely."

"Needs some weeding." And Brianna began to do so. "I found the money on the kitchen counter this morning, Maggie. It's too much."

"It was a good sale. You'll put some of it by."

"I'd rather you enjoyed it."

"I am, knowing you're that much closer to having her out."

Brianna sighed. "She isn't a burden to me." Catching her sister's expression, she shrugged. "Not as much as you think. Only when she's feeling poorly."

"Which is most of the time. Brie, I love you."

"I know you do."

"The money's the best way I know how to show it. Da wanted me to help you with her. And the good Lord knows I couldn't live with her as you do. She'd send me to the madhouse, or I'd send myself to prison by murdering her in her sleep."

"This business with Rogan Sweeney, you did it for her."

"I did not." Maggie bristled at the thought of it. "Because of her, perhaps, which is a different matter altogether. Once she's settled and you have your life back, you'll get married and give me a horde of nieces and nephews."

"You could have your own children."

"I don't want marriage." Comfortable, Maggie closed her eyes again. "No, indeed. I prefer coming and going as it suits me and answering to no one. I'll spoil your children, and they'll come running to Aunt Maggie whenever you're too strict with them." She opened one eye. "You could marry Murphy."

Brianna's laugh carried beautifully over the high grass. "It would shock him to know it."

"He was always sweet on you."

"He was, yes—when I was thirteen. No, he's a lovely man and I'm as fond of him as I would be of a brother. But he's not what I'm looking for in a husband."

"You've got it all planned then?"

"I've nothing planned," Brianna said primly, "and we're getting off the subject. I don't want you to join hands with Mr. Sweeney because you feel obliged to me. I might think it's the best thing you could do for your work, but I won't have you unhappy because you think I am. Because I'm not."

"How many times did you have to serve her a meal in bed this month?"

"I don't keep an accounting—"

"You should," Maggie interrupted. "In any case, it's done. I signed his contracts a week ago. I'm now being managed by Rogan Sweeney and Worldwide Galleries. I'll have a show in his Dublin gallery in two weeks."

"Two weeks. That's so fast."

"He doesn't seem to be a man to waste time. Come with me, Brianna." Maggie grabbed her sister's hands. "We'll make Sweeney pay for a fancy hotel and we'll eat out in restaurants and buy something foolish."

Shops. Food she hadn't cooked herself. A bed that didn't have to be made. Brianna yearned, but only for a moment. "I'd love to be with you, Maggie. But I can't leave her like that."

"The hell you can't. Jesus, she can stand her own company for a few days."

"I can't." Brianna hesitated then sat back wearily on her haunches. "She fell last week."

"Was she hurt?" Maggie's fingers tightened on her sister's. "Damn it, Brie, why didn't you tell me? How did it happen?"

"I didn't tell you because it turned out to be no great matter. She was outside, went out on her own while I was upstairs tidying rooms. Lost her footing, it seems. She bruised her hip, jarred her shoulder."

"You called Dr. Hogan?"

"Of course. I did. He said there was nothing to worry about. She'd lost her balance was all. And if she got more exercise, ate better and all the rest, she'd be stronger."

"Who didn't know that?" Damn the woman, Maggie thought. And damn the constant and incessant guilt that lived in her own heart. "And it's back to bed she went, I'll wager. And has stayed there ever since."

Brianna's lips twitched into a wry smile. "I haven't been able to budge her. She claims she has an inner-ear deficiency and wants to go into Cork to a specialist."

"Hah!" Maggie tossed back her head and glared at the sky. "It's typical. Never have I known anyone with more complaints than Maeve Concannon. And she's got you on a string, my girl." She jabbed a finger at Brianna.

"I won't deny it, but I haven't the heart to cut it."

"I do." Maggie stood, brushed at her knees. "The answer's money, Brie. It's what she's always wanted. God knows she made his life a misery because he couldn't hang on to it." In a gesture of protection, Maggie laid a hand on her father's headstone.

"That's true, and he made hers a misery as well. Two people less suited I've never seen. Marriages aren't always made in heaven, or in hell. Sometimes they're just stuck in purgatory."

"And sometimes people are too foolish or too righteous to walk away." The hand on the headstone stroked once, then dropped away. "I prefer fools to martyrs. Put the money by, Brie. There'll be more coming soon. I'll see to that in Dublin."

"Will you see her before you go?"

"I will," Maggie said grimly.

I think you'll enjoy her." Rogan dipped into the clotted cream for his scone and smiled at his grandmother. "She's an interesting woman."

"Interesting." Christine Rogan Sweeney lifted one sharp white brow. She knew her grandson well, could interpret every nuance of tone and expression. On the subject of Maggie Concannon, however, he was cryptic. "In what way?"

He wasn't sure of that himself and stalled for time by stirring his tea. "She's a brilliant artist; her vision is extraordinary. Yet she lives alone in a little cottage in Clare, and the decor is anything but aesthetically unique. She's passionate about her work, but reluctant to show it. She's by turns charming and rude—and both seem to be true to her nature."

"A contradictory woman."

"Very." He settled back, a man completely content in the gracious parlor, Sèvres cup in his hand, and his head resting against the brocade cushion of a Queen Anne chair. A fire burned quietly in the grate. The flowers and the scones were fresh.

He enjoyed these occasional teas with his grandmother as much as she did. The peace and order of her home were soothing, as was she with her perpetual dignity and softly faded beauty.

He knew she was seventy-three and took personal pride in the fact that she looked ten years younger. Her skin was pale as alabaster. Lined, yes, but the marks of age only added to the serenity of her face. Her eyes were brilliantly blue, her hair as soft and white as a first snowfall.

She had a sharp mind, unquestionable taste, a generous heart and a dry, sometimes biting wit. She was, as Rogan had often told her, his ideal woman.

It was a sentiment that flattered Christine as much as it concerned her.

He had failed her in only one way. That was to find a personal contentment that equalled his professional one.

"How are preparations for the show going?" she asked.

"Very well. It would be easier if our artist of the moment answered her damn phone." He brushed that irritation away. "The pieces that have been shipped in are wonderful. You'll have to come by the gallery and see for yourself."

"I may do that." But she was more interested in the artist than in the art. "Did you say she was a young woman?"

"Hmmm?"

"Maggie Concannon. Did you mention she was young?"

"Oh, middle twenties, I'd expect. Young, certainly, for the scope of her work."

Lord, it was like drawing teeth. "And flashy would you say? Like—what was her name—Miranda Whitfield-Fry, the one who did metal sculpture and wore all the heavy jewelry and colored scarves?"

"She's nothing like Miranda." Thank Christ. He remembered with a shudder how relentlessly, and embarrassingly, the woman had pursued him. "Maggie's more the boots and cotton shirt type. Her hair looks like she had a whack at it with kitchen shears."

"Unattractive then."

"No, very attractive—but in an unusual sense."

"Mannish?"

"No." He recalled, uncomfortably, the vicious sexual tug, the sensual scent of her, the feel of that quick, involuntary tremble under his hand. "Far from it."

Ah. Christine thought. She would definitely make time to meet the woman who put that scowl on Rogan's face. "She intrigues you."

"Certainly, I wouldn't have signed her otherwise." He caught Christine's look and raised a brow in an identical manner. "It's business, Grandmother. Just business."

"Of course." Smiling to herself, she poured him more tea. "Tell me what else you've been up to."

Rogan arrived at the gallery at eight the next morning. He'd enjoyed an evening at the theater, and a late supper with a sometimes companion. As always, he'd found Patricia charming and delightful. The widow of an old friend, she was, to his mind, more of a distant cousin than a date. They'd discussed the Eugene O'Neill play over salmon and champagne and had parted with a platonic kiss at just after midnight.

And he hadn't slept a wink.

It hadn't been Patricia's light laugh or her subtle perfume that had kept him tossing.

Maggie Concannon, he thought. Naturally the woman was in the forefront of his mind, since most of his time and effort was focused on her upcoming show. It was hardly any wonder that he was thinking of her—particularly since it was all but impossible to speak to her.

Her aversion to the phone had caused him to resort to telegrams, which he fired off to the west with blistering regularity.

Her one and only answer had been brief and to the point: Stop nagging.

Imagine, Rogan thought as he unlocked the elegant glass doors of the gallery. She'd accused him of nagging, like some spoiled, whiny child. He was a businessman, for God's sake, one about to give her career an astronomical boost. And she wouldn't even spare the time to pick up the damn phone and have a reasonable conversation.

He was used to artists. Sweet Mary knew he had dealt with their eccentricities, their insecurities, their often childish demands. It was his job to do so, and he considered himself adept. But Maggie Concannon was trying both his skill and his patience.

He relocked the doors behind him and breathed in the quietly scented air of the gallery. Built by his grandfather, the building was lofty and grand, a striking testament to art with its Gothic stonework and carved balusters.

The interior consisted of dozens of rooms, some small, some large, all flowing into the next with wide archways. Stairs curved up fluidly to a second story that housed a ballroom-size space along with intimate parlors fitted with antique sofas.

It was there he would show Maggie's work. In the ballroom he would have a small orchestra. While the guests enjoyed the music, the champagne, the canapes, they could browse among her strategically placed works. The larger, bolder pieces he would highlight, showcasing smaller pieces in more intimate settings.

Imagining it, refining the pictures in his mind, he walked through the lower gallery toward the office and storage rooms.

He found his gallery manager, Joseph Donahoe, pouring coffee in the kitchenette.

"You're here early." Joseph smiled, showing the flash of one gold tooth. "Coffee?"

"Yes. I wanted to check on the progress upstairs before heading into the office."

"Coming right along," Joseph assured him. Though the two men were of an age, Joseph's hair was thinning on top. He compensated for the loss by growing it long enough to tie in a streaming ponytail. His nose had been broken once by a wayward polo mallet and so listed a bit to the left. The result was the look of a pirate in a Savile Row suit.

The women adored him.

"You look a bit washed-out."

"Insomnia," Rogan said, and took his coffee black. "Did yesterday's shipment get unpacked?"

Joseph winced. "I was afraid you'd ask." He lifted his cup and muttered into it. "Hasn't come in."

"What?"

Joseph rolled his eyes. He'd worked for Rogan for more than a decade and knew that tone. "It didn't arrive yesterday. I'm sure it'll be along this morning. That's why I came in early myself."

"What is that woman doing? Her instructions were very specific, very simple. She was to ship the last of the pieces overnight."

"She's an artist, Rogan. She probably got struck by inspiration and worked past the time to post it. We've got plenty of time."

"I won't have her dragging her feet." Incensed, Rogan snapped up the kitchen phone. He didn't have to look up Maggie's number in his address book. He already knew it by heart. He stabbed buttons and listened to the phone ring. And ring. "Irresponsible twit."

Joseph took out a cigarette as Rogan slammed down the receiver. "We have more than thirty pieces," he said as he flicked an ornate enameled lighter. "Even without this last shipment, it's enough. And the work, Rogan. Even a jaded old hand like me is dazzled."

"That's hardly the point, is it?"

Joseph blew out smoke, pursed his lips. "Actually, it is, yes."

"We agreed on forty pieces, not thirty-five, not thirty-six. Forty. And by God, forty is what I'll have."

"Rogan—where are you going?" he called out when Rogan stormed from the kitchen.

"To goddamn Clare."

Joseph took another drag on his cigarette and toasted the air with his coffee cup. "Bon voyage."

The flight was a short one and didn't give Rogan's temper time to cool. The fact that the sky was gloriously blue, the air balmy, didn't change a thing. When he slammed the door on his rental car and headed away from Shannon Airport, he was still cursing Maggie.

By the time he arrived at her cottage, he was at full boil.

The nerve of the woman, he thought as he stalked up to her front door. Pulling him away from his work, from his obligations. Did she think she was the only artist he represented?

He pounded on her door until his fist throbbed. Ignoring manners, he pushed the door open. "Maggie!" he called out, striding from the living room to the kitchen. "Damn you." Without pausing, he stamped through the back door and headed for her workshop.

He should have known she'd be there.

She glanced up from a workbench and a mountain of shredded paper. "Good, I could use some help with this."

"Why the hell don't you answer the bloody phone? Why have the damn thing if you're going to ignore it?"

"I often ask myself the same thing. Pass me that hammer, will you?"

He lifted it from the bench, hefted the weight a moment as the very pleasant image of bopping her on the head with it flitted into his brain. "Where the devil's my shipment?"

"It's right here." She dragged a hand through her untidy hair before taking the hammer from him. "I'm just packing it up."

"It was supposed to be in Dublin yesterday."

"Well, it couldn't be because I hadn't sent it yet." With quick, expert moves, she began to hammer nails into the crate on the floor. "And if you've come all this way to check on it, I have to say you don't have enough to do with your time."

He lifted her off the floor and plunked her down on the workbench. The hammer clanked on concrete, barely missing his foot. Before she'd drawn the breath to spit at him, he caught her chin in his hand.

"I have more than enough to do with my time," he said evenly. "And baby-sitting for an irresponsible, scatterbrained woman interferes with my schedule. I have a staff at the gallery, one whose timetable is carefully, even meticulously thought out. All you had to do was follow instructions and ship the damn merchandise."

She slapped his hand away. "I don't give a tinker's damn about your schedules and timetables. You signed on an artist, Sweeney, not a bleeding clerk."

"And what artistic endeavor prevented you from following a simple direction?"

She bared her teeth, considered punching him, then simply pointed. "That."

He glanced over, froze. Only the blindness of temper could have prevented him from seeing it, being struck dumb by it on entering the building.

The sculpture stood on the far side of the room, fully three feet high, all bleeding colors and twisting, sinuous shapes. A tangle of limbs, surely, he thought, unashamedly sexual, beautifully human. He crossed to it to study it from a different angle.

He could almost, almost make out faces. They seemed to melt into imagination, leaving only the sensation of absolute fulfillment. It was impossible to see where one form began and the other left off, so completely, so perfectly were they merged.

It was, he thought, a celebration of the human spirit and the sexuality of the beast.

"What do you call it?"

"Surrender." She smiled. "It seems you inspired me, Rogan." Whipped by fresh energy, she pushed off the bench. She was light-headed, giddy, and felt glorious. "It took forever to get the colors right. You wouldn't believe what I've remelted and discarded. But I could see it, perfectly, and it had to be exact." She laughed and picked up her hammer to drive another nail. "I don't know when I've slept last. Two days, three." She laughed again, dragging her hands through her tousled hair. "I'm not tired. I feel incredible. Full of desperate energy. I can't seem to stop."

"It's magnificent, Maggie."

"It's the best work I've ever done." She turned to study it again, tapping the hammer against her palm. "Probably the best I'll ever do."

"I'll arrange for a crate." He tossed her a look over his shoulder. She was pale as wax, he noted, with the fatigue her bustling brain had yet to transmit to her body. "And handle the shipping personally."

"I was going to build one. It wouldn't take long."

"You can't be trusted."

"Of course I can." Her mood was so festive, she didn't even take offense. "And it'd be quicker for me to build one than for you to have one built. I already have the dimensions."

"How long?"

"An hour."

He nodded. "I'll use your phone and arrange for a truck. Your phone does work, I assume."

"Sarcasm"—chuckling, she crossed to him—"becomes you. So does that impeccably proper tie."

Before either of them had a chance to think, she grabbed his tie and hauled him toward her. Her warm mouth fixed on his, stunning him into immobility. Her free hand slid into his hair, gripped as her body pressed close. The kiss sizzled, sparked, smoldered. Then as quickly as she had initiated it, she broke away.

"Just a whim," she said, and smiled up at him. Her heart might have been jolting like a rabbit in her chest, but she would think about that later. "Blame it on sleep deprivation and excess energy. Now—"

He snagged her arm before she could turn away. She wouldn't get away so easily, he thought. Wouldn't paralyze him one moment and shrug it off the next.

"I have a whim of my own," he murmured. As he slid a hand around to cup the back of her neck, he watched her eyes register wary surprise. She didn't resist. He thought he saw a hint of amusement on her face before he lowered his mouth to hers.

The amusement faded quickly. This kiss was soft, sweet, sumptuous. As unexpected as rose petals in the blaze of a furnace, it cooled and soothed and aroused all at once. She thought she heard a sound, something between a whimper and a sigh. The fact that it had slipped from her own burning throat amazed her.

But she didn't draw away, not even when the sound came again, quiet and helpless and beguiled. No, she didn't pull away. His mouth was too clever, too gently persuasive. She opened herself to it and absorbed.

She seemed to melt against him, degree by slow degree. That first blast of heat had mellowed, ripened into a low, long burn. He forgot that he'd been angry, or that he'd been challenged, and knew only that he was alive.

She tasted dark, dangerous, and his mouth was full of her. His mind veered toward taking, toward conquering, toward ravishing. The civilized man in him, the one who had been raised to follow a strict code of ethics, stepped back, appalled.

Her head reeled. She placed a hand down on the workbench for balance as her legs buckled. One long breath followed by another helped clear her vision. And she saw him staring at her, a mixture of hunger and shock in his eyes.

"Well," she managed, "that's certainly something to think about."

It was foolish to apologize for his thoughts, Rogan told himself. Ridiculous to blame himself for the fact that his imagination had drawn erotic and vivid pictures of throwing her to the floor and tearing away flannel and denim. He hadn't acted on it. He'd only kissed her.

But he thought it was possible, even preferable, to blame her.

"We have a business relationship," he began tersely. "It would be unwise and possibly destructive to let anything interfere with that at this point."

She cocked her head, rocked back on her heels. "And sleeping together would confuse things?"

Curse her for making him sound like a fool. Curse her twice for leaving him shaken and horribly, horribly needy. "At this point I think we should concentrate on launching your show."

"Hmmm." She turned away on the pretext of tidying the workbench. In truth she needed a moment to settle herself. She wasn't promiscuous by any means, and certainly didn't tumble into bed with every man who attracted her. But she liked to think of herself as independent enough, liberated enough and smart enough to choose her lovers with care.

She had, she realized, chosen Rogan Sweeney.

"Why did you kiss me?"

"You annoyed me."

Her wide, generous mouth curved. "Since I seem to be doing that on a regular basis, we'll be spending a lot of time with our lips locked."

"It's a matter of control." He knew he sounded stiff and prim, and hated her for it.

"I'm sure you have just buckets of it. I don't." She tossed her head, folded her arms over her chest. "If I decide I want you, what are you going to do about it? Fight me off?"

"I doubt it'll come to that." The image brought on twinges of humor and desperation. "We both need to concentrate on the business at hand. This could be the turning point in your career."

"Yes." It would be wise to remember that, she thought. "So we'll use each other, professionally."

"We'll *enhance* each other, professionally," he corrected. Christ, he needed air. "I'll go in and call for that truck."

"Rogan." She waited until he reached the door and turned back to her. "I'd like to go with you."

"To Dublin? Today?"

"Yes. I can be ready to go by the time the truck arrives. I only need to make one stop, at my sister's."

She was as good as her word. Even as the shipment chugged away she was tossing a suitcase into the back of Rogan's rented car.

"If you'd just give me ten minutes," she said as Rogan started down the narrow lane, "I'm sure Brie has some tea or coffee on."

"Fine." He stopped the car by Blackthorn and went with Maggie up the walk.

She didn't knock, but stepped inside and headed straight toward the kitchen in the back. Brianna was there, a white bib apron tied at her waist and her hands coated with flour.

"Oh, Mr. Sweeney, hello. Maggie. You'll have to excuse the mess. We have guests and I'm making pies for dinner."

"I'm leaving for Dublin."

"So soon?" Brianna picked up a tea towel to dust off her hands. "I thought the show was next week."

"It is. I'm going early. Is she in her room?"

Brianna's polite smile strained a bit at the edges. "Yes. Why don't I go tell her you're here?"

"I'll tell her myself. Perhaps you could give Rogan some coffee."

"Of course." She cast one worried look at Maggie as her sister walked out of the kitchen into the adjoining apartment. "If you'll make yourself comfortable in the parlor, Mr. Sweeney, I'll bring you some coffee right away."

"Don't trouble." His curiosity was up. "I'll have a cup right here, if I won't be in your way." He added an easy smile. "And please, call me Rogan."

"You have it black as I recall."

"You have a good memory." And you're a bundle of nerves, he observed, watching Brianna reach for a cup and saucer.

"I try to remember the preferences of my guests. Would you have some cake? It's a bit of chocolate I made yesterday."

"The memory of your cooking makes it difficult to refuse." He took a seat at the scrubbed wood table. "You do it all yourself?"

"Yes, I . . ." She heard the first raised voice and fumbled. "I do. I've a fire laid in the parlor. Are you sure you wouldn't be more comfortable?"

The clash of voices from the next room rose, bringing a flush of embarrassment to Brianna's cheeks. Rogan merely lifted his cup. "Who's she shouting at this time?"

Brianna managed a smile. "Our mother. They don't get on very well."

"Does Maggie get along with anyone?"

"Only when it suits her. But she has a heart, a wonderful, generous heart. It's only that she guards it so carefully." Brianna sighed. If Rogan wasn't embarrassed by the shouting, neither would she be. "I'll cut you that cake."

"You never change." Maeve stared at her older child through narrowed eyes. "Just like your father."

"If you think that's an insult to me, you're wrong."

Maeve sniffed and brushed at the lace cuffs of her bed gown. The years and her own dissatisfactions had stolen the beauty of her face. It was puffy and pale, with lines dug deeply around the pursed mouth. Her hair, once as golden as sunlight, had faded to gray and was scraped back ruthlessly into a tight bun.

She was plumped onto a mountain of pillows, her Bible at one hand and a box of chocolates at the other. The television across the room murmured low.

"So, it's Dublin, is it? Brianna told me you were going off. Frittering money away on hotels, I imagine."

"It's my money."

"Oh, and you won't let me forget it." Bitterness reared as Maeve pushed up in bed. For her whole life, someone else had held the purse strings, her parents, her husband, and now, most demeaning of all, her own daughter. "To think of all he tossed away on you, buying you glass, sending you off to that foreign country. And for what? So you could play at being an artist and superior to the rest of us."

"He tossed nothing away on me. He gave me the chance to learn."

"While I stayed on the farm, working my fingers to the bone."

"You never worked a blessed day in your life. It was Brianna who did it all while you took to your bed with one ailment after another."

"Do you think I enjoy being delicate?"

"Oh, aye," Maggie said with relish. "I think you revel in it."

"It's my cross to bear." Maeve picked up her Bible, pressed it to her chest like a shield. She had paid for her sin, she thought. A hundred times over she had paid for it. Yet if forgiveness had come, comfort had not. "That and an ungrateful child."

"What am I supposed to be grateful for? The fact that you complained every day of your life? That you made your dissatisfaction for my father and your disappointment in me clear with every word, every look."

"I gave birth to you!" Maeve shouted. "I nearly died giving you life. And because I carried you in my womb, I married a man who didn't love me, and who I didn't love. I sacrificed everything for you."

"Sacrificed?" Maggie said wearily. "What sacrifices have you made?"

Maeve cloaked herself in the bitter rage of her pride. "More than you know. And my reward was to have children who have no love for me."

"Do you think because you got pregnant and married to give me a name, I should overlook everything you've done? Everything you haven't done?" Like love me even a little, Maggie thought, and ruthlessly pushed the ache away. "It was you on your back, Mother. I was the result, not the cause."

"How dare you speak to me that way?" Maeve's face flushed hot, her fingers dug into the blankets. "You never had any respect, any kindness, any compassion."

"No." Because her eyes were stinging, Maggie's voice was sharp as a whip. "And it's that lack I inherited from you. I only came today to tell you that you won't run Brie ragged while I'm gone. If I find you have, I'll stop the allowance."

"You'd take food out of my mouth?"

Maggie leaned over to tap the box of chocolates. "Yes. Be sure of it."

"Honor thy father and thy mother." Maeve hugged the Bible close. "You're breaking a commandment, Margaret Mary, and sending your soul to hell."

"Then I'll give up my place in heaven rather than live a hypocrite on earth."

"Margaret Mary!" Maeve shouted when Maggie had reached the door. "You'll never amount to anything. You're just like him. God's curse is on you, Maggie, for being conceived outside the sacrament of marriage."

"I saw no sacrament of marriage in my house," Maggie tossed back. "Only the agony of it. And if there was a sin in my conception, it wasn't mine."

She slammed the door behind her, then leaned back against it a moment to steady herself.

It was always the same, she thought. They could never be in the same room together without hurling insults. She had known, since she was twelve, why her mother disliked her, condemned her. Her very existence was the reason Maeve's life had turned from dream to harsh reality.

A loveless marriage, a seven-month baby and a farm without a farmer.

It was *that* her mother had thrown in her face when Maggie had reached puberty.

It was *that* they had never forgiven each other for.

Straightening her shoulders, she walked back into the kitchen. She didn't know her eyes were still angry and overbright or her face pale. She walked to her sister and kissed her briskly on the cheek.

"I'll call you from Dublin."

"Maggie." There was too much to say, and nothing to say. Brianna only squeezed her hands. "I wish I could be there for you."

"You could if you wished it enough. Rogan, are you ready?"

"Yes." He rose. "Good-bye, Brianna. Thank you."

"I'll just walk you—" Brianna broke off when her mother called out.

"Go see to her," Maggie said, and walked quickly out of the house. She was yanking at the door of Rogan's car when he laid a hand on her shoulder.

"Are you all right?"

"No, but I don't want to talk about it." With a final tug, she jerked the door open and climbed inside.

He hurried around the hood and slipped onto the driver's seat. "Maggie—"

"Don't say anything. Anything at all. There's nothing you can do or say to change what's always been. Just drive the car and leave me alone. It would be a great favor to me." She began to weep then, passionately, bitterly, while he struggled with the urge to comfort her and the wish to comply with her request.

In the end, he drove, saying nothing, but holding her hand. They were nearing the airport when her sobs died and her tensed fingers went limp. Glancing over, he saw she was sleeping.

She didn't awaken when he carried her inside his company jet, or when he settled her in a seat. Nor did she awaken all through the flight as he watched her. And wondered.

SIX

Maggie awoke in the dark. The only thing she was certain of in those first groggy minutes was that she wasn't in her own bed. The scent of the sheets, the texture of them was wrong. She didn't have to sleep on fine linen habitually to recognize the difference, or to notice the faint, restful scent of verbena that clung to the pillowslip in which she'd buried her face.

As an uncomfortable thought zeroed into her brain, she stretched out a cautious hand to make certain she was the only occupant of the bed. The mattress flowed on, a veritable lake of smooth sheets and cozy blankets. An empty lake, thank Jesus, she thought, and rolled over to the center of the bed.

Her last clear memory was of crying herself empty in Rogan's car, and the hollow feeling that had left her drifting like a broken reed in a stream.

A good purge, she decided, for she felt incredibly better—steady and rested and clean.

It was tempting to luxuriate in the soft dark on soft sheets with soft scents. But she decided she'd best find out where she was and how she'd arrived. After sliding her way over to the edge of the bed, she groped around the smooth wood of the night table, eased her fingers over and up until she located a lamp and its switch.

The light was gently shaded, a warm golden hue that subtly illuminated a large bedroom with coffered ceiling, dainty rosebud wallpaper and the bed itself, a massive four-poster.

The veritable queen of beds, she thought with a smile. A pity she'd been too tired to appreciate it.

The fireplace across the room was unlit, but scrubbed clean as a new coin and set for kindling. Long-stemmed pink roses, fresh as a summer morning, stood in a Waterford vase on a majestic bureau along with a silver brush set and gorgeous little colored bottles with fancy stoppers.

The mirror above it reflected Maggie, rumpled and heavy-eyed among the sheets.

You look a bit out of place, my girl, she decided, and grinning, tugged on the sleeve of her cotton nightshirt. Someone, it seemed, had had the good sense to change her before dumping her into the royal bed.

A maid perhaps, or Rogan himself. It hardly mattered, she thought practically, since the deed was done and she'd certainly benefited from it. In all likelihood, her clothes were gracing the carved rosewood armoire. As out of place there, she decided with a chuckle, as she was in the glorious lake of smooth linen sheets.

If she was in a hotel, it was certainly the finest that had ever had her patronage. She scrambled up, stumbled toward the closet door over a deep-piled Aubusson.

The bath was as sumptuous as the bedroom, all gleaming rose and ivory tiles, a huge tub fashioned for lounging and a separate shower constructed from a wavy glass block. With a sigh of pure greed, she stripped off her nightshirt and turned on the spray.

It was heaven, the hot water beating on the back of her neck, her shoulders, like the firm fingers of an expert masseuse. A far cry from the stingy trickle her own shower managed at home. The soap smelled of lemon and glided over her skin like silk.

She saw with some amusement that her few meager toiletries had been set out on the generous counter by the shell-shaped pink sinks. Her robe, such as it was, hung on a brass hook beside the door.

Well, someone was taking care of her, she realized, and at the moment she could find no cause for complaint.

After a steamy fifteen minutes while the water ran hot, she reached for one of the thick towels folded over a warming bar. It was big enough to wrap her from breast to calf.

She combed her wet hair back from her face, made use of the cream in a crystal decanter, then exchanged the towel for her tattered flannel robe.

Barefoot and curious, she set out to explore.

Her room was off a long wide hall. Low lights tossed shadows over the gleaming floor and its regal red runner. She heard not a sound as she wandered toward the stairs that curved graciously up to another story, and down. She chose down, letting her fingers play along the polished railing.

Quite obviously she wasn't a guest in a luxury hotel, but in a private home. Rogan's home, she concluded, with an envious glance at the art that graced the foyer and main hall. The man had a Van Gogh and a Matisse, she realized as her mouth watered.

She found the front parlor, with its wide windows open to the balmy night, a sitting room, its chairs and sofas arranged in conversation groupings. Across the hall was what she supposed would be called the music room, as it was dominated by a grand piano and a gilded harp.

Beautiful it all was, with enough artwork to keep Maggie entranced for days. But at the moment she had another priority.

She wondered how long she would have to search before she found the kitchen.

The light under a door drew her closer. When she looked in, she saw Rogan seated behind a desk, papers arranged in tidy piles before him. It was a two-level room, with his desk on the first and steps leading up to a small sitting area. The walls were lined with books.

Acres of them, she thought at a glance, in a room smelling of leather and beeswax. The room was done in burgundies and dark woods that suited the man as much as it suited the literature.

She watched him, interested in the way he scanned the page in front of him, made quick, decisive notes. He was, for the first time in their acquaintance, without a suit coat or tie. He'd been wearing them, certainly, she mused, but now his collar was unbuttoned, the sleeves of his crisp shirt rolled up to the elbows.

His hair, glinting darkly in the lamplight, was a bit mussed. As if he'd run his hands impatiently through it while he worked. Even as she watched he did so again, raking the fingers through, scowling a bit.

Whatever he was working on absorbed him, for he worked in a steady, undistracted rhythm that was, in some odd way, fascinating.

He wasn't a man to let his mind wander, she thought. Whatever he chose to do, he would do with the utmost concentration and skill.

She remembered the way he had kissed her. Concentration and skill indeed.

Rogan read the next clause in the proposal and frowned. The wording wasn't quite right. A modification . . . He paused, considered, crossed out a phrase and reworded it. The expansion of his factory in Limerick was crucial to his game plan, and needed to be implemented before the end of the year.

Hundreds of jobs would be created, and with the construction of moderate-income apartments that a subsidiary of Worldwide was planning, hundreds of families would have homes as well.

One branch of the business would feed directly into the other, he thought. It would be a small but important contribution to keeping the Irish—sadly, his country's biggest export—in Ireland.

His mind circled around the next clause, had nearly zeroed in, when he caught himself drifting. Something pulled at his brain, distracting it from the business at hand. Rogan glanced toward the doorway and saw it was not some*thing,* but some*one.*

He must have sensed her standing there, barefoot and sleepy-eyed in a ratty gray robe. Her hair was slicked back, shining red fire, in a style that should have been severe but instead was striking.

Unadorned and fresh-scrubbed, her face was like ivory with a blush of rose beneath. Her lashes were spiked with damp around her slumberous eyes.

His reaction was swift and brutal and human. Even as the heat blasted through him he checked it, ruthlessly.

"Sorry to interrupt." She flashed him a quick, cheeky smile that tortured his already active libido. "I was looking for the kitchen. I'm half-starved."

"It's hardly a wonder." He was forced to clear his throat. Her voice was husky, as sleepily sexy as her eyes. "When did you eat last?"

"I'm not certain." Leaning lazily on the doorjamb, she yawned. "Yesterday, I think. I'm still a bit foggy."

"No, you slept yesterday. All of yesterday—from the time we left your sister's—and all of today."

"Oh." She shrugged. "What time is it?"

"Just past eight—Tuesday."

"Well." She walked into the room and curled up in a big leather chair across from his desk, as if she'd been joining him there for years.

"Do you often sleep for thirty-odd hours straight?"

"Only when I've been up too long." She stretched her arms high to work out kinks she was just beginning to feel. "Sometimes a piece grabs you by the throat and it won't let you go until you've finished."

Resolutely, he shifted his gaze from the flesh the fall of her robe had revealed, and looked down blindly at the paperwork before him. He was appalled that he would react like some hormone-mad teenager. "It's dangerous, in your line of work."

"No, because you're not tired. You're almost unbearably alert. When you've simply worked too long, you lose the edge. You have to stop, rest. This is different. And when I'm done, I fall down and stay down until I've slept it off." She smiled again. "The kitchen, Rogan? I'm ravenous."

Instead of an answer, he reached for the phone and punched in a number. "Miss Concannon is awake," he said. "She'd like a meal. In the library, please."

"That's grand," she said when he replaced the receiver. "But I could have scrambled myself some eggs and saved your staff the bother."

"They're paid to bother."

"Of course." Her voice was dry as dust. "How smug you must be to have round-the-clock servants." She waved a hand before he could answer. "Best we don't get into that on an empty stomach. Tell me, Rogan, how exactly did I come to be in that big bed upstairs?"

"I put you there."

"Did you now?" If he was hoping for a blush or stutter, he'd be disappointed. "I'll have to thank you."

"You slept like a stone. At one point I nearly held a mirror up to your lips to be certain you were alive." She was certainly alive now, vibrant in the lamplight. "Do you want a brandy?"

"Better not, before I've eaten."

He rose, went to a sideboard and poured a single snifter from a decanter. "You were upset before we left."

She cocked her head. "Now, that's a fine and diplomatic way of phrasing it." The weeping spell didn't embarrass her. It was simply emotion, passion, as real and as human as laughter or lust. But she remembered that he had held her hand and had offered no useless words to stem the storm. "I'm sorry if I made you uncomfortable."

She had, miserably, but he shrugged it off. "You didn't want to talk about it."

"Didn't, and don't." She took a quiet breath because her voice had been sharp. He didn't deserve such rudeness after his kindness. "It's nothing to do with you, Rogan, just old family miseries. Since I'm feeling mellow, I'll tell you it was comforting to have you hold my hand. I didn't think you were the type to offer."

His eyes flicked back to hers. "It seems to me we don't know each other well enough to generalize."

"I've always considered myself a quick and accurate judge, but you may be right. So tell me"—she propped an elbow on the arm of the chair, cocked her chin on her fist—"who are you, Rogan Sweeney?"

He was relieved when the need to answer was postponed by the arrival of her dinner. A tidy, uniformed maid wheeled in a tray, settling it in front of Maggie with no more than a whisper of sound and a jingle of silverware. She bobbed once when Maggie thanked her, then disappeared the moment Rogan told her that would be all.

"Ah, what a scent." Maggie attacked the soup first, a rich, thick broth swimming with chunks of vegetables. "Do you want some?"

"No, I've eaten." Rather than go back around the desk, he sat in the chair beside hers. It was oddly cozy, he realized, to sit with her while she ate and the house seemed to settle quietly around them. "Since you're back among the living, perhaps you'd like to go by the gallery in the morning."

"Umm." She nodded, her mouth full of crusty roll. "When?"

"Eight—I have appointments midmorning, but I can take you in and leave a car at your disposal."

"A car at my disposal." Tickled, she pressed a fist to her mouth as she laughed. "Oh, I could get used to that quick enough. And what would I do with the car at my disposal?"

"What you like." God knew why her reaction annoyed him, but it did. "Or you can wander around Dublin on foot, if you prefer."

"A bit touchy this evening, are we?" She moved from the soup to the entrée of honeyed chicken. "Your cook's a treasure, Rogan. Do you think I can charm this recipe out of him—or her—for Brie?"

"Him," Rogan said. "And you're welcome to try. He's French, insolent and given to tantrums."

"Then we have all but nationality in common. Tell me, will I be moving to a hotel tomorrow?"

He'd thought about that, a great deal. It would certainly be more comfortable for him if she were tucked away in a suite at the Westbury. More comfortable, he thought, and much more dull. "You're welcome to stay in the guest room if it suits you."

"It suits me down to the ground." She studied him as she speared a tiny new potato. He looked relaxed here, she realized. Very much the complacent king of the castle. "Is it just you in this big house?"

"It is." He lifted a brow. "Does that worry you?"

"Worry me? Oh, you mean because you might come knocking on my door one lustful night?" She chuckled, infuriating him. "I'm able to say yes or no, Rogan, the same as you would be if I came knocking on yours. I only asked because it seems a lot of room for one man."

"It's my family home," he said stiffly. "I've lived here all my life."

"And a fine place it is." She pushed the tray back and rose to go to the small sideboard. Lifting the top of a decanter, she sniffed. Sighed at the fine scent of Irish whiskey. After pouring herself a glass, she came back and curled up her legs. *"Slainte,"* she said, and tossed the whiskey back. It set a good, strong fire kindling in her gut.

"Would you like another?"

"One'll do me. One warms the soul, two warms the brain, my father often said. I'm in the mood for a cool head." She set the empty glass on the tray, shifted her body more comfortably. Her frayed flannel robe slid open at the curve of her knee. "You haven't answered my question."

"Which was?"

"Who are you?"

"I'm a businessman, as you remind me with regularity." He settled back, making a determined effort not to let his mind or his gaze wander to her bare legs. "Third generation. Born and bred in Dublin, with love and respect for art nurtured in me from the cradle."

"And that love and respect was augmented by the idea of making a profit."

"Precisely." He swirled his brandy, sipped, and looked exactly like what he was. A man comfortable with his own wealth and content with his life. "While making a profit brings its own sense of satisfaction, there's another, more spiritual satisfaction that comes from developing and promoting a new artist. Particularly one you believe in passionately."

Maggie touched her tongue to her top lip. He was entirely too confident, she decided, much too sure of himself and his place in the world. All that tidy certainty begged for a bit of shaking.

"So, I'm here to satisfy you, Rogan?"

He met her amused eyes, nodded. "I have no doubt you will, Maggie, eventually. On every level."

"Eventually." She hadn't meant, really, to steer them onto this boggy ground, but it seemed irresistible, sitting with him in the quiet room with her body so rested, her mind so alert. "Your choice of time and place, then?"

"It's traditional, I believe, for the man to choose when to advance."

"Hah!" Bristling, she leaned over to jab a finger in his chest. Any thoughts she'd had of easing into romance vanished like smoke. "Stuff your traditions in your hat and wear it well. I don't cater to them. You might be interested to know that as we approach the twenty-first century, women are doing their own choosing. The fact is we've been doing so since time began, those of us sharp enough, and men are just catching on to it." She plopped back in her chair. "I'll have you, Rogan, in my time, and in my place."

It baffled him why such an incredible statement should both arouse him and make him uneasy. "Your father was right, Maggie, about you getting the brass. You have it to spare."

"And what of it? Oh, I know your type." Contempt colored her tone. "You like a woman to sit quietly by, mooning a bit, catering to your whims, to be sure, and hoping, while her romantic heart beats desperately in her breast, that you'll look twice in her direction. She'll be proper as a saint in public, never a sour word slipping through her rosy lips. Then, of course, when you've decided on that time and that place, she's to transform herself into a veritable tiger, indulging your most prurient fantasies until the lights switch on again and she turns into a doorstop."

Rogan waited to be sure she'd run down, then hid a smile in his brandy. "That sums it up amazingly well."

"Jackass."

"Shrew," he said pleasantly. "Would you care for some dessert?"

The chuckle tickled her throat, so she set it free. Who would have thought she'd actually come to like him? "No, damn you. I'll not drag that poor maid away again from her television or her flirtation with the butler or however she spends her evenings."

"My butler is seventy-six, and well safe from flirtations with a maid."

"A lot you know." Maggie rose again and wandered toward a wall of books. Alphabetized by author, she noted, and nearly snorted. She should have known. "What's her name?"

"Whose?"

"The maid's."

"You want to know my maid's name?"

Maggie stroked a finger down a volume of James Joyce. "No, I want to see if *you* know your maid's name. It's a test."

He opened his mouth, closed it again, grateful that Maggie's back was to him. What difference did it make if he knew the name of one of his maids? Colleen? Maureen? Hell! The domestic staff was his butler's domain. Bridgit? No, damn it, it was . . .

"Nancy." He thought—was nearly certain. "She's fairly new. I believe she's been here about five months. Would you like me to call her back in for an introduction?"

"No." Casually, Maggie moved from Joyce to Keats. "It was a curiosity to me, that's all. Tell me, Rogan, do you have anything in here other than classics? You know, a good murder mystery I might pass some time with?"

His library of first editions was considered one of the finest in the country, and she was criticizing it for lacking a potboiler. With an effort, he schooled his temper and his voice. "I believe you'll find some of Dame Agatha's work."

"The British." She shrugged. "Not bloodthirsty enough as a rule—unless they're sacking castles like those damn Cromwellians. What's this?" She bent down, peered. "This Dante's in Italian."

"I believe it is."

"Can you read it, or is it just for show?"

"I can fumble through it well enough."

She passed by it, hoping for something more contemporary. "I didn't pick up as much of the language as I should have in Venice. Plenty of slang, little of the socially correct." She glanced over her shoulder and grinned. "Artists are a colorful lot in any country."

"So I've noticed." He rose and crossed to another shelf of books. "This might be more what you're looking for." He offered Maggie a copy of Thomas Harris's *Red Dragon.* "I believe several people are murdered horribly."

"Wonderful." She tucked the book under her arm. "I'll say good night then so you can get back to work. I'm grateful for the bed and the meal."

"You're welcome." He sat behind his desk again, lifted a pen and ran it through his fingers while he watched her. "I'd like to leave at eight sharp. The dining room's down this hall and to the left. Breakfast will be served anytime after six."

"I can guarantee it won't be served to me at that hour, but I'll be ready at eight." On impulse she crossed to him, placed her hands on the arms of his chair and leaned her face close to his. "You know, Rogan, we're precisely what each other doesn't need or want—on a personal level."

"I couldn't agree more. On a personal level." Her skin, soft and white where the flannel parted at her throat, smelled like sin.

"And that's why, to my way of thinking, we're going to have such a fascinating relationship. Barely any common ground at all, wouldn't you say?"

"No more than a toehold." His gaze lowered to her mouth, lingered, rose to hers again. "A shaky one at that."

"I like dangerous climbs." She leaned forward a little more, just an inch, and nipped his bottom lip with her teeth.

A spear of fire arrowed straight to his loins. "I prefer having my feet on the ground."

"I know." She leaned back again, leaving him with a tingle on his lips and the heat in his gut. "We'll try it your way first. Good night."

She strolled out of the room without looking back. Rogan waited until he was certain she was well away before he lifted his hands and scrubbed them over his face.

Good Christ, the woman was tying him into knots, slippery tangled knots of pure lust. He didn't believe on acting on lust alone, at least not since his adolescence. He was, after all, a civilized man, one of taste and breeding.

He respected women, admired them. Certainly he'd developed relationships that had culminated in bed, but he'd always tried to wait until the relationships had developed before making love. Reasonably, mutually and discreetly. He wasn't an animal to be driven by instinct alone.

He wasn't even certain he liked Maggie Concannon as a person. So what kind of man would he be if he did what he was burning to do at this moment? If he stalked up those stairs, threw open the door to her bedroom and ravished her good and proper.

A satisfied man, he thought with grim humor.

At least until morning when he had to face her, and himself, and the business they had to complete.

Perhaps it was more difficult to take the high road. Perhaps he would suffer, as he was damn well certain she expected him to. But when the time came for him to take her to bed, he would have the upper hand.

That, most certainly, was worth something.

Even, he thought as he shoved papers aside, a miserably sleepless night.

Maggie slept like a baby. Despite the images evoked by the novel Rogan had given her, she'd dropped off to sleep just after midnight and had slept dreamlessly until nearly seven.

Flushed with energy and anticipation, she searched out the dining room and was pleased to see a full Irish breakfast warming on the sideboard.

"Good morning, miss." The same maid who had served her the night before scurried in from the kitchen. "Is there anything I can get for you?"

"Thank you, no. I can serve myself." Maggie picked up a plate from the table and moved toward the tempting scents on the sideboard.

"Shall I pour you coffee or tea, miss?"

"Tea would be lovely." Maggie took the lid off a silver warmer and sniffed appreciately at the thick rashers of bacon. "Nancy, is it?"

"No, miss, it's Noreen."

Failed that test, Squire Sweeney, Maggie mused. "Would you tell the cook, Noreen, that I've never had a better meal than my dinner last night."

"I'd be happy to, miss."

Maggie moved from server to server, heaping her plate. She often skipped meals altogether, so indifferent was her own cooking. But when food was available in such quantity, and food of such quality, she made up for it.

"Will Mr. Sweeney be joining me for breakfast?" she asked as she carried her plate back to the table.

"He's already eaten, miss. Mr. Sweeney breakfasts every day at half-six, precisely."

"A creature of habit, is he?" Maggie winked at the maid and slathered fresh jam on her warmed toast.

"He is, yes," Noreen answered, flushing a bit. "I'm to remind you, miss, he'll be ready to leave at eight."

"Thank you, Noreen, I'll keep it in mind."

"You've only to ring if you need anything."

Quiet as a mouse, Noreen faded back into the kitchen. Maggie applied herself to a breakfast she felt was fit for a queen and perused the copy of the *Irish Times* that had been neatly folded beside her plate.

A cozy way to live, she supposed, with servants only the snap of a finger away. But didn't it drive Rogan mad to know they were always about the house? That he was never alone?

The very idea made her wince. She'd go mad for sure, Maggie decided, without solitude. She looked over the room with its dark and glossy wainscoting, the glitter from the twin crystal chandeliers, the gleam from the silver on the antique sideboard, the sparkle of china and Waterford glass.

Yes, even in this lush setting, she'd go stark, raving mad.

She lingered over a second cup of tea, read the paper from back to front and cleaned every crumb from her plate. From somewhere in the house a clock chimed the hour. She debated having just one more serving of bacon, called herself a glutton and resisted.

She took a few moments to study the art on the walls. There was a watercolor she found particularly exquisite. Taking a last, leisurely turn around the room, she started out, down the hall.

Rogan stood in the foyer, immaculate in a gray suit and navy tie. He studied her, studied his watch. "You're late."

"Am I?"

"It's eight past the hour."

She lifted her brows, saw he was serious and dutifully muffled a chuckle. "I should be flogged."

He skimmed a gaze up her, from the half boots and dark leggings to the mannish white shirt that reached to midthigh and was cinched with two leather belts. Glittering translucent stones swung at her ears, and she had, for once, added a touch of makeup. She hadn't, however, bothered with a watch.

"If you don't wear a timepiece, how can you be on time?"

"You've a point there. Perhaps that's why I don't."

Still watching her, he took out a pad and his pen.

"What are you doing?"

"Noting down that we have to supply you with a watch, as well as a phone-answering machine and a calendar."

"That's very generous of you, Rogan." She waited until he opened the door and gestured her out. "Why?"

"The watch so you'll be prompt. The answering machine so I'll at least be able to leave a damn message when you ignore the phone, and the calendar so you'll know what the bloody day is when I request a shipment."

He'd bitten off the last word as if it were stringy meat, Maggie thought. "Since you're in such a bright and cheerful mood this morning, I'll risk telling you that none of those things will change me a whit. I'm irresponsible, Rogan. You've only to ask what's left of my family." She turned around, ignoring his hiss of impatience, and studied his house.

It overlooked a lovely, shady green—St. Stephen's, she was to learn later—and stood proudly, a trifle haughtily, against a dreamy blue sky.

Though the stone was aged, the lines were as graceful as a young woman's body. It was a combination of dignity and elegance Maggie knew only the rich could afford. Every window, of which there were many, glistened like diamonds in the sun. The lawn, smooth and green, gave way to a lovely front garden, tidy as a church and twice as formal.

"A pretty spot you have here. I missed it, you know, on my way in."

"I'm aware of that. You'll have to wait for the tour, Margaret Mary. I don't like to be late." He took her arm and all but dragged her to the waiting car.

"Do you get docked for tardiness, then?" She laughed when he said nothing, and settled back to enjoy the ride. "Are you by nature surly of a morning, Rogan?"

"I'm not surly," he snapped at her. Or he wouldn't be, he thought, if he'd gotten above two hours' sleep. And the responsibility for that, damn all women, fell solidly on her head. "I have a lot to accomplish today."

"Oh, to be sure. Empires to build, fortunes to win."

That did it. He didn't know why, but the light undertone of disdain broke the last link on control. He swerved to the side of the road, causing the driver who had been cruising behind him to blast rudely on his horn. Grabbing Maggie by the collar, he hauled her half out of her seat and crushed his mouth to hers.

She hadn't been expecting quite that reaction. But that didn't mean she couldn't enjoy it. She could meet him on even ground when he wasn't quite so controlled, quite so skillful. Her head might have spun, but the sensation of power remained. No seduction here, only raw needs, rubbing together like live wires and threatening to flare.

He dragged her head back and plundered her mouth. Just once, he promised himself. Only once to relieve some of this vicious tension that coiled inside him like a snake.

But kissing her didn't relieve it. Instead, the complete and eager response of her, the total verve of it, wrapped his tension only tighter until he couldn't breathe.

For a moment he felt as though he were being sucked into some velvet-lined, airless tunnel. And he was terrified that he'd never want or need light again.

He jerked away, fastened his hands like vises on the wheel. He eased back onto the road like a drunk trying to negotiate a straight line.

"I'm assuming that was an answer to something." Her voice was unnaturally quiet. It wasn't his kiss that had unnerved her nearly as much as the way he had ended it.

"It was that or throttle you."

"I prefer being kissed to strangled. Still, I'd like it better if you weren't angry about wanting me."

He was calmer now, concentrating on the road and making up the time she'd cost him that morning. "I explained myself before. The timing's inappropriate."

"Inappropriate. And who's in charge of propriety?"

"I prefer knowing whom I'm sleeping with. Having some mutual affection and respect."

Her eyes narrowed. "There's a long way between a kiss on the lips and a tumble in the sheets, Sweeney. I'll have you know I'm not one to leap onto the mattress at the blink of an eye."

"I never said—"

"Oh, didn't you, now?" She was all the more insulted because she knew how quickly she would have leaped onto a mattress with him. "As far as I can see, you've decided I'm plenty loose enough. Well, I won't be explaining my past history to you. And as for affection and respect, you've yet to earn them from me, boy-o."

"Fine, then. We're agreed."

"We're agreed you can go straight to hell. And your maid's name is Noreen."

That distracted him enough to have him taking his eyes off the road and staring. "What?"

"Your maid, you dolt, you narrow-nosed aristocrat. 'Tisn't Nancy. It's Noreen." Maggie folded her arms and stared resolutely out the side window.

Rogan only shook his head. "I'm grateful to you for clearing that up. God knows what an embarrassment it would have been to me if I'd had to introduce her to the neighbors."

"Blue-blooded snob," she muttered.

"Wasp-tongued viper."

They settled into an angry silence for the rest of the drive.

SEVEN

It was impossible not to be impressed by Worldwide Gallery, Dublin. The architecture alone was worth a visit to the place. Indeed, photographs of the building had appeared in dozens of magazines and art books around the world as a shining example of the Georgian style that was part of Dublin's architectural legacy.

Though Maggie had seen it reproduced in glossy pages, the sight of it, the sheer grandeur of it in three dimensions, took her breath away.

She'd spent hours of her free time during her apprenticeship in Venice haunting galleries. But nothing compared in splendor with Rogan's.

Yet she made no comment at all while he unlocked the imposing-looking front doors and gestured her inside.

She had to resist the urge to genuflect, such was the churchlike quiet, the play of light, the scented air in the main room. The Native American display was beautifully and carefully mounted—the pottery bowls, the gorgeous baskets, the ritual masks, shaman rattles and beadwork. On the walls were drawings at once primitive and sophisticated. Maggie's attention and her admiration focused on a buckskin dress the color of cream, adorned with beads and smooth, bright stones. Rogan had ordered it hung like a tapestry. Maggie's fingers itched to touch.

"Impressive" was all she said.

"I'm delighted you approve."

"I've never seen American Indian work outside of books and such." She leaned over a water vessel.

"That's precisely why I wanted to bring the display to Ireland. We too often focus on European history and culture and forget there's more to the world."

"Hard to believe people who could create this would be the savages we see in those old John Wayne movies. Then again"—she smiled as she straightened—"my ancestors were savage enough, stripping naked and painting themselves blue before they screamed into battle. I come from that." She tilted her head to study him, the perfectly polished businessman. "We both do."

"One could say that such tendencies become more diluted in some than in others over the centuries. I haven't had the urge to paint myself blue in years."

She laughed, but he was already checking his watch again.

"We're using the second floor for your work." He started toward the stairs.

"For any particular reason?"

"For several particular reasons." Impatience shimmering like a wave of heat around him, he paused until she joined him on the staircase. "I prefer a show like this to have some sense of a social occasion. People tend to appreciate art, at least feel it's more accessible, if they're relaxed and enjoying themselves." He stopped at the top of the steps, lifting a brow at her expression. "You've a problem with that?"

"I'd like people to take my work seriously, not think of it as a party favor."

"I assure you, they'll take it seriously." Particularly with the prices he'd decided to demand for it, the strategy he intended to employ. "And the marketing of your work is, after all, my province." He turned, sliding open double pocket doors, then stepped back so that Maggie could enter first.

She quite simply lost her voice. The wonderfully enormous room was flooded with light from the domed central skylight above. It poured down over the dark, polished floor and tossed back stunning reflections, almost mirrorlike, of the work Rogan had chosen to display.

In all of her dreams, in her wildest and most secret hopes, she'd never imagined that her work would be showcased so sensitively, or so grandly.

Thick-based pedestals of creamy white marble stood around the room, lifting the glass to eye level. Rogan had chosen only twelve pieces to grace the lofty space. A canny move, she realized, as it made each piece seem all the more unique. And there, in the center of the room, glistening like ice heated by a core of fire, was Maggie's *Surrender.*

There was a dull ache in her heart as she studied the sculpture. Someone would buy it, she knew. Within days someone would pay the price Rogan was asking and steal it completely and finally from her life.

The price of wanting more, she thought, seemed to be the loss of what you already had. Or perhaps of what you were.

When she said nothing, only walked through the room with her boots echoing, Rogan stuck his hands in his pockets. "The smaller pieces are displayed in what we call the upper sitting rooms. It's a more intimate space." He paused, waiting for some response, then hissed through his teeth when he received none. Damn the woman, he thought. What did she want? "We'll have an orchestra at the show. Strings. And champagne and canapés, of course."

"Of course," Maggie managed. She kept her back to him, wondering why she should stand in such a magnificent room and want to weep.

"I'll ask you to attend, at least for a short time. You needn't do or say anything that would compromise your artistic integrity."

Her heart was beating much too loudly for her to catch his tone of annoyance. "It looks . . ." She couldn't think of a word. Simply couldn't. "Fine," she said lamely. "It all looks fine."

"Fine?"

"Yes." She turned back, sober-eyed and, for the first time in recent memory, terrified. "You have a nice aesthetic sense."

"A nice aesthetic sense," he repeated, amazed at her tepid response. "Well, Margaret Mary, I'm so gratified. It's only taken three incredibly difficult weeks and the combined efforts of more than a dozen highly qualified people to make everything look 'fine.' "

She ran an unsteady hand through her hair. Couldn't he see she was speechless, that she was completely out of her realm and scared as a rabbit faced by a hound? "What do you want me to say? I've done my job and given you the art. You've done yours and utilized it. We're both to be congratulated, Rogan. Now perhaps I should look about in your more intimate rooms."

He stepped forward, blocking her path as she started for the doorway. The fury that rose up in him was so molten, so intense, he was surprised it didn't melt her glass into puddles of shine and color.

"You ungrateful peasant."

"A peasant, am I?" Emotions swirled inside her, contradictory and frightening. "You're right enough on that, Sweeney. And if I'm ungrateful because I don't fall at your feet and kiss your boots, then it's ungrateful I'll stay. I don't want or expect any more from you than what it said in your cursed contracts with your bloody exclusive clauses, and you'll get no more from me."

She could feel the hot tears boiling up, ready to erupt. She was certain that if she didn't get out of the room quickly, her lungs would quite simply collapse from the strain. In her desperation to escape, she shoved at him.

"I'll tell you what I expect." He snagged her shoulder, whirled her around. "And what I'll have."

"I beg your pardon," Joseph said from the doorway. "I seem to be interrupting."

He couldn't have been more amused, or more fascinated, as he watched his coolheaded boss spit fire and rage at the small, dangerous-eyed woman whose fists had already raised as if for a bout.

"Not at all." Using every ounce of willpower, Rogan released Maggie's arm and stepped back. In the wink of an eye, he had gone from fury to calmness. "Miss Concannon and I were just discussing the terms of our contract. Maggie Concannon, Joseph Donahoe, the curator of this gallery."

"A pleasure." All charm, Joseph stepped forward to take Maggie's hand. Though it trembled a bit, he kissed it lavishly, dashingly, and set his gold tooth flashing with a grin. "A pure pleasure, Miss Concannon, to meet the person behind the genius."

"And a pleasure for me, Mr. Donahoe, to meet a man so sensitive to art, and to the artist."

"I'll be leaving Maggie in your capable hands, Joseph. I have appointments."

"You'll be doing me an honor, Rogan." Joseph's eyes twinkled as he kept Maggie's hand lightly in his.

The gesture wasn't lost on Rogan, nor was the fact that Maggie made no move to break the contact. She was, in fact, smiling up at Joseph flirtatiously.

"You've only to tell Joseph when you require the car," Rogan said stiffly. "The driver's at your disposal."

"Thank you, Rogan," she said without looking at him. "But I'm sure Joseph can keep me entertained for some time."

"There's no way I'd rather spend the day," Joseph quickly put in. "Have you seen the sitting rooms, Miss Concannon?"

"I haven't, no. You'll call me Maggie, I hope."

"I will." His hand still linked with hers, Joseph drew her through the doorway. "I believe you'll appreciate what we've done here. With the showing only days away, we want to be certain you're happy. Any suggestions you have will be most welcomed."

"That'll be a change." Maggie paused, glanced over her shoulder to where Rogan remained standing. "Don't let us keep you from your business, Rogan. I'm sure it's pressing." With a toss of her head, she beamed at Joseph. "I know a Francis Donahoe, from near Ennis. A merchant he is, with the same look around the eyes as you. Would you be related?"

"I've cousins in Clare, on my father's side, and my mother's. They'd be Ryans."

"I know scores of Ryans. Oh." She stopped, sighed as she stepped through an archway into a tidy little room complete with fireplace and love seat. Several of her smaller pieces, including the one Rogan had bought at their first meeting, graced the antique tables.

"An elegant setting, I think." Joseph moved inside to switch on the recessed lighting. The glass jumped into life under the beams, seemed to pulse. "The ballroom makes a breathless statement. This, a delicate one."

"Yes." She sighed again. "Do you mind if I sit a moment, Joseph? For the truth is I have lost my breath." She settled on the love seat and closed her eyes. "Once when I was a child, my father bought a billy goat, with some idea of breeding. I was in the field with it one morning, paying it no mind, and it got its dander up. Butted me hard, he did, and sent me flying. I felt just that way when I stepped into that other room. As if something had butted me hard and sent me flying."

"Nervous, are you?"

She opened her eyes and saw the understanding in Joseph's. "I'm frightened to death. And damned if I'll let himself know it. He's so damned cocksure, isn't he?"

"He's confident, our Rogan. And with reason enough. He's got an uncanny sense for buying the right piece, or patronizing the right artist." A curious man, and one who enjoyed a good gossip, Joseph made himself comfortable beside her. He stretched out his legs, crossed them at the ankle in a posture inviting relaxation and confidence. "I noticed the two of you were butting heads, so to speak, when I interrupted."

"We don't seem to have a lot of common ground." Maggie smiled a little. "He's pushy, our Rogan."

"True enough, but usually in such a subtle way one doesn't know one's been pushed."

Maggie hissed through her teeth, "He hasn't been subtle with me."

"I noticed. Interesting. You know, Maggie, I don't think I'd be giving away any corporate secrets if I told you Rogan was determined to sign you with Worldwide. I've worked for him for more than ten years, and never recall seeing him more focused on a single artist."

"And I should be flattered." She sighed and closed her eyes again. "I am, most of the time, when I'm not busy being infuriated with his bossy ways. Always prince to peasant."

"He's used to having things his way."

"Well, he won't be having me his way." She opened her eyes and rose. "Will you show me the rest of the gallery?"

"I'd be happy to. And perhaps you'll tell me the story of your life."

Maggie cocked her head and studied him. A mischief maker, she thought, with his dreamy eyes and piratical demeaner. She'd always enjoyed a mischief-making friend. "All right, then," she said, and linked her arm through his as they strolled through the next archway. "There once was a farmer who wanted to be a poet. . . ."

There were just too damn many people in Dublin for Maggie's taste. You could hardly take a step without bumping into someone. It was a pretty city, she couldn't deny it, with its lovely bay and spearing steeples. She could admire the magnificence of its architecture, all the red brick and gray stone, the charm of its colorful storefronts.

She was told by her driver, Brian Duggin, that the early Dubliners had a sense of order and beauty as keen as their sense of profit. And so, she thought, the city suited Rogan even as he suited it.

She settled back in the quiet car to admire the dazzling front gardens and copper cupolas, the shady greens and the busy River Liffey, which split the city in two.

She felt her pulse quicken to the pace around her, respond to the crowds and the hurry. But the bustle excited her only briefly before it exhausted. The sheer number of people on O'Connell Street, where everyone seemed to be in a desperate rush to get somewhere else, made her yearn for the lazy, quiet roads of the west.

Still, she found the view from O'Connell Bridge spectacular, the ships moored at the quays, the majestic dome of the Four Courts glinting in the sun. Her driver seemed happy enough to obey her request simply to cruise, or to pull over and wait while she walked through parks and squares.

She stopped on Grafton Street among the smart shops and bought a pin for Brianna, a simple silver crescent with a curve of garnets. It would, Maggie thought as she tucked the box in her purse, suit her sister's traditional taste.

For herself, she mooned briefly over a pair of earrings, long twists of gold and silver and copper, accented top and bottom with fire opals. She had no business spending good money on such frivolous baubles. No business at all, she reminded herself, when she had no real guarantee when she might sell another piece.

So, of course, she bought the earrings, and sent her budget to the devil.

To round off her day, she visited museums, wandered along the river and had tea in a tiny shop off FitzWilliam Square. She spent her last hour watching the sunlight and reflections from Half Penny Bridge and sketching in a pad she'd picked up in an art store.

It was after seven when she returned to Rogan's house. He came out of the front parlor and stopped her before she'd reached the stairs.

"I'd begun to wonder if you'd had Duggin drive you all the way back to Clare."

"I thought of it once or twice." She pushed back her untidy hair. "It's been years since I've visited Dublin." She thought of the juggler she'd seen, and of course, of her father. "I'd forgotten how noisy it is."

"I assume you haven't eaten."

"I haven't, no." If she didn't count the biscuit she'd had with her tea.

"Dinner's ordered for seven-thirty, but I can have it put back until eight if you'd like to join us for cocktails."

"Us?"

"My grandmother. She's anxious to meet you."

"Oh." Maggie's mood plummeted. Someone else to meet, to talk to, to be with. "I wouldn't want to hold you up."

"It's not a problem. If you'd like to change, we'll be in the parlor."

"Change for what?" Resigned, she tucked her sketchbook under her arm. "I'm afraid I left all my formal attire at home. But if my appearance embarrasses you, I can have a tray in my room."

"Don't put words in my mouth, Maggie." Taking her firmly by the arm, Rogan steered her into the parlor. "Grandmother." He addressed the woman sitting regally in the high back brocaded chair. "I'd like you to meet Margaret Mary Concannon. Maggie, Christine Sweeney."

"An absolute delight." Christine offered a fine-boned hand, accented with one gleaming sapphire. Matching ones dripped from her ears. "I take full credit for you being here, my dear, as I bought the first piece of your work that intrigued Rogan."

"Thank you. You're a collector, then?"

"It's in the blood. Please sit. Rogan, get the child something to drink."

Rogan moved to the glittering decanters. "What would you like, Maggie?"

"Whatever you're having." Resigned to being polite for an hour or two, Maggie set her sketchpad and purse aside.

"It must be thrilling to be having your first major show," Christine began. Why, the girl was striking, she thought. All cream and fire, as eye-catching in a shirt and tights as dozens of women would attempt to be in diamonds and silks.

"To be honest, Mrs. Sweeney, it's hard for me to imagine it." She accepted the glass from Rogan and hoped its contents would be enough to brace her for an evening of making conversation.

"Tell me what you thought of the gallery."

"It's wonderful. A cathedral to art."

"Oh." Christine reached out again, squeezing Maggie's hand. "How my Michael would have loved to hear you say that. It's exactly what he wanted. He was a frustrated artist, you know."

"No." Maggie slanted Rogan a glance. "I didn't."

"He wanted to paint. He had the vision, but not the aptitude. So he created the atmosphere and the means to celebrate others who did." Christine's smoky silk suit rustled as she sat back. "He was a wonderful man. Rogan takes after him, in looks and temperament."

"That must make you very proud."

"It does. As I'm sure what you've done with your life has made your family proud of you."

"I don't know as pride's quite the word." Maggie sipped her drink, discovered Rogan had served her sherry and struggled not to grimace. Fortunately, the butler came to the doorway at that moment to announce dinner.

"Well, that's handy." Grateful, Maggie set her glass aside. "I'm starved."

"Then we'll go straight in." Rogan offered his grandmother his arm. "Julien is delighted you're enjoying his cuisine."

"Oh, he's a fine cook, that's the truth. I wouldn't have the heart to tell him I'm such a poor one myself I'll eat anything I don't have to prepare."

"We won't mention it." Rogan drew out a chair for Christine, then for Maggie.

"We won't," Maggie agreed. "Since I've decided to try to barter some of Brie's recipes for his."

"Brie is Maggie's sister," Rogan explained as the soup course was served. "She runs a B-and-B in Clare, and from personal experience, I can attest that her cuisine is excellent."

"So, your sister's an artist in the kitchen rather than the studio."

"She is," Maggie agreed, finding herself much more comfortable in Christine Sweeney's company than she'd expected to be. "It's a magic touch Brianna has with hearth and home."

"In Clare, you say." Christine nodded as Rogan offered her wine. "I know the area well. I come from Galway myself."

"You do?" Surprise and pleasure flitted across Maggie's face. It was another reminder to her of how much she missed home. "What part?"

"Galway City. My father was in shipping. I met Michael through his business deals with my father."

"My own grandmother—on my mother's side—came from Galway." Though under most circumstances, Maggie would rather eat than talk, she was enjoying the combination of excellent food and conversation. "She lived there until she married. That would be about sixty years ago. She was a merchant's daughter."

"Is that so. And her name?"

"She was Sharon Feeney before her marriage."

"Sharon Feeney." Christine's eyes brightened, as deep now and as sparkling as her sapphires. "Daughter of Colin and Mary Feeney?"

"Aye. You knew her, then?"

"Oh, I did. We lived minutes from each other. I was a bit younger than she, but we spent time together." Christine winked at Maggie, then looked at Rogan to draw him into the conversation. "I was madly in love with Maggie's great-uncle Niall, and used Sharon shamelessly to be around him."

"Surely you needed to use nothing and no one to get any man's attention," Rogan said.

"Oh, you've a sweet tongue." Christine laughed and patted his hand. "Mind yourself around this one, Maggie."

"He doesn't waste much sugar on me."

"It dissolves in vinegar," Rogan retorted in the most pleasant of tones.

Deciding to ignore him, Maggie turned back to Christine. "I haven't seen my uncle in years, but I've heard he was a fine, handsome man in his youth, and had a way with the ladies."

"He was, and he did." Christine laughed again, and the sound was young and gay. "I spent many a night dreaming of Niall Feeney when I was a girl. The truth is"—she turned her brilliant eyes on Rogan, and there was a hint of mischief in them that Maggie admired—"if Michael hadn't come along and swept me off my feet, I'd have fought to the death to marry Niall. Interesting, isn't it? You two might have been cousins had things worked out differently."

Rogan glanced at Maggie, lifted his wine. Horrifying was all he could think. Absolutely horrifying.

Maggie snickered and polished off her soup. "Niall Feeney never married, you know, and lives a bachelor's life in Galway. Perhaps, Mrs. Sweeney, you broke his heart."

"I'd like to think so." The bone-deep beauty so evident in Christine Sweeney's face was enhanced by a flattering blush. "But the sad truth is, Niall never noticed me."

"Was he blind, then?" Rogan asked, and earned a beaming smile from his grandmother.

"Not blind." Maggie sighed at the scents as the fish course was set before her. "But a man perhaps more foolish than most."

"And never married, you say?" Christine's inquiry, Rogan noted with a slight frown, was perhaps just a tad too casual.

"Never. My sister corresponds with him." A wicked twinkle gleamed in Maggie's eye. "I'll have her mention you in her next letter. We'll see if his memory's better than his youthful judgment."

Though her smile was a bit dreamy, Christine shook her head. "Fifty-five years it's been since I left Galway for Dublin, and for Michael. Sweet Mary."

The thought of the passing years brought a pleasant sadness, the same she might have felt on watching a ship sail out of port. She still missed her husband, though he'd been gone for more than a dozen years. In an automatic gesture Maggie found touching, Christine laid a hand over Rogan's.

"Sharon married a hotelier, did she not?"

"She did, yes, and was widowed for the last ten years of her life."

"I'm sorry. But she had her daughter to comfort her."

"My mother. But I don't know as she was a comfort." The dregs of bitterness interfered with the delicate flavor of the trout in Maggie's mouth. She washed them away with wine.

"We wrote for several years after Sharon married. She was very proud of her girl. Maeve, isn't it?"

"Aye." Maggie tried to envision her mother as a girl, and failed.

"A lovely child, Sharon told me, with striking golden hair. The temper of a devil, she would say, and the voice of an angel."

Maggie swallowed hurriedly, gaped. "The voice of an angel? My mother?"

"Why, yes. Sharon said she sang like a saint and wanted to be a professional. I believe she was, at least for a time." Christine paused, thinking, while Maggie simply stared. "Yes, I know she was. In fact she came up to Gort to sing, but I couldn't get down to see her. I had some clippings Sharon sent me, must have been thirty years past." She smiled, curious. "She no longer sings?"

"No." Maggie let out a quiet baffled breath. She had never heard her mother raise her voice in anything other than complaint or criticism. A singer? A professional, with a voice like an angel? Surely they must be speaking of different people.

"Well," Christine went on, "I imagine she was happy raising her family."

Happy? That was surely a different Maeve Feeney Concannon than had raised her. "I suppose," Maggie said slowly, "she made her choice."

"As we all do. Sharon made hers when she married and moved from Galway. I must say I missed her sorely, but she loved her Johnny, and her hotel."

With an effort, Maggie put thoughts of her mother aside. She would have to pick through them later, carefully. "I remember Gran's hotel from childhood. We worked there one summer, Brie and I, as girls. Tidying and fetching. I didn't take to it."

"A fortunate thing for the art world."

Maggie acknowledged Rogan's compliment. "Perhaps, but it was certainly a relief to me."

"I've never asked you how you became interested in glass."

"My father's mother had a vase—Venetian glass it was, flute-shaped, of pale, hazy green. The color of leaves in bud. I thought it was the most beautiful thing I'd ever seen. She told me it had been made with breath and fire." Maggie smiled at the memory, lost herself in it a moment, so that her eyes became as hazy as the vase she described. "It was like a fairy tale to me. Using breath and fire to create something you could hold in your hand. So she brought me a book that had pictures of a glass house, the workers, the pipes, the furnaces. I think from that moment there was nothing else I wanted to do but make my own."

"Rogan was the same," Christine murmured. "So sure at such a young age of what his life would be." She let her gaze wander from Maggie to her grandson and back. "And now you've found each other."

"So it would seem," Rogan agreed, and rang for the next course.

EIGHT

Maggie couldn't stay away from the gallery. There seemed to be no reason to. Joseph and the rest of the staff were welcoming enough, even going so far as asking for her opinion on some of the displays.

However much it might have pleased her, she couldn't improve on Rogan's eye for detail and placement. She left the staff to carry out his orders and set herself up unobtrusively to sketch the Native American artwork.

It fascinated her—the baskets and headdresses, the meticulous beading, the intricacies of the ritual masks. Ideas and visions leaped around in her head like gazelles, bounding, soaring, so that she rushed to transfer them to paper.

She preferred burying herself in work to everything else. Whenever she took too much time to think, her mind veered back to what Christine had told her about Maeve. Just how much, she'd wondered, was beneath the surface of her parents' lives that she'd been ignorant of? Her mother with a career, her father loving some other woman. And the two of them trapped—because of her—in a prison that had denied them their deepest wishes.

She needed to find out more, and yet she was afraid, afraid that whatever she learned would only further demonstrate the fact that she hadn't really known the people who had created her. Hadn't known them at all.

So she put that need aside and haunted the gallery.

When no one objected, she used Rogan's office as a temporary studio. The light was good, and as the room was tucked away in the back of the building, she was rarely disturbed. Roomy, it was not. Obviously Rogan had elected to utilize every space he could find for the showing of art.

She couldn't argue with that decision.

She covered his gleaming walnut desk with a sheet of plastic and thick pads of newspaper. The charcoal-and-pencil sketches she had made were only a start. She worked now by adding splashes of color. She'd picked up a few acrylics in a shop near the gallery, but often her impatience with the imperfections of her materials caused her to use other materials at hand, and she would dip her brush into coffee dregs or dampened ashes, or stroke bolder lines with lipstick or eyebrow pencils.

She considered her sketches merely a first step. While she believed herself an adequate enough draftsman, Maggie would never have termed herself a master with brush and paint. This was only a way to keep her vision alive from conception to execution. The fact that Rogan had arranged for several of her sketches to be matted and hung for the show embarrassed her more than pleased her.

Still, she reminded herself that people would buy anything if they were made to believe in its quality and value.

She'd become a cynic, she thought, narrowing her eyes as she studied her work. And a bean counter as well, tallying up profits before they were made. God help her, she'd been caught up in the gossamer dream Rogan had spun, and she'd hate herself, even more than she would hate him, if she went back home a failure.

Did failure run in her blood? she wondered. Would she be like her father and fail to achieve the goal that mattered most to her? She was so intent on her work, and on her darkening thoughts, that she hissed in surprise and annoyance as the office door opened.

"Out! Out! Do I have to lock the damn thing?"

"My thoughts exactly." Rogan closed the door at his back. "What the hell are you doing?"

"An experiment in nuclear physics," she snapped back. "What does it look like?" Frustrated by the interruption, she blew her choppy bangs out of her eyes and glared. "What are you doing here?"

"I believe this gallery, which includes this office, belongs to me."

"There's no forgetting that." Maggie dipped her brush in a mixture of paint she'd daubed on an old board. "Not with the first words out of everyone's mouth around here being Mr. Sweeney this and Mr. Sweeney that." Inspired by this little verbal foray, she washed color over the thick paper she'd tacked to another board.

As she did so his gaze dropped from her face to her hands, and for a moment he was struck speechless. "What in sweet hell are you about?" Dumbfounded, he lunged forward. His priceless and well-loved desk was covered with paint-splattered newspapers, jars of brushes, pencils and—unless he had very much mistaken the sharp smell—bottles of turpentine. "You're a madwoman. Do you realize this desk is a George II?"

"It's a sturdy piece," she responded, with no respect for the dead English king. "You're in my light." Distracted, she waved a paint-flecked hand at him. He avoided it out of instinct. "And well protected," she added. "I've a sheet of plastic under the newspaper."

"Oh well, that makes it all right, then." He grabbed a handful of her hair and tugged ruthlessly. "If you'd wanted a bloody easel," he said when they were nose to nose, "I'd have provided you with one."

"I don't need an easel, only a bit of privacy. So if you'd make yourself scarce, as you've done brilliantly for the past two days—" She gave him a helpful shove. They both looked down at the bold red smudges she'd transferred to his pinstriped lapel.

"Oops," she said.

"Idiot." His eyes narrowed into dangerous cobalt slits when she chuckled.

"I'm sorry. Truly." But the apology was diluted by a strangled laugh. "I'm messy when I work, and I forgot about my hands. But from what I've seen, you've a warehouse full of suits. You won't be missing this one."

"You think not." Quick as a snake, he dipped his fingers in paint and smeared it over her face. Her squeal of surprise was intensely satisfying. "The color becomes you."

She swiped the back of her hand over her cheek and spread the paint around. "So you want to play, do you?" Laughing, she snatched up a tube of canary yellow.

"If you dare," he said, torn between anger and amusement, "I'll make you eat it, tube and all."

"A Concannon never ignores a challenge." Her grin spread as she prepared to squeeze. Retaliation on both sides was interrupted as the office door opened.

"Rogan, I hope you're not—" The elegant woman in the Chanel suit broke off, pale blue eyes widening. "I beg your pardon." Obviously baffled, she smoothed back her soft swing of sable hair. "I didn't know you were . . . engaged."

"Your interruption's timely." Cool as a spring breeze, Rogan ripped a sheet of newspaper and rubbed at the paint on his fingertips. "I believe we were about to make fools of ourselves."

Perhaps, Maggie thought, setting aside the tube of paint with a ridiculous sense of regret. But it would have been fun.

"Patricia Hennessy, I'd like to present Margaret Mary Concannon, our featured artist."

This? Patricia thought, though her fragile, well-bred features revealed nothing but polite interest. This paint-smeared, wild-haired woman was M. M. Concannon? "How lovely to meet you."

"And you, Miss Hennessy."

"It's missus," Patricia told her with the faintest of smiles. "But please call me Patricia."

Like a single rose behind glass, Maggie thought, Patricia Hennessy was lovely, delicate and perfect. And, she mused, studying the elegant oval face, unhappy. "I'll be out of your way in a moment or two. I'm sure you want to talk to Rogan alone."

"Please don't hurry on my account." Patricia's smile curved her lips but barely touched her eyes. "I've just been upstairs with Joseph, admiring your work. You have an incredible talent."

"Thank you." Maggie snatched Rogan's handkerchief from his breast pocket.

"Don't—" The order died on his lips as she soaked the Irish linen in turpentine. With something resembling a snarl, he took it back and scrubbed the rest of the paint from his hands. "My office seems to have been temporarily transformed into an artist's garret."

"Sure and I've never worked in a garret in me life," Maggie announced, deliberately broadening her brogue. "I've annoyed himself by disturbing sacred ground here, don't you know. If you've been acquainted with Rogan long, you'll understand he's a finicky man."

"I'm not finicky," he said between his teeth.

"Oh, of course not," Maggie responded with a roll of the eyes. "A wild man he is, as unpredictable as the colors of a sunrise."

"A sense of organization and control is not generally considered a flaw. A complete lack of it normally is."

They'd turned toward each other again, effectively, if unintentionally, closing Patricia out, even in the small room. There was tension in the air, and it was obvious to Patricia. She couldn't forget the time when he had desired her keenly. She couldn't forget it because she was in love with Rogan Sweeney.

"I'm sorry if I've come at a bad time." She hated the fact that her voice was stiff with formality.

"Not at all." Rogan's scowl was easily transformed into a charming smile as he turned to her. "It's always a delight to see you."

"I just dropped in thinking you might be done with business for the day. The Carneys invited me for drinks and hoped you could join us."

"I'm sorry, Patricia." Rogan looked down at his ruined handkerchief, then dropped it onto the spread-out sheets of newspaper. "With the show tomorrow, I've dozens of details yet to see to."

"Nonsense." Maggie shot Rogan a wide grin. "I wouldn't want to interfere with your social hour."

"It's not your fault—I've simply other obligations. Give my apologies to Marion and George."

"I will." Patricia offered her cheek for Rogan to kiss. The scent of turpentine clashed with, then overwhelmed, her delicate floral perfume. "It was nice to meet you, Miss Concannon. I'm looking forward to tomorrow night."

"It's Maggie," she said, with a warmth that came from innate female understanding. "And thank you. We'll hope for the best. Good day to you, Patricia." Maggie hummed to herself as she cleaned her brushes. "She's lovely," she commented after Patricia left. "Old friend?"

"That's right."

"Old married friend."

He only lifted a brow at the implication. "An old widowed friend."

"Ah."

"A very significant response." For reasons he couldn't fathom, he became defensive. "I've known Patricia for more than fifteen years."

"My, you're a slow one, Sweeney." Propping a hip on the desk, Maggie tapped a pencil to her lips. "A beautiful woman, of obvious taste—a woman of your own class, I may add, and in fifteen years you haven't made a move."

"A move?" His tone iced like frost on glass. "A particularly unattractive phrase, but ignoring your infelicitous phrasing for the moment, how do you know I haven't?"

"Such things show." With a shrug, Maggie eased off the desk. "Intimate relationships and platonic ones give off entirely different signals." Her look softened. He was, after all, only a man. "I'll wager you think you're terribly good friends."

"Naturally I do."

"You dolt." She felt a rush of sympathy for Patricia. "She's more than half in love with you."

The idea, and the casually confident way Maggie presented it, took him aback. "That's absurd."

"The only thing absurd about it is that you haven't a clue." Briskly, she began to gather her supplies. "Mrs. Hennessy has my sympathy—or part of it. Hard for me to offer it all when I'm interested in you myself, and I don't fancy the idea of you popping from her bed to mine."

She was, he thought, exasperated, the damnedest woman. "This is a ridiculous conversation, and I have a great deal of work to do."

It was rather endearing, the way his voice could go so grandly formal. "On my account at that, so I shouldn't be holding you up. I'll spread these drawings out in the kitchen to dry, if that's all right with you."

"As long as they're out of my way." And their creator with them, he thought. He made the mistake of glancing down, focusing. "What have you done here?"

"Made a bit of a mess, as you've already pointed out, but it'll tidy quick enough."

Without a word, he picked up one of her drawings by the edges. He could see clearly what had inspired her, how she meant to employ the Native American art and turn it into something boldly and uniquely her own.

No matter how much or how often she exasperated him, he was struck time and again by her talent.

"You haven't been wasting time, I see."

"It's one of the little things we have in common. Do you want to tell me what you think?"

"That you understand pride and beauty very well."

"A good compliment, Rogan." She smiled over it. "A very good one."

"Your work exposes you, Maggie, and makes you all the more confusing. Sensitive and arrogant, compassionate, pitiless. Sensual and aloof."

"If you're saying I'm moody, I won't argue." The tug came again, quick and painful. She wondered if there would come a time when he would look at her the way he looked at her work. And what they would create between them when, and if, he did. "It's not a flaw to me."

"It only makes you difficult to live with."

"No one has to but myself." She lifted a hand, disconcerting him by stroking it down his cheek. "I'm thinking of sleeping with you, Rogan, and we both know it. But I'm not your proper Mrs. Hennessy, looking for a husband to guide the way."

He curled his fingers around her wrist, surprised and darkly pleased when her pulse bumped unsteadily. "What are you looking for?"

She should have had the answer. It should have been on the tip of her tongue. But she'd lost it somewhere between the question and the hard, fast stroke of her own heart. "I'll let you know when I find out." She leaned forward, rising on her toes to brush her mouth over his. "But that does fine for now."

She took the painting from him and gathered up others.

"Margaret Mary," he said as she started for the door. "I'd wash that paint from my face if I were you."

She twitched her nose, looked cross-eyed down at the red smear. "Bloody hell," she muttered, and slammed the door on her way out.

The parting shot may have soothed his pride, but he wasn't steady and bitterly resented that she could turn him inside out with so little effort. There was simply no time for the complications she could cause in his personal life. If there were time, he would simply drag her off to some quiet room and empty all of this frustration, this lust, this maddening hunger, into her until he was purged of it.

Surely once he'd taken control of her, or at least of the situation, he'd find his balance again.

But there were priorities, and his first, by legal contract and moral obligation, was to her art.

He glanced down at one of the paintings she'd left behind. It looked hurriedly executed, carelessly brilliant, with quick strokes and bold colors demanding attention.

Like the artist herself, he mused, it simply wouldn't be ignored.

Deliberately he turned his back on it and started out. But the image remained, teasing his brain just as the taste of her remained, teasing his senses.

"Mr. Sweeney. Sir."

Rogan stopped in the main room, bit back a sigh. The thin, grizzled-looking man standing there, clutching a ragged portfolio, was no stranger.

"Aiman." He greeted the roughly dressed man as politely as he would have a silk-draped client. "You haven't been in for a while."

"I've been working." A nervous tic worked around Aiman's left eye. "I've a lot of new work, Mr. Sweeney."

Perhaps he had been working, Rogan mused. He'd most certainly been drinking. The signs were all there in the flushed cheeks, the red-rimmed eyes, the trembling hands. Aiman was barely thirty, but drink had made him old, frail and desperate.

He stayed just inside the door, off to the side, so that visitors to the gallery wouldn't be distracted by him. His eyes pleaded with Rogan. His fingers curled and uncurled on the old cardboard portfolio.

"I was hoping you'd have time to look, Mr. Sweeney."

"I've a show tomorrow, Aiman. A large one."

"I know. I saw it in the paper." Nervously, Aiman licked his lips. He'd spent the last of the money he'd earned from sidewalk sales in the pub the night before. He knew it was crazy. Worse, he knew it was stupid. Now he desperately needed a hundred pounds for rent or he'd be out on the street within the week. "I could leave them with you, Mr. Sweeney. Come back on Monday. I've—I've done some good work here. I wanted you to be the first to see it."

Rogan didn't ask if Aiman was out of money. The answer was obvious and the question would only have humiliated the man. He had shown promise once, Rogan remembered, before fears and whiskey had leveled him.

"My office is a bit disrupted at the moment," Rogan said kindly. "Come upstairs and show me what you've done."

"Thank you." Aiman's bloodshot eyes brightened with a smile, with hope as pathetic as tears. "Thank you, Mr. Sweeney. I won't take up much of your time. I promise you."

"I was about to have a bit of tea." Unobtrusively, Rogan took Aiman's arm to steady him as they started upstairs. "You'll join me while we look over your work?"

"I'd be pleased to, Mr. Sweeney."

Maggie eased back so that Rogan wouldn't see her watching as he took the curve of the stairs. She'd been certain, absolutely certain, that he would boot the scruffy artist out the door. Or, she mused, have one of his underlings do his dirty work for him. Instead he'd invited the man to tea and had led him upstairs like a welcomed guest.

Who would have thought Rogan Sweeney had such kindness in him?

He'd buy some of the paintings as well, she realized. Enough so that the artist could keep his pride, and a meal or two in his belly. The gesture was more impressive to her, more important than a dozen of the grants and donations she imagined Worldwide made annually.

He cared. The realization shamed her even as it pleased her. He cared as much about the very human hands that created art as he did the art itself.

She went back into his office to tidy, and to try to assimilate this new aspect of Rogan with all the others.

Twenty-four hours later, Maggie sat on the edge of her bed in Rogan's guest room. She had her head between her knees and was cursing herself for being vilely ill. It was humiliating to admit, even to herself, that nerves could rule her. But there was no denying it, with the nasty taste of sickness still in her throat and her body shivering with the chills.

It won't matter, she told herself again. It won't matter a whit what they think. What I think is what counts.

Oh God, oh God, why did I let myself be pulled into this?

On long, careful breaths, she raised her head. The wave of dizziness slapped her, made her grit her teeth. In the cheval glass across the room, her image shot back at her.

She was wearing nothing but her underwear, and her skin was shockingly white against the lacy black she'd chosen. Her face was pasty-looking, her eyes red-rimmed. A shuddering moan escaped her as she lowered her head again.

A fine mess she looked. And it was nothing but a spectacle she was going to make of herself. She'd been happy in Clare, hadn't she? It was there she belonged, alone and unfettered. Just herself and her glass, with the quiet fields and the morning mists. It was there she would be if it hadn't been for Rogan Sweeney and all his fancy words tempting her away.

He was the devil, she thought, conveniently forgetting that she'd begun to change her mind about him. A monster he was, who preyed on innocent artists for his own greedy ends. He would squeeze her dry, then cast her aside like an empty tube of paint.

She would have murdered him if she'd had the strength to stand.

When the knock came softly at her door, she squeezed her eyes shut. Go away, she shouted in her mind. Go away and leave me to die in peace.

It came again, followed by a quiet inquiry. "Maggie, dear, are you nearly ready?"

Mrs. Sweeney. Maggie pressed the heels of her hands to her gritty eyes and bit back a scream. "No, I'm not." She fought to make her voice curt and decisive, but it came out in a whimper. "I'm not going at all."

With a swish of silk, Christine slipped into the room. "Oh, sweetheart." Instantly maternal, she hurried to Maggie and draped an arm over her shoulders. "It's all right, darling. It's just nerves."

"I'm fine." But Maggie abandoned pride and turned her face into Christine's shoulder. "I'm just not going."

"Of course you are." Briskly, Christine lifted Maggie's face to hers. She knew exactly which button needed to be pushed, and did so, ruthlessly. "You don't want them to think you're afraid, do you?"

"I'm not afraid." Maggie's chin came up, but the nausea swam like oil in her stomach. "I'm just not interested."

Christine smiled, stroked Maggie's hair and waited.

"I can't face it, Mrs. Sweeney," Maggie blurted out. "I just can't. I'll humiliate myself, and I hate that more than anything. I'd sooner be hanged."

"I understand completely, but you'll not humiliate yourself." She took

Maggie's frozen hands in hers. "It's true it's yourself on display as much as your work. That's the foolishness of the art world. They'll wonder about you, and talk about you and speculate. Let them."

"It's not that so much—though that's part of it. I'm not used to being wondered over, and I don't think I'll like it, but it's my work. . . ." She pressed her lips together. "It's the best part of me, Mrs. Sweeney. If it's found wanting. If it's not good enough—"

"Rogan thinks it is."

"A lot he knows," Maggie muttered.

"That's true. A lot he does know." Christine tilted her head. The child needed a bit of mothering, she decided. And mothering wasn't always kind. "Do you want me to go down and tell him you're too afraid, too insecure to attend the show?"

"No!" Helpless, Maggie covered her face with her hands. "He's trapped me. The tricky snake of a man. The damned greedy—I beg your pardon." Going stiff, Maggie lowered her hands.

Christine made certain to swallow the chuckle. "That's quite all right," she said soberly. "Now, you wait here and I'll go down and tell Rogan to go on without us. He's already wearing a trench in the hallway with his pacing."

"I've never seen anyone so obsessed with time."

"It's a Sweeney trait. Michael drove me mad with it, God bless him." She patted Maggie's hand. "I'll be right back up to help you dress."

"Mrs. Sweeney." Desperate, Maggie grabbed at Christine's sleeve. "Couldn't you just tell him I've died? They could make a lovely wake out of the showing. And as a rule, you make more of a profit off a dead artist than a live one."

"There, you see." Christine dislodged Maggie's clutching fingers. "You're feeling better already. Now run along and wash your face."

"But—"

"I'm standing in for your gran tonight," Christine said firmly. "I believe Sharon would have wanted me to. And I said go wash your face, Margaret Mary.

"Yes, ma'am. Mrs. Sweeney?" With no place else to go, Maggie got shakily to her feet. "You won't tell him . . . I mean, I'd be grateful to you if you didn't mention to Rogan that I'd . . ."

"On one of the most important evenings of her life, a woman's entitled to linger over dressing."

"I suppose." A ghost of a smile played around Maggie's mouth. "It makes me sound like a frivolous fool, but it's better than the alternative."

"Leave Rogan to me."

"There's just one other thing." She'd been putting this off, Maggie admitted. She might as well face it now when she was feeling as low as she imagined she could possibly feel. "Do you think you might be able to find those clippings you spoke of? The ones about my mother?"

"I think I could. I should have thought of it myself. Of course, you'd like to read them."

"I would, yes. I'd be grateful."

"I'll see that you get them. Now go fix your face. I'll scoot Rogan along." She sent Maggie a bolstering smile before closing the door.

When Christine found him, Rogan was still furiously pacing in the foyer. "Where the devil is she?" he demanded the moment he spotted his grandmother. "She's been primping up there for two hours."

"Well, of course she has." Christine gestured grandly. "The impression she makes tonight is vital, isn't it?"

"It's important, naturally." If she made the wrong one, his dreams would slide down the drain along with Maggie's. He needed her here, now, and ready to dazzle. "But why should it take her so long? She's only to put on her clothes and fuss with her hair."

"You've been a single man too long, my darling, if you truly believe such nonsense." Affectionately, Christine reached out to straighten his already perfect tie. "How handsome you look in a tuxedo."

"Grandmother, you're stalling."

"No, not at all." Beaming at him, she brushed at his spotless lapels. "I've just come down to tell you to go along without us. We'll follow when Maggie's ready."

"She should be ready now."

"But she's not. Besides, how much more effective might it be if she arrived just late enough to make an entrance? You appreciate the theater of these events, Rogan."

There was truth in that. "All right then." He checked his watch, swore lightly. If he didn't go within the minute he'd most certainly be late. It was his responsibility to be there, he reminded himself, to see to any last minute details, no matter how much he wanted to wait and take Maggie to the gallery himself. "I'll leave her in your more than capable hands. I'll have the car come back for you as soon as I've been dropped off. See that she's there within the hour, won't you?"

"You can count on me, darling."

"I always do." He kissed her on the cheek, stepped back. "By the way, Mrs. Sweeney, I haven't mentioned how beautiful you look."

"No, you haven't. I was quite deflated."

"You will be, as always, the most stunning woman in the room."

"Well said. Now, run along with you and leave Maggie to me."

"With pleasure." He shot one look up the stairs as he headed for the door. It was not a gentle look. "I wish you good luck with her."

As the door closed Christine let out a sigh. She thought she might need all the luck she could get.

NINE

No detail had been overlooked. The lighting was perfect, leaping and bounding off the curves and swirls of glass. The music, a waltz now, flowed as softly as happy tears through the room. Fizzing glasses of champagne crowded the silver trays carried gracefully by liveried waiters. The sound of clinking crystal and murmuring voices set up a gracious counterpoint to the weeping violins.

It was, in a word, perfect, not a detail missing. Except, Rogan thought grimly, the artist herself.

"It's wonderful, Rogan." Patricia stood beside him, elegant in a narrow white gown shivering with bugle beads. "You have a smashing success."

He turned to her, smiling. "So it would seem."

His eyes lingered on hers long enough, intensely enough, to make her uneasy. "What is it? Have I smudged my nose?"

"No." He lifted his own glass quickly, cursing Maggie for putting ridiculous thoughts in his head and making him wary of one of his oldest friends.

In love with him? Absurd.

"I'm sorry. I suppose my mind was wandering. I can't imagine what's keeping Maggie."

"I'm sure she'll be along any moment." Patricia laid a hand on his arm. "And in the meantime, everyone's being dazzled by our combined efforts."

"It's a lucky thing. She's always late," he added under his breath. "No more than a child's sense of time."

"Rogan, dear, there you are. I see my Patricia found you."

"Good evening, Mrs. Connelly." Rogan took Patricia's mother's delicate hand in his own. "I'm delighted to see you. No gallery showing can be a success without your presence."

"Flatterer." Pleased, she swept up her mink stole. Anne Connelly held on as tightly to her beauty as she did to her vanity. She considered it as much a woman's duty to preserve her looks as it was to make a home and bear children. Ann never, never neglected her duties, and as a result, she had the dewy skin and the youthful figure of a girl. She fought a constant battle with the years and had, for half a century, emerged the victor.

"And your husband?" Rogan continued. "Did Dennis come with you?"

"Naturally, though he's already off somewhere puffing on one of his cigars and discussing finance." She smiled when Rogan signaled for a waiter and offered her a glass of champagne. "Even his fondness for you doesn't change his apathy toward art. This is fascinating work." She gestured to the sculpture beside them, an explosion of color, mushrooming up from a twisted base. "Gorgeous and disturbing all at once. Patricia tells me she met the artist briefly yesterday. I'm dying to do so myself."

"She's yet to arrive," Rogan covered his own impatience smoothly. "You'll find Miss Concannon as contradictory and as interesting, I think, as her work."

"And I'm sure as fascinating. We haven't seen nearly enough of you lately, Rogan. I've badgered Patricia unmercifully about bringing you by." She shot her daughter a veiled look that spoke volumes.

Get a move on, girl, it said. *Don't let him slip away from you.*

"I'm afraid I've been so obsessed with getting this show together quickly that I've neglected my friends."

"You're forgiven, as long as we can expect you to dine with us one evening next week."

"I'd love to." Rogan caught Joseph's eye. "Excuse me just a moment, won't you?"

"Must you be so obvious, Mother?" Patricia murmured into her wine as Rogan slipped through the crowd.

"Someone has to be. Merciful heavens, girl, he treats you like a sister." Beaming a smile across the room at an acquaintance, Anne continued to speak in undertones. "A man doesn't marry a woman he thinks of as his sister, and it's time you were wed again. You couldn't ask for a better match. Keep loitering around, and someone else will scoop him up from under your nose. Now smile, will you? Must you always look as though you're in mourning?"

Dutifully, Patricia forced her lips to curve.

"Did you reach them?" Rogan demanded the moment he'd cornered Joseph.

"On the car phone." Joseph's gaze skimmed the room, brushed over Patricia, lingered, then moved on. "They'll be here any moment."

"More than an hour late. Typical."

"Be that as it may, you'll be pleased to know that we have sales on ten pieces already, and at least that many offers on *Surrender.*"

"That piece is not for sale." Rogan studied the flamboyant sculpture that stood in the center of the room. "We'll tour it first, in our galleries in Rome, Paris and New York, but along with the other pieces we've chosen it is not to be sold."

"It's your decision," Joseph said easily enough. "But I should tell you that General Fitzsimmons offered us twenty-five thousand pounds for it."

"Did he? Make sure that gets around, won't you?"

"Count on it. In the meantime I've been entertaining some of the art critics. I think you should . . ." Joseph trailed off when he saw Rogan's eyes darken as he looked intently at something over his shoulder. Joseph turned, saw the object of his boss's gaze and let out a low whistle. "She may be late, but she's certainly a showstopper."

Joseph looked back at Patricia and saw from the expression on her face that she, too, had noted Rogan's reaction. His heart bled a little for the woman. He knew from personal experience how miserable it was to love someone who thought of you as only a friend.

"Shall I go take her around?" Joseph asked.

"What? No—no. I'll do it myself."

Rogan had never imagined Maggie could look like that—sleek and stunning and sensual as sin. She'd chosen black, unrelieved and unadorned. The dress took all its style from the body it covered. It draped from throat to ankle, but no one would call it prim, not with the glossy black buttons that swirled the length of it, the buttons that she'd left daringly unfastened to the swell of her breast, and up to the top of one slim thigh.

Her hair was a tousled crown of fire, carelessly curled around her face. As he drew closer he saw that her eyes were already scanning, assessing and absorbing everything in the room.

She looked fearless, defiant and completely in control.

And so she was . . . now. The bout of nerves had served to embarrass her so much that she'd beaten them back with nothing more than sheer willfulness.

She was here. And she meant to succeed.

"You're impossibly late." The complaint was a last line of defense, delivered in a mutter as he took her hand and raised it to his lips. Their eyes met. "And incredibly beautiful."

"You approve of the dress?"

"That's not the word I would have chosen, but yes, I do."

She smiled then. "You were afraid I'd wear boots and torn jeans."

"Not with my grandmother standing guard."

"She's the most wonderful woman in the world. You're lucky to have her."

The emotional force of the statement more than the words caused Rogan to study her curiously. "I'm aware of that."

"You can't be. Not really, for you've never known any different." She took a deep breath. "Well." There were eyes on her already, dozens of them, bright with curiosity. "It's into the lions' den, isn't it? You needn't worry," she said before he could speak. "I'll behave. My future depends on it."

"This is only the beginning, Margaret Mary."

As he drew her into the room with its whirl of light and color, she was very much afraid he was right.

But behave she did. The evening seemed to go well as she shook hands, accepted compliments, answered questions. The first hour seemed to float by like a dream, what with the sparkle of wine, the glitter of glass and the flash of jewels. Drifting through it was easy, as Maggie felt slightly removed from the reality, somewhat disconnected, as much audience as actor in a sumptuously produced play.

"This, ah this." A bald man with a drooping mustache and a fussy British accent expounded on a piece. It was a series of glowing blue spears trapped within a sheer glass globe. *"Imprisoned,* you call it. Your creativity, your sexuality, fighting to set itself free. Man's eternal struggle, after all. It's triumphant, even as it's melancholy."

"It's the six counties," Maggie said simply.

The bald man blinked. "I beg your pardon."

"The six counties of Ireland," she repeated with a wicked rebel gleam in her eyes. "Imprisoned."

"I see."

Standing beside this would-be critic, Joseph muffled a laugh. "I found the use of color here so striking, Lord Whitfield. The translucence of it creates an unresolved tension between its delicacy and its boldness."

"Just so." Lord Whitfield nodded, cleared his throat. "Quite extraordinary. Excuse me."

Maggie watched him retreat with a broad smile. "Well, I don't think he'll be after buying it and setting it in his den, do you, Joseph?"

"You're a wicked woman, Maggie Concannon."

"I'm an Irishwoman, Joseph." She winked at him. "Up the rebels."

He laughed delightedly and, slipping an arm around her waist, led her around the room. "Ah, Mrs. Connelly." Joseph gave Maggie a subtle squeeze to signal her. "Looking stunning as always."

"Joseph, always a smooth word. And this—" Anne Connelly shifted her attention from Joseph, whom she considered a mere factotum to Maggie. "This is the creative drive. I'm thrilled to meet you, my dear. I'm Mrs. Dennis Connelly—Anne. I believe you met my daughter, Patricia, yesterday."

"I did, yes." Maggie found Anne's handclasp as delicate and soft as a brush of satin.

"She must be off with Rogan somewhere. They're a lovely couple, aren't they?"

"Very." Maggie lifted a brow. She knew a warning when she heard one. "Do you live in Dublin, Mrs. Connelly?"

"I do indeed. Only a few houses away from the Sweeney mansion. My family has been a part of Dublin society for generations. And you're from the west counties?"

"Clare, yes."

"Lovely scenery. All those charming quaint villages and thatched roofs. Your family are farmers, I'm told?" Anne lifted a brow, obviously amused.

"Were."

"This must be so exciting for you, particularly with your rural upbringing. I'm sure you've enjoyed your visit to Dublin. You'll be going back soon?"

"Very soon, I think."

"I'm sure you miss the country. Dublin can be very confusing to one unused to city life. Almost like a foreign land."

"At least I understand the language," Maggie said equably. "I hope you'll enjoy your evening, Mrs. Connelly. Excuse me, won't you?"

And if Rogan thought he would sell that woman anything that Maggie Concannon created, Maggie thought as she walked away, he'd hang for it.

Exclusive rights be damned. She'd smash every last piece into dust before she saw any in Anne Connelly's hands. Talking to her as though she were some slack-jawed milkmaid with straw in her hair.

She held her temper back as she made her way out of the ballroom and toward one of the sitting rooms. Each was crowded with people, talking, sitting, laughing, discussing her. Her head began to throb as she marched down the stairs. She'd get herself a beer out of the kitchen, she decided, and have a few minutes of peace.

She strode straight in, only to come up short when she saw a portly man puffing on a cigar and nursing a pilsner.

"Caught," he said, and grinned sheepishly.

"That makes two of us then. I was coming down for a quiet beer myself."

"Let me fetch you one." Gallantly, he heaved his bulk out of the chair and pulled a bottle out for her. "You don't want me to put out the cigar, do you?"

The plea in his voice made her laugh. "Not at all. My father used to smoke the world's worst pipe. Stunk to high heaven. I loved it."

"There's a lass." He found her a beer and a glass. "I hate these things." He jerked his thumb toward the ceiling. "M'wife drags me."

"I hate them, too."

"Pretty enough work, I suppose," he said as she drank. "Like the colors and shapes. Not that I know a damn thing about it. Wife's the expert. But I liked the look of it, and that should be enough, I'd say."

"And I."

"Everyone's always trying to explain it at these blasted affairs. What the artist had in mind and such. Symbolism." He rolled his tongue over the word as if it were a strange dish he wasn't quite ready to sample. "Don't know what the devil they're talking about."

Maggie decided the man was half-potted and that she loved him. "Neither do they."

"That's it!" He raised his glass and drank deeply. "Neither do they. Just blustering. But if I was to say that to Anne—that's my wife—she'd give me one of those looks."

He narrowed his eyes, lowered his brows and scowled. Maggie hooted with laughter.

"Who cares what they think anyway?" Maggie propped her elbow on the table and held a fist to her chin. "It's not as if anyone's life depended on it." Except mine, she thought, and pushed the idea away. "Don't you think affairs like this are just an excuse for people to get all dressed up and act important?"

"I do absolutely." So complete was his agreement that he rapped his glass sharply to hers. "As for me, do you know what I wanted to be doing tonight?"

"What?"

"Sitting in my chair, with my feet on the hassock and Irish in my glass, watching the television." He sighed, regretfully. "But I couldn't disappoint Anne—or Rogan, for that matter."

"You know Rogan, then?"

"Like my own son. A fine man he's turned out to be. He wasn't yet twenty when I saw him first. His father and I had business together, and the boy couldn't wait to be part of it." He gestured vaguely to encompass the gallery. "Smart as a whip, he is."

"And what business are you in?"

"Banking."

"Excuse me." A female voice interrupted them. They looked up to see Patricia standing in the doorway, her hands folded neatly.

"Ah, there's my love."

While Maggie looked on, goggle-eyed, the man lunged out of his chair and enfolded Patricia in a hug that could have felled a mule. Patricia's reaction, rather than stiff rejection or cool disgust, was a quick, musical laugh.

"Daddy, you'll break me in half."

Daddy? Maggie thought. Daddy? Patricia Henessy's father? Anne's husband? This delightful man was married to that—that icy stick of a woman? It only went to prove, she decided, that the words *till death do us part* were the most foolish syllables human beings were ever forced to utter.

"Meet my little girl." With obvious pride, Dennis whirled Patricia around. "A beauty, isn't she? My Patricia."

"Yes, indeed." Maggie rose, grinning. "It's nice to see you again."

"And you. Congratulations on the wonderful success of your show."

"Your show?" Dennis said blankly.

"We never introduced ourselves." Laughing now, Maggie stepped forward and offered Dennis her hand. "I'm Maggie Concannon, Mr. Connelly."

"Oh." He said nothing for a moment as he racked his brain trying to recall if he'd said anything insulting. "A pleasure," he managed to say as his brain stalled.

"It was, truly. Thank you for the best ten minutes I've had since I walked in the door."

Dennis smiled. This woman seemed downright human, for an artist. "I do like the colors, and the shapes," he offered hopefully.

"And that's the nicest compliment I've had all evening."

"Daddy, Mother's looking for you." Patricia brushed a stray ash from his lapel. The gesture, one she had carelessly used with her own father countless times, arrowed straight into Maggie's heart.

"I'd better let her find me, then." He looked back at Maggie, and when she grinned at him, he grinned back. "I hope we meet again, Miss Concannon."

"So do I."

"Won't you come up with us?" Patricia asked.

"No, not just now," Maggie answered, not wishing to socialize further with Patricia's mother.

The bright look faded the moment their footsteps died away on the polished floor. She sat down, alone, in the light-flooded kitchen. It was quiet there, so quiet she could nearly fool herself into believing the building was empty but for her.

She wanted to believe she was alone. More, she wanted to believe the sadness she suddenly felt was just that she missed the solitude of her own green fields and quiet hills, the endless hours of silence with only the roar of her own kiln and her own imagination to drive her.

But it wasn't only that. On this, one of the brightest nights of her life, she had no one. None of the chattering, brilliant crowd of people upstairs knew her, cared for her, understood her. There was no one abovestairs waiting for Maggie Concannon.

So she had herself, she thought, and rose. And that was all anyone needed. Her work was well received. It wasn't so difficult to cut through all the fancy and pompous phrases to the core. Rogan's people liked what she did, and that was the first step.

She was on her way, she told herself as she swung out of the kitchen. She was rushing down the path toward fame and fortune, the path that had eluded the Concannons for the last two generations. And she would do it all herself.

The light and the music sparkled down the staircase like fairy dust along the curve of a rainbow. She stood at the foot of the stairs, her hand clutched on the rail, her foot on the first tread. Then, with a jerk, she turned to hurry outside, into the dark.

When the clock struck one, Rogan yanked at his elegant black tie and swore. The woman, he thought as he paced the darkened parlor, deserved murder and no less. She'd vanished like smoke in the middle of a crowded party arranged for her benefit. Leaving him, he remembered with boiling resentment, to make foolish excuses.

He should have known that a woman of her temperament couldn't be trusted to behave reasonably. He certainly should have known better than to give her such a prominent place in his own ambitions, his hopes for the future of his business.

How in hell could he hope to build a gallery for Irish art when the first Irish artist he'd personally selected, groomed and showcased had fled her own opening like an irresponsible child?

Now it was the middle of the night, and he'd not had a word from her. The brilliant success of the show, his own satisfaction with a job well done, had clouded over like her precious west county sky. There was nothing he could do but wait.

And worry.

She didn't know Dublin. For all its beauty and charm there were still sections dangerous to a woman alone. And there was always the possibility of an accident—the thought of which brought on a vicious, throbbing headache at the base of his skull.

He'd taken two long strides toward the phone to telephone the hospitals when he heard the click of the front door. He pivoted and rushed into the hallway.

She was safe, and under the dazzle of the foyer chandelier, he could see she was unharmed. Visions of murder leaped back into his aching head.

"Where in the sweet hell have you been?"

She'd hoped he'd be out at some high-class club, clinking glasses with his friends. But since he wasn't, she offered him a smile and a shrug. "Oh, out and about. Your Dublin's a lovely city at night."

As he stared at her, his hands closed into ready fists. "You're saying you've been out sightseeing until one in the morning?"

"Is it so late then? I must have lost track. Well then, I'll say good night."

"No, you won't." He took a step toward her. "What you will do is give me an explanation for your behavior."

"That's something I don't have to explain to anyone, but if you'd be more clear, perhaps I'd make an exception."

"There were nearly two hundred people gathered tonight for your benefit. You were unbelievably rude."

"I was nothing of the kind." More weary than she wanted to admit, she strolled past him into the parlor, slipped out of the miserably uncomfortable heels and propped her tired feet on a tassled stool. "The truth is, I was so unbelievably polite, my teeth nearly fell out of my head. I hope to Christ I don't have to smile at another bloody soul for a month. I wouldn't mind one of your brandies now, Rogan. It's chilly out this time of night."

He noticed for the first time that she wore nothing over the thin black dress. "Where the devil is your wrap?"

"I didn't have one. You'll have to mark that down in your little book. Acquire Maggie a suitable evening wrap." She reached up for the snifter he'd poured.

"Damn it, your hands are frozen. Have you no sense?"

"They'll warm quick enough." Her brows arched as he stalked over to the fireplace and crouched down to start a fire. "What, no servants?"

"Shut up. The one thing I won't tolerate from you tonight is sarcasm. I've taken all I plan to take."

Flames licked into life to eat greedily at dry wood. In the shifting light Maggie saw that his face was tight with anger. The best way to meet temper, she'd always thought, was to match it.

"I've given you nothing to take." She sipped the brandy, would have sighed over the welcome heat of the liquor if she and Rogan hadn't been glaring at each other. "I went to your showing, didn't I? In a proper dress, with a proper foolish smile pasted on my face."

"It was your showing," he shot back. "You ungrateful, selfish, inconsiderate brat."

However weary her body, she wouldn't allow him to get away with such language. She stood rigidly and faced him. "I won't contradict you. I'm exactly as you say, and have been told so most of my life. Fortunately for both of us, it's only my work you have to be concerned about."

"Do you have any idea the time and effort and expense that went into putting that show together?"

"That's your province." Her voice was as stiff as her spine. "As you're always so quick to tell me. And I was there, stayed above two hours, rubbing elbows with strangers."

"You'd better learn that a patron is never a stranger, and that rudeness is never attractive."

The quiet, controlled tone cut through her defensive armor like a sword. "I never agreed to stay the whole evening. I needed to be alone, that's all."

"And to wander the streets all night? I'm responsible for you while you're here, Maggie. For God's sake, I'd nearly called out the garda."

"You're not responsible for me. I am." But she could see now that it wasn't simply anger darkening his eyes, but concern as well. "If I caused you worry, I'll apologize. I simply went for a walk."

"You went out strolling and left your first major show without a by-your-leave?"

"Yes." The snifter was out of her hand and hurtling toward the stone hearth before she realized it. Glass shattered, rained like bullets. "I had to get out! I couldn't breathe. I couldn't bear it. All those people, staring at me, at my work, and the music, the lights. Everything so lovely, so perfect. I didn't know it would scare me so. I thought I'd gotten over it since that first day you showed me the room, and my work set up like something out of a dream."

"You were frightened."

"Yes, yes, damn you. Are you happy to hear it? I was terrified when you opened the door and I looked inside and saw what you'd done. I could barely speak. You did this to me," she said furiously. "You opened this Pandora's box and let out all my hopes and my fears and my needs. You can't know what it's like to have needs, terrible ones, you don't even think you should have."

He studied her now, ivory and flame in a slim black dress. "Oh, but I can," he said quietly. "I can. You should have told me, Maggie." His voice was gentle now as he stepped toward her.

She threw up both hands to ward him off. "No, don't. I couldn't bear you to be kind just now. Especially when I know I don't deserve it. It was wrong of me to leave that way. It was selfish and ungrateful." She dropped her hands helplessly at her sides. "But there was no one for me up those stairs. No one. And it broke my heart."

She looked so delicate all at once, so he did what she asked and didn't touch her. He was afraid if he did, however gently, she might snap in his hands. "If you'd let me know how important it was to you, Maggie, I'd have arranged to have your family here."

"You can't arrange Brianna. God knows you can't bring my father back." Her voice broke, shaming her. With a strangled sound she pressed a hand to her mouth. "I'm overtired, that's all." She fought a bitter war to control her voice. "Overstimulated with all the excitement. I owe you an apology for leaving the way I did, and gratitude for all the work you did for me."

He preferred her raging or weeping to this stilted politeness. It left him no choice but to respond in kind. "The important thing is that the show was a success."

"Yes." Her eyes glittered in the firelight. "That's the important thing. If you'll excuse me now, I'll go up to bed."

"Of course. Maggie? One more thing."

She turned back. He stood before the fire, the flames leaping gold behind him. "Yes?"

"I was there for you, up those stairs. Perhaps next time you'll remember that, and be content."

She didn't answer. He heard only the rustle of her dress as she hurried across the hall and up the stairs, then the quick click of her bedroom door closing.

He stared at the fire, watched a log break apart, cut through by flame and heat. Smoke puffed once, stirred by the wind. He continued to stare as a shower of sparks rained against the screen, scattered over stone and winked out.

She was, he realized, every bit as capricious, moody and brilliant as that fire. As dangerous and as elemental.

And he was, quite desperately, in love with her.

TEN

"What do you mean, gone?" Rogan pushed away from his desk and scraped Joseph with a look of outrage. "Of course she's not gone."

"But she is. She stopped by the gallery to say good-bye only an hour ago." Reaching into his pocket, Joseph drew out an envelope. "She asked me to give you this."

Rogan took it, tossed it on his desk. "Are you saying she's gone back to Clare? The morning after her show?"

"Yes, and in a tearing hurry. I didn't have time to show her the reviews." Joseph reached up to fiddle with the tiny gold hoop in his ear. "She'd booked a flight to Shannon. Said she only had a moment to say good-bye and God bless, gave me the note for you, kissed me and ran out again." He smiled. "It was a bit like being battered by a small tornado." He lifted his shoulders, let them fall. "I'm sorry, Rogan, if I'd known you wanted her to stay, I'd have tried to stop her. I believe I'd have been flattened, but I'd have tried."

"It doesn't matter." He lowered carefully into his chair again. "How did she seem?"

"Impatient, rushed, distracted. Very much as usual. She wanted to be back home, was all she told me, back at work. I wasn't sure you knew, so I thought I'd come by and tell you in person. I have an appointment with General Fitzsimmons, and it was on my way."

"I appreciate it. I should be by the gallery by four. Give the general my regards."

"I'll give him the business," Joseph said with a flashing grin. "By the way, he went up another five thousand on *Surrender.*"

"Not for sale."

Rogan picked up the note on his desk after Joseph closed the door behind him. Ignoring his work, Rogan split the envelope with his ebony-handled letter opener. The creamy stationery from his own guest room was dashed over with Maggie's hurried and beautiful scrawl

Dear Rogan,

I imagine you'll be annoyed that I've left so abruptly, but it can't be helped. I need to be home and back at work, and I won't apologize for it. I will thank you. I'm sure you'll start firing wires my way, and I'll warn you in

advance I intend to ignore them, at least for a time. Please give my best to your grandmother. And I wouldn't mind if you thought of me now and again.

Maggie

Oh, one more thing. You might be interested to know that I'm taking home a half dozen of Julien's recipes—that's your cook's name, if you don't know. He thinks I'm charming.

Rogan skimmed the letter a second time before setting it aside. It was for the best, he decided. They would both be happier and more productive with the whole of Ireland between them. Certainly, he would be. It was difficult to be productive around a woman when you were in love with her, and when she frustrated you on every possible level.

And with any luck, any at all, these feelings that had grown in him would ease and fade with time and distance.

So . . . He folded the letter and set it aside. He was glad she'd gone back, satisfied that they'd accomplished the first stage of his plans for her career, happy that she'd inadvertently given him time to deal with his own confused emotions.

The hell, he thought. He missed her already.

The sky was the color of a robin's egg and clear as a mountain stream. Maggie sat on the little stoop at her front door, elbows on knees, and just breathed. Beyond her own garden gate and the trailing, flowering fuchsia, she could see the lush green of hill and valley. And farther, since the day was so clear, so bright, she glimpsed the distant dark mountains.

She watched a magpie dart across her line of vision, flashing over the hedge and up. Straight as an arrow he went, until even the shadow of him was lost in the green.

One of Murphy's cows lowed and was answered by another. There was a humming echo that would be his tractor, and the more insistent sealike roar of her furnaces, which she'd fired the moment she'd arrived.

Her flowers were brilliant in the sunshine, vivid red begonias tangled with the late-blooming tulips and dainty spears of larkspur. She could smell rosemary and thyme and the strong perfume of the wild roses that swayed like dancers in the mild, sweet breeze.

A wind chime she'd made out of scraps of glass sang musically above her head.

Dublin, with its busy streets, seemed very far away.

On the ribbon of road in the valley below, she saw a red truck, tiny and bright as a toy, rumble along, turn into a lane and climb toward a cottage.

Home for tea, she thought, and let out a sigh of pure contentment.

She heard the dog first, that full-throated echoing bark, then the rustle of brush that told her he'd flushed out a bird. Her sister's voice floated out on the air, amused, indulgent.

"Leave the poor thing alone, Con, you great bully."

The dog barked again and, moments later, leaped at the garden gate. His tongue lolled happily when he spotted Maggie.

"Get down from there," Brianna ordered. "Do you want her to come home and find her gate crashed in, and . . . Oh." She stopped, laying a hand on the wolfhound's massive head as she saw her sister. "I didn't know you were home." The smile came first as she tugged open the gate.

"I've just arrived." Maggie spent the next few minutes being greeted by Concobar, wrestling and accepting his lavish licks until he responded to Brianna's command to sit. Sit he did, his front paws over Maggie's feet, as if to ensure that she would stay put.

"I had a little time," Brianna began. "So I thought I'd come down and tend to your garden."

"It looks fine to me."

"You always think so. I've brought you some bread I baked this morning. I was going to put it in your freezer." Feeling awkward, Brianna held out the basket. There was something here, she realized. Something behind the cool, calm look in her sister's eyes. "How was Dublin?"

"Crowded." Maggie set the basket beside her on the stoop. The scent beneath the neat cloth was so tempting that she lifted the cloth aside and broke off a warm hunk of brown bread. "Noisy." She tore off a bit of bread and tossed it. Concobar nipped it midair, swallowed it whole and grinned. "Greedy bastard, aren't you?" She tossed him another piece before she rose. "I have something for you."

Maggie turned into the house, leaving Brianna standing on the path. When she came back, she handed Brianna a box and a manila envelope.

"You didn't have to get me anything—" Brianna began but stopped. It was guilt she felt, she realized. And guilt she was meant to feel. Accepting it, she opened the box. "Oh, Maggie, it's lovely. The loveliest thing I've ever had." She held the pin up to the sun and watched it glint. "You shouldn't have spent your money."

"It's mine to spend," Maggie said shortly. "And I hope you'll wear it on something other than an apron."

"I don't wear an apron everywhere," Brianna said evenly. She replaced the pin carefully in the box, slipped the box into her pocket. "Thank you. Maggie, I wish—"

"You haven't looked at the other." Maggie knew what her sister wished, and didn't care to hear it. Regrets that she hadn't been in Dublin for the show hardly mattered now.

Brianna studied her sister's face, found no sign of softening. "All right, then." She opened the envelope, drew out a sheet. "Oh! Oh my." However bright and lovely the pin, it was nothing compared with this. They both knew it. "Recipes. So many. Soufflés and pastries, and—oh, look at this chicken. It must be wonderful."

"It is." Maggie shook her head at Brianna's reaction, nearly sighed. "I've tasted it myself. And the soup there—the herbs are the trick to it, I'm told."

"Where did you get them?" Brianna caught her bottom lip between her teeth, studied the handwritten pages as if they were the treasure of all the ages.

"From Rogan's cook. He's a Frenchman."

"Recipes from a French chef," Brianna said reverently.

"I promised him you'd send a like number of your own in trade."

"Of mine?" Brianna blinked, as if coming out of a dream. "Why, he couldn't want mine."

"He can, and he does. I praised your Irish stew and your berry pie to the moon and back. And I gave him my solemn word you'd send them."

"I will, of course, but I can't imagine—thank you, Maggie. It's a wonderful gift." Brianna stepped forward for an embrace, then back again, cut to the quick by the coolness of Maggie's response. "Won't you tell me how it went for you? I kept trying to imagine it, but I couldn't."

"It went well enough. There were a lot of people. Rogan seems to know how to tickle their interest. There was an orchestra and waiters in white suits serving flutes of champagne and silver platters of fancy finger food."

"It must have been beautiful. I'm so proud of you."

Maggie's eyes chilled. "Are you?"

"You know I am."

"I know I needed you there. Damn it, Brie, I needed you there."

Con whined at the shout and looked uneasily from Maggie to his mistress.

"I would have been there if I could."

"There was nothing stopping you but her. One night of your life was all I asked. One. I had no one there, no family, no friends, no one who loved me. Because you chose her as you always have, over me, over Da, even over yourself."

"It wasn't a matter of choosing."

"It's always a matter of choosing," Maggie said coldly. "You've let her kill your heart, Brianna, just as she killed his."

"That's cruel, Maggie."

"Aye, it is. She'd be the first to tell you that cruel is just what I am. Cruel, marked with sin and damned to the devil. Well, I'm glad to be bad. I'd choose hell in a blink over kneeling in ashes and suffering silently for heaven as you do." Maggie stepped back, curled a stiff hand around the doorknob. "Well, I had my night without you, or anyone, and it went well enough. I should think they'll be some sales out of it. I'll have money for you in a few weeks."

"I'm sorry I hurt you, Maggie." Brianna's own pride stiffened her voice. "I don't care about the money."

"I do." Maggie shut the door.

For three days she was undisturbed. The phone didn't ring; no knock came at the door. Even if there had been a summons, she would have ignored it. She spent nearly every waking minute in the glass house, refining, perfecting, forming the images in her brain and on her sketchpad into glass.

Despite Rogan's claim as to their worth, she hung her drawings on clothespins or on magnets, so that a corner of the studio soon came to resemble a dark room, with prints drying.

She'd burned herself twice in her hurry, once badly enough to make her stop for some hastily applied first aid. Now she sat in her chair, carefully, meticulously, turning her sketch of an Apache breastplate into her own vision.

It was sweaty work, and viciously exacting. Bleeding color into color, shape into shape as she wanted required hundreds of trips to the glory hole.

But here, at least, she could be patient.

White-hot flames licked through open furnace doors, blasting out heat. The exhaust fan hummed like an engine to keep the fumes coating the glass—and not her lungs—to an iridescent hue.

For two days she worked with chemicals, mixing and experimenting like a mad scientist until she'd perfected the colors she desired. Copper for the deep turquoise, iron for the rich golden yellow, manganese for a royal, bluish purple. The red, the true ruby she wanted, had given her trouble, as it did any glass artist. She was working with that now, sandwiching that section between two layers of clear glass. She'd used copper again, with reducing agents in the melt to ensure a pure color. Though it was poisonous, and potentially dangerous even under controlled conditions, she'd chosen sodium cyanide.

Even with this the casing was necessary to prevent the red from going livery.

The first gather of the new section was blown, rotated, then carefully trailed from the iron. She used long tweezers to draw the molten, taffylike glass into a subtly feathery shape.

Sweat dripped down onto the cotton bandanna she'd tied around her brow as she worked the second gather, repeated the procedure.

Again and again, she went to the glory hole to reheat, not only to keep the glass hot, but to ensure against thermal strains that could break any vessel—and the heart of the artist.

To prevent searing her hands, she dripped water over the pipe. Only the tip needed to be kept hot.

She wanted the wall of the breastplate thin enough so that light could seep and be refracted throught it. This required additional trips for heating and careful patient work with tools for flattening and for adding the slight curve she envisioned.

Hours after she'd blown the first gather, she placed the vessel in the annealing oven and struck the pontil.

It wasn't until she'd set both temperature and time that she felt the cramps in her hands, the knots in her shoulders and neck.

And the emptiness in her belly.

No scraping out of a can tonight, she decided. She would celebrate with a meal and a pint at the pub.

Maggie didn't ask herself why, after pining for solitude, she now hurried toward company. She'd been home for three days and had spoken to no one but Brianna. And then only briefly and angrily.

Maggie was sorry for it now, sorry that she hadn't tried harder to understand Brianna's position. Her sister was always in the middle, the unlucky second child of a flawed marriage. Instead of leaping for her sister's throat, she should have taken her oversolicitousness toward their mother in stride. And she should have told Brianna what she'd learned from Christine Sweeney. It would be interesting to gauge Brianna's reaction to the news of their mother's past.

But that would have to wait. She wanted an undemanding hour with people she knew, over a hot meal and a cold beer. It would take her mind off the work that had been driving her for days, and off the fact that she'd yet to hear from Rogan.

Because the evening was fine and she wanted to work out the worst of her kinks, she straddled her bicycle and began the three-mile trek into the village.

The long days of summer had begun. The sun was brilliant and pleasantly warm, keeping many of the farmers out in their fields long after their supper was over. The curving narrow road was flanked on both sides by high hedgerows that provided no shoulder and gave Maggie the impression of riding down a long, sweet-smelling tunnel. She passed a car, gave the driver a wave and felt the breeze of its passing flutter her jeans.

Pedaling hard, more for the fun than because she was in a hurry, she burst out of the tunnel of hedges into the sheer breathless beauty of the valley.

The sun dashed off the tin roof of a hay barn and dazzled her eyes. The road was smoother now, if no wider, but she slowed, simply to enjoy the evening breeze and the lingering sunlight.

She caught the scent of honeysuckle, of hay, of sweet mown grass. Her mood, which had been manic and restless since her return, began to mellow.

She passed houses with clothes drying on the line and children playing in the yard, and the ruins of castles, majestic still with their gray stones and legends of ghostly inhabitants, a testament to a way to life that still lingered.

She took a curve, caught the bright flash that was the river flowing through high grass and turned away from it toward the village.

The houses were more plentiful now and stood closer together. Some of the newer ones made her sigh with disappointment. They were blocky and plain to her artist's eye, and usually drab in color. Only the gardens, lush and vivid, saved them from ugliness.

The long last curve took her into the village proper. She passed the butcher's, the chemist's, O'Ryan's little food store and the tiny, neat hotel that had once belonged to her grandfather.

Maggie paused to study the building a moment, trying to imagine her mother living there as a girl. A lovely girl, according to Christine Sweeney's report, with the voice of an angel.

If it were true, why had there been so little music in the house? And why, Maggie wondered, had there never been a mention, a hint of Maeve's talent?

She would ask, Maggie decided. And there was likely no place better than O'Malley's.

As she pulled her bike to the curb Maggie noticed a family of tourists wandering on foot, shooting videos and looking enormously pleased with themselves to be committing a quaint Irish village onto tape.

The woman held the small, clever little camera and laughed as she focused on her husband and two children. Maggie must have stepped into the frame, for the woman lifted her hand and waved.

"Good evening, miss."

"And to you."

To her credit, Maggie didn't even snicker when the woman whispered to her husband, "Isn't her accent wonderful? Ask her about food, John. I'm dying to get more of her on tape."

"Ah . . . excuse me."

Tourism couldn't hurt the village, Maggie decided, and turned back to play the game. "Can I help you with something this evening?"

"If you wouldn't mind. We were wondering about a place to eat in town. If you could recommend something."

"And sure I could do that." Because they looked so delighted with her, she layered a bit more west county into her speech. "Now, if you're after wanting something fancy, you couldn't do better but to drive along this road another, oh, fifteen minutes, and you could have the very king of meals at Dromoland Castle. It'll be hard on your wallet, but your taste buds will be in heaven."

"We're not dressed for a fancy meal," the woman put in. "Actually, we were hoping for something simple right here in the village."

"If you're in the mood for a bit of pub grub"—she winked at the two children, who were eyeing her as if she'd stepped off a light-flashing UFO—"you'll find O'Malley's to your liking, I'm sure. His chips are as good as anyone's."

"That means french fries," the woman translated. "We just arrived this morning, from America," she told Maggie. "I'm afraid we don't know much about the local customs. Are children permitted in the bars—pubs?"

"This is Ireland. Children are welcome anywhere, anywhere a'tall. That's O'Malley's there." She gestured toward the low plastered block building with dark trim. "I'm going there meself. They'd be pleased to have you and your family for a meal."

"Thank you." The man beamed at her, the children stared and the woman had yet to take the camera from in front of her face. "We'll give it a try."

"Enjoy your meal, then, and the rest of your stay." Maggie turned and sauntered down the sidewalk and into O'Malley's. It was dim, smoky and smelled of frying onions and beer.

"And how are you, Tim?" Maggie asked as she settled herself at the bar.

"And look who's dragged herself in." Tim grinned at her as he built a pint of Guinness. "And how are you, Maggie?"

"I'm fit and hungry as a bear." She exchanged greetings with a couple at a postage-stamp-sized table behind her and at the two men who nursed pints at the bar. "Will you fix me one of your steak sandwiches, Tim, with a pile of chips, and I'll have a pint of Harp while I'm waiting."

The proprietor stuck his head around the back of the bar and shouted out Maggie's order. "Well now, how was Dublin City?" he asked while he drew her a pint.

"I'll tell you." She propped her elbows on the bar and began to describe her trip for the patrons of the bar. While she talked the American family came in and settled at a table.

"Champagne and goose liver?" Tim shook his head. "Isn't that a wonder? And all those people come to see your glass. Your father'd be proud of you, Maggie girl. Proud as a peacock."

"I hope so." She sniffed deeply when Tim slid her plate in front of her. "But the truth is, I'd rather have your steak sandwich than a pound of goose liver."

He laughed heartily. "That's our girl."

"It turns out that the grandmother of the man who's managing things for me was a friend of my gran, Gran O'Reilly."

"You don't mean it?" With a sigh, Tim rubbed his belly. "Sure and it's a small world."

"It is," Maggie agreed, making it casual. "She's from Galway and knew Gran when they were girls. They wrote letters for years after Gran moved here, keeping up, you know?"

"That's fine. No friend like an old friend."

"Gran wrote her about the hotel and such, the family. Mentioned how it was my mother used to sing."

"Oh, that was a time ago." Remembering, Tim picked up a glass to polish. "Before you were born, to be sure. Fact is, now that I think of it, she sang here in this very pub one of the last times before she gave it up."

"Here? You had her sing here?"

"I did, yes. She had a sweet voice, did Maeve. Traveled all over the country. Hardly saw a bit of her for, oh, more than ten years, I'd say, then she came back to stay a time. It seems to me Mrs. O'Reilly was ailing. So I asked Maeve if maybe she'd like to sing an evening or two, not that we've as grand a place as some in Dublin and Cork and Donnegal where she'd performed."

"She performed? For ten years?"

"Oh well, I don't know as she made much of it at first. Anxious to be off and away was Maeve, as long as I remember. She wasn't happy making beds in a hotel in a village like ours, and let us know it." He winked to take the sting out of his words. "But she was doing well by the time she came back and sang here. Then she and Tom . . . well, they only had eyes for each other the moment he walked in and heard her singing."

"And after they married," Maggie said carefully, "she didn't sing any longer?"

"Didn't care to. Wouldn't talk of it. Fact is, it's been so long, till you brought it up, I'd nearly forgotten."

Maggie doubted her mother had forgotten, or could forget. How would she herself feel if some twist in her life demanded that she give up her art? she wondered. Angry, sad, resentful. She looked down at her hands, thought of how it would be if she couldn't use them again. What would she become if suddenly, just as she was about to make her mark, it was all taken away?

If relinquishing her career wasn't an excuse for the bitter years that had passed with her mother, at least it was a reason.

Maggie needed time to shift through it, to talk to Brianna. She toyed with her beer and began to put the pieces of the woman her mother had been together with the personality of the woman she'd become.

How much of both, Maggie wondered, had Maeve passed on to her daughter?

"You're to eat that sandwich," Tim ordered as he slid another pint down the bar. "Not study it."

"I am." To prove her point, Maggie took a healthy bite. The pub was warm and comforting. Time enough tomorrow, she decided, to wipe the film off old dreams. "Will you get me another pint, Tim?"

"That I'll do," he said, then lifted a hand when the pub door opened again. "Well, it's a night for strangers. Where've you been, Murphy?"

"Why, missing you, boy-o." Spotting Maggie, Murphy grinned and joined her at the bar. "I'm hoping I can sit by the celebrity."

"I suppose I can allow it," she returned. "This once, at any rate. So, Murphy, when are you going to court my sister?"

It was an old joke, but still made the pub patrons chuckle. Murphy sipped from Maggie's glass and sighed. "Now, darling, you know there's only room in my heart for you."

"I know you're a scoundrel." She took back her beer.

He was a wildly handsome man, trim and strong and weathered like an oak from the sun and wind. His dark hair curled around his collar, over his ears, and his eyes were as blue as the cobalt bottle in her shop.

Not polished like Rogan, she thought. Rough as a Gypsy was Murphy, but with a heart as wide and sweet as the valley he loved. Maggie had never had a brother, but Murphy was the nearest to it.

"I'd marry you tomorrow," he claimed, sending the pub, except for the Americans who looked on avidly, into whoops of laughter. "If you'd have me."

"You can rest easy, then, for I won't be having the likes of you. But I'll kiss you and make you sorry for it."

She made good on her word, kissing him long and hard until they drew back and grinned at one another. "Have you missed me, then?" Maggie asked.

"Not a whit. I'll have a pint of Guinness, Tim, and the same thing our celebrity's having." He stole one of her chips. "I heard you were back."

"Oh." Her voice cooled a little. "You saw Brie?"

"No, I *heard* you were back," he repeated. "Your furnace."

"Ah."

"My sister sent me some clippings, from Cork."

"Mmm. How is Mary Ellen?"

"Oh, she's fit. Drew and the children, too." Murphy reached in his pocket, frowned, patted another. "Ah, here we go." He took out two folded pieces of newspaper. " 'Clarewoman triumphs in Dublin,' " he read. " 'Margaret Mary Concannon impressed the art word at a showing at Worldwide Gallery, Dublin, Sunday night.' "

"Let me see that." Maggie snatched the clipping out of his hand. " 'Miss Concannon, a free-blown-glass artist, drew praise and compliments from attendees of the show with her bold and complex sculptures and drawings. The artist herself is a diminutive'—diminutive, hah!" Maggie editorialized.

"Give it back." Murphy tugged the clipping away and continued to read it aloud himself. " 'A diminutive young woman of exceptional talent and beauty.' Hah, yourself," Murphy added, sneering at her. " 'The green-eyed redhead of ivory complexion and considerable charm was as fascinating as her work to this art lover. Worldwide, one of the top galleries in the world, considers itself fortunate to display Miss Concannon's work.

" ' "I believe she's only begun to tap her creativity," stated Rogan Sweeney, president of Worldwide. "Bringing Miss Concannon's work to the attention of the world is a privilege." ' "

"He said that?" She reached for the clipping again, but Murphy held it out of reach.

"He did. It's here in black and white. Now let me finish. People want to hear."

Indeed, the pub had gone quiet. Every eye was on Murphy as he finished the review.

" 'Worldwide will be touring several of Miss Concannon's pieces over the next year, and will keep others, personally selected by the artist and Mr. Sweeney, on permanent display in Dublin.' " Satisfied, Murphy placed the clipping on the bar, where Tim craned over to see it.

"And there's pictures," he added, unfolding the second clipping. "Of Maggie with the ivory complexion and some of her fancy glass. Nothing to say, Maggie?"

She let out a long breath, dragged at her hair. "I guess I'd better say 'drinks for all my friends.' "

"You're quiet, Maggie Mae."

Maggie smiled over the nickname, one her father had used for her. She was more than comfortable in Murphy's lorry, with her bike stowed in the bed and the engine purring, as did all of Murphy's machinery, like a satisfied cat.

"I'm thinking I'm a wee bit drunk, Murphy." She stretched and sighed. "And that I like the feeling quite a lot."

"Well, you earned it." She was more than a wee bit drunk, which was why he'd hauled her bike into his lorry before she could think to argue. "We're all proud of you, and I for one will look upon that bottle you made me with more respect from now on."

" 'Tis a weed pot, I've told you, not a bottle. You put pretty twigs or wildflowers in it."

Why anyone would bring twigs, pretty or otherwise, into the house was beyond him. "So are you going back to Dublin, then?"

"I don't know—not for a time, anyway. I can't work there and work's what I want to do right now." She scowled at a tumble of furze, silvered now by the rising moon. "He never acted like it was a privilege, you know."

"What's that?"

"Oh, no, it was always that *I* should be privileged he'd taken a second look at me work. The great and powerful Sweeney giving the poor, struggling artist a chance for fame and fortune. Well, did I ask for fame and fortune, Murphy? That's what I want to know? Did I ask for it?"

He knew the tone, the belligerent, defensive slap of it, and answered cautiously. "I can't say, Maggie. But don't you want it?"

"Of course I do. Do I look like a fleabrain? But ask for it? No, I did not. I never once asked him for a blessed thing, except at the start to leave me alone. And did he? Hah!" She folded her arms across her chest. "Not much he did. He tempted me, Murphy, and the devil himself couldn't have been more sly and persuasive. Now I'm stuck, you see, and can't go back."

Murphy pursed his lips and pulled smoothly to a stop by her gate. "Well, are you wanting to go back?"

"No. And that's the worst of it. I want exactly what he says I can have, and want it so it hurts my heart. But I don't want things to change either, that's the hell of it. I want to be left alone to work and to think, and just to be. I don't know as I can have both."

"You can have what you want, Maggie. You're too stubborn to take less."

She laughed at that and turned to kiss him sloppily. "Oh, I love you, Murphy. Why don't you come out into the field and dance with me in the moonlight?"

He grinned, ruffled her hair. "Why don't I put your bike away and tuck you into bed?"

"I'll do it meself." She climbed out of the lorry, but he was quicker. He lifted out her bike and set it on the road. "Thank you for escorting me home, Mr. Muldoon."

"The pleasure was mine, Miss Concannon. Now get yourself to bed."

She wheeled her bike through the gate as he began to sing. Stopping just inside the garden, she listened as his voice, a strong, sweet tenor, drifted through the night quiet and disappeared.

"Alone all alone by the wave wash strand, all alone in a crowded hall. The hall it is gay, and the waves they are grand, but my heart is not here at all."

She smiled a little and finished the rest in her mind. *It flies far away, by night and by day, to the times and the joys that are gone.*

"Slievenamon" was the ballad, she knew. Woman of the Mountain. Well, she wasn't standing on a mountain, but she thought she understood the soul of the tune. The hall in Dublin had been gay, yet her heart hadn't been there. She'd been alone. All alone.

She wheeled her bike around the back, but instead of going inside, Maggie headed away from the house. It was true she was a little lightheaded and none too steady on her feet, but she didn't want to waste such a night in bed. Alone in bed.

And drunk or sober, day or night, she could find her way over the land that had once been hers.

She heard the hoot of an owl and the rustle of something that hunted or hid by night in the higher grass to the east. Overhead, the moon, just past full, shone like a bright beacon in a swimming sea of stars. The night whispered around her, secretly. A brook to the west babbled in answer.

This, this, was part of what she wanted. What she needed as much as breath was the glory of solitude. Having the green fields flowing around her, silvered now in moonlight and starlight, with only the faint glow in the distance that was the lamp in Murphy's kitchen.

She remembered walking here with her father, her child's hand clutched warmly in his. He hadn't talked of planting or plowing, but of dreams. Always, he had spoken of dreams.

He'd never really found his.

Sadder somehow, she thought, was that she was beginning to see that her mother had found hers, only to lose it again.

How would it be, she wondered, to have what you wanted as close as your fingertips, then have it slip away? Forever.

And wasn't that exactly what she herself was so afraid of?

She lay on her back on the grass, her head spinning with too much drink and too many dreams of her own. The stars wheeled in their angels' dance, and the moon, shiny as a silver coin, looked down on her. The air was sweetened by the lilt of a nightingale. And the night was hers alone.

She smiled, shut her eyes and slept.

ELEVEN

It was the cow that woke her. The big, liquid eyes studied the sleeping form curled in the pasture. There was little thought in a cow's head other than food and the need to be milked. So she sniffed once, twice, at Maggie's cheek, snorted, then began to crop grass.

"Oh God have mercy, what's the noise?"

Her head throbbing like a large drum being beaten, Maggie rolled over, bumped solidly into the cow's foreleg and opened bleary, bloodshot eyes.

"Sweet Jesus Christ!" Maggie's squeal reverberated in her head like a gong, causing her to catch hold of her ears as if they were about to explode as she scrambled away. The cow, as startled as she, mooed and rolled her eyes. "What are you doing here?" Keeping a firm hold on her head, Maggie made it to her knees. "What am I doing here?" When she dropped back on her haunches, she and the cow studied each other doubtfully. "I must've fallen asleep. Oh!" In pitiful defense against a raging hangover, she shifted her hands from her ears to her eyes. "Oh, the penance paid for one drink over the limit. I'll just sit right here for a minute, if you don't mind, until I have the strength to stand."

The cow, after one last roll of her eyes, began to graze again.

The morning was bright and warm, and full of sound. The drone of a tractor, the bark of a dog, the cheerful birdsong rolled in Maggie's sick head. Her mouth tasted as if she'd spent the night dining on a peat bog, and her clothes were coated with morning dew.

"Well, it's a fine thing to pass out in a field like a drunken hobo."

She made it to her feet, swayed once and moaned. The cow swished its tail in what might have been sympathy. Cautious, Maggie stretched. When her bones didn't shatter, she worked out the rest of the kinks and let her gritty eyes scan the field.

More cows, uninterested in their human visitor, grazed. In the next field, she could see the circle of standing stones, ancient as the air, that the locals called Druid's Mark. She remembered now kissing Murphy good night and, with his fading song playing in her head, wandering under the moon.

And the dream she'd had, sleeping under its silver light, came back to her so vividly, so breathlessly, that she forgot the throbbing in her head and the stiffness in her joints.

The moon, glowing with light, pulsing like a heartbeat. Flooding the sky, and the earth beneath it with cold white light. Then it had burned, hot as a torch until it ran with color, bled blues and reds and golds so lovely that even in sleep she had wept.

She had reached up, and up, and up, until she had touched it. Smooth it had been, and solid and cool as she cupped it in her hands. In that sphere she had seen herself, and deep, somewhere deep within those swimming colors, had been her heart.

The vision whirling in her head was more than a match for a hangover. Driven by it, she ran from the field, leaving the placid cows to their grazing and the morning to its birdsong.

Within the hour she was in her studio, desperate to turn vision into reality. She needed no sketch, not with the image so boldly imprinted in her mind. She'd eaten nothing, didn't need to. With the thrill of discovery glittering over her like a cloak, she made the first gather.

She smoothed it on the marble to chill and center it. Then she gave it her breath.

When it was heated and fluid again, she marvered the bubble over powdered colorants. Into the flames it went again until the color melted into the vessel wall.

She repeated the process over and over, adding glass, fire, breath, color.

Turning and turning the rod both against and with gravity, she smoothed the glowing sphere with paddles to maintain its shape.

Once she'd transferred the vessel from pipe to pontil, she heated it strongly in the glory hole. She would employ a wet stick now, holding it tightly to the mouth of her work so that the steam pressure enlarged the form.

All of her energies were focused. She knew that the water on the stick would vaporize. The pressure could blow out the vessel walls. She would have done with a pontil boy now, someone to be another pair of hands, to fetch tools, to gather more glass, but she had never hired anyone for the job.

She began to mutter to herself as she was forced to make the trips herself, back to the furnace, back to the marver, back to the chair.

The sun rose higher, streaming through the windows and crowning her in a nimbus of light.

That was how Rogan saw her when he opened the door. Sitting in the chair, with a ball of molten color under her hands and sunlight circling her.

She spared him one sharp glance. "Take off that damn suit coat and tie. I need your hands."

"What?"

"I need your hands, damn it. Do exactly what I tell you and don't talk to me."

He wasn't sure he could. He wasn't often struck dumb, but at that moment, with the blast of fire, the flash of sun, she looked like some sort of fierce, fiery goddess creating new worlds. He set his briefcase aside and stripped off his coat.

"You'll hold this steady," she told him as she slipped out of the chair. "And you'll turn the pontil just as I am. You see? Slowly, constantly. No jerks or pauses or I'll have to kill you. I need a prunt."

He was so stunned that she would trust him with her work that he sat in her chair without a word. The pipe was warm in his hands, heavier than he'd expected. She kept hers over his until she felt he had the rhythm.

"Don't stop," she warned him. "Believe me, your very life depends on it."

He didn't doubt her. She went to the furnace, gathered a prunt and came back.

"Do you see how I did that? Nothing to that part. I want you to do it for me next time." Once the wall was softened, she took jacks and pushed into the glass.

"Do it now." She took the pipe from him and continued to work it. "I can shear it off if you gather too much."

The heat from the furnace stole his breath. He dipped the pipe in, following her terse directions, rolled it under the melt. He watched the glass gather and cling, like hot tears.

"You'll bring it to me from the back of the bench and to the right." Anticipating him, she snatched up a pair of tongs and took control of the pontil even as he angled it toward her.

She repeated the process, sending off sparks from the wax, merging glass into glass, color into color. When she was satisfied with the interior design, she reblew the vessel, urging it into a sphere again, shaping it with air.

What Rogan saw was a perfect circle, the size perhaps of a soccer ball. The interior of the clear glass orb exploded with colors and shapes, bled and throbbed with them. If he had been a fanciful man, he would have said the glass lived and breathed just as he did. The colors swirled, impossibly vivid, at the center, then flowed to the most delicate hues as they trailed to the wall.

Dreams, he thought. It's a circle of dreams.

"Bring me that file," she snapped out.

"The what?"

"The file, blast it." She was already moving to a bench covered with fireproof pads. As she braced the pontil on a wooded vise, she held out her hand, like a surgeon demanding a scalpel. Rogan slapped a file into it.

He heard her slow steady breathing pause, hold, just as she struck the glass bond with the file. She struck the pontil. The ball rolled comfortably onto the pad. "Gloves," she ordered. "The heavy ones by my chair. Hurry up."

With her eyes still on the ball, she jerked the gloves on. Oh, she wanted to hold it. To cup it in her naked palms as she had in her dream. Instead, she chose a metal fork, covered with asbestos, and carried the sphere to the annealing oven.

She set the timer, then stood for a minute, staring blankly into space.

"It's the moon, you see," she said softly. "It pulls the tides, in the sea, in us. We hunt by it and harvest by it and sleep by it. And if we're lucky enough, we can hold it in our hands and dream by it."

"What will you call it?"

"It won't have a name. Everyone should see what they want most in it." As if coming out of a dream herself, she lifted a hand to her head. "I'm tired." She trudged wearily back to her chair, sat and let her head fall back.

She was milk pale, Rogan noticed, drained of the energized glow that had covered her while she'd worked. "Have you worked through the night again?"

"No, I slept last night." She smiled to herself. "In Murphy's field, under the bright, full moon."

"You slept in a field?"

"I was drunk." She yawned, then laughed and opened her eyes. "A little. And it was such a grand night."

"And who," Rogan asked as he crossed to her, "is Murphy?"

"A man I know. Who would have been a bit surprised to find me sleeping in his pasture. Would you get me a drink?" At his lifted brow, she laughed. "A soft one, if you will. From the refrigerator there. And help yourself," she added when he obliged her. "You make a passable pontil boy, Sweeney."

"You're welcome," he said, taking that for a thanks. As she tipped back the can he had given her, he scanned the room. She hadn't been idle, he noted. There were several new pieces tucked away, her interpretations of the Native American display. He studied a shallow wide-lipped dish, decorated with deep dull colors.

"Lovely work."

"Mmm. An experiment that turned out well. I combined opaque and transparent glass." She yawned again, broadly. "Then tin-fumed it."

"Tin-fumed? Never mind," he said when he saw that she was about to launch into a complicated explanation. "I wouldn't understand what you were talking about, anyway. Chemistry was never my forte. I'll just be pleased with the finished product."

"You're supposed to say it's fascinating, just as I am."

He glanced back at her and his lips twitched. "Been reading your reviews, have you? God help us now. Why don't you go get some rest? We'll talk later. I'll take you to dinner."

"You didn't come all this way to take me to dinner."

"I'd enjoy it just the same."

There was something different about him, she decided. Some subtle change somewhere deep in those gorgeous eyes of his. Whatever it was, he had it under control. A couple of hours with her ought to fix that, Maggie concluded, and smiled at him.

"We'll go in the house, have some tea and a bite to eat. You can tell me why you've come."

"To see you, for one thing."

Something in his tone told her to sharpen her work-dulled wits. "Well, you've seen me."

"So I have." He picked up his briefcase and opened the door. "I could use that tea."

"Good, you can brew it." She shot a look over her shoulder as she stepped outside. "If you know how."

"I believe I do. Your garden looks lovely."

"Brie's tended it while I was gone. What's this?" She tapped a foot against a cardboard box at her back door.

"A few things I brought with me. Your shoes for one. You left them in the parlor."

He handed her the briefcase and hauled the box into the kitchen. After dumping it on the table, he looked around the kitchen.

"Where's the tea?"

"In the cupboard above the stove."

While he went to work she slit the box open. Moments later she was sitting down, holding her belly as she laughed.

"Trust you never to forget a thing. Rogan, if I won't answer the phone, why should I listen to a silly answering machine?"

"Because I'll murder you if you don't."

"There's that." She rose again and pulled out a wall calendar. "French Impressionists," she murmured, studying the pictures above each month. "Well, at least it's pretty."

"Use it," he said simply, and set the kettle to boil. "And the machine, and this." He reached into the box himself and pulled out a long velvet case. Without ceremony he flipped it open and took out a slim gold watch, its amber face circled by diamonds.

"God, I can't wear that. It's a lady's watch. I'll forget I have it on and shower with it."

"It's waterproof."

"I'll break it."

"Then I'll get you another." He took her arm, began to unbutton the cuff of her shirt. "What the hell is this?" he demanded when he hit the bandage. "What have you done?"

"It's a burn." She was still staring at the watch and didn't see the fury light in his eyes. "I got a bit careless."

"Damn it, Maggie. You've no right to be careless. None at all. Am I to be worried about you setting yourself afire now?"

"Don't be ridiculous. You'd think I severed my hand." She would have pulled her hand away, but his grip tightened. "Rogan, for pity sake, a glass artist gets a burn now and again. It's not fatal."

"Of course not," he said stiffly. He forced back the anger he was feeling at her carelessness and clasped the watch on her wrist. "I don't like to hear you've been careless." He let her hand go, slipped his own in his pockets. "It's not serious, then?"

"No." She watched him warily when he went to answer the kettle's shrill. "Shall I make us a sandwich?"

"As you like."

"You didn't say how long you'd be staying."

"I'll go back tonight. I wanted to speak with you in person rather than try to reach you by phone." In control again, he finished making the tea and brought the pot to the table. "I've brought the clippings you asked my grandmother about."

"Oh, the clippings." Maggie stared at his briefcase. "Yes, that was good of her. I'll read them later." When she was alone.

"All right. And there was something else I wanted to give you. In person."

"Something else." She sliced through a loaf of Brianna's bread. "It's a day for presents."

"This wouldn't qualify as a present." Rogan opened his briefcase and took out an envelope. "You may want to open this now."

"All right, then." She dusted off her hands, tore open the envelope. She had to grab the back of a chair to keep her balance as she read the amount on the check. "Mary, mother of God."

"We sold every piece we'd priced." More than satisfied by her reaction, he watched her sink into the chair. "I would say the showing was quite successful."

"Every piece," she echoed. "For so much."

She thought of the moon, of dreams, of changes. Weak, she laid her head on the table.

"I can't breathe. My lungs have collapsed." Indeed, she could hardly talk. "I can't get my breath."

"Sure you can." He went behind her, massaged her shoulders. "Just in and out. Give yourself a minute to let it take hold."

"It's almost two hundred thousand pounds."

"Very nearly. With the interest we'll generate from touring your work, and offering only a portion of it to the market, we'll increase the price." The strangled sound she made caused him to laugh. "In and out, Maggie love. Just push the air out and bring it in again. I'll arrange for shipping for those pieces you've finished. We'll set the tour for the fall, because you've so much completed already. You may want to take some time off to enjoy yourself. Have a holiday."

"A holiday." She sat up again. "I can't think about that yet. I can't think at all."

"You've time." He patted her head, then moved around her to pour the tea. "You'll have dinner with me tonight, to celebrate?"

"Aye," she murmured. "I don't know what to say, Rogan. I never really believed it would . . . I just didn't believe it." She pressed her hands to her mouth. For a moment he was afraid she would begin to sob, but it was laughter, wild and jubilant, that burst out of her mouth. "I'm rich! I'm a rich woman, Rogan Sweeney." She popped out of the chair to kiss him, then whirled away. "Oh, I know it's a drop in the bucket to you, but to me—to me, it's freedom. The chains are broken, whether she wants them to be or not."

"What are you talking about?"

She shook her head, thinking of Brianna. "Dreams, Rogan, wonderful dreams. Oh, I have to tell her. Right away." She snatched up the check and impulsively stuffed it in her back pocket. "You'll stay, please. Have your tea, make some food. Make use of the phone you're so fond of. Whatever you like."

"Where are you going?"

"I won't be long." There were wings on her feet as she whirled back and kissed him again. Her lips missed his in her hurry and caught his chin. "Don't go." With that she was racing out of the door and across the fields.

She was puffing like a steam engine by the time she scrambled over the stone fence that bordered Brianna's land. But then, she'd been out of breath before she'd begun the race. She barely missed trampling her sister's pansies—a sin she would have paid for dearly—and skidded on the narrow stone path that wound through the velvety flowers.

She drew in air to shout, but didn't waste it as she spotted Brianna in the little path of green beyond the garden, hanging linen on the line.

Clothespins in her mouth, wet sheets in her hands, Brianna stared across the nodding columbines and daisies while Maggie pressed her hands to her thudding heart. Saying nothing, Brianna snapped the sheet expertly and began to clip it to the line.

There was hurt in her sister's face still, Maggie observed. And anger. All chilled lightly with Brianna's special blend of pride and control. The wolfhound gave a happy bark and started forward, only to stop short at Brianna's quiet order. He settled, with what could only be a look of regret at Maggie, back at his mistress's feet. She took another sheet from the basket beside her, flicked it and clipped it neatly to dry.

"Hello, Maggie."

So the wind blew cold from this quarter, Maggie mused, and tucked her hands into her back pockets. "Hello, Brianna. You've guests?"

"Aye. We're full at the moment. An American couple, an English family and a young man from Belgium."

"A virtual United Nations." She sniffed elaborately. "You've pies baking."

"They're baked and cooling on the windowsill." Because she hated confrontations of any kind, Brianna kept her eyes on her work as she spoke. "I thought about what you said, Maggie, and I want to say I'm sorry. I should have been there for you. I should have found a way."

"Why didn't you?"

Brianna let out a quick breath, her only sign of agitation. "You never make it easy, do you?"

"No."

"I have obligations—not only to her," she said before Maggie could speak. "But to this place. You're not the only one with ambitions, or with dreams."

The heated words that burned on Maggie's tongue cooled, then slid away. She turned to study the back of the house. The paint was fresh and white; the windows, open to the summer afternoon, were glistening. Lace curtains billowed, romantic as a bridal veil. Flowers crowded the ground and poured out of pots and tin buckets.

"You've done fine work here, Brianna. Gran would have approved."

"But you don't."

"You're wrong." In an apology of her own, she laid a hand on her sister's arm. "I don't claim I understand how you do it, or why you want to, but that's not for me to say. If this place is your dream, Brie, you've made it shine. I'm sorry I shouted at you."

"Oh, I'm used to that." Despite her resigned tone, it was clear that she had thawed. "If you'll wait till I've finished here, I'll put on some tea. I've a bit of trifle to go with it."

Maggie's empty stomach responded eagerly, but she shook her head. "I haven't time for it. I left Rogan back at the cottage."

"Left him? You should have brought him along with you. You can't leave a guest kicking his heels that way."

"He's not a guest, he's . . . well, I don't know what we'd call him, but that doesn't matter. I want to show you something."

Though her sense of propriety was offended, Brianna took out the last pillowslip. "All right, show me. Then get back to Rogan. If you've no food in the house, bring him here. The man's come all the way from Dublin after all, and—"

"Will you stop worrying about Sweeney?" Maggie cut in impatiently, and pulled the check out of her pocket. "And look at this?"

One hand on the line, Brianna glanced at the paper. Her mouth dropped open and the clothespin fell out to plop on the ground. The pillowslip floated after it.

"What is it?"

"It's a check, are you blind? A big, fat, beautiful check. He sold all of it, Brie. All he'd set out to sell."

"For so much?" Brianna could only gape at all the zeros. "For so much? How can that be?"

"I'm a genius." Maggie grabbed Brianna's shoulders and whirled her around. "Don't you read my reviews? I have untapped depths of creativity." Laughing, she dragged Brianna into a lively hornpipe. "Oh, and there's something more about my soul and my sexuality. I haven't memorized it all yet."

"Maggie, wait. My head's spinning."

"Let it spin. We're rich, don't you see?" They tumbled to the ground together, Maggie shrieking with laughter and Con jumping in frantic circles around them. "I can buy that glass lathe I've been wanting, and you can have that new stove you've been pretending you don't need. And we'll have a holiday. Anywhere in the world, anywhere a'tall. I'll have a new bed." She plopped back on the grass to wrestle with Con. "And you can add a whole wing onto Blackthorn if you've a mind to."

"I can't take it in. I just can't take it in."

"We'll find a house." Pushing herself up again, Maggie hooked an arm around Con's neck. "Whatever kind she wants. And hire someone to fetch and carry for her."

Brianna shut her eyes and fought back the first guilty flare of elation. "She might not want—"

"It will be what she wants. Listen to me." Maggie grabbed Brianna's hands and squeezed. "She'll go, Brie. And she'll be well taken care of. She'll have whatever pleases her. Tomorrow we'll go into Ennis and talk to Pat O'Shea. He sells houses. We'll set her up as grandly as we can, and as quickly. I promised Da I'd do my best by both of you, and that's what I'm going to do."

"Have you no consideration?" Maeve stood on the garden path, a shawl around her shoulders despite the warmth of the sun. The dress beneath it was starched and pressed—by Brianna's hand, Maggie had no doubt. "Out here shouting and shrieking while a body's trying to rest." She pulled the shawl closer and jabbed a finger at her younger daughter. "Get up off the ground. What's wrong with you? Behaving like a hoyden, and you with guests in the house."

Brianna rose stiffly, brushed at her slacks. "It's a fine day. Perhaps you'd like to sit in the sun."

"I might as well. Call off that vicious dog."

"Sit, Con." Protectively, Brianna laid a hand on the dog's head. "Can I bring you some tea?"

"Yes, and brew it properly this time." Maeve shuffled to the chair and table Brianna had set up beside the garden. "That boy, that Belgian, he's clattered up the stairs twice today. You'll have to tell him to mind the racket. It's what comes when parents let their children traipse all over the country."

"I'll have the tea in a moment. Maggie, will you stay?"

"Not for tea. But I'll have a word with Mother." She sent her sister a steely look to prevent any argument. "Can you be ready to drive into Ennis by ten tomorrow, Brie?"

"I—yes, I'll be ready."

"What's this?" Maeve demanded as Brie walked toward the kitchen door. "What are the two of you planning?"

"Your future." Maggie took the chair beside her mother's, kicked out her legs. She'd wanted to go about it differently. After what she'd begun to learn, she'd hoped she and her mother could find a meeting ground somewhere beyond the old hurts. But already the old angers and guilts were working in her. Remembering last night's moon and her thoughts about lost dreams, she spoke quietly. "We're after buying you a house."

Maeve made a sound of disgust and plucked at the fringe of her shawl. "Nonsense. I'm content here, with Brianna to look after me."

"I'm sure you are, but it's about to end. Oh, I'll hire you a companion. You needn't worry that you'll have to learn to do for yourself. But you won't be using Brie any longer."

"Brianna understands the responsibilities of a child to her mother."

"More than," Maggie agreed. "She's done everything in her power to make you content, Mother. It hasn't been enough, and maybe I've begun to understand that."

"You understand nothing."

"Perhaps, but I'd like to understand." She took a deep breath. Though she couldn't reach out to her mother, physically or emotionally, her voice softened. "I truly would. I'm sorry for what you gave up. I learned of the singing only—"

"You won't speak of it." Maeve's voice was frigid. Her already pale skin whitened further with the shock of a pain she'd never forgotten, never forgiven. "You will never speak of that time."

"I wanted only to say I'm sorry."

"I don't want your sorrow." With her mouth tight, Maeve looked aside. She couldn't bear to have the past tossed in her face, to be pitied because she had sinned and lost what had mattered most to her. "You will not speak of it to me again."

"All right." Maggie leaned forward until Maeve's gaze settled on her. "I'll say this. You blame me for what you lost, and maybe that comforts you somehow. I can't wish myself unborn. But I'll do what I can. You'll have a house, a good one, and a respectable, competent woman to see to your needs, someone I hope can be a friend to you as well as a companion. This I'll do for Da, and for Brie. And for you."

"You've done nothing for me in your life but cause me misery."

So there would be no softening, Maggie realized. No meeting on new ground. "So you've told me, time and again. We'll find a place close enough so that Brie can visit you, for she'll feel she should. And I'll furnish the place as well, however you like. You'll have a monthly allowance—for food, for clothes, for whatever it is you need. But I swear before God you'll be out of his house and into your own before a month is up."

"Pipe dreams." Her tone was blunt and dismissive, but Maggie sensed a little frisson of fear beneath. "Like your father, you are full of empty dreams and foolish schemes."

"Not empty, and not foolish." Again, Maggie drew the check out of her pocket. This time she had the satisfaction of seeing her mother's eyes go wide and blank. "Aye, it's real, and it's mine. I earned it. I earned it because Da had the faith in me to let me learn, to let me try."

Maeve's eyes flicked to Maggie's, calculating. "What he gave you belonged to me as well."

"The money for Venice, for schooling and for the roof over my head, that's true. What else he gave me had nothing to do with you. And you'll get your share of this." Maggie tucked the check away again. "Then I'll owe you nothing."

"You owe me your life," Maeve spat.

"Mine meant little enough to you. I may know why that is, but it doesn't change how it makes me feel inside. Understand me, you'll go without complaint, without making your last days with Brianna a misery for her."

"I'll not go at all." Maeve dug in her pocket for a lace-edged hanky. "A mother needs the comfort of her child."

"You've no more love for Brianna than you do for me. We both know it, Mother. She might believe differently, but here, now, let's at least be honest. You've played on her heart, it's true, and God knows she's deserving of any love you have in that cold heart of yours." After a long breath, she pulled out the trump card she'd been holding for five years. "Would you have me tell her why Rory McAvery went off to America and broke her heart?"

Maeve's hands gave a quick little jerk. "I don't know what you're talking about."

"Oh, but you do. You took him aside when you saw he was getting serious in his courting. And you told him that you couldn't in good conscience let him give his heart to your daughter. Not when she'd given her body to another. You convinced him, and he was only a boy, after all, that she'd been sleeping with Murphy."

"It's a lie." Maeve's chin thrust out, but there was fear in her eyes. "You're an evil, lying child, Margaret Mary."

"You're the liar, and worse, much worse than that. What kind of a woman is it that steals happiness from her own blood because she has none herself? I heard from Murphy," Maggie said tersely. "After he and Rory beat each other to bloody pulps. Rory didn't believe his denial. Why should he, when Brianna's own mother had tearfully told him the tale?"

"She was too young to marry," Maeve said quickly. "I wouldn't have her making the same mistake as I did, ruining her life that way. The boy wasn't right for her, I tell you. He'd never have amounted to anything."

"She loved him."

"Love doesn't put bread on the table." Maeve fisted her hands, twisting the handkerchief in them. "Why haven't you told her?"

"Because I thought it would only hurt her more. I asked Murphy to say nothing, knowing Brianna's pride, and how it would be shattered. And maybe because I was angry that he would have believed you, that he didn't love her enough to see the lie. But I will tell her now. I'll walk right into that kitchen and tell her now. And if I have to, I'll drag poor Murphy over to stand with me. You'll have no one then."

She hadn't known the flavor of revenge would be so bitter. It lay cold and distasteful on Maggie's tongue as she continued. "I'll say nothing if you do as I say. And I'll promise you that I will provide for you as long as you live and do whatever I can to see that you're content. I can't give you back what you had, or wanted to have before you conceived me. But I can give you something that might make you happier than you've been since. Your own home. You've only to agree to my offer in order to have everything you've always wanted—money, a fine house and a servant to tend you."

Maeve pressed her lips together. Oh, it crushed the pride to bargain with the girl. "How do I know you'll keep your word?"

"Because I give it to you. Because I swear these things to you on my father's soul." Maggie rose. "That will have to content you. Tell Brianna I'll be by to pick her up at ten tomorrow." And with these words, Maggie turned on her heel and walked away.

TWELVE

She took her time walking back, again choosing the fields rather than the road. As she went she gathered wildflowers, the meadowsweet and valerian that sunned themselves among the grass. Murphy's well-fed cows, their udders plump and nearly ready for milking, grazed unconcernedly as she climbed over the stone walls that separated pasture from plowed field and field from summer hay.

Then she saw Murphy himself, atop his tractor, with young Brian O'Shay and Dougal Finnian with him, all to harvest the waving hay. They called it *comhair* in Irish, but Maggie knew that here, in the west, the word meant much more than its literal translation of "help." It meant community. No man was alone here, not when it came to haying, or opening a bank of peat or sowing in the spring.

If today O'Shay and Finnian were working Murphy's land, then tomorrow, or the day after, he would be working theirs. No one would have to ask. The tractor or plow or two good hands and a strong back would simply come, and the work would be done.

Stone fences might separate one man's fields from another, but the love of the land joined them.

She lifted a hand to answer the salute of the three farmers and, gathering her flowers, continued on to her home.

A jackdaw swooped overhead, complaining fiercely. A moment later Maggie saw why as Con barreled through the verge of the hay, his tongue lolling happily.

"Helping Murphy again, are you?" She reached down to ruffle his fur. "And a fine farmer you are, too. Go on back, then."

With a flurry of self-important barks, Con raced back toward the tractor. Maggie stood looking around her, the gold of the hay, the green of the pasture with its lazy cows and the shadows cast by the sun on the circle of stones that generations of Concannons, and now Murphy, had left undisturbed for time out of mind. She saw the rich brown of the land where potatoes had been dug. And over it all, a sky as blue as a cornflower in full blossom.

A quick laugh bubbled up in her throat, and she found herself racing the rest of the way.

Perhaps it was the pure pleasure of the day, coupled with the giddy excitement of her first major success that made her blood pump fast. It might have been the sound of birds singing as if their hearts would break, or the scent of wildflowers gathered by her own hands. But when she stopped just outside her own door and looked into her own kitchen, she was breathless with more than a quick scramble over the fields.

He was at the table, elegant in his English suit and handmade shoes. His briefcase was open, his pen out. It made her smile to see him work there, amid the clutter, on a crude wooden table he might have used for firewood at home.

The sun streamed through the windows and open door, flashing gold off his pen as he wrote in his neat hand. Then his fingers tapped over the keys of a calculator, hesitated, tapped again. She could see his profile, the faint line of concentration between the strong black brows, the firm set of his mouth.

He reached for his tea, sipped as he studied his figures. Set it down again. Wrote, read.

Elegant, he was. And beautiful, she thought, in a way so uniquely male, and as wonderfully competent and precise as the handy little machine he used to run his figures. Not a man to run across sunny fields or lie dreaming under the moon.

But he was more than she'd first imagined him to be, much more, she now understood.

The overpowering urge came over her to loosen that careful knot in his tie, unbutton that snug collar and find the man beneath.

Rarely did Maggie refuse her own urges.

She slipped inside. Even as her shadow fell over his papers, she was straddling his lap and fastening her mouth to his.

Shock, pleasure and lust speared into him like a three-tipped arrow, all sharp, all true to aim. The pen had clattered from his fingers and his hands had dived into her hair before he took the next breath. Through a haze he felt the tug on his tie.

"What?" he managed in something like a croak. The need for dignity had him clearing his throat and pressing her back. "What's all this?"

"You know. . . ." She punctuated her words by feathering light kisses over his face. He smelled expensive, she realized, all fine soap and starched linen. "I've always thought a tie a foolish thing, a sort of punishment for a man for simply being a man. Doesn't it choke you?"

It didn't, unless his heart was in his throat. "No." He shoved her hands away, but the damage was already done. Under her quick fingers, his tie was loose and his collar undone. "What are you about, Maggie?"

"That should be obvious enough, even to a Dubliner." She laughed at him, her eyes wickedly green. "I brought you flowers."

The latter were, at that moment, crushed between them. Rogan glanced down at the bruised petals. "Very nice. They could use some water, I imagine."

She tossed back her head and laughed. "It's always first things first with you, isn't it? But Rogan, from where I'm sitting, I'm aware there's something on your mind other than fetching a vase."

He couldn't deny his obvious, and very human reaction. "You'd harden a dead man," he muttered, and put his hands firmly on her hips to lift her away. She only wriggled closer, torturing him.

"Now, that's a pretty compliment, to be sure. But you're not dead, are you?" She kissed him again, using her teeth to prove her point. "Are you thinking you've work to finish up, and no time to waste?"

"No." His hands were still on her hips, but the fingers had dug in and had begun to knead. She smelled of wildflowers and smoke. All he could see was her face, the white skin with its blush of rose, dusting of gold freckles, the depthless green of her eyes. He made an heroic effort to level his voice. "But I'm thinking this is a mistake." A groan sounded in his throat when she moved her lips to his ear. "That there's a time and a place."

"And that you should choose it," she murmured as her nimble fingers flipped open the rest of the buttons on his shirt.

"Yes—no." Good God, how was a man supposed to think? "That we should both choose it, after we've set some priorities."

"I've only one priority at the moment." Her hands cruised up his chest, crushing wildflower petals against his skin. "I'm going to have you now, Rogan." Her laugh came again, low and challenging, before her lips sank into his. "Go ahead, fight me off."

He hadn't meant to touch her. That was his last coherent thought before his hands streaked up and filled themselves with her breasts. Her throaty moan spilled into his mouth like wine, rich and drugging.

Then he was tugging away her shirt and shoving back from the table all at once. "To hell with it," he muttered against her greedy mouth, and was lifting her.

Her arms and legs wrapped around him like silken rope, her shirt dangling from one wrist where the buttons held. Beneath, she wore a plain cotton camisole as erotic to him as ivory lace.

She was small and light, but with the blood trumpeting in his brain, he thought he could have carried a mountain. Her busy mouth never paused, racing from cheek to jaw to ear and back, while sexy little whimpers purred in her throat.

He started out of the kitchen, stumbled over a loose throw rug and knocked her back against the doorjamb. She only laughed, breathlessly now, and tightened the vise of her legs around his waist.

Their lips fused again in a rough, desperate kiss. With the doorway and her own limbs bracing her, he tore his mouth free to fasten it on her breast, suckling greedily through cotton.

The pleasure of it, dark and damning, lanced like a spear through her system. This was more, she realized as the blood sizzling through her veins began to hum like an engine. More than she'd expected. More than she might have been ready for. But there was no turning back.

He whirled away from the wall.

"Hurry," was all she could say as he strode toward the stairs. "Hurry."

Her words pumped like a pulse of his blood. *Hurry. Hurry.* Against his thundering heart, hers beat in furious response. With Maggie clinging like a burr, he all but leaped up the stairs, leaving a trail of broken flowers in their wake.

He turned unerringly to the left, into the bedroom where the sun poured gold and the fragrant breeze lifted the open curtains. He fell with her onto already tumbled sheets.

If it was madness that overcame him, it ruled her as well. There was no thought, or need, in either of them for gentle caresses, for soft words or slow hands. They tore at each other, mindless as beasts, dragging at clothes, pulling, tugging, kicking off shoes, all the while feeding greedily with violent kisses.

Her body was like an engine, fueled to race. She bucked and rolled and reared while her breath seared out in burning gasps. Seams ripped, needs exploded.

His hands were smooth. Another time they might have glided over her body like water. But now they grasped and bruised and plundered, bringing her unspeakable pleasure that tore through her overcharged system like lightning tears a darkened sky. He filled his palms with her breast again, and now, without barriers, drew the rigid tips into his mouth.

She cried out, not in pain at the rough scrape of his teeth and tongue, but in glory as the first harsh, vicious orgasm struck like a blow.

She hadn't expected it to slap her so quick and hard, nor had she ever experienced the utter helplessness that followed so fast on the heels of the storm. Before she could do more than wonder, fresh needs coiled whiplike inside her.

She spoke in Gaelic, half-remembered words she hadn't known she'd held in her heart. She'd never believed, never, that hunger could swallow her up and leave her trembling. But she shook under his hands, under the wild demand of his mouth. For another dazed interlude she was totally vulnerable, her bones molten and her mind reeling, stunned into surrender by the punch of her own climax.

He never felt the change. He knew only that she vibrated beneath him like a plucked bow. She was wet and hot and unbearably arousing. Her body was smooth, soft, supple, all the lovely dips and curves his to explore. He knew only the desperate desire to conquer, to possess, and so gorged himself on the flavor of her flesh until it seemed the essence of her raced through his veins like his own blood.

He clasped her limp hand in his and ravaged until she cried out once again, and his name was like a sob in the air.

With the room spinning like a carousel around her, she dragged her hands from his, tangled her fingers in his hair. Need spurted through her again, voraciously. She thrust her hips up.

"Now!" The demand broke from her throat. "Rogan, for God's sake—"

But he had already plunged inside her, deep and hard. She arched back, arched up, in glorious welcome as fresh pleasure geysered through her in one lancing, molten flash. Her body mated with his, matching rhythms, stroke for desperate stroke. The bite of her nails on his back was unfelt.

With vision blurred and dimmed, he watched her, saw each stunning sensation flicker over her face. It won't be enough, he thought dizzily. Even as the sorrow nicked through the burnished shield of passion, she opened her eyes and said his name again.

So he drowned in that sea of green, and burying his face in the fire of her hair, surrendered. With one last flash of glorious greed, he emptied himself into her.

In a war of any kind, there are casualties. No one, Maggie thought, knew the glory, the sorrow or the price of battle better than the Irish. And if, as she was very much afraid at the moment, her body was paralyzed for life as the result of this wonderful little war, she wouldn't count the cost.

The sun was still shining. Now that her heart had ceased to crash like thunder in her head, she heard the twitter of birds, the roar of her furnace, and the hum of a bee buzzing by the window.

She lay across the bed, her head clear off the mattress and dragged down by gravity. Her arms were aching. Perhaps because they were still wrapped like vises around Rogan, who was splayed over her, still as death.

She felt, when she held her own breath, the quicksilver race of his heart. It was, she decided, a wonder they hadn't killed each other. Content with his weight, and the drouzy feel of cobwebs in her brain, she watched the sun dance on the ceiling.

His own mind cleared slowly, the red haze mellowing, then fading completely until he became aware again of the quiet light and the small, warm body beneath his. He shut his eyes again and lay still.

What were the words he should say? he wondered. If he told her that he'd discovered, to his own shock and confusion, that he loved her, why should she believe it? To say those words now, when they were both still sated and dazed from sex, would hardly please a woman like Maggie, or make her see the bare truth of them.

What words were there, after a man had tossed a woman down and plundered like an animal? Oh, he'd no doubt she'd enjoyed it, but that hardly changed the fact that he'd completely lost control, of his mind, of his body, of whatever it was that separated the civilized from the wild.

For the first time in his life, he'd taken a woman without finesse, without care and, he thought with a sudden start, without a thought about the consequences.

He started to shift, but she murmured in protest and tightened her already fierce grip.

"Don't go away."

"I'm not." He realized her head was unsupported and, cupping a hand beneath it, rolled to reverse their positions. And nearly sent them over the other edge. "How do you sleep on a bed this size? Hardly big enough for a cat."

"Oh, it's done well enough for me. But I'm thinking of buying another now that I've money to spare. A fine big one, like the one in your house."

He thought of a Chippendale four-poster in the tiny loft and smiled. Then his thoughts veered back and wiped the smile away. "Maggie." Her face was glowing, her eyes half-shut. There was a smug little smile on her face.

"Rogan," she said in the same serious tone, then laughed. "Oh, you're not going to start telling me you're sorry to have trampled my honor or some such thing? If anyone's honor was trampled, after all, it was yours. And I'm not a bit sorry for it."

"Maggie," he said again, and brushed the tousled hair from her cheek.

"What a woman you are. It's hard to be sorry for trampling, or for being trampled when I—" He broke off. He'd lifted her hand as he spoke, started to kiss her fingers, when his gaze landed on the dark smudges on her arm. Appalled, he started. "I've hurt you."

"Mmm. Now that you mention it, I'm beginning to feel it." She rolled her shoulder. "I must have hit the doorway pretty hard. Now, you were about to say?"

He shifted off of her. "I'm terribly sorry," he said in an odd voice. "It's inexcusable. An apology's hardly adequate for my behavior."

Her head tilted, and she took a good long look at him. Breeding, she thought again. How else could a buck-naked man sitting on a rumpled bed appear so dignified. "Your behavior?" she repeated. "I'd say it was more *our* behavior, Rogan, and that it was well done on both parts." Laughing at him, she pushed herself up and locked her arms around his neck. "Do you think a few bruises will wilt me like a rose, Rogan? They won't, I promise you, especially when I earned them."

"The point is—"

"The point is we tumbled each other. Now stop acting as though I'm a fragile blossom that can't admit to having enjoyed a good, hot bout of sex. Because I enjoyed it very much, and so, my fine fellow, did you."

He trailed a fingertip over the faint bruise above her wrist. "I'd rather I hadn't marked you."

"Well, it's not a brand that's permanent."

No, it wasn't. But there was something else, in his carelessness, that could be. "Maggie, I wasn't thinking before, and I certainly didn't leave Dublin today planning on ending up like this. It's a little late to be thinking of being responsible now." In frustration he dragged a hand through his hair. "Could I have gotten you pregnant?"

She blinked, sat back on her haunches. Let out a long breath. Born in fire. She remembered her father had told her she'd been born in fire. And this was what he'd meant. "No." She said it flatly, her emotions too mixed and unsteady for her to explore. "The timing's wrong. And I'm responsible for myself, Rogan."

"I should have seen to it." He reached over to rub his knuckles down her cheek. "You dazzled me, Maggie, sitting on my lap with your wildflowers. You dazzle me now."

Her smile came back, lighting her eyes first, then curving her lips. "I was coming across the fields away from my sister's and toward home. The sun was bright, Murphy was haying in his field, and there were flowers at my feet. I haven't felt so happy since before my father died five years ago. Then I saw you in the kitchen, working. And it may be I was dazzled as well."

She knelt again, rested her head on his shoulder. "Must you go back to Dublin tonight, Rogan?"

All the minute and tedious details of his schedule ran like a river through his brain. Her scent, mixed with his own, settled over them like a mist. "I can rearrange some things, leave in the morning."

She leaned back, smiled. "And I'd rather not go out to dinner."

"I'll cancel the reservations." He glanced around the room. "Don't you have a phone up here?"

"For what? So it can ring in my ear and wake me up?"

"I can't think why I asked." He eased away to tug on the wrinkled slacks of his suit. "I'll go down, make some calls." He looked back to where she knelt in the center of the narrow, rumpled bed. "Very quick calls."

"They could wait," she shouted after him.

"I don't intend to be interrupted by anything until morning." He hurried down, sentimentally scooping up a tattered meadowsweet as he went.

Upstairs, Maggie waited five minutes, then six before climbing out of bed. She stretched, wincing a bit at the aches. She considered the robe that was tossed carelessly over a chair, then humming to herself, strolled downstairs without it.

He was still on the phone, the receiver cocked on his shoulder as he made notes in his book. The light, softer now, pooled at his feet. "Reschedule that for eleven. No, eleven," he repeated. "I'll be back in the office by ten. Yes, and contact Joseph, will you, Eileen? Tell him I'm having another shipment sent from Clare. Concannon's work, yes. I . . ."

He heard the sound behind him, glanced back. Maggie stood like some flame-crowned goddess, all alabaster skin, sleek curves and knowing eyes. His secretary's voice buzzed in his ear like an annoying fly.

"What? The what?" His eyes, their expression dazed at first, then heated, skimmed up, then down, then up again to lock on Maggie's face. "I'll deal with it when I get back." His stomach muscles quivered when Maggie stepped forward and jerked down the zipper of his slacks. "No," he said in a strangled voice. "You can't reach me anymore today. I'm . . ." The breath hissed between his teeth when Maggie took him in her long, artist's fingers. "Sweet Jesus. Tomorrow," he said with the last of his control. "I'll see you tomorrow."

He slapped the receiver into the cradle, where it jiggled then slipped off to crash against the counter.

"I interrupted your call," she began, then laughed when he dragged her against him.

It was happening again. He could almost stand outside himself and watch the animal inside take over. With one desperate yank, he pulled her head back by the hair and savaged her throat, her mouth. The need to take her was raging, some fatal drug that stabbed into his veins, speeding up his heartbeat and clouding his mind.

He would hurt her again. Even knowing it, he couldn't stop. With a sound, part rage, part triumph, he pushed her back on the kitchen table.

He had the dark, twisted satisfaction of seeing her eyes widen in surprise. "Rogan, your papers."

He jerked her hips from the edge of the wood, raising them with his hands. His eyes were warrior bright on hers as he drove himself into her.

Her hand flailed out, knocked the cup from its saucer and sent both flying to the floor. China shattered, even as the jolting table sent his open briefcase crashing to the ground.

Stars seemed to explode in front of Maggie's eyes as she gave herself up to the delirium. She felt the rough wood on her back, the sweat that bloomed up to slicken her skin. And when he braced her legs higher and thrust himself deep, she could have sworn she felt him touch her heart.

Then she felt nothing at all but the wild wind that tossed her up and up and over that jagged-edged peak. She gasped for air like a woman drowning, then expelled it on a long, languorous moan.

Later, sometime later, when she found she could speak, she was cradled in his arms. "Did you finish your calls, then?"

He laughed and carried her out of the kitchen.

It was early when he left her. A sunshower tossed wavering rainbows into the morning sky. She'd made some sleepy offer to brew him tea, then had drifted off again. So he'd gone to the kitchen alone.

There'd been a miserable jar of hardening instant coffee in her cupboard. Though he'd winced, Rogan had settled for it, and for the single egg in her refrigerator.

He was gathering up, and trying to sort out, his scattered papers when she stumbled into the kitchen. She was heavy-eyed and rumpled, and barely grunted at him as she headed for the kettle.

So much, he thought, for loverlike farewells.

"I used what appeared to be your last clean towel."

She grunted again and scooped out tea.

"And you ran out of hot water in the middle of my shower."

This time she only yawned.

"You don't have any eggs."

She muttered something that sounded like "Murphy's hens."

He tapped his wrinkled papers together and stacked them in his briefcase. "I've left the clippings you wanted on the counter. There'll be a truck by this afternoon to pick up the shipment. You'll need to crate it before one o'clock."

When she made no answer at all to this, he snapped his briefcase closed. "I have to go." Annoyed, he strode to her, took her chin firmly in hand and kissed her. "I'll miss you, too."

He was out the front door before she could gather her wits and chase after him. "Rogan! For pity's sake, hold up a moment. I've barely got my eyes open."

He turned just as she launched herself at him. Off balance, he nearly tumbled them both into the flower bed. Then she was caught close and they were kissing each other breathless in the soft, luminous rain.

"I will miss you, damn it." She pressed her face into his shoulder, breathed deep.

"Come with me. Go throw some things in a bag and come with me."

"I can't." She drew back, surprised at how sorry she was to have to refuse. "I've some things I need to do. And I—I can't really work in Dublin."

"No," he said after a long moment. "I don't suppose you can."

"Could you come back? Take a day or two."

"It's not possible now. In a couple of weeks, perhaps I could."

"Well, that's not so long." It seemed like eternity. "We can both get what needs to be done done, and then . . ."

"And then." He bent to kiss her. "You'll think of me, Margaret Mary."

"I will."

She watched him go, carrying his briefcase to the car, starting the engine, backing out into the road.

She stood for a long time after the sound of the car had faded, until the rain stopped and the sun gilded the morning.

THIRTEEN

Maggie walked across the empty living room, took a long look out of the front window, then retraced her steps. It was the fifth house she had considered in a week, the only one not currently occupied by hopeful sellers, and the last one she intended to view.

It was on the outskirts of Ennis, a bit farther away than Brianna might have liked—and not far enough to Maggie's taste. It was new, which was in its favor, a box of a house with the rooms all on one floor.

Two bedrooms, Maggie mused as she walked through yet again. A bath, a kitchen with room for eating, a living area with plenty of light and tidy brick hearth.

She took one last glance, set her fists on her hips. "This is it."

"Maggie, it's certainly the right size for her." Brianna nibbled her lip as she scanned the empty room. "But shouldn't we have something closer to home?"

"Why? She hates it there in any case."

"But—"

"And this is closer to more conveniences. Food shops, the chemist, places to eat out if she's of a mind to."

"She never goes out."

"It's time she did. And since she won't have you jumping at every snap of her finger, she'll have to, won't she?"

"I don't jump." Spine stiff, Brianna walked to the window. "And the fact of the matter is, she's likely to refuse to move here in any case."

"She won't refuse." Not, Maggie thought, with the ax I hold over her head. "If you'll let go of that guilt you love wrapping about you for a moment, you'll admit this is best for everyone. She'll be happier in her own place—or as happy as a woman of her nature can be. You can give her whatever she wants out of the house if that eases your conscience, or I'll give her money to buy new. Which is what she'd rather."

"Maggie, the place is charmless."

"And so is our mother." Before Brianna could retort, Maggie crossed to her and swung an arm around the stiffened shoulders. "You'll make a garden, right outside the door there. We'll have the walls painted or papered or whatever it takes."

"It could be made nice."

"No one's better suited to do that than you. You'll draw out whatever money it takes until the two of you are satisfied."

"It's not fair, Maggie, that you should bear all this expense."

"Fairer than you might think." The time had come, Maggie decided, to speak to Brianna about their mother. "Did you know she used to sing? Professionally?"

"Mother?" The idea was so farfetched, Brianna laughed. "Where did you get a notion like that?"

"It's true. I learned of it by accident, and I've checked to be sure." Reaching into her purse, Maggie pulled out the yellowed clippings. "You can see for yourself, she was even written up a few times."

Speechless, Brianna scanned the newsprint, stared at the faded photo. "She sang in Dublin," she murmured. "She had a living. 'A voice as clear and sweet as church bells on Easter morning,' it says. But how can this be? She's never once spoken of it. Nor Da either."

"I've thought of it quite a lot in the last few days." Turning away, Maggie walked to the window again. "She lost something she wanted, and got something she didn't. All this time she's punished herself, and all of us."

Dazed, Brianna lowered the clipping. "But she never sang at home. Not a note. Ever."

"I'm thinking she couldn't bear to, or considered her refusal penance for her sin. Probably both." A weariness came over Maggie and she struggled to fight it back. "I'm trying to excuse her for it, Brie, to imagine how devastated she must have been when she learned she was pregnant with me. And being what she is, there'd have been nothing for her but marriage."

"It was wrong of her to blame you, Maggie. It always was. That's no less true today."

"Perhaps. Still, it gives me more of an understanding as to why she's never loved me. Never will."

"Have you . . ." Carefully Brianna folded the clippings and slipped them into her own purse. "Have you spoken to her of it?"

"I tried to. She won't talk about it. It could have been different." Maggie whirled back, hating the burden of guilt she couldn't shake. "It could have been. If she couldn't have the career she wanted, there could have been music still. Did she have to shut off everything because she couldn't have it all?"

"I don't know the answer. Some people aren't content with less than all."

"It can't be changed," Maggie said firmly. "But we'll give her this. We'll give all of us this."

How quickly money dribbled away, Maggie thought a few days later. It seemed the more you had, the more you needed. But the deed to the house was now in Maeve's name, and the details, the dozens of them that came from establishing a home, were being dealt with, one by one.

A pity the details of her own life seemed to hang in limbo.

She'd barely spoken to Rogan, she thought as she sulked at her kitchen table. Oh, there'd been messages relayed through his Eileen and Joseph, but he rarely bothered to contact her directly. Or to come back, as he'd said he would.

Well, that was fine, she thought. She was busy in any case. There were any number of sketches that were begging to be turned into glass. If she was a bit late getting started this morning, it was only because she'd yet to decide which project to pursue first.

It certainly wasn't because she was waiting for the blasted phone to ring.

She got up and started to the door when she saw Brianna through the window, the devoted wolfhound at her heels.

"Good. I hoped I'd catch you before you started for the day." Brianna took the basket from her arm as she stepped into the kitchen.

"You did, just. Is it going well?"

"Very." Brisk and efficient, Brianna uncovered the steaming muffins she'd brought along. "Finding Lottie Sullivan's like a gift from God." She smiled, thinking of the retired nurse they'd hired as Maeve's companion. "She's simply wonderful, Maggie. Like part of the family already. Yesterday, when I was working on the front flower beds, Mother was carrying on about how it was too late in the year for planting and how the paint on the outside of the house was the wrong color. And, oh, just being contrary. And Lottie was standing there laughing, disagreeing with everything she said. I swear, the two of them were having the time of their lives."

"I wish I'd seen it." Maggie broke open a muffin. The smell of it, and the picture Brianna had put in her head, almost made up for postponing her morning's work. "You found a treasure there, Brie. Lottie'll keep her in line."

"It's more than that. She really enjoys doing it. Every time Mother says something horrid, Lottie just laughs and winks and goes about her business. I never thought I'd say it, Maggie, but I really believe this is going to work."

"Of course it's going to work." Maggie tossed a bit of muffin to the patiently hopeful Con. "Did you ask Murphy if he'd help move her bed and the other things she wants?"

"I didn't have to. Word's out that you've bought her a house near Ennis. I've had a dozen people drop by in the last two weeks, casuallike. Murphy already offered his back and his lorry."

"Then she'll be moved tidily in with Lottie before the next week is up. I've bought us a bottle of champagne, and we're going to drink ourselves drunk when it's done."

Brianna's lips twitched, but her voice was sober. "It's not something to celebrate."

"Then I'll just drop in, casuallike," Maggie said with a sly grin. "With a bottle of bubbly under me arm."

Though Brianna smiled back, her heart wasn't in it. "Maggie, I tried to talk to her about her singing." She was sorry to see the light go out of her sister's eyes. "I thought I should."

"Of course you did." Losing her appetite for the muffin, Maggie tossed the rest to Con. "Did you have better luck than I?"

"No. She wouldn't talk to me, only got angry." It wasn't worth recounting the verbal blows punch by punch, Brianna thought. To do so would only serve to spread the unhappiness more thickly. "She went off to her room, but she took the clippings with her."

"Well, that's something. Perhaps they'll comfort her." Maggie jolted when the phone rang and scrambled out of her chair so quickly that Brianna gaped. "Hello. Oh, Eileen, is it?" The disappointment in her voice was unmistable. "Yes, I've the photos you sent for the catalog. They look more than fine. Perhaps I should tell Mr. Sweeney myself that—oh, a meeting. No, that's all right, then, you can tell him I approved of them. You're welcome. Good-bye."

"You answered the phone," Brianna commented.

"Of course I did. It rang, didn't it?"

The waspish tone of her sister's voice had Brianna's brow arching. "Were you expecting a call?"

"No. Why would you think so?"

"Well, the way you went leaping up, like you were after snatching a child from in front of a car."

Oh, had she? Maggie thought. Had she done that? It was humiliating. "I don't like the damn thing ringing my ears off, that's all. I've got to get to work." With that as a fare-thee-well, she stalked out of the kitchen.

It didn't matter a tinker's damn to her whether he called or not, Maggie told herself. Maybe it had been three weeks since he'd gone back to Dublin, maybe she'd only spoken to him twice in all that time, but it hardly mattered to her. She was much too busy to be bothered chattering over the phone, or entertaining him if he came to see her.

As he'd bloody well said he would, she added silently, and slammed the shop door behind her.

She didn't need Rogan Sweeney's company, or anyone's. She had herself.

Maggie picked up her pipe and went to work.

The Connellys' formal dining room would have reminded Maggie of a set she had seen on the glossy soap opera that had been on television the day her father died. Everything gleamed and sparkled and shone. Wine of the very best vintage glimmered gold in the crystal, shooting rainbows into the facets. Candles, slim and white, added to the elegance of light showered down from the five-tiered chandelier.

The people surrounding the lace-decked table were every bit as polished as the room. Anne, in sapphire silk and her grandmother's diamonds, was the picture of the gracious hostess. Dennis, flushed from the good meal and better company, beamed at his daughter. Patricia looked particularly lovely, and as delicate as the pastel pink and creamy pearls she wore.

Across from her, Rogan sipped at his wine and struggled to keep his mind from wandering west, toward Maggie.

"It's so nice to have a quiet family meal." Anne picked at the miserly portion of pheasant on her plate. The scale had warned her that she'd added two pounds in the last month, and that would never do. "I hope you're not disappointed I didn't invite a party, Rogan."

"Of course not. It's a pleasure, a rare one for me these days, to spend a quiet evening with friends."

"Exactly what I've been telling Dennis," Anne went on. "Why, we've hardly seen you in months. You work much too hard, Rogan."

"A man can't work too hard at something he loves," Dennis put in.

"Ah, you and your man's work." Anne laughed lightly and barely resisted kicking her husband smartly under the table. "Too much business makes a man tense, I say. Especially if he has no wife to soothe him."

Knowing just where this was leading, Patricia did her best to change the subject. "You had a wonderful success with Miss Concannon's showing, Rogan. And I've heard the American Indian art has been very well received."

"Yes, on both counts. The American art is moving to the Cork gallery this week, and Maggie's—Miss Concannon's—moves on to Paris shortly. She's finished some astonishing pieces this past month."

"I've seen a few of them. I believe Joseph covets the globe. The one with all the colors and shapes inside. It's quite fascinating really." Patricia folded her hands in her lap as the dessert course was served. "I wonder how it was done."

"As it happens, I was there when she made it." He remembered the heat, the bleeding colors, the sizzling sparks. "And I still can't explain it to you."

The look in his eyes put Anne on full alert. "Knowing too much about the artistic process can spoil the enjoyment, don't you think? I'm sure it's all routine to Miss Concannon, after all. Patricia, you haven't told us about your little project? How is the day school going?"

"It's coming along nicely, thank you."

"Imagine our little Patricia starting a school." Anne smiled indulgently.

Rogan realized with a guilty start that he hadn't asked Patricia about her pet project in weeks. "Have you found a location, then?"

"Yes, I have. It's a house off Mountjoy Square. The building will require some renovation, of course. I've hired an architect. The grounds are more than suitable, with plenty of space for play areas. I hope to have it ready for children by next spring."

And she could imagine it. The babies and toddlers whose mothers needed a reliable place to leave their children while they worked. The older children who would come after school and before the close of business. It would fill some of the ache, she thought, and the emptiness that throbbed inside her. She and Robert hadn't had children. They had been so sure there was plenty of time. So sure.

"I'm sure Rogan could help you with the business end of it, Patricia," Anne went on. "After all, you've no experience."

"She's my daughter, isn't she?" Dennis interjected with a wink. "She'll do fine."

"I'm sure she will." Again Anne itched to connect her foot with her husband's shin.

She waited until she was in the parlor with her daughter and the men were lingering over glasses of port in the dining room—a custom Anne refused to believe was outdated. She dismissed the maid who had wheeled in coffee, and rounded on her daughter.

"What are you waiting for, Patricia? You're letting the man slip between your fingers."

"Please, don't start this." Already Patricia could feel the dull, insistent throb of a headache in progress.

"You want to be a widow all your life, I suppose." Grim-eyed, Anne added cream to her cup. "I'm telling you it's been time enough."

"You've been telling me that since a year after Robbie died."

"And it's no more than the truth." Anne sighed. She'd hated to watch her daughter grieve, had wept long and hard herself, not only over the loss of the son-in-law she'd loved, but for the pain she'd been unable to erase from Patricia's eyes. "Darling, as much as we all wish it wasn't so, Robert's gone."

"I know that. I've accepted it and I'm trying to move on."

"By starting a day-care service for other people's children?"

"Yes, in part. I'm doing that for myself, Mother. Because I need work, the satisfaction of it."

"I've finished trying to talk you out of that." In a gesture of peace,

Anne raised her hands. "And if it's what you want, truly, then it's what I want as well."

"Thank you for that." Patricia's face softened as she leaned over to kiss her mother's cheek. "I know that you only want the best for me."

"I do. Which is exactly why I want Rogan for you. No, don't close up on me, girl. You can't tell me you don't want him as well."

"I care for him," Patricia said carefully. "Very much. I always have."

"And he for you. But you're standing back, all too patiently, and waiting for him to take the next step. And while you're waiting he's becoming distracted. A blind woman could see that he's interested in more than that Concannon woman's art. And she's not the type to wait," Anne added with a wag of the finger. "Oh, no, indeed. She'll see a man of Rogan's background and means and snap him up before he can blink."

"I very much doubt Rogan can be snapped up," Patricia said dryly. "He knows his own mind."

"In most areas," Anne agreed. "But men need to be guided, Patricia. Allured. You haven't set yourself out to allure Rogan Sweeney. You've got to make him see you as a woman, not as his friend's widow. You want him, don't you?"

"I think—"

"Of course you do. Now see to it that he wants you, too."

Patricia said little when Rogan drove her home. Home to the house she'd shared with Robert, the house she couldn't give up. She no longer walked into a room expecting to find him waiting for her, or suffered those silvery slashes of pain at odd moments when she suddenly remembered their life together.

It was simply a house that held good memories.

But did she want to live in it alone for the rest of her life? Did she want to spend her days caring for other women's children while there were none of her own to brighten her life?

If her mother was right and Rogan was what she wanted, then what was wrong with a little allure.

"Won't you come in for a while?" she asked when he walked her to the door. "It's early still, and I'm restless."

He thought of his own empty house, and the hours before the workday began. "If you'll promise me a brandy."

"On the terrace," she agreed, and walked inside.

The house reflected the quiet elegance and faultless taste of its mistress.

Though he'd always felt completely at home there, Rogan thought of Maggie's cluttered cottage and narrow rumpled bed.

Even the brandy snifter reminded him of Maggie. He thought of the way she'd smashed one against the hearth in a rage of passion. And of the package that had come days later, holding the one she'd made to replace it.

"It's a lovely night," Patricia said, and snagged his wandering attention.

"What? Oh, yes. Yes, it is." He swirled the brandy, but didn't drink.

A crescent moon rode the sky, misted by clouds, then glowing white and thin as the breeze nudged them clear. The air was warm and fragrant, disturbed only by the muffled sound of traffic beyond the hedges.

"Tell me more about the school," he began. "What architect have you chosen?" She named a firm he approved of. "They do good work. We've used them ourselves."

"I know. Joseph recommended them. He's been wonderfully helpful, though I feel guilty taking his mind off his work."

"He's well able to do a half-dozen things at once."

"He never seems to mind my dropping into the gallery." Testing him, herself, Patricia moved closer. "I've missed you."

"Things have been hectic." He tucked her hair behind her ear, an old gesture, an old habit he wasn't even aware of. "We'll have to make some time. We haven't been to the theater in weeks, have we?"

"No." She caught his hand, held it. "But I'm glad we have time now. Alone."

A warning signal sounded in his head. He dismissed it as ridiculous and smiled at her. "We'll make more. Why don't I come by that property you've bought, look it over for you?"

"You know I value your opinion." Her heart beat light, quick, in her chest. "I value you."

Before she could change her mind, she leaned forward and pressed her mouth to his. If there had been alarm in his eyes, she refused to see it.

No sweet, platonic kiss this time. Patricia curled her fingers into his hair and poured herself into it. She wanted, desperately wanted, to feel something again.

But his arms didn't come around her. His lips didn't heat. He stood, still as a statue. It wasn't pleasure, nor was it desire that trembled between them. It was the chilly air of shock.

She drew back, saw the astonishment and, worse, much worse, the regret in his eyes. Stung, she whirled away.

Rogan set his untouched brandy down. "Patricia."

"Don't." She squeezed her eyes tight. "Don't say anything."

"Of course I will. I have to." His hands hesitated over her shoulders and finally settled gently. "Patricia, you know how much I . . ." What words were there? he thought frantically. What possible words? "I care about you," he said, and hated himself.

"Leave it at that." She gripped her hands together until her fingers ached. "I'm humiliated enough."

"I never thought—" He cursed himself again and, because he felt so miserable, cursed Maggie for being right. "Patty," he said helplessly. "I'm sorry."

"I'm sure you are." Her voice was cool again, despite his use of her old nickname. "And so am I, for putting you in such an awkward position."

"It's my fault. I should have understood."

"Why should you?" Chilled, she stepped away from his hands, made herself turn. In the dappled starlight, her face was fragile as glass, her eyes as blank. "I'm always there, aren't I? Dropping by, available for whatever evening you might have free. Poor Patricia, at such loose ends, dreaming up her little projects to keep herself busy. The young widow who's content with a pat on the head and an indulgent smile."

"That's not at all true. It's not the way I feel."

"I don't know how you feel." Her voice rose, cracked, alarming them both. "I don't know how I feel. I only know I want you to go, before we say things that would embarrass us both more than we already are."

"I can't leave you this way. Please come inside, sit down. We'll talk."

No, she thought, she would weep and complete her mortification. "I mean it, Rogan," she said flatly. "I want you to go. There's nothing for either of us to say but good night. You know the way out." She swept past him, into the house.

Damn all women, Rogan thought as he strode into the gallery the following afternoon. Damn them for their uncanny ability to make a man feel guilty and needy and idiotic.

He'd lost a friend, one who was very dear to him. Lost her, he thought, because he'd been blind to her feelings. Feelings, he remembered with growing resentment, that Maggie had seen and understood in the blink of an eye.

He stalked up the stairs, furious with himself. Why was it he had no idea how to handle two of the women who meant so much to him?

He'd broken Patricia's heart, carelessly. And Maggie, God curse her, had the power to break his.

Did people never fall in love with anyone who was eager to return it?

Well, he wouldn't be fool enough to toss his feelings at Maggie's feet and have her crush them. Not now. Not after he'd inadvertently done some crushing of his own. He could get along very well on his own, thank you.

He stepped into the first sitting room and scowled. They'd put a few more pieces of her work on display. A mere glimpse of what would be toured over the next twelve months. The globe she'd created in front of his eyes gleamed back at him, seeming to contain all the dreams she'd claimed were held inside, dreams that now mocked at him as he stared into its depths.

It was just as well she hadn't answered the phone when he'd called the night before. Perhaps he'd needed her at that moment while the miserable guilt over Patricia had clawed at him. He'd needed to hear her voice, to soothe himself with it. Instead he'd heard his own, clipped and precise on the answering machine. She'd refused to make the recording herself.

So instead of a quiet, perhaps intimate late-night conversation, he'd left a terse message that would, no doubt, annoy Maggie as much as it annoyed him.

God, he wanted her.

"Ah, just the man I wanted to see." Cheerful as a robin, Joseph popped into the room. "I've sold *Carlotta.*" Joseph's self-satisfied smile faded into curiosity when Rogan turned. "Bad day, is it?"

"I've had better. *Carlotta,* you say? To whom?"

"To an American tourist who strolled in this morning. She was absolutely enthralled by *Carlotta.* We're having her shipped—the painting, that is—to someplace called Tucson."

Joseph sat on the corner of the love seat and lighted a celebratory cigarette. "The American claimed that she adores primitive nudes, and our *Carlotta* was certainly primitive. I'm quite fond of nudes myself, but Carlotta was never my type. Too heavy at the hip—and the brush strokes. Well, the artist lacked subtlety, shall we say."

"It was an excellent oil," Rogan said absently.

"Of its type. Since I prefer something a bit less obvious, I won't be sorry to ship *Carlotta* off to Tucson." He pulled a little flip-top ashtray out of his pocket and tapped his cigarette in it. "Oh, and that watercolor series, from the Scotsman? Arrived an hour ago. It's beautiful work, Rogan. I think you've discovered another star."

"Blind luck. If I hadn't been checking on the factory in Inverness, I never would have seen the paintings."

"A street artist." Joseph shook his head. "Well, not for long, I can guarantee that. There's a wonderfully mystical quality to the work, rather fragile and austere." His tooth flashed in a grin. "And a nude as well, to make up for the loss of *Carlotta*. More to my taste, I'll have to say. She's elegant, rather delicate and just a bit sad-eyed. I fell hopelessly in love."

He broke off, flushing a little around the collar as he saw Patricia in the doorway. His heart trembled hopelessly. Out of your reach, boy-o, he reminded himself. Way out of your reach. His smile was dashing as he rose.

"Hello, Patricia. How lovely to see you."

Rogan turned, decided he should be flogged for putting those shadows under her eyes.

"Hello, Joseph. I hope I'm not disturbing you."

"Not at all. Beauty is always welcome here." He took her hand, kissed it, and called himself an idiot. "Would you like tea?"

"No, don't trouble."

"It's no problem, no problem at all. It's near to closing."

"I know. I'd hoped . . ." Patricia braced herself. "Joseph, would you mind? I need to have a moment alone with Rogan."

"Of course not." Fool. Dolt. Imbecile. "I'll just go on down. I'll put the kettle on if you change your mind."

"Thank you." She waited until he'd gone, then shut the door. "I hope you don't mind my coming, since it's so near closing."

"No, of course not." Rogan wasn't prepared, again, he discovered, to handle himself. "I'm glad you came."

"No, you're not." She smiled a little as she said it, to ease the sting. "You're standing there, frantically trying to think of what to say, how to behave. I've known you too long, Rogan. Can we sit?"

"Yes, of course." He started to offer a hand, then let it fall back to his side. Patricia lifted a brow at the movement. She sat, folded her hands in her lap. "I've come to apologize."

Now his distress was complete. "Please, don't. There's no need."

"There's every need. You'll do me the courtesy of hearing me out."

"Patty." He sat as well, felt his stomach lurch. "I've made you cry." It was all too obvious now that they were close. However careful her makeup, he could see the signs.

"Yes, you did. And after I'd finished crying, I began to think. For myself." She sighed. "I've had much too little practice thinking for myself, Rogan. Mother and Daddy took such close care of me. And they had such expectations. I was always afraid I couldn't meet them."

"That's absurd—"

"I've asked you to hear me out," she said in a tone that had him staring in surprise. "And you will. You were always there, from the time I was what—fourteen, fifteen? And then there was Robbie. I was so in love there was no need to think, no room for it. It was all him, and putting the house together, making a home. When I lost him, I thought I would die, too. God knows I wanted to."

There was nothing else Rogan could do but take her hand. "I loved him, too."

"I know you did. And it was you who got me through it. You who helped me grieve, then move past the grieving. I could talk about Robbie with you, and laugh or cry. You've been the best of friends to me, so it was natural that I'd love you. It seemed sensible for me to wait until you began to see me as a woman instead of an old friend. Then, wouldn't it be natural enough for you to fall in love with me, ask me to marry you?"

His fingers moved restlessly under hers. "If I'd paid closer attention—"

"You'd have still seen nothing I didn't wish you to see," she finished. "For reasons I'd rather not discuss, I decided I'd take the next step myself, last night. When I kissed you, I expected to feel, oh, stardust and moonbeams. I threw myself into kissing you, expecting it to be everything I'd been waiting for, all those wonderful, terrifying tugs and pulls. I wanted so much to feel them again. But I didn't."

"Patricia, it's not that I—" He broke off, eyes narrowing. "I beg your pardon?"

She laughed, confusing him all the more. "When I'd finished my well-deserved bout of weeping, I thought through the whole episode. It wasn't just you who was taken by surprise, Rogan. I realized I'd felt nothing at all when I'd kissed you."

"Nothing at all," he repeated after a moment.

"Nothing more than embarrassment for having put us both in such a potentially dreadful situation. It came to me that while I love you dearly, I'm not in love with you at all. I was simply kissing my closest friend."

"I see." It was ridiculous to feel as though his manhood had been impugned. But he was, after all, a man. "That's lucky, isn't it?"

She did know him well. Laughing, she pressed his hand to her cheek. "Now I've insulted you."

"No, you haven't. I'm relieved we've sorted this out." Her bland look had him cursing. "All right, damn it, you have insulted me. Or at least nicked my masculine pride." He grinned back at her. "Friends, then?"

"Always." She let out a long breath. "I can't tell you how relieved I am that *that's* over. You know, I think I'll take Joseph up on that tea. Can you join us?"

"Sorry. We've just gotten in a shipment from Inverness I want to look over."

She rose. "You know, I have to agree with Mother on one thing. You're working too hard, Rogan. It's beginning to show. You need a few days to relax."

"In a month or two."

Shaking her head, she leaned down to kiss him. "You always say that. I wish I thought you meant it this time." She tilted her head, smiled. "I believe your villa in the south of France is an excellent place not only to relax, but for creative inspiration. The colors and the textures would undoubtedly appeal to an artist."

He opened his mouth, closed it again. "You do know me too well," he murmured.

"I do. Give it some thought." She left him brooding and went down to the kitchen. Since Joseph was in the main gallery with a few lingering clients, she began to brew the tea herself.

Joseph came in just as she was pouring the first cup. "I'm sorry," he said. "They wouldn't be hurried along, nor could they be seduced into parting with a single pound. Here I thought I'd end the day by selling that copper sculpture. You know, the one that looks a bit like a holly shrub, but they got away from me."

"Have some tea and console yourself."

"I will, thanks. Have you—" He stopped when she turned to him and he saw her face in the full light. "What is it? What's wrong?"

"Why, nothing." She brought the cups to the table, nearly dropping them both when he caught her by the arms.

"You've been crying," he said in a tight voice. "And there're shadows under your eyes."

On an impatient breath she set the jostling cups down. "Why are cosmetics so damn expensive if they don't do the job? A woman can't indulge herself in a good weeping spell if she can't depend on her powder." She started to sit, but his hands remained firm on her shoulders. Surprised, she looked up at him. What she saw in his eyes had her fumbling. "It's nothing—really nothing. Just some foolishness. I'm . . . I'm fine now."

He didn't think. He'd held her before, of course. They'd danced together. But there was no music now. Only her. Slowly, he lifted a hand, brushed a thumb gently over the faint smudges under her eyes. "You still miss him. Robbie."

"Yes. I always will." But her husband's face, so well loved, blurred. She saw only Joseph. "I wasn't crying for Robbie. Not really. I'm not sure exactly what I was crying for."

She was so lovely, he thought. Her eyes so soft and confused. And her skin—he'd never dared touch her like this before—was like silk. "You mustn't cry, Patty," he heard himself say. Then he was kissing her, his mouth homing to hers like an arrow, his hand scooping up into that soft swing of hair.

He lost himself, drowning in the scent of her, aching at the way her lips parted in surprise to allow him one long, full-bodied taste of her.

Her body gave to his, a delicate sway of fragility that aroused unbearable and conflicting needs. To take, to protect, to comfort and to possess.

It was her sigh, part shock, part wonder, that snapped him back like a faceful of ice water.

"I—I beg your pardon." He fumbled over the words, then went rigid with regret when she only stared at him. Emotions churned sickly inside of him as he stepped back. "That was inexcusable."

He turned on his heel and walked away before her head stopped spinning.

She took one step after him, his name on her lips. Then she stopped, pressed her hand to her racing heart and let her shaking legs buckle her into a chair.

Joseph? Her hand crept up from her breast to her flushed cheek. Joseph, she thought again, staggered. Why, it was ridiculous. They were no more than casual friends who shared an affection for Rogan and for art. He was . . . well, the closest thing she knew to a bohemian, she decided. Charming, certainly, as every woman who walked into the gallery would attest.

And it had only been a kiss. Just a kiss, she told herself as she reached for her cup. But her hand trembled and spilled tea onto the table.

A kiss, she realized with a jolt, that had given her those moonbeams, the stardust, and all the wonderful and terrifying tugs and pulls she had hoped for.

Joseph, she thought again, and raced out of the kitchen to find him.

She caught a glimpse of him outside and darted past Rogan with barely a word.

"Joseph!"

He stopped, swore. Here it was, he thought bitterly. She'd slap him down good and proper, and—since he hadn't made a quick enough exit—in public as well. Resigned to facing the music, he turned, tossed his streaming hair back over his shoulder.

She skidded to a halt inches in front of him. "I—" She completely forgot what she'd hoped to say.

"You've every right to be angry," he told her. "It hardly matters that I never meant—that is, I'd only wanted to . . . Goddamn it, what do you expect? You come in looking so sad and beautiful. So lost. I forgot myself, and I've apologized for it."

She had been feeling lost, she realized. She wondered if he would understand what it was like to know just where you were, and to believe you knew where you were going, but to be lost just the same. She thought he might.

"Will you have dinner with me?"

He blinked, stepped back. Stared. "What?"

"Will you have dinner with me?" she repeated. She felt giddy, almost reckless. "Tonight. Now."

"You want to have dinner?" He spoke slowly, spacing each word. "With me? Tonight?"

He looked so baffled, so leery, that she laughed. "Yes. Actually, no, that isn't what I want at all."

"All right, then." He nodded stiffly and headed down the street.

"I don't want dinner," she called out, loudly enough to have heads turn. Almost reckless? she thought. Oh, no, completely reckless. "I want you to kiss me again."

That stopped him. He turned back, ignored the wink and encouraging word from a man in a flowered shirt. Like a blind man feeling his way, he walked toward her. "I'm not sure I caught that."

"Then I'll speak plainly." She swallowed a foolish bubble of pride. "I want you to take me home with you, Joseph. And I want you to kiss me again. And unless I've very much mistaken what we're both feeling, I want you to make love with me." She took the last step toward him. "Did you understand that, and is it agreeable to you?"

"Agreeable?" He took her face in his hands, stared hard into her eyes. "You've lost your mind. Thank God." He laughed and swooped her against him. "Oh, it's more than agreeable, Patty darling. Much more."

FOURTEEN

Maggie dozed off at her kitchen table, her head on her folded arms.

Moving day had been sheer hell.

Her mother had complained constantly, relentlessly, about everything from the steady fall of rain to the curtains Brianna had hung at the wide front window of the new house. But it was worth the misery of the day to see Maeve at last settled in her own place. Maggie had kept her word, and Brianna was free.

Still, Maggie hadn't expected the wave of guilt that swamped her when

Maeve had wept—her back bent, her face buried in her hands and the hot fast tears leaking through her fingers. No, she hadn't expected to feel guilty, or to feel so miserably sorry for the woman who'd barely finished cursing her before she collapsed into sobs.

In the end it was Lottie, with her brisk, unflappable cheerfulness, who had taken control. She scooted both Brianna and Maggie out of the house, telling them not to worry, no, not to worry a bit, as the tears were as natural as the rain. And what a lovely place it was, she'd gone on to say, all the while nudging and pushing them along. Like a dollhouse and just as tidy. They'd be fine. They'd be cozy as cats.

She'd all but shoved them into Maggie's lorry.

So it was done, and it was right. But there would be no opening of champagne bottles that night.

Maggie had downed one bracing whiskey and simply folded into a heap of exhausted emotions at the table while the rain drummed on the roof and dusk deepened the gloom.

The phone didn't awaken her. It rang demandingly while she dozed. But Rogan's voice stabbed through the fatigue and had her jolting up, shaking off sleep.

"I'll expect to hear from you by morning, as I've neither the time nor the patience to come fetch you myself."

"What?" Groggy, she blinked like an owl and stared around the darkened room. Why, she'd have sworn he'd been right there, badgering her.

Annoyed that her nap had been interrupted, and that the interruption reminded her she was hungry and there was no more to eat in the house than would satisfy a bird, she pushed away from the table.

She'd go down to Brie's, she decided. Raid her kitchen. Perhaps they could cheer each other up. She was reaching for a cap when she saw the impatient red blip on the answering machine.

"Bloody nuisance," she muttered, but stabbed the buttons until the tape rewound, then played.

"Maggie." Again, Rogan's voice filled the room. It made her smile as she realized he had been the one to wake her after all. "Why the devil don't you ever answer this thing? It's noon. I want you to call the moment you come in from your studio. I mean it. There's something I need to discuss with you. So—I miss you. Damn you, Maggie, I miss you."

The message clicked off, and before she could feel too smug about it, another began.

"Do you think I've nothing better to do than spend my time talking to this blasted machine?"

"I don't," she answered back, "but you're the one who put it here."

"It's half four now, and I need to go by the gallery. Perhaps I didn't make myself clear. I need to speak with you, today. I'll be at the gallery until six, then you can reach me at home. I don't give a damn how wrapped up you are in your work. Damn you for being so far away."

"The man spends more time damning me than anything else," she muttered. "And you're just as far away from me as I am from you, Sweeney."

As if in answer, his voice came again. "You irresponsible, idiotic, insensitive brat. Am I supposed to worry now that you've blown yourself up with your chemicals and set your hair on fire? Thanks to your sister, who does answer her phone, I know perfectly well you're there. It's nearly eight, and I have a dinner meeting. Now you listen to me, Margaret Mary. Get yourself to Dublin, and bring your passport. I won't waste my time explaining why, just do as you're told. If you can't arrange a flight, I'll send the plane for you. I expect to hear from you by morning, as I've neither the time nor the patience to fetch you myself."

"*Fetch me?* As if you could." She stood for a moment, scowling at the machine. So she was supposed to get herself to Dublin, was she? Just because he demanded it. Never a please or a will you, just do what you're told.

Ice would flow in hell before she'd give him the satisfaction.

Forgetting her hunger, she stormed from the room and up the stairs. Get herself to Dublin, she fumed. The nerve of the man, ordering her about.

She yanked the suitcase out of her closet and heaved it onto the bed.

Did he think she was so eager to see him that she'd drop everything and scramble off to do his bidding? He was going to find out differently. Oh, yes, she decided as she tossed clothes into the case. She was going to tell him differently, in person. Face-to-face.

She doubted he'd thank her for it.

"Eileen, I'll need Limerick to fax me those adjusted figures before the end of the day." Behind his desk, Rogan checked off a line of his list, rubbed at the tension at the base of his neck. "And I'll want to see the report on the construction there the moment it comes in."

"It was promised by noon." Eileen, a trim brunette who managed the office as skillfully as she did her husband and three children, jotted a note. "You've a two o'clock meeting with Mr. Greenwald. That's *re* the changes in the London catalog."

"Yes, I've got that. He'll want martinis."

"Vodka," Eileen said. "Two olives. Should I see about a cheese tray to keep him from staggering out?"

"You'd better." Rogan drummed his fingers on the desk. "Has there been no call from Clare?"

"None this morning." She shot a quick, interested look from under her lashes. "I'll be sure to let you know the moment Miss Concannon calls."

He made a sound, the vocal equivalent of a shrug. "Go ahead and put that call through to Rome if you will."

"Right away. Oh, and I have that draft of the letter to Inverness on my desk if you want to approve it."

"Fine. And we'd best send a wire to Boston. What's the time there?" He started to check his watch when a blur of color in the doorway stopped him. "Maggie."

"Aye. Maggie." She tossed her suitcase down with a thud and fisted her hands on her hips. "I've a few choice words for you, Mr. Sweeney." She bit down on her temper long enough to nod at the woman rising from the chair in front of Rogan's desk. "You'd be Eileen?"

"Yes. It's a pleasure to meet you at last, Miss Concannon."

"It's nice of you to say so. I must say you look remarkably well for a woman who works for a tyrant." Her voice rose on the last word.

Eileen's lips twitched. She cleared her throat, closed her steno pad. "It's nice of you to say so. Is there anything else, Mr. Sweeney?"

"No. Hold my calls please."

"Yes, sir." Eileen walked out, closing the door discreetly behind her.

"So." Rogan leaned back in his chair, tapped his pen against his palm. "You got my message."

"I got it."

She walked across the room. No, Rogan thought, she swaggered across it, hands still fisted on hips, eyes flashing.

He wasn't ashamed to admit that his mouth watered at the sight of her.

"Who in this wide world do you think you are?" She slapped her palms on his desk, rattling pens. "I signed my work to you, Rogan Sweeney, and aye, I slept with you—to my undying regret. But none of it gives you the right to order me about or swear at me every five minutes."

"I haven't spoken to you in days," he reminded her. "So how can I have sworn at you?"

"Over your hideous machine—which I tossed into the garbage this very morning."

Very calmly, he made a note on a pad.

"Don't start that."

"I'm merely noting down that you need a replacement for your answering machine. You had no trouble getting a flight in, I see."

"No trouble? You've been nothing but trouble to me since the moment you walked into my glass house. Nothing but. You think you can just take over everything, not just my work—which is bad enough—but me as well. I'm here to tell you that you can't. I won't—where in the hell are you going? I haven't finished."

"I never thought you had." He continued to the door, locked it, turned back.

"Unlock that door."

"No."

The fact that he was smiling as he came back toward her didn't help her nerves. "Don't you put your hands on me."

"I'm about to. In fact, I'm about to do something I haven't done in the twelve years I've worked in this office."

Her heart began a fast hard tattoo in her throat. "You are not."

So, he thought, he'd finally shocked her. He watched her gaze slide to the door, then made his grab. "You can rage at me once I've finished with you."

"Finished with me?" Even as she took a swing at him he was crushing his mouth to hers. "Get off me, you ham-handed brute."

"You like my hands." And he used them to tug her sweater up. "You told me so."

"That's a lie. I won't have this, Rogan." But the denial ended in a moan as his lips skimmed hot over her throat. Then, "I'll shout down the roof," once she got her breath back.

"Go ahead." He bit her, none too gently. "I like it when you shout."

"Curse you," she muttered, and went willingly when he lowered her to the floor.

It was fast and hot, a frantic coupling that was over almost as soon as it had begun. But the speed didn't diminish the power. They lay tangled together a moment longer, limbs vibrating. Rogan turned his head to press a kiss to her jaw.

"Nice of you to drop by, Maggie."

She summoned up the strength to bounce her fist off his shoulder. "Get off of me, you brute." She would have shoved him, but he was already shifting, drawing her with him until she was straddled across his lap.

"Better?"

"Than what?" She grinned, then remembered she was furious with him. Pushing away, she sat on the rug and tidied her clothes. "You've a nerve, you do, Rogan Sweeney."

"Because I dragged you to the floor?"

"No." She snapped her jeans. "It'd be foolish to say that when it's obvious I enjoyed it."

"Very obvious."

She sent him a steely look as he rose and offered her a hand.

"That's neither here nor there. Who do you think you are, ordering me about, telling me what to do without a will you or a won't you?"

He bent down and pulled her to her feet. "You're here, aren't you?"

"I'm here, you swine, to tell you that I won't tolerate it. Here it's been nearly a month since you walked away from my door, whistling, and—"

"You missed me."

She hissed at him. "I did not. I have more than enough to keep my time filled. Oh, straighten that silly tie. You look like a drunkard."

He obliged her. "You missed me, Margaret Mary, though you never bothered to say so whenever I managed to reach you by phone."

"I can't talk on the phone. How am I supposed to say anything to someone I can't see? And you're evading the issue."

"What is the issue?" He leaned back comfortably against his desk.

"I won't be given orders. I'm not one of your servants or one of your staff, so get that through your head. Mark it down in that fancy leather notebook of yours if you need reminding. But don't you ever tell me what to do again." She let out a short, satisfied breath. "Now that I've made that clear, I'll be on my way."

"Maggie. If you'd no intention to stay, why did you pack a suitcase?"

He had her there. Patiently he waited while annoyance, dismay and confusion flitted across her face.

"Maybe I've a mind to stay in Dublin for a day or two. I can come and go as I please, can't I?"

"Mmm. Did you bring your passport?"

She eyed him warily. "And what if I did?"

"Good." He circled around his desk, sat. "It'll save time. I thought you might have been stubborn and left it at home. It would have been a nuisance to go back and get it." He leaned back, smiling. "Why don't you sit down? Shall I ask Eileen to bring in some tea?"

"I don't want to sit, and I don't want tea." Folding her arms, she turned away from him and stared hard at the Georgia O'Keeffe on the wall. "Why didn't you come back?"

"There were a couple of reasons. One, I've been swamped here. I had several matters I wanted to clear up so I'd have a block of free time. Second, I wanted to stay away from you for a while."

"Oh, did you?" She kept her eyes trained on the bold colors. "Did you now?"

"Because I didn't want to admit how much I wanted to be with you." He waited, shook his head. "No response to that, I see. No I-wanted-to-be-with-you-as-well?"

"I did. Not that I don't have a life of my own. But there were odd moments when I would have liked your company."

And he would, it seemed, have to settle for that. "You're about to get it. Would you sit now, Maggie? There are some things we need to discuss."

"All right, then." She turned back, sat in front of his desk. He looked perfect there, she thought. Dignified, competent, in charge. Not at all like a man who would have indulged in a wild tussle on the office rug. The idea made her smile.

"What?"

"I was just wondering what your secretary might be thinking out there."

He lifted a brow. "I'm sure she assumes we're having a civilized business discussion."

"Hah! She looked like a sensible woman to me, but you go right on believing that." Pleased by the way his eyes flickered to the door, she propped her ankle on her knee. "So, what business are we about to discuss?"

"Ah—your work over the last few weeks has been exceptional. As you know, we held back ten pieces from the first showing with the purpose of touring them over the next year. I would like to keep a few of your newest pieces in Dublin, but the rest is already on its way to Paris."

"So your very efficient and very sensible Eileen told me." She began to tap her fingers on her ankle. "You didn't call me all the way to Dublin to tell me again—nor do I think you called me here for a spot of hot sex on the office rug."

"No, I didn't. I would have preferred discussing the plans with you over the phone, but you never bothered to return my calls."

"I was out a good deal of the time. You may have exclusive rights to my work, but not to me, Rogan. I do have my own life, as I've already explained."

"A number of times." He could feel the temper seeping back into him. "I'm not interfering with your life. I'm managing your career. And to that purpose, I'll be traveling to Paris to oversee the display, and the showing."

Paris. She'd barely had an hour with him and he was already talking about leaving. Distressed by her own plummeting heart, she spoke crisply.

" 'Tis a wonder you keep your business thriving, Rogan. I'd think you'd be hiring people capable of handling details like that without you feeling the need to peek over their shoulders."

"I assure you, I have very competent people. As it happens, I have a vested interest in your work, and I want to handle those details myself. I want it done right."

"Which means you want it done your way."

"Precisely. And I want you to come with me."

The sarcastic little comment that had sprung to her lips slipped off. "With you? To Paris?"

"I realize you have some artistic or possibly moral objection to promoting your own work, but you did well enough at the Dublin show. It would be advantageous to have you appear, however briefly, at your first international show."

"My first international show," she repeated, dumbfounded as the phrase sank into her head. "I don't—I don't speak French."

"That won't be a problem. You'll have a look at the Paris gallery, dispense a bit of charm and have plenty of time to see the sights." He waited for her answer, received nothing but a blank stare. "Well?"

"When?"

"Tomorrow."

"Tomorrow." The first skitter of panic had her pressing a hand to her stomach. "You want me to go with you to Paris tomorrow?"

"Unless you've some pressing previous engagement."

"I don't, no."

"Then it's settled." The relief was almost brutal. "After we've satisfied ourselves that the Paris show is successful, I'd like you to go south with me."

"South?"

"I've a villa on the Mediterranean. I want to be alone with you, Maggie. No distractions, no interruptions. Just you."

Her eyes lifted to his. "The block of time you've been working on for these weeks?"

"Yes."

"I wouldn't have shouted at you if you'd explained it to me."

"I had to explain it to myself first. Will you come?"

"Yes, I'll come with you." She smiled. "You'd only to ask."

An hour later she burst into the gallery, only to stop and simmer with frustration as she waited for Joseph to finish with a client. While he charmed a woman old enough to be his mother, Maggie wandered around the main room, noting that the American Indian display had been replaced by a selection of metal sculptures. Intrigued by the shapes, she lost her sense of urgency in admiration.

"A German artist," Joseph said from behind her. "This particular work is, I feel, both visceral and joyous. A celebration of elemental forces."

"Earth, fire, water, the suggestion of wind in the feathering of the copper." She put on an airy accent to match his. "Powerful indeed in scope, but with an underlying mischief that suggests satire."

"And it can be yours for a mere two thousand pounds."

"A bargain. A pity I'm without a farthing to me name." She turned, laughing, and kissed him. "You're looking fit, Joseph. How many hearts have you broken since I left you?"

"Nary a one. Since mine belongs to you."

"Hah! A good thing for us both that I know you're full of blarney. Have you a minute to spare?"

"For you, days. Weeks." He kissed her hand. "Years."

"A minute will do me. Joseph, what do I need for Paris?"

"A tight black sweater, a short skirt and very high heels."

"That'll be the day. Really, I'm to go, and I haven't a clue what I'll need. I tried to reach Mrs. Sweeney, but she's out today."

"So I'm your second choice. You devastate me." He signaled to one of his staff to take the room. "All you need for Paris, Maggie, is a romantic heart."

"Where can I buy one?"

"You have your own. You can't hide it from me—I've seen your work."

She grimaced, then slipped her arm through his. "Listen now, I'd not admit this to just anyone, but I've never traveled. In Venice I only had to worry about learning and not wearing anything that would catch fire. And paying the rent. If I'm going to have a trip to Paris, I don't want to make a fool of myself."

"You won't. You'll be going with Rogan, I take it, and he knows Paris as well as a native. You've only to act a bit arrogant, a bit bored, and you'll fit right in."

"I've come to you for fashion advice. Oh, it's humiliating to say it, but I can't go looking like this. Not that I want to paint myself up like a mannequin, but I don't want to look like Rogan's country cousin either."

"Hmm." Joseph took the question seriously, drawing her back to arm's length for a slow, careful study. "You'd do just fine as you are, but . . ."

"But?"

"Buy yourself a silk blouse, very tailored, but soft. Vivid colors, my girl, no pastels for you. Slacks of the same type. Use your eye for color. Go for the clash. And that short skirt is a must. You've got that black dress?"

"I didn't bring it with me."

He clucked his tongue like a maiden aunt. "You should always be prepared. All right, that's out, so go for glitter this time. Something that dazzles the eye." He tapped the sculpture beside them. "These metal tones would suit you. Don't go for classic, go for bold." Pleased with the thought, he nodded. "How's that?"

"Confusing. I'm ashamed to find it matters to me."

"There's nothing shameful about it. It's simply a matter of presentation."

"That may be, but I'd be grateful to you if you didn't mention this to Rogan."

"Consider me your confessor, darling." He looked over her shoulder, and Maggie saw joy leap into his eyes.

Patricia came in, hesitated, then crossed the glossy tiles. "Hello, Maggie. I didn't know you were coming to Dublin."

"Neither did I." What change was this? Maggie wondered. Gone was the shadowed sadness, the fragile reserve. It only took a moment, seeing the way Patricia's eyes lighted on Joseph's, to give her the answer. Aha, she thought. So there's where the wind blows.

"I'm sorry to interrupt. I just wanted to tell Joseph . . ." Patricia sputtered to a halt. "Ah, that is, I was passing by and remembered the business we'd discussed. The seven o'clock appointment?"

"Yes." Joseph dipped his hands into his pockets to keep them from reaching for her. "Seven o'clock."

"I'm afraid I have to make it seven-thirty. I've a bit of a conflict. I wanted to be sure that wouldn't upset the schedule."

"I'll adjust it."

"Good. That's good." She stood for a moment, staring foolishly at him before she remembered Maggie and her manners. "Will you be in town long?"

"No, actually, I'm leaving tomorrow." The way the air was sizzling, Maggie thought, it was a wonder the sculptures didn't melt. "In fact, I'm leaving now."

"Oh, no, please, don't run off on my account. I've got to go." Patricia sent one more longing look in Joseph's direction. "I've people waiting for me. I just wanted to—well, good-bye."

Maggie waited one beat. "Are you just going to stand here?" she hissed at Joseph as Patricia headed for the door.

"Hmm? What? Excuse me." He made the dash to the door in two seconds flat. She watched Patricia turn, blush, smile. Then they were in each other's arms.

The romantic heart Maggie refused to believe she had, swelled. She waited until Patricia hurried out and Joseph stood staring after her like a man recently struck by lightning.

"So your heart belongs to me, does it?"

The dazed look cleared from his eyes. "She's beautiful, isn't she?"

"There's no denying it."

"I've been in love with her so long, even before she married Robbie. I never thought, never believed . . ." He laughed a little, still dazzled by love. "I thought it was Rogan."

"So did I. It's plain to see you make her happy." She kissed his cheek. "I'm glad for you."

"It's—we're trying to keep it between us. At least until . . . for a while. Her family . . . I can guarantee her mother won't approve of me."

"The hell with her mother."

"Patricia said nearly the same thing." It brought a smile to his lips to remember it. "But I'll not be the cause of any trouble there. So I'd appreciate it if you'd say nothing."

"Not to Rogan either?"

"I work for him, Maggie. He's a friend, yes, but I work for him. Patricia's the widow of one of his oldest friends, a woman he's escorted himself. A great many people thought she'd become his wife."

"I don't believe Rogan was among them."

"Be that as it may, I'd rather tell him myself when the time's right."

"It's your business, Joseph. Yours and Patricia's. So we'll trade confession for confession."

"I'm grateful to you."

"No need. If Rogan's stiff-necked enough to disapprove, he deserves to be fooled."

FIFTEEN

Paris was hot, muggy and crowded. The traffic was abominable. Cars, buses, motorbikes screeched and swerved and sped, their drivers seemingly bent on challenging each other to endless roadway duels. Along the sidewalks, people strolled and swaggered in a colorful pedestrian parade. Women in those short skirts Joseph seemed so fond of looked lean and bored and impossibly chic. Men, equally fashionable, watched them from little café tables where they sipped red wine or strong black coffee.

Flowers bloomed everywhere—roses, gladiolus, marigolds, snapdragons, begonias tumbling out of vendors' stalls, sunning on banks, spilling out of the arms of young girls whose legs flashed bright as blades in the sunshine.

Boys skated by with yards of golden bread spearing up out of bags. Packs of tourists aimed cameras like so many shotguns to blast away at their shutter view of Paris life.

And there were dogs. The city seemed a veritable den of them, prancing on leashes, skulking in alleyways, darting by shops. Even the lowliest cur appeared exotic, wonderfully foreign and arrogantly French.

Maggie took it all in from her window overlooking the Place de la Concorde.

She was in Paris. The air was full of sound and scent and gaudy light. And her lover was sleeping like a stone in the bed behind her.

Or so she thought.

He'd been watching her watch Paris for some time. She leaned out of the grand window, heedless of the cotton nightshirt falling off her left shoulder. She'd acted wholly indifferent to the city when they'd arrived the evening before. Her eyes had widened at the lush lobby of the Hôtel de Crillon, but she'd made no comment when they'd checked in.

She'd said little more when they entered the plush and lofty suite, and wandered away when Rogan tipped the bellman.

When he asked her if the room suited her, she'd simply shrugged and said it would do well enough.

It made him laugh and drag her off to bed.

But she wasn't quite so blasé now, he noted. He could all but see the excitement shimmering around her as she stared out at the street and absorbed the bustling life of the city. Nothing could have pleased him more than to give her Paris.

"If you lean out much farther, you'll stop traffic."

She jolted and, dragging her hair from her eyes, looked around to where he lay among rumpled sheets and a mountain of pillows.

"A bomb couldn't stop that traffic. Why do they want to kill each other?"

"It's a matter of honor. What do you think of the city in daylight?"

"It's crowded. Worse than Dublin." Then she relented and grinned at him. "It's lovely, Rogan. Like an old, bad-tempered woman holding court. There's a vendor down there with an ocean of flowers. And every time someone stops to look or buy, he ignores them, like it's beneath his dignity to notice them. But he takes their money, and counts every coin."

She crawled back into bed and stretched herself over him. "I know exactly how he feels," she murmured. "Nothing makes you more irritable than selling what you love."

"If he didn't sell them, they'd die." He tipped up her chin. "If you didn't sell what you love, part of you would die, too."

"Well, the part that needs to eat would without a doubt. Are you going to call up one of those fancy waiters and have him bring us breakfast?"

"What would you like?"

Her eyes danced. "Oh, everything. Starting with this . . ."

She tugged the sheets away and fell on him.

Quite a bit later she stepped out of the shower, wrapping herself in the plush white robe that had hung on the back of the door. She found Rogan at a table by the parlor window, pouring coffee and reading the paper.

"That newspaper's in French." She sniffed at a basket of croissants. "You read French and Italian?"

"Mmm." His brows were knit over the financial pages. He was thinking of calling his broker.

"What else?"

"What else what?"

"What else do you read—speak. Language I mean."

"Some German. Enough Spanish to get by."

"Gaelic?"

"No." He turned the page, scanning for news of art auctions. "Do you?"

"My father's mother spoke it, so I learned." Her shoulders moved restlessly as she slathered jam onto a steaming croissant. "It's not much good, I suppose, except for cursing. It won't get you the best table in a French restaurant."

"It's valuable. We've lost a considerable amount of our heritage." Which was something he thought about, often. "It's a pity that there are only pockets in Ireland where you can hear Irish spoken." Because this reminded him of an idea he'd been toying with, he folded his paper and set it aside. "Say something in Gaelic."

"I'm eating."

"Say something for me, Maggie, in the old tongue."

She made a little sound of impatience, but obliged him. It was musical, exotic and as foreign to him as Greek.

"What did you say?"

"That you've a pleasing face to see of a morning." She smiled. "You see it's a language as useful for flattery as it is for cursing. Now say something to me in French."

He did more than speak. He leaned over, touched his lips softly to hers, then murmured, *"Me reveiller à côté de toi, c'est le plus beau de tous les rêves."* Her heart did a long, slow swirl in her chest.

"What does it mean?"

"That waking beside you is more lovely than any dream."

She lowered her eyes. "Well. It seems French is a tongue more given to pretty sounds than plain English."

Her quick, unplanned feminine reaction both amused and allured. "I've touched you. I should have tried French before."

"Don't be foolish." But he *had* touched her, deeply. She combated the uneasy weakness by attacking her meal. "What am I eating?"

"Eggs Benedict."

"It's good," she said with her mouth full. "A bit on the rich side, but good. What are we after doing today, Rogan?"

"You're still blushing, Maggie."

"I'm not." She met his eyes narrowly, in a dare. "I'd like to know what the plans are. I'm assuming this time you'll discuss them with me first instead of just tugging me along like an idiot dog."

"I'm growing very fond of that wasp you call a tongue," he said pleasantly. "I'm probably losing my mind. And before you sting me again, I thought you'd enjoy seeing some of the city. You'd no doubt enjoy the Louvre. So I've left the morning quite clear for sight-seeing, or shopping, or whatever you'd like. Then we'll go by the gallery later this afternoon."

The notion of strolling through the great museum pleased her. She topped off Rogan's coffee, then heated up her own cup of tea. "I'd like to wander about, I suppose. As for shopping, I'll want to find something to take back for Brie."

"You should have something for Maggie as well."

"Maggie doesn't need anything. Besides, I can't afford it."

"That's absurd. You've no need to deny yourself a present or two. You've earned it."

"I've spent what I've earned." She grimaced over her cup. "Do they have the nerve to call this tea?"

"What do you mean you've spent it?" He set down his fork. "Only a month ago I gave you a check in the six figures. You can hardly have frittered that away."

"Frittered?" She gestured dangerously with her knife. "Do I look like a fritterer?"

"Good God, no."

"And what's that supposed to mean? That I haven't the taste or style to spend my money well?"

He held up a hand for peace. "It means nothing more than no. But if you've wasted the money I gave you, I'd like to know how."

"I wasted nothing, as if it were your business to begin with."

"You are my business. If you can't manage your money, I'll do it for you."

"You'll not. Why you pompous, penny-pinching ass, 'tis mine, isn't it? And it's gone, or most of it. So you'll just have to see that you sell my work and get me more."

"That's precisely what I'll do. Now, where did it go?"

"Away." Infuriated, embarrassed, she shoved back from the table. "I've expenses, don't I? I needed supplies, and I was foolish enough to buy a dress."

He folded his hands. "You spent, in a month's time, nearly two hundred thousand pounds on supplies and a dress."

"I had a debt to pay," she raged at him. "And why should I have to explain to you? It says nothing of how I spend my money in your bloody contract."

"The contract has nothing to do with it," he said patiently, because he could see it wasn't anger so much as mortification that was driving her. "I'm asking you where the money went. But you're certainly under no legal obligation to tell me."

His reasonable tone only pinched harder at her humiliation. "I bought my mother a house, though she'll never thank me for it. And I had to furnish it for her, didn't I? She'd have taken every stick and cushion from Brianna otherwise." Frustrated, she dragged both hands through her hair and sent it into fiery tufts. "And I had to hire Lottie, and see they had a car. And she'll have to be paid every week, so I gave Brie enough for six months in salary and for food and such. Then there was the lien, though Brie will be furious when she finds I've paid it off. But it was mine to pay, as Da took it out for me. So it's done. I kept my word to him and I won't have you telling me what I should or shouldn't do with my own money."

She'd stormed around the room while she spoke and came to a halt now by the table where Rogan continued to sit, silently, patiently.

"If I might summarize?" he said. "You bought a house for your mother, furnished it, purchased a car and hired a companion for her. You've paid off a lien, which will displease your sister, but which you felt was your responsibility. You've given Brianna enough to keep your mother for six months, bought supplies. And with what was left, you bought yourself a dress."

"That's right. That's what I said. What of it?"

She stood there, trembling with fury, her eyes sharp and bright and eager for battle. He could, he mused, tell her he admired her incredible generosity, her loyalty to her family. But he doubted that she'd appreciate the effort.

"That explains it." He picked up his coffee again. "I'll see that you get an advance."

She wasn't at all sure she could speak. When she did, her voice came out in a dangerous hiss. "I don't want your bloody advance. I don't want it. I'll earn my own keep."

"Which you're doing—and quite well. It's not charity, Maggie, or even a loan. It's a simple business transaction."

"Be damned to your business." Her face was pink with embarrassment now. "I'll not take a penny until I've earned it. I've just gotten myself out of debt. I won't go into it again."

"God, you're stubborn." He tapped his fingers on the table as he thought her reaction through, trying to understand her display of passion. If it was pride she needed so badly, he could help her keep it. "Very well, we'll do this another way entirely. We've had several offers on your *Surrender,* which I've turned down."

"Turned down?"

"Mmm. The last, I believe, was thirty thousand."

"Pounds!" The word erupted from her. "I was offered thirty thousand pounds for it, and you turned it down? Are you mad? It may seem like little or nothing to you, Rogan Sweeney, but I could live handsomely on that amount for more than a year. If this is how you manage—"

"Be quiet." And because he said it so casually, so absently, she did just that. "I refused the offer because I intended to buy the piece myself, after we'd toured it. I'll simply buy it now and it will continue on the tour as part of my collection. We'll make it thirty-five thousand."

He tossed off the amount as though it was loose change casually dropped on a bureau.

Something inside her was trembling like the heart of a frightened bird. "Why?"

"I can't, ethically, purchase it for myself at the same amount offered by a client."

"No, I mean why do you want it?"

He stopped his mental calculations and looked up at her. "Because it's beautiful work, intimate work. And because whenever I look at it, I remember making love with you the first time. You didn't want to sell it. Did you think I couldn't see that in your face the day you showed it to me? Did you really think I couldn't understand how much it hurt you to give it up?"

Unable to speak, she simply shook her head and turned away.

"It was mine, Maggie, even before you finished it. As much, I think, as it was yours. And it'll go to no one else. I never intended it to go to anyone else."

Still silent, she walked to the window. "I don't want you to pay me for it."

"Don't be absurd—"

"I don't want your money," she said quickly, while she could. "You're right—that piece was terribly special to me, and I'd be grateful if you'd accept it." She let out a long breath, staring hard through the glass. "I'd be pleased to know it was yours."

"Ours," he said in a tone that drew her gaze back to his like a magnet. "As it was meant to be."

"Ours, then." She sighed. "How can I stay angry with you?" she said quietly. "How can I fight what you do to me?"

"You can't."

She was afraid he was right about that. But she could, at least, take a stand on a smaller matter. "I'm grateful to you for offering an advance, but I don't want it. It's important to me to take only what I make, when I make it. I've enough left to get by. I want no more than that for now. What needed to be done is done. From this point on, what comes will be mine."

"It's only money, Maggie."

"So easy to say when you've more than you've ever needed." The edge in her voice, so much like her mother's, stopped her cold. She took a deep breath and let out what was in her own heart. "Money was like an open wound in my house—the lack of it, my father's skill for losing it, and my mother's constant nagging for more. I don't want to depend on pounds for my happiness, Rogan. And it frightens and shames me that I might."

So, he thought, studying her, this was why she'd fought him every step of the way. "Didn't you tell me once that you didn't pick up your pipe each day thinking about the profit on the other end of it?"

"Yes, but—"

"Do you think of it now?"

"No. Rogan—"

"You're arguing against shadows, Maggie." He rose to cross to her. "The woman you are has already decided that the future will be very different from the past."

"I can't go back," she murmured. "Even if I wanted to, I couldn't go back."

"No, you can't. You'll always be one to go forward." He kissed her softly on the brow. "Will you get dressed now, Maggie? Let me give you Paris."

He did. For nearly a week he gave her everything the city had to offer, from the magnificence of Notre Dame to the intimacy of dim cafés. He bought her flowers from the tight-lipped street vendor every morning until the suite smelled like a garden. They strolled along the Seine in the moonlight, Maggie with her shoes in her hand and the river's breeze on her cheeks. They danced in clubs to poorly played American music, and dined on glorious food and wine at Maxim's.

She watched him pore over the sidewalk art, searching always for another diamond in the rough. And though he winced when she bought an undoubtedly bad painting of the Eiffel Tower, she only laughed and told him art was in the soul, not always in the execution.

The hours she spent in the Paris gallery were just as exciting to her. While Rogan ordered, directed and arranged, she saw her work shine under his vigilant eye.

A vested interest, he'd said. She couldn't deny that he tended his interests well. He was as passionate and attentive to her art during those afternoons as he was to her body during the nights.

When it was done, and the last piece was set to shine under the lights, she thought that the show was every bit as much a result of his efforts as of her own.

But partnership didn't always equal harmony.

"Damn it, Maggie, if you keep fussing in there we'll be late." For the third time in as many minutes, Rogan knocked on the bedroom door she'd locked.

"And if you keep bothering me, we'll be later still," she called out. "Go away. Better yet, go on to the gallery yourself. I can get myself there when I'm ready."

"You can't be trusted," he muttered, but her ears were sharp.

"I don't need a keeper, Rogan Sweeney." She was breathless from struggling to reach the low zipper of her dress. "I've never seen a man so ruled by the hands of a clock."

"And I've never seen a woman more careless of time. Would you unlock this door? It's infuriating to have to shout through it."

"All right, all right." By nearly dislocating her arm, she managed to fasten the dress. She wriggled her feet into ridiculously high bronze heels, cursed herself for being fool enough to take Joseph's advice, then twisted the lock. "I wouldn't have taken so long if they made women's clothes with the same consideration they make men's. Your zippers are within easy reach." She stopped, tugged once on the short hem of the dress. "Well? Is it all right or not?"

He said nothing at all, only twirled his finger to indicate he wanted her to circle. Rolling her eyes to heaven, she complied.

The dress was strapless, nearly backless, with a skirt that halted teasingly at midthigh. It glittered, bronze, copper, gold, sparking fire at every breath. Her hair echoed the tone so that she seemed like a candle flame, slim and bright.

"Maggie. You take my breath away."

"The seamstress wasn't generous with material."

"I admire her parsimony."

When he continued to stare, she lifted her brows. "You said we were in a hurry."

"I've changed my mind."

Her brows lifted higher as he started toward her. "I'm warning you, if you get me out of this dress, it'll be your responsibility to get me back in."

"As attractive as that sounds, it'll have to wait. I've a present for you, and it seems that the fates guided my hand. I believe this will complement your dress nicely."

He reached into the inside pocket of his tux and took out a slim velvet box.

"You've already bought me a present. That huge bottle of scent."

"That was for me." He leaned over to sniff her bare shoulder. The smoky perfume might have been created with her in mind. "Very much for me. This is for you."

"Well, since it's too small to be another answering machine, I'll take it." But when she opened the box, the chuckle died in her throat. Rubies, square flames of them, simmered with white-hot diamonds in a three-tiered choker tied together by twists of glinting gold. No delicate bauble, but a bold flash, a lightning flash of color and heat and gleam.

"Something to remember Paris by," Rogan told her as he slipped it from the box. The necklace ran like blood and water through his fingers.

"It's diamonds. Rogan, I can't wear diamonds."

"Of course you can." He brought it to her throat, his eyes on hers as he fastened the clasp. "Not alone, perhaps. They'd be cold and wouldn't suit you. But with the other stones . . ." He stepped back to take in the effect. "Yes, exactly right. You look like a pagan goddess."

She couldn't stop her hand from reaching up, from running across the gems. They felt warm against her skin. "I don't know what to say to you."

"Say thank you, Rogan. It's lovely."

"Thank you, Rogan." Her smile bloomed and spread. "It's a great deal more than lovely. It's dazzling."

"And so are you." He leaned into the kiss, then patted her bottom. "Now get a move on, or we'll be late. Where's your wrap?"

"I haven't got one."

"Typical," he murmured, and pulled her out the door.

Maggie thought she handled her second showing with a great deal more panache than she had the first. Her stomach wasn't nearly as jittery, her temper not nearly as short. If she did, once or twice, think wistfully of escape, she covered it well.

And if she pined for something she couldn't have, she reminded herself that success sometimes had to be enough in itself.

"Maggie."

She turned from the heavily accented ramblings of a Frenchman whose eyes had rarely left her cleavage and stared dumbstruck at her sister.

"Brianna?"

"It certainly is." Smiling, Brianna gathered her astonished sister in an embrace. "I would have been here an hour ago, but there was a delay at the airport."

"But how? How are you here at all?"

"Rogan sent his plane for me."

"Rogan?" Baffled, Maggie scanned the room until she found him. He only smiled at her, then at Brianna, before returning his attention to an enormous woman in fuchsia lace. Maggie nudged her sister to a corner of the room. "You came on Rogan's plane?"

"I thought I would have to let you down again, Maggie." More than a little overwhelmed by the sight of Maggie's work glittering in a roomful of exotic strangers, Brianna slipped her hand into her sister's. "I was trying to think of how to manage it. Mother's fine with Lottie, of course, and I knew I could leave Con with Murphy. I even asked Mrs. McGee if she'd look after Blackthorn for a day or two. But then there was the how to get here."

"You wanted to come," Maggie said softly. "You wanted to."

"Of course I did. I wanted nothing more than to be with you. But I never imagined it would be like this." Brie stared at the white-coated waiter who offered her champagne from his silver tray. "Thank you."

"I didn't think it mattered to you." To clear the emotion from her throat, Maggie drank deeply. "I was, just now, standing here thinking I wished it mattered to you."

"I'm proud of you, Maggie, so proud. I've told you."

"I didn't believe you. Oh God." She felt the tears well up and blinked them furiously away.

"You should be ashamed of yourself, thinking so little of my feelings," Brie scolded.

"You never showed any interest," Maggie fired back.

"I showed all the interest I could. I don't understand what you do, but that doesn't mean it doesn't make me proud that you do it." Coolly, Brianna tipped back her glass. "Oh," she murmured, staring at the bubbling wine, "but that's lovely. Who'd have thought anything could taste like that?"

With a hoot of laughter, Maggie kissed her sister hard on the mouth. "Jesus save us, Brie, what are we doing here? The two of us, drinking champagne in Paris."

"I for one am going to enjoy it. I have to thank Rogan. Do you think I could interrupt him for a moment?"

"After you've told me the rest. When did you call him?"

"I didn't, he called me. A week ago."

"He called you?"

"Aye, and before I could wish him good morning, he was telling me what I would do and how I would do it."

"That's Rogan."

"He said he'd be sending the plane, and that I was to meet his driver at the airport in Paris. I tried to get a word in, but he rolled right over me. The driver would take me to the hotel. Have you ever seen the like of that place, Maggie? It's like a palace."

"I nearly swallowed my tongue when I walked in. Go on."

"Then, I was to get myself ready, and the driver would bring me here. Which he did, though I thought for certain he'd kill me along the way. And there was this in the hotel room, with a note from him telling me it would please him if I'd wear it." She brushed a hand down the misty blue silk of the evening suit she wore. "I wouldn't have taken it, but he put the request in such a way I'd have felt rude not to."

"He's good at that. And you look wonderful in it."

"I *feel* wonderful in it. I confess, my head's still spinning from planes and cars and all this. All of this," she said again, staring around the room. "These people, Maggie, they're all here for you."

"I'm glad you are. Shall I take you around so you can charm them for me?"

"They're charmed already, just seeing the two of you." Rogan stepped beside them and took Brianna's hand. "It's delightful to see you again."

"I'm grateful to you for arranging it. I can't begin to thank you."

"You just have. You don't mind if I introduce you around? Mr. LeClair—there, the rather flamboyant-looking man by Maggie's *Momentum?* He's just confessed to me that he's fallen in love with you."

"He certainly falls easily, but I'll be pleased to meet him. I'd like to wander about as well. I've never seen Maggie's work shown like this."

It took only minutes before Maggie was able to draw Rogan aside again. "Don't tell me I need to circulate," she said before he could do just that. "I have something I need to say to you."

"As long as you say it quickly. It doesn't do for me to monopolize the artist."

"It won't take long for me to tell you that this was the kindest thing anyone has ever done for me. I'll never forget it."

He ignored the distraction of the rapid French a woman chattered at his shoulder and took Maggie's hand to his lips. "I didn't want you unhappy again, and it was the simplest thing in the world to arrange for Brianna to be here."

"It might have been simple." She remembered the ragged artist he'd escorted up the elegant steps of the gallery. That, too, had been simple. "That doesn't make it any less kind. And to show you what it means to me, I'll not only stay through the whole evening, until the last guest toddles out the door, I'll talk to every one of them."

"Nicely?"

"Nicely. No matter how often I hear the word *visceral.*"

"That's my girl." He kissed the tip of her nose. "Now get to work."

SIXTEEN

If Paris had staggered her, the south of France with its sweep of beaches and snow-covered mountains left Maggie awestruck. There was no rattle of traffic here in Rogan's sparkling villa overlooking the searing blue waters of the Mediterranean, no crowds bustling toward shops or cafés.

The people who dotted the beach were no more than part of the painting that encompassed water and sand, bobbing boats and an endless, cloudless sky.

The countryside, which she could see from one of the many terraces that graced the villa, spread out in neat square fields bordered by stone fences like the ones she saw from her own doorway in Clare. But here, the ground rose up in terraced slopes, from orchards on sunny embankments to the higher green of the forests and on to the foothills of the magnificent Alps.

Rogan's grounds were lush with blooms and flowering herbs, exotic with olive and box trees and the sparkle of fountains. The quiet was disturbed only by the call of gulls and the music of falling water.

Content, Maggie lounged in one of the padded chaises on a sun-washed terrace and sketched.

"I thought I'd find you here." Rogan stepped out and dropped a kiss, both casual and intimate, on the top of her head.

"It's impossible to stay inside on such a day." She squinted up at him until he took the shaded glasses she'd tossed on a table and slipped them on her nose. "Did you finish your business?"

"For now." He sat beside her, shifting so as not to block her view. "I'm sorry I've been so long. One call seemed to lead to another."

"No matter. I like being on my own."

"I've noticed." He peeked into the sketchbook. "A seascape?"

"It's irresistible. And I thought I'd draw some of the scenery, so Brie could see it. She had such a wonderful time in Paris."

"I'm sorry she could only stay one day."

"One lovely day. It's hard to believe I strolled along the Left Bank with my sister. The Concannon sisters in Paris." It still made her laugh to think of it. "She'll not forget it, Rogan." Tucking her pencil behind her ear, Maggie took his hand. "Neither will I."

"You've thanked me, both of you. And the truth is I did nothing more than make a few calls. Speaking of calls, one that kept me away just now was from Paris." Reaching over, Rogan selected a sugared grape from the basket of fruit beside them. "You've an offer, Maggie, from the Comte de Lorraine."

"De Lorraine?" Lips pursed, she searched her memory. "Ah, the skinny old man with a cane who talked in whispers."

"Yes." Rogan was amused to hear her describe one of the wealthiest men in France as a skinny old man. "He'd like to commission you to make a gift for his granddaughter's wedding this December."

Her hackles rose instinctively. "I'll take no commissions, Rogan. I made that clear from the start."

"You did, yes." Rogan took another grape and popped it into Maggie's mouth to keep her quiet. "But it's my obligation to inform you of any requests. I'm not suggesting you agree, though it would be quite an impressive feather in your—and Worldwide's—cap. I'm simply fulfilling my duties as your manager."

Eyeing him, Maggie swallowed the grape. His tone, she noted, was as sugarcoated as the fruit. "I'll not do it."

"Your choice, naturally." He waved the entire matter away. "Shall I ring for something cold? Lemonade perhaps, or iced tea?"

"No." Maggie took the pencil from behind her ear, tapped it on her pad. "I'm not interested in made-to-order."

"And why should you be?" he responded, all reason. "Your Paris showing was every bit as successful as the one in Dublin. I have every confidence that this will continue in Rome and beyond. You're well on your way, Margaret Mary." He leaned down and kissed her. "Not that the comte's request has anything to do with made-to-order. He's quite willing to leave it completely in your hands."

Cautious, Maggie tipped down her glasses and studied him over the tip. "You're trying to sweet-talk me into it."

"Hardly." But, of course, he was. "I should add, however, that the comte—a very well-respected art connoisseur, by the way—is willing to pay handsomely."

"I'm not interested." She shoved her glasses in place again, then swore. "How much is handsome?"

"Up to the equivalent of fifty thousand pounds. But I know how adamant you are about the money angle, so you needn't give it a thought. I told him it was unlikely you'd be interested. Would you like to go down to the beach? Take a drive?"

Before he could rise, Maggie snagged his collar. "Oh, you're a sneaky one, aren't you, Sweeney?"

"When needs be."

"It would be whatever I choose to make? Whatever came to me?"

"It would." He traced a finger over her bare shoulder, which was beginning to turn the color of a peach in the sun. "Except . . ."

"Ah, here we are."

"Blue," Rogan said, and grinned. "He wants blue."

"Blue, is it?" The laugh began to shake her. "Any particular shade?"

"The same as his granddaughter's eyes. He claims they are as blue as the summer sky. It seems she's his favorite, and after he saw your work in Paris, nothing would do but that she have something made for her alone from your lovely hands."

"His words or yours?"

"A bit of both," Rogan answered, kissing one of those lovely hands.

"I'll think about it."

"I'd hoped you would." No longer concerned with blocking her view, he leaned over to nibble at her lips. "But think about it later, will you?"

"Excusez-moi, monsieur." A bland-faced servant stood on the edge of the terrace, his hands at his sides and his eyes discreetly aimed toward the sea.

"Oui, Henri?"

"Vous et mademoiselle, voudriez-vous déjeuner sur la terrasse maintenant?"

"Non, nous allons déjeuner plus tard."

"Très bien, monsieur." Henri faded away, silent as a shadow into the house.

"And what was that about?" Maggie asked.

"He wanted to know if we wanted lunch. I said we'd eat later." When Rogan started to lean down again, Maggie stopped him with a hand slapped to his chest. "Problem?" Rogan murmured. "I can call him back and tell him we're ready after all."

"No, I don't want you to call him." It made her uneasy to think of Henri, or any of the other servants, lurking in a corner, waiting to serve. She wriggled off the chaise. "Don't you ever want to be alone?"

"We are alone. That's exactly why I wanted to bring you here."

"Alone? You must have six people puttering around the house. Gardeners and cooks, maids and butlers. If I were to snap my fingers right now, one of them would come running."

"Which is exactly the purpose in having servants."

"Well, I don't want them. Do you know one of those little maids wanted to wash out my underwear?"

"That's because it's her job to tend to you, not because she wanted to riffle your drawers."

"I can tend to myself. Rogan, I want you to send them away. All of them."

He rose at that. "You want me to fire the help?"

"No, for pity's sake, I'm not a monster, tossing innocent people out on the street. I want you to send them off, that's all. On a holiday, or whatever you'd call it."

"I can certainly give the staff a day off, if you'd like."

"Not a day, the week." She blew out a breath, seeing his puzzlement. "It doesn't make any sense to you, and why should it? You're so used to them, you don't even see them."

"His name was Henri, the cook is Jacques, the maid who so cheekily offered to wash your lingerie is Marie." Or possibly, he thought, Monique.

"I wasn't after starting a quarrel." She came forward, her hands reaching for his. "I can't relax as you do with all these people hovering about. I'm just not used to it—I don't think I want to be. Do this for me, please, Rogan. Give them a few days off."

"Wait here a moment."

When he left, she stood on the terrace, feeling foolish. Here she was, she mused, lounging in a Mediterranean villa with anything she could ask for within her reach. And she still wasn't satisfied.

She'd changed, she realized. In the few short months since she met Rogan, she had changed. She not only wished for more now, she coveted more of what she didn't have. She wanted the ease and the pleasure money could bring, and not just for her family. She wanted it for herself.

She'd worn diamonds and had danced in Paris.

And she wanted to do so again.

Yet, deep within her, there remained that small, hot need to be only herself, to need nothing and no one. If she lost that, Maggie thought with a whip of panic, she would have lost everything.

She snatched up her sketch pad, flipped pages. But for a moment, a terrifying moment, her mind was as blank as the sheet in front of her. Then she began to draw frantically, with a violent intensity that burst from her like a gale.

It was herself she drew. The two parts, twisted together, pulled apart and so desperately trying to meet again. But how could they, when one was so completely opposed to the other?

Art for art's sake, solitude for sanity, independence for pride. And on the other side—ambition, hungers and needs.

She stared at the completed sketch, dumbfounded that it had poured out of her so swiftly. And now that it had, she was oddly calm. Perhaps it was those two opposing forces that made her what she was. And perhaps if she were ever really at peace, she'd be less than she could be.

"They've gone."

Her mind still drifting, she looked blankly up at Rogan. "What? Who's gone?"

On a half laugh, he shook his head. "The staff. That's what you wanted, isn't it?"

"The staff? Oh." Her mind cleared, settled. "You've sent them off? All of them?"

"I did, though God alone knows how we'll eat over the next few days. Still—" He broke off when she leaped into his arms. As she'd shot at him like a bullet from a gun, he staggered back, overbalancing to keep them from crashing through the beveled-glass door behind him and nearly tumbling them over the railing.

"You're a wonderful man, Rogan. A prince of a man."

He shifted her in his arms and looked wearily at the drop over the rail. "I was nearly a dead man."

"We're alone? Completely?"

"We are, and I've earned the undying gratitude of everyone from the butler down. The parlor maid wept with joy." As he supposed she should, with the holiday bonus he'd given her and the rest of the servants. "So now they're off to the beach or to the country or to wherever their hearts lead them. And we've the house to ourselves."

She kissed him, hard. "And we're about to use every inch of it. We'll start with that sofa in the room just through there."

"Will we?" Amused, he made no protest as she began unbuttoning his shirt. "You're full of demands today, Margaret Mary."

"The business with the servants was a request. The sofa's a demand."

He cocked a brow. "The chaise is closer."

"So it is." She laughed as he lowered her to it. "So it is."

Over the next few days they sunned on the terrace, walked on the beach or swam lazy laps in the lagoonlike pool to the music of the fountains. There were ill-prepared meals to be eaten in the kitchen, and afternoon drives through the countryside.

There were also, to Maggie's mind, entirely too many telephones.

It might have been a holiday, but Rogan was never farther than a phone or a fax away from business. There was something about a factory in Limerick, something else about an auction in New York, and unintelligible mutters about property he was looking for in order to add another branch to Worldwide Galleries.

It might have annoyed her if she hadn't begun to see that his work was as much a part of his identity as her work was to hers. All differences aside, she could hardly complain about him spending an hour or two closeted in his office when he took her absorption in her sketches in stride.

If she had believed in a man and woman finding the kind of harmony that was needed to last a lifetime, she might have believed she'd found it with Rogan.

"Let me see what you've done."

With a contented yawn, Maggie offered him her sketchbook. The sun was setting, drowning colors sweeping the western sky. Between them the bottle of wine he'd chosen from his cellar nestled in a silver bucket frosty with ice. Maggie lifted her glass, sipped and settled back to enjoy her last evening in France.

"You'll be busy when you get home," Rogan commented as he studied each sketch. "How will you choose which one to work on first?"

"It will choose me. And as much as I've enjoyed being lazy, I'm itching to get back and fire up my furnace."

"I can have the ones you've drawn up for Brianna matted and framed. For simple pencil sketches they're quite good. I particularly like . . ." He trailed off when he turned a page and came across something entirely different from a sketch of the sea or a landscape. "And what have we here?"

Almost too lazy to move, she glanced over. "Oh, yes, that. I don't do portraits often, but that one was irresistible."

It was himself, stretched over the bed, his arm flung out as if he'd been reaching for something. For her.

Taken by surprise and not entirely pleased, he frowned down at the sketch. "You drew this while I was asleep."

"Well, I didn't want to wake you and spoil the moment." She hid her grin in her glass. "You were sleeping so sweetly. Perhaps you'd like to hang that one in your Dublin gallery."

"I'm naked."

"*Nude* is the word, I'll remind you. When it's art. And you look very artistic nude, Rogan. I've signed it, you see, so you may get a nice price for it."

"I think not."

She tucked her tongue in her cheek. "As my manager it's your duty to market my work. You're always saying so yourself. And this, if I do say so, is one of my finest drawings. You'll note the light, and the way it plays on the muscles of your—"

"I see," he said in a strangled voice. "And so would everyone else."

"No need to be modest. You've a fine form. I think I captured it even better in this other one."

His blood, quite simply, ran cold. "Other one?"

"Aye. Let's see now." She reached over to flip pages herself. "Here we are. Shows a bit more . . . contrast when you're standing, I think. And a bit of that arrogance comes through as well."

Words failed him. She'd drawn him standing on the terrace, one arm resting on the rail behind him, the other cupping a brandy snifter. And a smile—a particularly smug smile—on his face. It was all he was wearing.

"I never posed for this. And I've never stood naked on the terrace drinking brandy."

"Artistic license," she said airily, delighted that she'd flummoxed him so completely. "I know your body well enough to draw it from memory. It would have spoiled the theme to bother with clothes."

"The theme? Which is?"

"Master of the house. I thought that's what I'd title it. Both of them actually. You might offer them as a set."

"I won't be selling them."

"And why not? I'd like to know? You've sold several of my other drawings that aren't nearly as well done. Those I didn't want you to sell, but I'd signed on the dotted line, so you did. I *want* you to market these." Her eyes danced. "In fact, I insist, as I believe is my right, contractually speaking."

"I'll buy them myself, then."

"What's your offer? My dealer tells me my price is rising."

"You're blackmailing me, Maggie."

"Oh, aye." She toasted him then sipped more wine. "You'll have to meet my price."

He glanced at the sketch again before firmly closing the book. "Which is?"

"Let's see now. . . . I think if I was taken upstairs and made love to until moonrise, we might have a deal."

"You've a shrewd business sense."

"I've learned it from a master." She started to stand, but he shook his head and scooped her into his arms.

"I want no slipping through loopholes on this deal. I believe your terms were that you be taken upstairs."

"Right you are. I suppose that's why I need a manager." She wound a lock of his hair around her fingers as he carried her into the house. "You know, of course, if I'm not satisfied with the rest of the terms, the deal's off."

"You'll be satisfied."

At the top of the stairs he stopped to kiss her. Her response was, as always, fast and urgent, and as always, it quickened his blood. He stepped into the bedroom, where the softened light of sunset swam through the windows. Soon the light would go gray with dusk.

Their last night alone would not be spent in the dark.

Thinking this, he laid her on the bed, and when she reached for him, he slipped away to light candles. They were scattered through the room, some stubs, some slim tapers, all burned down to varying lengths. Maggie knelt on the bed while Rogan struck the flames and sent the light dancing gold.

"Romance." She smiled and felt oddly touched. "It seems a spot of blackmail's been well worth the effort."

He paused, a flaring match between his fingers. "Have I given you so little romance, Maggie?"

"I was only joking." She tossed back her breeze-ruffled hair. His voice had been much too serious. "I've no need for romance. Honest lust is quite good enough for me."

"Is that what we have?" Thoughtfully he set the match to the wick then shook it out. "Lust."

Laughing, she held out her arms. "If you'd stop wandering about the room and come over here, I'll show you exactly what we have."

She looked dazzling in the candle glow with the last colors of day bleeding through the windows beside the bed. Her hair afire, her skin kissed by her days in the sun and her eyes aware, mocking and unquestionably inviting.

On other days and other nights he would have dived into that invitation, accepted it, reveled in it and the firestorm they could make between them. But his mood had shifted. He crossed slowly to her, taking her hands before they could tug him eagerly into the bed with her, lifting them to his lips as his eyes watched her.

"That wasn't the bargain, Margaret Mary. I was to make love to you. It's time I did." He kept her hands in his, drawing her arms down to her sides as he leaned forward to toy with her lips. "It's time you let me."

"What foolishness is that?" Her voice wasn't steady. He was kissing her as he had once before, slowly, gently, and with the utmost concentration. "I've done more than let you a great many times before."

"Not like this." He felt her hands flex against his, her body draw back. "Are you so afraid of tenderness, Maggie?"

"Of course I'm not." She couldn't get her breath, yet she could hear it, feel it coming slow and heavy through her lips. Her whole body was tingling, yet he was barely touching her. Something was slipping away from her. "Rogan, I don't want to—"

"To be seduced?" He took his lips from hers, let them roam leisurely over her face.

"No, I don't." But her head tilted back as he skimmed his mouth down her throat.

"You're about to be."

He released her hands then to draw her closer. No fevered embrace this time, but an inescapable possession. Her arms seemed impossibly heavy as she wound them 'round his neck. She could do no more than cling as he stroked her hair, her face, with gentle fingertips that felt no more substantial than a whisper on the air.

His mouth came back to hers in a moist, deep, sumptuous kiss that went on endlessly, endlessly, until she was as pliant as wax in his arms.

He'd cheated both of them, Rogan realized as he laid her back on the bed. By letting only the fire take them, he'd kept them both from experiencing all the warm, waiting wells of tenderness.

Tonight it would be different.

Tonight he would take her through a labyrinth of dreams before the flames.

The taste of him seeped into her, stunning her, staggering her with tenderness. The greed that had always been so much a part of their lovemaking had mellowed into a lazy patience she could neither resist nor refuse. Long before he opened her blouse and skimmed those smooth, clever fingertips over her skin, she was floating.

Limply her hands slid from his shoulders. Her breath caught and expelled as he laved his tongue over her, seeking small secret tastes, lingering over them. Savoring. Drifting on that slow sweep of sensation, she was aware of every pulse point he awakened, of the long, quiet pull from deep inside her. So different from an explosion. So much more devastating.

She murmured his name when he cupped a hand under her head and lifted her melting body to his.

"You're mine, Maggie. No one else will ever take you here."

She should have objected to this new demand for exclusivity. But she couldn't. For his mouth was journeying over her again as if he had years, decades, to complete the exploration.

The candlelight flickered dreamily against her heavy lids. She could smell the flowers she'd picked only that morning and had placed in a blue vase by the window. She heard the breeze heralding the Mediterranean night with the scents of blossoms and water in its wake. Beneath his fingers and lips her skin softened and her muscles quivered.

How could he not have known he'd wanted her like this? All the fires banked, only glowing embers and drifting smoke. She moved under his hands helplessly, unable to do anything but absorb what he gave her, follow where he led. Even as the blood pounded in his head, in his loins, he kept the caresses light, teasing, waiting for her, watching her slide from one into the next melting sensation.

When she trembled, when a new sighing moan slipped through her lips, he took her hands again, braceleting them in one of his so that he was free to urge her over the first edge.

Her body bowed, her lashes fluttered. He watched as that first velvet fist took her breath. Then she went fluid again, languid and limp. Her pleasure welled inside of him.

The sun sank. Candles guttered. He guided her up again, a higher peak that made her cry out weakly. The sound echoed away into sighs and murmurs. When her heart was so full that it, too, seemed to weep, he slipped into her, taking her tenderly while the moon rose.

Perhaps she slept. She knew she dreamed. When she opened her eyes again, the moon was up and the room was empty. Languid as a cat, she considered curling up again. But even as she nuzzled into the pillow she knew she would not sleep without him.

She rose, floating a little as though her mind was dazed with wine. She found a robe, a thin swatch of silk that Rogan had insisted on giving her. It settled smoothly against her skin as she went to find him.

"I should have known you'd be here."

He was in the kitchen, standing shirtless in front of the gleaming stove in the brilliant white-and-black kitchen. "Thinking of your stomach?"

"And of yours, my girl." He turned off the fire under the skillet before he turned. "Eggs."

"What else?" It was all either of them could competently cook. "I won't be surprised if we're cackling when we get back to Ireland tomorrow." Because she felt unexpectedly awkward, she raked a hand through her hair once, then twice. "You should have made me get up and fix it."

"Made you?" He reached up for plates. "That would be a first."

"What I mean is, I'd have done it. After all, I don't feel I did my part before."

"Before?"

"Upstairs. In bed. I didn't exactly do my share."

"A bargain's a bargain." He scooped eggs into plates. "And from my point of view, you did very well indeed. Watching you unravel was an incredible pleasure for me." One he intended to experience again, very soon. "Why don't you sit down and eat. The moon'll be up for some time yet."

"I suppose it will." More at ease, she joined him at the table. "And this may just give me my energy back. Do you know," she said with her mouth full. "I'd no idea that sex could make you so weak."

"It wasn't just sex."

Her fork paused halfway to her lips at his tone. There was hurt beneath the sharp annoyance, and she was sorry to have caused it. Amazed that she could. "I didn't mean it that way, Rogan. Not so impersonally. When two people are fond of each other—"

"I'm a great deal more than fond of you, Maggie. I'm in love with you."

The fork slipped from her fingers and clattered on the plate. Panic tore at her throat in sharp, hungry fangs. "You're not."

"I am." He said it calmly, though he was cursing himself for making his declaration in a brightly lit kitchen over badly cooked eggs. "And you're in love with me."

"It's not—I'm not—you can't tell me what I am."

"I can when you're too foolish to say so yourself. What's between us is far more than physical attraction. If you weren't so pigheaded, you'd stop pretending it was."

"I'm not pigheaded."

"You are, but I find that's one of the things I like about you." He was thinking coolly now, pleased to be back in control. "We might have discussed all this under more atmospheric circumstances, but knowing you, it hardly matters. I'm in love with you, and I want you to marry me."

SEVENTEEN

Marriage? The word stuck in her throat, threatened to choke her. She didn't dare repeat it.

"You're out of your mind."

"Believe me, I've considered the possibility." He picked up his fork and ate with the appearance of sanity. But the hurt, unexpected and raw, scraped at him. "You're stubborn, often rude, more than occasionally self-absorbed and not a little temperamental."

For a moment her mouth moved like a guppy's. "Oh, am I?"

"You most certainly are, and a man would have to have taken leave of his senses to want that sort of baggage for a lifetime. But"—he poured out the tea he'd had steeping—"there you are. I believe it's customary to use the bride's church, so we'll be married in Clare."

"Customary? Hang your customs, Rogan, and you with them." Was this panic she felt, skidding along her spine like jagged ice? Surely not, she told herself. It had to be temper. She had nothing to fear. "I'm not marrying you or anyone. Ever."

"That's absurd. Of course you'll marry me. We're amazingly well suited, Maggie."

"A moment ago I was stubborn and temperamental and rude."

"So you are. And it suits me." He took her hand, ignored her resistance and tugged it to his lips. "And it suits me beautifully."

"Well, it doesn't suit me. Not at all. Perhaps I've softened toward your arrogance, Rogan, but that's changing by the second. Understand me." She yanked her hand free of his. "I'll be no man's wife."

"No man's but mine."

She hissed out a curse. When he only grinned at that, she took a hard grip on her temper. A fight, she thought, might be satisfying, but it would solve nothing. "You brought me here for this, didn't you?"

"No, actually, I didn't. I'd thought to take more time before tossing my feelings at your feet." Very carefully, very deliberately, he shifted his plate aside. "Knowing very well you'd kick them back at me." His eyes stayed on hers, level, patient. "You see I know you very well, Margaret Mary."

"You don't." Temper, and the panic she didn't want to admit, leaked out of her, leaving room for sorrow. "I've reasons for keeping my heart whole, Rogan, and for not ever considering the possibility of marriage."

It interested and soothed him to understand that it wasn't marriage to him that seemed to appall her, but marriage itself. "What are they?"

She lowered her gaze to her cup. After a moment's hesitation she added her usual three cubes of sugar and stirred. "You lost your parents."

"Yes." His brow furrowed. This certainly wasn't the tack he'd expected her to take. "Almost ten years ago."

"It's hard losing family. It strips away a whole layer of security, exposes you to the simple cold fact of mortality. You loved them?"

"Very much. Maggie—"

"No, I'd like to hear what you have to say about this. It's important. They loved you?"

"Yes, they did."

"How did you know it?" She drank now, holding the cup in two hands. "Was it because they gave you a good life, a fine home?"

"It had nothing to do with material comfort. I knew they loved me because I felt it, because they showed it. And I could see they loved each other as well."

"There was love in your house. And laughter? Was there laughter, Rogan?"

"Quite a bit of it." He could remember it still. "I was devastated when they died. So sudden, so brutally sudden . . ." His voice tapered off, then strengthened again. "But after, when the worst of it had passed, I was glad they'd gone together. Each of them would have been only half-alive without the other."

"You've no notice how lucky you are, what a gift you were given growing up in a loving, happy home. I've never known that. I never will. There was no love between my parents. There was anger and blame and guilt and there was duty, but no love. Can you imagine what it was like, growing up in a house where the two people who had made you cared nothing for each other? Were only there because their marriage was a prison barring them in with conscience and church law."

"No, I can't." He covered her hand with his. "I'm sorry you can."

"I swore, when I was a little girl, I swore I'd never be locked in a prison like that."

"Marriage isn't only a prison, Maggie," he said gently. "My own parents' was a joy."

"And you may make one for yourself one day. But not I. You make what you know, Rogan. And you can't change what you've come from. My mother hates me."

He would have protested, but she'd said it so matter-of-factly, so simply, he could not.

"Even before I was born she hated me. The fact that I grew inside her ruined her life, which she tells me as often as possible. All these years I never knew how deep it truly went, until your grandmother told me my mother had had a career."

"A career?" He cast his mind back. "The singing? What does that have to do with you?"

"Everything. What choice did she have but to give up her career? What career would she have had left as a single, pregnant woman in a country like ours? None." Cold, she shivered and let out a shaky breath. It hurt to say it aloud this way, to say it all aloud. "She wanted something for herself. I understand that, Rogan. I know what it is to have ambitions. And I can imagine, all too well, what it would be like to have them dashed. You see, they never would have married if I hadn't been conceived. A moment of passion, of need, that was all. My father more than forty, and she past thirty. She dreaming, I suppose, of romance and he seeing a lovely woman. She was lovely then. There are pictures. She was lovely before the bitterness ate it all away. And I was the seed of it, the seven-month baby that humiliated her and ruined her dreams. And his, too. Aye, and his."

"You can hardly blame yourself for being born, Maggie."

"Oh, I know that. Don't you think I know? Up here?" Suddenly fierce, she tapped her head. "But in my heart—can't you see? I know that my very existence and every breath I take burdened the lives of two people beyond measure. I came from passion only, and every time she looked at me, it reminded her that she'd sinned."

"That's not only ridiculous, it's foolish."

"Perhaps it is. My father said he'd loved her once, and perhaps it was true." She could imagine him, walking into O'Malley's, seeing Maeve, hearing her and letting his romantic heart take flight.

But it had crashed soon enough. For both of them.

"I was twelve when she told me that I hadn't been conceived within marriage. That's how she puts it. Perhaps she'd begun to see that I was making that slow shift from girl to woman. I'd begun to look at boys, you see. Had practiced my flirting on Murphy and one or two others from the village. She caught me at it, standing by the hay barn with Murphy, trying out a kiss. Just a kiss, that was all, beside the hay on a warm summer afternoon, both of us young and curious. It was my first kiss, and it was lovely—soft and shy and harmless.

"And she found us." When Maggie shut her eyes, the scene played back vividly. "She went white, bone white, and screamed and raged, dragged me into the house. I was wicked, she said, and sinful, and because my father wasn't home to stop her, she whipped me."

"Whipped you?" Shock had him rising out of his chair. "Are you telling me she hit you because you'd kissed a boy?"

"She beat me," Maggie said flatly. "It was more than the back of her hand that I'd been used to. She took a belt and laid into me until I thought she'd kill me. While she did she shouted scripture and raged about the branding of sin."

"She had no right to treat you so." He knelt in front of her, cupped her face in his hands.

"No, no one has such a right, but it doesn't stop them. I could see the hate in her then, and the fear, too. The fear, I came to understand, was that I would end up as she had, with a baby in my belly and emptiness in my heart. I'd known always that she didn't love me as mothers were meant to love their children. I'd known that she was easier, a bit softer on Brie. But until that day, I hadn't known why."

She couldn't sit any longer. Rising, she went to the door that led out to a little stone patio decked with clay pots filled with brilliant geraniums.

"There's no need for you to talk about this anymore," Rogan said from behind her.

"I'll finish." The sky was studded with stars, the breeze a gentle whisper through the trees. "She told me that I was marked. And she beat me so that the mark would be on the outside as well, so that I would understand what a burden a woman bears because it's she who carries the child."

"That's vile, Maggie." Unable to clamp down on his own emotions, he whirled her around, his hands hard on her shoulders, his eyes icy blue and furious. "You were just a girl."

"If I was, I stopped being one that day. Because I understood, Rogan, that she meant exactly what she said."

"It was a lie, a pitiful one."

"Not to her. To her it was sterling truth. She told me I was her penance, that God had punished her for her night of sin, with me. She believed that, fully, and every time she looked at me she was reminded of it. That even the pain and misery of birthing me wasn't enough. Because of me she was trapped in a marriage she despised, bound to a man she couldn't love and mother to a child she'd never wanted. And, as I've found out just recently, the ruin of everything she really wanted. Perhaps the ruin of everything she was."

"She's the one who should have been whipped. No one has the right to abuse a child so, and worse to use some warped vision of God as the strap."

"Funny, my father said nearly the same thing when he came home and saw what she'd done. I thought he would strike her. It's the only time in my life I'd ever seen him close to violence. They had a horrible fight. It was almost worse than the beating to listen to it. I went up to the bedroom to get away from the worst of it, and Brie came in with salve. She tended to me like a little mother, talking nonsense all the while the shouts and curses boomed up the stairs. Her hands were shaking."

She didn't object when Rogan drew her into his arms, but her eyes remained dry, her voice calm. "I thought he would go then. They said such vicious things to each other, I thought no two people could live under the same roof after. I thought if he'd just take us with him, if Brie and I could just go with him, anywhere at all, it would be all right again. Then I heard him say that he was paying, too. That he was paying for ever having believed that he loved and wanted her. That he'd go to his grave paying. Of course, he didn't go."

Maggie pulled away again. Stepped back. "He stayed more than ten years longer, and she never touched me again. Not in any way. But neither of us forgot that day—I think neither of us wanted to. He tried to make up for it by giving me more, loving me more. But he couldn't. If he'd left her, if he'd taken us and left her, it would have changed things. But that he couldn't do, so we lived in that house, like sinners in hell. And I knew no matter how he loved me that there were times he must have thought if it hadn't been—if *I* hadn't been, he'd have been free."

"Do you honestly blame the child, Maggie?"

"The sins of the fathers . . ." She shook her head. "One of my mother's favorite expressions that. No, Rogan, I don't blame the child. But it doesn't change the results." She took a deep breath. She was better for having said it all. "I'll never risk locking myself in that prison."

"You're too smart a woman to believe what happened to your parents happens to everyone."

"Not to everyone, no. One day, now that she's not hobbled by my mother's demands, Brie will marry. She's a woman who wants family."

"And you don't."

"I don't," she said, but the words sounded hollow. "I've my work, and a need to be alone."

He caught her chin in his hand. "You're afraid."

"If I am, I've a right to be." She shook free of him. "What kind of wife or mother would I make with what I've come from?"

"Yet you've just said your sister will be both."

"It affected her differently than it did me. She has as much need for people and for a home as I have to do without them. You were right enough when you said I was stubborn and rude and self-absorbed. I am."

"Maybe you've had to be. But that's not all you are, Maggie. You're compassionate and loyal and loving. It's not just part of you I fell in love with, but the whole. I want to spend my life with you."

Something trembled inside her, fragile as crystal struck by a careless hand. "Haven't you listened to a word I've said?"

"Every word. Now I know that you don't just love me. You need me."

She dragged both hands through her hair, fingers digging in and pulling in frustration. "I don't need anyone."

"Of course you do. You're afraid to admit it, but that's understandable." He was sorry, bitterly, for the child she'd been. But he couldn't allow that to change his plans for the woman. "You've locked yourself in a prison, Maggie. Once you admit those needs, the door will open."

"I'm happy with the way things are. Why do you have to change them?"

"Because I want more than a few days a month with you. I want a life with you, children with you." He skimmed a hand over her hair to cup the back of her neck. "Because you're the first and only woman I've ever loved. I won't lose you, Maggie. And I won't let you lose me."

"I've given you all I can give, Rogan." Her voice was shaky, but she held her ground. "It's more than I've given anyone else. Be content with what I'm able to give, for if you can't, I'll have to end it."

"Can you?"

"I'll have to."

His hand squeezed once at the base of her neck, then released and fell away. "Stubborn," he said with a trace of amusement to hide the ache. "Well, so am I. I can wait for you to come to me. No, don't tell me you won't," he went on as she opened her mouth to protest. "It will only make it more difficult on you when you do. We'll leave things as they are, Maggie. With one alteration."

The relief she'd felt shifted into wariness. "Which is?"

"I love you." He pulled her into his arms, covered her mouth with his. "You'll have to get used to hearing it."

She was glad to be home. At home she could savor the solitude, enjoy her own company and the long, long days where the light clung to the sky until ten. At home, she didn't have to think of anything but work. To prove it, she gave herself three days in her glass house, three days without interruption.

She was productive, pleased with the results she saw cooling in the annealing oven. And she was, for the first time in her memory, lonely.

That was on his head, she thought as she watched the twilight grow and deepen and slip beautifully toward night. He'd tricked her into enjoying his company, into enjoying the whirl of cities and people. He'd made her want too much.

She wanted him too much.

Marriage. The thought made her shudder as she gathered what she wanted from the kitchen table. That, at least, he could never make her want. She was certain, given a little time, he would see it her way. If not . . .

She stepped outside, shut the door. It was best not to think about any if-nots. Rogan was, above all, a sensible man.

She took the walk to Brianna's slowly as night settled around her. A slow mist gathered at her feet, and a breeze holding a warning chill whispered through the trees.

Like a welcoming beacon, the light in Brianna's kitchen glowed against the night. Maggie shifted the sketches she'd framed and quickened her steps.

As she approached, a low growl sounded out of the shadows of the sycamore. Maggie called out softly and was answered by a happy bark. Con leaped out of the shadows, through the mist, and would have jumped on her to show his love and devotion had she not held out a hand to stop him.

"I'd rather not be knocked over, thank you." She rubbed his head, his neck, while his swinging tail tore the thin fog like rags. "Guarding your princess tonight, are you? Well, let's go in and find her."

The moment Maggie opened the kitchen door, Con shot through in a blur of fur and muscle. He paused across the room at the door that led into the hallway, tail thumping.

"Out there, is she?" Maggie set the sketches aside and walked to the door. She heard voices through it, a soft laugh, a British accent. "She has guests," she said to Con, and disappointed the dog thoroughly when she backed away from the door. "We won't disturb her, so you're stuck with me." To make the prospect a bit more hopeful, she went to the cupboard where Brianna kept Con's biscuits. "Well, what trick will you do for me, boy-o?"

Con eyed the biscuit she was holding, smacked his lip. With restrained dignity he padded to Maggie, sat and lifted a paw.

"Well done, lad."

Once he had a treat between his teeth, Con pranced to the rug in front of the kitchen hearth, circled three times, then settled down with a sigh to enjoy himself.

"I could do with something myself."

A quick snoop around the kitchen revealed a treasure. A square of gingerbread, half-gone, rested under a protecting cloth. Maggie ate one slice while the kettle was heating, and sat down to another with a homey pot of tea.

When Brianna came in, Maggie was scraping crumbs from the plate.

"I wondered when you'd come by." Brianna reached down to pet the dog, who'd risen to press himself against her legs.

"It would have been sooner, if I'd known this was waiting. You've guests, I see."

"Yes, a couple from London, a student from Derry and two sweet ladies down from Edinburgh. How did you enjoy your holiday?"

"It was a beautiful place, hot, sunny days, warm nights. I drew you some pictures so you'd see for yourself." She gestured to them.

Brie lifted the pictures and her face lit up with joy. "Oh, they're wonderful."

"I thought you'd like them more than a postcard."

"I do. Thank you, Maggie. I've some clippings about your show in Paris."

Maggie was surprised. "Oh, how did you get them?"

"I asked Rogan to send them to me. Would you like to see?"

"Not now, no. They'll just give me a nervous stomach, and my work's going too well."

"Will you be going to Rome when the show moves on?"

"I don't know. I haven't thought about it. All that part of it seems a long way from here."

"Like a dream." Brianna sighed as she sat down. "I can hardly believe I was in Paris."

"You could travel more now, if you'd like."

"Mmm." Perhaps there were places she'd like to see, but home held her. "Alice Quinn had a boy. David they're calling him. He was christened just yesterday. He wailed all through the service."

"And Alice probably fluttered around like a bird."

"No, she held little David and soothed him, then took him off to nurse. Marriage and motherhood have changed her. You wouldn't think it was the same Alice."

"Marriage always changes people."

"Often for the better." But Brianna knew what Maggie was thinking. "Mother's getting along well."

"I didn't ask."

"No," Brianna said evenly. "But I'm telling you. Lottie's badgered her into sitting out in the garden every day, and into taking walks."

"Walking?" Despite herself, Maggie's interest was snagged. "Mother, walking?"

"I don't know how she does it, but Lottie has a way with her. The last time I visited, Mother was holding yarn while Lottie balled it. When I came in, she tossed it down and began to rant about how the woman would drive her into the grave. Claimed she fired Lottie twice, but Lottie wouldn't go. All the while Mother complained, Lottie rocked in her chair, smiling and rolling her yarn."

"If the woman drives Lottie away—"

"No, let me finish." Brianna leaned forward, her eyes dancing. "I stood there, making excuses and apologies and waiting for the worst. And after a while Lottie stopped rocking. 'Maeve,' she said, 'stop pestering the girl. You sound like a magpie.' And she handed the yarn back to her and told me how she was after teaching Mother to knit."

"Teaching her to—oh, that'll be the day."

"The thing was, Mother kept muttering under her breath and arguing with Lottie. But she seemed to be enjoying it. You were right about her having her own place, Maggie. She may not realize it yet, but she's happier there than she's been most of her life."

"The point is she's out of here." Restless, Maggie rose to prowl around the kitchen. "I don't want you deluding yourself into thinking I did it out of the goodness of my heart."

"But you did," Brianna said quietly. "If you want no one but me to know it, that's your choice."

"I didn't come here to talk about her, but to see how you were getting on. Have you moved into the room off the kitchen?"

"Yes. It gives me another room upstairs free for guests."

"It gives you some privacy."

"There's that. I've a place for a desk in there so I can do the books and the paperwork. I like having a window right over the garden. Murphy said I could have a door put in, if I want, so I could come in and out without going through the rest of the house."

"Good." Maggie lifted a jar of currants, set it down again. "Have you enough for the labor?"

"I've enough. It's been a good summer. Maggie, won't you tell me what's troubling you?"

"Nothing is," Maggie answered abruptly. "I've a lot on my mind, that's all."

"Have you quarreled with Rogan?"

"No." It couldn't be called a quarrel, she thought. "Why should you assume I'd be thinking of him?"

"Because I saw you together, saw how much you care for each other."

"That should be enough, shouldn't it?" Maggie demanded. "I care for him and he for me. The business we have together is successful and will likely continue to be. That should be enough."

"I don't know the answer to that. Are you in love with him?"

"I'm not." Wouldn't be. "He thinks I am, but I can't be responsible for what the man thinks. Nor will I change my life for him, or anyone. He's already made it change." She hugged her arms close, feeling suddenly cold. "And, damn him, I can't go back."

"Back to what?"

"To being what I was, what I thought I was. He's made me want more. I know I always did, but he's made me admit it. It's not enough for me to believe in my work, I need him to. He's made himself a part of it, and if I fail, I don't fail alone. When I succeed, the satisfaction isn't mine alone either. And I think I've compromised myself because I've given part of me, the best of me, into his hands."

"Is it your art you're talking about, Maggie, or is it your heart?" Brianna stared hard at her sister as she asked the question.

Maggie sat again, defeated. "I don't have one without the other. So it seems I've given him a piece of both."

Rogan would have been surprised to hear it. He'd decided, after a great deal of thought, to treat his relationship with Maggie as he would any business merger with a reluctant company. He'd made his offer. Now it was time to stand back, to distance himself while the other party considered.

There was no professional reason to contact her. The show in Paris would remain for another two weeks before moving to Rome. The pieces had been chosen, the groundwork laid.

For the foreseeable future, she had her work and he had his. Any business contact could be made through his staff.

He would, in other words, let her stew.

It was important to his pride and his plans not to let her know how much her rejection of his feelings had hurt. Apart, they could each evaluate their future objectively. Together, they would simply end up in bed. That was no longer enough.

Patience and a firm hand were what was required. Rogan was sure of it. And if Maggie remained so foolishly obstinate after a reasonable amount of time, he'd use whatever means were at his disposal.

Rogan knocked briskly on his grandmother's door. It wasn't their usual time for visiting, but after being back in Dublin for a week, he needed the comfort of family.

He nodded at the maid who opened the door. "Is my grandmother at home?"

"Yes, Mr. Sweeney. She's in the front parlor. I'll tell her you're here."

"No need." He strode down the hall and through the open parlor doors. Christine rose immediately and opened her arms to him.

"Rogan! What a lovely surprise."

"I had a meeting canceled, so I thought I'd drop in and see how you were." He drew her back, lifting a brow as he studied her face. "You look exceptionally well."

"I feel exceptionally well." She laughed and led him to a chair. "Shall I get you a drink?"

"No. I don't have very long, and I only came for the company."

"I've heard how well it went in Paris." Christine sat beside him, smoothed down the skirt of her linen dress. "I had lunch with Patricia last week, and she told me it was a rousing success."

"It was. Though I can't say how Patricia would know." He thought of his friend with a lingering trickle of guilt. "She's well?"

"Oh, very. Blooming, you could say. And I believe she said Joseph had told her about the Paris business. She's working very hard on her day school, and Joseph is giving her a bit of help."

"Good. I haven't had much time at the gallery this past week, I'm afraid. The fact is the expansion in Limerick is taking most of my efforts."

"How is that going?"

"Well enough. I've had some complications, so I'll have to take a trip down to sort them out."

"But you've hardly gotten back."

"It shouldn't take more than a day or two." He cocked his head, watching his grandmother tug at her skirt, brush at her hair. "Is something wrong?"

"No." She smiled brightly and forced her hands to still. "Not at all, though there is something I want to discuss with you. You see . . ." She trailed off, calling herself a miserable coward. "How is Maggie? Did she enjoy France?"

"She seemed to."

"It's a beautiful time of year to holiday at the villa. Was the weather good?"

"It was. Is it weather you want to discuss, Grandmother?"

"No, I was just—are you sure you don't want that drink?"

A trickle of alarm skidded down his back. "If something's wrong, I want you to tell me."

"There's nothing wrong, darling. Nothing at all wrong."

To his amazement she blushed like a schoolgirl. "Grandmother—"

He was interrupted by a clatter on the stairs and a shout. "Chrissy? Where have you gone off to, girl?"

Rogan stood slowly as a man popped into the doorway. He was burly of chest, bald as an egg and dressed in an ill-fitting suit the color of marigolds. His face was round and wrinkled. It beamed like a moon.

"There you are, my darling girl. I thought I'd lost you."

"I was about to ring for tea." Christine's blush deepened as the man strode into the room and kissed both her fluttering hands.

"Rogan, this is Niall Feeney. Niall, my grandson, Rogan."

"So, this be himself." Rogan found his hand enveloped and pumped heartily. "Well, it's delighted I am to be meeting you at long last. Chrissy's told me all about you, lad. Why, you're the very apple of her eye."

"I'm—pleased to meet you, Mr. Feeney."

"No, no, now, none of that formality between us. Not with all our family connections." He winked and laughed until his belly jiggled.

"Connections?" Rogan said weakly.

"Aye, with me growing up no farther than a toad could spit from Chrissy here. Fifty years pass, begad, and now fate has it that you're handling all that pretty glass my niece makes."

"Your niece?" Realization struck like a fist. "You're Maggie's uncle."

"I am indeed." Niall sat, very much at home, his substantial belly sagging over his belt. "Proud as a peacock of the girl, I'll say, though I don't understand a bloody thing about what she's doing. I have to take Chrissy's word that it's fine."

"Chrissy," Rogan repeated in a small voice.

"Isn't it lovely, Rogan?" Christine's nervous smile hurt her face. "It seems Brianna wrote to Niall in Galway to tell him Maggie and you were working together. Of course, she mentioned that you were my grandson. Niall wrote me back, and one thing led to another. He's come to visit awhile."

"Visit. In Dublin?"

"A fine city it is, to be sure." Niall smacked a hand on the delicate arm of the sofa. "With the prettiest girls in all of Ireland." He winked at Christine. "Though, in truth, I've only eyes for one."

"Go on with you, Niall."

Rogan stared at the pair of them, all but billing and cooing before his eyes. "I believe I'll have that drink after all," he said. "A whiskey."

EIGHTEEN

It was a very subdued Rogan who left his grandmother's parlor and swung by the gallery just past closing. He didn't want to believe he'd seen what he knew he'd seen. Just as Maggie had once said, when a couple is intimate, they throw off signals.

His grandmother, for God's sake, was flirting with Maggie's moon-faced uncle from Galway.

No, he decided as he let himself into the gallery, it didn't bear thinking of. Signals there might have been, but undoubtedly he'd read them incorrectly. His grandmother was, after all, over seventy, a woman of faultless taste, unblemished character, impeccable style.

And Niall Feeney was . . . was simply indescribable, Rogan decided.

What he needed was a couple of hours of perfect peace and quiet in his gallery office—away from people and phones and anything remotely personal.

He shook his head as he crossed the room. He was sounding entirely too much like Maggie.

The raised voices stopped him before his hand met the knob. An argument was in full swing on the other side of the door. While manners might have urged him to retreat, curiosity turned the tide.

He opened the door on Joseph and Patricia in full steam.

"I tell you, you're not using the head God gave you," Joseph shouted. "I won't be the cause of an estrangement between you and your mother."

"I don't give a bloody pin for what my mother thinks," Patricia shouted right back, causing Rogan's mouth to fall open. "This has nothing to do with her."

"The fact that you could say so proves my point. You're not using your head. She's—Rogan." Joseph's furious face went still as a stone. "I didn't expect you in."

"Obviously." Rogan looked cautiously from Joseph to Patricia. "I seem to have interrupted."

"Perhaps you can talk your way through that pride of his." Eyes glinting with emotion, Patricia tossed back her hair. "I can't."

"This has nothing to do with Rogan." Joseph's voice was quiet, with the steel of warning beneath.

"Oh, no, we mustn't let anyone know." The first tear spilled over. Patricia dashed it away. "We should keep sneaking around like—like adulterers. Well, I won't do it any longer, Joseph. I'm in love with you and I don't care who knows." She whirled on Rogan. "Well? What do you have to say about it?"

He held up a hand as if to regain his balance. "I think I should leave you alone."

"No need." She fumbled for her purse. "He won't listen to me. It was my mistake to believe he would. That he was the only one who really would."

"Patricia."

"Don't Patricia me in that tone," she snapped at Joseph. "All my life I've been told what to do and how to do it. What's proper, what's acceptable, and I'm sick to death of it. I tolerated the criticism over opening my school, and the damnable unspoken belief of my friends and family that I'd fail. Well, I won't fail." She whirled on Rogan again as if he'd spoken. "Do you hear, I won't fail. I'll do exactly what I wish, and I'll do it well. What I won't tolerate is criticism of my choice of lovers. Not from you, not from my mother, and most certainly not from the lover I've chosen."

Chin up, she looked back at Joseph with tear-drenched eyes. "If you don't want me, then be honest and say so. But don't you dare tell me what's best for me."

Joseph stepped toward her, but she was already darting out the door. "Patty! Damn it." Better to let her go, Joseph told himself. Better for her. "I'm sorry, Rogan," he said stiffly. "I would have found a way to have avoided that scene if I'd known you were coming in."

"Since you didn't, perhaps you might explain it." Equally stiff, Rogan rounded his desk and sat, assuming the position of authority. "In fact, I insist."

Joseph didn't bat an eye at Rogan's seamless switch from friend to employer. "It's obvious I've been seeing Patricia."

"I believe the term she used was *sneaking about.*"

The color washed back into Joseph's face. "We—I thought it best if we were discreet."

"Did you?" A fire kindled in Rogan's eyes. "And treating a woman like Patricia like one of your casual affairs was your idea of discretion?"

"I was prepared for your disapproval, Rogan." Beneath his tailored jacket, Joseph's shoulders were rigid as steel. "I expected it."

"And well you should have," Rogan said evenly.

"So I did, just as I expected the reaction I got from her mother when Patricia talked me into dining with them last evening." His hands tightened into fists. "A gallery manager without a drop of blue in his blood. She might as well have said it, for it was in her eyes. Her daughter could do better. And by Christ she can. But I won't stand here and have you say that what's between us is a casual affair." His voice had risen to a shout by the time he was finished.

"Then what is it?"

"I'm in love with her. I've been in love with her since the first time I saw her, nearly ten years ago. But then there was Robert . . . and there was you."

"There was never me." Baffled, Rogan rubbed his hands over his face. Was the world going mad? he wondered. His grandmother and Maggie's uncle, himself and Maggie and now Joseph and Patricia. "When did this happen?"

"The week before you left for Paris." Joseph remembered those giddy hours, those wonderful days and nights before reality had set in. "I didn't plan it, but that hardly changes anything. I realize you may want to make other arrangements now."

Rogan dropped his hands. "What other arrangements?"

"For managing the gallery."

What he needed, Rogan thought, was to go home and find a bottle of aspirin. "Why?" he asked wearily.

"I'm your employee."

"You are, and I hope you'll remain so. Your private life has nothing to do with your work here. Good Christ, do I look like some kind of monster who would fire you for claiming to be in love with a friend of mine?" He indulged his now throbbing head a moment by pressing the heels of his hands to his eyes. "I walk in here—into my own office, I'll remind you—and find the two of you snapping like terriers. Before I can take the next breath, Patricia's clawing at me for not believing her capable of running a school." He shook his head and dropped his hands. "I never thought she was incapable of anything. She's one of the most intelligent women I know."

"You just got caught in the backlash," Joseph murmured, and gave in to the desperate need for a cigarette.

"So it seems. You've a right to tell me it's none of my business, but as someone who's known you for ten years, and Patricia longer than that, I do take an interest. What the devil were you fighting about?"

Joseph huffed out smoke. "She wants to elope."

"Elope?" If Joseph had told him Patricia wanted to dance naked in St. Stephen's Square, he'd have been no more staggered. "Patricia?"

"She's cooked up some mad scheme about us driving up to Scotland. It seems she had a row with her mother and came storming straight over here."

"I've never known Patricia to storm anywhere. Her mother's not in favor of the relationship, I take it."

"Anything but." He offered a weak smile. "The truth is, she thinks Patricia should hang out for you."

Rogan was hardly surprised at this news. "She's doomed to disappointment there," he said. "I've other plans. If it helps matters, I'll make them clear to her."

"I don't know as it could hurt." Joseph hesitated, then sat as he was used to, on the corner of Rogan's desk. "You don't mind, then? It doesn't bother you?"

"Why should it? And as far as Anne's concerned, Dennis will bring her around."

"That's what Patricia said." Joseph studied the cigarette smoldering between his fingers, then pulled out his little flip-top ashtray and crushed it out. "She seemed to think if we just ran off and got married, her mother would soon fall in with the idea as if it had been hers all along."

"I'd lay odds on it. She wasn't keen on Robbie at first either."

"Wasn't she?" Joseph had the look of a man who was beginning to see the light.

"Not at all sure he was good enough for her darling daughter." Speculating, Rogan rocked back in his chair. "It didn't take long for her to begin to dote on him. Of course, he didn't wear an earring."

Joseph's grin flashed as he lifted a hand to his ear. "Patty likes it."

"Hmm," was all Rogan could think of to say. "Anne might be a bit difficult." He ignored Joseph's rude snort. "But in the end, all she wants is her daughter's happiness. If you're the answer to that, Anne will want you as well. You know, we could manage well enough around here if you took a sudden trip to Scotland."

"I couldn't. It wouldn't be fair to her."

"Your business, of course. But . . ." Rogan stretched back in his chair again. "It seems to me a woman might find a wild ride over the border, a ceremony in some musty chapel and a honeymoon in the Highlands very romantic."

"I don't want her to regret it." Joseph was beginning to sound less certain.

"The woman who walked out of here just now looked to me to know her own mind."

"She does, and she's come to know mine all too quickly." He pushed away from the desk. "I'd better go find her." He stopped at the door, tossed a grin over his shoulder. "Rogan, can you spare me for a week?"

"Take two. And kiss the bride for me."

The wire that came three days later, telling Rogan that Mr. and Mrs. Joseph Donahoe were well and happy, proved to him that he wasn't a hard-hearted man. In fact, he liked to believe he'd done his part to speed the two lovers on their way.

But there were two other lovers he'd have given much to see go their separate paths. In fact, he fantasized daily about booting Niall Feeney all the way back to Galway. At first Rogan tried to ignore the situation. When more than a week had passed and Niall was still cozily ensconced in Christine Sweeney's home, he tried patience. After all, he told himself, how long would a woman of his grandmother's taste and sensibilities be duped by a charmless, borish west-county sharpie?

After two weeks, he decided it was time to try reason.

Rogan waited in the parlor—the parlor, he reminded himself that reflected the style and breeding of a lovely, sensible and generous woman.

"Why, Rogan." Christine glided into the room looking, her grandson thought, entirely too attractive for a woman of her age. "What a lovely surprise. I thought you were on your way to Limerick."

"I am. I've just stopped in on the way to the airport." He kissed her, glanced over her shoulder to the doorway. "So . . . you're alone?"

"Yes, Niall's out running some errands. Do you have time for a bite to eat before you go? Cook's baked some lovely tarts. Niall's charmed her so, that she's been baking treats daily."

"Charmed her?" As his grandmother sat Rogan rolled his eyes.

"Oh, yes. He's always popping into the kitchen to tell her what a way she has with soup, or the duck or some dish or other. She can't do enough for him."

"He certainly looks like a man who eats well."

Christine's smile was indulgent. "Oh, he loves his food, Niall does."

"I'm sure it goes down easy, when it's free."

The comment had Christine raising a brow. "Would you have me bill a friend for a meal, Rogan?"

"Of course not. He's been in town some time now," he said, changing tacks. "I'm sure he must miss his home, and his business."

"Oh, he's retired. As Niall says, a man can't work all his life."

"If he's worked at all," Rogan said under his breath. "Grandmother, I'm sure it's been nice for you to visit with a friend from your childhood, but—"

"It has. It's been truly wonderful. Why, I feel young again." She laughed. "Like a girl. Just last night we went dancing. I'd forgotten what a fine dancer Niall is. And when we go to Galway—"

"We?" Rogan felt himself pale. "*We* go to Galway?"

"Yes, next week we're planning to take a long drive back to the west. A bit of nostalgia for me. Of course, I'm interested in seeing Niall's home."

"But you can't. It's absurd. You can't go traisping off to Galway with the man."

"Why ever not?"

"Because it's—you're my grandmother, for God's sake. I won't have you . . ."

"Won't have me what?" she asked very quietly.

The tone, reflecting the sort of anger she rarely directed at him, had Rogan reining in. "Grandmother, I realize you've let yourself be swept away by the man, by the memories. I'm sure there's no harm in it. But the idea of you going off with a man you haven't seen for more than fifty years is ludicrous."

How young he is, Christine thought. And how distressingly proper. "I believe, at my age, I'd enjoy doing something ludicrous. However, I don't believe taking a trip back to my childhood home with a man I'm very fond of, a man I knew long before you were born, fits into that category. Now, perhaps," she said, holding up a hand before he could speak, "you find that the idea of my having a relationship, an adult, satisfying relationship with Niall, does fit that category."

"You're not telling me—you're not saying—you haven't actually . . ."

"Slept with him?" Christine leaned back, tapping her well-manicured nails on the arm of the love seat. "That's certainly my business, isn't it? And I don't require your approval."

"Of course not." He heard himself beginning to babble. "I'm just concerned, naturally."

"Your concern is noted." She rose, regally. "I'm sorry that you're shocked by my behavior, but it can't be helped."

"I'm not shocked—damn, of course I'm shocked. You can't just . . ." He could hardly say the words, could he? In his grandmother's parlor. "Darling, I know nothing about the man."

"I know about him. I haven't any definite plans on how long we'll be in Galway, but we will be stopping in to see Maggie and her family on the way. Shall I give her your regards?"

"You can't have thought this through."

"I know my own mind and heart better, it seems, than you think. Have a safe trip, Rogan."

Dismissed, he had no choice but to kiss her cheek and leave. The moment he was in the car, he yanked at the phone. "Eileen, reschedule Limerick for tomorrow. . . . Yes, there's a problem," he muttered. "I have to go to Clare."

When the first touch of fall caressed the air and gilded the trees, it seemed a sin not to enjoy it. After two solid weeks of work, Maggie decided she deserved a day off. She spent the morning in the garden, weeding with a vigor that would have made Brianna proud. To reward herself, she decided to bike to the village for a late lunch at O'Malley's.

There was a bite to the air, and the layered clouds to the west promised rain before nightfall. She pulled on her cap, pumped up her rear tire, which was going flat, then guided the bike around the house and through the gate.

She set off at a leisurely pace, dreaming a bit over the harvesting in the fields. The fuchsia continued to bloom in teardrops of red despite the threat of early frost. The landscape would change as soon as winter set it, become barren and swept by a bitter wind. But it would still be beautiful. The nights would lengthen, urging people to their fires. The rains would come, sweeping across the Atlantic with the wail of the wind.

She looked forward to it, and to the work she would do in the chilly months ahead.

She wondered if she could convince Rogan to come west during the winter, and if she did, would he find charm in the rattling windows and smoky fires. She hoped that he would. And when he stopped punishing her, she hoped that they could go back to the way things had been before that last night in France.

He'd see reason, she told herself, and leaned low over the bike against the wind. She'd make him see it. She'd even forgive him for being high-handed, overconfident and dictatorial. The moment they were together again, she would be calm and cool and sweet-tongued. They'd put this foolish disagreement behind them, and—

She had time to squeal, barely, and to swerve into the hedgerows as a car barreled around the curve. Brakes screamed, the car veered, and Maggie ended up bottom first in the blackthorn.

"Jesus, Mary and Joseph, what kind of a blind, ignorant fool is it who tries to run down innocent people?" She shoved the cap back that had fallen over her eyes and glared. "Oh, of course. It would be you."

"Are you hurt?" Rogan was out of the car and beside her in an instant. "Don't try to move."

"I can move, curse you." She batted his exploring hands away. "What do you mean driving at that horrible speed? This isn't a raceway."

The heart that had lodged hard in his throat freed itself. "I wasn't driving that fast. You were in the middle of the road, daydreaming. If I'd come around that turn a second sooner, I'd have flattened you like a rabbit."

"I wasn't daydreaming. Minding my own business was what I was doing, not expecting some jackeen to come speeding along in a fancy car." She brushed off the seat of her pants, then kicked her bike. "Now see what you've done. I've a puncture."

"You're lucky it's the tire that's flat and not yourself."

"What are you doing?" she demanded.

"I'm putting this excuse for transportation in the car." Once he'd done so, he turned back to her. "Come on, I'll drive you back home."

"I wasn't going home. If you had any sense of direction, you'd see I was going to the village, where I was going to have a meal."

"That'll have to wait." He took her arm in the proprietary manner she forgot she'd found amusing.

"Oh, will it? Well, you can drive me to the village or nowhere at all, because I'm hungry."

"I'll drive you home," he said again. "I have something to discuss with you, privately. If I'd been able to get through to you this morning, I could have told you I was coming and you wouldn't have been riding that bike in the middle of the road."

With this, he slammed the car door behind her and skirted the hood.

"If you'd been able to get through this morning, and had had this nasty way about you, I'd have told you not to bother to come at all."

"I've had a difficult morning, Maggie." He resisted the urge to rub at the headache drumming behind his temples. "Don't push me."

She began to, then saw that he'd said no more than the truth. There was trouble in his eyes. "Is it a problem at work?"

"No. Actually, I do have some complications with a project in Limerick. I'm on my way there."

"So you're not staying."

"No." He glanced at her. "I'm not staying. But it isn't the factory expansion I need to speak with you about." He stopped at her gate, shut off the car. "If you've nothing to eat, I'll run into the village and bring something back."

"It's not a problem. I can make do." She relented enough to close a hand over his. "I'm glad to see you, even though you nearly ran me down."

"I'm glad to see you." He lifted the hand to his lips. "Even though you nearly ran into me. I'll get your bike out."

"Just leave it in front." After striding up the walk, she turned. "Have you a proper kiss for me?"

It was hard to resist that quick flash of smile, or the way she reached up to link her hands behind his head. "I've a kiss for you, proper or not."

It was easy to meet the heat, to draw the energy in. What was difficult was to check the need, that instant desire to back her through the door and take it all.

"Perhaps I was daydreaming a bit before," she said, tugging on his lips. "I was thinking of you, and wondering how much longer you'd punish me."

"How do you mean?"

"By staying away from me." She spoke airily as she pushed through the door.

"I wasn't punishing you."

"Just staying away, then."

"Distancing myself, to give you time to think."

"And time to miss you."

"To miss me. And to change your mind."

"I have missed you, but I haven't changed my mind or anything else. Why don't you sit? I need to get some more turf for the fire."

"I love you, Maggie."

That stopped her, had her closing her eyes a moment before she turned back. "I believe you might, Rogan, and though something in me warms to it, it changes nothing." She hurried out.

He hadn't come to beg, he reminded himself. He'd come to ask her to help him with a problem. Though from her reaction, he believed things were changing more than she was ready to admit.

He paced to the window, to the sagging sofa, back again.

"Will you sit?" she demanded when she came back with her arms piled with turf blocks. "You'll wear out the floor. What's this business in Limerick?"

"A few complications, that's all." He watched as she knelt at the hearth and expertly stacked fuel. It occurred to him that he'd never seen anyone build a turf fire before. A restful sight, he mused, that drew a man close to seek that warm red heart. "We're expanding the factory."

"Oh, and what do you make at your factory?"

"China. For the most part the inexpensive sort that's fashioned into mementos."

"Mementos?" She paused at her work, leaned back on her haunches. "Souvenirs, you mean? Not those little bells and teacups and such in the tourist shops?"

"They're very well done."

She tossed back her head and laughed. "Oh, it's rich. I've hired myself a man who makes little plates with shamrocks all over them."

"Have you any idea what percent of our economy depends on tourism, on the sale of little plates with shamrocks on them, or hand-knit sweaters, linen, lace, bloody postcards?"

"No." She snorted behind her hand. "But I'm sure you can tell me, down to the pence. Tell me, Rogan, do you do much business in plaster leprechauns, or plastic shillelaghs?"

"I didn't come here to justify my business to you, or to discuss the fact that this expansion—which will allow us to manufacture some of the finest china produced in Ireland—will create more than a hundred new jobs in a part of the country that desperately needs them."

She waved a hand to stop him. "I'm sorry, I've insulted you. I'm sure there's a rising need for thimbles and ashtrays and cups that say 'Erin Go

Bragh.' It's just hard for me, you see, to picture a man who wears such wonderful suits owning a place that makes them."

"The fact that I do makes it possible for Worldwide to subsidize and offer grants to a number of artists each year. Even if they are snobs."

She rubbed the back of her hand over her nose. "That puts me in my place. And since I don't want to waste what time we have arguing, we'll say no more about it. Are you going to sit, or just stand there and glower at me? Not that you don't look fine, even with a scowl on your face."

He surrendered on a long breath. "Your work's going well?"

"Very well." She shifted, crossing her legs on the rug. "I'll show you what's new before you go, if there's time."

"We're a little behind at the gallery. I suppose I should tell you that Joseph and Patricia have eloped."

"Yes, I know. I've had a card from them."

He tilted his head. "You don't seem at all surprised."

"I'm not. They were crazy in love with each other."

"I seem to recall you claiming Patricia was crazy in love with me."

"Not at all. I said she was half in love with you, and I'll stand by that. I imagine she wanted to be in love with you—it would have been so convenient after all. But it was Joseph all along. That's not what's troubling you, is it?"

"No. I admit it took me by surprise, but it doesn't trouble me. I've come to realize I took Joseph's skills for granted. He'll be back tomorrow, and I'm grateful for it."

"Then what is it?"

"Have you had a letter from your uncle Niall?"

"Brianna has. She's the one who gets them, as she's the one who'll remember to answer back. He wrote to tell her he'd be visiting Dublin and might pass through on his way back home. Have you seen him?"

"Seen him?" On a sound of disgust, Rogan pushed out of the chair again. "I can't get near my grandmother without stepping all over him. He's settled himself in her house for two weeks past. We've got to decide what to do about it."

"Why should we do anything?"

"Are you listening to me, Maggie? They've been living together. My grandmother and your uncle—"

"Great-uncle, actually."

"Whatever the devil he is to you, they've been having a flaming affair."

"Have they?" Maggie let out a roar of approving laughter. "Well, that's wonderful."

"Wonderful? It's insane. She's been acting like some giddy girl, going dancing, staying out half the night, sharing her bed with a man whose suits are the color of fried eggs."

"So you object to his taste in clothes?"

"I object to him. I'll not have him waltzing into my grandmother's house and planting himself in the parlor as if he belongs there. I don't know what his game is, but I won't have him exploiting her generous heart, her vulnerability. If he thinks he'll get his hands on one penny of her money—"

"Hold that." She sprang up like a tiger. " 'Tis my blood you're speaking of, Sweeney."

"This is no time to be overly sensitive."

"Overly sensitive." She jabbed him in the chest. "Look who's talking. You're jealous because your granny's got someone besides you in her life."

"That's ridiculous."

"It's true as the day. Do you think a man couldn't be interested in her, but for her money?"

Familial pride stiffened his spine. "My grandmother is a beautiful, intelligent woman."

"I'll not disagree with that. And my Uncle Niall is no fortune hunter. He retired from his business most comfortably set. He may not have a villa in France or wear suits tailored by the bloody British, but he's done well enough and has no need to play gigolo. And I won't have you speak of me kin in such a way in me own house."

"I didn't mean to offend you. I've come to you because, as their family, it's up to us to do something about the situation. Since they're planning a trip to Galway within the next few days, and passing by here on the way, I'd hoped you might speak with him."

"Certainly I'll speak with him. He's my kin, isn't he? I'd hardly ignore him. But I won't help you interfere. You're the snob, Rogan, and a prude as well."

"Prude?"

"You're offended by the idea of your grandmother having a rich and full sex life."

He winced, hissed through his teeth. "Oh please. I don't want to imagine it."

"Nor should you, since it's her private business." Her mouth twitched. "Still . . . it's interesting."

"Don't." Defeated, he sank into the chair again. "If there's one picture I don't want in my mind, it's that."

"Actually, I can't quite get it there myself. Now, wouldn't it be a strange thing if they married? Then we'd be in the way of cousins after all." Laughing, she slapped his back when he choked. "Could you use a whiskey, darling?"

"I could. Maggie." He took several deep breaths. "Maggie," he called again as she rummaged through in the kitchen. "I don't want her to be hurt."

"I know." She came back, holding two glasses. "It's knowing that that kept me from bloodying your nose when you spoke so of Uncle Niall. Your gran's a fine woman, Rogan, and a wise one."

"She's—" Finally, he said it aloud. "She's all I have left of my family."

Maggie's eyes gentled. "You're not losing her."

He let out a breath, stared into his glass. "I suppose you think I'm being a fool."

"No, I don't—exactly." She smiled when his eyes lifted to hers. "A man can be expected to be a bit jittery when his granny takes on a boyfriend."

Rogan winced. She laughed.

"Why not let her be happy? If it eases your mind, I'll look the situation over when they stop here."

"That's something at least." He touched his glass to hers, and they tossed the whiskey back together. "I have to go."

"You've hardly been here. Why don't you come to the pub with me and we'll have a meal together. Or"—she slipped her arms around him—"we'll stay here and go hungry."

No, he thought as he lowered his mouth to hers. They wouldn't be hungry for long.

"I can't stay." He set the empty glass aside to take her by her shoulders. "If I did we'd only end up in bed. That wouldn't solve anything."

"There doesn't have to be anything to solve. Why must you make it complicated? We're good together."

"We are." He framed her face in his hands. "Very good together. That's only one of the reasons I want to spend my life with you. No, don't draw away. Nothing you told me changes what we can have. Once you realize that, you'll come to me. I can wait."

"You'll just go, then stay away again? So, it's marriage or nothing?"

"It's marriage." He kissed her again. "And everything. I'll be in Limerick for almost a week. The office knows where to reach me."

"I won't call."

He traced a thumb over her lips. "But you'll want to. That's enough for now."

NINETEEN

"You're being pigheaded, Maggie."

"You know, I'm tired of having that particular word applied to me." With goggles protecting her eyes, Maggie experimented with lamp work. For nearly a week everything she'd free-blown had dissatisfied her. For a change of pace she had set up a half-dozen torches, three clamped to each side of a bench, and was heating a tube of glass in the cross fire.

"Well, if it's applied to you often enough, it may be true," Brianna shot back. "It's family. You can spare one evening for family."

"It isn't a matter of time." She meant this, though for some reason, Maggie felt time was breathing down her neck like a snarling dog. "Why should I subject myself to having dinner with her?" Carefully, brows knit, she began to pull and rotate the softened glass. "I can tell you I have no appetite for it. Nor will she."

" 'Tisn't just Mother who'll be coming. Uncle Niall and Mrs. Sweeney will be there. And Lottie, of course. It would be rude of you not to come."

"I've been told I'm that, as well as pigheaded." As with everything else she'd touched over the last few days, the glass refused to follow the vision in her head. The vision itself blurred, infuriating her as much as it frightened her. Pure obstinancy kept her working.

"You haven't seen Uncle Niall since Da's wake. And he's bringing Rogan's grandmother, for heaven's sake. You told me you liked her very much."

"I do." Damn it, what was wrong with her hands? What was wrong with her heart? She fused one rod to the other, burned it off, returned, burned it off. "Perhaps one of the reasons I don't want to be there is so she'll not be subjected to one of our happy family meals."

The sarcasm was as hot as one of Maggie's points of flame. Brianna faced it down with ice. "It wouldn't cost you much to put aside your feelings for one night. If Uncle Niall and Mrs. Sweeney are going out of their way to visit us before going on to Galway, we'll welcome them. All of us."

"Stop badgering me, will you? You're pecking away at me like a damn duck. Can't you see I'm working?"

"You hardly do anything else, so it's necessary to interrupt you if I want a word. They'll be here shortly, Maggie, and I'll not make excuses for you." In a gesture similar to her sister's habitual stance, Brianna folded her arms. "I'll stand right here and keep pecking until you do what's expected of you."

"All right, all right. Jesus. I'll come to the damn dinner."

Brianna smiled serenely. She'd never expected less. "At half seven. I'm serving my guests earlier so we'll have a private family meal."

"And oh, what a jolly time that will be."

"It'll go well enough if you promise to hold that nasty tongue of yours. I'm only asking for the smallest of efforts."

"I'll smile. I'll be polite. I won't eat with me fingers." With a bitter sigh, Maggie shoved up her goggles and held the figure on the end of the tube out of the flames.

"What have you done there?" Curious, Brianna stepped closer.

"Gone mad."

"It's pretty. Is it a unicorn?"

"Aye, a unicorn—only needs a touch of gold on the horn to make it complete." She laughed, turning the mythical figure in the air. "It's a joke, Brie, a poor one. On me. It'll be swans next, I'm sure. Or those little dogs with puffs for tails." She set her work aside, briskly turned off her torches. "Well, that's that, I suppose. I'll hardly do anything worthwhile today, so I'll be along to your dinner party. God help you."

"Why don't you rest awhile, Maggie? You look awfully tired."

"Perhaps I will, after I crate up a few pieces." She tossed the goggles aside, rubbed her hands over her face. She was tired, Maggie realized. Outrageously so. "You needn't worry, Brie, you'll not have to send out the dogs for me. I've said I'll be there."

"I'm grateful." Brianna reached down to squeeze her sister's hand. "I have to go back, make certain everything's in place. Half seven, Maggie."

"I know."

She waved her sister out. To keep her mind on practical matters, she took one of the crates she'd made and packed it with padding. After spreading bubble wrap over a table, she turned to the shelves at the back of the shop. There was only one piece there, the last she'd completed before Rogan's visit.

Tall and sturdy, the trunk speared up, then curved, flooding down in slim, graceful limbs that almost seemed to sway. It would stand, she thought, like the willow that had inspired it. And it would bend, yielding, even as it remained true to itself. The color was a deep, pure blue that flooded up from the base and paled gently to the delicate tips.

She wrapped it carefully, for it was more than a sculpture. This was the last work she'd been able to draw successfully from her heart. Nothing she had attempted since then had gelled. Day after day she had labored only to remelt and remelt. Day after day she came closer to releasing the panic that jittered inside her.

His fault, she told herself as she secured the top of the crate. His fault for tempting her with fame and fortune, for exposing her vanity to such a stunning and fast success. Now she was blocked, dried up. As hollow as the tube she'd fashioned into a unicorn.

He'd made her want too much. Want him too much. Then he had walked away and let her see, brutally, what it was like to have nothing.

She wouldn't give up, nor would she give in. Maggie promised herself she would have her pride at least. While her furnace roared mockingly she sat in her chair, felt the familiarity of its shape.

It was only that she'd been working too hard, surely. She'd been pushing herself to do better and better work with each piece. The pressure of holding on to success had blocked her, that was all. She couldn't suppress the idea that as the tour moved on from Paris it would be found wanting. That *she* would be found wanting.

That she would never again pick up the pipe just for herself, just for the pleasure of it. Rogan had changed all that. He had, as she'd told him he would, changed her.

And how was it, she thought, closing her eyes, how could it be that a man could make you love him by going away?

"You've done well for yourself, haven't you, darling?" Niall, stuffed into one of his bright-hued suits like a happy sausage, beamed at Brianna. "I always said you were a clever lass. Takes after me dear sister, does Brianna, Chrissy."

"You have a lovely home." Christine accepted the glass Brianna offered. "And your gardens are simply breathtaking."

"Thank you. They give me pleasure."

"Rogan told me how he enjoyed his brief stay here." Christine sighed, content with the warmth of the fire and the glow of the lamp. "I can see why."

"She's got the touch." Niall gave Brianna a bone-crushing squeeze around the shoulders. "In the blood, you know. Blood runs true."

"So it seems. I knew your grandmother quite well."

"Chrissy was underfoot all the time." Niall winked. "Thought I didn't notice her. Shy was what I was."

"You never had a shy moment in your life," Christine said with a laugh. "You thought I was a nuisance."

"If I did, I've changed me mind." He leaned over and under Brianna's curious eye, kissed Christine firmly on the mouth.

"It took you more than fifty years."

"Seems like yesterday."

"Well . . ." Disconcerted, Brianna cleared her throat. "I suppose I should check on . . . I believe that's Mother and Lottie," she continued when raised voices boomed down the hallway.

"You drive like a blind woman," Maeve complained. "I'll walk back to Ennis before I get into that car with you again."

"If you can do better, you should drive yourself. Then you'd have a sense of independence." Obviously unconcerned, Lottie strolled into the parlor, unwrapping a thick scarf from around her neck. "It's a chilly night," she announced, rosy-cheeked and smiling.

"And you dragging me out in it'll put me in bed for a week."

"Mother." Shoulders braced against embarrassment, Brianna helped Maeve off with her coat. "I'd like you to meet Mrs. Sweeney. Mrs. Sweeney, this is my mother, Maeve Concannon, and our friend Lottie Sullivan."

"I'm delighted to meet you both." Christine rose to offer her hand to both women. "I was a friend of your mother's, Mrs. Concannon. We were girls together in Galway. I was Christine Rogan then."

"She spoke of you," Maeve said shortly. "I'm pleased to meet you." Her gaze shifted to her uncle, narrowed. "Well, Uncle Niall, is it? You haven't graced us with your presence for many a day."

"It warms my heart to see you, Maeve." He enveloped her in an embrace, patting her stiff back with a beefy hand. "I hope the years have been kind to you."

"Why would they?" The moment she was freed, Maeve sat in a chair by the fire. "This fire's drawing poorly, Brianna."

It wasn't, but Brianna walked over to make minute adjustments to the flue.

"Stop fussing," Niall ordered with a casual wave of his hand. "It's drawing fine. We all know Maeve lives to complain."

"Doesn't she, now?" Lottie spoke pleasantly while she pulled her knitting needles from the basket she'd brought along. "I pay no mind to it myself. But that comes from raising four children, I suppose."

Unsure what step to take, Christine focused on Lottie. "What lovely wool, Mrs. Sullivan."

"Thank you. I'm partial to it myself. Had you a nice trip from Dublin, then?"

"A lovely one, yes. I'd forgotten how beautiful this part of the country was."

"Nothing but fields and cows," Maeve tossed out, annoyed that the conversation was circling out of her control. "It's fine to live in Dublin and pass through on a fine autumn day. Come winter, you wouldn't think it so lovely." She might have continued the theme, but Maggie came in.

"Why, it's Uncle Niall, big as life." With a laugh, she went into his arms.

"Little Maggie Mae, all grown up."

"As I've been for some time." She stepped back, laughed again. "Well, you've lost nearly all of it now." She rubbed an affectionate hand over his head.

"It was such a fine head, you see, the good Lord saw no need to cover it with hair. I've heard about how well you're doing, darling. I'm proud of you."

"Mrs. Sweeney's telling you that so she can brag upon her grandson. It's lovely seeing you," Maggie said to Christine. "I hope you won't let this one run you ragged in Galway."

"I find I can keep up. I was hoping, if it's not inconvenient to you, that I could have a look at your glass house tomorrow before we go."

"Sure I'd be glad to show you. Hello, Lottie, are you well?"

"Fit as a fiddle." Her needles clacked musically. "I was hoping you'd come by the house and tell us about your trip to France."

This statement drew an audible sniff from Maeve. Schooling her features, Maggie turned. "Mother."

"Margaret Mary. You've been busy with your own doings, as usual, I see."

"I have."

"Brianna finds time to come by twice a week to see that I have all I need."

Maggie nodded. "Then it isn't necessary for me to do the same."

"I'll serve dinner now, if everyone's ready," Brianna cut in.

"I'm always ready for a meal," Niall kept Christine's hand in his, using his free one to give Maggie's shoulder a squeeze as they went into the dining room.

There was linen on the table, and fresh flowers, with the warmth of candles flickering on the sideboard. The food was beautifully prepared and plentiful. It should have been a pleasant, congenial evening. But, of course, it wasn't.

Maeve picked at her food. The lighter the mood at the table became, the darker grew her own. She envied Christine her fine, well-cut dress, the gleam of pearls around her throat, the quiet, expensive scent that drifted from her skin. And the skin itself, soft and pampered by wealth.

Her mother's friend, Maeve thought. Her childhood playmate, class to class. The life Christine Sweeney had led should have been hers, she thought. Would have been hers, but for one mistake. But for Maggie.

She could have wept from the rage of it, from the shame of it. From the helpless loss of it.

All around her the conversation bubbled like some expensive wine, frothy and foolish talk about flowers and old times, about Paris and Dublin. About children.

"How lovely for you to have such a large family," Christine was saying to Lottie. "I was always sorry that Michael and I couldn't have more children. Though we doted on our son, then on Rogan."

"A son," Maeve muttered. "A son doesn't forget his mother."

"It's true, it's a special bond." Christine smiled, hoping to soften the harshness around Maeve's mouth. "But I confess, I always wanted a daughter of my own. You're blessed with two, Mrs. Concannon."

"Cursed, more like."

"Try the mushrooms, Maeve." Deliberately Lottie spooned some onto Maeve's plate. "They're fried to a turn. You've a find hand, Brianna."

"I learned the knack of these from my gran," Brianna began. "I was always pestering her to show me how to cook."

"And blaming me because I didn't choose to strap myself to the stove," Maeve tossed back her head. "I'd no liking for it. I'll wager you don't spend much time in the kitchen, Mrs. Sweeney."

"Not a great deal, I'm afraid." Aware her voice had chilled, Christine made the effort to lighten it again. "And I'll have to admit that none of my efforts there can come close to what you've served us tonight, Brianna. Rogan was right to praise your cooking."

"She makes a living from it. Bedding and boarding strangers."

"Leave her alone." Maggie spoke quietly, but the look in her eyes was as sharp as a shout. "God knows she bedded and boarded you as well."

"As was her duty. There's no one at this table would deny that it's a daughter's obligation to tend to her mother. Which is more than you've ever done, Margaret Mary."

"Or ever will do, so count your blessings that Brie tolerates you."

"I haven't a blessing to count, with my own children tossing me out of my own house. Then leaving me, sick and alone."

"Why, you haven't been sick a day, Maeve," Lottie said complacently. "And how can you be alone when I'm there, day and night?"

"And you draw a weekly wage to be there. It should be my own blood tending me, but no. My daughters turn their backs, and my uncle, with his fine house in Galway, pays no mind at all."

"Enough to see you haven't changed, Maeve." Niall regarded her with pity. "Not a whit. I apologize, Chrissy, for my niece's poor behavior."

"I think we'll have our dessert in the parlor." Pale and quiet, Brianna rose. "If you'd like to go in and sit, I'll serve it."

"Much cozier," Lottie agreed. "I'll help you, Brianna."

"If you'll excuse me, Uncle Niall, Mrs. Sweeney, I'd like a word with my mother before we join you." Maggie kept her seat, waiting until the room emptied out. "Why would you do it?" Maggie asked Maeve. "Why would you spoil it for her? Would it have been so hard to give her the illusion for one evening that we were a family?"

Embarrassment only sharpened Maeve's tongue. "I've no illusions, and no need to impress Mrs. Sweeney from Dublin."

"You impressed her just the same—badly. It reflects on us all."

"Do you think you can be better than the rest of us, Margaret Mary? Better because you traipse off to Venice or Paris?" With her knuckles whitening on the edge of the table, Maeve leaned forward. "Do you think I don't know what you've been doing with that woman's grandson? Whoring yourself without an ounce of shame. Ah, he sees you've got the money and the glory you always wanted. You've only had to sell body and soul to get it."

Maggie clasped her hands beneath the table to try to stem the shaking. "My work's what I sell, so perhaps you've a point about my soul. But my body's mine. I've given it to Rogan freely."

Maeve paled as her suspicions were confirmed. "And you'll pay for it, as I did. A man of his class wants nothing more from the likes of you than what he finds in the dark."

"You know nothing about it. Nothing about him."

"But I know you. What will happen to your fine career when you discover a baby in your belly?"

"If I found myself with a child to raise, I pray God I'd do a better job than you. I wouldn't give everything up and wrap myself and the child in sackcloth for the rest of my days."

"And that you know nothing about," Maeve said sharply. "But go on this way, and you will. You'll know what it's like to see your life stop and your heart break."

"But it didn't have to. Other musicians have families."

"I was given a gift." To her own misery, Maeve felt tears burn her eyes. "And because I was arrogant, as you are, it was taken from me. There's been no music in me since the moment I made you."

"There could have been," Maggie whispered. "If you'd wanted it badly enough."

Wanted it? Even now Maeve could feel the old scar throb over her heart. "What good is wanting?" she demanded. "All your life you've wanted, and now you risk having it taken away for the thrill of having a man between your legs."

"He loves me," Maggie heard herself say.

"A man speaks easily of loving in the dark. You'll never be happy. Born in sin, live in sin, die in sin. And alone. Just as I'm alone."

"You've made hating me your life's work, and a fine job you've done of it." Slowly, unsteadily, Maggie rose. "Do you know what frightens me, frightens me down to the bone? You hate me because you see yourself when you look at me. God help me if you're right."

She fled out of the room, and into the night.

The hardest pill to swallow was apology. Maggie postponed downing it, distracting herself by showing Christine and Niall her studio. In the cool light of morning, the nastiness of the previous evening blurred a little. She was able to soothe herself by explaining various tools and techniques, even, when Niall insisted, trying to coach him through blowing his first bubble.

"It's not a trumpet." Maggie clasped a hand on the pipe as he started to lift it high. "Showing off like that will do no more than have hot glass spilling all over you."

"I believe I'll stick with me golf." He winked and turned the pipe back to her. "One artist in the family's enough."

"And you really make your own glass." Christine wandered around the shop, in tailored slacks and a silk blouse. "From sand."

"And a few other things. Sand, soda, lime. Feldspar, dolomite. A bit of arsenic."

"Arsenic." Christine's eyes widened.

"And this and that," Maggie said with a smile. "I guard my formulas closely, like a sorcerer with a spell. Depending on what color you want, you add other chemicals. Various colorants change in different base glasses. Cobalt, copper, manganese. Then there are the carbonates and the oxides. The arsenic's an excellent oxide."

Christine looked dubiously at the chemicals Maggie showed her. "I'd think it would be simpler to melt down used or commercial glass."

"But it's not yours then, is it?"

"I didn't realize you had to be a chemist as well as an artist."

"Our Maggie was always a bright one." Niall swung an arm over her shoulder. "Sarah was always writing me with how bright she was in school, how sweet Brianna's disposition."

"That was it," Maggie said with a laugh. "I was bright. Brie was sweet."

"She said Brie was bright as well," Niall said staunchly.

"But I'll wager she never said I was sweet." Maggie turned to nuzzle her face in his coat. "I'm so glad to see you again. I didn't realize how glad I would be."

"I've neglected you since Tom died, Maggie Mae."

"No. We all had our own lives, and Brie and I both understood that Mother didn't make it easy for you to visit. As to that . . ." She pulled back, took a deep breath. "I'd like to apologize for last evening. I shouldn't have provoked her, and I certainly shouldn't have left without saying good night."

"There's no need for apologies from you, or from Brianna as I've told her already today." Niall patted Maggie's cheek. "Maeve had settled on her mood before she arrived. You provoked nothing. You're not to blame for the way she's chosen to go through life, Maggie."

"Whether I am or not, I'm sorry the evening was uncomfortable."

"I would have called it illuminating," Christine said calmly.

"I suppose it was," Maggie agreed. "Uncle Niall, did you ever hear her sing?"

"I did. Lovely as a nightingale, to be sure. And restless, like one of those big cats you see caged in the zoo. She was never an easy girl, Maggie, happy only when the people would hush and listen to her music."

"Then there was my father."

"Then there was Tom. From what I'm told they were blind and deaf to everything but each other. Maybe to each other as well." He stroked the big hand down her hair. "It could be neither of them saw what was inside until they were bound. And when they did, what they saw was different than they'd hoped. She let that sour her."

"Do you think if they hadn't met, she'd have been different?"

He smiled a little and kept his hand gentle. "We're tossed by the winds of fate, Maggie Mae. Once we end where they blow us, we make of ourselves what we will."

"I'm sorry for her," Maggie said softly. "I never thought I could be."

"And you've done well by her." He kissed Maggie's brow. "Now it's time to make yourself what you will."

"I'm working on it." She smiled again. "Very hard on it."

Satisfied that the timing was right, Christine spoke up. "Niall, would you be a darling and give me a moment with Maggie?"

"Girl talk, is it?" His round face creased in smiles. "Take your time, I'll go for a walk."

"Now then," Christine began as soon as the door shut behind Niall. "I have a confession. I didn't go into the parlor right after last night. I came back, thinking I might be able to smooth things over."

Maggie lowered her eyes to stare at the floor. "I see."

"What I did, rudely, was listen. It took all my control not to barge into that room and give your mother a piece of my mind."

"It would only have made things worse."

"Which was why I didn't give in to the urge—though it would have been greatly satisfying." Christine took Maggie by the arms, gave her a little shake. "She has no idea what she has in you."

"Perhaps she knows too well. I've sold part of what I am because there's a need in me, just as there is in her, for more."

"You've earned more."

"If I've earned it, or been given it as a gift, it doesn't change things. I wanted to be content with what I had, Mrs. Sweeney. I wanted so much to be, because otherwise I'd be admitting there hadn't been enough. That my father had failed us, and he didn't. Before Rogan walked through that door, I was content, or I'd talked myself into believing I could be. But the door's open now and I've had a taste of it. I haven't done a decent hour's work in a week."

"Why do you think that is?"

"He's pushed me into a corner, that's why. It can't be for myself anymore. *I* can't be for myself anymore. He's changed that. I don't know what to do. I always know what to do."

"Your work comes through your heart. That's plain for anyone who's seen it. Maybe you're blocking off your heart, Maggie."

"If I am, it's because I have to. I won't do what she did. Nor what my father did. I won't be the cause of misery, or the victim of it."

"I think you *are* the victim of it, my dear Maggie. You're letting yourself feel guilty for succeeding, guiltier yet for harboring the ambition to succeed. And I think you're refusing to let out what's in your heart, because once you do, you won't be able to take it back again, even though holding it in is making you unhappy. You're in love with Rogan, aren't you?"

"If I am, he brought it on himself."

"I'm sure he'll deal with it admirably."

Maggie turned away to shuffle tools on a bench. "He's never met her. I think I made sure he wouldn't so he couldn't see I was like her. Moody and mean, dissatisfied."

"Lonely," Christine said softly, and drew Maggie's eyes back to hers. "She's a lonely woman, Maggie, through no one's fault but her own. It'll be no one's but yours if you're lonely, too." Coming forward, she took

Maggie's hands. "I didn't know your father, but there must be some of him in you as well."

"He dreamed. So do I."

"And your grandmother, with her quick mind and ready temper. She's in you as well. Niall, with his wonderful lust for life. All of that's in you. None of it makes up the whole. Niall's right about that, Maggie. So right. You'll make yourself what you will."

"I thought I had. I thought I knew exactly who I was and wanted to be. Now it's all mixed up in my head."

"When your head won't give you the answer, it's best to listen to your heart."

"I don't like the answer it's giving me."

Christine laughed. "Then, my dear child, you can be absolutely sure it's the right one."

TWENTY

By midmorning, her solitude tucked around her, Maggie took up her pipe again. Two hours later the vessel she had blown was tossed back into the melt for cullet.

She pored over her sketches, rejected them, tried others. After scowling at the unicorn she'd set on a shelf, she turned to her torches for lamp work. But she'd hardly taken up a rod of glass before the vision faded. She watched the tip of the rod dip, melt, begin to droop. Hardly thinking of what she was doing, she began dropping the bits of molten glass into a container of water.

Some broke, others survived. She took one out by the tip to study. Though it had been formed by fire, it was cool now, shaped like a tear. A Prince Rupert's drop, no more than a glass artist's novelty, one a child could create.

Rubbing the one drop between her fingers, she took it to her polariscope. Through the lens the internal stresses in the drop exploded into a dazzling rainbow of colors. So much, she thought, inside so little.

She slipped the drop into her pocket, fished several more out of the bucket. Moving with studied care, she shut down her furnaces. Ten minutes later she was striding into her sister's kitchen.

"Brianna. What do you see when you look at me?"

Blowing a stray hair out of her eyes, Brianna looked up and continued to knead her bread dough. "My sister, of course."

"No, no. Try for once not to be so literal-minded. What is it you see in me?"

"A woman who seems to be on the edge of something, always. One who has enough energy to tire me to the bone. And anger." Brianna stared down at her hands again. "Anger that makes me sad and sorry."

"Selfishness?"

Startled, Brianna glanced up again. "No, not that. Not ever. That's one flaw I've never seen in you."

"But others?"

"You've enough of them. What, do you want to be perfect?"

The dismissive tone had Maggie wincing. "You're still upset with me about last evening."

"I'm not, no." With renewed vigor Brianna began to pound the dough. "With myself, with circumstances, with fate, if you like. But not with you. It wasn't your doing, and God knows you warned me it wouldn't work. But I wish you wouldn't always leap to defend me."

"I can't help it."

"I know." Brianna smoothed the dough into a mound and slipped it into a bowl for a second rising. "She was better behaved after you'd gone. And a little embarrassed, I think. Before she left she told me I'd cooked a nice meal. Not that she ate any of it, but at least she said it."

"We've had worse evenings."

"That's God's truth. Maggie, she said something else."

"She says lots of things. I didn't come to go over all of that."

"It was about the candlesticks," Brianna continued, and had Maggie lifting both brows.

"What of them?"

"The ones I had on the sideboard, the ones you'd made me last year. She said what pretty work they were."

With a laugh, Maggie shook her head. "You've been dreaming."

"I was awake and standing in my own hallway. She looked at me, and she told me. And she kept standing there, looking at me until I understood that she couldn't say it to you herself, but she wanted you to know."

"Why should she?" Maggie said unsteadily.

"I think it was a kind of apology, for whatever passed between you in the dining room. The best she could make. When she saw I understood her, she started in on Lottie again, so the two of them left the way they'd come in. Arguing."

"Well." Maggie had no idea how to react, how to feel. Restlessly, her fingers reached into her pocket to toy with the smooth glass drops.

"It's a small step, but a step it is." Brisk, Brianna began to dust flour on her hands in preparation for kneading the next loaf. "She's happy in the house you gave her, even if she doesn't know it yet."

"You could be right." Her breath hitched a bit as she released it. "I hope you are. But don't be planning any more family meals in the near future."

"That I won't."

"Brianna . . ." Maggie hesitated, ended by looking helplessly at her sister. "I'm driving to Dublin today."

"Oh, you'll have a long day, then. You're needed at the gallery?"

"No. I'm going to see Rogan. I'm either going to tell him I'm not going to see him again, or that I'll marry him."

"Marry him?" Brianna bobbled the next ball of dough. "He's asked you to marry him?"

"The last night we were in France. I told him no, absolutely no. I meant it. I might still. That's why I'm driving, to give myself time to think it through. I've realized that it has to be one or the other." She fingered the glass drops in her pocket. "So I'm going, and I wanted to tell you."

"Maggie—" Brianna was left with her hands full of dough, staring at the swinging back door.

The worst part was not finding him home—and knowing she should have checked before making the drive. At the gallery, his butler had said, but when she arrived there, cursing Dublin traffic all the way, he was already gone and on the way to his office.

Again, she missed him, by no more than five minutes, she was informed. He was heading to the airport and a flight to Rome. Would she care to put through a call to his car phone?

She would not, Maggie decided, stumble through one of the biggest decisions of her life over the telephone. In the end, she got back in her lorry and made the long, lonely drive back to Clare.

It was easy to call herself a fool. And to tell herself she was better off not having found him at all. Exhausted by the hours of driving, she slept like the dead until noon the next day.

Then she tried to work.

"I want the *Seeker* in the forefront, and the *Triad* centered, precisely."

Rogan stood in the sun-washed showroom of Worldwide Gallery,

Rome, watching his staff arrange Maggie's work. The sculptures stood up well in the gilded rococo decor. The heavy red velvet he'd chosen to drape the pedestals and tables added a royal touch. Something he was sure Maggie would have complained about, but which suited the clientele of this particular gallery.

He checked his watch, muttered to himself under his breath. He had a meeting in twenty minutes. There was no help for it, he thought as he called out another order for a minute adjustment. He was going to be late. Maggie's influence, he supposed. She'd corrupted his sense of time.

"The gallery opens in fifteen minutes," he reminded the staff. "Expect some press, and see that they each receive a catalog." He scanned the room one last time, noting the placement of each piece, the fold of every drape. "Well done."

He stepped outside into the bright Italian sun, where his driver waited. "I'm running late, Carlo." Rogan shifted into his seat and opened his briefcase.

Carlo grinned, tucked the chauffeur's cap lower on his brow and flexed his fingers like a concert pianist preparing to launch into an arpeggio. "Not for long, signore."

To Rogan's credit, he barely lifted a brow as the car leaped like a tiger from the curb, snarling and growling at the cars it cut off. Bracing himself in the corner of the seat, Rogan turned his attention to a printout of figures from his Roman branch.

It had been an excellent year, he decided. Far from the staggering boom of the mideighties, but quite good enough. He thought perhaps it was best that the days when a painting could demand hundreds of millions of pounds at auction were over. Art, with so high a price tag, was too often hidden away in a vault until it was as soulless as gold bullion.

Still, it had been a profitable year. Profitable enough, he thought, that he could implement his idea of opening another smaller branch of Worldwide, one that displayed and sold only the works of Irish artists. It had been a germ in his mind for the last few years, but lately, just lately, it had grown.

A small, even cozy gallery—very accessible, from the decor to the art itself. A place that invited browsing, with good-quality art priced in a range that invited owning.

Yes, he thought the time was perfect. Absolutely perfect.

The car screeched to a halt, all but rearing up like a stallion. Carlo hurried out to open Rogan's door. "You are on time, signore."

"You are a magician, Carlo."

Rogan spent thirty minutes with the head of the Roman branch, twice that in a board meeting, then granted back-to-back interviews to promote the Concannon tour. Several hours were devoted to studying Rome's proposed acquisitions and to meeting artists. He planned to fly to Venice that evening and lay the groundwork for the next stop of the tour. Gauging his time, he slipped away to place a few calls to Dublin.

"Joseph."

"Rogan, how's Rome?"

"Sunny. I've finished up here. I should be in Venice by seven at the latest. If there's time, I'll go by the gallery there tonight. Otherwise, I'll do the preliminaries tomorrow."

"I have your schedule here. You'll be back in a week?"

"Sooner, if I can manage it. Anything I should know?"

"Aiman was in. I bought two of his street sketches. They're reasonably good."

"That's fine. I've an idea we might be able to sell more of his work after the first of the year."

"Oh?"

"A project I'll discuss with you when I get back. Anything else?"

"I saw your grandmother and her friend off to Galway."

Rogan grunted. "Brought him by the gallery, did she?"

"He wanted to see some of Maggie's work—in the proper setting. He's quite the character."

"He certainly is."

"Oh, and speaking of Maggie, she was by earlier this week."

"By there? In Dublin? What for?"

"Didn't say. She sort of dashed in and out. I didn't even speak with her myself. She did send a shipment, with what seems to be a message for you."

"What message?"

" 'It's blue.' "

Rogan's fingers paused on his notebook. "The message is blue?"

"No, no, the message reads, 'It's blue.' It's a gorgeous piece, rather delicate and willowy. Apparently she thought you'd know what she meant."

"I do." He smiled to himself, rubbing the bridge of his nose. "It's for the Comte de Lorraine, Paris. A wedding present for his granddaughter. You'll want to contact him."

"I will, then. Oh, and it seems Maggie was by your office, and the house as well. I suppose she was looking for you for some reason."

"It would seem so." He debated a moment, then acted on instinct. "Joseph, do me a favor? Contact the gallery in Venice. Tell them I'll be delayed a few days."

"I'll be glad to. Any reason?"

"I'll let you know. Give Patricia my best. I'll be in touch."

Maggie drummed her fingers on a table in O'Malley's, tapped her foot, blew out a long breath. "Tim, will you give me a bookmaker's sandwich to go with this pint? I can't wait for Murphy all bloody afternoon on an empty stomach."

"Happy to do it. Got a date, do you?" He grinned at her from over the bar, wriggled his eyebrows.

"Hah. The day when I date Murphy Muldoon's the day I lose what's left of my mind. He said he had some business in the village and would I meet him here." She tapped the box on the floor with her. "I've got his birthday present for his mother."

"Something you made, then?"

"Aye. And if he's not here by the time I've finished eating, he'll have to come fetch it himself."

"Alice Muldoon," said David Ryan, who sat at the bar puffing a cigarette. "She be living down to Killarney now, wouldn't she?"

"She would," Maggie agreed. "And has been these past ten years or more."

"Didn't think I'd seen her about. Married again, did she, after Rory Muldoon passed over?"

"She did." Tim took up the story while he built a pint of Guinness. "Married a rich doctor name of Colin Brennan."

"Kin to Daniel Brennan." Another patron picked up the tale, musing over his bowl of stew. "You know, he that runs a food store in Clarecastle."

"No, no." Tim shook his head as he walked over to serve Maggie her sandwich. " 'Tisn't kin to Daniel Brennan but to Bobby Brennan from Newmarket on Fergus."

"I think you're wrong about that." David pointed with the stub of his cigarette.

"I'll wager two pounds on it."

"Done. We'll ask Murphy himself."

"If he ever gets here," Maggie muttered, and bit into her sandwich. "You'd think I have nothing better to do than to sit here twiddling my thumbs."

"I knew a Brennan once." The old man at the end of the bar spoke up, paused, blew a lazy smoke ring. "Frankie Brennan, he was, from Ballybunion, where I lived as a boy. One night he was walking home from the pub. Had a fill of porter, he did, and never had the head for it."

He blew another smoke ring. Time passed, but no one spoke. A story was in the making.

"So he went walking home, reeling a bit, and cut across a field to shorten the way. There was a fairy hill, and in his drunken state, he trod right over it. Well, a man should know better, drunk or sober, but Frankie Brennan got less than his share when the Lord passed out sense. Now, of course, the fairies had to teach him manners and respect, and so they tugged off all his clothes as he went staggering across the field. And he arrived home, stark naked, but for his hat and one shoe." He paused again, smiled. "Never did find the other shoe."

Maggie gave an appreciative hoot of laughter and propped her feet on the empty chair across from her. They could keep Paris and Rome and the rest, she thought. She was just where she wanted to be.

Then Rogan walked in.

His entrance gained him some glances, appraisals. It wasn't often a man in so fine a suit strolled into O'Malley's on a cloudy afternoon. Maggie, the pint glass nearly to her lips, froze like stone.

"Good day to you. Is there something I can get you?" Tim asked.

"A pint of Guinness, thank you." Rogan leaned back against the bar, smiled at Maggie while Tim turned the tap. "Good day to you, Margaret Mary."

"What are you doing here?"

"Why, I'm about to have a pint." Still smiling, he slid coins across the bar. "You're looking well."

"I thought you were in Rome."

"I was. Your work shows well there."

"Would you be Rogan Sweeney, then?" Tim slid the glass to Rogan.

"I would, yes."

"I'm O'Malley, Tim O'Malley." After wiping his hand over his apron, Tim took Rogan's and pumped. "I was a great friend of Maggie's father. He'd have been pleased with what you're doing for her. Pleased and proud. We've a scrapbook started, my Deirdre and I."

"I can promise you you'll be adding to it, Mr. O'Malley, for some time to come."

"If you've come to see if I've work to show you," Maggie called out, "I haven't. And I won't if you breathe down my neck."

"I haven't come to see your work." With a nod to Tim, Rogan walked to Maggie. He sat beside her, took her chin in his hand and kissed her softly. And kissed her long. "I've come to see you."

She let out the breath she'd forgotten she was holding. A frowning glance at the bar had the curious onlookers turning their attention elsewhere. Or pretending to.

"You took your sweet time."

"Time enough for you to miss me."

"I've hardly worked at all since you left." Because it was difficult to admit, she kept her eyes trained on her glass. "I've started and stopped, started and stopped. Nothing's coming out the way I want it to. I don't care for this feeling, Rogan. I don't care for it at all."

"What feeling is that?"

She shot him a look from under her lashes. "I've been missing you. I came to Dublin."

"I know." He toyed with the ends of her hair. It had grown a bit, he noted, and wondered how long it would be before she whacked away again with her scissors as she said she sometimes did. "Was it so hard to come to me, Maggie?"

"Yes, it was. As hard as anything I've done. Then you weren't there."

"I'm here now."

He was. And she wasn't sure she could speak for the pounding of her heart. "There are things I want to tell you. I don't—" She broke off as the door opened, and Murphy came in. "Oh, his timing's perfect."

Murphy signaled to Tim before heading toward Maggie. "You've had lunch, then." In a casual gesture, he scraped up a chair and snatched one of her chips. "Did you bring it?"

"I did. And you've kept me waiting half the day."

"It's barely one o'clock." Eyeing Rogan, Murphy ate another of Maggie's chips. "You'd be Sweeney, would you?"

"I would."

" 'Twas the suit," Murphy explained. "Maggie said how it was you dressed like every day was Sunday. I'm Murphy Muldoon, Maggie's neighbor."

The first kiss, Rogan remembered, and shook hands as cautiously as Murphy. "It's good to meet you."

"And you." Murphy leaned his chair on its back legs as he did his measuring. "You could almost say I'm a brother to Maggie. As she's no man to look out for her."

"And she's not needing one," Maggie tossed out. She would have kicked Murphy's chair out from under him if he hadn't been quick enough to drop it in place again. "I'll look out for myself very well, thank you."

"So she's often told me." Rogan addressed Murphy. "But need or not, she has one."

The message passed, male to male. After a moment's consideration, Murphy nodded. "That's fine, then. Did you bring it or not, Maggie?"

"I said I did." In an impatient move, she bent to grab the box from the floor and set it on the table between them. "If it wasn't for my fondness of your mother, I'd bash it over your head."

"She'll be grateful you restrained yourself." As Tim plunked down another beer Murphy opened the box. "This is grand, Maggie. She'll be pleased."

Rogan imagined so. The pale pink bowl was as fluid as water, its sides waving up to end in delicate crests. The glass was so thin, so fragile, he could see the shadow of Murphy's hands through it.

"You'll wish her a happy birthday for me as well."

"I will." Murphy skimmed a callused finger over the glass before setting it back in the box. "Fifty pounds, was it?"

"It was." Maggie held out a hand, palm up. "Cash."

Feigning reluctance, Murphy scratched his cheek. "It seems mighty dear for one little bowl, Maggie Mae—that you can't even eat from. But my mother likes foolish, useless things."

"Keep talking, Murphy, and the price'll go up."

"Fifty pounds." Shaking his head, Murphy reached for his wallet. He counted out the bills in her outstretched hand. "You know I could've gotten her a whole set of dishes for that. And maybe a fine new skillet."

"And she'd have knocked you in the head with it." Satisfied, Maggie tucked the bills away. "No woman wants a skillet for her birthday, and any man who thinks she does deserves the consequences."

"Murphy." David Ryan shifted on his stool. "If you've finished your transaction there, we've a question for you."

"Then I'll have to answer it." Taking up his beer, Murphy rose. " 'Tis a fine suit, Mr. Sweeney." He walked away to settle the wager of the Brennans.

"Fifty pounds?" Rogan murmured, nodding toward the box Murphy had left on the table. "You and I are both aware that you could get more than twenty times that."

"What of it?" Instantly defensive, she shoved her glass aside. "It's my work, and I'll ask for it what I please. You've got your damned exclusive clause, Sweeney, so you can sue me if you like for breaking it, but you'll not have the bowl."

"I didn't—"

"I gave my word to Murphy," she barreled on. "And a deal's done.

You can have your cursed twenty-five percent of the fifty pounds. But if I choose to make something for a friend—"

"It wasn't a complaint." He wrapped his hand around her fisted one. "It was a compliment. You have a generous heart, Maggie."

With the wind so successfully stripped from her sails, she sighed. "The papers say I'm not to make anything that doesn't go to you."

"The papers say that," he agreed. "I imagine you'll go on snarling about it, and you'll go on slipping your friends gifts when it suits you." She shot him a look from under her lashes, so blatantly guilty, he laughed. "I see I could have sued you a time or two over the last few months. We can make what we'd call a side deal. I won't take my percentage of your fifty pounds, and you'll make something for my grandmother for Christmas."

She nodded, lowered her lashes again. "It isn't just about money, is it, Rogan? I'm afraid sometimes that it is, that I've let it be. Because I like the money, you see. I like it very much, and all that goes with it."

"It's not just about money, Maggie. It's not just about champagne showings or newspaper clippings or parties in Paris. Those are just trimmings. What it's about really is what's inside you, and all that you are that goes into creating the beautiful, the unique and the startling."

"I can't go back, you see. I can't go back to the way things were, before you." She looked at him then, studying his face feature by feature while his hand lay warm over hers. "Will you take a drive with me? There's something I want to show you."

"I have a car outside. I've already put your bike in it."

She had to smile. "I should have known you would."

With a fall wind in the air, and the leaves a riot of color, they drove toward Loop Hea. Away from the narrow road, spilling back like the sea itself, were harvested fields and the deep, sweet green so special to Ireland. Maggie saw the tumbled stone sheds that looked no different than they had when she had traveled this road nearly five years before. The land was there, and the people tended it, as they always had. Always would.

When she heard the sea, smelled the first sharp sting of it on the air, her heart lurched. She squeezed her eyes tight, opened them again. And read the sign.

LAST PUB UNTIL NEW YORK

Shall we sail over to New York, Maggie, and have a pint?

When the car stopped, she said nothing, only got out to let the wind slap cool over her skin. Reaching for Rogan's hand, she held it as they walked down the beaten path to the sea.

The war continued, wave against rock in the echoing crash and hiss that was eternal. The mist had rolled in, so that there was no border between sea and sky, just a wide, wide cup of soft gray.

"I haven't been here in almost five years. I didn't know I'd ever come again to stand like this." She pressed her lips together, wishing the fist around her heart would loosen, just a little. "My father died here. We'd come out together, just us two. It was winter and bitter cold, but he loved this spot more than any other I can think of. I'd sold some pieces that day to a merchant in Ennis, and we'd celebrated in O'Malleys."

"You were alone with him?" The horror of it slashed Rogan like a rapier. He could do nothing for her but pull her into his arms and hold on. "I'm sorry, Maggie. So sorry."

She brushed her cheek over the soft wool of Rogan's coat, caught the scent of him in it. She let her eyes close. "We talked, about my mother, their marriage. I'd never understood why he stayed. Maybe I never will. But there was something in him that yearned, and that wanted for me and Brianna whatever that yearning was. I think I have the same longing, but that I might have the chance to grab hold of it."

She drew back so that she could look at his face as she spoke. "I've something for you." Watching him, she took one of the glass drops from her pocket, held it out in her palm.

"It looks like a tear."

"Aye." She waited while he held it to the light and studied it.

He rubbed a thumb over the smooth glass. "Are you giving me your tears, Maggie?"

"Perhaps I am." She took another one out of her pocket. "It comes from dropping hot glass in water. When you do, some shatter right away, but others hold and form. Strong." She crouched and chose a rock. While Rogan watched she struck the glass with rock. "Strong enough that it won't break under a hammer." She rose again, holding the undamaged drop. "It holds, you see. Does nothing more than bounce away from the blow and shine. But there's this thin end here and it only takes a careless twist." She took the slim, trailing end between her fingers. The glass turned to harmless dust. "It's gone, you see. Like it never was."

"A tear comes from the heart," Rogan said. "And neither should be handled carelessly. I won't break yours, Maggie, nor you mine."

"No." She took a long breath. "But we'll hammer away often enough. We're as different as that water and hot glass, Rogan."

"And as able to make something strong between us."

"I think we might. Yet I wonder how long you'd last in a cottage in Clare, or I in a house full of servants in Dublin."

"We could move to the midlands," he said, and watched her smile. "Actually, I've given that particular matter some thought. The idea, Maggie, is negotiation and compromise."

"Ah, the businessman, even at such a time."

He ignored the sarcasm. "I've plans to open a gallery in Clare to spotlight Irish artists."

"In Clare?" Pushing back her windblown hair, she stared at him. "A branch of Worldwide here in Clare? You'd do that for me?"

"I would. I'm afraid I'll spoil the heroics by telling you I'd thought of the idea long before I met you. The conception had nothing to do with you, but the location does. Or I should say it has to do with us." As the wind picked up he pulled her jacket together and buttoned it. "I believe I can live in a west-county cottage for part of the year, just as you could live with servants for the other."

"You've thought this all through."

"I have, yes. Certain aspects are, of course, negotiable." He studied the glass drop again before slipping it into his pocket. "There is one, however, that is not."

"And that would be?"

"Exclusivity again, Maggie, in the form of a marriage contract. A lifetime term with no escape clauses."

The fist around her heart squeezed all the tighter. "You're a hard bargainer, Sweeney."

"I am."

She looked out to sea again, the ceaseless rush of water, the indominable rock, and the magic they made between them. "I've been happy alone," she said quietly. "And I've been unhappy without you. I never wanted to depend on anyone, or to let myself care so much I could be made unhappy. But I depend on you, Rogan." Gently she lifted a hand to his cheek. "And I love you."

The sweetness of hearing it swarmed through him. He guided her palm over his lips. "I know."

And the fist, so tight around her heart, loosened. "You know." She laughed, shook her head. "Oh, it must be a fine thing to always be right."

"It's never been a finer thing." He lifted her off her feet, spun her around once before their lips met and clung. The wind swooped down, ribboned around them, smelling of the sea. "If I can make you unhappy, Maggie, then I can make you happy as well."

She squeezed her arms tight around him. "If you don't, I'll make your life hell. I swear it. God, I never wanted to be a wife."

"You'll be mine, and glad of it."

"I'll be yours." She lifted her face to the wind. "And glad of it."

BORN IN ICE

Dear Reader,

Ireland holds a special place in my heart. The rolling green fields under heavy skies, the criss-crossing gray of stone fences, the majestic tumble of a ruined castle, most likely sacked by those damned Cromwellians. I love the way the sun can shine gold through the rain, and the flowers bloom wildly in gardens and fields. It's a land of violent cliffs and dim, smoky pubs. Of magic and legend and heartbreak. There is a beauty even in the air.

And the west of Ireland is the most stunning landscape of a stunning country.

There, the traffic jams are often the cows being led to field by the farmer. There, a winding country road, closed in tight with hedgerows of wild fuchsia, can lead you anywhere. There, the River Shannon gleams like silver and the sea crashes like thunder.

But beyond the countryside, the most magnificent thing in Ireland are the Irish. True, it's a land of poets and warriors and dreamers, but it is also a land that opens its arms to strangers. Irish hospitality is simple and kind. That is, or should be, the definition of the word welcome.

In writing Born in Ice, *Brianna Concannon's story, I hoped to reflect that incomparable generosity of spirit, the simplicity of an open door, and the strength of love. So come and sit for a while in front of the fire, take a drop of whiskey in your tea. Put your feet up and let your worries rest. I'd like to tell you a story.*

Nora Roberts

To all my ancestors
who traveled across the foam

I've been a wild rover for many the year.

THE WILD ROVER

PROLOGUE

The wild wind raced cursing across the Atlantic and pounded its fists over the fields of the west counties. Hard, needle-point bullets of rain beat on the ground and sliced through a man's flesh to batter his bones. Flowers that had bloomed brilliantly from spring through autumn blackened under the killing frost.

In cottages and pubs, people gathered around fires and talked of their farms and their roofs, the loved ones who had emigrated to Germany or the States. It hardly mattered whether they had left the day before, or a generation. Ireland was losing its people, as it had all but lost its language.

There was occasional talk about The Troubles, that endless war in the north. But Belfast was far from the village of Kilmilhil, in miles, and in emotion. People worried more about their crops, their animals, and the weddings and wakes that would come with winter.

A few miles out of the village, in a kitchen warmed with the heat and scents of baking, Brianna Concannon looked out of the window as the ice-edged rain attacked her garden.

"I'll lose the columbine, I'm thinking. And the foxglove." It broke her heart to think of it, but she'd dug up what she could and stored the plants in the crowded little cabin out back. The gale had come so quickly.

"You'll plant more in spring." Maggie studied her sister's profile. Brie worried about her flowers like a mother over her babes. With a sigh, Maggie rubbed her own bulging belly. It still astonished her that it was she who was married and carrying a child, and not her home-loving sister. "You'll love every minute of it."

"I suppose. What I need is a greenhouse. I've been looking at pictures. I think it could be done." And she could probably afford it by spring, if she was careful. Daydreaming a little about the plants that would flourish in their new glass enclosure, she slipped a fresh batch of cranberry muffins from the oven. Maggie had brought her the berries all the way from a Dublin market. "You'll take this home with you."

"I will, yes." Maggie grinned and snatched one from the basket, tossing it from hand to hand to cool it enough before she bit in. "After I've eaten my fill. I swear to you, Rogan all but weighs every morsel I put in my mouth."

"He wants you and the baby healthy."

"Oh, he does. And I think he's worrying about how much of me is baby and how much is fat."

Brianna eyed her sister. Maggie had grown round and soft, and there was a rosy contentment about her as she approached the last trimester of her pregnancy that was a sharp contrast to the bundle of energy and nerve Brianna was accustomed to.

She's happy, Brianna thought, in love. And knows her love is well returned. "You have put on more than a few, Margaret Mary," Brianna said and watched wicked humor rather than temper light Maggie's eyes.

"I'm having a contest with one of Murphy's cows, and I'm winning." She finished off the muffin, reached shamelessly for another. "In a few weeks I'll not be able to see past my belly to the end of my pipe to blow glass. I'll have to switch to lamp work."

"You could take a vacation from your glass," Brianna pointed out. "I know Rogan's told you you've enough done already for all of his galleries."

"And what would I do, besides die of boredom? I've got an idea for a special piece for the new gallery here in Clare."

"Which won't open until spring."

"By then Rogan will have made good on his threat to tie me to the bed if I make a move toward my shop." She sighed, but Brie suspected Maggie didn't mind the threat so much. Didn't mind Rogan's subtle domineering ways. She was afraid she was mellowing. "I want to work while I can," Maggie added. "And it's good to be home, even in such weather. I suppose you've got no guests coming."

"As it happens, I do. A Yank, next week." Brianna freshened Maggie's cup of tea, then her own, before sitting down. The dog, who had been waiting patiently beside her chair, laid his big head in her lap.

"A Yank? Just one? A man?"

"Mmmm." Brianna stroked Concobar's head. "It's a writer. He's booked a room, wants board as well, for an indefinite period. He's paid a month in advance."

"A month! At this time of year?" Amused, Maggie looked out as the wind shook the kitchen windows. Welcoming weather it wasn't. "And they say artists are eccentric. What sort of writer is he, then?"

"A mystery type. I've read a few, and he's good. He's won awards and had films made from them."

"A successful writer, a Yank, spending the dead of winter at a B-and-B in Clare County. Well, they'll have plenty to say about that at the pub."

Maggie licked crumbs from her fingers and studied her sister with an artist's eye. Brianna was a lovely woman, all rose and gold with creamy skin and a fine, trim figure. A classic oval face, a mouth that was soft, unpainted, and often too serious. Pale green eyes that tended to dream, long, fluid limbs, hair that held quiet fire—thick, slippery hair that often escaped its pins.

And she was soft-hearted, Maggie thought. Entirely too naive, despite her contact with strangers as the owner of a B-and-B, about what went on out in the world beyond her own garden gate.

"I don't know as I like it, Brie, you alone in the house with a man for weeks at a time."

"I'm often alone with guests, Maggie. That's how I make my living."

"You rarely have only one, and in the middle of winter. I don't know when we might have to go back to Dublin, and—"

"Not be here to look after me?" Brianna smiled, more amused than offended. "Maggie, I'm a grown woman. A grown businesswoman who can look after herself."

"You're always too busy looking after everyone else."

"Don't start on about Mother." Brianna's lips tightened. "I do very little now that she's settled with Lottie in the cottage."

"I know exactly what you do," Maggie tossed back. "Running every time she wags her finger, listening to her complaints, dragging her off to the doctor's every time she imagines herself with a new fatal disease." Maggie held up a hand, furious at herself for being sucked, yet again, into the anger and the guilt. "That's not my concern just now. This man—"

"Grayson Thane," Brianna supplied, more than grateful the topic had turned away from their mother. "A respected American author who has designs on a quiet room in a well-run establishment in the west of Ireland. He doesn't have designs on his landlady." She picked up her tea, sipped. "And he's going to pay for my greenhouse."

ONE

It wasn't unusual for Brianna to have a guest or two at Blackthorn Cottage during the worst of winter's storms. But January was slow, and more often than not her home was empty. She didn't mind the solitude, or the hell-hound howl of the wind, or even the leaden sky that spewed rain and ice day after bitter day. It gave her time to plan.

She enjoyed travelers, expected or not. From a business standpoint the pounds and pence counted. But beyond that, Brianna liked company, and the opportunity to serve and make a temporary home for those who passed her way.

She had, in the years since her father died and her mother moved out, turned the house into the home she had longed for as a child, with turf fires and lace curtains and the scents of baking coming from the kitchen. Still, it had been Maggie, and Maggie's art, that had made it possible for Brianna to expand, bit by bit. It wasn't something Brianna forgot.

But the house was hers. Their father had understood her love and her need for it. She tended her legacy as she would a child.

Perhaps it was the weather that made her think of her father. He had died on a day very much like this. Now and again, at odd moments when she found herself alone, she discovered she still carried little pockets of grief, with memories, good and bad, tucked into them.

Work was what she needed, she told herself, turning away from the window before she could brood for long.

With the rain pelting down, she decided to postpone a trip into the village and instead tackle a task she had put off for too long. No one was expected that day, and her single reservation wasn't due until the end of the week. With her dog trooping behind her, Brianna carted broom, bucket, rags, and an empty carton up to the attic.

She cleaned up here with regularity. No dust was allowed in Brianna's house for long. But there were boxes and trunks she had ignored in her day-to-day routine. No more, she told herself and propped open the attic door. This time she would make a clean sweep. And she would not allow sentiment to prevent her from dealing with leftover memories.

If the room was cleaned out properly once and for all, she thought, she might be able to afford the materials and labor necessary to remodel it. A cozy loft room it could be, she mused, leaning on her broom. With one of those ceiling windows, and perhaps a dormer. Soft yellow paint to bring the sun inside. Polish and one of her hooked rugs on the floor.

She could already see it, the pretty bed covered by a colorful quilt, a sugan chair, a little writing table. And if she had . . .

Brianna shook her head and laughed at herself. She was getting ahead of herself.

"Always dreaming, Con," she murmured, rubbing the dog's head. "And what's needed here is elbow grease and ruthlessness."

Boxes first, she decided. It was time to clean out old papers, old clothes.

Thirty minutes later she had neat piles. One she would take to the church for the poor; another would be rags. The last she would keep.

"Ah, look at this, Con." Reverently she took out a small white christening gown, gently shaking out the folds. Faint wisps of lavender haunted the air. Tiny buttons and narrow edges of lace decorated the linen. Her grandmother's handiwork, Brianna knew, and smiled. "He saved it," she murmured. Her mother would never had given such sentimental thought to future generations. "Maggie and I would have worn this, you see. And Da packed it away for our children."

There was a pang, so familiar she barely felt it. There was no babe sleeping in a cradle for her, no soft bundle waiting to be held and nursed and loved. But Maggie, she thought, would want this. Taking care, she folded the gown again.

The next box was filled with papers that made her sigh. She would have to read them, scan them at least. Her father had saved every scrap of correspondence. There would be newspaper clippings as well. His ideas, he would have said, for new ventures.

Always a new venture. She set aside various articles he'd clipped out, on inventions, foresting, carpentry, shopkeeping. None on farming, she noticed with a smile. A farmer he'd never been. She found letters from relatives, from companies he'd written to in America, in Australia, in Canada. And here the proof of purchase for the old truck they'd had when she'd been a child. One document stopped her, made her frown in puzzlement. It looked like some sort of stock certificate. Triquarter Mining, in Wales. From the date it seemed he'd purchased it only a few weeks before he died.

Triquarter Mining? Another venture, Da, she mused, spending money we barely had. Well, she would have to write to this Triquarter company and see what was to be done. It was unlikely the stock was worth more than the paper it was printed on. Such had always been Tom Concannon's luck with business deals.

That bright brass ring he'd forever reached for had never fit the palm of his hand.

She dug further into the box, amused herself with letters from cousins and uncles and aunts. They had loved him. Everyone had loved him. Almost, she corrected, thinking of her mother.

Pushing that thought aside, she took out a trio of letters tied with a faded red ribbon. The return address was New York, but that was no surprise. The Concannons had a number of friends and relations in the States. The name, however, was a mystery to her. Amanda Dougherty.

Brianna unfolded the letter, scanned the neat, convent-school writing. As her breath caught in her throat, she read again, carefully, word for word.

My darling Tommy,

I told you I wouldn't write. Perhaps I won't send this letter, but I need to pretend, at least, that I can talk to you. I've been back in New York for only a day. Already you seem so far away, and the time we had together all the more precious. I have been to confession and received my penance. Yet in my heart, nothing that passed between us is a sin. Love cannot be a sin. And I will always love you. One day, if God is kind, we will find a way to be together. But if that never happens, I want you to know that I'll treasure every moment we were given. I know it's my duty to tell you to honor the sacrament of your marriage, to devote yourself to the two babies you love so much. And I do. But, however selfish it is, I also ask that sometime, when spring comes to Clare, and the Shannon is bright with sunlight, you think of me. And how for those few short weeks, you loved me. And I love you . . .

Always,
Amanda

Love letters, she thought dully. To her father. Written, she saw, staring at the date, when she was an infant.

Her hands chilled. How was a woman, a grown woman of twenty-eight years, supposed to react when she learned her father had loved a woman other than his wife? Her father, with his quick laugh, his useless schemes. These were words written for no one's eyes but his. And yet, how could she not read them?

With her heart pounding thickly in her chest, Brianna unfolded the next.

My darling Tommy,

I have read and read your letter until I can see every word in my head. My heart breaks to think of you so unhappy. I, too, often look out to sea and picture you gazing across the water toward me. There is so much I wish to tell you, but I'm afraid it will only add to your heartache. If there is no love with your wife, there must be duty. There is no need for me to tell you that your children are your first concern. I know, have known all along, that they are first in your heart, and in your thoughts. God bless you, Tommy, for thinking also of me. And for the gift you gave me. I thought my life would be empty, now it will never be anything but full and rich. I love you now even more than I did when we parted. Don't grieve when you think of me. But think of me.

Always,
Amanda

Love, Brianna thought as her eyes welled with tears. There was such love here, though so little had been said. Who had she been, this Amanda? How had they met? And how often had her father thought of this woman? How often had he wished for her?

Dashing a tear away, Brianna opened the last letter.

My darling,

I have prayed and prayed before writing this. I've asked the Holy Mother to help me know what is right. What is fair to you, I can't be sure. I can only hope that what I tell you will give you joy, not grief.

I remember the hours we spent together in my little room at the inn overlooking the Shannon. How sweet and gentle you were, how blinded we both were by the love that swept through us. I have never known, nor will I know again, that deep, abiding love. So am I grateful that though we can never be together, I will have something precious to remind me that I was loved. I'm carrying your child, Tommy. Please be happy for me. I'm not alone, and I'm not afraid. Perhaps I should be ashamed. Unmarried, pregnant by another woman's husband. Perhaps the shame will come, but for now, I am only full of joy.

I have known for weeks, but could not find the courage to tell you. I find it now, feeling the first quickening of the life we made inside me. Do I have to tell you how much this child will be loved? I have already imagined holding our baby in my arms. Please, my darling, for the sake of our child, let there be no grief or guilt in your heart. And, for the sake of our child, I am going away. Though I will think of you every day, every night, I will not write again. I will love you all of my life, and whenever I look at the life we created in those magic hours near the Shannon, I will love you more.

Give whatever you feel for me to your children. And be happy.

Always,
Amanda

A child. As her eyes swam with tears, Brianna covered her mouth with her hand. A sister. A brother. Dear God. Somewhere, there was a man or woman bound to her by blood. They would be close in age. Perhaps share the same coloring, the same features.

What could she do? What could her father have done, all those years ago? Had he searched for the woman and his baby? Had he tried to forget?

No. Gently Brianna smoothed the letters. He hadn't tried to forget. He'd kept her letters always. She closed her eyes, sitting in the dimly lit attic. And, she thought, he had loved his Amanda. Always.

She needed to think before she told Maggie what she'd found. Brianna thought best when she was busy. She could no longer face the attic, but there were other things that could be done. She scrubbed and polished and baked. The simple hominess of chores, the pleasure of the scents they created, lightened her spirits. She added turf to the fires, brewed tea, and settled down to sketch out ideas for her greenhouse.

The solution would come, in time, she told herself. After more than twenty-five years, a few days of thought would hurt no one. If a part of the delay was cowardice, a weak need to avoid the whip of her sister's emotions, she recognized it.

Brianna never claimed to be a brave woman.

In her practical way, she composed a polite, businesslike letter to Triquarter Mining in Wales and set it aside to be posted the next day.

She had a list of chores for the morning, rain or shine. By the time she'd banked the fires for the night, she was grateful Maggie had been too busy to drop by. Another day, perhaps two, Brianna told herself, and she would show her sister the letters.

But tonight she would relax, let her mind empty. An indulgence was what she needed, Brianna decided. In truth her back was aching just a bit from overdoing her scrubbing. A long bath with some of the bubbles Maggie had brought her from Paris, a cup of tea, a book. She would use the big tub upstairs and treat herself like a guest. Rather than her narrow bed in the room off the kitchen, she would sleep in splendor in what she thought of as the bridal suite.

"We're kings tonight, Con," she told the dog as she poured bubbles lavishly under the stream of water. "A supper tray in bed, a book written by our soon-to-be guest. A very important Yank, remember," she added as Con thumped his tail on the floor.

She slipped out of her clothes and into the hot, fragrant water. The sigh rose up from her toes. A love story might be more appropriate to the moment, she thought, than a thriller with the title of *The Bloodstone Legacy*. But Brianna settled back in the tub and eased into the story of a woman haunted by her past and threatened by her present.

It caught her. So much so that when her water had chilled, she held the book in one hand, reading, as she dried off with the other. Shivering, she tugged on a long flannel nightgown, unpinned her hair. Only ingrained habit had her setting the book aside long enough to tidy the bath. But she didn't bother with the supper tray. Instead, she snuggled into bed, pulling the quilt up close.

She barely heard the wind kick at the windows, the rain slash at them. Courtesy of Grayson Thane's book, Brianna was in the sultry summer of the southern United States, hunted by a murderer.

It was past midnight when fatigue defeated her. She fell asleep with the book still in her hands, the dog snoring at the foot of the bed and the wind howling like a frightened woman.

She dreamed, of course, of terror.

Grayson Thane was a man of impulses. Because he recognized it, he generally took the disasters that grew from them as philosophically as the triumphs. At the moment he was forced to admit that the impulse to drive from Dublin to Clare, in the dead of winter, in the face of one of the most bad-tempered storms he'd ever experienced, had probably been a mistake.

But it was still an adventure. And he lived his life by them.

He'd had a flat outside of Limerick. A puncture, Gray corrected. When in Rome, speak the lingo. By the time he'd changed the tire, he'd looked and felt like a drowned rat, despite the macintosh he'd picked up in London the week before.

He'd gotten lost twice, finding himself creeping down narrow, winding roads that were hardly more than ditches. His research had told him that getting lost in Ireland was part of its charm.

He was trying hard to remember that.

He was hungry, soaked to the skin, and afraid he would run out of gas—petrol—before he found anything remotely like an inn or village.

In his mind he went over the map. Visualizing was a talent he'd been born with, and he could, with little effort, reproduce every line of the careful map his hostess had sent him.

The trouble was, it was pitch dark, the rain washed over his windshield like a roaring river, and the wind was buffeting his car on this godforsaken excuse for a road as if the Mercedes was a Tinkertoy.

He wished violently for coffee.

When the road forked, Gray took his chances and guided the car to the left. If he didn't find the inn or something like in it another ten miles, he'd sleep in the damn car and try again in the morning.

It was a pity he couldn't see any of the countryside. He had a feeling in the dark desolation of the storm it would be exactly what he was looking for. He wanted his book here, among the cliffs and fields of western Ireland, with the fierce Atlantic threatening, and the quiet villages huddled against it. And he might just have his tired, world-weary hero arriving in the teeth of a gale.

He squinted into the gloom. A light? He hoped to Christ it was. He caught a glimpse of a sign, swinging hard in the wind. Gray reversed, aimed the headlights, and grinned.

The sign read "Blackthorn Cottage." His sense of direction hadn't failed him after all. He hoped his hostess proved out the legend of Irish hospitality—he was two days early after all. And it was two in the morning.

Gray looked for a driveway, saw nothing but soaked hedges. With a shrug, he stopped the car in the road, pocketed the keys. He had all he'd need for the night in a knapsack on the seat beside him. Swinging it with him, he left the car where it was and stepped into the storm.

It slapped him like an angry woman, all teeth and nails. He staggered, almost plowed through the drenched hedges of fuchsia, and through more luck than design all but ran into the garden gate. Gray opened it, then fought it closed again. He wished he could see the house more clearly. There was only an impression of shape and size through the dark, with that single light shining in the window upstairs.

He used it like a beacon and began to dream of coffee.

No one answered his knock. With the wind screaming, he doubted anyone would hear a battering ram. It took him less than ten seconds to decide to open the door himself.

Again, there were only impressions. The storm at his back, the warmth within. There were scents—lemon, polish, lavender, and rosemary. He wondered if the old Irishwoman who ran the inn made her own potpourri. He wondered if she'd wake up and fix him a hot meal.

Then he heard the growl—deep, feral—and tensed. His head whipped up, his eyes narrowed. Then his mind, for one stunning moment, blanked.

Later, he would think it was a scene from a book. One of his own perhaps. The beautiful woman, the long white gown billowing, her hair spilling like fired gold down her shoulders. Her face was pale in the swaying light of the candle she held in one hand. Her other hand was clutched at the collar of a dog that looked and snarled like a wolf. A dog whose shoulders reached her waist.

She stared down at him from the top of the steps, like a vision he had conjured. She might have been carved from marble, or ice. She was so still, so utterly perfect.

Then the dog strained forward. With a movement that rippled her gown, she checked him.

"You're letting the rain in," she said in a voice that only added to the fantasy. Soft, musical, lilting of the Ireland he'd come to discover.

"Sorry." He fumbled behind him for the door, shutting it so that the storm became only a backdrop.

Her heart was still thudding. The noise and Con's response had wakened her from a dream of pursuit and terror. Now, Brianna stared down at a man in black, shapeless but for his face, which was shadowed. When he stepped closer, she kept her trembling hand tight on Con's collar.

A long, narrow face, she saw now. A poet's face with its dark, curious eyes and solemn mouth. A pirate's face, hardened by those prominent bones and the long sun-streaked hair that curled damp around it.

Silly to be afraid, she scolded herself. He was just a man, after all.

"Are you lost, then?" she asked him.

"No." He smiled, slow, easy. "I'm found. This is Blackthorn Cottage?"

"It is, yes."

"I'm Grayson Thane. I'm a couple days early, but Miss Concannon's expecting me."

"Oh." Brianna murmured something to the dog Gray didn't catch, but it had the effect of relaxing those bunched canine muscles. "I was looking for you on Friday, Mr. Thane. But you're welcome." She started down the steps, the dog at her side, the candlelight wavering. "I'm Brianna Concannon." She offered a hand.

He stared at it a moment. He'd been expecting a nice, homey woman with graying hair tucked back in a bun. "I woke you," he said foolishly.

"We usually sleep here in the middle of the night. Come in by the fire." She walked to the parlor, switching on the lights. After setting the candle aside, blowing it out, she turned to take his wet coat. "It's a terrible night for traveling."

"So I discovered."

He wasn't shapeless under the mac. Though he wasn't as tall as Brianna's uneasy imagination had made him, he was lean and wiry. Like a boxer, she thought, then smiled at herself. Poet, pirate, boxer. The man was a writer, and a guest. "Warm yourself, Mr. Thane. I'll make you some tea, shall I? Or would you rather I . . ." She'd started to offer to show him to his room, and remembered that she was sleeping in it.

"I've been dreaming of coffee for the last hour. If it isn't too much trouble."

"It's not a problem. No problem at all. Make yourself comfortable."

It was too pretty a scene to spend alone, he decided. "I'll just come in the kitchen with you. I feel bad enough about dragging you out of bed at this hour." He held out a hand for Con to sniff. "This is some dog. For a minute I took him for a wolf."

"A wolfhound, he is." Her mind was busy figuring details. "You're welcome to sit in the kitchen. Are you hungry, then?"

He rubbed Con's head and grinned down at her. "Miss Concannon, I think I love you."

She flushed at his compliment. "Well, you give your heart easily then, if for no more than a bowl of soup."

"Not from what I've heard of your cooking."

"Oh?" She led the way into the kitchen and hung his dripping coat on a hook by the rear door.

"A friend of a cousin of my editor stayed here a year or so ago. The word was that the hostess of the Blackthorn cooked like an angel." He hadn't heard she looked like one as well.

"That's a fine compliment." Brianna put on the kettle, then ladeled soup into a pot for heating. "I'm afraid I can only offer you plain fare tonight, Mr. Thane, but you'll not go to your bed hungry." She took soda bread from a bin and sliced it generously. "Have you traveled long today?"

"I started out late from Dublin. I'd planned to stay another day, but I had the itch." He smiled, taking the bread she set on the table and biting into the first piece before she could offer him butter. "It was time to get on the road. Do you run this place alone?"

"I do. I'm afraid you'll have a lack of company this time of year."

"I didn't come for company," he said, watching as she measured out coffee. The kitchen was beginning to smell like heaven.

"For work, you said. I think it must be wonderful to be able to tell stories."

"It has its moments."

"I like yours." It was simply said as she reached into a cupboard for a stoneware bowl glazed in deep blue.

He raised a brow. People usually began to ask dozens of questions at this point. How do you write, where do you get your ideas—the most hated of questions—how do you get published? And questions were usually followed up by the deathless information that the inquirer had a story to tell.

But that was all she said. Gray found himself smiling again. "Thanks. Sometimes I do, too." He leaned forward, sniffed deeply when she set the bowl of soup in front of him. "It doesn't smell like plain fare to me."

"It's vegetable, with a bit of beef. I can make you a sandwich if you like."

"No, this is great." He sampled, sighed. "Really great." He studied her again. Did her skin always look so soft and flushed? he wondered. Or was it sleepiness? "I'm trying to be sorry I woke you," he said and continued to eat. "This is making it tough."

"A good inn's always open to a traveler, Mr. Thane." She set his coffee beside him, signaled the dog who immediately stood from his perch beside the kitchen table. "Help yourself to another bowl if you like. I'll tend to your room."

She hurried out, quickening her steps as she came to the stairs. She'd have to change the sheets on the bed, the towels in the bath. It didn't occur to her to offer him one of the other rooms. As her only guest, he was entitled to the best she had.

She worked quickly and was just plumping the pillows in their lace-edged cases when she heard the sound at the door.

Her first reaction was distress to see him standing in the doorway. Her next was resignation. It was her home, after all. She had a right to use any part of it.

"I was giving myself a bit of a holiday," she began and tugged at the quilt.

Odd, he thought, that a woman performing the simple task of tucking in sheets should look so outrageously sexy. He must be more tired than he'd thought.

"I seemed to have dragged you from your bed in more ways than one. It wasn't necessary for you to move out."

"This is the room you're paying for. It's warm. I've built the fire up, and you've your own bath. If you—"

She broke off because he'd come up behind her. The prickling down her spine had her stiffening, but he only reached for the book on the night table.

Brianna cleared her throat and stepped back. "I fell asleep reading it," she began, then went wide-eyed in distress. "I don't mean to say it put me to sleep. I just—" He was smiling, she noted. No, he was grinning at her. The corners of her mouth tugged in response. "It gave me nightmares."

"Thank you."

She relaxed again, automatically turning sheets and quilt down in welcome. "And you coming in from the storm had me imagining the worst. I was sure the killer had popped right out of the book, bloody knife in hand."

"And who is he?"

She cocked a brow. "I can't say, but I've my suspicions. You've a clever way of twisting the emotions, Mr. Thane."

"Gray," he said, handing her the book. "After all, in a convoluted sort of way, we're sharing a bed." He took her hand before she could think of how to respond, then left her unsettled by raising it to his lips. "Thanks for the soup."

"You're welcome. Sleep well."

He didn't doubt he would. Brianna had hardly gone out and closed his door when he stripped off his clothes and tumbled naked into the bed. There was a faint scent of lilacs in the air, lilacs and some summer meadow scent he recognized as Brianna's hair.

He fell asleep with a smile on his face.

TWO

It was still raining. The first thing Gray noticed when he pried his eyes open in the morning was the gloom. It could have been any time from dawn to dusk. The old clock on the stone mantel said nine-fifteen. He was optimistic enough to bet it was A.M.

He hadn't studied the room the night before. Travel fatigue, and the pretty sight of Brianna Concannon making his bed, had fuzzed his brain. He did so now, warm under the pooling quilt. The walls were papered so that tiny sprigs of violets and rosebuds climbed from floor to ceiling. The fire, gone cold now, had been set in a stone hearth, and bricks of turf were set in a painted box beside it.

There was a desk that looked old and sturdy. Its surface was polished to a high gloss. A brass lamp, an old inkwell, and a glass bowl of potpourri stood on it. A vase of dried flowers was centered on a mirrored dresser. Two chairs, covered in a soft rose, flanked a small occasional table. There was a braided rug on the floor that picked up the muted tones of the room and prints of wildflowers on the wall.

Gray leaned against the headboard, yawned. He didn't need ambience when he worked, but he appreciated it. All in all, he thought he'd chosen well.

He considered rolling over, going back to sleep. He hadn't yet closed the cage door behind him—an analogy he often used for writing. Chilly, rainy mornings anywhere in the world were meant to be spent in bed. But he thought of his landlady, pretty, rosy-cheeked Brianna. Curiosity about her had him gingerly setting his feet on the chilly floor.

At least the water ran hot, he thought as he stood groggily under the shower. And the soap smelled lightly, and practically, of a pine forest. Traveling as he did, he'd faced a great many icy showers. The simple hominess of the bath, the white towels with their charming touch of embroidery suited his mood perfectly. Then again, his surroundings usually suited him, from a tent in the Arizona desert to plush hotels on the Riviera. Gray liked to think he twisted his setting to fit his needs—until, of course, his needs changed.

For the next few months he figured the cozy inn in Ireland would do just fine. Particularly with the added benefit of his lovely landlady. Beauty was always a plus.

He saw no reason to shave, and pulled on jeans and a tattered sweatshirt. Since the wind had died considerably, he might take a tramp over the fields after breakfast. Soak up a little atmosphere.

But it was breakfast that sent him downstairs.

He wasn't surprised to find her in the kitchen. The room seemed to have been designed for her—the smoky hearth, the bright walls, the neat-as-a-pin counters.

She'd scooped her hair up this morning, he noted. He imagined she thought the knot on top of her head was practical. And perhaps it was, he mused, but the fact that strands escaped to flutter and curl around her neck and cheeks made the practical alluring.

It probably was a bad idea all around to be allured by his landlady.

She was baking something, and the scent of it made his mouth water. Surely it was the scent of food and not the sight of her in her trim white apron that had his juices running.

She turned then, her arms full of a huge bowl, the contents of which she continued to beat with a wooden spoon. She blinked once in surprise, then smiled in cautious welcome. "Good morning. You'll want your breakfast."

"I'll have whatever I'm smelling."

"No, you won't." In a competent manner he had to admire, she poured the contents of a bowl into a pan. "It's not done yet, and what it is is a cake for tea."

"Apple," he said, sniffing the air. "Cinnamon."

"Your nose is right. Can you handle an Irish breakfast, or will you be wanting something lighter?"

"Light isn't what I had in mind."

"Fine, then, the dining room's through the door there. I'll bring you in some coffee and buns to hold you."

"Can I eat in here?" He gave her his most charming smile and leaned against the doorjamb. "Or does it bother you to have people watch you cook?" Or just watch her, he thought, do anything at all.

"Not at all." Some of her guests preferred it, though most liked to be served. She poured him coffee she already had heating. "You take it black?"

"That's right." He sipped it standing, watching her. "Did you grow up in this house?"

"I did." She slid fat sausages in a pan.

"I thought it seemed more of a home than an inn."

"It's meant to. We had a farm, you see, but sold off most of the land. We kept the house, and the little cottage down the way where my sister and her husband live from time to time."

"From time to time?"

"He has a home in Dublin as well. He owns galleries. She's an artist."

"Oh, what kind?"

She smiled a little as she went about the cooking. Most people assumed artist meant painter, a fact which irritated Maggie always. "A glass artist. She blows glass." Brianna gestured to the bowl in the center of the kitchen table. It bled with melting pastels, its rim fluid, like rain-washed petals. "That's her work."

"Impressive." Curious, he moved closer, ran a finger tip around the wavy rim. "Concannon," he murmured, then chuckled to himself. "Damn me, M. M. Concannon, the Irish sensation."

Brianna's eyes danced with pleasure. "Do they call her that, really? Oh, she'll love it." Pride flashed in. "And you recognized her work."

"I ought to, I just bought a—I don't know what the hell it is. A sculpture. Worldwide Galleries, London, two weeks ago."

"Rogan's gallery. Her husband."

"Handy." He went to the stove to top off his cup himself. The frying sausages smelled almost as good as his hostess. "It's an amazing piece. Icy white glass with this pulse of fire inside. I thought it looked like the Fortress of Solitude." At her blank look, he laughed. "You're not up on your American comic books, I take it. Superman's private sanctum, in the Arctic, I think."

"She'll like that, she will. Maggie's big on private sanctums." In an unconscious habit she tucked loose hair back into pins. Her nerves were humming a little. She supposed it was due to the way he stared at her, that frank and unapologetic appraisal that was uncomfortably intimate. It was the writer in him, she told herself and dropped potatoes into the spitting grease.

"They're building a gallery here in Clare," she continued. "It'll be open in the spring. Here's porridge to start you off while the rest is cooking."

Porridge. It was perfect. A rainy morning in an Irish cottage and porridge in a thick brown bowl. Grinning, he sat down and began to eat.

"Are you setting a book here, in Ireland?" She glanced over her shoulder. "Is it all right to ask?"

"Sure. That's the plan. Lonely countryside, rainy fields, towering cliffs." He shrugged. "Tidy little villages. Postcards. But what passions and ambitions lie beneath."

Now she laughed, turning bacon. "I don't know if you'll find our village passions and ambitions up to your scope, Mr. Thane."

"Gray."

"Yes, Gray." She took an egg, broke it one-handed into the sizzling skillet. "Now, mine ran pretty high when one of Murphy's cows broke through the fence and trampled my roses last summer. And as I recall, Tommy Duggin and Joe Ryan had a bloody fistfight outside O'Malley's pub not long back."

"Over a woman?"

"No, over a soccer game on the television. But then, they were a wee bit drunk at the time, I'm told, and made it up well enough once their heads stopped ringing."

"Well, fiction's nothing but a lie anyway."

"But it's not." Her eyes, softly green and serious, met his as she set a plate in front of him. "It's a different kind of truth. It would be your truth at the time of the writing, wouldn't it?"

Her perception surprised and almost embarrassed him. "Yes. Yes, it would."

Satisfied, she turned back to the stove to heap sausage, a rasher of bacon, eggs, potato pancakes onto a platter. "You'll be a sensation in the village. We Irish are wild for writers, you know."

"I'm no Yeats."

She smiled, pleased when he transferred healthy portions of food onto his plate. "But you don't want to be, do you?"

He looked up, crunching into his first slice of bacon. Had she pegged him so accurately so quickly? he wondered. He, who prided himself on his own aura of mystery—no past, no future.

Before he could think of a response, the kitchen door crashed open and a whirlwind of rain and woman came in. "Some knothead left his car smack in the middle of the road outside the house, Brie." Maggie stopped, dragged off a dripping cap, and eyed Gray.

"Guilty," he said, lifting a hand. "I forgot. I'll move it."

"No rush now." She waved him back into his seat and dragged off her coat. "Finish your breakfast, I've time. You'd be the Yank writer, would you?"

"Twice guilty. And you'd be M. M. Concannon."

"I would."

"My sister, Maggie," Brianna said as she poured tea. "Grayson Thane."

Maggie sat with a little sigh of relief. The baby was kicking up a storm of its own. "A bit early, are you?"

"Change of plans." She was a sharper version of Brianna, Gray thought. Redder hair, greener eyes—edgier eyes. "Your sister was kind enough not to make me sleep in the yard."

"Oh, she's a kind one, Brie is." Maggie helped herself to a piece of the bacon on the platter. "Apple cake?" Maggie asked, sniffing the air.

"For tea." Brianna took one pan out of the oven, slipped another in. "You and Rogan are welcome to some."

"Maybe we'll come by." She took a bun from the basket on the table and began to nibble. "Plan to stay awhile, do you?"

"Maggie, don't harass my guest. I've some extra buns if you want to take some home."

"I'm not leaving yet. Rogan's on the phone, will be as far as I can tell until doomsday's come and gone. I was heading to the village for some bread."

"I've plenty to spare."

Maggie smiled, bit into the bun again. "I thought you might." She turned those sharp green eyes on Gray. "She bakes enough for the whole village."

"Artistic talent runs in the family," Gray said easily. After heaping strawberry jam on a piece of bread, he passed the jar companionably to Maggie. "You with glass, Brianna with cooking." Without shame, he eyed the cake cooling on top of the stove. "How long until tea?"

Maggie grinned at him. "I may like you."

"I may like you back." He rose. "I'll move the car."

"If you'd just pull it into the street."

He gave Brianna a blank look. "What street?"

"Beside the house—the driveway you'd call it. Will you need help with your luggage?"

"No, I can handle it. Nice to have met you, Maggie."

"And you." Maggie licked her fingers, waited until she heard the door shut. "Better to look at than his picture in back of his books."

"He is."

"You wouldn't think a writer would have a build like that—all tough and muscled."

Well aware Maggie was looking for a reaction, Brianna kept her back turned. "I suppose he's nicely put together. I wouldn't think a married woman going into her sixth month of pregnancy would pay his build much mind."

Maggie snorted. "I've a notion every woman would pay him mind. And if you haven't, we'd best be having more than your eyes checked."

"My eyes are fine, thank you. And aren't you the one who was worried about me being alone with him?"

"That was before I decided to like him."

With a little sigh Brianna glanced toward the kitchen doorway. She doubted she had much time. Brianna moistened her lips, kept her hands busy with tidying the breakfast dishes. "Maggie, I'd be glad if you could find time to come by later. I need to talk to you about something."

"Talk now."

"No, I can't." She glanced at the kitchen doorway. "We need to be private. It's important."

"You're upset."

"I don't know if I'm upset or not."

"Did he do something? The Yank?" Despite her bulk, Maggie was out of her chair and ready to fight.

"No, no. It's nothing to do with him." Exasperated, Brianna set her hands on her hips. "You just said you liked him."

"Not if he's upsetting you."

"Well, he's not. Don't press me about it now. Will you come by later, once I'm sure he's settled?"

"Of course I will." Concerned, Maggie brushed a hand over Brianna's shoulder. "Do you want Rogan to come?"

"If he can. Yes," Brianna decided, thinking of Maggie's condition. "Yes, please ask him to come with you."

"Before tea, then—two, three o'clock?"

"That would be good. Take the buns, Maggie, and the bread. I want to help Mr. Thane settle in."

There was nothing Brianna dreaded more than confrontations, angry words, bitter emotions. She had grown up in a house where the air had always simmered with them. Resentments boiling into blowups. Disappointments flashing into shouts. In defense she had always tried to keep her own feelings controlled, steering as far to the opposite pole as possible from the storms and rages that had served as her sister's shield to their parents' misery.

She could admit, to herself, that she had often wished to wake one morning and discover her parents had decided to ignore church and tradition and go their separate ways. But more often, too often, she had prayed for a miracle. The miracle of having her parents discover each other again, and reigniting the spark that had drawn them together so many years before.

Now, she understood, at least in part, why that miracle could never have happened. Amanda. The woman's name had been Amanda.

Had her mother known? Brianna wondered. Had she known that the husband she'd come to detest had loved another? Did she know there was a child, grown now, who was a result of that reckless, forbidden love?

She could never ask. Would never ask, Brianna promised herself. The horrible scene it would cause would be more than she could bear.

Already she had spent most of the day dreading sharing what she'd discovered with her sister. Knowing, for she knew Maggie well, that there would be hurt and anger and soul-deep disillusionment.

She'd put it off for hours. The coward's way, she knew, and it shamed her. But she told herself she needed time to settle her own heart before she could take on the burden of Maggie's.

Gray was the perfect distraction. Helping him settle into his room, answering his questions about the nearby villages and the countryside. And questions he had, by the dozen. By the time she pointed him off toward Ennis, she was exhausted. His mental energy was amazing, reminding her of a contortionist she'd once seen at a fair, twisting and turning himself into outrageous shapes, then popping out only to twist and turn again.

To relax, she got down on hands and knees and scrubbed the kitchen floor.

It was barely two when she heard Con's welcoming barks. The tea was steeping, her cakes frosted, and the little sandwiches she'd made cut into neat triangles. Brianna wrung her hands once, then opened the kitchen door to her sister and brother-in-law.

"Did you walk over, then?"

"Sweeney claims I need exercise." Maggie's face was rosy, her eyes dancing. She took one long, deep sniff of the air. "And I will, after tea."

"She's greedy these days." Rogan hung his coat and Maggie's on hooks by the door. He might have worn old trousers and sturdy walking shoes, but nothing could disguise what his wife would have termed the Dublin in him. Tall, dark, elegant, he would be in black tie or rags. "It's lucky you asked us for tea, Brianna. She's cleaned out our pantry."

"Well, we've plenty here. Go sit by the fire and I'll bring it out."

"We're not guests," Maggie objected. "The kitchen'll do for us."

"I've been in it all day." It was a lame excuse. There was no more appealing room in the house for her. But she wanted, needed, the formality of the parlor for what needed to be done. "And there's a nice fire laid."

"I'll take the tray," Rogan offered.

The minute they were settled in the parlor, Maggie reached for a cake.

"Take a sandwich," Rogan told her.

"He treats me more like a child than a woman who's carrying one." But she took the sandwich first. "I've been telling Rogan about your very attractive Yank. Long gold-tipped hair, sturdy muscles, and big brown eyes. Isn't he joining us for tea?"

"We're early for tea," Rogan pointed out. "I've read his books," he said to Brianna. "He has a clever way of plunging the reader into the turmoil."

"I know." She smiled a little. "I fell asleep last night with the light on. He's gone out for a drive, to Ennis and about. He was kind enough to post a letter for me." The easiest way, Brianna thought, was often through the back door. "I found some papers when I was up in the attic yesterday."

"Haven't we been through that business before?" Maggie asked.

"We left a lot of Da's boxes untouched. When Mother was here, it seemed best not to bring it up."

"She'd have done nothing but rant and rave." Maggie scowled into her tea. "You shouldn't have to go through his papers on your own, Brie."

"I don't mind. I've been thinking I might turn the attic into a loft room, for guests."

"More guests." Maggie rolled her eyes. "You're overrun with them now, spring and summer."

"I like having people in the house." It was an old argument, one they would never see through the same eyes. "At any rate, it was past time to go through things. There were some clothes as well, some no more than rags now. But I found this." She rose and went to a small box. She took out the lacy white gown. "It's Granny's work, I'm sure. Da would have saved it for his grandchildren."

"Oh." Everything about Maggie softened. Her eyes, her mouth, her voice. She held out her hands, took the gown into them. "So tiny," she murmured. Even as she stroked the linen, the baby inside her stirred.

"I thought your family might have one put aside as well, Rogan, but—"

"We'll use this. Thank you, Brie." One look at his wife's face had decided him. "Here, Margaret Mary."

Maggie took the handkerchief he offered and wiped her eyes. "The books say it's hormones. I always seem to be spilling over."

"I'll put it back for you." After replacing the gown, Brianna took the next step and offered the stock certificate. "I found this as well. Da must have bought it, or invested, whatever it is, shortly before he died."

A glance at the paper had Maggie sighing. "Another of his moneymaking schemes." She was nearly as sentimental over the stock certificate as she'd been over the baby gown. "How like him. So he thought he'd go into mining, did he?"

"Well, he'd tried everything else."

Rogan frowned over the certificate. "Would you like me to look into this company, see what's what?"

"I've written to them. Mr. Thane's posting the letter for me. It'll come to nothing, I imagine." None of Tom Concannon's schemes ever had. "But you might keep the paper for me until I hear back."

"It's ten thousand shares," Rogan pointed out.

Maggie and Brianna smiled at each other. "And if it's worth more than the paper it's printed on, he'll have broken his record." Maggie shrugged and treated herself to a cake. "He was always after investing in something, or starting a new business. It was his dreams that were big, Rogan, and his heart."

Brianna's smile dimmed. "I found something else. Something I need to show you. Letters."

"He was famous for writing them."

"No," Brianna interrupted before Maggie could launch into one of her stories. Do it now, she ordered herself when her heart shied back. Do it quickly. "These were written to him. There are three of them, and I think it's best if you read them for yourself."

Maggie could see Brianna's eyes had gone cool and remote. A defense, she knew, against anything from temper to heartache. "All right, Brie."

Saying nothing, Brianna picked up the letters, put them in Maggie's hand.

Maggie had only to look at the return address on the first envelope for her heartbeat to thicken. She opened the letter.

Brianna heard the quick sound of distress. The fingers she'd locked together twisted. She saw Maggie reach out, grip Rogan's hand. A change, Brianna thought with a little sigh. Even a year before Maggie would have slapped any comforting hand aside.

"Amanda." There were tears in Maggie's voice. "It was Amanda he said before he died. Standing there at the cliffs at Loop Head, at that spot he loved so much. We would go there and he would joke about how we'd hop in a boat and our next stop would be a pub in New York." Now the tears spilled over. "In New York. Amanda was in New York."

"He said her name." Brianna's fingers went to her mouth. She stopped herself, barely, before she gave into her childhood habit of gnawing her nails. "I remember now that you said something about that at his wake. Did he say anything more, tell you anything about her?"

"He said nothing but her name." Maggie dashed at tears with a furious hand. "He said nothing then, nothing ever. He loved her, but he did nothing about it."

"What could he do?" Brianna asked. "Maggie—"

"Something." There were more tears and more fury when Maggie lifted her head. "Anything. Sweet Jesus, he spent his life in hell. Why? Because the Church says it's a sin to do otherwise. Well, he'd sinned already, hadn't he? He'd committed adultery. Do I blame him for that? I don't know that I can, remembering what he faced in this house. But by God, couldn't he have followed through on it? Couldn't he have finally followed through?"

"He stayed for us." Brianna's voice was tight and cold. "You know he stayed for us."

"Is that supposed to make me grateful?"

"Will you blame him for loving you?" Rogan asked quietly. "Or condemn him for loving someone else?"

Her eyes flashed. But the bitterness that rose up in her throat died into grief. "No, I'll do neither. But he should have had more than memories."

"Read the others, Maggie."

"I will. You were barely born when these were written," she said as she opened the second letter.

"I know," Brianna said dully.

"I think she loved him very much. There's a kindness here. It isn't so much to ask, love, kindness." Maggie looked at Brianna then, for some sign. She saw nothing but that same cool detachment. With a sigh, she opened the final letter while Brianna sat stiff and cold. "I only wish he . . ." Her words faltered. "Oh, my God. A baby." Instinctively her hand went to cover her own. "She was pregnant."

"We have a brother or sister somewhere. I don't know what to do."

Shock and fury had Maggie lurching to her feet. Teacups rattled as she pushed back to stalk around the room. "What to do? It's been done, hasn't it? Twenty-eight years ago to be exact."

Distressed, Brianna started to rise, but Rogan covered her hand. "Let her go," he murmured. "She'll be better for it after."

"What right did she have to tell him this and then go away?" Maggie demanded. "What right did he have to let her? And now, are you thinking it falls to us? To us to follow it through? This isn't some abandoned fatherless child we're speaking of now, Brianna, but a person grown. What have they to do with us?"

"Our father, Maggie. Our family."

"Oh, aye, the Concannon family. God help us." Overwhelmed, she leaned against the mantel, staring blindly into the fire. "Was he so weak, then?"

"We don't know what he did, or could have done. We may never know." Brianna took a careful breath. "If Mother had known—"

Maggie interrupted with a short, bitter laugh. "She didn't. Do you think she wouldn't have used a weapon like this to beat him into the ground? God knows she used everything else."

"Then there's no point in telling her now, is there?"

Slowly Maggie turned. "You want to say nothing?"

"To her. What purpose would it serve to hurt her?"

Maggie's mouth thinned. "You think it would?"

"Are you so sure it wouldn't?"

The fire went out in Maggie as quickly as it had flared. "I don't know. How can I know? I feel as if they're both strangers now."

"He loved you, Maggie." Rogan rose now to go to her. "You know that."

"I know that." She let herself lean. "But I don't know what I feel."

"I think we should try to find Amanda Dougherty," Brianna began, "and—"

"I can't think." Maggie closed her eyes. There were too many emotions battering inside her to allow her to see, as she wanted, the right direction to take. "I need to think about this, Brie. It's rested this long. It can rest awhile longer."

"I'm sorry, Maggie."

"Don't take this on your shoulders as well." A bit of the bite and briskness came back into Maggie's voice. "They're burdened enough. Give me a few days, Brie, then we'll decide together what's to be done."

"All right."

"I'd like to keep the letters, for now."

"Of course."

Maggie crossed over, laid a hand on Brianna's pale cheek. "He loved you, too, Brie."

"In his way."

"In every way. You were his angel, his cool rose. Don't worry. We'll find a way to do what's best."

Gray didn't mind when the leaden sky began to spit rain again. He stood on a parapet of a ruined castle looking out on a sluggish river. Wind whistled and moaned through chinks in the stone. He might have been alone, not simply in this spot, but in this country, in the world.

It was, he decided, the perfect place for murder.

The victim could be lured here, could be pursued up ancient winding stone steps, could flee helplessly up, until any crumb of hope would dissolve. There would be no escape.

Here, where old blood had been spilled, where it seeped into stone and earth so deep, yet not so deep, fresh murder would be done. Not for God, not for country. But for pleasure.

Gray already knew his villain, could picture him there, slicing down so that the edge of his knife glinted silver in the dull light. He knew his victim, the terror and the pain. The hero, and the woman he would love, were as clear to Gray as the slow run of the river below.

And he knew he would have to begin soon to create them with words. There was nothing he enjoyed in writing more than making his people breathe, giving them flesh and blood. Discovering their backgrounds, their hidden fears, every twist and turn of their pasts.

It was, perhaps, because he had no past of his own. He had made himself, layer by layer, as skillfully and as meticulously as he crafted his characters. Grayson Thane was who he had decided to be, and his skill in storytelling had provided a means to become who and what he wanted, in some style.

He would never consider himself a modest man, but considered himself no more than a competent writer, a spinner of tales. He wrote to entertain himself first, and acknowledged his luck in hitting some chord in the public.

Brianna had been right. He had no desire to be a Yeats. Being a good writer meant he could make a living and do as he chose. Being a great one would bring responsibilities and expectations he had no desire to face. What Gray didn't choose to face, he simply turned his back on.

But there were times, such as this, when he wondered what it might be like to have roots, ancestry, a full-blooded devotion to family or country. The people who had built this castle that still stood, those who had fought there, died there. What had they felt? What had they wished for? And how could battles fought so long ago still ring, as clear as the fatal music of sword against sword, in the air?

He'd chosen Ireland for this, for the history, for the people whose memories were long and roots were deep. For people, he admitted, like Brianna Concannon.

It was an odd and interesting bonus that she should be so much what he was looking for in his heroine.

Physically she was perfect. That soft, luminous beauty, the simple grace and quiet manner. But beneath the shell, in contrast to that open-handed hospitality, was a remoteness, and a sadness. Complexities, he thought, letting the rain slap his cheeks. He enjoyed nothing better than contrasts and complexities—puzzles to be solved. What had put that haunted look in her eyes, that defensive coolness in her manner?

It would be interesting to find out.

THREE

He thought she was out when he came back. As focused as a hound on a scent, Gray headed to the kitchen. It was her voice that stopped him—soft, quiet, and icy. Without giving a thought to the ethics of eavesdropping, he shifted and moved to the doorway of the parlor.

He could see her on the phone. Her hand twisted in the cord, a gesture of anger or nerves. He couldn't see her face, but the stiff set of her back and shoulders was indication enough of her mood.

"I've just come in, Mother. I had to pick up a few things in the village. I've a guest."

There was a pause, Gray watched as Brianna lifted a hand, rubbed it hard at her temple.

"Yes, I know. I'm sorry it upsets you. I'll come around tomorrow. I can—"

She broke off, obviously interrupted by some sharp comment on the other end of the phone. Gray pushed back an urge to move into the room and soothe those tensed shoulders.

"I'll take you wherever you want to go tomorrow. I never said I was too busy, and I'm sorry you're not feeling well. I'll do the marketing, yes, it's no problem. Before noon, I promise. I have to go now. I have cakes in the oven. I'll bring you some, shall I? Tomorrow, Mother, I promise." She muttered a good-bye and turned. The weary distress on her face turned to shock when she saw Gray, then a flush crept into her cheeks. "You move quietly," she said with the faintest trace of annoyance in the tone. "I didn't hear you come in."

"I didn't want to interrupt." He had no shame about listening to her conversation, nor about watching her varying reactions flicker over her face. "Your mother lives nearby?"

"Not far." Her voice was clipped now, edged with the anger that stirred inside her. He'd listened to her personal misery and didn't think it important enough to apologize for. "I'll get your tea now."

"No hurry. You've got cakes in the oven."

She leveled her eyes at his. "I lied. I should tell you that I open my home to you, but not my private life."

He acknowledged this with a nod. "I should tell you, I always pry. You're upset, Brianna. Maybe you should have some tea."

"I've had mine, thank you." Her shoulders remained stiff as she crossed the room and started to move past him. He stopped her with the faintest of brushes of his hand on her arm. There was curiosity in his eyes—and she resented it. There was sympathy—she didn't want it.

"Most writers have as open an ear as a good bartender."

She shifted. It was only the slightest movement, but it put distance between them, and made her point. "I've always wondered about people who find it necessary to tell their personal problems to the man who serves them ale. I'll bring your tea into the parlor. I've too much to do in the kitchen for company."

Gray ran his tongue around his teeth as she walked away. He had, he knew, been put ever so completely in his place.

Brianna couldn't fault the American for curiosity. She had plenty of her own. She enjoyed finding out about the people who passed through her home, hearing them talk about their lives and their families. It might have been unfair, but she preferred not to discuss hers. Much more comfortable was the role of onlooker. It was safer that way.

But she wasn't angry with him. Experience had taught her that temper solved nothing. Patience, manners, and a quiet tone were more effective shields, and weapons against most confrontations. They had served her well through the evening meal, and by the end of it, it seemed to her that she and Gray had resumed their proper positions of landlandy and guest. His casual invitation to join him at the village pub had been just as casually refused. Brianna had spent a pleasant hour finishing his book.

Now, with breakfast served and the dishes done, she prepared to drive to her mother's and devote the rest of the morning to Maeve. Maggie would be annoyed to hear it, Brianna thought. But her sister didn't understand that it was easier, certainly less stressful to simply meet their mother's need for time and attention. Inconvenience aside, it was only a few hours out of her life.

Hardly a year earlier, before Maggie's success had made it possible to set Maeve up with a companion in her own home, Brianna had been at her beck and call twenty-four hours a day, tending to imaginary illnesses, listening to complaints on her own shortcomings.

And being reminded, time after time, that Maeve had done her duty by giving Brianna life.

What Maggie couldn't understand, and what Brianna continued to be guilty about, was that she was willing to pay any price for the serenity of being the sole mistress of Blackthorn Cottage.

And today the sun was shining. There was a teasing hint of far-off spring in the mild breeze. It wouldn't last, Brianna knew. That made the luminous light and soft air all the more precious. To enjoy it more fully, she rolled down the windows of her ancient Fiat. She would have to roll them up again and turn on the sluggish heater when her mother joined her.

She glanced over at the pretty little Mercedes Gray had leased—not in envy. Or perhaps with just the slightest twinge of envy. It was so efficiently flashy and sleek. And suited its driver, she mused, perfectly. She wondered what it would be like to sit behind the wheel, just for a moment or two.

Almost in apology she patted the steering wheel of her Fiat before turning the key. The engine strained, grumbled, and coughed.

"Ah, now, I didn't mean it," she murmured and tried the key again. "Come on, sweetheart, catch hold, will you? She hates it when I'm late."

But the engine merely stuttered, then died off with a moan. Resigned,

Brianna got out and lifted the hood. She knew the Fiat often displayed the temperament of a cranky old woman. Most usually she could coax it along with a few strokes or taps with the tools she carried in the trunk.

She was hauling out a dented toolbox when Gray strolled out the front door.

"Car trouble?" he called.

"She's temperamental." Brianna tossed back her hair and pushed up the sleeves of her sweater. "Just needs a bit of attention."

Thumbs tucked in the front pocket of his jeans, he crossed over, glanced under the hood. It wasn't a swagger—but it was close. "Want me to take a look?"

She eyed him. He still hadn't shaved. The stubble should have made him look unkempt and sloppy. Instead, the combination of it and the gold-tipped hair pulled back in a stubby ponytail fit Brianna's image of an American rock star. The idea made her smile.

"Do you know about cars then, or are you offering because you think you should—being male, that is."

His brow shot up, and his lips quirked as he took the toolbox from her. He had to admit he was relieved she wasn't angry with him any longer.

"Step back, little lady," he drawled in a voice thick with the rural South. "And don't worry that pretty head of yours. Let a man handle this."

Impressed, she tilted her head. "You sounded just as I imagined Buck sounded in your book."

"You've a good ear." He flashed her a grin before he ducked under the hood. "He was a pompous red-necked ass, wasn't he?"

"Mmm." She wasn't sure, even though they were discussing a fictional character, if it was polite to agree. "Usually it's the carburetor," she began. "Murphy promised to rebuild it when he has a few hours to spare."

Already head and shoulders under the hood, Gray simply turned his head and gave her a dry look. "Well, Murphy's not here, is he?"

She had to admit he was not. Brianna bit her lip as she watched Gray work. She appreciated the offer, truly she did. But the man was a writer, not a mechanic. She couldn't afford to have him, with all good intentions, damage something.

"Usually if I just prop open that hinge thing there with a stick"—to show him, she leaned in alongside Gray and pointed—"then I get in and start it."

He turned his head again, was eye to eye and mouth to mouth with her. She smelled glorious, as fresh and clean as the morning. As he stared, color flushed into her cheeks, her eyes widened fractionally. Her quick and obviously unplanned reaction to him might have made him smile, if his system hadn't been so busy going haywire.

"It's not the carburetor this time," he said and wondered what she would do if he pressed his lips just where the pulse in her throat was jumping.

"No?" She couldn't have moved if her life had been threatened. His eyes had gold in them, she thought foolishly, gold streaks along the brown, just as he had in his hair. She fought to get a breath in and out. "Usually it is."

He shifted, a test for both of them, until their shoulders brushed. Those lovely eyes of hers clouded with confusion, like a sea under uncertain skies. "This time it's the battery cables. They're corroded."

"It's . . . been a damp winter."

If he leaned just the slightest bit toward her now, his mouth would be on hers. The thought of it shot straight to her stomach, flipped over. It would be rough—he would be rough, she was certain. Would he kiss like the hero in the book she had finished the night before? With teeth nipping, tongue thrusting? All fierce demand and wild urgency while his hands . . .

Oh, God. She'd been wrong, Brianna discovered. She could move if her life was threatened. If felt as if it had been, though he hadn't moved, hadn't so much as blinked. Giddy from her own imagination, she jerked back, only to make a small, distressed sound in her throat when he moved with her.

They stood, almost embracing, in the sunlight.

What would he do? she wondered. What would *she* do?

He wasn't sure why he resisted. Perhaps it was the subtle waves of fear vibrating from her. It might have been the shock of discovering he had his own fear, compressed in a small tight ball in the pit of his stomach.

It was he who took a step back, a very vital step back.

"I'll clean them off for you," he said. "And we'll try her again."

Her hands reached for each other until her fingers were linked. "Thank you. I should go in and call my mother, let her know I'll be a little late."

"Brianna." He waited until she stopped retreating, until her eyes lifted to his again. "You have an incredibly appealing face."

As compliments went, she wasn't sure how this one fit. She nodded. "Thank you. I like yours."

He cocked his head. "Just how careful do you want to be about this?"

It took her a moment to understand, and another to find her voice. "Very," she managed. "I think very."

Gray watched her disappear into the house before he turned back to the job at hand. "I was afraid of that," he muttered.

Once she was on her way—the Fiat's engine definitely needed an overhaul—Gray took a long walk over the fields. He told himself he was absorbing atmosphere, researching, priming himself to work. It was a pity he knew himself well enough to understand he was working off his response to Brianna.

A normal response, he assured himself. She was, after all, a beautiful woman. And he hadn't been with a woman at all for some time. If his libido was revving, it was only to be expected.

There had been a woman, an associate with his publishing house in England, whom he might have tumbled for. Briefly. But he'd suspected that she'd been much more interested in how their relationship might have advanced her career than in enjoying the moment. It had been distressingly easy for him to keep their relationship from becoming intimate.

He was becoming jaded, he supposed. Success could do that to you. Whatever pleasure and pride it brought carried a price. A growing lack of trust, a more jaundiced eye. It rarely bothered him. How could it when trust had never been his strong point in any case? Better, he thought, to see things as they were rather than as you wanted them to be. Save the *I wants* for fiction.

He could turn his reaction to Brianna around just that way. She would be his prototype for his heroine. The lovely, serene, and composed woman, with secrets in her eyes and ice floes, banked fires, and conflicts stirring beneath the shell.

What made her tick? What did she dream of? What did she fear? Those were questions he would answer as he built a woman out of words and imagination.

Was she jealous of her stunningly successful sister? Did she resent her demanding mother? Was there a man she wanted and who wanted her?

Those were questions he needed to answer as he discovered Brianna Concannon.

Gray began to think he would need to combine them all before he could tell his tale.

He smiled to himself as he walked. He would tell himself that, he thought, because he wanted to know. And he had no qualms whatsoever about prying into someone's private thoughts and experiences. And no guilt about hording his own.

He stopped, turned a slow circle as he looked around him. Now this, he decided, was a place a person could lose himself in. Roll after roll of glistening green fields bisected with gray stone walls, dotted with fat cows. The morning was so clear, so shining, that he could see the glint of window glass in cottages in the distance, the flap of clothes hung out on lines to dry in the breeze.

Overhead the sky was a bowl of swimming blue—postcard perfect. Yet already, at the west rim of that bowl, clouds were swarming together; their purple-edged tips threatened storm.

Here, in what seemed to be the center of a crystalized world, he could smell grass and cow, hints of the sea carried on the air, and the faint, faint scent of smoke from a cottage chimney. There was the sound of wind in the grass, the swish of cows' tails, and the steady trumpet of a bird who celebrated the day.

He almost felt guilty about bringing even fictional murder and mayhem to such a place. Almost.

He had six months, Gray thought. Six months before his next book hit the stands and he flung himself, as cheerfully as possible, into the fun house ride of book tours and press. Six months to create the story that was already growing inside his head. Six months to enjoy this little spot in the world, and the people in it.

Then he would leave it, as he had left dozens of other spots, hundreds of other people, and go on to the next. Going on was something he excelled at.

Gray swung over a wall and crossed the next field.

The circle of stones caught his eye and his imagination immediately. He had seen greater monuments, had stood in the shadow of Stonehenge and felt the power. This dance was hardly more than eight feet, the king stone no taller than a man. But finding it here, standing silent among grazing, disinterested cows, seemed wonderful to him.

Who had built it, and why? Fascinated, Gray rounded the outside circumference first. Only two of the lintels remained in place, the others having fallen off in some long-ago night. At least he hoped it had been at night, during a storm, and the sound of them crashing to earth would have vibrated like a roar of a god.

He laid a hand on the king stone. It was warm from the sun, but carried an underlying iciness that thrilled. Could he use this, he wondered? Somehow weave this place and the echoes of ancient magic into his book?

Would there be murder done here? He stepped into the circle, into the center. A sacrifice of sorts, he mused. A self-serving ritual where blood would splash the thriving green grass, stain the base of the stones.

Or perhaps it would be love done here. A desperate and greedy tangle of limbs—the grass cool and damp beneath, the full white moon swimming overhead. The stones standing guard as the man and woman lost themselves in need.

He could imagine both with equal clarity. But the second appealed more, so much more, he could all but see Brianna lying on the grass, her hair fanned out, her arms lifted up. Her skin would be pale as milk, soft as water.

Her slim hips would arch, her slender back bow. And when he drove himself into her, she would cry out. Those neat, rounded nails would score his back. Her body would plunge like a mustang under his, faster, deeper, stronger, until . . .

"Good morning to you."

"Jesus." Gray jolted back. His breathing was unsteady, his mouth dust dry. Later, he promised himself, later it would be amusing, but for now he fought to rip himself out of erotic fantasy and focus on the man approaching the circle of stones.

He was dark, strikingly handsome, dressed in the rough, sturdy clothes of a farmer. Perhaps thirty, Gray judged, one of the stunning Black Irish who claimed jet hair and cobalt eyes. The eyes seemed friendly enough, a little amused.

Brianna's dog was prancing happily at his heels. Recognizing Gray, Con galloped into the circle to greet him.

"An interesting spot," the man said in a musical west county brogue.

"I didn't expect to find it here." Rubbing Con's head, Gray came through a space between stones. "It isn't listed on any of the tourist maps I have."

"It isn't, no. It's our dance, you see, but we don't mind sharing it occasionally. You'd be Brie's Yank." He offered a big, work-roughened hand. "I'm Murphy Muldoon."

"Of the rose-trampling cows."

Murphy winced. "Christ, she'll never forget it. And didn't I replace every last bush? You'd think the cows had stepped on her firstborn." He looked down at Con for support. The dog sat, tilted his head, and kept his own counsel. "You've settled into Blackthorn, then?"

"Yes. I'm trying to get a feel for the area." Gray glanced around again. "I guess I crossed over onto your land."

"We don't shoot trespassers often these days," Murphy said easily.

"Glad to hear it." Gray studied his companion again. There was something solid here, he thought, and easily approachable. "I was in the village pub last night, O'Malley's, had a beer with a man named Rooney."

"You mean you bought him a pint." Murphy grinned.

"Two." Gray grinned back. "He earned them, with the payment of village gossip."

"Some of which was probably truth." Murphy took out a cigarette, offered one.

After shaking his head, Gray tucked his hands in his pockets. He only smoked when he was writing. "I believe your name was mentioned."

"I won't doubt you."

"What young Murphy is missing," Gray began in such a deadly mimic of Rooney that Murphy snorted with laughter, "is a good wife and strong sons to be working the land with him. He's after perfection, is Murphy, so he's spending his nights alone in a cold bed."

"This from Rooney who spends most of his nights in the pub complaining that his wife drives him to drink."

"He did mention that." Gray eased into the question he was most interested in. "And that since the jackeen had snapped Maggie out from under your nose, you'd be courting her younger sister before long."

"Brie?" Murphy shook his head as he expelled smoke. "It'd be like cuddling my baby sister." He smiled still, but his eyes were sharp on Gray's. "Is that what you wanted to know, Mr. Thane?"

"Gray. Yes, that's what I wanted to know."

"Then I'll tell you the way's clear there. But mind your step. I'm protective of my sisters." Satisfied his point was made, Murphy took another comfortable drag. "You're welcome to come back to the house for a cup of tea."

"I appreciate the offer, but I'll take a raincheck. There are things I need to get done today."

"Well, then, I'll let you get to them. I enjoy your books," he said in such an offhand way that Gray was doubly complimented. "There's a bookstore in Galway you may like to visit if you travel that way."

"I intend to."

"You'll find it then. Give my best to Brianna, will you? And you might mention that I've not a scone left in my pantry." His grin flashed. " 'Twill make her feel sorry for me."

After whistling for the dog who fell into place beside him, he walked away with the easy grace of a man crossing his own land.

It was midafternoon when Brianna returned home, frazzled, drained, and tense. She was grateful to find no trace of Gray but for a note hastily scrawled and left on her kitchen table.

Maggie called. Murphy's out of scones.

An odd message, she thought. Why would Maggie call to tell her Murphy wanted scones? With a sigh Brianna set the note aside. Automatically she put on the kettle for tea before setting out the ingredients she needed to go with the free-range chicken she'd found—like a prize—at the market.

Then she sighed, gave in. Sitting down again, she folded her arms on the table, laid her head on them. She didn't weep. Tears wouldn't help, wouldn't change anything. It had been one of Maeve's bad days, full of snipes and complaints and accusations. Maybe the bad days were harder now, because over the last year or so there had been nearly as many good ones.

Maeve loved her little house, whether or not she ever admitted to it. She was fond of Lottie Sullivan, the retired nurse Brianna and Maggie had hired as her companion. Though the devil would never be able to drag that simple truth from Maeve's lips. She had found as much contentment as Brianna imagined she was capable of.

But Maeve never forgot, never, that Brianna was responsible for nearly every bite of bread their mother enjoyed. And Maeve could never seem to stop resenting that.

This had been one of the days when Maeve had paid her younger daughter back by finding fault with everything. With the added strain of the letters Brianna had found, she was simply exhausted.

She closed her eyes and indulged herself for a moment by wishing. She wished her mother could be happy. She wished Maeve could recapture whatever joy and pleasure she'd had in her youth. She wished, oh, she wished most of all that she could love her mother with an open and generous heart instead of with cold duty and dragging dispair.

And she wished for family, for her home to be filled with love and voices and laughter. Not simply for the transient guests who came and went, but for permanence.

And, Brianna thought, if wishes were pennies, we'd all be as rich as Midas. She pushed back from the table, knowing the fatigue and depression would fade once she began to work.

Gray would have a fine roast chicken for dinner, stuffed with herbed bread and ladeled with rich gravy.

And Murphy, bless him, would have his scones.

FOUR

In a matter of days Brianna had grown accustomed to Gray's routine and adjusted her schedule accordingly. He liked to eat, rarely missing a meal—though she soon discovered he had little respect for timetables. She understood he was hungry when he began to haunt her kitchen. Whatever the time, she fixed him a plate. And had to admit she appreciated watching him enjoy her cooking.

Most days he went out on what she thought of as his rambles. If he asked, she gave him directions, or made suggestions on some sight he might like to see. But usually he set out with a map, a notebook, and a camera.

She saw to his rooms when he was out. Anyone who tidies up after another begins to learn things. Brianna discovered Grayson Thane was neat enough when it came to what belonged to her. Her good guest towels were never tossed on the floor in a damp heap; there were never any wet rings on her furniture from a forgotten glass or cup. But he had a careless disregard for what he owned. He might scrape off his boots before he came in out of the mud and onto her floors. Yet he never cleaned the expensive leather or bothered to polish them.

So she did it herself.

His clothes carried labels from fine shops around the world. But they were never pressed and were often tossed negligently over a chair or hung crookedly in the wardrobe.

She began to add his laundry to her own, and had to admit it was pleasant to hang his shirts on the line when the day was sunny.

He kept no mementos of friends or family, made no attempt to personalize the room he now lived in. There were books, boxes of them—mysteries, horror novels, spy thrillers, romances, classics, nonfiction books on police procedures, weapons and murder, psychology, mythology, witchcraft, auto mechanics—that made her smile—and subjects as varied as architecture and zoology.

There seemed to be nothing that didn't interest him.

She knew he preferred coffee but would drink tea in a pinch if it was strong enough. He had the sweet tooth of a ten-year-old boy—and the energy of one.

He was nosy—there was to be no question he wouldn't ask. But there was an innate kindness in him that made him hard to rebuff. He never failed to offer to do some chore or errand for her—and she'd seen him sneaking tidbits of food to Con when he thought she wasn't looking.

All in all, it was an excellent arrangement—he provided her company, income, and the work she loved. She gave him a smoothly running base. Yet she could never quite relax around him. He had never referred to that one moment of mind-numbing attraction between them. But it was there—in the way her pulse jumped if she walked into a room and found him there unexpectedly. In the way her body heated when he turned those gilded eyes in her direction and simply looked at her.

Brianna blamed herself for it. It had been a long, long time since she had been deeply attracted to a man. Not since Rory McAvery had left her with a scar on her heart and a hole in her life had she felt such a wicked stirring for any man.

Since she was feeling it for a guest, Brianna had decided it was her responsibility to still it.

But as she smoothed the quilt on his bed, fluffed his pillows, she wondered where his ramblings were taking him today.

He hadn't gone far. Gray had decided to travel on foot that morning and wandered down the narrow road under gloomy, threatening skies. He passed a couple of outbuildings, saw a tractor shelter, hay bales stacked out of the weather. Murphy's, he imagined and began to wonder what it would be like to be a farmer.

Owning land, he mused, being responsible for it. Plowing, planting, tending, watching things grow. Keeping an eye on the sky, sniffing the air for a turn in the weather.

Not a life for Grayson Thane, he thought, but imagined some would find it rewarding. There'd been that simple pride of ownership in Murphy Muldoon's walk—a man who knew his feet were planted on his own.

But owning land—or anything—meant being tied to it. He'd have to ask Murphy how he felt about that.

Gray could see the valley from this spot, and the rise of hills. From the distance came the quick, happy bark of a dog. Con, perhaps, out looking for adventure before heading home to lay his head in Brianna's lap.

Gray had to envy the dog the privilege.

Grimacing, Gray tucked his hands in his pockets. He'd been working hard to keep those hands off his subtly sexy landlady.

He told himself she didn't wear those prim aprons or pin her hair up in those fall-away knots to charm him. But it worked. It was unlikely she fussed around the house smelling of wildflowers and cloves to drive him crazy. But he was suffering.

Beyond the physical—which was difficult enough—there was that air of secrets and sadness. He'd yet to slip through that thin wall of reserve and discover what was troubling her. Whatever it was haunted her eyes.

Not that he intended to get involved, Gray assured himself. He was just curious. Making friends was something he did easily by way of sincere interest and a sympathetic nature. But close friends, the kind a man kept in touch with through the years, worried over, missed when he was away, weren't in the master plan.

Grayson Thane traveled light, and he traveled frequently.

The little cottage with the boldly painted front door had Gray pausing. An addition had been framed in on the south side that was as big as the original house. The earth that had been displaced was now a hill of mud that would have delighted any five-year-old.

The little place down the road? he wondered. Where Brianna's sister and brother-in-law lived from time to time? He decided the magenta door was Maggie's doing and went through the gate for a closer look.

For the next few minutes he pleased himself poking through the new construction. Someone knew what they were doing here, he thought. The frame was sturdy, the materials top of the line. Adding on for the baby, he assumed, working his way to the rear. It was then he spotted the building out in the back.

Her glass shop. Pleased with his new discovery, he stepped off the planking and crossed the dew-dampened lawn. Once he reached it, Gray cupped his hands against the window and peered in. He could see furnaces, benches, tools that whetted his curiosity and imagination. Shelves were loaded with works in progress. Without a qualm he stepped back and reached for the door.

"Are you wanting your fingers broken?"

He turned. Maggie stood in the rear doorway of the cottage, a steaming cup in one hand. She wore a bagging sweater, worn cords, and a scowl. Gray grinned at her.

"Not especially. Is this where you work?"

"It is. How do you treat people who pop uninvited into your studio?"

"I haven't got a studio. How about a tour?"

She didn't bother to muffle the oath, or the sigh. "You're a bold one, aren't you? All right, then, since I don't seem to be doing anything else. The man goes off," she complained as she crossed the grass. "Doesn't even wake me. Leaves me a note is all he does, telling me to eat a decent breakfast and keep my feet up."

"And did you?"

"I might have if I hadn't heard somebody tramping around my property."

"Sorry." But still he grinned at her. "When's the baby due?"

"In the spring." Despite herself she softened. It took only the mention of the baby. "I've weeks yet, and if the man keeps trying to pamper me, I'll have to murder him. Well, come in, then, since you're here."

"I see that gracious hospitality runs in the family."

"It doesn't." Now a smile tugged at her lips. "Brianna got all the niceness. Look," she said as she opened the door. "Don't touch, or I will break those fingers."

"Yes, ma'am. This is great." He started to explore the minute he stepped in, moving to the benches, bending down to check out the furnace. "You studied in Venice, didn't you?"

"I did, yes."

"What started you off? God, I hate when people ask me that. Never mind." He laughed at himself and strolled toward her pipes. His fingers itched to touch. Cautious, he looked back at her, measured. "I'm bigger than you."

She nodded. "I'm meaner." But she relented enough to take up a pontil herself and hand it to him.

He hefted it, twirled it. "Great murder weapon."

"I'll keep that in mind the next time someone interrupts my work."

"So what's the process?" He glanced toward drawings spread out on a bench. "You sketch out ideas?"

"Often." She sipped at her tea, eyeing him. In truth, there was something about the way he moved, light and fluid without any fuss, that made her yearn for her sketchpad. "After a quick lesson?"

"Always. It must get pretty hot in here when the furnaces are fired. You melt the stuff in there, and then what?"

"I make a gather," she began. For the next thirty minutes she took him step by step through the process of hand-blowing a vessel.

The man was full of questions, she thought. Intriguing questions, she admitted, the kind that made you go beyond the technical processes and into the creative purpose behind them. She might have been able to resist that, but his enthusiasm was more difficult. Instead of hurrying him along, she found herself answering those questions, demonstrating, and laughing with him.

"Keep this up and I'll draft you as pontil boy." Amused, she rubbed a hand over her belly. "Well, come in and have some tea."

"You wouldn't have any of Brianna's cookies—biscuits."

Maggie's brow arched. "I do."

A few moments later Gray was settled at Maggie's kitchen table with a plate of gingersnaps. "I swear she could market these," he said with his mouth full. "Make a fortune."

"She'd rather give them to the village children."

"I'm surprised she doesn't have a brood of her own." He waited a beat. "I haven't noticed any man coming around."

"And you're the noticing sort, aren't you, Grayson Thane?"

"Goes with the territory. She's a beautiful woman."

"I won't disagree." Maggie poured boiling water into a warmed teapot.

"You're going to make me yank it out," he muttered. "Is there someone or not?"

"You could ask her yourself." Miffed, Maggie set the pot on the table, frowned at him. Oh, he had a talent, she thought, for making you want to tell him what he wanted to know. "No," she snapped out and slapped a mug on the table in front of him. "There's no one. She brushes them off, freezes them out. She'd rather spend all her time tending to her guests or running out to Ennis every time our mother sniffles. Self-sacrificing is what our Saint Brianna does best."

"You're worried about her," Gray murmured. "What's troubling her, Maggie?"

" 'Tis family business. Let it alone." Belatedly she poured his cup, then her own. She sighed then, and sat. "How do you know she's troubled?"

"It shows. In her eyes. Just like it's showing in yours now."

"It'll be settled soon enough." Maggie made a determined effort to push it aside. "Do you always dig into people?"

"Sure." He tried the tea. It was strong enough to stand up and dance. Perfect. "Being a writer's a great cover for just being nosy." Then his eyes changed, sobered. "I like her. It's impossible not to. It bothers me to see her sad."

"She can use a friend. You've a talent for getting people to talk. Use it on her. But mind," she added before Gray could speak, "she's soft feelings underneath. Bruise them, and I'll bruise you."

"Point taken." And time, he thought, to change the subject. He kicked back, propping a booted foot on his knee. "So, what's the story with our pal Murphy? Did the guy from Dublin really steal you out from under his nose?"

It was fortunate that she'd swallowed her tea, or she might have choked. Her laugh started deep and grew into guffaws that had her eyes watering.

"I missed a joke," Rogan said from the doorway. "Take a breath, Maggie, you're turning red."

"Sweeney." She sucked in a giggling breath and reached for his hand. "This is Grayson Thane. He was wondering if you stepped over Murphy's back to woo me."

"Not Murphy's," Rogan said pleasantly, "but I had to step all over

Maggie's—ending with her head, which needed some sense knocked into it. It's nice meeting you," he added, offering Gray his free hand. "I've spent many entertaining hours in your stories."

"Thanks."

"Gray's been keeping me company," Maggie told him. "And now I'm in too fine a mood to yell at you for not waking me this morning."

"You needed sleep." He poured tea, winced after the first sip. "Christ, Maggie, must you always brew it to death?"

"Yes." She leaned forward, propped her chin on her hand. "What part of America are you from, Gray?"

"No part in particular. I move around."

"But your home?"

"I don't have one." He bit into another cookie. "I don't need one with the way I travel."

The idea was fascinating. Maggie tilted her head and studied him. "You just go from place to place, with what—the clothes on your back?"

"A little more than that, but basically. Sometimes I end up picking up something I can't resist—like that sculpture of yours in Dublin. I rent a place in New York, kind of a catchall for stuff. That's where my publisher and agent are based, so I go back about once, maybe twice a year. I can write anywhere," he said with a shrug. "So I do."

"And your family?"

"You're prying, Margaret Mary."

"He did it first," she shot back to Rogan.

"I don't have any family. Do you have names picked out for the baby?" Gray asked, neatly turning the subject.

Recognizing the tactic, Maggie frowned at him. Rogan gave her knee a squeeze under the table before she could speak. "None that we can agree on. We hope to settle on one before the child's ready to go to university."

Smoothly Rogan steered the conversation into polite, impersonal topics until Gray rose to leave. Once she was alone with her husband, Maggie drummed her fingers on the table.

"I'd have found out more about him if you hadn't interfered."

"It's none of your business." He leaned over and kissed her mouth.

"Maybe it is. I like him well enough. But he gets a look in his eyes when he speaks of Brianna. I'm not sure I like *that*."

"That's none of your business, either."

"She's my sister."

"And well able to take care of herself."

"A lot you'd know about it," Maggie grumbled. "Men always think they know women, when what they know is a pitiful nothing."

"I know you, Margaret Mary." In a neat move he scooped her out of the chair and into his arms.

"What are you about?"

"I'm about to take you to bed, strip you naked, and make incredibly thorough love with you."

"Oh, are you?" She tossed back her hair. "You're just trying to distract me from the subject at hand."

"Let's see how well I can do."

She smiled, wound her arms around his neck. "I suppose I should at least give you the chance."

When Gray strolled back into Blackthorn Cottage, he found Brianna on her hands and knees rubbing paste wax into the parlor floor in slow, almost loving circles. The little gold cross she sometimes wore swung like a pendulum from its thin chain and caught quick glints of light. She had music on, some lilting tune she was singing along with in Irish. Charmed, he crossed over and squatted down beside her.

"What do the words mean?"

She jolted first. He had a way of moving that no more than stirred the air. She blew loose hair out of her eyes and continued to polish. "It's about going off to war."

"It sounds too happy to be about war."

"Oh, we're happy enough to fight. You're back earlier than usual. Are you wanting tea?"

"No, thanks. I just had some at Maggie's."

She looked up then. "You were visiting Maggie?"

"I thought I'd take a walk and ended up at her place. She gave me a tour of her glass house."

Brianna laughed, then seeing he was serious, sat back on her haunches. "And how in sweet heaven did you manage such a feat as that?"

"I asked." And grinned. "She was a little cranky about it at first, but she fell in." He leaned toward Brianna, sniffed. "You smell of lemon and beeswax."

"That's not surprising." She had to clear her throat. "It's what I'm polishing the floor with." She made a small, strangled sound when he took her hand.

"You ought to wear gloves when you do heavy work."

"They get in my way." She shook her hand, but he held on. Though she tried to look firm, she only managed to look distressed. "You're in my way."

"I'll get out of it in a minute." She looked so damned pretty, he thought, kneeling on the floor with her polishing rag and her flushed cheeks. "Come out with me tonight, Brie. Let me take you to dinner."

"I've a—I've mutton," she said, fumbling, "for making Dingle Pies."

"It'll keep, won't it?"

"It will, yes, but . . . If you're tired of my cooking—"

"Brianna." His voice was soft, persuasive. "I want to take you out."

"Why?"

"Because you've got a pretty face." He skimmed his lips over her knuckles and made her heart stick in her throat. "Because I think it might be nice for you to have someone else do the cooking and the washing up for one night."

"I like to cook."

"I like to write, but it's always a kick to read something someone else has sweated over."

"It's not the same."

"Sure it is." Head tilted, he aimed that sudden razor-sharp gaze at her. "You're not afraid to be alone with me in a public restaurant, are you?"

"What a foolish thing to say." What a foolish thing, she realized, for her to feel.

"Fine then, it's a date. Seven o'clock." Wise enough to know when to retreat, Gray straightened and strolled out.

She told herself not to worry over her dress, then fretted about it just the same. In the end she chose the simple hunter green wool that Maggie had brought her back from Milan. With its long sleeves and high neck, it looked plain, even serviceable, until it was on. Cannily cut, the thin, soft wool had a way of draping over curves and revealing every bit as much as it concealed.

Still, Brianna told herself, it suited a dinner out, and that it was a sin she'd yet to wear it when Maggie had gone to the trouble and expense. And it felt so lovely against her skin.

Annoyed at the continued flutter of nerves, she picked up her coat, a plain black with a mended lining, and draped it over her arm. It was simply the offer of a meal, she reminded herself. A nice gesture from a man she'd been feeding for more than a week.

Taking one last steadying breath, she stepped out of her room into the kitchen, then started down the hall. He'd just come down the stairs. Self-conscious, she paused.

He stopped where he was, one foot still on the bottom step, his hand on the newel post. For a moment they only stared at each other in one of those odd, sliding instants of awareness. Then he stepped forward and the sensation rippled away.

"Well, well." His lips curved into a slow, satisfied smile. "You make a picture, Brianna."

"You're wearing a suit." And looked gorgeous in it.

"I drag one on now and again." He took her coat, slipped it over her shoulders.

"You never said where we were going."

"To eat." He put an arm around her waist and swept her out of the house.

The interior of the car made her sigh. It smelled of leather, and the leather was soft as butter. She skimmed her fingers over the seat as he drove.

"It was kind of you to do this, Gray."

"Kindness had nothing to do with it. I had an urge to go out, and I wanted you with me. You never come into the pub at night."

She relaxed a little. So that's where they were going. "I haven't lately. I do like stopping in now and then, seeing everyone. The O'Malleys had another grandchild this week."

"I know. I was treated to a pint to celebrate."

"I just finished a bunting for the baby. I should have brought it with me."

"We're not going to the pub. What's a bunting?"

"It's a kind of sacque; you button the baby into it." As they passed through the village she smiled. "Look, there's Mr. and Mrs. Conroy. More than fifty years married, and they still hold hands. You should see them dance."

"That's what I was told about you." He glanced at her. "You won contests."

"When I was a girl." She shrugged it off. Regrets were a foolish indulgence. "I was never serious about it. It was just for fun."

"What do you do for fun now?"

"Oh, this and that. You drive well for a Yank." At his bland look, she chuckled. "What I mean is that a lot of your people have some trouble adjusting to our roads and driving on the proper side."

"We won't debate which is the proper side, but I've spent a lot of time in Europe."

"You don't have an accent I can place—I mean other than American. I've made kind of a game out of it, you see, from guessing with my guests."

"It might be because I'm not from anywhere."

"Everyone's from somewhere."

"No, they're not. There are more nomads in the world than you might think."

"So, you're claiming to be a gypsy." She pushed her hair back and studied his profile. "Well, that's one I didn't think of."

"Meaning?"

"The night you came. I thought you looked a bit like a pirate—then a poet, even a boxer, but not a gypsy. But that suits, too."

"And you looked like a vision—billowing white gown, tumbled hair, courage and fear warring in your eyes."

"I wasn't afraid." She glimpsed the sign just before he turned off the road. "Here? Drumoland Castle? But we can't."

"Why not? I'm told the cuisine's exquisite."

"Sure and it is, and very dear."

He laughed, slowing to enjoy the view of the castle, gray and glorious on the slope of the hill, glinting under lights. "Brianna, I'm a very well paid gypsy. Stunning, isn't it?"

"Yes. And the gardens . . . you can't see them well now, and the winter's been so harsh, but they've the most beautiful gardens." She looked over the slope of lawn to a bed of dormant rosebushes. "In the back is a walled garden. It's so lovely it doesn't seem real. Why didn't you stay at a place like this?"

He parked the car, shut it off. "I nearly did, then I heard about your inn. Call it impulse." He flashed a grin at her. "I like impulses."

He climbed out of the car, took her hand to lead her up the stone steps into the great hall.

It was spacious and lush, as castles should be, with dark wood and deep red carpets. There was the smell of woodsmoke from the fire, the glint of crystal, the lonely sound of harp music.

"I stayed in a castle in Scotland," he began, moving toward the dining room with his fingers twined with hers. "And one in Cornwall. Fascinating places, full of shades and shadows."

"You believe in ghosts?"

"Of course." His eyes met hers as he reached out to take her coat. "Don't you?"

"I do, yes. We have some, you know, at home."

"The stone circle."

Even as she felt surprise, she realized she shouldn't. He would have been there, and he would have felt it. "There, yes, and other places."

Gray turned to the maître d'. "Thane," he said simply.

They were welcomed, shown to their table. As Gray accepted the wine list, he glanced at Brianna. "Would you like wine?"

"That would be nice."

He took a brief glance, smiled up at the sommelier. "The Chassagne-Montrachet."

"Yes, sir."

"Hungry?" he asked Brianna, who was all but devouring the menu.

"I'm trying to memorize it," she murmured. "I dined here once with Maggie and Rogan, and I've come close to duplicating this chicken in honey and wine."

"Read it for pleasure," he suggested. "We'll get a copy of the menu for you."

She eyed him over the top. "They won't give one to you."

"Sure they will."

She gave a short laugh and chose her meal at random. Once they'd placed their orders and sampled the wine, Gray leaned forward. "Now, tell me."

She blinked. "Tell you what?"

"About the ghosts."

"Oh." She smiled a little, running a finger down her wineglass. "Well, years ago, as it happened, there were lovers. She was betrothed to another, so they met in secret. He was a poor man, a simple farmer so they say, and she the daughter of the English landlord. But they loved, and made desperate plans to run off and be together. This night, they met at the stone circle. There, they thought, at that holy place, that magic place, they would ask the gods to bless them. She carried his child now, you see, and they had no time to lose. They knelt there, at the center, and she told him she was with child. It's said they wept together, with joy and with fear as the wind whispered cold and the old stones sheltered them. And there they loved each other a last time. He would go, he told her, and take his horse from his plow, gather whatever he could, and come back for her. They would leave that very night."

Brianna sighed a little, her eyes dreamy. "So he left her there, in the center of the circle of stones. But when he reached his farm, they were waiting for him. The men of the English landlord. They cut him down so that his blood stained the land, and they burned his house, his crops. His only thought as he lay dying was of his love."

She paused, with the innate timing of one who knows and spins tales. The harpist in the far corner plucked softly at a ballad of ill-fated love. "And she waited there, in the center of the circle of stones. While she waited, she grew cold, so cold she began to tremble. Her lover's voice came across the fields to her, like tears in the air. She knew he was dead. And knowing, she laid down, closed her eyes, and sent herself to him. When they found her the next morning, she was smiling. But she was cold, very cold, and her heart was not beating. There are nights, if you stand in the center of the circle of stones, you can hear them whisper their promises to each other and the grass grows damp with their tears."

Letting out a long breath, Gray sat back and sipped at his wine. "You have talent, Brianna, for storytelling."

"I tell you only as it was told to me. Love survives, you see. Through fear, through heartache, even through death."

"Have you heard them whispering?"

"I have. And I've wept for them. And I've envied them." She sat back, shook off the mood. "And what ghosts do you know?"

"Well, I'll tell you a story. In the hills not far from the field of Culloden a one-armed Highlander roams."

Her lips curved. "Is this truth, Grayson, or made up?"

He took her hand, kissed it. "You tell me."

FIVE

She'd never had an evening quite like it. All the elements added up to one wonderful memory—the gorgeous man who seemed fascinated by her every word, the romantic trappings of a castle, without the medieval inconveniences, glorious French food, delicate wine.

She wasn't sure how she would ever pay him back for it—particularly for the menu Gray had charmed out of the maître d'.

She began the only way she knew, by planning a special breakfast.

When Maggie came in, the kitchen was filled with sizzling scents, and Brianna was singing.

"Well, you're having a fine morning, I see."

"I am, yes." Brianna flipped over a thick slab of spiced toast. "Will you have some breakfast, Maggie? There's more than enough."

"I've eaten already." It was said with some regret. "Is Gray about?"

"He isn't down yet. Usually he's sniffing at the skillets by this time of day."

"Then we're alone for the moment."

"Yes." Her light mood plummeted. Carefully Brianna set the last piece of bread on the platter and put the meal into the oven to keep warm. "You've come to talk about the letters."

"I've kept you worrying over it long enough, haven't I? I'm sorry for that."

"We both needed to think." Brianna folded her hands over her apron, faced her sister. "What do you want to do, Maggie?"

"What I want to do is nothing, to pretend I've never read them, that they don't exist."

"Maggie—"

"Let me finish," she snapped out and began to roam the kitchen like an ill-tempered cat. "I want to go on as we are, and to keep my memories of Da my own. I don't want to wonder or worry about a woman he knew and bedded a lifetime ago. I don't want to think about a grown brother or sister somewhere. You're my sister," she said passionately. "You're my family. I tell myself this Amanda made a life for herself and her child somewhere, somehow, and they wouldn't thank us for poking into it now. I want to forget it. I want it to go away. That's what I want, Brianna."

She stopped, leaning back on the counter and sighing. "That's what I want," she repeated, "but it's not what must be done. He said her name—almost the last thing he said in life was her name. She has the right to know that. I have the right to curse her for it."

"Sit down, Maggie. It can't be good for you to be so upset."

"Of course I'm upset. We're both upset. We have different ways of dealing with it." With a shake of her head she waved Brianna off. "I don't need to sit. If the baby isn't used to my temper by now, he'll have to learn." Still she made an effort, taking a couple of calming breaths. "We'll need to hire an investigator, a detective, in New York. That's what you want, isn't it?"

"I think it's what we have to do," Brianna said carefully. "For ourselves. For Da. How will we go about it?"

"Rogan knows people. He'll make calls. He's wonderful at making calls." Because she could see Brianna needed it, she managed a smile. "That'll be the easy part. As to finding them, I don't know how long that might take. And God only knows what we'll do if and when we're faced with them. She might have married, this Amanda, and have a dozen children and a happy life."

"I've thought of that. But we have to find out, don't we?"

"We do." Stepping forward, Maggie laid her hands gently on Brianna's cheeks. "Don't worry so, Brie."

"I won't if you won't."

"It's a pact." Maggie kissed her lightly to seal it. "Now go feed your lazy Yank. I've fired my furnace and have work to do."

"Nothing heavy."

Maggie tossed back a grin as she turned for the door. "I know my limits."

"No, you don't, Margaret Mary," Brianna called out as the door slammed shut. She stood for a moment, lost in thought until Con's steady tail thumping roused her. "Want out, do you? Fine, then. Go see what Murphy's up to."

The minute she opened the door, Con streaked out. After one satisfied bark, he was loping toward the fields. She closed the door on the damp air and debated. It was after ten, and she had chores. If Gray wasn't coming down to breakfast, she'd take it up to him.

A glance at the menu on the table had her smiling again. She was humming as she arranged the breakfast tray. Hefting it, she carried it upstairs. His door was closed and made her hesitate. She knocked softly, got no response, and began to gnaw her lip. Perhaps he was ill. Concerned, she knocked again, more loudly, and called his name.

She thought she heard a grunt, and shifting the tray, eased the door open.

The bed looked as though it had been the scene of a small war. The sheets and blankets were tangled into knots, the quilt trailing over the footboard onto the floor. And the room was stone cold.

Stepping over the threshold, she saw him, and stared.

He was at the desk, his hair wild, his feet bare. There was a heap of books piled beside him as his fingers raced over the keys of a small computer. At his elbow was an ashtray overflowing with cigarette butts. The air reeked of them.

"Excuse me." No response. The muscles in her arms were beginning to ache from the weight of the tray. "Grayson."

"What?" The word shot out like a bullet, taking her back a step. His head whipped up.

It was the pirate again, she thought. He looked dangerous and inclined to violence. As his eyes focused on her, without any sign of recognition, she wondered if he might have gone mad during the night.

"Wait," he ordered and attacked the keyboard again. Brianna waited, baffled, for nearly five full minutes. He leaned back then, rubbed his hands hard over his face like a man just waking from a dream. Or, she thought, a nightmare. Then he turned to her again, with that quick, familiar smile. "Is that breakfast?"

"Yes, I . . . It's half past ten, and when you didn't come down . . ."

"Sorry." He rose, took the tray from her, and set it on the bed. He picked up a piece of English bacon with his fingers. "I got it in the middle of the night. It was the ghost story that clicked it, I think. Christ, it's cold in here."

"Well, 'tis no wonder. You're after catching your death with nothing on your feet and the fire out."

He only smiled as she knelt at the hearth and began to arrange new turf. She'd sounded like a mother scolding a foolish child. "I got caught up."

"That's all fine and good, but it's not healthy for you to be sitting here in the cold, smoking cigarettes instead of eating a decent meal."

"Smells better than decent." Patient, he crouched down beside her, ran a carelessly friendly hand down her back. "Brianna, will you do me a favor?"

"If I can, yes."

"Go away."

Stunned, she turned her head. Even as she gaped at him, he was laughing and taking her hands in his.

"No offense, honey. It's just that I tend to bite if my work's interrupted, and it's cooking for me right now."

"I certainly don't mean to be in your way."

He winced, bit back on annoyance. He was trying to be diplomatic, wasn't he? "I need to hang with it while it's moving, okay? So just forget I'm up here."

"But your room. You need the linens changed, and the bath—"

"Don't worry about it." The fire was glowing now, and so was the impatience inside him. He raised her to her feet. "You can shovel it out when I hit a dry spell. I'd appreciate it if you'd drop some food off outside the door now and again, but that's all I'll need."

"All right, but—" He was already guiding her to the door. She huffed. "You don't have to be booting me out, I'm going."

"Thanks for breakfast."

"You're—" He shut the door in her face. "Welcome," she said between her teeth.

For the rest of that day and two more she didn't hear a peep out of him. She tried not to think of the state of the room, if he'd remembered to keep the fire going or if he bothered to sleep. She knew he was eating. Each time she brought up a fresh tray, the old one was outside the door. He rarely left so much as a crumb on a plate.

She might have been alone in the house—if she hadn't been so aware of him. She doubted very much that he gave her a moment's thought.

She'd have been right. He did sleep now and again, catnaps that were ripe with dreams and visions. He ate, fueling his body as the story fueled his mind. It was storming through him. In three days he had more than a hundred pages. They were rough, sometimes static, but he had the core of it.

He had murder, gleeful and sly. He had hopelessness and pain, desperation and lies.

He was in heaven.

When it finally ground to a halt, he crawled into bed, pulled the covers over his head, and slept like the dead.

When he woke, he took a long look at the room and decided a woman as strong as Brianna was unlikely to faint at the sight of it. The sight of him, however, as he studied himself in the bathroom mirror, was another matter. He rubbed a hand over the stubble on his chin. He looked, he decided, like something that had crawled out of a bog.

He peeled off his shirt, winced at the smell of it, and himself, and stepped into the shower. Thirty minutes later he was pulling on fresh clothes. He felt a little light-headed, more than a little stiff from lack of exercise. But the excitement was still on him. He pushed open the bedroom window and took a deep gulp of the rainy morning.

A perfect day, he thought. In the perfect place.

His breakfast tray was outside the door, the food gone cold. He'd slept through that, he realized, and lifting it, hoped he could charm Brianna into heating it up for him again.

And maybe she'd go for a walk with him. He could use some company. Maybe he could talk her into driving into Galway, spending the day with him in crowds. They could always—

He stopped in the kitchen doorway, and his grin spread from ear to ear. There she was, up to her wrists in bread dough, her hair scooped up, her nose dusted with flour.

It was such a wonderful picture, and his mood was high. He set the tray down with a rattle that had her jolting and looking up. She had just begun to smile when he strode to her, framed her face firmly in his hands, and kissed her hard on the mouth.

Her hands fisted in the dough. Her head spun. Before she could react, he'd pulled away. "Hi. Great day, isn't it? I feel incredible. You can't count on it coming like that, you know. And when it does, it's like this train highballing right through your head. You can't stop it." He picked up a piece of cold toast from his tray, started to bite in. It was halfway to his mouth before it hit him. His eyes locked on hers again. He let the toast fall back to the plate.

The kiss had merely been a reflection of his mood, light, exuberant. Now, some sort of delayed reaction was setting in, tightening his muscles, skimming up his spine.

She simply stood there, staring at him, her lips still parted in shock, her eyes huge with it.

"Wait a minute," he murmured and moved to her again. "Wait just a minute."

She couldn't have moved if the roof had caved in. She could barely breathe as his hands framed her face again, gently this time, like a man experimenting with texture. His eyes stayed open, the expression in them not entirely pleased as he leaned toward her this time.

She felt his lips brush hers, soft, lovely. The kind of touch that shouldn't have kindled a fire in the blood. Yet her blood heated. He turned her, just enough so that their bodies met, tipped her head back just enough so that the kiss would deepen.

Some sound, distress or pleasure, hummed in her throat before her fisted hands went limp.

Hers was a mouth to savor, he realized. Full, generous, yielding. A man shouldn't hurry a mouth such as this. He scraped his teeth lightly over her bottom lip and thrilled to the low, helpless purr that answered him. Slowly, watching her eyes glaze and close, he traced her lips with his tongue, dipped inside.

So many subtle flavors.

It was wonderful, the way he could feel her skin warm, her bones soften, her heart pound. Or maybe it was his heart. Something was roaring in his head, throbbing in his blood. It wasn't until greed began to grow, with the crafty violence that mated with it, that he drew back.

She was trembling, and instinct warned him that if he let himself go, he'd hurt them both. "That was better than I imagined it would be," he managed. "And I've got a hell of an imagination."

Staggered, she braced a hand on the counter. Her knees were shaking. Only fear of mortification kept her voice from shaking as well. "Is this how you always behave when you come out of your cave?"

"I'm not always lucky enough to have a beautiful woman handy." He tilted his head, studying her. The pulse in her throat was still jumping, and her skin was still flushed. But, unless he was off the mark, she was already rebuilding that thin, defensive wall. "That wasn't ordinary. There isn't any point in pretending it was."

"I'm not ordinarily kissed by a guest while I'm making bread. I wouldn't know what's ordinary for you, would I?" His eyes changed, darkening with a hint of temper. When he stepped forward, she stepped back. "Please, don't."

Now those dark eyes narrowed. "Be more specific."

"I have to finish this. The dough needs to rise again."

"You're evading, Brianna."

"All right, don't kiss me like that again." She let out a choppy breath, drew another in. "I don't have the right defenses."

"It doesn't have to be a battle. I'd like to take you to bed, Brianna."

To occupy her nervous hands, she snatched up a towel and rubbed at the dough clinging to her fingers. "Well, that's blunt."

"It's honest. If you're not interested, just say so."

"I don't take things as casually as you, with a yes or a no, and no harm done." Fighting for calm, she folded the towel neatly, set it aside. "And I've no experience in such matters."

Damn her for being cool when his blood was raging. "What matters?"

"The one you're speaking of. Now, move aside so I can get back to my bread."

He simply took her arm and stared into her eyes. A virgin? he wondered, letting the idea circle around and take root. A woman who looked like this, who responded like this?

"Is something wrong with the men around here?" He said it lightly, hoping to cut some of the tension. But the result was a flash of pain in her eyes that made him feel like a slug.

"It's my business, isn't it, how I live my life?" Her voice had chilled. "Now, I've respected your wishes and your work these past days. Would you do me the same and let me get on with mine?"

"All right." He let her go, stepped back. "I'm going out for a while. Do you want me to pick up anything for you?"

"No, thank you." She plunged her hands into the dough again and began to knead. "It's raining a bit," she said evenly. "You might want a jacket."

He walked to the doorway, turned back. "Brianna." He waited until she'd lifted her head. "You never said whether or not you were interested. I'll have to assume you're thinking about it."

He strode out. She didn't let out her next breath until she heard the door close behind him.

Gray worked off excess energy with a long drive and a visit to the Cliffs of Moher. To give them both time to settle, he stopped in for lunch at a pub in Ennis. He walked off a heavy dose of fish and chips by wandering along the narrow streets. Something in a shop window caught his eyes, and following impulse he stepped inside and had it boxed.

By the time he returned to Blackthorn, he'd nearly convinced himself that what he'd experienced in the kitchen with Brianna was more a result of his joy over his work than chemistry.

Still, when he stepped into his room and found her kneeling on the edge of his bathroom floor, a bucket beside her and a rag in her hand, the scales tipped the other way. If a man wasn't dazzled with sex, why else would such a picture make his blood pump?

"Do you have any idea how often I come across you in that position?"

She looked over her shoulder. "It's an honest living." She blew her hair back. "I'll tell you this, Grayson Thane, you live like a pig when you're working."

He cocked a brow. "Is that the way you talk to all your guests?"

He had her there. She flushed a little and slapped her rag back on the floor. "I'll be done here soon if you've a mind to get back to it. I've another guest coming in this evening."

"Tonight?" He scowled at the back of her head. He liked having the place to himself. Having her to himself. "Who?"

"A British gentleman. He called shortly after you left this morning."

"Well, who is he? How long's he staying?" And what the hell did he want?

"A night or two," she said easily. "I don't interrogate my guests, as you should know."

"It just seems to me that you should ask questions. You can't just let strangers waltz into your home."

Amused, she sat back and shook her head at him. A combination of the scruffy and elegant, she thought, with his gold-tipped hair pulled back piratelike, those lovely eyes of his sulky, the pricey boots, worn jeans, and crisp shirt. "That's exactly what I do. I believe you waltzed in yourself, in the dead of night, not so long ago."

"That's different." At her bland look, he shrugged. "It just is. Look, would you get up and stop that? You could eat off the damn floor."

"Obviously today's rambling didn't put a smile on your face."

"I was fine." He prowled the room, then snarled. "You've been messing with my desk."

"I cleaned off an inch of dust and cigarette ash, if that's what you're meaning. I didn't touch your little machine there except to lift it up and set it down again." Though she'd been tempted, sorely, to open the lid and take a peek at the works.

"You don't have to clean up after me all the time." He hissed out a breath, stuffed his hands in his pockets when she simply stood, bucket in hand, and looked at him. "Goddamn it, I thought I'd figured this out. It's not doing my ego any good to know you're not even trying to tie me up in knots." He closed his eyes, let out a breath. "Okay, let's try this again. I brought you a present."

"Did you? Why?"

"Why the hell not?" He snatched the bag he'd put on the bed and handed it to her. "I saw it. I thought you'd like it."

"That was kind of you." She slipped the box from the bag and began to work at the tape that held it closed.

She smelled of soap and flowers and disinfectant. Gray set his teeth. "Unless you want me to toss you on the bed you've just tidied up, you'd be wise to step back."

She looked up, startled, her hands freezing on the box.

"I'm serious."

Cautious, she moistened her lips. "All right." She took a step back, then another. "Is this better?"

The absurdity of it finally struck. Helpless to do otherwise, he grinned at her. "Why do you fascinate me, Brianna?"

"I have no idea. None at all."

"That might be why," he murmured. "Open your present."

"I'm trying." She loosened the tape, turned back the lid, and dug into the tissue paper. "Oh, it's lovely." Pleasure lit her face as she turned the porcelain cottage in her hands. It was delicately made, the front door open in welcome, a tidy garden with each tiny petal perfect. "It looks as though you could move right in."

"It made me think of you."

"Thank you." Her smile was easier now. "Did you buy it to soften me up?"

"Tell me if it worked first."

Now she laughed. "No, I won't. You have advantage enough as it is."

"Do I?"

Warned by the purr in his tone, she concentrated on replacing the cottage in the bed of tissue. "I have dinner to tend to. Will you be wanting a tray?"

"Not tonight. The first wave's past."

"The new guest is expected by five, so you'll have company with your meal."

"Terrific."

Gray had been prepared to dislike the British gentlemen on sight, rather like a stud dog, he realized, exercising territorial rights. But it was difficult to feel threatened or irritated with the tidy little man with the shiny bald pate and the snooty public school accent.

His name was Herbert Smythe-White, of London, a retired widower who was in the first stages of a six-month tour of Ireland and Scotland.

"Pure indulgence," he told Gray over dinner. "Nancy and I weren't blessed with children, you see. She's been gone nearly two years now, and I find myself brooding about the house. We'd planned to make a trip like this, but work always kept me too busy." His smile was laced with regret. "I decided to make it myself as a sort of tribute to her. I think she would have liked that."

"Is this your first stop?"

"It is. I flew into Shannon, leased a car." He chuckled, taking off his wire-rimmed glasses and polishing the lenses on a handkerchief. "I'm armed with the tourist's weapons of maps and guidebooks. I'll take a day or two here before heading north." He set his glasses back on his prominent nose. "I'm very much afraid I'm taking the best first, however. Miss Concannon sets an excellent table."

"You won't get an argument from me." They were sharing the dining room and a succulent salmon. "What work were you in?"

"Banking. I'm afraid I spent too much of my life worried about figures." He helped himself to another spoonful of potatoes in mustard sauce. "And you, Mr. Thane. Miss Concannon tells me you're a writer. We practical sorts always envy the creative ones. I've never taken enough time to read for pleasure, but will certainly pick up one of your books now that we've met. Are you traveling, also?"

"Not at the moment. I'm based here for now."

"Here, at the inn?"

"That's right." He glanced up as Brianna came in.

"I hope you've room for dessert." She set a large bowl of trifle on the table.

"Oh, my dear." Behind his polished lenses, Smythe-White's eyes danced with pleasure, and perhaps a little greed. "I'll be a stone heavier before I leave the room."

"I put magic in it, so the calories don't count." She dished generous portions into bowls. "I hope your room's comfortable, sir. If there's anything you need, you've only to ask."

"It's exactly what I want," he assured her. "I must come back when your garden's in bloom."

"I hope you will." She left them a coffeepot and a decanter of brandy.

"A lovely woman," Smythe-White commented.

"Yes, she is."

"And so young to be running an establishment alone. One would think she'd have a husband, a family."

"She's nothing if not efficient." The first spoonful of trifle melted on Gray's tongue. *Efficient* wasn't the word, he realized. The woman was a culinary witch. "She has a sister and brother-in-law just down the road.

And it's a close community. Someone's always knocking on the kitchen door."

"That's fortunate. I imagine it could be a lonely place otherwise. Still, I noticed as I was driving in that neighbors are few and far between." He smiled again. "I'm afraid I'm spoiled by the city, and not at all ashamed that I enjoy the crowds and the pace. It may take me awhile to grow accustomed to the night quiet."

"You'll have plenty of it." Gray poured brandy into a snifter, then, at his companion's nod, into a second. "I was in London not long ago. What part are you from?"

"I have a little flat near Green Park. Didn't have the heart to keep the house after Nancy went." He sighed, swirled brandy. "Let me offer some unsolicited advice, Mr. Thane. Make your days count. Don't invest all your efforts in the future. You miss too much of the now."

"That's advice I live on."

Hours later it was thoughts of leftover trifle that pulled Gray away from his warm bed and a good book. The house moaned a bit around him as he dug up a pair of sweats, pulled them on. He padded downstairs in his bare feet with greedy dreams of gorging.

It certainly wasn't his first middle-of-the-night trip to the kitchen since he'd settled into Blackthorn. None of the shadows or creaking boards disturbed him as he slipped down the hall and into the dark kitchen. He turned on the stove light, not wanting to awaken Brianna.

Then he wished he hadn't thought of her, or of the fact that she was sleeping just a wall beyond. In that long, flannel nightgown, he imagined, with the little buttons at the collar. So prim it made her look exotic—certainly it made a man, a red-blooded one, wonder about the body all that material concealed.

And if he kept thinking along those lines, all the trifle in the country wouldn't sate his appetite.

One vice at a time, pal, he told himself. And got out a bowl. A sound from the outside made him pause, listen. Just as he was about to dismiss it as old house groans, he heard the scratching.

With the bowl in one hand, he went to the kitchen door, looked out, and saw nothing but night. Suddenly the glass was filled with fur and fangs. Gray managed to stifle a yelp and keep himself from overbalancing onto his butt. On something between a curse and a laugh, he opened the door for Con.

"Ten years off my life, thanks very much." He scratched the dog's ears, and since Brianna wasn't around to see, decided to share the trifle with his canine companion.

"What do you think you're up to?"

Gray straightened, rapped his head against the cupboard door he'd failed to close. A spoonful of trifle plopped into the dog's bowl and was gobbled up.

"Nothing." Gray rubbed his throbbing head. "Jesus Christ, between you and your wolf I'll be lucky if I live to see my next birthday."

"He's not to be eating that." Brianna snatched the bowl away from Gray. "It isn't good for him."

"*I* was going to eat it. Now I'll settle for a bottle of aspirin."

"Sit down and I'll have a look at the knot on your head, or the hole in it, whatever the case may be."

"Very cute. Why don't you just go back to bed and—"

He never finished the thought. From his stance between them, Con abruptly tensed, snarled, and with a growl bursting from his throat leaped toward the hallway door. It was Gray's bad luck that he happened to be in the way.

The force of a hundred and seventy pounds of muscle had him reeling back and smashing into the counter. He saw stars as his elbow cracked against the wood, and dimly heard Brianna's sharp command.

"Are you hurt?" Her tone was all soothing maternal concern now. "Here now, Grayson, you've gone pale. Sit down. Con, heel!"

Ears ringing, stars circling in front of his eyes, the best Gray could do was slide into the chair Brianna held out for him. "All this for a fucking bowl of cream."

"There now, you just need to get your breath back. Let me see your arm."

"Shit!" Gray's eyes popped wide as she flexed his elbow and pain radiated out. "Are you trying to kill me just because I want to get you naked?"

"Stop that." The rebuke was mild as she tut-tutted over the bruise. "I've got some witch hazel."

"I'd rather have morphine." He blew out a breath and stared narrow-eyed at the dog. Con continued to stand, quivering and ready at the doorway. "What the hell is with him?"

"I don't know. Con, stop being a bloody fool and sit." She dampened a cloth with witch hazel. "It's probably Mr. Smythe-White. Con was out roaming when he got in. They haven't been introduced. It's likely he caught a scent."

"It's lucky the old man didn't get a yen for trifle then."

She only smiled and straightened up to look at the top of Gray's head. He had lovely hair, she thought, all gilded and silky. "Oh, Con wouldn't hurt him. He'd just corner him. There, you'll have a fine bump, you will."

"You don't have to sound so pleased about it."

"It'll teach you not to give the dog sweets. I'll just make you an ice pack and—" She squealed as Gray yanked her into his lap. The dog's ears pricked up, but he merely wandered over and sniffed at Gray's hands.

"He likes me."

"He's easily charmed. Let me up or I'll tell him to bite you."

"He wouldn't. I just gave him trifle. Let's just sit here a minute, Brie. I'm too weak to bother you."

"I don't believe that for a minute," she said under her breath, but relented.

Gray cradled her head on his shoulder and smiled when Con rested his on her lap. "This is nice."

"It is."

She felt a little crack around her heart as he held her quietly in the dim light from the stove while the house settled in sleep around them.

SIX

Brianna needed a taste of spring. It was chancy, she knew, to begin too early, but the mood wouldn't pass. She gathered the seeds she'd been hording and her small portable radio and carted them out to the little shed she'd rigged as a temporary greenhouse.

It wasn't much, and she'd have been the first to admit it. No more than eight feet square with a floor of hard-packed dirt, the shed was better used for storage than planting. But she'd imposed on Murphy to put in glass and a heater. The benches she'd built herself with little skill and a great deal of pride.

There wasn't room, nor was there equipment for the kind of experimentation she dreamed of. Still, she could give her seeds an early start in the peat pots she'd ordered from a gardening supply catalog.

The afternoon was hers, after all, she told herself. Gray was closeted with his work, and Mr. Smythe-White was taking a motor tour of the Ring of Kerry. All the baking and mending were done for the day, so it was time for pleasure.

There was little that made her happier than having her hands in soil. Grunting a bit, she hefted a bag of potting mix onto the bench.

Next year, she promised herself, she'd have a professional greenhouse. Not a large one, but a fine one nonetheless. She'd take cuttings and root them, force bulbs so that she could have spring any time of year she liked. Perhaps she'd even attempt some grafting. But for the moment she was content to baby her seeds.

In days, she mused, humming along with the radio, the first tender sprigs would push through the soil. True it was a horrid expense, the luxury of fuel to warm them. It would have been wiser to use the money to have her car overhauled.

But it wouldn't be nearly so much fun.

She sowed, gently patting dirt, and let her mind drift.

How sweet Gray had been the night before, she remembered. Cuddling with her in the kitchen. It hadn't been so frightening, nor, she admitted, so exciting, as when he'd kissed her. This had been soft and soothing, and so natural it had seemed, just for a moment, that they'd belonged there together.

Once, long ago, she'd dreamed of sharing small, sweet moments like that with someone. With Rory, she thought with an old, dull pang. Then she'd believed she'd be married, have children to love, a home to tend to. What plans she'd made, she thought now, all rosy and warm with happy ever after at the end of them.

But then, she'd only been a girl, and in love. A girl in love believed anything. Believed everything. She wasn't a girl now.

She'd stopped believing when Rory had broken her heart, snapped it into two aching halves. She knew he was living near Boston now, with a wife and a family of his own. And, she was sure, with no thought whatever of the young sweet springtime when he'd courted her, and promised her. And pledged to her.

That was long ago, she reminded herself. Now she knew that love didn't always endure, and promises weren't always kept. If she still carried a seed of hope inside that longed to bloom, it hurt no one but herself.

"Here you are!" Eyes dancing, Maggie burst into the shed. "I heard the music. What in the world are you up to in here?"

"I'm planting flowers." Distracted, Brianna swiped the back of her hand over her cheek and smeared it with soil. "Close the door, Maggie, you're letting the heat out. What is it? You look about to burst."

"You'll never guess, not in a thousand years." With a laugh, Maggie swung around the small shed, grabbing Brianna's arms to twirl her. "Go ahead. Try."

"You're having triplets."

"No! Praise God."

Maggie's mood was infectious enough to have Brianna chuckle and fall into the rhythm of the impromptu jig. "You've sold a piece of your glass for a million pounds, to the president of the United States."

"Oh, what a thought. Maybe we should send him a brochure. No, you're miles off, you are, miles. I'll give you a bit of a hint then. Rogan's grandmother called."

Brianna blew her tumbling hair out of her eyes. "That's a hint?"

"It would be if you'd put your mind to it. Brie, she's getting married. She's marrying Uncle Niall, next week, in Dublin."

"What?" Brianna's mouth fell open on the word. "Uncle Niall, Mrs. Sweeney, married?"

"Isn't it grand? Isn't it just grand? You know she had a crush on him when she was a girl in Galway. Then after more than fifty years they meet again because of Rogan and me. Now, by all the saints in heaven, they're going to take vows." Tossing back her head, she cackled. "Now as well as being husband and wife, Rogan and I will be cousins."

"Uncle Niall." It seemed to be all Brianna could manage.

"You should have seen Rogan's face when he took the call. He looked like a fish. His mouth opening and closing and not a word coming out." Snorting with laughter, she leaned against Brianna's workbench. "He's never gotten accustomed to the idea that they were courting. More than courting, if it comes to that—but I suppose it's a difficult thing for a man to imagine his white-haired granny snuggled up in sin."

"Maggie!" Overcome, Brianna covered her mouth with her hand. Giggles turned into hoots of laughter.

"Well, they're making it legal now, with an archbishop no less officiating." She took a deep breath, looked around. "Have you anything to eat out here?"

"No. When is it to be? Where?"

"Saturday next, in her Dublin house. A small ceremony, she tells me, with just family and close friends. Uncle Niall's eighty if he's a day, Brie. Imagine it."

"I think I can. Oh, and I do think it's grand. I'll call them after I've finished here and cleaned up."

"Rogan and I are leaving for Dublin today. He's on the phone right now, God bless him, making arrangements." She smiled a little. "He's trying to be a man about it."

"He'll be happy for them, once he gets used to it." Brianna's voice was vague as she began to wonder what sort of gift she should buy the bride and groom.

"It's to be an afternoon ceremony, but you may want to come out the night before so you'll have some time."

"Come out?" Brianna focused on her sister again. "But I can't go, Maggie. I can't leave. I have a guest."

"Of course you'll go." Maggie straightened from the bench, set her jaw. "It's Uncle Niall. He'll expect you there. It's one bloody day, Brianna."

"Maggie, I have obligations here, and no way to get to Dublin and back."

"Rogan will have the plane take you."

"But—"

"Oh, hang Grayson Thane. He can cook his own meals for a day. You're not a servant."

Brianna's shoulders stiffened. Her eyes turned cool. "No, I'm not. I'm a businesswoman who's given her word. I can't dance off for a weekend in Dublin and tell the man to fend for himself."

"Then bring him along. If you're worried the man will fall over dead without you to tend him, bring him with you."

"Bring him where?" Gray pushed open the door, eyed both women cautiously. He'd seen Maggie go dashing into the shed from his bedroom window. Curiosity had eventually brought him out, and the shouting had done the rest.

"Shut the door," Brianna said automatically. She fought back embarrassment that he should have walked in on a family argument. She sighed once. The tiny shed was now crowded with people. "Was there something you needed, Grayson?"

"No." He lifted a hand, brushing his thumb over the dirt on her cheek—a gesture that had Maggie's eyes narrowing. "You have dirt on your face, Brie. What are you up to?"

"I'm trying to put in some seeds—but there's hardly room for them now."

"Mind your hands, boy-o," Maggie muttered.

He only grinned and stuck them in his pockets. "I heard my name mentioned. Is there a problem?"

"There wouldn't be if she wasn't so stubborn." Maggie tossed up her chin and decided to dump the blame at Gray's feet. "She needs to go to Dublin next weekend, but she won't leave you."

Gray's grin turned into a satisfied smile as his gaze shifted from Maggie to Brianna. "Won't she?"

"You've paid for room and board," Brianna began.

"Why do you need to go to Dublin?" he interrupted.

"Our uncle's getting married," Maggie told him. "He'll want her there, and that's as it should be. I say if she won't leave you behind, she should take you along."

"Maggie, Gray doesn't want to be going off to a wedding, with people he doesn't know. He's working, and he can't just—"

"Sure he does," Gray cut her off. "When do we leave?"

"Good. You'll stay at our house there. That's settled." Maggie brushed her hands together. "Now, who's going to tell Mother?"

"I—"

"No, let me," Maggie decided before Brianna could answer. She smiled. "She'll really hate it. We'll have the plane take her out Saturday morning so you won't be badgered by her the whole trip. Have you a suit, Gray?"

"One or two," he murmured.

"Then you're set, aren't you?" She leaned forward, kissed Brianna firmly on both cheeks. "Plan to leave Friday," she ordered. "I'll call you from Dublin."

Gray ran his tongue around his teeth as Maggie slammed out. "Bossy, isn't she?"

"Aye." Brianna blinked, shook her head. "She doesn't mean it. It's just that she's always sure she's right. And she has a deep fondness for Uncle Niall and for Rogan's grandmother."

"Rogan's grandmother."

"That's who he's marrying." She turned back to her potting, hoping to clear her mind with work.

"That sounds like a story."

"Oh, 'tis. Gray, it's kind of you to be so obliging, but it's not necessary. They won't miss me, really, and it's a lot of trouble for you."

"A weekend in Dublin's no trouble for me. And you want to go, don't you?"

"That's not the point. Maggie put you in a difficult position."

He put a hand under her chin, lifted it. "Why do you have such a hard time answering questions? You want to go, don't you? Yes or no."

"Yes."

"Okay, we go."

Her lips started to curve, until he leaned toward them. "Don't kiss me," she said, weakening.

"Now, that's a lot of trouble for me." But he reined himself in, leaned back. "Who hurt you, Brianna?"

Her lashes fluttered down, shielding her eyes. "It may be I don't answer questions because you ask too many of them."

"Did you love him?"

She turned her head, concentrated on her pots. "Yes, very much."

It was an answer, but he found it didn't please him. "Are you still in love with him?"

"That would be foolish."

"That's not an answer."

"Yes, it is. Do I breathe down your neck when you're working?"

"No." But he didn't step back. "But you have such an appealing neck." To prove it, he bent down to brush his lips over the nape. It didn't hurt his ego to feel her tremble. "I dreamed of you last night, Brianna. And wrote of it today."

Most of her seeds scattered on the workbench instead of in the soil. She busied herself rescuing them. "Wrote of it?"

"I made some changes. In the book you're a young widow who's struggling to build on a broken past."

Despite herself, she was drawn and turned to look at him. "You're putting me in your book?"

"Pieces of you. Your eyes, those wonderful, sad eyes. Your hair." He lifted a hand to it. "Thick, slippery hair, the color of the coolest sunset. Your voice, that soft lilt. Your body, slim, willowy, with a dancer's unconscious grace. Your skin, your hands. I see you when I write, so I write of you. And beyond the physical, there's your integrity, your loyalty." He smiled a little. "Your tea cakes. The hero's just as fascinated with her as I am with you."

Gray set his hands on the bench on either side of her, caging her in. "And he keeps running into that same shield you both have. I wonder how long it'll take him to break it down."

No one had ever said such words about her before, such words to her. A part of her yearned to wallow in them, as if they were silk. Another part stood cautiously back.

"You're trying to seduce me."

He lifted a brow. "How'm I doing?"

"I can't breathe."

"That's a good start." He leaned closer until his mouth was a whisper from hers. "Let me kiss you, Brianna."

He already was in that slow, sinking way he had that turned all her muscles to mush. Mouth to mouth. It was such a simple thing, but it tilted everything in her world. Further and further until she was afraid she would never right it again.

He had skill, and with skill a patience. Beneath both was the shimmer of repressed violence she once sensed in him. The combination seeped into her like a drug, weakening, dizzying.

She wanted, as a woman wanted. She feared, as innocence feared.

Gently he took the fingers she gripped on the edge of the bench, soothed them open. With his mouth skimming over hers, he lifted her arms.

"Hold me, Brianna." God he needed her to. "Kiss me back."

Like a crack of a whip, his quiet words spurred her. Suddenly she was clinging to him, her mouth wild and willing. Staggered, he rocked back, gripping her. Her lips were hot, hungry, her body vibrating like a plucked harp string. The eruption of her passion was like lava spewing through ice, frenzied, unexpected, and dangerous.

There was the elemental smell of earth, the wail of Irish pipes from the radio, the succulent flavor of woman in his mouth, and the quivering temptation of her in his arms.

Then he was blind and deaf to all but her. Her hands were fisted in his hair, her panting breaths filling his mouth. More, only wanting more, he slammed her back against the shed wall. He heard her cry out—in shock, pain, excitement—before he muffled the sound, devouring it, devouring her.

His hands streaked over her, hotly possessive, invasive. And her pants turned to moans: Please . . . She wanted to beg him for something. Oh, please. Such an ache, a deep, grinding, glorious ache. But she didn't know the beginning of it, or how it would end. And the fear was snapping like a wolf behind it—fear of him, of herself, of what she'd yet to know.

He wanted her skin—the feel and taste of her flesh. He wanted to pound himself inside of her until they were both empty. The breath was tearing through his lungs as he gripped her shirt, his hands poised to rip and rend.

And his eyes met hers.

Her lips were bruised and trembling, her cheeks pale as ice. Her eyes were wide with terror and need warring in them. He looked down, saw his knuckles were white from strain. And the marks his greedy fingers had put on her lovely skin.

He jerked back as if she'd slapped him, then held up his hands. He wasn't sure what or who he was warding off.

"I'm sorry," he managed while she stood pressed back into the wall, gulping air. "I'm sorry. Did I hurt you?"

"I don't know." How could she know where there was nothing but this horrible pulsing ache. She hadn't dreamed she could feel like this. Hadn't known it was possible to feel so much. Dazed, she brushed at the dampness on her cheeks.

"Don't cry." He dragged an unsteady hand through his hair. "I feel filthy enough about this."

"No, it's not—" She swallowed the tears. She had no idea why she should shed them. "I don't know what happened to me."

Of course she didn't, he thought bitterly. Hadn't she told him she was innocent? And he'd gone at her like an animal. In another minute he would have dragged her down on the dirt and finished the job.

"I pushed you, and there's no excuse for it. I can only tell you I lost my head and apologize for it." He wanted to go back to her, brush the tangled hair from her face. But didn't dare. "I was rough, and frightened you. It won't happen again."

"I knew you would be." She was steadier now, perhaps because he seemed so shaken. "All along I knew. It wasn't that, Grayson. I'm not the fragile sort."

He found he could smile after all. "Oh, but you are, Brianna. And I've never been quite so clumsy. This may seem like an awkward time to tell you, but you don't have to be afraid of me. I won't hurt you."

"I know. You—"

"And I'm going to try my damnedest not to rush you," he interrupted. "But I want you."

She discovered she had to concentrate to breath evenly again. "We can't always have what we want."

"I've never believed that. I don't know who he was, Brie, but he's gone. I'm here."

She nodded. "For now."

"There's only now." He shook his head before she could argue. "This is as odd a place for philosophy as it is for sex. We're both a little wired up, right?"

"I suppose you could say that."

"Let's go inside. This time I'll make *you* some tea."

Her lips curved. "Do you know how?"

"I've been watching you. Come on." He held out a hand. She looked at it, hesitated. After another cautious glance at his face—it was calm now, without that odd feral light that was so frightening and exciting—she slipped her hand into his.

"Maybe it's a good thing we've got a chaperone tonight."

"Oh?" She turned her head as they stepped outside.

"Otherwise you might sneak up to my room tonight and take advantage of me."

She let out a short laugh. "You're too clever for anyone to take advantage of you."

"Well, you could try." Relieved neither of them were trembling now, he slung a companionable arm around her shoulders. "Why don't we have a bit of cake with the tea?"

She slid her eyes toward him as they reached the kitchen door. "Mine, or the one the woman makes in your book?"

"Hers is only in my imagination, darling. Now, yours—" He froze when he pushed the door open. Instinctly he shoved Brianna behind him. "Stay here. Right here."

"What? Are you—oh, sweet Jesus." Over his shoulder she could see the chaos of her kitchen. Tins had been turned over, cupboards emptied. Flour and sugar, spices and tea were swept onto the floor.

"I said stay here," he repeated as she tried to shove by him.

"I'll not. Look at this mess."

He blocked her with an arm across the doorway. "Do you keep money in your tins? Jewelry?"

"Don't be daft. Of course I don't." She blinked up at him. "You think someone was after stealing something? I've nothing to steal and no one would."

"Well, someone did, and they could still be in the house. Where's that damn dog?" he muttered.

"He'd be off with Murphy," she said dully. "He goes off to visit most afternoons."

"Run over to Murphy's then, or to your sister's. I'll take a look around."

She drew herself up. "This is my home, I'll remind you. I'll look myself."

"Stay behind me," was all he said.

He checked her rooms first, ignoring her expected shriek of outrage when she saw the pulled-out drawers and tumbled clothes.

"My things."

"We'll see if there's anything missing later. Better check the rest."

"What sort of mischief is this?" she demanded, her temper heating as she trailed behind Gray. "Oh, damn them," she swore when she saw the parlor.

It had been a quick, hurried, and frantic search, Gray mused. Anything but professional and foolishly risky. He was thinking it through when another idea slammed into him.

"Shit." He took the stairs two at a time, burst into the mess of his own room, and bolted straight for his laptop. "Somebody will die," he muttered, booting it up.

"Your work." Brianna stood pale and furious in the doorway. "Did they harm your work?"

"No." He skimmed through page after page until he was satisfied. "No, it's here. It's fine."

She let out a little sigh of relief before turning away to check Mr. Smythe-White's room. His clothes had been turned out of the drawers and closet, his bed pulled apart. "Mary, Mother of God, how will I explain this to him?"

"I think it's more to the point to ask what they were looking for. Sit down, Brianna," Gray ordered. "Let's think this through."

"What's to think about?" But she did sit, on the edge of the tilted mattress. "I've nothing of value here. A few pounds, a few trinkets." She rubbed her eyes, impatient with herself for the tears she couldn't manage to stem. "It wouldn't have been anyone from the village or nearby. It had to be a vagrant, a hitchhiker perhaps, hoping to find a bit of cash. Well . . ." She let out a shaky breath. "He'll have been disappointed in what he found here." She looked up abruptly, paling again. "You? Did you have any?"

"Mostly traveler's checks. They're still here." He shrugged. "He got a few hundred pounds, that's all."

"A few—hundred?" She bolted off the bed. "He took your money?"

"It's not important. Brie—"

"Not important?" she cut in. "You're living under my roof, a guest in my home, and had your money stolen. How much was it? I'll make it good."

"You certainly will not. Sit down and stop it."

"I said I'll make it good."

Patience snapped, he took her firmly by the shoulders and shoved her down on the bed. "They paid me five million for my last book, before foreign and movie rights. A few hundred pounds isn't going to break me." His eyes narrowed when her lips quivered again. "Take a deep breath. Now. Okay, another."

"I don't care if you've gold dripping from your fingers." Her voice broke, humiliating her.

"You want to cry some more?" He sighed lustily, sat down beside her, and braced for it. "Okay, let it rip."

"I'm not going to cry." She sniffled, used the heels of her hands to dry her cheeks. "I've got too much to do. It'll take hours to put things right here."

"You'll need to call the police."

"For what?" She lifted her hands, let them fall. "If anyone saw a stranger lurking about, my phone would already be ringing. Someone needed money, and they took it." She scanned the room, wondering how much her other guest might have lost, and how big a hole it would put in her precious savings. "I want you to say nothing to Maggie about this."

"Goddamn it, Brie—"

"She's six months along. I won't have her upset. I mean this." She gave him a steady look through eyes still shimmering with tears. "Your word, please."

"Fine, whatever you want. I want yours that you'll tell me exactly what's missing."

"I will. I'll phone to Murphy and tell him. He'll ask about. If there's something to know, I'll know it by nightfall." Calm again, she rose. "I need to start putting things in order. I'll start with your room so you can get to your work."

"I'll see to my own room."

"It's for me to—"

"You're pissing me off, Brianna." He unfolded himself slowly until he stood toe to toe with her. "Let's get this straight. You're not my maid, my mother, or my wife. I can hang up my own clothes."

"As you please."

Swearing, he grabbed her arm before she could walk out on him. She didn't resist, but stood very still, looking just over his shoulder. "Listen to me. You have a problem here and I want to help you. Can you get that through your head?"

"Want to help, do you?" She inclined her head and spoke with all the warmth of a glacier. "You might go borrow some tea from Murphy. We seem to be out."

"I'll call him for you," Gray said evenly. "And ask him to bring some over. I'm not leaving you alone here."

"Whatever suits you. His number's in the book in the kitchen by the . . ." She trailed off as the image of her lovely little room flashed into her head. She closed her eyes. "Gray, would you leave me alone for a little while? I'll be better for it."

"Brianna." He touched her cheek.

"Please." She'd crumble completely, humiliatingly, if he was kind now. "I'll be fine again once I'm busy. And I'd like some tea." Opening her eyes, she managed to smile. "Truly, I would."

"All right, I'll be downstairs."

Grateful, she got to work.

SEVEN

Gray sometimes toyed with the idea of buying himself a plane. Something very much along the lines of the sleek little jet Rogan had left at his and Brianna's disposal for the trip to Dublin might be just the ticket. He could have it custom-decorated to suit him, play with the engine himself occasionally. There was nothing to stop him from learning how to fly it.

It would certainly be an interesting toy, he mused as he settled into the comfortable leather seat beside Brianna. And having his own transportation would eliminate the minor headache of arranging for tickets and being at the mercy of the hiccups of the airlines.

But owning something—anything—equaled the responsibility of maintaining that something. That was why he rented or leased, but had never actually owned a car. And though there was something to be said for the privacy and convenience of a neat little Lear, he thought he would miss the crowds and company and all the odd expected glitches of a commercial flight.

But not this time. He slipped his hand over Brianna's as the plane began to taxi.

"Do you like to fly?"

"I haven't done it very often." The anticipation of spearing up into the sky still gave her stomach an intriguing little flip. "But yes, I think I do. I like looking down." She smiled at herself as she watched the ground tilt away below. It fascinated her, always, to picture herself above her own home, the hills, streaking through the clouds to somewhere else. "I suppose it's second nature to you."

"It's fun, thinking about where you're going."

"And where you've been."

"I don't think about that much. I've just been there."

As the plane climbed, he put a hand under her chin, turned her face toward his to study it. "You're still worried."

"It doesn't feel right, going off like this, and so luxuriously, too."

"Catholic guilt." The gilt in his eyes deepened when he grinned. "I've heard of that particular phenomenon. It's like if you're not doing something constructive, and actually enjoying not doing it, you're going to hell. Right?"

"Nonsense." She sniffed, irritated that it was even partially true. "I've responsibilities."

"And shirking them." He tsked and fingered the gold cross she wore. "That's like the near occasion of sin, isn't it? What is the near occasion of sin, exactly?"

"You are," she said, batting his hand away.

"No kidding?" The idea of that appealed enormously. "I like it."

"You would." She tucked a loose pin into place. "And this has nothing to do with that. If I'm feeling guilty, it's because I'm not used to just packing up and going on a moment's notice. I like to plan things out."

"Takes half the fun out of it."

"It stretches out the fun to my way of thinking." But she gnawed on her lip. "I know it's important that I be in Dublin for the wedding, but leaving home just now . . ."

"Murphy's dog-sitting," Gray reminded her. "And keeping an eye on the place." A sharp eye, Gray was certain, since he'd talked to Murphy privately. "Old Smythe-White left days ago, so you don't have any customers to worry about."

"Guests," she said automatically, brow creasing. "I can't imagine he'll be recommending Blackthorn after what happened. Though he was terribly good about it."

"He didn't lose anything. 'Never travel with cash, you know,' " Gray said in a mimic of Smythe-White's prissy voice. " 'It's an invitation for trouble.' "

She smiled a little, as he'd hoped. "He may not have had anything stolen, but I doubt he spent a peaceful night knowing his room had been broken into, his possessions pawed through." Which was why she'd refused to charge him for his stay.

"Oh, I don't know. I haven't had any trouble." He unfastened his seat belt and rose to wander into the galley. "Your brother-in-law's a classy guy."

"He is, yes." Her brow furrowed when Gray came back with a bottle of champagne and two glasses. "You're not going to open that. 'Tis only a short flight and—"

"Sure I'm going to open it. Don't you like champagne?"

"I like it well enough, but—" Her protest was cut off by the cheerful sound of a popping cork. She sighed, as a mother might seeing her child leap into a mud puddle.

"Now then." He sat again, poured both glasses. After handing her one, he tapped crystal to crystal and grinned. "Tell me about the bride and groom. Did you say they were eighty?"

"Uncle Niall, yes." Since there could be no putting the cork back into the bottle, she sipped. "Mrs. Sweeney's a few years younger."

"Imagine that." It tickled him. "Entering the matrimonial cage at their age."

"Cage?"

"It has a lot of restrictions and no easy way out." Enjoying the wine, he let it linger on his tongue before swallowing. "So, they were childhood sweethearts?"

"Not exactly," she murmured, still frowning over his description of marriage. "They grew up in Galway. Mrs. Sweeney was friends with my grandmother—she was Uncle Niall's sister, you see. And Mrs. Sweeney had a bit of a crush on Uncle Niall. Then my grandmother married and moved to Clare. Mrs. Sweeney married and went to Dublin. They lost track of each other. Then Maggie and Rogan began working together, and Mrs. Sweeney made the connection between the families. I wrote of it to Uncle Niall, and he brought himself down to Dublin." She smiled over it, hardly noticing when Gray refilled her glass. "The two of them have been close as bread and jam ever since."

"The twists and turns of fate." Gray raised his glass in toast. "Fascinating, isn't it?"

"They love each other," she said simply, sighed. "I only hope—" She cut herself off and stared out the window again.

"What?"

"I want them to have a fine day, a lovely one. I'm worried my mother will make it awkward." She turned to him again. However it embarrassed her, it was best he knew so that he wouldn't be too shocked if there was a scene. "She wouldn't go out to Dublin today. Wouldn't sleep in Maggie's Dublin house. She told me she'd come tomorrow, do her duty, then go back immediately."

He lifted a brow. "Not happy in cities?" he asked, though he sensed it was something entirely different.

"Mother's not a woman who finds contentment easily anywhere at all. I should tell you she may be difficult. She doesn't approve, you see, of the wedding."

"What? Does she think those crazy kids are too young to get married?"

Brianna's lips curved, but her eyes didn't reflect it. "It's money marrying money, as she sees it. And she . . . well, she has strong opinions about the fact that they've been living together in a way outside the sacrament."

"Living together?" He couldn't stop the grin. "In a way?"

"Living together," she said primly. "And as Mother will tell you, if you give her the chance, age hardly absolves them from the sin of fornication."

He choked on his wine. He was laughing and whooping for air when he caught the glint of Brianna's narrowed gaze. "Sorry—I can see that wasn't meant to be a joke."

"Some people find it easy to laugh at another's beliefs."

"I don't mean to." But he couldn't quite get the chuckles under control. "Christ, Brie, you've just told me the man's eighty and his blushing bride is right behind him. You don't really believe they're going to some firey hell because they . . ." He decided he'd better find a delicate way of putting it. "They've had a mature, mutually satisfying physical relationship."

"No." Some of the ice melted from her eyes. "No, I don't, of course. But Mother does, or says she does, because it makes it easier to complain. Families are complicated, aren't they?"

"From what I've observed. I don't have one to worry about myself."

"No family?" The rest of the ice melted into sympathy. "You lost your parents?"

"In a manner of speaking." It would have been more apt, he supposed, to say they had lost him.

"I'm sorry. And you've no brothers, no sisters?"

"Nope." He reached for the bottle again to top off his glass.

"But you've cousins, surely." Everyone had someone, she thought. "Grandparents, or aunts, uncles."

"No."

She only stared, devastated for him. To have no one. She couldn't conceive of it. Couldn't bear it.

"You're looking at me like I'm some foundling bundled in a basket on your doorstep." It amused him, and oddly, it touched him. "Believe me, honey, I like it this way. No ties, no strings, no guilts." He drank again, as if to seal the words. "Simplifies my life."

Empties it, more like, she thought. "It doesn't bother you, having no one to go home to?"

"It relieves me. Maybe it would if I had a home, but I don't have one of those, either."

The gypsy, she recalled, but she hadn't taken him literally until now. "But, Grayson, to have no place of your own—"

"No mortgage, no lawn to mow or neighbor to placate." He leaned over her to glance out the window. "Look, there's Dublin."

But she looked at him, felt for him. "But when you leave Ireland, where will you go?"

"I haven't decided. That's the beauty of it."

"You've got a great house." Less than three hours after landing in Dublin, Gray stretched his legs out toward the fire in Rogan's parlor. "I appreciate your putting me up."

"It's our pleasure." Rogan offered him a snifter of after-dinner brandy. They were alone for the moment, as Brianna and Maggie had driven to his grandmother's to help the bride with last-minute arrangements.

Rogan still had trouble picturing his grandmother as a nervous bride-to-be. And more trouble yet, imagining the man even now haranguing the cook as his future step-grandfather.

"You don't look too happy about it."

"What?" Rogan glanced back at Gray, made himself smile. "No, I'm sorry, it's nothing to do with you. I'm a bit uneasy about tomorrow, I suppose."

"Giving-the-bride-away jitters?"

The best Rogan could come up with was a grunt.

Reading his host well, Gray tucked his tongue in his cheek and stirred the unease. "Niall's an interesting character."

"A character," Rogan muttered. "Indeed."

"Your grandmother had stars in her eyes at dinner."

Now Rogan sighed. She had never looked happier. "They're besotted with each other."

"Well . . ." Gray swirled his brandy. "There are two of us and one of him. We could overpower him, drag him off to the docks, and put him on a ship bound for Australia."

"Don't think I haven't considered it." But he smiled now, easier. "There's no picking family, is there? And I'm forced to admit the man adores her. Maggie and Brie are delighted, so I find myself outgunned and outvoted."

"I like him," Gray said in grinning apology. "How can you not like a man who wears a jacket the shade of a Halloween pumpkin with tasseled alligator shoes?"

"There you are." Rogan waved an elegant hand. "In any case, we're pleased to be able to provide you with a wedding during your stay in Ireland. You're comfortable at Blackthorn?"

"Brianna has a knack for providing the comfortable."

"She does."

Gray's expression sobered as he frowned into his drink. "Something happened a few days ago that I think you should know. She didn't want me to mention it, particularly to Maggie. But I'd like your take on it."

"All right."

"The cottage was broken into."

"Blackthorn?" Startled, Rogan set his brandy aside.

"We were outside, in that shed she uses for potting. We might have been in there for half an hour, maybe a little longer. When we went back in, someone had tossed the place."

"Excuse me?"

"Turned it upside down," Gray explained. "A fast, messy search, I'd say."

"That doesn't make sense." But he leaned forward, worried. "Was anything taken?"

"I had some cash in my room." Gray shrugged it off. "That seems to be all. Brianna claims none of the neighbors would have come in that way."

"She'd be right." Rogan sat back again, picked up his brandy but didn't drink. "It's a closely knit community, and Brie's well loved there. Did you inform the garda?"

"She didn't want to, didn't see the point. I did speak with Murphy, privately."

"That would tend to it," Rogan agreed. "I'd have to think it was some stranger passing through. But even that seems out of place." Dissatisfied with any explanation, he tapped his fingers against the side of his glass. "You've been there some time now. You must have gotten a sense of the people, the atmosphere."

"Next stop Brigadoon," Gray murmured. "Logic points to a one-shot deal, and that's how she's handling it." Gray moved his shoulders. "Still, I don't think it would hurt for you to keep an eye out when you come back."

"I'll do that." Rogan frowned into his brandy. "You can be sure of it."

"You've a fine cook, Rogan me boy." Niall strolled in carting a tray loaded with china and a huge chocolate torte. He was a large man, sporting his thirty extra pounds like a badge of honor. And did indeed look somewhat like a jolly jack-o'-lantern in his orange sport coat and lime-green tie. "A prince of a man, he is." Niall set down the tray and beamed. "He's sent out this bit of sweet to help calm my nerves."

"I'm feeling nervous myself." Grinning, Gray rose to cut into the torte himself.

Niall boomed out with a laugh and slapped Gray heartily on the back. "There's a lad. Good appetite. Why don't we tuck into this, then have a few games of snooker?" He winked at Rogan. "After all, it's my last night as a free man. No more carousing with the boy-os for me. Any whiskey to wash this down with?"

"Whiskey." Rogan looked at the wide, grinning face of his future grandfather. "I could use a shot myself."

They had several. And then a few more. By the time the second bottle was opened, Gray had to squint to see the balls on the snooker table, and then they still tended to weave. He ended by closing one eye completely.

He heard the balls clack together, then stood back. "My point, gentlemen. My point." He leaned heavily on his cue.

"Yank bastard can't lose tonight." Niall slapped Gray on the back and nearly sent him nose first onto the table. "Set 'em up again, Rogan me boy. Let's have another."

"I can't see them," Rogan said slowly before lifting a hand in front of his face and peering at it. "I can't feel my fingers."

"Another whiskey's what you need." Like a sailor aboard a pitching deck, Niall made his way to the decanter. "Not a drop," he said sadly as he upended the crystal. "Not a bleeding drop left."

"There's no whiskey left in Dublin." Rogan pushed himself away from the wall that was holding him up, then fell weakly back. "We've drank it all. Drunk it all. Oh, Christ. I can't feel my tongue, either. I've lost it."

"Let's see." Willing to help, Gray laid his hands heavily on Rogan's shoulders. "Stick it out." Eyes narrowed, he nodded. " 'S okay, pal. It's there. Fact is, you've got two of 'em. That's the problem."

"I'm marrying my Chrissy tomorrow." Niall stood, teetering dangerously left, then right, his eyes glazed, his smile brilliant. "Beautiful little Chrissy, the belle of Dublin."

He pitched forward, falling like a redwood. With their arms companionably supporting each other, Rogan and Gray stared down at him.

"What do we do with him?" Gray wondered.

Rogan ran one of his two tongues around his teeth. "Do you think he's alive?"

"Doesn't look like it."

"Don't start the wake yet." Niall lifted his head. "Just get me on me feet, lads. I'll dance till dawn." His head hit the floor again with a thud.

"He's not so bad, is he?" Rogan asked. "When I'm drunk, that is."

"A prince of a man. Let's haul him up. He can't dance on his face."

"Right." They staggered over. By the time they'd hefted Niall to his knees, they were out of breath and laughing like fools. "Get up, you dolt. It's like trying to shift a beached whale."

Niall opened his bleary eyes, tossed back his head, and began, in a wavering but surprisingly affecting tenor, to sing.

"And it's all for me grog, me jolly, jolly grog. It's all for me beer and tobacco." He grunted his way up on one foot, nearly sent Gray flying. "Well, I spent all me tin on lassies drinking gin. Far across the Western ocean I must wander."

"You'll be lucky to wander to bed," Rogan told him.

He simply switched tunes. "Well, if you've got a wingo, take me up to ringo where the waxies singo all the day."

Well insulated by whiskey, Rogan joined in as the three of them teetered on their feet. "If you've had your fill of porter and you can't go any further—"

That struck Gray as wonderfully funny, and he snickered his way into the chorus.

With the harmony and affection of the drunk, they staggered their way down the hall. By the time they reached the base of the stairs, they were well into a whiskey-soaked rendition of "Dicey Riley."

"Well, I wouldn't say it was only poor old Dicey Riley who'd taken to the sup, would you, Brie?" Maggie stood halfway down the stairs with her sister, studying the trio below.

"I wouldn't, no." Folding her hands neatly at her waist, Brianna shook her head. "From the looks of them, they've dropped in for several little drops."

"Christ, she's beautiful, isn't she?" Gray mumbled.

"Yes." Rogan grinned brilliantly at his wife. "Takes my breath away. Maggie, my love, come give me a kiss."

"I'll give you the back of my hand." But she laughed as she started down. "Look at the lot of you, pitiful drunk. Uncle Niall, you're old enough to know better."

"Getting married, Maggie Mae. Where's my Chrissy?" He tried to turn a circle in search and had his two supporters tipping like dominoes.

"In her own bed sleeping, as you should be. Come on, Brie, let's get these warriors off the field."

"We were playing snooker." Gray beamed at Brianna. "I won."

"Yank bastard," Niall said affectionately, then kissed Gray hard on the mouth.

"Well, that's nice, isn't it?" Maggie managed to get an arm around Rogan. "Come on, now, that's the way. One foot in front of the other." Somehow they managed to negotiate the steps. They dumped Niall first.

"Get Rogan off to bed, Maggie," Brianna told her. "I'll tuck this one in, then come back and pull off Uncle Niall's shoes."

"Oh, what heads they'll have tomorrow." The prospect made Maggie smile. "Here we go, Sweeney, off to bed. Mind your hands." Since she considered him harmless in his current state, the order came out with a chuckle. "You haven't a clue what to do with them in your state."

"I'll wager I do."

"Oh, but you smell of whiskey and cigars." Brianna sighed and draped Gray's arm over her shoulders, braced him. "The man's eighty, you know. You should have stopped him."

"He's a bad influence, that Niall Feeney. We had to toast Chrissy's eyes, and her lips, and her hair, and her ears. I think we toasted her toes, too, but things get blurry about then."

"And small wonder. Here's your door. Just a bit farther, now."

"You smell so good, Brianna." With what he thought was a smooth move, he sniffed doglike at her neck. "Come to bed with me. I could show you things. All sorts of wonderful things."

"Mmm-hmm. Down you go. That's the way." Efficiently, she lifted his legs onto the bed and began to take off his shoes.

"Lie down with me. I can take you places. I want to be inside you."

Her hands fumbled at that. She looked up sharply, but his eyes were closed, his smile dreamy. "Hush, now," she murmured. "Go to sleep."

She tucked a blanket around him, brushed the hair from his brow, and left him snoring.

Suffering was to be expected. Overindulgence had to be paid for, and Gray was always willing to pay his way. But it seemed a little extreme to have to take a short, vicious trip to hell because of one foolish evening.

His head was cracked in two. It didn't show, a fact that relieved him considerably when he managed to crawl into the bathroom the following morning. He looked haggard, but whole. Obviously the jagged break in his skull was on the inside.

He'd probably be dead by nightfall.

His eyes were small, hard balls of fire. The inside of his mouth had been swabbed with something too foul to imagine. His stomach clutched and seized like a nervous fist.

He began to hope he'd be dead long before nightfall.

Since there was no one around, he indulged himself in a few whimpers as he stepped under the shower. He'd have sworn the smell of whiskey was seeping out of his pores.

Moving with the care of the aged or infirm, he climbed out of the tub, wrapped a towel around his waist. He did what he could to wash the hideous taste out of his mouth.

When he stepped into the bedroom, he yelped, slapped his hands over his eyes in time—he hoped—to keep them from bursting out of his head. Some sadist had come in and opened his drapes to the sunlight.

Brianna's own eyes had gone wide. Her mouth had fallen open. Other than the towel hanging loosely at his hips, he wore nothing but a few lingering drops of water from his shower.

His body was . . . the word *exquisite* flashed into her mind. Lean, muscled, gleaming. She found herself linking her fingers together and swallowing hard.

"I brought you a breakfast tray," she managed. "I thought you might be feeling poorly."

Cautious, Gray spread his fingers just enough to see through. "Then it wasn't the wrath of God." His voice was rough, but he feared the act of clearing it might do permanent damage. "For a minute I thought I was being struck down for my sins."

"It's only porridge, toast, and some coffee."

"Coffee." He said the word like a prayer. "Could you pour it?"

"I could. I brought you some aspirin."

"Aspirin." He could have wept. "Please."

"Take them first then." She brought him the pills with a small glass of water. "Rogan looks as sad as you," she said as Gray gobbled down the pills—and she fought to keep her hand from stroking over all that wet, curling dark hair. "Uncle Niall's fit as a fiddle."

"Figures." Gray moved cautiously toward the bed. He eased down, praying his head wouldn't roll off his neck. "Before we go any further, do I have anything to apologize for?"

"To me?"

"To anyone. Whiskey's not my usual poison, and I'm fuzzy on details after we started on the second bottle." He squinted up at her and found she was smiling at him. "Something funny?"

"No—well, yes, but it's not very kind of me to find it funny." She did give in then, sleeking a hand over his hair as she might over that of a child who had overindulged in cakes. "I was thinking it was sweet of you to offer to apologize right off that way." Her smile warmed. "But no, there's nothing. You were just drunk and silly. There was no harm in it."

"Easy for you to say." He supported his head. "I don't make a habit of drinking like that." Wincing, he reached for the coffee with his free hand. "In fact, I don't believe I've ever had that much at one time, or will again."

"You'll feel better when you've had a bite to eat. You have a couple of hours before you have to drive over for the wedding—if you're up to it."

"Wouldn't miss it." Resigned, Gray picked up the porridge. It smelled safe. He took a tentative bite and waited to see if his system would accept it. "Aren't I going with you?"

"I'm leaving in a few minutes. There's things to be done. You'll come over with Rogan and Uncle Niall—since it's doubtful the three of you can get into any trouble on such a short drive."

He grunted and scooped up more porridge.

"Do you need anything else before I go?"

"You've hit most of the vital points." Tilting his head, he studied her. "Did I try to talk you into going to bed with me last night?"

"You did."

"I thought I remembered that." His smile was quick and easy. "I can't imagine how you resisted me."

"Oh, I managed. I'll be off, then."

"Brianna." He sent her one quick, dangerous look. "I won't be plastered next time."

Christine Rogan Sweeney might have been on the verge of becoming a great-grandmother, but she was still a bride. No matter how often she told herself it was foolish to be nervous, to feel so giddy, her stomach still jumped.

She was to be married in only a few minutes more. To pledge herself to a man she loved dearly. And to take his pledge to her. And she would be a wife once again, after so many years a widow.

"You look beautiful." Maggie stood back as Christine turned in front of the chevel glass. The pale rose suit gleamed with tiny pearls on the lapels. Against Christine's shining white hair sat a jaunty, matching hat with a fingertip veil.

"I feel beautiful." She laughed and turned to embrace Maggie, then Brianna. "I don't care who knows it. I wonder if Niall could be as nervous as I am."

"He's pacing like a big cat," Maggie told her. "And asking Rogan for the time every ten seconds."

"Good." Christine drew in a long breath. "That's good, then. It is nearly time, isn't it?"

"Nearly." Brianna kissed her on each cheek. "I'll be going down now to make sure everything's as it should be. I wish you happiness . . . Aunt Christine."

"Oh, dear." Christine's eyes filled. "How sweet you are."

"Don't do that," Maggie warned. "You'll have us all going. I'll signal when we're ready, Brie."

With a quick nod Brianna hurried out. There were caterers, of course, and a houseful of servants. But a wedding was a family thing, and she wanted it perfect.

The guests were milling in the parlor—swirls of color, snatches of laughter. A harpist was playing in soft, dreamy notes. Garlands of roses had been twined along the banister, and pots of them were artistically decked throughout the house.

She wondered if she should slip into the kitchen, just to be certain all was well, when she spotted her mother and Lottie. Fixing a bright smile on her face, she went forward.

"Mother, you look wonderful."

"Foolishness. Lottie nagged me into spending good money on a new dress." But she brushed a hand fussily along the soft linen sleeve.

"It's lovely. And so's yours, Lottie."

Maeve's companion laughed heartily. "We splurged sinfully, we did. But it isn't every day you go to such a fancy wedding. The archbishop," she said with a whisper and a wink. "Imagine."

Maeve sniffed. "A priest's a priest no matter what hat he's wearing. Seems to me he'd think twice before officiating at such a time. When two people have lived in sin—"

"Mother." Brianna kept her voice low, but icily firm. "Not today. Please, if you'd only—"

"Brianna." Gray stepped up, took her hand, kissed it. "You look fabulous."

"Thank you." She struggled not to flush as his fingers locked possessively around hers. "Mother, Lottie, this is Grayson Thane. He's a guest at Blackthorn. Gray, Maeve Concannon and Lottie Sullivan."

"Mrs. Sullivan." He took Lottie's hand, making her giggle when he kissed it. "Mrs. Concannon. My congratulations on your lovely and talented daughters."

Maeve only scowled. His hair was as long as a girl's, she observed. And his smile had more than a bit of the devil in it. "A Yank, are you?"

"Yes, ma'am. I'm enjoying your country very much. And your daughter's hospitality."

"Paying tenants don't usually come to family weddings."

"Mother—"

"No, they don't," Gray said smoothly. "That's another thing I find charming about your country. Strangers are treated as friends, and friends never as strangers. May I escort you to your seats?"

Lottie was already hooking her arm through his. "Come ahead, Maeve.

How often are we going to get an offer from a fine-looking young man like this? You're a book writer, are you?"

"I am." He swept both women off, sending a quick, smug smile to Brianna over his shoulder.

She could have kissed him. Even as she sighed in relief, Maggie signaled from the top of the stairs.

As the harpist switched to the wedding march, Brianna slipped to the back of the room. Her throat tightened as Niall took his place in front of the hearth and looked toward the stairs. Perhaps his hair was thin and his waist thick, but just then he looked young and eager and full of nerves.

The room hummed with anticipation as Christine walked slowly down the stairs, turned, and with her eyes bright behind her veil, went to him. The archbishop blessed them, and the ceremony began.

"Here." Gray slipped up beside Brianna a few moments later and offered his handkerchief. "I had a feeling you'd need this."

"It's beautiful." She dabbed at her eyes. The words sighed through her. *To love. To honor. To cherish.*

Gray heard *Till death do us part.* A life sentence. He'd always figured there was a reason people cried at weddings. He put an arm around her shoulders and gave her a friendly squeeze. "Buck up," he murmured. "It's nearly over."

"It's only beginning," she corrected and indulged herself by resting her head on his shoulder.

Applause erupted when Niall thoroughly, and enthusiastically, kissed the bride.

EIGHT

Trips on private planes, champagne, and glossy society weddings were all well and good, Brianna supposed. But she was glad to be home. Though she knew better than to trust the skies or the balmy air, she preferred to think the worst of the winter was over. She dreamed of her fine new greenhouse as she tended her seedlings in the shed. And planned for her converted attic room while she hung the wash.

In the week she'd been back from Dublin, she all but had the house to herself. Gray was closeted in his room working. Now and again he popped off for a drive or strolled into the kitchen sniffing for food.

She wasn't sure whether to be relieved or miffed that he seemed too preoccupied to try to charm more kisses from her.

Still, she was forced to admit that her solitude was more pleasant knowing he was just up the stairs. She could sit by the fire in the evening, reading or knitting or sketching out her plans, knowing he could come wandering down to join her at any time.

But it wasn't Gray who interrupted her knitting one cool evening, but her mother and Lottie.

She heard the car outside without much surprise. Friends and neighbors often stopped in when they saw her light on. She'd set her knitting aside and started for the door when she heard her mother and Lottie arguing outside it.

Brianna only sighed. For reasons that escaped her, the two women seemed to enjoy their bickering.

"Good evening to you." She greeted them both with a kiss. "What a fine surprise."

"I hope we're not disturbing you, Brie." Lottie rolled her merry eyes. "Maeve had it in her head we would come, so here we are."

"I'm always pleased to see you."

"We were out, weren't we?" Maeve shot back. "Too lazy to cook, she was, so I have to drag myself out to a restaurant no matter how I'm feeling."

"Even Brie must tire of her own cooking from time to time," Lottie said as she hung Maeve's coat on the hall rack. "As fine as it is. And it's nice to get out now and again and see people."

"There's no one I need to see."

"You wanted to see Brianna, didn't you?" It pleased Lottie to score a small point. "That's why we're here."

"I want some decent tea is what I want, not that pap they serve in the restaurant."

"I'll make it." Lottie patted Brianna's arm. "You have a nice visit with your ma. I know where everything is."

"And take that hound to the kitchen with you." Maeve gave Con a look of impatient dislike. "I won't have him slobbering all over me."

"You'll keep me company, won't you, boy-o?" Cheerful, Lottie ruffled Con between the ears. "Come along with Lottie, now, there's a good lad."

Agreeable, and ever hopeful for a snack, Con trailed behind her.

"I've a nice fire in the parlor, Mother. Come and sit."

"Waste of fuel," Maeve muttered. "It's warm enough without one."

Brianna ignored the headache brewing behind her eyes. "It's comforting with one. Did you have a nice dinner?"

Maeve gave a snort as she sat. She liked the feel and the look of the fire, but was damned if she would admit it. "Dragged me off to a place in Ennis and orders pizza, she does. Pizza of all things!"

"Oh, I know the place you're speaking of. They have lovely food. Rogan says the pizza tastes just as it does in the States." Brianna picked up her knitting again. "Did you know that Murphy's sister Kate is expecting again?"

"The girl breeds like a rabbit. What's this—four of them?"

" 'Twill be her third. She's two boys now and is hoping for a girl." Smiling, Brianna held up the soft pink yarn. "So I'm making this blanket for luck."

"God will give her what He gives her, whatever color you knit."

Brianna's needles clicked quietly. "So He will. I had a card from Uncle Niall and Aunt Christine. It has the prettiest picture of the sea and mountains on it. They're having a lovely time on their cruise ship, touring the islands of Greece."

"Honeymoons at their age." And in her heart Maeve yearned to see the mountains and foreign seas herself. "Well, if you've enough money you can go where you choose and do what you choose. Not all of us can fly off to warm places in the winter. If I could, perhaps my chest wouldn't be so tight with cold."

"Are you feeling poorly?" The question was automatic, like the answers to the multiplication tables she'd learned in school. It shamed her enough to have her look up and try harder. "I'm sorry, Mother."

"I'm used to it. Dr. Hogan does no more than cluck his tongue and tell me I'm fit. But I know how I feel, don't I?"

"You do, yes." Brianna's knitting slowed as she turned over an idea. "I wonder if you'd feel better if you could go away for some sun."

"Hah. And where am I to find sun?"

"Maggie and Rogan have that villa in the south of France. It's beautiful and warm there, they say. Remember, she drew me pictures."

"Went off with him to that foreign country before they were married."

"They're married now," Brianna said mildly. "Wouldn't you like to go there, Mother, you and Lottie, for a week or two? Such a nice rest in the sunshine you could have, and the sea air's always so healing."

"And how would I get there?"

"Mother, you know Rogan would have the plane take you."

Maeve could imagine it. The sun, the servants, the fine big house overlooking the sea. She might have had such a place of her own if . . . If.

"I'll not ask that girl for any favors."

"You needn't. I'll ask for you."

"I don't know as I'm fit to travel," Maeve said, for the simple pleasure of making things difficult. "The trip to Dublin and back tired me."

"All the more reason for you to have a nice vacation," Brianna returned, knowing the game well. "I'll speak to Maggie tomorrow and arrange it. I'll help you pack, don't worry."

"Anxious to see me off, are you?"

"Mother." The headache was growing by leaps and bounds.

"I'll go, all right." Maeve waved a hand. "For my health, though the good Lord knows how it'll affect my nerves to be among all those foreigners." Her eyes narrowed. "And where is the Yank?"

"Grayson? He's upstairs, working."

"Working." She huffed out a breath. "Since when is spinning a tale working, I'd like to know. Every other person in this county spins tales."

"Putting them on paper would be different, I'd think. And there are times when he comes down after he's been at it for a while he looks as though he's been digging ditches. He seems that tired."

"He looked frisky enough in Dublin—when he had his hands all over you."

"What?" Brianna dropped a stitch and stared.

"Do you think I'm blind as well as ailing?" Spots of pink rode high on Maeve's cheeks. "Mortified I was to see the way you let him carry on with you, in public, too."

"We were dancing," Brianna said between lips that had gone stiff and cold. "I was teaching him some steps."

"I saw what I saw." Maeve set her jaw. "And I'm asking you right now if you're giving your body to him."

"If I'm . . ." The pink wool spilled onto the floor. "How can you ask me such a thing?"

"I'm your mother, and I'll ask what I please of you. No doubt half the village is talking of it, you being here alone night after night with the man."

"No one is talking of it. I run an inn, and he's my guest."

"A convenient path to sin—I've said so since you insisted on starting this business." She nodded as if Grayson's presence there only confirmed her opinion. "You haven't answered me, Brianna."

"And I shouldn't, but I'll answer you. I haven't given my body to him, or to anyone."

Maeve waited a moment, then nodded again. "Well, a liar you've never been, so I'll believe you."

"I can't find it in me to care what you believe." It was temper she knew that had her knees trembling as she rose. "Do you think I'm proud and happy to have never known a man, to have never found one who would love me? I've no wish to live my life alone, or to forever be making baby things for some other woman's child."

"Don't raise your voice to me, girl."

"What good does it do to raise it?" Brianna took a deep breath, fought for calm. "What good does it do not to? I'll help Lottie with the tea."

"You'll stay where you are." Mouth grim, Maeve angled her head. "You should thank God on your knees for the life you lead, my girl. You've a roof over your head and money in your pocket. It may be I don't like how you earn it, but you've made some small success out of your choice in what many would consider an honest living. Do you think a man and babies can replace that? Well, you're wrong if you do."

"Maeve, what are you badgering the girl about now?" Wearily Lottie came in and set down the tea tray.

"Stay out of this, Lottie."

"Please." Cooly, calmly, Brianna inclined her head. "Let her finish."

"Finish I will. I had something once I could call mine. And I lost it." Maeve's mouth trembled once, but she firmed it, hardened it. "Lost any chance I had to be what I'd wanted to be. Lust and nothing more, the sin of it. With a baby in my belly what could I be but some man's wife?"

"My father's wife," Brianna said slowly.

"So I was. I conceived a child in sin and paid for it my whole life."

"You conceived two children," Brianna reminded her.

"Aye, I did. The first, your sister, carried that mark with her. Wild she was and will always be. But you were a child of marriage and duty."

"Duty?"

With her hands planted on either arm of her chair, Maeve leaned forward, and her voice was bitter. "Do you think I wanted him to touch me again? Do you think I enjoyed being reminded why I would never have my heart's desire? But the Church says marriage should produce children. So I did my duty by the Church and let him plant another child in me."

"Duty," Brianna repeated, and the tears she might have shed were frozen in her heart. "With no love, no pleasure. Is that what I came from?"

"There was no need to share my bed with him when I knew I carried you. I suffered another labor, another birth, and thanked God it would be my last."

"You never shared a bed with him. All those years."

"There would be no more children. With you I had done what I could to absolve my sin. You don't have Maggie's wildness. There's a coolness in you, a control. You'll use that to keep yourself pure—unless you let some man tempt you. It was nearly so with Rory."

"I loved Rory." She hated knowing she was so near tears. For her father, she thought, and the woman he had loved and let go.

"You were a child." Maeve dismissed the heartbreak of youth. "But you're a woman now, and pretty enough to draw a man's eye. I want you to remember what can happen if you let them persuade you to give in. The one upstairs, he'll come and he'll go as he pleases. Forget that, and you could end up alone, with a baby growing under your apron and shame in your heart."

"So often I wondered why there was no love in this house." Brianna took in a shuddering breath and struggled to steady her voice. "I knew you didn't love Da, couldn't somehow. It hurt me to know it. But then when I learned from Maggie about your singing, your career, and how you'd lost that, I thought I understood, and could sympathize for the pain you must have felt."

"You could never know what it is to lose all you've ever wanted."

"No, I can't. But neither can I understand a woman, any woman, having no love in her heart for the children she carried and birthed." She lifted her hands to her cheeks. But they weren't wet. Dry and cold they were, like marble against her fingers. "Always you've blamed Maggie for simply being born. Now I see I was nothing more than a duty to you, a sort of penance for an earlier sin."

"I raised you with care," Maeve began.

"With care. No, it's true you never raised your hand to me the way you did with Maggie. It's a miracle she didn't grow to hate me for that alone. It was heat with her, and cold discipline with me. And it worked well, made us, I suppose, what we are."

Very carefully she sat again, picked up her yarn. "I've wanted to love you. I used to ask myself why it was I could never give you more than loyalty and duty. Now I see it wasn't the lack in me, but in you."

"Brianna." Appalled, and deeply shaken, Maeve got to her feet. "How can you say such things to me? I've only tried to spare you, to protect you."

"I've no need of protection. I'm alone, aren't I, and a virgin, just as you wish it. I'm knitting a blanket for another woman's child as I've done before, and will do again. I have my business, as you say. Nothing has changed here, Mother, but for an easing of my conscience. I'll give you no less than I've always given you, only I'll stop berating myself for not giving more."

Dry-eyed again, she looked up. "Will you pour the tea, Lottie? I want to tell you about the vacation you and Mother will be taking soon. Have you been to France?"

"No." Lottie swallowed the lump in her throat. Her heart bled for both the women. She sent a look of sorrow toward Maeve, knowing no way to comfort. With a sigh she poured the tea. "No," she repeated. "I've not been there. Are we going, then?"

"Yes, indeed." Brianna picked up the rhythm of her knitting. "Very soon if you like. I'll be talking to Maggie about it tomorrow." She read the sympathy in Lottie's eyes and made herself smile. "You'll have to go shopping for a bikini."

Brianna was rewarded with a laugh. After setting the teacup on the table beside Brianna, Lottie touched her cold cheek. "There's a girl," she murmured.

A family from Helsinki stayed the weekend at Blackthorn. Brianna was kept busy catering to the couple and their three children. Out of pity, she scooted Con off to Murphy. The towheaded three-year-old couldn't seem to resist pulling ears and tail—an indignity which Concobar suffered silently.

Unexpected guests helped keep her mind off the emotional upheaval her mother had stirred. The family was loud, boisterous, and as hungry as bears just out of hibernation.

Brianna enjoyed every moment of them.

She bid them good-bye with kisses for the children and a dozen tea cakes for their journey south. The moment their car passed out of sight, Gray crept up behind her.

"Are they gone?"

"Oh." She pressed a hand to her heart. "You scared the life out of me." Turning, she pushed at the stray wisps escaping her topknot. "I thought you'd come down to say good-bye to the Svensons. Little Jon asked about you."

"I still have little Jon's sticky fingerprints over half my body and most of my papers." With a wry grin Gray tucked his thumbs in his front pockets. "Cute kid, but, Jesus, he never stopped."

"Three-year-olds are usually active."

"You're telling me. Give one piggyback ride and you're committed for life."

Now she smiled, remembering. "You looked very sweet with him. I imagine he'll always remember the Yank who played with him at the Irish inn." She tilted her head. "And he was holding the little lorry you bought him yesterday when he left."

"Lorry—oh, the truck, right." He shrugged. "I just happened to see it when I was taking a breather in the village."

"Just happened to see it," she repeated with a slow nod. "As well as the two dolls for the little girls."

"That's right. Anyway, I usually get a kick out of OPKs."

"OPKs?"

"Other people's kids. But now"—he slipped his hands neatly around her waist—"we're alone again."

In a quick defensive move she pressed a hand to his chest before he could draw her closer. "I've errands to do."

He looked down at her hand, lifted a brow. "Errands."

"That's right, and I've a mountain of wash to do when I get back."

"Are you going to hang out the wash? I love to watch you hang it on the line—especially when there's a breeze. It's incredibly sexy."

"What a foolish thing to say."

His grin only widened. "There's something to be said for making you blush, too."

"I'm not blushing." She could feel the heat in her cheeks. "I'm impatient. I need to be off, Grayson."

"How about this, I'll take you where you need to go." Before she could speak, he lowered his mouth, brushed it lightly over hers. "I've missed you, Brianna."

"You can't have. I've been right here."

"I've missed you." He watched her lashes lower. Her shy, uncertain responses to him gave him an odd sense of power. All ego, he thought, amused at himself. "Where's your list?"

"My list?"

"You've always got one."

Her gaze shifted up again. Those misty-green eyes were aware, and just a little afraid. Gray felt the surge of heat spear up from the balls of his feet straight to the loins. His fingers tightened convulsively on her waist before he forced himself to step back, let out a breath.

"Taking it slow is killing me," he muttered.

"I beg your pardon?"

"Never mind. Get your list and whatever. I'll drive you."

"I don't have a list. I've only to go to my mother's and help her and Lottie pack for their trip. There's no need for you to take me."

"I could use the drive. How long will you be there?"

"Two hours, perhaps three."

"I'll drop you off, pick you up. I'm going out anyway," he continued before she could argue. "It'll save petrol."

"All right. If you're sure. I'll just be a minute."

While he waited, Gray stepped into the path of the front garden. In the month he'd been there, he'd seen gales, rain, and the luminous light of the Irish sun. He'd sat in village pubs and listened to gossip, traditional music. He'd wandered down lanes where farmers herded their cows from field to field, and had walked up the winding steps of ruined castles, hearing the echos of war and death. He'd visited grave sites and had stood on the verge of towering cliffs looking out on the rolling sea.

Of all the places he'd visited, none seemed quite so appealing as the view from Brianna's front garden. But he wasn't altogether certain if it was the spot or the woman he was waiting for. Either way, he decided, his time here would certainly be one of the most satisfying slices of his life.

After he dropped Brianna off at the tidy house outside Ennis, he went wandering. For more than an hour he clambered over rocks at the Burren, taking pictures in his head. The sheer vastness delighted him, as did the Druid's Altar that drew so many tourists with their clicking cameras.

He drove aimlessly, stopping where he chose—a small beach deserted but for a small boy and a huge dog, a field where goats cropped and the wind whispered through tall grass, a small village where a woman counted out his change for his candy bar purchase with curled, arthritic fingers, then offered him a smile as sweet as sunlight.

A ruined abbey with a round tower caught his eye and had him pulling off the road to take a closer look. The round towers of Ireland fascinated him, but he'd found them primarily on the east coast. To guard, he supposed, from the influx of invasions across the Irish Sea. This one was whole, undamaged, and set at a curious slant. Gray spent some time circling, studying, and wondering how he could use it.

There were graves there as well, some old, some new. He had always been intrigued by the way generations could mingle so comfortably in death when they rarely managed it in life. For himself, he would take the Viking way—a ship out to sea and a torch.

But for a man who dealt in death a great deal, he preferred not to linger his thoughts overmuch on his own mortality.

Nearly all of the graves he passed were decked with flowers. Many of them were covered with plastic boxes, misty with condensation, the blossoms within all no more than a smear of color. He wondered why it didn't amuse him. It should have. Instead he was touched, stirred by the devotion to the dead.

They had belonged once, he thought. Maybe that was the definition of family. Belong once, belong always.

He'd never had that problem. Or that privilege.

He wandered through, wondering when the husbands, the wives, the children came to lay the wreaths and flowers. On the day of death? The day of birth? The feast day of the saint the dead had been named for? Or Easter maybe. That was a big one for Catholics.

He'd ask Brianna, he decided. It was something he could definitely work into his book.

He couldn't have said why he stopped just at that moment, why he looked down at that particular marker. But he did, and he stood, alone, the breeze ruffling his hair, looking down at Thomas Michael Concannon's grave.

Brianna's father? he wondered and felt an odd clutch around his heart. The dates seemed right. O'Malley had told him stories of Tom Concannon when Gray had sipped at a Guinness at the pub. Stories ripe with affection, sentiment, and humor.

Gray knew he had died suddenly, at the cliffs at Loop Head, with only Maggie with him. But the flowers on the grave, Gray was certain, were Brianna's doing.

They'd been planted over him. Though the winter had been hard on them, Gray could see they'd been recently weeded. More than a few brave blades of green were spearing up, searching for the sun.

He'd never stood over a grave of someone he'd known. Though he often paid visits to the dead, there'd been no pilgrimage to the resting place of anyone he'd cared for. But he felt a tug now, one that made him crouch down and brush a hand lightly over the carefully tended mound.

And he wished he'd brought flowers.

"Tom Concannon," he murmured. "You're well remembered. They talk of you in the village, and smile when they say your name. I guess that's as fine an epitaph as anyone could ask for."

Oddly content, he sat beside Tom awhile and watched sunlight and shadows play on the stones the living planted to honor the dead.

He gave Brianna three hours. It was obviously more than enough as she came out of the house almost as soon as he pulled up in front of it. His smile of greeting turned to a look of speculation as he got a closer look.

Her face was pale, as he knew it became when she was upset or moved.

Her eyes, though cool, showed traces of strain. He glanced toward the house, saw the curtain move. He caught a glimpse only, but Maeve's face was as pale as her daughter's, and appeared equally unhappy.

"All packed?" he said, keeping his tone mild.

"Yes." She slipped into the car, her hands tight around her purse—as if it was the only thing that kept her from leaping up. "Thank you for coming for me."

"A lot of people find packing a chore." Gray pulled the car out and for once kept his speed moderate.

"It can be." Normally, she enjoyed it. The anticipation of going somewhere, and more, the anticipation of returning home. "It's done now, and they'll be ready to leave in the morning."

God, she wanted to close her eyes, to escape from the pounding headache and miserable guilt into sleep.

"Do you want to tell me what's upset you?"

"I'm not upset."

"You're wound up, unhappy, and as pale as ice."

"It's personal. It's family business."

The fact that her dismissal stung surprised him. But he only shrugged and lapsed into silence.

"I'm sorry." Now she did close her eyes. She wanted peace. Couldn't everyone just give her a moment's peace? "That was rude of me."

"Forget it." He didn't need her problems in any case, he reminded himself. Then he glanced at her and swore under his breath. She looked exhausted. "I want to make a stop."

She started to object, then kept her eyes and mouth closed. He'd been good enough to drive her, she reminded herself. She could certainly bear a few minutes longer before she buried all this tension in work.

He didn't speak again. He was driving on instinct, hoping the choice he made would bring the color back to her cheeks and the warmth to her voice.

She didn't open her eyes again until he braked and shut the engine off. Then she merely stared at the castle ruins. "You needed to stop here?"

"I wanted to stop here," he corrected. "I found this my first day here. It's playing a prominent part in my book. I like the feel of it."

He got out, rounded the hood, and opened her door. "Come on." When she didn't move, he leaned down and unfastened her seat belt himself. "Come on. It's great. Wait till you see the view from the top."

"I've wash to do," she complained and heard the sulkiness of her own voice as she stepped out of the car.

"It's not going anywhere." He had her hand now and was tugging her over the high grass.

She didn't have the heart to point out that the ruins weren't likely to go anywhere, either. "You're using this place in your book?"

"Big murder scene." He grinned at her reaction, the uneasiness and superstition in her eyes. "Not afraid are you? I don't usually act out my scenes."

"Don't be foolish." But she shivered once as they stepped between the high stone walls.

There was grass growing wild on the ground, bits of green pushing its way through chinks in the stone. Above her, she could see where the floors had been once, so many years ago. But now time and war left the view to the sky unimpeded.

The clouds floated silently as ghosts.

"What do you suppose they did here, right here?" Gray mused.

"Lived, worked. Fought."

"That's too general. Use your imagination. Can't you see it, the people walking here? It's winter, and it's bone cold. Ice rings on the water barrels, frost on the ground that snaps like dry twigs underfoot. The air stings with smoke from the fires. A baby's crying, hungry, then stops when his mother bares her breast."

He drew her along with him, physically, emotionally, until she could almost see it as he did.

"Soldiers are drilling out there, and you can hear the ring of sword to sword. A man hurries by, limping from an old wound, his breath steaming out in cold clouds. Come on, let's go up."

He pulled her toward narrow, tight winding stairs. Every so often there would be an opening in the stone, a kind of cave. She wondered if people had slept there, or stored goods. Or tried to hide, perhaps, from the enemy who would always find them.

"There'd be an old woman carrying an oil lamp up here, and she has a puckered scar on the back of her hand and fear in her eyes. Another's bringing fresh rushes for the floors, but she's young and thinking of her lover."

Gray kept her hand in his, stopping when they came to a level midway. "It must have been the Cromwellians, don't you think, who sacked it. There'd have been screams, the stench of smoke and blood, that nasty thud of metal hacking into bone, and that high-pitched shriek a man makes when the pain slices him. Spears driving straight through bellies, pinning a body to the ground where the limbs would twitch before nerves died. Crows circling overhead, waiting for the feast."

He turned, saw her eyes were wide and glazed—and chuckled. "Sorry, I get caught up."

"It's not just a blessing to have an imagination like that." She shivered again and fought to swallow. "I don't think I want you to make me see it so clear."

"Death's fascinating, especially the violent type. Men are always hunting men. And this is a hell of a spot for murder—of the contemporary sort."

"Your sort," she murmured.

"Mmm. He'll toy with the victim first," Gray began as he started to climb again. He was caught up in his own mind, true, but he could see Brianna was no longer worrying over whatever had happened at her mother's. "Let the atmosphere and those smoky ghosts stir into the fear like a slow poison. He won't hurry—he likes the hunt, craves it. He can scent the fear, like any wolf, he can scent it. It's the scent that gets in his blood and makes it pump, that arouses him like sex. And the prey runs, chasing that thin thread of hope. But she's breathing fast. The sound of it echoes, carries on the wind. She falls—the stairs are treacherous in the dark, in the rain. Wet and slick, they're weapons themselves. But she claws her way up them, air sobbing in and out of her lungs, her eyes wild."

"Gray—"

"She's nearly as much of an animal as he, now. Terror's stripped off layers of humanity, the same as good sex will, or true hunger. Most people think they've experienced all three, but it's rare even to know one sensation fully. But she knows the first now, knows that terror as if it was solid and alive, as if it could wrap its hands around her throat. She wants a bolt hole, but there's nowhere to hide. And she can hear him climbing, slowly, tirelessly behind her. Then she reaches the top."

He drew Brianna out of the shadows onto the wide, walled ledge where sunlight streamed.

"And she's trapped."

She jolted when Gray swung her around, nearly screamed. Roaring with laughter, he lifted her off her feet. "Christ, what an audience you are."

" 'Tisn't funny." She tried to wiggle free.

"It's wonderful. I'm planning on having him mutilate her with an antique dagger, but . . ." He hooked his arm under Brianna's knees and carried her to the wall. "Maybe he should just dump her over the side."

"Stop!" Out of self-preservation she threw her arms around him and clung.

"Why didn't I think of this before? Your heart's pounding, you've got your arms around me."

"Bully."

"Got your mind off your troubles, didn't it?"

"I'll keep my troubles, thank you, and keep out of that twisted imagination of yours."

"No, no one does." He snuggled her a little closer. "That's what fiction's all about, books, movies, whatever. It gives you a break from reality and lets you worry about someone else's problems."

"What does it do for you who tells the tale?"

"Same thing. Exactly the same thing." He set her on her feet and turned her to the view. "It's like a painting, isn't it?" Gently, he drew her closer until her back was nestled against him. "As soon as I saw this place, it grabbed me. It was raining the first time I came here, and it almost seemed as if the colors should run."

She sighed. Here was the peace she'd wanted after all. In his odd roundabout way he'd given it to her. "It's nearly spring," she murmured.

"You always smell of spring." He bent his head to rub his lips over the nape of her neck. "And taste of it."

"You're making my legs weak again."

"Then you'd better hold on to me." He turned her, cupped a hand at her jaw. "I haven't kissed you in days."

"I know." She built up her courage, kept her eyes level. "I've wanted you to."

"That was the idea." He touched his lips to hers, stirred when her hands slipped up his chest to frame his face.

She opened for him willingly, her little murmur of pleasure as arousing as a caress. With the wind swirling around them, he drew her closer, careful to keep his hands easy, his mouth gentle.

All the strain, the fatigue, the frustration had vanished. She was home, was all that Brianna could think. Home was always where she wanted to be.

On a sigh she rested her head on his shoulder, curved her arms up his back. "I've never felt like this."

Nor had he. But that was a dangerous thought, and one he would have to consider. "It's good with us," he murmured. "There's something good about it."

"There is." She lifted her cheek to his. "Be patient with me, Gray."

"I intend to. I want you, Brianna, and when you're ready . . ." He stepped back, ran his hands down her arms until their fingers linked. "When you're ready."

NINE

Gray wondered if his appetite was enhanced due to the fact that he had another hunger that was far from satisfied. He thought it best to take it philosophically—and help himself to a late-night feast of Brianna's bread-and-butter pudding. Making tea was becoming a habit as well, and he'd already set the kettle on the stove and warmed the pot before he scooped out pudding into a bowl.

He didn't think he'd been so obsessed with sex since his thirteenth year. Then it had been Sally Anne Howe, one of the other residents of the Simon Brent Memorial Home for Children. Good old Sally Anne, Gray thought now, with her well-blossomed body and sly eyes. She'd been three years older than he, and more than willing to share her charms with anyone for smuggled cigarettes or candy bars.

At the time he thought she was a goddess, the answer to a randy adolescent's prayers. He could look back now with pity and anger, knowing the cycle of abuse and the flaws in the system that had made a pretty young girl feel her only true worth was nestled between her thighs.

He'd had plenty of sweaty dreams about Sally Anne after lights out. And had been lucky enough to steal an entire pack of Marlboros from one of the counselors. Twenty cigarettes had equaled twenty fucks, he remembered. And he'd been a very fast learner.

Over the years, he'd learned quite a bit more, from girls his own age, and from professionals who plied their trade out of darkened doorways that smelled of stale grease and sour sweat.

He'd been barely sixteen when he'd broken free of the orphanage and hit the road with the clothes on his back and twenty-three dollars worth of loose change and crumpled bills in his pocket.

Freedom was what he'd wanted, freedom from the rules, the regulations, the endless cycle of the system he'd been caught in most of his life. He'd found it, and used it, and paid for it.

He'd lived and worked those streets for a long time before he'd given himself a name, and a purpose. He'd been fortunate enough to have possessed a talent that had kept him from being swallowed up by other hungers.

At twenty he'd had his first lofty, and sadly autobiographical, novel under his belt. The publishing world had not been impressed. By twenty-two, he'd crafted out a neat, clever little whodunit. Publishers did not come clamoring, but a whiff of interest from an assistant editor had kept him holed up in a cheap rooming house battering at a manual typewriter for weeks.

That, he'd sold. For peanuts. Nothing before or since had meant as much to him.

Ten years later, and he could live as he chose, and he felt he'd chosen well.

He poured the water into the pot, shoveled a spoonful of pudding into his mouth. As he glanced over at Brianna's door, spotted the thin slant of light beneath it, he smiled.

He'd chosen her, too.

Covering his bases, he set the pot with two cups on a tray, then knocked at her door.

"Yes, come in."

She was sitting at her little desk, tidy as a nun in a flannel gown and slippers, her hair in a loose braid over one shoulder. Gray gamely swallowed the saliva that pooled in his mouth.

"Saw your light. Want some tea?"

"That would be nice. I was just finishing up some paperwork."

The dog uncurled himself from beside her feet and walked over to rub against Gray. "Me, too." He set down the tray to ruffle Con's fur. "Murder makes me hungry."

"Killed someone today, did you?"

"Brutally." He said it with such relish, she laughed.

"Perhaps that's what makes you so even-tempered all in all," she mused. "All those emotional murders purging your system. Do you ever—" She caught herself, moving a shoulder as he handed her a cup.

"Go ahead, ask. You rarely ask anything about my work."

"Because I imagine everyone does."

"They do." He made himself comfortable. "I don't mind."

"Well, I was wondering if you ever make one of the characters someone you know—then kill them off."

"There was this snotty French waiter in Dijon. I garotted him."

"Oh." She rubbed a hand over her throat. "How did it feel?"

"For him, or me?"

"For you."

"Satisfying." He spooned up pudding. "Want me to kill someone for you, Brie? I aim to please."

"Not at the moment, no." She shifted, and some of her papers fluttered to the floor.

"You need a typewriter," he told her as he helped her gather them up.

"Better yet, a word processor. It would save you time writing business letters."

"Not when I'd have to search for every key." While he read her correspondence, she cocked a brow, amused. " 'Tisn't very interesting."

"Hmm. Oh, sorry, habit. What's Triquarter Mining?"

"Oh, just a company Da must have invested in. I found the stock certificate with his things in the attic. I've written them once already," she added, mildly annoyed. "But had no answer. So I'm trying again."

"Ten thousand shares." Gray pursed his lips. "That's not chump change."

"It is, if I think I know what you're saying. You had to know my father—he was always after a new moneymaking scheme that cost more than it would ever earn. Still, this needs to be done." She held out a hand. "That's just a copy. Rogan took the original for safekeeping and made that for me."

"You should have him check it out."

"I don't like to bother him with it. His plate's full with the new gallery—and with Maggie."

He handed her back the copy. "Even at a dollar a share, it's fairly substantial."

"I'd be surprised if it was worth more than a pence a share. God knows he couldn't have paid much more. More likely it is that the whole company went out of business."

"Then your letter would have come back."

She only smiled. "You've been here long enough to know the Irish mails. I think—" They both glanced over as the dog began to growl. "Con?"

Instead of responding, the dog growled again, and the fur on his back lifted. In two strides Gray was at the windows. He saw nothing but mist.

"Fog," he muttered. "I'll go look around. No," he said when she started to rise. "It's dark, it's cold, it's damp, and you're staying put."

"There's nothing out there."

"Con and I will find out. Let's go." He snapped his fingers, and to Brianna's surprise, Con responded immediately. He pranced out at Gray's heels.

She kept a flashlight in the first kitchen drawer. Gray snagged it before he opened the door. The dog quivered once, then as Gray murmured, "go," leaped into the mist. In seconds the sound of his racing feet was muffled to silence.

The fog distorted the beam from the flash. Gray moved carefully, eyes and ears straining. He heard the dog bark, but from what direction or distance he couldn't say.

He stopped by Brianna's bedroom windows, playing the light on the ground. There, in her neat bed of perennials, was a single footprint.

Small, Gray mused, crouching down. Nearly small enough to be a child's. It could be as simple as that—kids out on a lark. But when he continued to circle the house, he heard the sound of an engine turning over. Cursing, he quickened his pace. Con burst through the mist like a diver spearing through the surface of a lake.

"No luck?" To commiserate, Gray stroked Con's head as they both stared out into the fog. "Well, I'm afraid I might know what this is about. Let's go back."

Brianna was gnawing on her nails when they came through the kitchen door. "You were gone so long."

"We wanted to circle the whole way around." He set the flashlight on the counter, combed a hand through his damp hair. "This could be related to your break-in."

"I don't see how. You didn't find anyone."

"Because we weren't quick enough. There's another possible explanation." He jammed his hands in his pockets. "Me."

"You? What do you mean?"

"I've had it happen a few times. An overenthusiastic fan finds out where I'm staying. Sometimes they come calling like they were old pals—sometimes they just trail you like a shadow. Now and again, they break in, look for souvenirs."

"But that's dreadful."

"It's annoying, but fairly harmless. One enterprising woman picked the lock on my hotel room at the Paris Ritz, stripped, and crawled into bed with me." He tried for a grin. "It was . . . awkward."

"Awkward," Brianna repeated after she'd managed to close her mouth. "What—no, I don't think I want to know what you did."

"Called security." His eyes went bright with amusement. "There are limits to what I'll do for my readers. Anyway, this might have been kids, but if it was one of my adoring fans, you might want me to find other accommodations."

"I do not." Her protective instincts snapped into place. "They've no right to intrude on your privacy that way, and you'll certainly not leave here because of it." She let out a huff of breath. "It's not just your stories, you know. Oh, they draw people in—it all seems so real, and there's always something heroic that rises above all the greed and violence and grief. It's your picture, too."

He was charmed by her description of his work and answered absently. "What about it?"

"Your face." She looked at him then. "It's such a lovely face."

He didn't know whether to laugh or wince. "Really?"

"Yes, it's . . ." She cleared her throat. There was a gleam in his eyes she knew better than to trust. "And the little biography on the back—more the lack of it. It's as if you came from nowhere. The mystery of it's appealing."

"I did come from nowhere. Why don't we go back to my face?"

She took a step in retreat. "I think there's been enough excitement for the night."

He just kept moving forward until his hands were on her shoulders and his mouth lay quietly on hers. "Will you be able to sleep?"

"Yes." Her breath caught, expelled lazily. "Con will be with me."

"Lucky dog. Go on, get some sleep." He waited until she and the dog were settled, then did something Brianna hadn't done in all the years she'd lived in the house.

He locked the doors.

The best place to spread news or to garner it was, logically, the village pub. In the weeks he'd been in Clare County, Gray had developed an almost sentimental affection for O'Malley's. Naturally, during his research, he'd breezed into a number of public houses in the area, but O'Malley's had become, for him, as close to his own neighborhood bar as he'd ever known.

He heard the lilt of music even as he reached for the door. Murphy, he thought. Now, that was lucky. The moment Gray stepped in, he was greeted by name or a cheery wave. O'Malley began to build him a pint of Guinness before he'd planted himself in a seat.

"Well, how's the storytelling these days?" O'Malley asked him.

"It's fine. Two dead, no suspects."

With a shake of his head, O'Malley slipped the pint under Gray's nose. "Don't know how it is a man can play with murder all the day and still have a smile on his face of an evening."

"Unnatural, isn't it?" Gray grinned at him.

"I've a story for you." This came from David Ryan who sat on the end of the bar and lighted one of his American cigarettes.

Gray settled back amid the music and smoke. There was always a story, and he was as good a listener as he was a teller.

"Was a maid who lived in the countryside near Tralee. Beautiful as a sunrise, she was, with hair like new gold and eyes as blue as Kerry."

Conversation quieted, and Murphy lowered his music so that it was a backdrop for the tale.

"It happened that two men came a-courting her," David went on. "One was a bookish fellow, the other a farmer. In her way, the maid loved them both; for she was as fickle of heart as she was lovely of face. So, enjoying the attention, as a maid might, she let them both dangle for her, making promises to each. And there began to grow a blackness in the heart of the young farmer, side by side with his love of the maid."

He paused, as storytellers often do, and studied the red glow at the end of his cigarette. He took a deep drag, expelled smoke.

"So one night he waited for his rival along the roadside, and when the bookish fellow came a-whistling—for the maid had given him her kisses freely—the farmer leaped out and bore the young lover to the ground. He dragged him, you see, in the moonlight across the fields, and though the poor sod still breathed, he buried him deep. When dawn came, he sowed his crop over him and put an end to the competition."

David paused again, drew deep on his cigarette, reached for his pint.

"And?" Gray asked, caught up. "He married the maid."

"No, indeed he didn't. She ran off with a tinker that very day. But the farmer had the best bloody crop of hay of his life."

There were roars of laughter as Gray only shook his head. He considered himself a professional liar and a good one. But the competition here was fierce. Amid the chuckles, Gray picked up his glass and went to join Murphy.

"Davey's a tale for every day of the week," Murphy told him, gently running his hands along the buttons of his squeeze box.

"I imagine my agent would scoop him up in a heartbeat. Heard anything, Murphy?"

"No, nothing helpful. Mrs. Leery thought she might have seen a car go by the day of your troubles. She thinks it was green, but didn't pay it any mind."

"Someone was poking around the cottage last night. Lost him in the fog." Gray remembered in disgust. "But he was close enough to leave a footprint in Brie's flower bed. Might have been kids." Gray took a contemplative sip of beer. "Has anyone been asking about me?"

"You're a daily topic of conversation," Murphy said dryly.

"Ah, fame. No, I mean a stranger."

"Not that I've heard. You'd better to ask over at the post office. Why?"

"I think it might be an overenthusiastic fan. I've run into it before.

Then again . . ." He shrugged. "It's the way my mind works, always making more out of what's there."

"There's a dozen men or more a whistle away if anyone gives you or Brie any trouble." Murphy glanced up as the door to the pub opened. Brianna came in, flanked by Rogan and Maggie. His brow lifted as he looked back at Gray. "And a dozen men or more who'll haul you off to the altar if you don't mind that gleam in your eye."

"What?" Gray picked up his beer again, and his lips curved. "Just looking."

"Aye. I'm a rover," Murphy sang, "and seldom sober, I'm a rover of high degree. For when I'm drinking, I'm always thinking, how to gain my love's company."

"There's still half a pint in this glass," Gray muttered, and rose to walk to Brianna. "I thought you had mending."

"I did."

"We bullied her into coming out," Maggie explained and gave a little sigh as she levered herself onto a stool.

"Persuaded," Rogan corrected. "A glass of Harp, Brie?"

"Thank you, I will."

"Tea for Maggie, Tim," Rogan began and grinned as his wife muttered. "A glass of Harp for Brie, a pint of Guiness for me. Another pint, Gray?"

"This'll do me." Gray leaned against the bar. "I remember the last time I went drinking with you."

"Speaking of Uncle Niall," Maggie put in. "He and his bride are spending a few days on the island of Crete. Play something bright, will you, Murphy?"

Obligingly, he reeled into "Whiskey in the Jar" and set her feet tapping.

After listening to the lyrics, Gray shook his head. "Why is it you Irish always sing about war?"

"Do we?" Maggie smiled, sipping at her tea as she waited to join in the chorus.

"Sometimes it's betrayal or dying, but mostly it's war."

"Is that a fact?" She smiled over the rim of her cup. "I couldn't say. Then again, it might be that we've had to fight for every inch of our own ground for centuries. Or—"

"Don't get her started," Rogan pleaded. "There's a rebel's heart in there."

"There's a rebel's heart inside every Irish man or woman. Murphy's a fine voice, he does. Why don't you sing with him, Brie?"

Enjoying the moment, she sipped her Harp. "I'd rather listen."

"I'd like to hear you," Gray murmured and stroked a hand down her hair.

Maggie narrowed her eyes at the gesture. "Brie has a voice like a bell," she said. "We always wondered where she got it, until we found out our mother had one as well."

"How about 'Danny Boy'?"

Maggie rolled her eyes. "Count on a Yank to ask for it. A Brit wrote that tune, outlander. Do 'James Connolly,' Murphy. Brie'll sing with you."

With a resigned shake of her head, Brianna went to sit with Murphy.

"They make lovely harmony," Maggie murmured, watching Gray.

"Mmm. She sings around the house when she forgets someone's there."

"And how long do you plan to be there?" Maggie asked, ignoring Rogan's warning scowl.

"Until I'm finished," Gray said absently.

"Then onto the next?"

"That's right. Onto the next."

Despite the fact that Rogan now had his hand clamped at the back of her neck, Maggie started to make some pithy comment. It was Gray's eyes rather than her husband's annoyance that stopped her. The desire in them had stirred her protective instincts. But there was something more now. She wondered if he was aware of it.

When a man looked at a woman that way, more than hormones were involved. She'd have to think it over, Maggie decided, and see how it set with her. In the meantime she picked up her tea again, still watching Gray.

"We'll see about that," she murmured. "We'll just see about it."

One song became two, and two, three. The war songs, the love songs, the sly and the sad. In his mind Gray began to craft a scene.

The smoky pub was filled with noise and music—a sanctuary from the horrors outside. The woman's voice drawing the man who didn't want to be drawn. Here, he thought, just here was where his hero would lose the battle. She would be sitting in front of the turf fire, her hands neatly folded in her lap, her voice soaring, effortless and lovely, her eyes as haunted as the tune.

And he would love her then, to the point of giving his life if need be. Certainly of changing it. He could forget the past with her, and look toward the future.

"You look pale, Gray." Maggie tugged on his arm until he backed onto a stool. "How many pints have you had?"

"Just this." He scrubbed a hand over his face to bring himself back. "I was just . . . working," he finished. That was it, of course. He'd only been thinking of characters, of crafting the lie. Nothing personal.

"Looked like a trance."

"Same thing." He let out a little breath, laughed at himself. "I think I'll have another pint after all."

TEN

With the pub scene he'd spun in his imagination replaying in his head, Gray did not spend a peaceful night. Though he couldn't erase it, neither could he seem to write it. At least not well.

The one thing he despised was even the idea of writer's block. Normally he could shrug it off, continue working until the nasty threat of it passed. Much, he sometimes thought, like a black-edged cloud that would then hover over some other unfortunate writer.

But this time he was stuck. He couldn't move into the scene, nor beyond it, and spent a great deal of the night scowling at the words he'd written.

Cold, he thought. He was just running cold. That's why the scene was cold.

Itchy was what he was, he admitted bitterly. Sexually frustrated by a woman who could hold him off with no more than one quiet look.

Served him right for obsessing over his landlady when he should be obsessing about murder.

Muttering to himself, he pushed away from his desk and stalked to the window. It was just his luck that Brianna should be the first thing he saw.

There she was below his window, neat as a nun in some prim pink dress, her hair all swept up and pinned into submission. Why was she wearing heels? he wondered and leaned closer to the glass. He supposed she'd call the unadorned pumps sensible shoes, but they did senselessly wonderful things to her legs.

As he watched, she climbed behind the wheel of her car, her movements both practical and graceful. She'd set her purse on the seat beside her first, he thought. And so she did. Then carefully buckle her seat belt, check her mirrors. No primping in the rearview for Brianna, he noted. Just a quick adjustment to be certain it was aligned properly. Now turn the key.

Even through the glass he could hear the coughing fatigue of the engine. She tried it again and a third time. By then Gray was shaking his head and heading downstairs.

"Why the hell don't you get that thing fixed?" he shouted at her as he strode out the front door.

"Oh." She was out of the car by now and trying to lift the hood. "It was working just fine a day or two ago."

"This heap hasn't worked fine in a decade." He elbowed her aside, annoyed that she should look and smell so fresh when he felt like old laundry. "Look, if you need to go to the village for something, take my car. I'll see what I can do with this."

In automatic defense against the terse words, she angled her chin. "Thank you just the same, but I'm going to Ennistymon."

"Ennistymon?" Even as he placed the village on his mental map, he lifted his head from under the hood long enough to glare at her. "What for?"

"To look at the new gallery. They'll be opening it in a couple of weeks, and Maggie asked if I'd come see." She stared at his back as he fiddled with wires and cursed. "I left you a note and food you can heat since I'll be gone most of the day."

"You're not going anywhere in this. Fan belt's busted, fuel line's leaking, and it's a pretty good bet your starter motor's had it." He straightened, noted that she wore earrings today, thin gold hoops that just brushed the tips of her lobes. They added a celebrational air that irritated him unreasonably. "You've got no business driving around in this junkyard."

"Well, it's what I have to drive, isn't it? I'll thank you for your trouble, Grayson. I'll just see if Murphy can—"

"Don't pull that ice queen routine on me." He slammed the hood hard enough to make her jolt. Good, he thought. It proved she had blood in her veins. "And don't throw Murphy up in my face. He couldn't do any more with it than I can. Go get in my car, I'll be back in a minute."

"And why would I be getting in your car?"

"So I can drive you to goddamn Ennistymon."

Teeth set, she slapped her hands on her hips. "It's so kind of you to offer, but—"

"Get in the car," he snapped as he headed for the house. "I need to soak my head."

"I'd soak it for you," she muttered. Yanking open her car door, she snatched out her purse. Who'd asked him to drive her, she'd like to know? Why she'd rather walk every step than sit in the same car with such a man. And if she wanted to call Murphy, well . . . she'd damn well call him.

But first she wanted to calm down.

She took a deep breath, then another, before walking slowly among her flowers. They soothed her, as always, the tender green just beginning to bud. They needed some work and care, she thought, bending down to tug out an invading weed. If tomorrow was fine, she'd begin. By Easter, her garden would be in its glory.

The scents, the colors. She smiled a little at a brave young daffodil.

Then the door slammed. Her smile gone, she rose, turned.

He hadn't bothered to shave, she noted. His hair was damp and pulled back by a thin leather thong, his clothes clean if a bit ragged.

She knew very well the man had decent clothes. Why, didn't she wash and iron them herself?

He flicked a glance at her, tugged the keys out of his jeans pocket. "In the car."

Oh, he needed a bit of a coming down, he did. She walked to him slowly, ice in her eyes and heat on her tongue. "And what do you have to be so cheerful about this morning?"

Sometimes, even a writer understood that actions can speak louder than words. Without giving either of them time to think he hauled her against him, took one satisfied look at the shock that raced over her face, then crushed her mouth with his.

It was rough and hungry and full of frustration. Her heart leaped, seemed to burst in her head. She had an instant to fear, a moment to yearn, then he was yanking her away again.

His eyes, oh, his eyes were fierce. A wolf's eyes, she thought dully, full of violence and stunning strength.

"Got it?" he tossed out, furious with her, with himself when she only stared. Like a child, he thought, who'd just been slapped for no reason.

It was a feeling he remembered all too well.

"Christ, I'm going crazy." He scrubbed his hands over his face and fought back the beast. "I'm sorry. Get in the car, Brianna. I'm not going to jump you."

His temper flashed again when she didn't move, didn't blink. "I'm not going to fucking touch you."

She found her voice then, though it wasn't as steady as she might have liked. "Why are you angry with me?"

"I'm not." He stepped back. Control, he reminded himself. He was usually pretty good at it. "I'm sorry," he repeated. "Stop looking at me as if I'd just punched you."

But he had. Didn't he know that anger, harsh words, hard feelings wounded her more than a violent hand? "I'm going inside." She found her defenses, the thin walls that blocked out temper. "I need to call Maggie and tell her I can't be there."

"Brianna." He started to reach out, then lifted both hands in a gesture that was equal parts frustration and a plea for peace. "How bad do you want me to feel?"

"I don't know, but I imagine you'll feel better after some food."

"Now she's going to fix me breakfast." He closed his eyes, took a steadying breath. "Even-tempered," he muttered, and looked at her again. "Isn't that what you said I was, not too long ago? You were more than a little off the mark. Writers are miserable bastards, Brie. Moody, mean, selfish, self-absorbed."

"You're none of those things." She couldn't explain why she felt bound to come to his defense. "Moody, perhaps, but none of the others."

"I am. Depending on how the book's going. Right now it's going badly, so I behaved badly. I hit a snag, a wall. A goddamn fortress, and I took it out on you. Do you want me to apologize again?"

"No." She softened, reached out and laid a hand on his stubbled cheek. "You look tired, Gray."

"I haven't slept." He kept his hands in his pockets, his eyes on hers. "Be careful how sympathetic you are, Brianna. The book's only part of the reason I'm feeling raw this morning. You're the rest of it."

She dropped her hand as if she'd touched an open flame. Her quick withdrawal had his lips curling.

"I want you. It hurts wanting you this way."

"It does?"

"That wasn't supposed to make you look pleased with yourself."

Her color bloomed. "I didn't mean to—"

"That's part of the problem. Come on, get in the car. Please," he added. "I'll drive myself insane trying to write today if I stay here."

It was exactly the right button to push. She slipped into the car and waited for him to join her. "Perhaps if you just murdered someone else."

He found he could laugh after all. "Oh, I'm thinking about it."

Worldwide Gallery of Clare County was a gem. Newly constructed, it was designed like an elegant manor house, complete with formal gardens. It wasn't the lofty cathedral of the gallery in Dublin, nor the opulent palace of Rome, but a dignified building specifically conceived to house and showcase the work of Irish artists.

It had been Rogan's dream, and now his and Maggie's reality.

Brianna had designed the gardens. Though she hadn't been able to plant them herself, the landscapers had used her scheme so that brick walkways were flanked with roses, and wide, semi-circular beds were planted with lupins and poppies, dianthus and foxglove, columbine and dahlias, and all of her favorites.

The gallery itself was built of brick, soft rose in color, with tall, graceful windows trimmed in muted gray. Inside the grand foyer, the floor was tiled in deep blue and white, with a Waterford chandelier overhead and the sweep of mahogany stairs leading to the second floor.

" 'Tis Maggie's," Brianna murmured, caught by the sculpture that dominated the entranceway.

Gray saw two figures intwined, the cool glass just hinting of heat, the form strikingly sexual, oddly romantic.

"It's her *Surrender*. Rogan bought it himself before they were married. He wouldn't sell it to anyone."

"I can see why." He had to swallow. The sinuous glass was an erotic slap to his already suffering system. "It makes a stunning beginning to a tour."

"She has a special gift, doesn't she?" Gently, with fingertips only, Brianna stroked the cool glass that her sister had created from fire and dreams. "Special gifts make a person moody, I suppose." Smiling a little, she looked over her shoulder at Gray. He looked so restless, she thought. So impatient with everything, especially himself. "And difficult, because they'll always ask so much of themselves."

"And make life hell for everyone around them when they don't get it." He reached out, touched her instead of the glass. "Don't hold grudges, do you?"

"What's the point in them?" With a shrug, she turned a circle, admiring the clean and simple lines of the foyer. "Rogan wanted the gallery to be a home, you see, for art. So there's a parlor, a drawing room, even a dining room, and sitting rooms upstairs." Brianna took his hand and drew him toward open double doors. "All the paintings, the sculptures, even the furniture, are by Irish artists and craftsmen. And—oh."

She stopped dead and stared. Cleverly arranged over the back and side of a low divan was a soft throw in bold teal that faded into cool green. She moved forward, ran her hand over it.

"I made this," she murmured. "For Maggie's birthday. They put it here. They put it here, in an art gallery."

"Why shouldn't they? It's beautiful." Curious, he took a closer look. "Did you weave this?"

"Yes. I don't have much time for weaving, but . . ." She trailed off, afraid she might weep. "Imagine it. In an art gallery, with all these wonderful paintings and things."

"Brianna."

"Joseph."

Gray watched the man stride across the room and envelope Brianna in a hard and very warm embrace. Artistic type, Gray thought with a scowl. Turquoise stud in the ear, ponytail streaming down the back, Italian suit. The look clicked. He remembered seeing the man at the wedding in Dublin.

"You get lovelier every time I see you."

"You get more full of nonsense." But she laughed. "I didn't know you were here."

"I just came in for the day, to help Rogan with a few details."

"And Patricia?"

"She's in Dublin still. Between the baby and the school, she couldn't get away."

"Oh, the baby, and how is she?"

"Beautiful. Looks like her mother." Joseph looked at Gray then, held out a hand. "You'd be Grayson Thane? I'm Joseph Donahue."

"Oh, I'm sorry. Gray, Joseph manages Rogan's gallery in Dublin. I thought you'd met at the wedding."

"Not technically." But Gray shook in a friendly manner. He remembered Joseph had a wife and daughter.

"I'll have to get it out of the way and tell you I'm a big fan."

"It's never in the way."

"It happens I brought a book along with me, thinking I could pass it along to Brie to pass it to you. I was hoping you wouldn't mind signing it for me."

Gray decided he could probably learn to like Joseph Donohue after all. "I'd be glad to."

"It's kind of you. I should tell Maggie you're here. She wants to tour you about herself."

"It's a lovely job you've done here, Joseph. All of you."

"And worth every hour of insanity." He gave the room a quick, satisfied glance. "I'll fetch Maggie. Wander around if you like." He stopped at the doorway, turned, and grinned. "Oh, be sure to ask her about selling a piece to the president."

"The president?" Brianna repeated.

"Of Ireland, darling. He offered for her *Unconquered* this morning."

"Imagine it," Brianna whispered as Joseph hurried off. "Maggie being known to the president of Ireland."

"I can tell you she's becoming known everywhere."

"Yes, I knew it, but it seems . . ." She laughed, unable to describe it. "How wonderful this is. Da would have been so proud. And Maggie, oh, she must be flying. You'd know how it feels, wouldn't you? The way it is when someone reads your books."

"Yeah, I know."

"It must be wonderful, to be talented, to have something to give that touches people."

"Brie." Gray lifted the end of the soft teal throw. "What do you call this?"

"Oh, anyone can do that—just takes time. What I mean is art, something that lasts." She crossed to a painting, a bold, colorful oil of busy Dublin. "I've always wished . . . it's not that I'm envious of Maggie. Though I was, a little, when she went off to study in Venice and I stayed home. But we both did what we needed to do. And now, she's doing something so important."

"So are you. Why do you do that?" he demanded, irritated with her. "Why do you think of what you do and who you are as second place. You can do more than anyone I've ever known."

She smiled, turning toward him again. "You just like my cooking."

"Yes, I like your cooking." He didn't smile back. "And your weaving, your knitting, your flowers. The way you make the air smell, the way you tuck the corners of the sheets in when you make the bed. How you hang the clothes on the line and iron my shirts. You do all of those things, more, and make it all seem effortless."

"Well it doesn't take much to—"

"It does." He cut her off, his temper rolling again for no reason he could name. "Don't you know how many people can't make a home, or don't give a damn, who haven't a clue how to nurture. They'd rather toss away what they have instead of caring for it. Time, things, children."

He stopped himself, stunned by what had come out of him, stunned it had been there to come out. How long had that been hiding? he wondered. And what would it take to bury it again?

"Gray." Brianna lifted a hand to his cheek to soothe, but he stepped back. He'd never considered himself vulnerable, or not in too many years to count. But at the moment he felt too off balance to be touched.

"What I mean is what you do is important. You shouldn't forget that. I want to look around." He turned abruptly to the side doorway of the parlor and hurried through.

"Well." Maggie stepped in from the hallway. "That was an interesting outburst."

"He needs family," Brianna murmured.

"Brie, he's a grown man, not a babe."

"Age doesn't take away the need. He's too alone, Maggie, and doesn't even know it."

"You can't take him in like a stray." Tilting her head, Maggie stepped closer. "Or can you?"

"I have feelings for him. I never thought I'd have these feelings for anyone again." She looked down at her hands that she'd clutched together in front of her, deliberately loosened then. "No, that's not true. It's not what I felt for Rory."

"Rory be damned."

"So you always say." And because of it, Brianna smiled. "That's family." She kissed Maggie's cheek. "Tell me, how does it feel having the president buy your work?"

"As long as his money's good." Then Maggie threw back her head and laughed. "It's like going to the moon and back. I can't help it. We Concannons just aren't sophisticated enough to take such things in stride. Oh, I wish Da . . ."

"I know."

"Well." Maggie took a deep breath. "I should tell you that the detective Rogan hired hasn't found Amanda Dougherty as yet. He's following leads, whatever that may mean."

"So many weeks, Maggie, the expense."

"Don't start nagging me about taking your housekeeping money. I married a rich man."

"And everyone knows you wanted only his wealth."

"No, I wanted his body." She winked and hooked her arm through Brianna's. "And your friend Grayson Thane has one a woman wouldn't sneeze at, I've noticed."

"I've noticed myself."

"Good, shows you haven't forgotten how to look. I had a card from Lottie."

"So did I. Do you mind if they stay the third week?"

"For myself, Mother could stay in that villa for the rest of her natural life." She sighed at Brianna's expression. "All right, all right. It's happy I am that she's enjoying herself, though she won't admit to it."

"She's grateful to you, Maggie. It's just not in her to say so."

"I don't need her to say so anymore." Maggie laid a hand on her belly. "I have my own, and it makes all the difference. I never knew I could feel so strongly about anyone. Then there was Rogan. After that, I thought I could never feel so strongly about anything or anyone else. And now, I do. So maybe I understand a little how if you didn't love, and didn't want the child growing in you, it could blight your life as much as loving and wanting it can brighten it."

"She didn't want me, either."

"What makes you say such a thing?"

"She told me." It was a load lifted, Brianna discovered, to say it aloud. "Duty. 'Twas only duty, not even to Da, but to the Church. It's a cold way to be brought into the world."

It wasn't anger Brianna needed now, Maggie knew, and bit back on it. Instead, she cupped Brianna's face. "It's her loss, Brie. Not yours. Never yours. And for myself, if the duty hadn't been done, I'd have been lost."

"He loved us. Da loved us."

"Yes, he did. And that's been enough. Come, don't worry on it. I'll take you upstairs and show you what we've been up to."

From the back of the hallway, Gray let out a long breath. The acoustics in the building were much too good for secrets to be told. He thought he understood now some of the sadness that haunted Brianna's eyes. Odd that they should have the lack of a mother's care in common.

Not that the lack haunted him, he assured himself. He'd gotten over that long ago. He'd left the scared, lonely child behind in the cheerless rooms of the Simon Brent Memorial Home for Children.

But who, he wondered, was Rory? And why had Rogan hired detectives to look for a woman named Amanda Dougherty?

Gray had always found the very best way to find the answers was to ask the questions.

"Who's Rory?"

The question snapped Brianna out from her quiet daydream as Gray drove easily down narrow winding roads away from Ennistymon. "What?"

"Not what, who?" He nipped the car closer to the edge as a loaded VW rounded a curve on his side of the road. Probably an inexperienced Yank, he thought with a superior degree of smugness. "Who's Rory?" he repeated.

"You've been listening to pub gossip, have you?"

Rather than warn him off, the coolness in her voice merely egged him on. "Sure, but that's not where I heard the name. You mentioned him to Maggie back at the gallery."

"Then you were eavesdropping on a private conversation."

"That's redundant. It's not eavesdropping unless it's a private conversation."

She straightened in her seat. "There's no need to correct my grammar, thank you."

"That wasn't grammar, it was . . . never mind." He let it, and her, stew a moment. "So, who was he?"

"And why would it be your business?"

"You're only making me more curious."

"He was a boy I knew. You're taking the wrong road."

"There is no wrong road in Ireland. Read the guidebooks. Is he the one who hurt you?" He flicked a glance in her direction, nodded. "Well, that answers that. What happened?"

"Are you after putting it in one of your books?"

"Maybe. But it's personal first. Did you love him?"

"I loved him. I was going to marry him."

He caught himself scowling over that and tapping a finger against the steering wheel. "Why didn't you?"

"Because he jilted me two paces from the altar. Does that satisfy your curiosity?"

"No. It only tells me that Rory was obviously an idiot." He couldn't stop the next question, was surprised he wanted to. "Do you still love him?"

"That would be remarkably idiotic of me as it was ten years ago."

"But it still hurts."

"Being tossed aside hurts," she said tersely. "Being the object of pity in the community hurts. Poor Brie, poor dear Brie, thrown over two weeks before her wedding day. Left with a wedding dress and her sad little trousseau while her lad runs off to America rather than make her a wife. Is that enough for you?" She shifted to stare at him. "Do you want to know if I cried? I did. Did I wait for him to come back? I did that as well."

"You can punch me if it makes you feel better."

"I doubt it would."

"Why did he leave?"

She made a sound that came as much from annoyance as memory. "I don't know. I've never known. That was the worst of it. He came to me and said he didn't want me, wouldn't have me, would never forgive me for what I'd done. And when I tried to ask him what he meant, he pushed me away, knocked me down."

Gray's hands tightened on the wheel. "He what?"

"He knocked me down," she said calmly. "And my pride wouldn't let me go after him. So he left, went to America."

"Bastard."

"I've often thought so myself, but I don't know why he left me. So, after a time, I gave away my wedding dress. Murphy's sister Kate wore it the day she married her Patrick."

"He isn't worth the sadness you carry around in your eyes."

"Perhaps not. But the dream was. What are you doing?"

"Pulling over. Let's walk out to the cliffs."

"I'm not dressed for walking over rough ground," she protested, but he was already out of the car. "I've the wrong shoes, Gray. I can wait here if you want a look."

"I want to look with you." He tugged her out of the car, then swung her up in his arms.

"What are you doing? Are you mad?"

"It's not far, and think of what nice pictures those nice tourists over there are going to take home of us. Can you speak French?"

"No?" Baffled, she angled back to look at his face. "Why?"

"I was just thinking if we spoke French, they'd think we were—French, you know. Then they'd tell Cousin Fred back in Dallas the story about this romantic French couple they'd seen near the coast." He kissed her lightly before setting her on her feet near the verge of a rocky slope.

The water was the color of her eyes today, he noted. That cool, misty green that spoke of dreaming. It was clear enough that he could see the sturdy humps of the Aran Islands, and a little ferryboat that sailed between Innismore and the mainland. The smell was fresh, the sky a moody blue that could, and would, change at any moment. The tourists a few yards away were speaking in a rich Texas twang that made him smile.

"It's beautiful here. Everything. You've only to turn your head in this part of the world to see something else breathtaking." Deliberately, he turned to Brianna. "Absolutely breathtaking."

"Now you're trying to flatter me to make up for prying into my business."

"No, I'm not. And I haven't finished prying, and I like to pry, so it'd be hypocritical to apologize. Who's Amanda Dougherty, and why is Rogan looking for her?"

Shock flashed over her face, had her mouth tremble open and closed. "You're the most rude of men."

"I know all that already. Tell me something I don't know."

"I'm going back." But as she turned, he simply took her arm.

"I'll carry you back in a minute. You'll break your ankle in those shoes. Especially if you're going to flounce."

"I don't flounce as you so colorfully put it. And this is none of your . . ." She trailed off, blew out a huff of breath. "Why would I waste my time telling you it's none of your business?"

"I haven't got a clue."

Her gaze narrowed on his face. Bland was what it was, she noted. And stubborn as two mules. "You'll just keep hammering at me until I tell you."

"Now you're catching on." But he didn't smile. Instead he tucked away a tendril of hair that fluttered into her face. His eyes were intense, unwavering. "That's what's worrying you. She's what's worrying you."

"It's nothing you'd understand."

"You'd be surprised what I understand. Here, sit." He guided her to a rock, urged her down, then sat beside her. "Tell me a story. It comes easier that way."

Perhaps it would. And perhaps it would help this heaviness in her heart to say it all. "Years ago, there was a woman who had a voice like an angel—or so they say. And ambition to use it to make her mark. She was discontent with her life as an innkeeper's daughter and went roaming, paying her way with a song. One day she came back, for her mother was ailing and she was a dutiful daughter if not a loving one. She sang in the village pub for her pleasure, and the patron's pleasure, and a few pounds. It was there she met a man."

Brianna looked out to sea as she imagined her father catching sight of her mother, hearing her voice.

"Something hot flashed between them. It might have been love, but not the lasting kind. Still, they didn't, or couldn't resist it. And so, before long, she found herself with child. The Church, her upbringing, and her own beliefs left her no choice but to marry, and give up the dream she'd had. She was never happy after that, and had not enough compassion in her to make her husband happy. Soon after the first child was born, she conceived another. Not out of that flash of something hot this time, but out of a cold sense of duty. And that duty satisfied, she refused her husband her bed and her body."

It was her sigh that had Gray reaching out, covering her hand with his. But he didn't speak. Not yet.

"One day, somewhere near the River Shannon, he met another. There was love there, a deep, abiding love. Whatever their sin, the love was greater. But he had a wife, you see, and two small daughters. And he, and the woman who loved him, knew there was no future for them. So she left him, went back to America. She wrote him three letters, lovely letters full of love and understanding. And in the third she told him that she was carrying his child. She was going away, she said, and he wasn't to worry, for she was happy to have a part of him inside her growing."

A sea bird called, drew her gaze up. She watched it wing off toward the horizon before she continued her story.

"She never wrote to him again, and he never forgot her. Those memories may have comforted him through the chill of his dutiful marriage and all the years of emptiness. I think they did, for it was her name he said before he died. He said Amanda as he looked out to the sea. And a lifetime after the letters were written, one of his daughters found them, tucked in the attic where he'd kept them tied in a faded red ribbon."

She shifted to Gray then. "There's nothing she can do, you see, to turn back the clock, to make any of those lives better than they might have been. But doesn't a woman who was loved so deserve to know she was never forgotten? And hasn't the child of that woman, and that man, a right to know his own blood?"

"It may hurt you more to find them." He looked down at their joined hands. "The past has a lot of nasty trapdoors. It's a tenuous tie, Brianna, between you and Amanda's child. Stronger ones are broken every day."

"My father loved her," she said simply. "The child she bore is kin. There's nothing else to do but look."

"Not for you," he murmured as his eyes scanned her face. There was strength there mixed with the sadness. "Let me help you."

"How?"

"I know a lot of people. Finding someone's mostly research, phone tag, connections."

"Rogan's hired a detective in New York."

"That's a good start. If he doesn't turn up something soon, will you let me try?" He lifted a brow. "Don't say it's kind of me."

"All right I won't, though it is." She brought their joined hands to her cheek. "I was angry with you for pushing me to tell you. But it helped." She tilted her face toward his. "You knew it would."

"I'm innately nosy."

"You are, yes. But you knew it would help."

"It usually does." He stood, scooped her from the rock. "It's time to go back. I'm ready to work."

ELEVEN

The chain the story had around his throat kept Gray shackled to his desk for days. Curiosity turned the key in the lock now and again as guests came and went from the cottage.

He'd had it to himself, or nearly so, for so many weeks, he thought he might find the noise and chatter annoying. Instead it was cozy, like the inn itself, colorful, like the flowers that were beginning to bloom in Brianna's garden, bright as those first precious days of spring.

When he didn't leave his room, he would always find a tray outside his door. And when he did, there was a meal and some new company in the parlor. Most stayed only a night, which suited him. Gray had always preferred quick, uncomplicated contacts.

But one afternoon he came down, stomach rumbling, and tracked Brianna to the front garden.

"Are we empty?"

She glanced up from under the brim of her garden hat. "For a day or two, yes. Are you ready for a meal?"

"It can wait until you're finished. What are you doing there?"

"Planting. I want pansies here. Their faces always look so arrogant and smug." She sat back on her heels. "Have you heard the cuckoo calling, Grayson?"

"A clock?"

"No." She laughed and patted earth tenderly around roots. "I heard the cuckoo call when I walked with Con early this morning, so we're in for fine weather. And there were two magpies chattering, which means prosperity will follow." She bent back to her work. "So, perhaps another guest will find his way here."

"Superstitious, Brianna. You surprise me."

"I don't see why. Ah, there's the phone now. A reservation."

"I'll get it." As he was already on his feet, he beat her to the parlor phone. "Blackthorn Cottage. Arlene? Yeah, it's me. How's it going, beautiful?"

With a faint frown around her mouth, Brianna stood in the doorway and wiped her hands on the rag she'd tucked in her waistband.

"Any place I hang my hat," he said in response to her question of whether he was feeling at home in Ireland. When he saw Brianna start to step back and fade from the room, he held out a hand in invitation. "What's it like in New York?" He watched Brianna hesitate, step forward. Gray linked his fingers with hers and began to nuzzle her knuckles. "No, I haven't forgotten that was coming up. I haven't given it much thought. If the spirit moves me, sweetheart."

Though Brianna tugged on her hand and frowned, he only grinned and kept his grip firm.

"I'm glad to hear that. What's the deal?" He paused, listening and smiling into Brianna's eyes. "That's generous, Arlene, but you know how

I feel about long-term commitments. I want it one at a time, just like always."

As he listened, he made little sounds of agreement, hums of interest, and nipped his way down to Brianna's wrist. It didn't do his ego any harm to feel her pulse scrambling.

"It sounds more than fine to me. Sure, push the Brits a bit further if you think you can. No, I haven't seen the London *Times*. Really? Well, that's handy, isn't it? No, I'm not being a smartass. It's great. Thanks. I—what? A fax? Here?" He snickered, leaned forward, and gave Brianna a quick, friendly kiss on the mouth. "Bless you, Arlene. No, just send it through the mail, my ego can wait. Right back at you, beautiful. I'll be in touch."

He said his good-byes and hung up with Brianna's hand still clutched in his.

When she spoke, the chill in her voice lowered the temperature of the room by ten degrees. "Don't you think it's rude to be flirting with one woman on the phone and kissing another?"

His already pleased expression brightened. "Jealous, darling?"

"Certainly not."

"Just a little." He caught her other hand before she could evade and brought both to his lips. "Now that's progress. I almost hate to tell you that was my agent. My very married agent, who though dear to my heart and my bankbook is twenty years older than I and the proud grandmother of three."

"Oh." She hated to feel foolish almost as much as she hated to feel jealous. "I suppose you want that meal now."

"For once, food's the last thing on my mind." What was on it was very clear in his eyes as he tugged her closer. "You look really cute in that hat."

She turned her head just in time to avoid his mouth. His lips merely skimmed over her cheek. "Was it good news then, her calling?"

"Very good. My publisher liked the sample chapters I sent them a couple weeks ago and made an offer."

"That's nice." He seemed hungry enough to her, the way he was nibbling at her ear. "I suppose I thought you sold books before you wrote them, like a contract."

"I don't do multiples. Makes me feel caged in." So much so that he had just turned down a spectacular offer for three projected novels. "We deal one at a time, and with Arlene in my corner, we deal nicely."

A warmth was spreading in her stomach as he worked his way leisurely down her neck. "Five million you told me. I can't imagine so much."

"Not this time." He cruised up her jaw. "Arlene strong-armed them up to six point five."

Stunned, she jerked back. "Million? American dollars?"

"Sounds like Monopoly money, doesn't it?" He chuckled. "She's not satisfied with the British offer—and since my current book is steady at number one on the London *Times*, she's squeezing them a bit." Absently he nipped her by the waist, pressed his lips to her brow, her temple. "*Sticking Point* opens in New York next month."

"Opens?"

"Mmm. The movie. Arlene thought I might like to go to the premiere."

"Of your own movie. You must."

"There's no musts. Seems like old news. *Flashback*'s now."

His lips teased the corner of her mouth and her breath began to hitch. "*Flashback*?"

"The book I'm working on. It's the only one that matters." His eyes narrowed, lost focus. "He has to find the book. Shit, how could I have missed that? It's the whole thing." He jerked back, dragged a hand through his hair. "Once he finds it, he won't have any choice, will he? That's what makes it personal."

Every nerve ending in her body was humming from the imprint of his lips. "What are you talking about? What book?"

"Deliah's diary. That's what links past and present. There'll be no walking away after he reads it. He'll have to—" Gray shook his head, like a man coming out, or moving into a trance. "I've got to get to work."

He was halfway up the stairs, and Brianna's heart was still thudding dully. "Grayson?"

"What?"

He was already steeped in his own world, she noted, torn between amusement and irritation. That impatient gleam was in his eyes, eyes she doubted were even seeing her. "Don't you want some food?"

"Just leave a tray when you have a chance. Thanks."

And he was gone.

Well. Brianna set her hands on her hips and managed to laugh at herself. The man had all but seduced her into a puddle, and didn't even know it. Off he went with Deliah and her diary, murder and mayhem, leaving her system ticking like an overwound watch.

For the best, she assured herself. All that hand kissing and nibbling had weakened her. And it was foolish, wasn't it, to go weak over a man who would be gone from her home and her country as carelessly as he'd gone from her parlor.

But oh, she thought as she walked to the kitchen, it made her wonder what it would be like. What it would be like to have all that energy, all that attention, all that skill focused only on her. Even for a short time. Even for only one night.

She would know then, wouldn't she, what it felt like to give pleasure to a man? And to take it. Loneliness might be bitter after, but the moment might be sweet.

Might. Too many mights, she warned herself, and fixed Gray a generous plate of cold lamb and cheese croquettes. She carried it up, taking it into his room without speaking.

He didn't acknowledge her, nor did she expect it now. Not when he was hulked over his little machine, his eyes slitted, his fingers racing. He did grunt when she poured the tea and set a cup at his elbow.

When she caught herself smiling, checking an urge to run a hand down that lovely gold-tipped hair, she decided it was a very good time to walk over to Murphy's and ask him about fixing her car.

The exercise helped work out those last jittery frissons of need. It was her time of year, the spring, when the birds called, the flowers bloomed, and the hills glowed so green your throat ached to look at them.

The light was gilded, the air so clear that she could hear the *putt-putt* of Murphy's tractor two fields over. Charmed by the day, she swung the basket she carried and sang to herself. As she climbed over a low stone wall, she smiled at the spindly legged foal that nursed greedily while his mother cropped grass. She spent a moment in admiration, another few stroking both mother and baby before wandering on.

Perhaps she would walk to Maggie's after seeing Murphy, she thought. It was only a matter of weeks now before the baby was due. Someone needed to tend Maggie's garden, do a bit of wash.

Laughing, she stopped, crouching down when Con raced over the field toward her.

"Been farming, have you? Or just chasing rabbits. No, 'tisn't for you," she said, hooking the basket higher as the dog sniffed around it. "But I've a fine bone at home waiting." Hearing Murphy's hail, she straightened, waved her arm in greeting.

He shut off his tractor and hopped down as she walked over the newly turned earth.

"A fine day for planting."

"The finest," he agreed and eyed the basket. "What have you there, Brie?"

"A bribe."

"Oh, I'm made of stronger stuff than that."

"Sponge cake."

He closed his eyes and gave an exaggerated sigh. "I'm your man."

"That you are." But she held the basket tantalizingly out of reach. " 'Tis my car again, Murphy."

Now his look was pained. "Brianna, darling, it's time for the wake there. Past time."

"Couldn't you just take a peek?"

He looked at her, then at the basket. "The whole of the sponge cake?"

"Every crumb."

"Done." He took the basket, set it up on the tractor seat. "But I'm warning you, you'll need a new one before summer."

"If I do, I do. But I've my heart set on the greenhouse, so the car has to last a wee bit longer. Did you have time to look at my drawings for the greenhouse, Murphy?"

"I did. Could be done." Taking advantage of the break, he pulled out a cigarette, lighted it. "I made a few adjustments."

"You're a darling man, Murphy." Grinning, she kissed his cheek.

"So all the ladies tell me." He tugged on a loose curl of hair. "And what would your Yank think if he came across you charming me in my own field?"

"He's not my Yank." She shifted as Murphy only lifted one black brow. "You like him, don't you?"

"Hard not to like him. Is he worrying you, Brianna?"

"Maybe a little." She sighed, gave up. There was nothing in her heart and mind she couldn't tell Murphy. "A lot. I care for him. I'm not sure what to do about it, but I care for him, so much. It's different than even it was with Rory."

At the mention of the name, Murphy scowled and stared down at the tip of his cigarette. "Rory's not worth a single thought in your head."

"I don't spend time thinking of him. But now, with Gray, it brings it back, you see. Murphy . . . he'll leave, you know. As Rory left." She looked away. She could say it, Brianna thought, but she couldn't deal with the sympathy in Murphy's eyes when she did. "I try to understand that, to accept it. I tell myself it'll be easier for at least I'll know why. Not knowing, my whole life with Rory, what was lacking in me—"

"There's nothing lacking in you," Murphy said shortly. "Put it aside."

"I have. I did—or nearly. But I . . ." Overwhelmed, she turned away to stare out over the hills. "But what is it in me, or not in me, that sends a man away? Do I ask too much from him, or not enough? Is there a coldness in me that freezes them out?"

"There's nothing cold about you. Stop blaming yourself for someone else's cruelty."

"But I've only myself to ask. Ten years, it's been. And this is the first time since I've felt any stirring. It frightens me because I don't know how I'll live through heartbreak again. He's not Rory, I know, and yet—"

"No, he's not Rory." Furious at seeing her so lost, so unhappy, Murphy tossed his cigarette down and ground it out. "Rory was a fool who couldn't see what he had, and wanted to believe whatever lies he heard. You should thank God he's gone."

"What lies?"

The heat stirred in Murphy's eyes, then cooled. "Whatever. The day's wasting, Brie. I'll come look at your car tomorrow."

"What lies?" She put a hand on his arm. There was a faint ringing in her ears, a hard fist in her belly. "What do you know about it, Murphy, that you haven't told me?"

"What would I know? Rory and I were never mates."

"No, you weren't," she said slowly. "He never liked you. He was jealous, he was, because we were close. He couldn't see that it was like having a brother. He couldn't see that," she continued, watching Murphy carefully. "And once or twice we argued over it, and he said how I was too free with kisses when it came to you."

Something flickered over Murphy's face before he checked it. "Well, didn't I tell you he was a fool?"

"Did you say something to him about it? Did he say something to you?" She waited, then the chill that was growing in her heart spread and cloaked her. "You'll tell me, by God you will. I've a right. I wept my heart out over him. I suffered from the pitying looks of everyone I knew. I watched your sister marry in the dress I'd made with my own hands to be a bride. For ten years there's been an emptiness in me."

"Brianna."

"You'll tell me." Rigid, braced, she faced him. "For I can see you have the answer. If you're my friend, you'll tell me."

"That isn't fair."

"Is doubting myself all this time any fairer?"

"I don't want to hurt you, Brianna." Gently he touched a hand to her cheek. "I'd cut off my arm before."

"I'll hurt less knowing."

"Maybe. Maybe." He couldn't know, had never known. "Maggie and I both thought—"

"Maggie?" she broke in, stunned. "Maggie knows as well?"

Oh, he was in it now, he realized. And there was no way out without sinking the lot of them. "Her love for you is so fierce, Brianna. She'd do anything to protect you."

"And I'll tell you what I've told her, time and again. I don't need protecting. Tell me what you know."

Ten years, he thought, was a long time for an honest man to hold a secret. Ten years, he thought, was longer still for an innocent woman to hold blame.

"He came after me one day while I was out here, working the fields. He went for me, out of the blue, it seemed to me. And not being fond of him, I went for him as well. Can't say my heart was in it much until he said what he did. He said you'd been . . . with me."

It embarrassed him still, and beneath the embarrassment, he discovered, there remained that sharp-edged rage that had never dulled with time.

"He said that we'd made a fool of him behind his back and he'd not marry a whore. I bloodied his face for that," Murphy said viciously, his fist curling hard in memory. "I'm not sorry for it. I might have broken his bones as well, but he told me he'd heard it from your mother's own lips. That she'd told him you'd been sneaking off with me, and might even be carrying my child."

She was dead pale now, her heart crackling with ice. "My mother said this to him?"

"She said—she couldn't, in good conscience, let him marry you in church when you'd sinned with me."

"She knew I hadn't," Brie whispered. "She knew we hadn't."

"Her reasons for believing it, or saying it, are her own. Maggie came by when I was cleaning myself up, and I told her before I could think better of it. At first I thought she'd go deal with Maeve with her fists, and I had to hold her there until she'd calmed a bit. We talked, and it was Maggie's thinking that Maeve had done it to keep you at home."

Oh, yes, Brianna thought. At home, that had never been a home. "Where I'd tend her, and the house, and Da."

"We didn't know what to do, Brianna. I swear to you I'd have dragged you away from the altar meself if you'd gone ahead and tried to marry that snake-bellied bastard. But he left the very next day, and you were hurting so. I didn't have the heart, nor did Maggie, to tell you what he'd said."

"You didn't have the heart." She pressed her lips together. "What you didn't have, Murphy, you nor Maggie, was the right to keep it from me. You didn't have the right any more than my mother did to say such things."

"Brianna."

She jerked back before he could touch her. "No, don't. I can't talk to you now. I can't talk to you." She turned and raced away.

She didn't weep. The tears were frozen in her throat, and she refused to let them melt. She ran across the fields, seeing nothing now, nothing but the haze of what had been. Or what had nearly been. All innocence had been shattered now. All illusions crushed to dust. Her life was lies. Conceived on them, bred on them, nurtured with them.

By the time she reached the house, her breath was sobbing in her lungs. She stopped herself, fisting her hands hard until her nails dug into flesh.

The birds still sang, and the tender young flowers she'd planted herself continued to dance in the breeze. But they no longer touched her. She saw herself as she'd been, shocked and appalled as she'd felt Rory's hand strike her to the ground. All these years later she could visualize it perfectly, the bafflement she'd felt as she'd stared up at him, the rage and disgust in his face before he'd turned and left her there.

She'd been marked as a whore, had she? By her own mother. By the man she had loved. What a fine joke it was, when she had never felt the weight of a man.

Very quietly she opened the door, closed it behind her. So her fate had been decided for her on that long-ago morning. Well, now, this very day, she would take her fate into her own hands.

Deliberately she walked up the stairs, opened Gray's door. Closed it tight at her back. "Grayson?"

"Huh?"

"Do you want me?"

"Sure. Later." His head came up, his glazed eyes only half focused. "What? What did you say?"

"Do you want me?" she repeated. Her spine was as stiff as the question. "You've said you did, and acted as you did."

"I . . ." He made a manful attempt to pull himself out of imagination into reality. She was pale as ice, he noted, and her eyes glittered with cold. And, he noted, hurt. "Brianna, what's going on?"

"A simple question. I'd thank you for an answer to it."

"Of course I want you. What's the—what in hell are you doing?" He was out of the chair like a shot, gaping as she began to briskly unbutton her blouse. "Cut it out. Goddamn it, stop that now."

"You said you want me. I'm obliging you."

"I said stop." In three strides he was to her, yanking her blouse together. "What's gotten into you? What's happened?"

"That's neither here nor there." She could feel herself beginning to shake and fought it back. "You've been trying to persuade me into bed, now I'm ready to go. If you can't spare the time now, just say so." Her eyes flared. "I'm used to being put off."

"It's not a matter of time—"

"Well, then." She broke away to turn down the bed. "Would you prefer the curtains open or closed? I've no preference."

"Leave the stupid curtains." The neat way she folded down the covers did what it always did. It made his stomach tighten into a slippery fist of lust. "We're not going to do this."

"You don't want me, then." When she straightened, her open blouse shifted, giving him a tantalizing peek of pale skin and tidy white cotton.

"You're killing me," he murmured.

"Fine. I'll leave you to die in peace." Head high, she marched for the door. He merely slammed a hand on it to keep it shut.

"You're not going anywhere until you tell me what's going on."

"Nothing, it seems, at least with you." She pressed herself back against the door, forgetting now to breathe slowly, evenly, to keep the wrenching pain out of her voice. "Surely there's a man somewhere who might spare a moment or two to give me a tumble."

He bared his teeth. "You're pissing me off."

"Oh, well, that's a pity. I do beg your pardon. It's sorry I am to have bothered you. It's only that I thought you'd meant what you'd said. That's my problem, you see," she murmured as tears glistened in her eyes. "Always believing."

He would have to handle the tears, he realized, and whatever emotional tailspin she was caught in, without touching her. "What happened?"

"I found out." Her eyes weren't cold now, but devastated and desperate. "I found out that there's never been a man who's loved me. Not really loved me ever. And that my own mother lied, lied hatefully, to take away even that small chance of happiness. She told him I'd slept with Murphy. She told him that, and that I might be carrying a child. How could he marry me believing that? How could he believe it loving me?"

"Hold on a minute." He paused, waiting for her quick blur of words to register. "You're saying that your mother told the guy you were going to marry, this Rory, that you'd been having sex with Murphy, might be pregnant?"

"She told him that so that I couldn't escape this house." Leaning her head back she closed her eyes. "This house as it was then. And he believed her. He believed I could have done that, believed it so that he never asked me if it was true. Only told me he wouldn't have me, and left. And all this time, Maggie and Murphy have known it, and kept it from me."

Tread carefully, Gray warned himself. Emotional quicksand. "Look, I'm on the outside here, and I'd say, being a professional observer, that your sister and Murphy kept their mouths shut to keep you from hurting more than you already were."

"It was my life, wasn't it? Do you know what it's like not to know why you're not wanted, to go through life only knowing you weren't, but never why?"

Yeah, he knew, exactly. But he didn't think it was the answer she wanted. "He didn't deserve you. That should give you some satisfaction."

"It doesn't. Not now. I thought you would show me."

He stepped cautiously back as the breath clogged in his lungs. A beautiful woman, one who had, from the first instant, stirred his blood. Innocent. Offering. "You're upset," he managed in a tight voice. "Not thinking clearly. And as much as it pains me, there are rules."

"I don't want excuses."

"You want a substitute." The quick violence of the statement surprised both of them. He hadn't realized that little germ had been in his head. But he lashed out as it grew. "I'm not a goddamn stand-in for some whiny, wimp-hearted jerk who tossed you over a decade ago. Yesterday sucks. Well, welcome to reality. When I take a woman to bed, she's going to be thinking about me. Just me."

What little color that had seeped back into her cheeks drained. "I'm sorry. I didn't mean it that way, didn't mean it to seem that way."

"That's exactly how it seems, because that's exactly what it is. Pull yourself together," he ordered, deadly afraid she would start to cry again. "When you figure out what you want, let me know."

"I only . . . I needed to feel as if something, you, wanted me. I thought—I hoped I'd have something to remember. Just once, to know what it was like to be touched by a man I cared for." The color came back, humiliation riding her cheeks as Gray stared at her. "Doesn't matter. I'm sorry. I'm very sorry."

She yanked open the door and fled.

She was sorry, Gray thought, staring into the space where she'd been. He could all but see the air vibrate in her wake.

Good going, pal, he thought in disgust as he began to pace the room. Nice job. It always makes someone feel better when you kick them while they're down.

But damn it, damn it, she'd made him feel exactly as he'd told her. A convenient substitute for some lost love. He felt miserable for her, facing that kind of betrayal, that kind of rejection. There was nothing he understood better. But he'd patched himself up, hadn't he? So could she.

She'd wanted to be touched. She'd just needed to be soothed. Head pounding, he stalked to the window and back. She'd wanted him—a little sympathy, a little understanding. A little sex. And he'd brushed her off.

Just like the ever-popular Rory.

What was he supposed to do? How could he have taken her to bed when all that hurt and fear and confusion had been shimmering around her? He didn't need other people's complications.

He didn't want them.

He wanted her.

On an oath he rested his head against the window glass. He could walk away. He'd never had any trouble walking away. Just sit down again, pick up the threads of his story, and dive into it.

Or . . . or he could try something that might clear the frustration out of the air for both of them.

The second impulse was more appealing, a great deal more appealing, if a great deal more dangerous. The safe route was for cowards, he told himself. Snatching up his keys, he walked downstairs and out of the house.

TWELVE

If there was one thing Gray knew how to do with style, it was set scenes. Two hours after he'd left Blackthorn Cottage, he was back in his room and putting the final touch on the details. He didn't think past the first step. Sometimes it was wiser—safer certainly—not to dwell on how the scene might unfold or the chapter close.

After a last glance around, he nodded to himself, then went downstairs to find her.

"Brianna."

She didn't turn from the sink where she was meticulously frosting a chocolate cake. She was calmer now, but no less ashamed of her behavior. She had shuddered more than once over the past two hours over the way she'd thrown herself at him.

Thrown herself, she remembered again, and not been caught.

"Yes, dinner's ready," she said calmly. "Would you want it down here?"

"I need you to come upstairs."

"All right, then." Her relief that he didn't ask for a cozy meal in the kitchen was tremendous. "I'll just fix a tray for you."

"No." He laid a hand on her shoulder, uneasy when he felt her muscles stiffen. "I need you to come upstairs."

Well, she would have to face him sooner or later. Carefully wiping her hands on her apron, she turned. She read nothing in his face of condemnation, or the anger he'd speared at her earlier. It didn't help. "Is there a problem?"

"Come up, then you tell me."

"All right." She followed behind him. Should she apologize again? She wasn't sure. It might be best just to pretend nothing had been said. She gave a little sigh as they approached his room. Oh, she hoped it wasn't the plumbing. The expense just now would . . .

She forgot about plumbing as she stepped inside. She forgot about everything.

There were candles set everywhere, the soft light streaming like melted gold against the twilight gray of the room. Flowers spilled out of a half dozen vases, tulips and roses, freesia and lilacs. In a silver bucket rested an iced bottle of champagne, still corked. Music came from somewhere. Harp music. She stared, baffled, at the portable stereo on his desk.

"I like the curtains open," he said.

She folded her hands under her apron where only she would know they trembled. "Why?"

"Because you never know when you might catch a moonbeam."

Her lips curved, ever so slightly at the thought. "No, I mean why have you done all this?"

"To make you smile. To give you time to decide if it's what you really want. To help persuade you that it is."

"You've gone to such trouble." Her eyes skimmed toward the bed, then quickly, nervously, onto the vase of roses. "You didn't have to. I've made you feel obliged."

"Please. Don't be an idiot. It's your choice." But he moved to her, took the first pin from her hair, tossed it aside. "Do you want me to show you how much I want you?"

"I—"

"I think I should show you, at least a little." He took out another pin, a third, then simply combed his hands through her tumbling hair. "Then you can decide how much you'll give."

His mouth skimmed over hers, gentle as air, erotic as sin. When her lips trembled apart, he slipped his tongue between them, teasing hers.

"That should give you the idea." He moved his lips along her jaw, up to her temple, then back to nip at the corner of her mouth. "Tell me you want me, Brianna. I want to hear you say it."

"I do." She couldn't hear her own voice, only the hum of it in her throat where his mouth now nestled. "I do want you. Gray, I can't think. I need—"

"Just me. You only need me tonight. I only need you." Coaxing, he smoothed his hands down her back. "Lie down with me, Brianna." He lifted her, cradled her. "There are so many places I want to take you."

He laid her down on the bed where the sheets and quilt had been folded down in invitation. Her hair spilled like fired gold over the crisp linen, subtle waves of it catching glints from the candlelight. Her eyes were stormy with the war of doubts and needs.

And his stomach trembled, looking at her. From desire, yes, but also from fear.

He would be her first. No matter what happened after, through her life, she would remember tonight, and him.

"I don't know what to do." She closed her eyes, excited, embarrassed, enchanted.

"I do." He laid beside her, dipped his mouth to hers once more. She was trembling beneath him, a fact that had a hot ball of panic tightening in his gut. If he moved too fast. If he moved too slow. To soothe them both he pried her nervous fingers apart, kissed them one by one. "Don't be afraid, Brianna. Don't be afraid of me. I won't hurt you."

But she was afraid, and not only of the pain she knew went hand in hand with the loss of innocence. She was afraid of not being capable of giving pleasure, and of not being able to feel the full truth of it.

"Think of me," he murmured, deepening the kiss degree by shuddering degree. If he did nothing else, he swore he would exorcise the last ghost of her heartache. "Think of me." And when he repeated it, he knew, from somewhere hidden inside, that he needed this moment as much as she.

Sweet, she thought hazily. How odd that a man's mouth could taste so sweet, and could be firm and soft all at once. Fascinated by the taste and texture, she traced his lips with the tip of her tongue. And heard his quiet purr in answer.

One by one her muscles uncoiled as his flavor seeped into her. And how lovely it was to be kissed as if you would be kissed until time stopped. How solid and good his weight was, how strong his back when she dared let her hands roam.

He stiffened, bit back a moan as her hesitant fingers skimmed over his hips. He was already hard and shifted slightly, worried that he might frighten her.

Slowly, he ordered himself. Delicately.

He slipped the top strap of her apron over her head, untied the one around her waist and drew it off. Her eyes fluttered open, her lips curved.

"Will you kiss me again?" Her voice was honey thick now, and warm. "It makes everything go gold behind my eyes when you do."

He rested his brow on hers, waited a moment until he thought he could give her the gentleness she'd asked for. Then he took her mouth, swallowed her lovely, soft sigh. She seemed to melt beneath him, the tremblings giving way to pliancy.

She felt nothing but his mouth, that wonderful mouth that feasted so sumptuously on hers. Then his hand cupped her throat as if testing the speed of the pulse that fluttered there before he trailed down.

She hadn't been aware that he'd unfastened her blouse. As his fingers traced the soft swell of her breast above her bra, her eyes flew open. His were steady on hers, with a concentration so focused it brought the trembles back. She started to protest, to make some sound of denial. But his touch was so alluring, just a skim of fingertips against flesh.

It wasn't fearful, she realized. It was soothing, and just as sweet as the kiss. Even as she willed herself to relax again, those clever fingers slipped under the cotton and found the sensitive point.

Her first gasp ripped through him—the sound of it, the arousing sensation of her body arching in surprise and pleasure. He was barely touching her, he thought as his blood pounded. She had no idea how much more there was.

God, he was desperate to show her.

"Relax." He kissed her, kissed her, as his fingers continued to arouse and his free hand circled back to unhook the barrier. "Just feel it."

She had no choice. Sensations were tearing through her, tiny arrows of pleasure and shock. His mouth swallowed her strangled breaths as he tugged away her clothes and left her bare to the waist.

"God, you're so beautiful." His first look at that milk-pale skin, the small breasts that fit so perfectly into the cups of his palms, nearly undid him. Unable to resist, he lowered his head and tasted.

She moaned, long, deep, throaty. The movements of her body under his were pure instinct, he knew, and not designed to deliberately claw at his control. So he pleased her, gently, and found his own pleasure growing from hers.

His mouth was so hot. The air was so thick. Each time he tugged, pulled, laved, there was an answering flutter in the pit of her stomach. A flutter that built and built into something too close to pain, too close to pleasure to separate them.

He was murmuring to her, lovely, soft words that circled like rainbows in her head. It didn't matter what he said—she would have told him if she could. Nothing mattered as long as he never, never stopped touching her.

He tugged his own shirt over his head, craving the feel of flesh against flesh. When he lowered himself to her again, she made a small sound and wrapped her arms around him.

She only sighed again when his mouth roamed lower, over torso, over ribs. Her skin heated, muscles jerking, quivering under his lips and hands. And he knew she was lost in that dark tunnel of sensations.

Carefully he unhooked her slacks, baring new flesh slowly, exploring it gently. As her hips arched once in innocent agreement, he clamped his teeth and fought back the tearing need to take, just take and satisfy the grinding in his taut body.

Her nails dug into his back, drawing out a groan of dark delight from him as his hand skimmed down her bared hip. He knew she'd stiffened again and begged whatever god was listening for strength.

"Not until you're ready," he murmured, and brought his lips patiently back to hers again. "I promise. But I want to see you. All of you."

He shifted, knelt back. There was fear in her eyes again, though her body was quivering with suppressed needs. He couldn't steady his hands or his voice, but he kept them gentle.

"I want to touch all of you." His eyes stayed on hers as he unsnapped his jeans. "All of you."

When he stripped, her gaze was drawn inexorably down. And her fear doubled. She knew what was to happen. She was, after all, a farmer's daughter, however poor a farmer he'd been. There would be pain, and blood, and . . .

"Gray—"

"Your skin's so soft." Watching her, he skimmed a finger up her thigh. "I've wondered what you'd look like, but you're so much lovelier than I imagined."

Unsettled, she'd crossed an arm over her breast. He left it there and went back to where he'd begun. With soft, slow, drugging kisses. And next caresses, patient, skilled hands that knew where a woman longed to be touched. Even when the woman didn't. Helplessly she yielded beneath him again, her breathing quickening into catchy pants as his hand roamed over the flat of her stomach toward the terrible, glorious heat.

Yes, he thought, fighting delirium. Open for me. Let me. Just let me.

She was damp and hot where he cupped her. The groan tore from his throat when she writhed and tried to resist.

"Let go, Brianna. Let me take you there. Just let go."

She was clinging to the edge of some towering cliff by no more than her fingertips. Terror welled inside her. She was slipping. No control. There was too much happening inside her body all at once for her burning flesh to hold it all in. His hand was like a torch against her, firing her, searing her mercilessly until she would have no choice but to tumble free into the unknown.

"Please." The word sobbed out. "Oh, sweet God, please."

Then the pleasure, the molten flood of it washed through her, over her, stealing her breath, her mind, her vision. For one glorious moment she was blind and deaf to everything but herself and the velvet shocks convulsing her.

She poured into his hand, making him moan like a dying man. He shuddered, even as she did, then with his face buried against her skin took her soaring again.

Straining against the chain of his own control, he waited until she was at peak. "Hold me. Hold on to me," he murmured, dizzy with his own needs as he struggled to ease gently into her.

She was so small, so tight, so deliciously hot. He used every ounce of willpower he had left not to thrust greedily inside as he felt her close around him.

"Only for a second," he promised her. "Only for a second, then it'll be good again."

But he was wrong. It never stopped being good. She felt him break the barrier of her innocence, fill her with himself, and felt nothing but joy.

"I love you." She arched up to meet him, to welcome him.

He heard the words dimly, shook his head to deny them. But she was wrapped around him, drawing him into a well of generosity. And he was helpless to do anything but drown.

Coming back to time and place was, for Brianna, like sliding weightlessly through a thin, white cloud. She sighed, let the gentle gravity take her until she was once more in the big old bed, candlelight flickering red and gold on her closed lids, and the truly incredible pleasure of Gray's weight pinning her to the mattress.

She thought hazily that no books she had read, no chatter she had heard from other women, no secret daydreaming could have taught her how simply good it was to have a man's naked body pressed onto hers.

The body itself was an amazing creation, more beautiful than she'd imagined. The long, muscled arms were strong enough to lift her, gentle enough to hold her as if she were a hollowed-out egg, easily broken.

The hands, wide of palm, long of finger, knew so cleverly just where to touch and stroke. Then there were the broad shoulders, the long, lovely, lean back, narrow hips leading down to hard thighs, firm calves.

Hard. She smiled to herself. Wasn't it a miracle that something so hard, so tough and strong should be covered with smooth, soft skin?

Oh, indeed, she thought, a man's body was a glorious thing.

Gray knew if she kept touching him he'd go quietly mad. If she stopped, he was certain he'd whimper.

Those pretty tea-serving hands of hers were gliding over him, whispering touches, exploring, tracing, testing, as if she were memorizing each muscle and curve.

He was still inside her, couldn't bear to separate himself. He knew he should, should ease away and give her time to recover. However much he'd fought not to hurt her, there was bound to be some discomfort.

And yet, he was so content—she seemed so content. All those nerves that had sizzled through him at the thought of taking her the first time—her first time—had melted away into lazy bliss.

When those skimming caresses caused him to stir again, he forced himself to move, propping up on his elbows to look down at her.

She was smiling. He couldn't have said why he found that so endearing, so perfectly charming. Her lips curved, her eyes warmly green, her skin softly flushed. Now, with that first rush of needs and nerves calmed, he could enjoy the moment, the lights, the shadows, the rippling pleasure of fresh arousal.

He pressed his lips to her brow, her temples, her cheeks, her mouth. "Beautiful Brianna."

"It was beautiful for me." Her voice was thick, still raspy with passion. "You made it beautiful for me."

"How do you feel now?"

He would ask, she thought, both in kindness and in curiosity. "Weak," she said. And with a quick laugh, "Invincible. Why do you suppose such a natural thing as this should make such a difference in a life?"

His brows drew together, smoothed out again. Responsibility, he thought, it was his responsibility. He had to remind himself she was a grown woman, and the choice had been hers. "Are you comfortable with that difference?"

She smiled up at him, beautifully, touched a hand to his cheek. "I've waited so long for you, Gray."

The quick inner defense signal flashed on. Even steeped in her, warm, damn, half aroused, it flashed. Step carefully, cautioned a cool, controlled part of his mind. *Warning: Intimacy Ahead.*

She saw the change in his eyes, a subtle but distinct distancing even as he took the hand against his cheek and shifted it so that his lips pressed to her palm.

"I'm crushing you."

She wanted to say—no, stay—but he was already moving away.

"We haven't had any champagne." Easy with his nakedness, he rolled out of bed. "Why don't you go have a bath while I open the bottle?"

She felt odd suddenly, and awkward, where she'd felt nothing but natural with him atop and inside her. Now she fumbled with the sheets.

"The linen," she began, and found herself flushing and tongue-tied. It would be soiled, she knew, with her innocence.

"I'll take care of it." Seeing her color deepen and understanding, he moved to the bed again and cupped her chin in his hand. "I can change sheets, Brie. And even if I didn't know how before, I'd have picked it up watching you." His mouth brushed hers, his voice thickening. "Do you know how often I've been driven insane watching you smooth and tuck my sheets?"

"No." There was a quick lick of pleasure and desire. "Really?"

He only laughed and laid his brow on hers. "What wonderful good deed did I do to deserve this? To earn you?" He drew back, but his eyes had kindled again, making her heart drum slow and hard against her ribs. "Go have your bath. I'm wanting to make love with you again," he said, slipping into a brogue that made her lips quirk. "If you'd like it."

"I would, yes." She drew a deep breath, bracing herself to climb naked from the bed. "Very much I would. I won't be long."

When she went into the bath, he took a deep breath himself. To steady his system, he told himself.

He'd never had anyone like her. It wasn't just that he'd never tasted innocence before—that would have been enormous enough. But she was unique to him. Her responses, that hesitation and eagerness playing at odds with each other. With her absolute trust shining over all.

"I love you," she'd said.

It wouldn't do to dwell on that. Women tended to romanticize, emotionalize sex in most cases. Certainly a woman experiencing sex for the first time would be bound to mix lust with love. Women used words, and required them. He knew that. That was why he was very careful when choosing his.

But something had spurted through him when she'd whispered that overrated and overused phrase. Warmth and need and, for an instant, just a heartbeat, a desperate desire to believe it. And to echo her words.

He knew better, and though he would do anything and everything in his power to keep her from hurt, anything and everything to make her happy while they were together, there were limits to what he could and would give to her. To anyone.

Enjoy the moment, he reminded himself. That's all there was. He hoped he could teach her to enjoy it as well.

She felt odd as she wrapped the towel around her freshly scrubbed body. Different. It was something that could never be explained to a man, she supposed. They lost nothing when they gave themselves the first time. There was no sharp tearing of self to admit another. But it wasn't pain she remembered, even the soreness between her thighs didn't bring the violence of invasion to mind. It was the unity she thought of. The sweet and simple bond of mating.

She studied herself in the misty mirror. She looked warm, she decided. It was the same face, surely, that she'd glimpsed countless times in countless mirrors. Yet wasn't there a softness here she'd never noticed before? In the eyes, around the mouth? Love had done that. The love she held in her heart, the love she'd tasted for the first time with her body.

Perhaps it was only the first time that a woman felt so aware of herself, so stripped of everything but flesh and soul. And perhaps, she thought, because she was older than most, the moment was all the more overwhelming and precious.

He wanted her. Brianna closed her eyes, the better to feel those long, slow ripples of delight. A beautiful man with a beautiful mind and kind heart wanted her.

All of her life she'd dreamed of finding him. Now she had.

She stepped into the bedroom, and saw him. He'd put fresh linen on the bed and had laid one of her white flannel gowns at the foot of it. He stood now in jeans unsnapped and relaxed on his hips, with champagne bubbling in glasses and candlelight simmering in his eyes.

"I'm hoping you'll wear it," he said when she saw her gaze rest on the prim, old-fashioned nightgown. "I've imagined getting you out of it since that first night. I watched you come down the stairs, a candle in one hand, a wolfhound in the other, and my head went spinning."

She picked up a sleeve. How much she wished it was silk or lace or something that would make a man's blood heat. " 'Tisn't very alluring, I think."

"You think wrong."

Because she had nothing else, and it seemed to please him, she slipped the gown over her head, letting the towel fall away as the flannel slid down. His muffled groan had her smiling over uncertainly.

"Brianna, what a picture you are. Leave the towel," he murmured as she bent to retrieve it. "Come here. Please."

She stepped forward, that half smile on her face and nerves threatening to swallow her, to take the glass he held out. She sipped, discovered the frothy wine did nothing to ease her dry throat. He was looking at her, she thought, the way she imagined a tiger might look at a lamb just before he pounced.

"You haven't had dinner," she said.

"No." Don't frighten her, idiot, he warned himself and struggled back the urge to devour. He took a slow sample of champagne, watching her, wanting her. "I was just thinking I wanted it. Thinking we could eat up here, together. But now . . ." He reached out to curl a damp tendril of her hair around his finger. "Can you wait?"

So it was to be simple again, she thought. And again her choice. "I can wait for dinner." She could barely get the words passed the heat in her throat. "But not for you."

She stepped, quite naturally, into his arms.

THIRTEEN

An elbow in the ribs brought Brianna groggily out of sleep. Her first view of the morning after a night of love was floor. If Gray took up another inch of the bed, she'd be on it.

It took her only seconds, and a shiver in the chilly morning air, to realize she hadn't even the stingiest corner of sheet or blanket covering her.

Gray, on the other hand, was cozily wrapped beside her, like a contented moth in a cocoon.

Sprawled over the mattress, he slept like the dead. She wished she could have said his snuggled position, and the elbow lodged near her kidney, was loverlike, but it smacked plainly of greed. Her tentative pushes and tugs didn't budge him.

So that was the way of it, she thought. The man was obviously unaccustomed to sharing.

She might have stayed to tussle for her share—just on principle—but the sun was shining through the windows. And there were chores to do.

Her efforts to slip quietly from the bed so as not to disturb him proved unnecessary. The minute her feet were on the floor, he grunted, then shifted to lay claim to her small slice of mattress.

Still, the dregs of romance remained in the room. The candles had guttered out in their own wax sometime during the night. The champagne bottle was empty in its silver bucket, and flowers scented the air. The open curtain caught sunbeams, rather than moonbeams.

He'd made it perfect for her, she remembered. Had known how to make it perfect.

This morning business wasn't quite the way she'd imagined it. In sleep, he didn't look like an innocent boy dreaming, but like a man well satisfied with himself. There hadn't been any gentle caresses or murmured good mornings to acknowledge their first day together as lovers. Just a grunt and a shove to send her on her way.

The many moods of Grayson Thane, she mused. Perhaps she could write a book on that subject herself.

Amused, she tugged her discarded nightgown over her head and headed downstairs.

She could do with some tea, she decided, to get the blood moving again. And since the sky looked promising, she'd do a bit of wash and hang it out to catch the morning air.

She thought the house could do with an airing as well and tossed open windows as she walked. Through the one in the parlor, she spotted Murphy bent under the hood of her car.

She watched him a moment, her emotions tangling. Her anger with him warred with loyalty and affection. Anger was already losing as she walked outside and moved along the garden path.

"I didn't expect to see you," she began.

"I said I'd have a look." He glanced back. She was standing in her nightgown, her hair tangled from the night, her feet bare. Unlike Gray, his blood didn't kindle. She was simply Brianna to him, and he took the moment to search out any sign of temper or forgiveness. He saw neither, so went back to his business.

"Your starter motor's in a bad way," he muttered.

"So I've been told."

"Your engine's sick as an old horse. I can get some parts, patch it back together. But it's good money after bad as I see it."

"If it could last me through the summer, into the autumn . . ." She trailed off as he cursed under his breath. She simply couldn't keep her heart cool from him. He'd been her friend as long as she remembered. And it was friendship, she knew, that had caused him to do what he'd done.

"Murphy, I'm sorry."

He straightened then, and turned to her, with everything he felt naked in his eyes. "So am I. I never meant to cause you hurt, Brie. God's witness."

"I know that." She took the step, crossing to him and slipping her arms around him. "I shouldn't have been so hard, Murphy. Not on you. Never on you."

"You scared me, I'll admit it." His arms went tight around her. "I spent the night worrying over it—afraid you wouldn't forgive me, and not bake me scones anymore."

She laughed as he'd hoped. Shaking her head, she kissed him under the ear. "I was so angry at the thought of it all more than at you. I know you acted out of caring. And Maggie, too." Secure with her head on his shoulder, Brianna closed her eyes. "But my mother, Murphy, what did she act out of?"

"I can't say, Brie."

"You wouldn't say," she murmured and eased back to study his face. Such a handsome one, she thought, with all that goodness inside. It wasn't right for her to ask him to condemn or defend her mother. And she wanted to see him smile again. "Tell me, did Rory hurt you very much?"

Murphy made a sound of derision, purely male, Brianna thought. "Soft hands is what he had, and not a bit of style. Wouldn't have laid the first one on me if I'd been expecting it."

She tucked her tongue in her cheek. "No, I'm sure of it. And did you bloody his nose for me, Murphy darling?"

"That and more. His nose was broke when I'd finished with him, and he'd lost a tooth or two."

"That's a hero for you." She kissed him lightly on both cheeks. "I'm sorry she used you that way."

He shrugged that off. "I'm glad I was the one who plowed a fist in his face, and that's the truth. Never liked the bastard."

"No," Brianna said softly. "You nor Maggie, either. It seems you both saw something I didn't, or I was seeing something that was never there."

"Don't worry at it now, Brie. It was years ago." He started to pat her and remembered the grease on his hands. "Get back now, you'll make yourself filthy. What are you doing out here in your bare feet?"

"Making up with you." She smiled, then looked toward the road at the sound of a car. When she spotted Maggie, Brianna folded her hands, lifted a brow. "Warned her, did you?" she muttered to Murphy.

"Well, I thought it best." And he thought it best now to step neatly back out of the line of fire.

"So." Maggie walked around the nodding columbine, her eyes on Brianna's face. "I thought you might want to talk to me."

"I do, yes. Did you think I had no right to know, Maggie?"

"It wasn't rights I was worried about. 'Twas you."

"I loved him." The long breath she took was part relief that the emotion was fully past tense. "I loved him longer than I would had I known the whole of it."

"Maybe that's true, and I'm sorry for it. I couldn't bear to tell you." To all three of their discomfort, Maggie's eyes filled. "I just couldn't. You were so hurt already, so sad and lost." Pressing her lips together, she struggled with the tears. "I didn't know what was best."

"It was both of our decision." Murphy ranged himself with Maggie. "There was no bringing him back for you, Brie."

"Do you think I would have wanted him back?" A shimmer of heat, and more of pride seeped through as she tossed back her hair. "Do you think so little of me? He believed what she told him. No, I'd not have had him back." She let out a quick huff of breath, drew in another more slowly. "And, I'm thinking, had it been me in your position, Margaret Mary, I might have done the same. I'd have loved you enough to have done the same."

She rubbed her hands together, then held one out. "Come inside, I'm going to make some tea. Have you had breakfast, Murphy?"

"Nothing to speak of."

"I'll call you when it's ready then." With Maggie's hand in hers, she turned and saw Gray standing in the doorway. There was no way to stop the color that flooded her cheeks, a combination of pleasure and embarrassment, that sent her pulse scrambling. But her voice was steady enough, her nod of greeting easy. "Good morning to you, Grayson. I was about to start breakfast."

So, she wanted to play it cool and casual, Gray noted, and returned the nod. "Looks like I'll have company eating it. Morning, Maggie."

Maggie sized him up as she walked with Brianna to the house. "And to you, Gray. You look . . . rested."

"The Irish air agrees with me." He moved aside to let them through the door. "I'll see what Murphy's up to."

He strolled down the walk and stopped by the open hood of the car. "So, what's the verdict?"

Murphy leaned on the car and watched him. "You could say it's still out."

Understanding that neither of them were discussing engines, Gray tucked his thumbs in his front pockets and rocked back on his heels. "Still looking out for her? Can't blame you for that, but I'm not Rory."

"Never thought you were." Murphy scratched his chin, considered. "She's a sturdy piece of work, our Brie, you know. But even sturdy women can be damaged if handled carelessly."

"I don't intend to be careless." He lifted a brow. "Thinking of beating me up, Murphy?"

"Not yet." And he smiled. "I like you, Grayson. I hope I won't be called upon to break any of your bones."

"That goes for both of us." Satisfied, Gray glanced toward the engine. "Are we going to give this thing a decent burial?"

Murphy's sigh was long and heartfelt. "If only we could."

In harmony they ducked under the hood together.

In the kitchen Maggie waited until coffee was scenting the air and Con was chomping happily at his breakfast. Brianna had dressed hastily and, with her apron in place, was busy slicing bacon.

"I've gotten a late start," Brianna began, "so there's no time for fresh muffins or buns. But I've plenty of bread."

Maggie sat at the table, knowing her sister preferred that she stay out of the way. "Are you all right, Brianna?"

"Why wouldn't I be? Will you be wanting sausage, too?"

"Doesn't matter. Brie . . ." Maggie dragged a hand through her hair. "He was your first, wasn't he?" When Brianna set her slicing knife aside and said nothing, Maggie pushed away from the table. "Did you think I wouldn't know, just seeing you together? The way he looks at you." She rubbed her hands absently over her weighted belly as she paced. "The way you look."

"Have I a sign around my neck that says fallen woman?" Brianna said coolly.

"Damn it, you know that's not my meaning." Exasperated, Maggie stopped to face her. "Anyone with wit could see what was between you." And their mother had wit, Maggie thought grimly. Maeve would be back in a matter of days. "I'm not trying to interfere, or to give advice if advice isn't welcome. I just want to know . . . I need to know that you're all right."

Brianna smiled then and let her stiff shoulders relax. "I'm fine, Maggie. He was very good to me. Very kind and gentle. He's a kind and gentle man."

Maggie touched a hand to Brianna's cheek, brushed at her hair. "You're in love with him."

"Yes."

"And he?"

"He's used to being on his own, to coming and going as he pleases, without ties."

Maggie tilted her head. "And you're after changing that?"

With a little hum in her throat, Brianna turned back to her cooking. "You don't think I can?"

"I think he's a fool if he doesn't love you. But changing a man's like walking through molasses. A lot of effort for little progress."

"Well, it's not so much changing him as letting him see what choices there are. I can make a home for him, Maggie, if he'll let me." Then she shook her head. "Oh, it's too soon to be thinking so far. He's made me happy. That's enough for now."

Maggie hoped that was true. "What will you do about Mother?"

"As far as Gray's concerned, I won't let her spoil it." Brianna's eyes frosted as she turned to add cubed potatoes to the pan. "As to the other, I haven't decided. But I will handle it myself, Maggie. You understand me?"

"I do." Giving in to eight months of pregnancy, she sat again. "We heard from the New York detective yesterday."

"You did? Did he find her?"

"It's a more complicated business than we might have thought. He found a brother—a retired policeman who still lives in New York."

"Well, that's a start then, isn't it?" Eager for more, Brianna began to whip up batter for griddle cakes.

"More of a stop, I'm afraid. The man refused to admit he even had a sister at first. When the detective pressed—he had copies of Amanda's birth certificate and such—this Dennis Dougherty said he hadn't seen nor heard from Amanda in more than twenty-five years. That she was no sister to him and so forth as she'd gotten herself in trouble and run off. He didn't know where, or care to know."

"That's sad for him, isn't it?" Brianna murmured. "And her parents? Amanda's parents?"

"Dead, both of them. The mother only last year. There's a sister as well, married and living out in the West of the States. He's talked to her as well, Rogan's man, and though she seems softer of heart, she hasn't been any real help."

"But she must know," Brianna protested. "Surely she'd know how to find her own sister."

"That doesn't seem to be true. It appears there was a family ruckus when Amanda announced she was pregnant, and she wouldn't name the father." Maggie paused, pressed her lips together. "I don't know if she was protecting Da, or herself, or the child if it comes to it. But according to the sister, there were bitter words on all sides. They were lace-curtain Irish and saw a pregnant unwed daughter as a smear on the family name. They wanted her to go away, have the child, and give it up. It seems she refused and simply went away altogether. If she contacted her parents again, the brother isn't saying, and the sister isn't aware of it."

"So we have nothing."

"Next to it. He did find out—the detective—that she'd visited Ireland all those years ago with a woman friend. He's working now on tracking her down."

"Then we'll be patient." She brought a pot of tea to the table and frowned at her sister. "You look pale."

"I'm just tired. Sleeping's not as easy as it once was."

"When do you see the doctor again?"

"This very afternoon." Maggie drummed up a smile as she poured herself a cup.

"Then I'll take you. You shouldn't be driving."

Maggie sighed. "You sound like Rogan. He's coming all the way back from the gallery to take me himself."

"Good. And you're staying right here with me until he comes to get you." More concerned than pleased when she got no argument, Brianna went to call the men to breakfast.

She spent the day happily enough, fussing over Maggie, welcoming an American couple who had stayed at her inn two years earlier. Gray had gone off with Murphy to look for car parts. The sky stayed clear, the air warm. Once she had seen Maggie safely off with Rogan, Brianna settled down for an hour of gardening in her herb bed.

Freshly washed linens were billowing on the line, music was trilling out through the open windows, her guests were enjoying tea cakes in her parlor, and her dog was snoozing in a patch of sunlight beside her.

She couldn't have been happier.

The dog's ears pricked, and her own head came up when she heard the sound of cars. "That's Murphy's truck," she said to Con, and indeed, the dog was already up, tail wagging. "The other I don't recognize. Do you think we have another guest?"

Pleased with the prospect, Brianna rose, dusted the garden dirt from her apron and started around the house. Con raced ahead of her, already barking happily in greeting.

She spotted Gray and Murphy, both of them wearing silly grins as the dog welcomed them as if it had been days rather than hours since they'd parted. Her gaze skimmed over the neat, late-model blue sedan parked in front of Murphy's truck.

"I thought I heard two cars." She looked around anxiously. "Did they go inside already?"

"Who?" Gray wanted to know.

"The people who were driving this. Is there luggage? I should brew some tea fresh."

"I was driving it," Gray told her. "And I wouldn't mind some tea."

"You're a brave one, boy-o," Murphy said under his breath. "I don't have time for tea meself," he went on, preparing to desert. "My cows'll be looking for me by now." He rolled his eyes at Gray, shook his head, and climbed back into his truck."

"Now, what was that?" Brianna wondered as Murphy's truck backed into the road. "What have the pair of you been up to, and why would you be driving this car when you've already got one?"

"Someone had to drive it, and Murphy doesn't like anyone else behind the wheel of his truck. What do you think of it?" In the way of men Gray ran a hand along the front fender of the car as lovingly as he would over a smooth, creamy shoulder.

"It's very nice, I'm sure."

"Runs like a top. Want to see the engine?"

"I don't think so." She frowned at him. "Are you tired of your other one?"

"My other what?"

"Car." She laughed and shook back her hair. "What are you about, Grayson?"

"Why don't you sit in it? Get the feel of it?" Encouraged by her laugh, he took her arm and tugged her toward the driver's side. "It only has about twenty thousand miles on it."

Murphy had warned him that bringing back a new car would be as foolish as spitting into the wind.

Willing to humor him, Brianna climbed in and set her hands on the wheel. "Very nice. It feels just like a car."

"But do you like it?" He propped his elbows on the base of the window and grinned at her.

"It's a fine car, Gray, and I'm sure you'll enjoy the driving of it."

"It's yours."

"Mine? What do you mean it's mine?"

"That old crate of yours is going to junkyard heaven. Murphy and I agreed it was hopeless, so I bought you this."

He yelped when she jerked open the door and caught him smartly on the shin. "Well, you can just take it back where it came from." Her voice was ominously cool as he rubbed his throbbing shin. "I'm not ready to buy a new car, and when I am I'll decide for myself."

"You're not buying it. I'm buying it. I bought it." He straightened and faced the ice with what he was certain was sheer reason. "You needed reliable transportation, and I've provided it. Now stop being so stiff-necked."

"Stiff-necked, is it? Well, 'tis you who's being arrogant, Grayson Thane. Going out and buying a car without a by-your-leave. I won't have

it best. When she sat down with her accounts, it was with a light heart. She was nearly ready to buy her material for the greenhouse.

He found her at her little desk, bundled in her robe, tapping a pen against her lips, her eyes dreamy.

"Are you thinking of me?" he murmured, bending down to nuzzle her neck.

"Actually, I was thinking of southern exposure and treated glass."

"Second place to a greenhouse." He'd worked his way around to her jaw when his gaze skimmed over a letter she had spread open. "What's this? An answer from that mining company."

"Yes, at last. They've gotten their bookkeeping together. We'll get a thousand pounds when we turn in the stock."

He drew back frowning. "A thousand? For ten thousand shares? That doesn't seem right."

She only smiled and rose to take down her hair. Normally it was a ritual he enjoyed, but this time he only continued to stare at the papers on her desk.

"You didn't know Da," she told him. "It's a great deal more than I expected. A fortune really, as his schemes usually cost much more than they ever gained."

"A tenth of a pound per share." He picked up the letter himself. "What do they say he paid for it?"

"Half of that, as you can see. I can't remember anything he ever did that earned as well. I've only to tell Rogan to send them the certificate."

"Don't."

"Don't?" She paused, the brush in her hand. "Why shouldn't we?"

"Has Rogan looked into the company?"

"No, he's enough on his mind with Maggie and the gallery opening next week. I only asked him to hold the certificate."

"Let me call my broker. Look, it can't hurt to get a prospectus on the company, a little information. A few days won't matter to you, will they?"

"No. But it seems a lot of bother for you."

"A phone call. My broker loves to bother." Setting the letter down again, he crossed to her and took the brush. "Let me do that." He turned her to face the mirror and began to draw the brush through her hair. "Just like a Titian painting," he murmured. "All these shades within shades."

She stood very still, watching him in the glass. It shocked her to realize how intimate it was, how arousing, to have him tend to her hair. The way his fingers combed through after the brush. Much more than her scalp began to tingle.

Then his eyes lifted, met hers in the glass. Excitement arrowed into her when she saw the flare of need in his.

"No, not yet." He held her as she was when she started to turn to him. He set the brush down, then drew her hair away from her face.

"Watch," he murmured, then slid his fingers down her to the belt of her robe. "Do you ever wonder how we look together?"

The idea was so shocking, so thrilling, she couldn't speak. His eyes stayed on hers as he unbelted the robe, drew it away. "I can see it in my head. Sometimes it gets in the way of my work, but it's hard to mind."

His hands trailed up lightly over her breasts, making her shiver before he began to unbutton the high-necked gown.

Speechless, helpless, she watched his hands move over her, felt the heat spread under her skin, over it. Her legs seemed to melt away so that she had no choice but to lean back against him. As if in a dream she saw him tug the gown from her shoulder, press his lips to the bared skin.

A jolt of pleasure, a flash of heat.

Her breath came out on a little purr of agreement as the tip of his tongue teased the curve of her neck.

It was so stunning to see as well as to feel. Though her eyes went wide when he slipped the gown up, over her head and away, she didn't protest. Couldn't.

She stared in amazement at the woman in the glass. At herself, she thought hazily. It was herself she watched, for she could feel that light, devastating touch as his hands curved up to take her breasts.

"So pale," he said in a voice that had roughened. "Like ivory, tipped with rose petals." Eyes dark and intense, he rubbed his thumbs over her nipples, felt her tremble, heard her moan.

It was beautifully erotic to watch her body curve back, to feel the soft, yielding weight of her sag against him as she went pliant with pleasure. Almost experimentally he took his hand down her torso, feeling each muscle quiver under his palm. The scent of her hair streamed through his senses, the silk of those long white limbs, and the sight of them trembling in the glass.

He wanted to give, to give to her as he'd never wanted to give to anyone before. To soothe and excite, to protect and inflame. And she, he thought, pressing his lips to her throat again, was so perfect, so outrageously generous.

A touch, he thought, at his touch all that cool dignity and calm manner melted away.

"Brianna." His breath was backing up in his lungs, but he held on until her clouded eyes lifted once more to the reflection of his. "Watch what happens to you when I take you up."

She started to speak, but his hand glided smoothly down, cupping her, finding her already hot and wet. Even as she choked out his name, half in protest, half in disbelief, he stroked her, gently at first, persuasively. But his eyes were fierce with concentration.

It was staggering, shocking to see his hand possess her there, and to feel those long slow strokes that evoked an answering pull and tug in her center. Her own eyes showed her that she was moving against him now, willingly, eagerly, almost pleadingly. Any thought of modesty was forgotten, abandoned as she lifted her arms, hooking them back around his neck, her hips responding to his increasing rhythm.

And she was like a moth pinned by a sharp sweet spear of pleasure. Her body was still shuddering when he lifted her, carrying her to the bed to show her more.

FOURTEEN

"The opening's tomorrow, and he's barred me from the place." With her chin on her fist, Maggie glared at Brianna's back. "And he's plopped me down in your kitchen so you can be my keeper."

Patiently Brianna finished icing the petit fours she'd baked for tea. She had eight guests, counting Gray, including three active children. "Margaret Mary, didn't the doctor tell you to stay off your feet, and that since the baby's dropped, you could deliver earlier than you'd thought?"

"What does he know?" Cranky as a child herself, Maggie scowled. "I'm going to be pregnant for the rest of my life. And if Sweeney thinks he's keeping me from the opening tomorrow, he'd best think again."

"Rogan never said he intended to do that. He didn't want you . . ." She'd nearly said underfoot and took more care with her words. "Overdoing today."

"It's my gallery, too," she muttered. Her back was paining her like a toothache, and she was having twinges. Just twinges, she assured herself. Probably the mutton she'd eaten that afternoon.

"Of course it is," Brianna soothed. "And we'll all be there tomorrow for the opening. The advertisements in the papers were lovely. It'll be a great success, I know."

Maggie only grunted. "Where's the Yank?"

"He's working. Locked himself in as defense against the little German girl who kept wandering into his room." She smiled over it. "He's a darling with children. He played Chutes and Ladders with her last night, so she's fallen in love with him and won't leave him in peace."

"And you're thinking what a fine father he'll make."

Brianna pokered up. "I didn't say that. But he would. You should see how he—" She broke off when she heard the front door open. "If that's more guests, I'll have to give them my room and sleep in the parlor."

"You can just stop playing musical beds and sleep in Gray's," Maggie commented, then winced when she recognized the voices coming down the hall. "Ah, perfect. I'd hoped she'd changed her mind and stayed in France."

"Stop it," Brianna warned and took out more cups for tea.

"The world travelers are back," Lottie said cheerfully as she trailed Maeve into the kitchen. "Oh, what a fine place you have there, Maggie. Like a palace it is. What a wonderful time we had."

"Speak for yourself." Maeve sniffed and set her purse on the counter. "Bunch of foreign half-naked people running around on the beach."

"Some of the men were built beautifully." Lottie giggled. "There was an American widower who flirted with Maeve."

"Dallying." Maeve waved a hand, but her cheeks had flushed. "I paid no mind to his kind." Sitting down, Maeve gave Maggie a hard stare. She covered the spurt of concern with a curl of the lip. "Peaked you are. You'll soon appreciate what a mother suffers when you go into labor."

"Thank you so much."

"Ah, the girl's as strong as a horse." Lottie's voice was bracing as she patted Maggie's hand. "And young enough to have a half dozen children."

Maggie rolled her eyes and managed a laugh. "I don't know which of you depresses me more."

"It's nice you're back in time for the gallery opening tomorrow." Brianna tactfully changed subjects as she served the tea.

"Hah. What would I be doing wasting time at some art place?"

"We wouldn't miss it." Lottie aimed a stern look in Maeve's direction. "Maeve, you know very well you said you'd be pleased to see Maggie's work, and the rest."

Maeve shifted uncomfortably. "What I said was I was surprised there was so much fuss over bits of glass." She frowned at Brianna before Lottie could embarrass her further. "Your car wasn't out front. Has it fallen apart at last?"

"I'm told it was hopeless. I've a new one, the blue one out there."

"A new one." Maeve set her cup down with a clatter. "Squandering your money on a new car?"

" 'Tis her money," Maggie began heatedly, but Brianna cut her off with a look.

"It's not new, except to me. It's a used car, and I didn't buy it." She braced herself. "Grayson bought it for me."

For a moment there was silence. Lottie stared down at her tea with her lips pursed. Maggie prepared to leap to her sister's defense and fought to ignore the twinges.

"Bought it for you?" Maeve's voice was hard as stone. "You accepted such a thing from a man? Have you no care for what people will think, or say?"

"I imagine people will think it was a generous thing, and say the same." She set aside her frosting knife and picked up her tea. Her hands would shake in a moment. She knew it, hated it.

"What they will think is that you sold yourself for it. And have you? Is that what you've done?"

"No." The word was frigidly calm. "The car was a gift, and accepted as such. It has nothing to do with our being lovers."

There, she thought. She'd said it. Her stomach was clutched, her hands fit to tremble, but she'd said it.

White around the lips, her eyes burning blue, Maeve shoved away from the table. "You've whored yourself."

"I haven't. I've given myself to a man I care for and admire. Given myself for the first time," she said and was surprised that her hands remained steady. "Though you've told it differently."

Maeve's gaze cut to Maggie, full of bitterness and temper.

"No, I didn't tell her," Maggie said calmly enough. "I should have, but I didn't."

"It hardly matters how I found out." Brianna folded her hands together. There was a coldness inside her, a horrible chill, but she would finish this. "You saw that I lost whatever happiness I might have had with Rory."

"He was nothing," Maeve shot back. "A farmer's son who never would have made a man. You'd have had nothing with him but a houseful of crying children."

"I wanted children." An ache shot through the ice. "I wanted a family and a home, but we'll never know if I would have found that with him. You saw to that and dragged a good, fine man into your lies. To keep me safe, Mother? I don't think so. I wish I could think so. To keep me tied. Who would have tended to you and this house if I had married Rory? We'll never know that, either."

"I did what was best for you."

"What was best for you."

Because her legs felt weak, Maeve sat again. "So, this is the way you pay me back for it. By giving yourself in sin to the first man who strikes your fancy."

"By giving myself in love to the first and only man who's touched me."

"And what will you do when he plants a baby in your belly and goes off whistling?"

"That's my concern."

"She's talking like you now." Enraged, Maeve turned on Maggie. "You've turned her against me."

"You've done that yourself."

"Don't bring Maggie into this." In a protective move Brianna laid a hand on her sister's shoulder. "This is you and me, Mother."

"Any chance of getting a . . ." High on an afternoon of successful writing, Gray breezed into the kitchen and trailed off as he spotted the company. Though he felt the weight of tension in the room, he tried a friendly smile. "Mrs. Concannon, Mrs. Sullivan, it's good to have you back."

Maeve's hands curled into fists. "Bloody bastard, you'll burn in hell with my daughter beside you."

"Mind your tongue in my house." Brianna's sharp order shocked them all more than Maeve's bitter prediction. "I beg your pardon, Gray, for my mother's rudeness."

"You'll beg no one's pardon on my account."

"No," Gray agreed, nodding at Maeve. "There's no need. You can say what you like to me, Mrs. Concannon."

"Did you promise her love and marriage, a lifetime of devotion to get her on her back? Do you think I don't know what men say to have their way?"

"He promised me nothing," Brianna began, but Gray cut her off with one sharp look.

"No, I didn't make promises. Brianna's not someone I would lie to. And she's not someone I'd turn from if I was told something about her I didn't like."

"You've shared family business with him, too?" Maeve whirled on Brianna. "It's not enough for you to condemn your soul to hell?"

"Will you forever be damning your children to hell?" Maggie fired up before Brianna could speak. "Because you couldn't find happiness, must you try to keep us both from finding it? She loves him. If you could see through your own bitterness, you'd know that, and that's what would matter to you. But she's been at your beck and call all her life and you can't stand the thought that she might find something, someone for herself."

"Maggie, enough," Brianna murmured.

" 'Tisn't enough. You won't say it, never would. But she'll hear it from me. She's hated me from the moment I was born, and she's used you. We're not daughters to her, but by turns a penance and a crutch. Has she once, even once wished me happy with Rogan, or with the baby?"

"And why should I?" Maeve shot back, lips trembling. "And have my good wishes tossed back in my face. You've never given me the love that's a mother's right."

"I would have." Maggie's breath began to hitch as she shoved back from the table. "God knows I've wanted to. And Brianna's tried. Have you ever been grateful for all she put aside for your comfort? Instead you ruined whatever chance she had for the home and family she wanted. Well, you'll not do it again, not this time. You won't come into her house and speak to her or the man she loves this way."

"I'll speak as I choose to my own flesh and blood."

"Stop it, the pair of you." Brianna's voice was sharp as a whiplash. She was pale, icily so, and the trembling she'd managed to fight back had grown to shudders. "Must you strike at each other this way, always? I won't be the club you use to hurt each other. I've guests in the parlor," she said, drawing an unsteady breath. "And I prefer they not be subjected to the misery of my family. Maggie, you sit down and calm yourself."

"Fight your own battles, then," Maggie said furiously. "I'll leave." Even as she said it, the pain struck and had her gripping the back of the chair.

"Maggie." Panicked, Brianna grabbed her. "What is it? Is it the baby?"

"Just a twinge." But it built into a wave that stunned her.

"You've gone white. Sit down now. Sit, don't argue with me."

Lottie, a retired nurse, rose briskly. "How many twinges have you had, darling?"

"I don't know. On and off all afternoon." She let out a relieved breath when the pain passed. "It's nothing, really. I've two weeks yet, or nearly that."

"The doctor said anytime now," Brianna reminded her.

"What does a doctor know?"

"True, true." Smiling easily, Lottie skirted the table and began to massage Maggie's shoulders. "Anything else paining you, love?"

"My back a bit," Maggie admitted. "It's been nagging me all day."

"Mmmm. Well, you just breathe easy now and relax. No, no more tea for her just now, Brianna," she said before Brianna could pour. "We'll see by and by."

"I'm not in labor." Maggie's head went giddy at the idea. "It's just the mutton."

"Might be, yes. Brie, you haven't given your young man any tea."

"I'm fine." Gray looked from one woman to the other, wondering what move to make. Retreat, he decided, would probably be best for all of them. "I think I'll go back to work."

"Oh, I do enjoy your books," Lottie said cheerfully. "Two of them I read while we were on our holiday. I wonder how you can think up such tales and write them down in all those nice words."

She chattered on, keeping him and everyone as they were until Maggie caught her breath. "There you are, only about four minutes apart, I'd say. Breathe it out, love, that's a girl. Brie, I think you should call Rogan now. He'll want to meet us at the hospital."

"Oh." For an instant Brianna couldn't think, much less move. "I should call the doctor."

"That'll be fine." Lottie took Maggie's hand, held it tight as Brianna dashed off. "Now, don't you worry. I've helped bring many a baby into this world. Do you have a case packed, Maggie, at home?"

"In the bedroom, yes." She shuddered out a breath as the contraction passed. Odd, she felt calmer now. "In the closet."

"The young man will go fetch it for you. Won't you, dear?"

"Sure." He'd be glad to. It would get him out of the house, away from the terrifying prospect of childbirth. "I'll go get it right now."

"It's all right, Gray." With the new calm cloaking her, Maggie managed a chuckle. "I'm not going to deliver on the kitchen table."

"Right." He gave her an uncertain smile, and fled.

"I'm going to get your jacket now," Lottie told Maggie, and sent Maeve a telling look. "Don't forget your breathing."

"I won't. Thank you, Lottie. I'll be fine."

"You're scared." Gently Lottie bent down to cup Maggie's cheek. " 'Tis natural. But what's happening to you is just as natural. Something only a woman can do. Only a woman can understand. The good Lord knows if a man could do it, there'd be fewer people in the world."

The thought made Maggie smile. "I'm only a little scared. And not just of the pain. Of knowing what to do after."

"You'll know. You'll be a mother soon, Margaret Mary. God bless you."

Maggie closed her eyes when Lottie left the room. She could feel the changes inside her body, the magnitude of them. She imagined the changes in her life, the enormity of them. Yes, she would be a mother soon. The child she and Rogan had created would be in her arms instead of her womb.

I love you, she thought. I swear to you I'll only show you love.

The pain began to well again, drawing a low moan from her throat. She squeezed her eyes tighter, concentrated on breathing. Through the haze of pain she felt a hand cover hers. Opening her eyes she saw her mother's face, and tears, and perhaps for the first time in her life, a true understanding.

"I wish you happy, Maggie," Maeve said slowly. "With your child."

For a moment at least, the gap was bridged. Maggie turned her hand over and gripped her mother's palm to palm.

When Gray hurried back, the overnight bag clutched in his hand, Lottie was helping Maggie toward Brianna's car. Every guest in the house was outside, waving them off.

"Oh, thank you for being quick." Brianna snatched the case, then looked around distractedly. "Rogan's on his way to the hospital. He hung up before I could even say good-bye. The doctor said to bring her right in. I have to go with her."

"Of course you do. She'll be fine."

"Yes, she'll be fine." Brianna nibbled on her thumb nail. "I have to leave—all the guests."

"Don't worry about things here. I'll take care of it."

"You can't cook."

"I'll take the lot of them out to dinner. Don't worry, Brie."

"No, it's silly of me. I'm so distracted. I'm so sorry, Gray."

"Don't." Steadier himself, he took her face in his hands. "Don't even think about any of that now. Just go help your sister have a baby."

"I will. Could you call Mrs. O'Malley, please? Her number's in my book. She'll come tend to things until I get home again. And if you'd call Murphy. He'd want to know. And—"

"Brie, go. I'll call the whole county." Despite the audience, he gave her a quick, hard kiss. "Have Rogan send me a cigar."

"Yes. All right, yes, I'm going." She hurried to the car.

Gray stood back and watched her drive away, with Lottie and Maeve following behind.

Families, he thought, with a shake of the head and a shudder. Thank Christ he didn't have to worry about one.

But he worried about her. As afternoon became evening and evening became night. Mrs. O'Malley had come, bustling into the kitchen barely half an hour after his SOS call. Rattling pans, she chattered cheerfully about the childbirth experience, until queasy, Gray had retreated to his room.

He fared better when Murphy came down and shared a glass of whiskey with him in toast to Maggie and the baby.

But as the inn grew quiet and the hour late, Gray wasn't able to work or sleep—two activities he'd always used for escape.

Being wakeful gave him too much time to think. However much he wanted to avoid it, the kitchen scene played over and over in his head. What kind of trouble had he caused Brianna simply by wanting her, then acting on the wanting? He hadn't considered her family, or her religion. Did she believe as her mother did?

It made him uneasy to think of souls and eternal damnation. Anything eternal made him uneasy, and damnation certainly topped the list.

Or had Maggie spoken Brianna's mind. That was hardly less disturbing. All that talk of love. From his point of view love could be every bit as dangerous as damnation, and he preferred to dwell on neither on a personal level.

Why couldn't people keep things simple? he wondered as he wandered into Brianna's room. Complications were part and parcel of fiction, but in reality life was so much smoother one day at a time.

But it was stupid, he admitted, and incredibly naive to pretend that Brianna Concannon wasn't a complication. Hadn't he admitted already that she was unique? Restless, he lifted the top off a small bottle on her dresser. And smelled her.

He just wanted to be with her—for the time being, he told himself. They enjoyed each other, liked each other. At this particular time and this particular place, they suited each other well.

Of course, he could back off any time. Of course he could. With a little snarl he shot the top back in the bottle.

But her scent remained with him.

She wasn't in love with him. Maybe she thought she was, because he was her first. That was natural. And maybe, just maybe, he was a little more involved with her than he'd ever been with anyone else. Because she was unlike anyone else. So that was natural, too.

Still and all, when his book was finished, they would have to be finished as well. He'd be moving on. Lifting his head, he stared at himself in the mirror. No surprises there, he thought. It was the same face. If there was a faint light of panic in the eyes, he chose to ignore it.

Grayson Thane looked back at him. The man he'd made from nothing. A man he was comfortable with. A man, he told himself now, who moved through life as he chose to move. Free, no baggage, no regrets.

There were memories. He could block the unpleasant ones. He'd been doing that for years. One day, he thought, he'd look back and remember Brianna, and that would be enough.

Why the hell hadn't she called?

He checked himself, turned away from the mirror before he could see something he preferred to avoid. No need for her to call, he told himself and poked through the books on her shelf. It was her business, family business, and he had no part in it. Wanted no part in it.

He was curious, that was all, about Maggie and the baby. If he was waiting up, it was only to satisfy that curiosity.

Feeling better, he chose a book, stretched out on her bed, and began to read.

Brianna found him there at three A.M. She staggered in on a wave of joy and fatigue to see him asleep on top of her blankets, an open book on his chest. She beamed at him, foolishly, she knew. But it was a night for foolishness.

Quietly she undressed, folded her clothes over a chair, slipped into a nightgown. In the adjoining bath she scrubbed the tiredness from her face. She caught her own grinning reflection in the mirror, and laughed.

Padding back into the bedroom, she bent down to pet Con, who was curled on the rug at the foot of the bed. With a sigh she turned off the light and laid down without bothering to turn down the covers.

He turned to her instantly, his arm draping over her, his face nuzzling her hair. "Brie." His voice was thick with sleep. "Missed you."

"I'm back now." She shifted, curving to him. "Just sleep."

"Hard to sleep without you. Too many old dreams without you."

"Shh." She stroked him, felt herself start to drift. "I'm right here."

He came fully awake with a snap, blinking, confused. "Brie." He cleared his throat and pushed himself up. "You're back."

"Yes. You fell asleep reading."

"Oh. Yeah." After scrubbing his hands over his face, he squinted to see her in the dim light. It came flooding back. "Maggie?"

"She's fine, she's wonderful. Oh, it was beautiful to see, Gray." Excited all over again, she sat up, wrapped her arms around her knees. "She was cursing Rogan, vowing all sorts of hideous revenge on him. He just kept kissing her hands and telling her to breathe. Then she'd laugh, tell him she loved him, and curse him all over again. I've never seen a man so nervous and awed and loving all at once."

She sighed again, not even aware her cheeks were wet. "There was all this confusion and chattering, arguing, just as you'd expect. Whenever they tried to boot us out, Maggie would threaten to get up and leave herself. 'My family stays,' says she, 'or I go with them.' So we stayed. And it was so . . . marvelous."

Gray wiped her tears himself. "Are you going to tell me what she had?"

"A boy." Brianna sniffled. "The most beautiful boy. He has black hair, like Rogan's. It curls around his little head like a halo. And he has Maggie's eyes. They're blue now, of course, but the shape of them's Maggie's. And he wailed so, like he was cursing the lot of us for bringing him into this mess. His little fingers all clenched into fists. Liam, they named him. Liam Matthew Sweeney. They let me hold him." She rested her head on Gray's shoulder. "He looked at me."

"Are you going to tell me he smiled at you?"

"No." But she smiled. "No, that he didn't. He looked at me, very serious like, as if he was after wondering what he was to make of all this business. I've never held a life so new before. It's like nothing else, nothing else in the world." She turned her face into his throat. "I wish you could have been there."

To his amazement, he found he wished the same. "Well, somebody had to mind the ranch. Your Mrs. O'Malley came on the fly."

"Bless her. I'll call her up tomorrow to give her the news and thank her."

"She doesn't cook as well as you."

"You don't think so?" She grinned to herself, delighted. "I hope you didn't say so."

"I'm the soul of diplomacy. So." He kissed Brianna's temple. "She had a boy. What's the weight?"

"Seven pounds, one ounce."

"And the time—you know, when she had it?"

"Oh, it was about half one."

"Shit, looks like the German copped the pool."

"Pardon?"

"The pool. We had a baby pool going. Sex, weight, time of birth. I'm pretty sure the German guy—Krause—hit the closest."

"A betting pool, is it? And whose idea was that?"

Gray ran his tongue around his teeth. "Murphy's," he said. "The man'll bet on anything."

"And what was your guess?"

"Girl, seven and a half pounds, straight up midnight." He kissed her again. "Where's my cigar?"

"Rogan sent you along a fine one. It's in my purse."

"I'll take it down to the pub tomorrow. Somebody's bound to be handing out free drinks."

"Oh, you can bet on that as well." She took a little breath, locked her fingers together. "Grayson, about this afternoon. My mother."

"You don't have to say anything about that. I walked in at a bad moment, that's all."

"It's not all, and it's foolish to pretend it is."

"All right." He'd known she'd insist on hashing it out, but he couldn't bear to see her mood lowered. "We won't pretend. Let's not think about it tonight, though. We'll talk about it later, as much as you need to. Tonight's for celebrating, don't you think?"

Relief warmed her. Her emotions had ridden on a roller coaster long enough that day. "I do, yes."

"I bet you haven't eaten."

"I haven't."

"Why don't I get us some of the cold chicken that's left over from dinner? We'll eat in bed."

FIFTEEN

It was easy enough to avoid serious subjects over the next week. Gray buried himself in his work, and Brianna's time was stretched thin between her guests and her new nephew. Whenever she had a spare minute, she found some excuse to dart down to Maggie's cottage and fuss over the new mother and baby. Maggie was too enraptured with her son to do more than give a few token complaints about missing the opening of her new gallery.

Gray had to admit the kid was a winner. He'd wandered down to the cottage himself a time or two when he needed to stretch his legs and clear his mind.

Early evening was the best time, when the light took on that luminous glow so special to Ireland, and the air was so clear he could see for miles across the emerald hills with the sun striking down on the thin ribbon of river in the distance making it flash like a silver sword.

He found Rogan, dressed in a T-shirt and old jeans, in the front garden, plucking industriously at weeds. An interesting look, Gray mused, for a man who could likely afford a platoon of gardeners.

"Hiya, Pop." Grinning, Gray leaned on the garden gate.

Rogan shifted back on the worn heels of his boots. "Ah, a man. Come in and join me. I've been evicted. Women." He jerked his head toward the cottage. "Maggie and Brie and Murphy's sister Kate up for a visit, and some of the village ladies. Discussing breast feeding and delivery room war stories."

"Yeah." Gray gave the cottage a pained look as he swung through the gate. "It sounds to me more like you escaped than got kicked out."

"True enough. Being outnumbered I can't get near Liam. And Brianna pointed out that Maggie shouldn't be doing the gardening yet, and it's getting overrun. Then she lifted her brow at me in that way of hers. So I took the hint." He looked longingly back at the cottage. "We could try sneaking into the kitchen for a beer."

"It's safer out here." Gray sat down, folded his legs. Companionably, he reached out and pulled a weed. At least it looked like a weed. "I've been wanting to talk to you anyway. About that stock certificate."

"Which stock certificate is that?"

"The Triquarter Mining thing."

"Ah, yes. That business slipped my mind with all that's been going on. Brianna heard from them, didn't she?"

"She heard from someone." Gray scratched his chin. "I had my broker do a little digging. It's interesting."

"Thinking of investing, are you?"

"No, and couldn't if I were. There is no Triquarter Mining—not in Wales or anywhere else he can locate."

Rogan's brow creased. "Folded, did they?"

"It doesn't appear there ever was a Triquarter Mining—which should mean the certificate you're holding is worthless."

"Odd then, that someone would be willing to pay a thousand pounds for it. Your man might have missed something. The company might be quite small, not appear on any of the standard lists."

"I thought of that. So did he. He was curious enough to dig a little deeper, even called the number that was printed on the letterhead."

"And?"

"It isn't a working number. It occurs to me that anyone can have a sheet of letterhead printed up. Just as anyone can rent a post office box, like the one Brianna wrote to in Wales."

"True enough. But it doesn't explain why someone would be willing to pay for something that doesn't exist." Rogan frowned into middle distance. "I've got some business in Dublin. Though I'm not sure Brie will forgive me for taking Maggie and Liam away, we need to leave at the end of the week. It should only take a few days, and I can look into this myself while I'm there."

"I figure it's worth a trip to Wales." Gray shrugged as Rogan looked at him. "You're a little encumbered right now, but I'm not."

"You're thinking of going to Wales yourself?"

"I've always wanted to play detective. It's kind of a coincidence, don't you think, that shortly after Brie found the certificate and sent off a letter, the cottage was broken into." He moved his shoulders again. "I make my living tying coincidences into plots."

"And will you tell Brianna what you're up to?"

"Pieces of it anyway. I've been thinking about taking a quick trip to New York—Brianna might like a weekend in Manhattan."

Now Rogan's brows lifted. "I imagine she would—if you could convince her to leave the cottage during high season."

"I think I've got that worked out."

"And New York is a distance from Wales."

"Wouldn't be hard to detour there on the way back to Clare, though. Add a couple days onto the trip. I thought about going on my own, but if I had to talk to anyone official, I think I'd need her—or Maggie or their mother." He grinned again. "I think Brie's the obvious choice."

"When would you leave?"

"A couple of days."

"You move fast," Rogan commented. "Do you think you can get Brianna to move as quickly?"

"It'll take a lot of charm. I've been saving up."

"Well, if you manage it, keep in touch with me. I'll do what I can to look into the matter from my end. Oh, and if you need extra ammunition, you could mention we've several of Maggie's pieces displayed in Worldwide New York."

The sound of women's laughter filled the air. They came outside, still circling Maggie, who had Liam in the crook of her arm. There were introductions, greetings, a lot of last-minute cooing over the baby before the visitors hopped on bicycles and peddled off.

"Let's have him." Gray reached out and took the baby from Maggie's arms. He always got a kick out of the way Liam stared up at him with solemn blue eyes. "Hey, aren't you talking yet? Rogan, I think it's time we got this kid away from the women, took him down to the pub for a pint."

"He's had his pint for the evening, thank you," Maggie put in. "Mother's milk."

Gray tickled the baby's chin. "How come he's wearing a dress? These women are making a sissy out of you, kid."

" 'Tisn't a dress." Brianna leaned forward to kiss the top of Liam's head. "A sacque is what it is. He'll be wearing trousers soon enough.

Rogan, you've only to heat that dish I brought down when you're ready for dinner." She scowled down at his gardening attempt. "It's no good playing with the weeds. You have to get the roots."

He grinned, kissed her. "Yes, ma'am."

Waving him away, she laughed. "I'm going. Gray, give the baby back. The Sweeneys have had more than enough company for the day. You'll put your feet up?" she said to Maggie.

"I will. Make her do the same," she ordered Gray. "She's been running two households for days."

Gray snatched Brianna's hand. "I could carry you back."

"Don't be foolish. You take care." She let her hand stay in Gray's as they walked through the garden gate and onto the road. "He's grown so much already," she murmured. "And he does smile now, right at you. Do you ever wonder what goes through a baby's mind when he's looking at you?"

"I figure he's wondering if this life is going to be much different from the last."

Surprised, she turned her head. "Do you believe in that sort of thing? Really?"

"Sure. One trip through never made sense to me. We'd never get it right with one try. And being in a place like this, you can feel the echo of old souls every time you take a breath."

"Sometimes I feel I've walked along here before." Idly she reached out, trailing her hand along the red blossoms of fuchsia that lined the road. "Right here, but in a different time, in a different skin."

"Tell me a story."

"There's a stillness to the air, a peace. The road's only a path, very narrow but well trod. And I can smell turf fires burning. I'm tired, but it's good, because I'm going home to someone. Someone's waiting for me just up ahead. Sometimes I can almost see him standing there, lifting his hand to wave at me."

She stopped, shook her head at her own nonsense. "It's foolish. Just imagining."

"Doesn't have to be." He bent down, plucked a wildflower from the side of the road, and handed it to her. "The first day I walked here, I couldn't look at it all fast enough, long enough. It wasn't just because it was new. It was like remembering." On impulse he turned, took her into his arms, and kissed her.

So was this, he realized. Now and then, when he held her, when his mouth was on hers, there was a picture of it at the edge of his mind.

Like remembering.

He brushed off the feeling. It was time, he decided, to start charming her into doing what he wanted. "Rogan told me he needs to go back to Dublin for a while. Maggie and Liam will go with him."

"Oh." There was a sharp, quick stab of regret before she found acceptance. "Well, they have a life there as well. I tend to forget when they're here."

"You'll miss them."

"I will, yes."

"I need to take a little trip myself."

"A trip?" Now there was a jolt of panic she fought to control. "Where are you going?"

"New York. The premiere, remember?"

"Your movie." She managed a smile. "It's exciting for you."

"It could be. If you'd go with me."

"Go with you?" Now she stopped dead in the road to gape at him. "To New York City?"

"A couple of days. Three or four." He scooped her into his arms again and led her into an impromptu waltz. "We could stay at the Plaza like Eloise."

"Eloise? Who—"

"Never mind. I'll explain later. We'll take the Concorde, be there before you know it. We could visit Worldwide there," he added as extra incentive. "Do all the tourist things, eat in ridiculously expensive restaurants. You might get some new menus out of it."

"But I couldn't. Really." Her head was spinning, and had nothing to do with the quick circles of the dance. "The inn—"

"Mrs. O'Malley said she'd be glad to pinch hit."

"To—"

"To help out," he elaborated. "I want you with me, Brianna. The movie's important, but it won't be any fun without you. It's a big moment for me. I don't want it to just be an obligation."

"But, New York—"

"A wink away on the SST. Murphy's happy to look after Con. Mrs. O'Malley's bustling to take care of the inn."

"You've talked to them already." She tried to stop the whirling dance, but Gray kept spinning her.

"Sure. I knew you wouldn't go until everything was tidy."

"I wouldn't. And I can't—"

"Do this for me, Brianna." Ruthlessly he pulled out his best weapon. The trust. "I need you there."

Her breath came out on a long, slow sigh. "Grayson."

"Is that a yes?"

"I must be mad." And she laughed. "Yes."

Two days later Brianna found herself on the Concorde, streaking across the Atlantic. Her heart was in her throat. Had been since she'd closed her suitcase. She was going to New York. Just like that. She'd left her business in the hands of another. Capable hands, to be sure, but not her hands.

She'd agreed to go to another country, to cross an entire ocean with a man who wasn't even kin, in a plane that was a great deal smaller than she'd imagined.

Surely she must have gone mad.

"Nervous?" He took her hand, brought it to his lips.

"Gray, I should never have done this. I don't know what got into me." Of course, she knew. He had. He had gotten into her in every possible way.

"Are you worried about your mother's reaction?"

That had been hideous. The hard words, the accusations and predictions. But Brianna shook her head. She'd resigned herself to Maeve's feelings on Gray, and their relationship.

"I just packed and left," she murmured.

"Hardly." He laughed at her. "You made at least a dozen lists, cooked enough meals for a month and stuck them in the freezer, cleaned the cottage from top to bottom—" He broke off because she didn't merely look nervous. She looked terrified. "Honey, relax. There's nothing to be scared of. New York isn't nearly as bad as it's made out to be."

It wasn't New York. Brianna turned her head, burying her face against his shoulder. It was Gray. She understood, if he didn't, that there was no one else in the world she would have done this for, but family. She understood, if he didn't, that he had become as intricate and vital a part of her life as her own flesh and blood.

"Tell me about Eloise again."

He kept her hand in his, soothing. "She's a little girl who lives at the Plaza with her Nanny, her dog Weenie, and her turtle Skipperdee."

Brianna smiled, closed her eyes, and let him tell her the story.

There was a limo waiting for them at the airport. Thanks to Rogan and Maggie, Brianna had experienced a limo before and didn't feel a complete dolt. In the plush backseat she found an elaborate bouquet of three dozen white roses and a chilled bottle of Dom Pérignon.

"Grayson." Overwhelmed, she buried her face in the blossoms.

"All you have to do is enjoy yourself." He popped the cork on the champagne, let it fizz to the rim. "And I, your genial host, will show you all there is to see in the Big Apple."

"Why do they call it that?"

"I haven't got a clue." He handed her a flute of wine, tapped his against it. "You are the most beautiful woman I've ever known."

She flushed, fumbled, and pushed a hand through her travel-touseled hair. "I'm sure I'm looking my best."

"No, you look best in your apron." When she laughed, he leaned closer, nibbled on her ear. "In fact, I was wondering if you'd wear it for me sometime."

"I wear it every day."

"Uh-uh. I mean *just* the apron."

Now color flooded her cheeks and she cast a distracted glance at the back of the driver's head through the security glass. "Gray—"

"Okay, we'll deal with my prurient fantasies later. What do you want to do first?"

"I—" She was still stuttering over the idea of standing in her kitchen in nothing but her apron.

"Shopping," he decided. "After we check in, and I make a couple of calls, we'll hit the streets."

"I should buy some souveniers. And there's that toy store, that important one."

"F.A.O. Schwartz."

"Aye. They'd have something wonderful for Liam, wouldn't they?"

"Absolutely. But I was thinking more about Fifth and Forty-seventh."

"What's that?"

"I'll take you."

He barely gave her time to gawk, at the palacelike structure of the hotel itself, at the opulent lobby of the Plaza with its red carpeting and dazzling chandeliers, the spiffy uniforms of the staff, the magnificently ornate floral arrangements, and the glorious little display windows filled with stunning jewels.

They rode the elevator to the top, and she walked into the sumptuous suite so high up that it had a view of the lush green island of Central Park. He whirled her in, and by the time she'd freshened up from traveling, he was waiting impatiently to whirl her out again.

"Let's walk. It's the best way to see New York." He took her purse, crossed the strap from her shoulder to her hip. "Carry it like this, with your hand on it. Are those shoes comfortable?"

"Yes."

"Then you're set."

She was still trying to catch her breath when he pulled her out.

"It's a great town in the spring," he told her as they began to walk down Fifth.

"So many people." She watched a woman dash by, legs flashing under short, shimmering silk. And another in baggy red leather with a trio of earrings dangling from her left lobe.

"You like people."

She stared at a man marching along, barking orders into a cellular phone. "Yes."

Gray shifted her out of the path of a zipping bike. "Me, too. Now and then."

He pointed out things to her, promised her as much time as she wanted in the grand toy store, enjoyed watching her gawk at store windows and the wonderfully varied people who hurried along the streets.

"I went to Paris once," she told him, smiling at a sidewalk vender who hawked hot dogs. "To see Maggie's show there. I thought then I'd never in my life see anything as grand as that." Laughing, she squeezed his hand hard. "But this is."

She loved it. The constant and almost violent noise of traffic, the glittering offerings displayed in shop after shop, the people, self-absorbed and rushing away on their own business, and the towering buildings, spearing up everywhere and turning the streets into canyons.

"Here."

Brianna stared at the building on the corner, each window dripping with jewels and gems. "Oh, what is it?"

"It's a bazaar, darling." Zooming on the excitement of just being there with her, he yanked open the door. "A carnival."

The air inside was alive with voices. Shoppers bumped along the aisles, peering into display cases. She saw diamonds, ring after ring flashing through glass. Colored stones like rainbows, the seductive gleam of gold.

"Oh, what a place." She was pleased to wander along the aisle with him. It seemed otherworldly, all the sellers and buyers haggling over the price of ruby necklaces and sapphire rings. What a story she'd have to tell when she got back to Clare.

She stopped with Gray by a display case and chuckled. "I doubt very much I'll find my souveniers in here."

"I will. Pearls, I think." He wagged a finger at the saleswoman to hold her off and studied the wares himself. "Pearls would suit."

"Are you buying a gift?"

"Exactly. This one." He gestured to the clerk. He'd already had an image in his mind, and the three strands of milky pearls fit it perfectly.

He listened with half an ear as the clerk touted the beauty and worth of the necklace. Traditional, she said, simple and elegant. An heirloom. And, of course, a bargain.

Gray took the necklace himself, tested the weight, studied the glowing orbs. "What do you think, Brianna?"

"It's stunning."

"Of course it is," the clerk said, sensing a sale rather than a browse. "You won't find another to compare with it, certainly not at this price. A classic look like this, you can wear with anything, evening dress, day wear. A little cashmere sweater, silk blouse. Simple little black dress."

"Black wouldn't suit her," Gray said, looking at Brianna. "Midnight blue, pastels, moss green maybe."

Brianna stomach began to jitter as the clerk picked up the theme. "You know you're right. With her coloring, you want jewel tones or pastels. Not every woman can wear both. Try it on. You'll see for yourself how beautifully they drape."

"Gray, no." Brianna took a step back, bumped solidly into another shopper. "You can't. It's ridiculous."

"Dearie," the clerk broke in. "When a man wants to buy you a necklace like this, it's ridiculous to quibble. At forty percent off retail, too."

"Oh, I think you can do better than that," Gray said off-handedly. It wasn't the money, he'd hardly glanced at the tiny ticket tagged discreetly to the pave diamond clasp. It was the sport. "Let's see how they look."

Brianna stood, her eyes filled with distress, as Gray fastened the necklace around her. It lay like a miracle against her plain cotton blouse. "You can't buy me something like this." She refused, however much her fingers itched, to reach up and stroke the pearls.

"Sure I can." He leaned over, gave her a casual kiss. "Let me enjoy myself." Straightening, he studied her through narrowed eyes. "I think it's pretty much what I'm looking for." He shot the clerk a look. "Do better."

"Dearie, I'm practically giving it away now. Those pearls are perfectly matched, you know."

"Mmm-hmm." He turned the little tabletop mirror toward Brianna. "Take a look," he suggested. "Live with them for a minute. Let me see that pin there, the diamond heart."

"Oh, that's a nice piece. You've got a good eye." Revved, the clerk reached for it, lay it on the counter on a black velvet pad. "Twenty-four brilliant cut stones. Top quality."

"Pretty. Brie, don't you think Maggie would like it? A new mom present."

"Ah." She was having a hard time keeping her mouth from hanging open. First the sight of herself in the mirror with pearls around her neck, then the idea that Gray would buy diamonds for her sister. "She'd adore it, how couldn't she? But you can't—"

"What kind of deal are you going to make me for both?"

"Well . . ." the clerk drummed her fingers on her breast. As if pained, she picked up a calculator and started running figures. She wrote an amount on a pad that had Brianna's heart stopping.

"Gray, please."

He just waved her to silence. "I think you can do better than that."

"You're killing me here," the woman said.

"See if you can stand a little more pain."

She grumbled, muttering about profit margins and the quality of her merchandise. But she juggled figures, sliced a bit, then patted a hand over her heart. "I'm cutting my own throat."

Gray winked at her, took out his wallet. "Box them up. Send them to the Plaza."

"Gray, no."

"Sorry." He unclasped the pearls, handed them negligently to the delighted clerk. "You'll have them by tonight. It's not smart to walk around with them."

"That's not what I mean, and you know it."

"You have such a lovely voice," the clerk said to distract her. "Are you Irish?"

"I am, yes. You see—"

"It's her first trip to the States. I want her to have something special to remember it by." He took Brianna's hand, kissing her fingers in a way that made even the clerk's cynical heart sigh. "I want that very much."

"You don't have to buy me things."

"That's part of the beauty of it. You never ask."

"And what part of Ireland are you from, dearie?"

"County Clare," Brianna murmured, knowing she'd lost again. "It's in the west."

"I'm sure it's lovely. And you're going to . . ." After taking Gray's credit card, the clerk read the name and yelped. "Grayson Thane. God, I read all your books. I'm your biggest fan. Wait until I tell my husband. He's your biggest fan, too. We're going to see your movie next week. Can't wait. Can I have your autograph? Milt's just not going to believe it."

"Sure." He took the pad she shoved at him. "This you, Marcia?" He tapped the business card displayed on the counter.

"That's me. Do you live in New York? It never says where on the back of your books."

"No, I don't." He smiled at her, handing her back the pad to distract her from asking more questions.

" 'To Marcia,' " she read, " 'a gem among gems. Fondly, Grayson Thane.' " She beamed at him now, but not so brightly she forgot to have him sign the credit slip. "You come back any time you're looking for something special. And don't you worry, Mr. Thane. I'll have these sent out to your hotel right away. You enjoy your necklace, dearie. And you enjoy New York."

"Thanks, Marcia. Give my best to Milt." Pleased with himself, he turned back to Brianna. "Want to look around some more?"

Numb, she merely shook her head. "Why do you do that?" she managed when they were on the street again. "How do you make it impossible to say no when I mean no."

"You're welcome," he said lightly. "Are you hungry? I'm hungry. Let's get a hot dog."

"Gray." She stopped him. "It's the most beautiful thing I've ever had," she said solemnly. "And so are you."

"Good." He grabbed her hand and led her to the next corner, calculating that he'd softened her up enough so that she'd let him buy her the perfect dress for the premiere.

She argued. She lost. To balance things out Gray backed off when she insisted on paying for her trinkets for Ireland herself. He amused himself helping her figure her change with the unfamiliar American money she'd gotten at the airport bank. It fascinated him that she seemed more dazzled by the toy store than by the jewelry or dress shops they'd visited. And when inspiration hit, he discovered her even more enthralled with a kitchen specialty store.

Delighted with her, he carted her bags and boxes back to the hotel, then charmed her into bed, spinning out time with long, luxurious lovemaking.

He wined and dined her at Le Cirque, then in a rush of nostalgic romanticism, took her dancing at the Rainbow Room, enjoying as much as she the out-of-time decor and big band sound.

Then he loved her again, until she slept exhausted beside him, and he lay wakeful.

He lay wakeful a long time, smelling the roses he'd given her, stroking the silk of her hair, listening to her quiet, even breathing.

Somewhere during that twilight time of half sleep, he thought of how many hotels he'd slept in alone. How many mornings he'd awakened alone, with only the people he created inside his head for company.

He thought of how he preferred it that way. He always had. And how, with her curled beside him, he wasn't quite able to recapture that sensation of solitary contentment.

Surely he would again, when their time was up. Even half dreaming he warned himself not to dwell on tomorrow, and certainly not on yesterday.

Today was where he lived. And today was very nearly perfect.

SIXTEEN

By the following afternoon Brianna was still dazzled enough with New York to try to look everywhere at once. She didn't care if she appeared so obviously the tourist, snapping pictures with her camera, staring up, her neck craned back, to see the very top of the spearing buildings. If she gawked, what of it? New York was a noisy and elaborate sideshow designed to stun the senses.

She pored over the guidebook in their suite, making careful lists and dutifully crossing off each sight she'd seen.

Now she had to face the prospect of a business lunch with Gray's agent.

"Arlene's terrific," Gray assured Brianna as he hustled her along the street. "You'll like her."

"But this lunch." Though she slowed her pace, he didn't allow her to hang back as she would have preferred. "It's like a business meeting. I should wait for you somewhere, or perhaps join you when you've finished. I could go to Saint Patrick's now, and—"

"I told you I'd take you to Saint Pat's after lunch."

And he would, she knew. He was more than willing to take her anywhere. Everywhere. Already that morning she'd stood at the top of the Empire State Building, marvelling. She'd had a subway ride, eaten breakfast in a deli. Everything she'd done, everything she'd seen was whirling around in her head like a kaleidoscope of color and sound.

Still, he promised more.

But the prospect of having lunch with a New York agent, an obviously formidable woman, was daunting. She'd have found some firm way of excusing herself, perhaps even inventing a headache or fatigue, if Gray hadn't seemed so excited by the idea.

She watched as he casually stuffed a bill into a tin cup of a man dozing against the side of a building. He never missed one. Whatever the hand-printed sign might say—homeless, out of work, Vietnam vet—it got his attention. And his wallet.

Everything got his attention, she mused. He missed nothing and saw everything. And those small acts of kindness to strangers others seemed not even to admit existed were an innate part of him.

"Hey, bud, need a watch? Got some nice watches here. Only twenty bucks." A slim black man opened a briefcase to display an array of Gucci and Cartier knockoffs. "Got a real nice watch for the lady here."

To Brianna's dismay, Gray stopped. "Yeah? They got works?"

"Hey." The man grinned. "What do I look like? They keep the time, man. Look just like the ones you pay a thousand for down on Fifth."

"Let's see." Gray chose one while Brianna bit her lip. The man looked dangerous to her, the way his eyes were shifting right and left. "Get hassled much on this corner?"

"Nah. I got a rep. Nice watch there, quality, look pretty on the lady. Twenty bucks."

Gray gave the watch a shake, held it to his ear. "Fine." He passed the man a twenty. "Couple of beat cops heading this way," he said mildly and tucked Brianna's hand in his arm.

When she looked back, the man was gone.

"Were they stolen?" she asked, awed.

"Probably not. Here you go." He fastened the watch on her wrist. "It might run for a day—or a year. You can never tell."

"Then why did you buy it?"

"Hey, the guy's got to make a living, doesn't he? The restaurant's up here."

That distracted her enough to have her tug on the jacket of her suit. She felt drab and countrified, and foolish with her little I Love New York bag holding her Empire State souveniers.

Nonsense, she assured herself. She met new people all the time. She enjoyed new people. The problem was, she thought as Gray ushered her into the Four Seasons, this time it was Gray's people.

She tried not to stare as he led her up the steps.

"Ah, Mr. Thane." The maître d' greeted him warmly. "It's been too long. Ms. Winston is already here."

They crossed the room with its long gleaming bar, the linen-decked tables already filled with the lunch crowd. A woman rose as she spotted Gray.

Brianna saw the gorgeous red suit first, the glint of gold at the lapel and at the ears. Then the short, sleek blond hair, the quick flashing smile before the woman was enveloped by Gray's enthusiastic embrace.

"Good to see you, beautiful."

"My favorite globe trotter." Her voice was husky, with a hint of gravel.

Arlene Winston was tiny, barely topping five feet, and athletically trim from her thrice weekly workouts. Gray had said she was a grandmother, but her face was almost unlined, the tawny eyes sharp in contrast to the soft complexion and pixie features. With her arm still around Gray's waist, she held out a hand to Brianna.

"And you're Brianna. Welcome to New York. Has our boy been showing you a good time?"

"He has, yes. It's a wonderful city. I'm pleased to meet you, Mrs. Winston."

"Arlene." She cupped Brianna's hand briefly between the two of hers, patted. However friendly the gesture, Brianna wasn't unaware of the quick and thorough measuring. Gray simply stood back beaming.

"Isn't she gorgeous?"

"She certainly is. Let's sit. I hope you don't mind, I've ordered champagne. A little celebration."

"The Brits?" Gray asked, settling.

"There is that." She smiled as their glasses were filled from the bottle of spring water already on the table. "Do you want to get this business out of the way now, or wait until after lunch?"

"Let's get it out of the way."

Obliging, Arlene dismissed the waiter, then reached into her briefcase and took out a file of faxes. "Here's the British deal."

"What a woman," Gray said and winked at her.

"The other foreign offers are in there—and the audio. We've just started to pitch to the movie people. And I have your contract." She shifted, letting Gray look over the papers while she smiled at Brianna. "Gray tells me you're an incredible cook."

"He likes to eat."

"Doesn't he though? You run a B-and-B, delightfully from what I hear. Blackthorn, it's called."

"Blackthorn Cottage, yes. It's not a large place."

"Homey, I imagine." Arlene studied Brianna over her water glass. "And quiet."

"Quiet, certainly. People come to the west for the scenery."

"Which, I'm told, is quite spectacular. I've never been to Ireland, but Gray's certainly whetted my curiosity. How many people can you manage?"

"Oh, I've four guest rooms, so it varies depending on the size of families. Eight's comfortable, but I sometimes have twelve or more with children."

"And you cook for them all, run the place by yourself?"

"It's a bit like running a family," Brianna explained. "Most people stay only a night or two, going on their way."

Casually Arlene drew Brianna out, weighing each word, every inflection, judging. Gray was more than a client to her, much more. An interesting woman, she decided. Reserved, a bit nervous. Obviously capable, she mused, tapping a perfectly manicured nail against the cloth as she pumped Brianna for details of the countryside.

Neat as a pin, she observed, well mannered, and . . . ah . . . she watched Brianna's gaze wander—just for a fraction—and rest on Gray. And saw what she wanted to see.

Brianna looked back, saw Arlene's lifted brows, and struggled not to blush. "Grayson said you have grandchildren."

"I certainly do. And after a glass of champagne, I'm likely to drag out all their pictures."

"I'd love to see them. Really. My sister just had a baby." Everything about her warmed, her eyes, her voice. "I've pictures of my own."

"Arlene." Gray looked up from the file, focused again. "You're a queen among agents.

"And don't you forget it." She handed him a pen even as she signaled for the wine and the menus. "Sign the contracts, Gray, and let's celebrate."

Brianna calculated that she had sipped more champagne since meeting Grayson than she had in the whole of her life before him. While she toyed with a glass, she studied the menu and tried not to wince over the prices.

"We have drinks with Rosalie late this afternoon," Gray was saying, referring to the meeting scheduled with his editor, "then the premiere. You're going, aren't you?"

"Wouldn't miss it," Arlene assured him. "I'll have the chicken," she added, passing her menu to the hovering waiter. "Now," she continued after their orders were placed. "Tell me how the book's going."

"It's going well. Incredibly well. I've never had anything fall into place like this. I've nearly got the first draft finished."

"So quickly?"

"It's streaming out." His gaze rested on Brianna. "Almost like magic. Maybe it's the atmosphere. It's a magical place, Ireland."

"He works hard," Brianna put in. "Sometimes he doesn't come out of his room for days at a time. And it doesn't do to disturb him. He'll snap at you like a terrier."

"And do you snap back?" Arlene wanted to know.

"Not usually." Brianna smiled as Gray covered her hand with his own. "I'm used to that sort of behavior with my sister."

"Oh, yes, the artist. You'd have experience with the artistic temperament."

"I do, indeed," Brianna said with a laugh. "Creative people have a more difficult time than the rest of us, I think. Gray needs to keep the door of his world closed while he's in it."

"Isn't she perfect?"

"I believe she is," Arlene said complacently.

A patient woman, she waited until after the meal before making her next move. "Will you have dessert, Brianna?"

"I couldn't, thank you."

"Gray will. Never gains an ounce," she said with a shake of her head. "You order something sinful, Gray. Brianna and I will go into the ladies' room where we can talk about you in private."

When Arlene rose, Brianna had little choice but to follow suit. She cast one confused glance at Gray over her shoulder as they walked away.

The ladies' lounge was as glamorous as the barroom. The counter was set with bottles of scent, lotions, even cosmetics. Arlene sat before the mirror, crossed her legs, and gestured for Brianna to join her.

"Are you excited about the premiere tonight?"

"Yes. It's a big moment for him, isn't it? I know they've made movies of his books before—I've seen one. The book was better."

"Thatta girl." Arlene laughed, tilted her head. "Do you know Gray has never brought a woman with him to meet me before you?"

"I . . ." Brianna fumbled, wondered how best to respond.

"I find that a very telling thing. Our relationship goes beyond business, Brianna."

"I know. He's so fond of you. He speaks of you like family."

"I am family. Or as close as he'll let himself come to it. I love him dearly. When he told me he was bringing you to New York, I was more than surprised." Casually Arlene opened her compact, dabbed powder under her eyes. "I wondered just how some little Irish tart had gotten her hooks in my boy."

When Brianna's mouth opened, her eyes iced, Arlene held up a hand.

"An overprotective mother's first reaction. And one that shifted as soon as I got a look at you. Forgive me."

"Of course." But Brianna's voice was stiff and formal.

"Now you're annoyed with me, and you should be. I've adored Gray for more than a decade, worried about him, harassed him, soothed him. I'd hoped he could find someone he could care for, someone who would make him happy. Because he's not."

She snapped her compact closed and, out of habit, took out a tube of lipstick. "Oh, he's probably the most well-adjusted person I know, but there's a lack of happiness in some corner of his heart."

"I know," Brianna murmured. "He's too alone."

"He was. Do you know the way he looks at you? He's almost giddy. That might have concerned me, if I hadn't seen the way you look at him."

"I love him," Brianna heard herself say.

"Oh, my dear, I can see that." She reached out to clasp Brianna's hand. "Has he told you about himself?"

"Very little. He holds that in, pretends it isn't there."

Arlene's lips thinned as she nodded. "He's not one to share. I've been as close to him as anyone can be for a long time, and I know next to nothing myself. Once, after his first million-dollar sale, he got a little drunk and told me more than he'd meant to." She shook her head. "I don't feel I can tell you. Something like a priest in confession—you'd understand that."

"Yes."

"I'll say this. He had a miserable childhood and a difficult life. Despite it, maybe because of it, he's a kind and generous man."

"I know he is. Sometimes too generous. How do you make him stop buying you things?"

"You don't. Because he needs to do it. Money's not important to Gray. The symbol of it is vital, but the money itself is nothing more than a means to an end. And I'm about to give some unsolicited advice and tell you not to give up, to be patient. Gray's only home in his work. He sees to that. I wonder if he realizes yet you're making him a home in Ireland."

"No." Brianna relaxed enough to smile. "He doesn't. Neither did I until a bit ago. Still, his book's almost finished."

"But you're not. And you've got someone very much on your side now, if you feel the need for it."

Hours later, as Gray tugged up the zipper of her dress, Brianna thought over Arlene's words. It was a lover's gesture, she thought as Gray planted a kiss on her shoulder. A husband's.

She smiled at him in the mirror. "You look wonderful, Grayson."

So he did in the black suit, tieless, with that casual sophistication she'd always associated with movie and music stars.

"Who's going to look at me when you're around?"

"All the women?"

"There's a thought." He draped the pearls around her throat, grinning as he clasped them. "Nearly perfect," he judged, turning her to face him.

The tone of the midnight blue warmed against her creamy skin. The neckline was a low scoop that skimmed the soft curve of breasts and left her shoulders bare. She'd put her hair up so that he could play with the tendrils that escaped to tickle her ears and the nape of her neck.

She laughed as he turned her in a slow circle. "Earlier you said I was perfect."

"So I did." He took a box out of his pocket, flipped open the top. There were more pearls inside, two luminous teardrops that dripped from single flashing diamonds.

"Gray—"

"Shh." He slipped the earrings over her lobes. A practiced move, she thought wryly, smoothly and casually done. "*Now*, you're perfect."

"When did you get these?"

"I picked them out when we bought the necklace. Marcia was delighted when I called and had her send them over."

"I bet she was." Helpless to do otherwise, she lifted a hand and stroked an earring. It was real, she knew, yet she couldn't imagine it—Brianna Concannon standing in a luxurious New York hotel, wearing pearls and diamonds while the man she loved smiled at her.

"It's no use telling you that you shouldn't have done it?"

"No use at all. Say thank you."

"Thank you." Accepting, she pressed her cheek to his. "This is your night, Grayson, and you've made me feel like a princess."

"Just think how nifty we'll look if any of the press bothers to snap a picture."

"Bothers to?" She grabbed her bag as he pulled her toward the door. "It's your movie. You wrote it."

"I wrote the book."

"That's what I said."

"No." He slipped an arm around her shoulders as they walked to the elevator. She may have looked like a glamorous stranger, he noted, but she still smelled like Brianna. Soft, sweet, and subtle. "You said it was my movie. It's not. It's the director's movie, the producer's movie, the actors' movie. And it's the screenwriter's movie." As the doors opened he led her inside, pushed the button for lobby. "The novelist is way down on the list, honey."

"That's ridiculous. It's your story, your people."

"Was." He smiled at her. She was becoming indignant for him, and he found it charming. "I sold it, so whatever they've done—for better or worse—you won't hear me complain. And the spotlight most certainly will not be on 'based on the novel written by' tonight."

"Well, it should be. They'd have nothing without you."

"Damn right."

She cut him a glance as they stepped into the lobby. "You're making fun of me."

"No, I'm not. I'm adoring you." He kissed her to prove it, then led her outside where their limo was waiting. "The trick to surviving a Hollywood sale is not to take it too personally."

"You could have written the screenplay yourself."

"Do I look like a masochist?" He almost shuddered at the thought. "Thanks, but working with an editor is as close as I ever want to come to writing by committee." He settled back as the car cruised through traffic. "I get paid well, I get my name on the screen for a few seconds, and if the movie's a hit—and the early buzz seems to indicate this one will be—my sales soar."

"Don't you have any temperament?"

"Plenty of it. Just not about this."

Their picture was snapped the moment they alighted at the theater. Brianna blinked against the lights, surprised and more than a little disconcerted. He'd indicated that he'd be all but ignored, yet a microphone was thrust at him before they'd taken two steps. Gray answered questions easily, avoided them just as easily, all the while keeping a firm grip on Brianna as they made their way toward the theater.

Dazzled, she looked around. There were people here she'd only seen in glossy magazines, on movie and television screens. Some loitered in the lobby, as ordinary people might, catching a last smoke, chatting over drinks, gossiping or talking shop.

Here and there, Gray introduced her. She made whatever responses seemed right and filed away names and faces for the people back in Clare.

Some dressed up, some dressed down. She saw diamonds, and she saw denim. There were baseball caps and thousand-dollar suits. She smelled popcorn, as she might in any theater on any continent, and that bubble gum scent of candy along with subtle perfumes. And over it all was a thin, glossy coat of glamour.

When they took their seats in the theater, Gray draped his arm over the back of her chair, turned so that his mouth was at her ear. "Impressed?"

"Desperately. I feel I've walked into a movie instead of coming to see one."

"That's because events like this have nothing to do with reality. Wait until the party after."

Brianna let out a careful breath. She'd come a long way from Clare, she thought. A long, long way.

She didn't have much time to chew over it. The lights dimmed, the screen lit. In only moments she felt the sharp, silvery thrill of seeing Gray's name flash, hold, then fade.

"That's wonderful," she whispered. "That's a wonderful thing."

"Let's see if the rest is as good."

She thought it was. The action swept by, that edge-of-the-seat pace that had her immersed. It didn't seem to matter that she'd read the book, already knew the twists of plot, recognized whole blocks of Gray's words in the dialogue. Her stomach still clenched, her lips still curved, her eyes still widened. Once Gray pressed a handkerchief into her hands so she could dry her cheeks.

"You're the perfect audience, Brie. I don't know how I've watched a movie without you."

"Shh." She sighed, took his hand, and held it through the breathless climax and through the closing credits while applause echoed from the walls.

"I'd say we've got a hit."

"They won't believe me," Brianna said as they stepped out of the elevator in the Plaza hours later. "*I* wouldn't believe me. I danced with Tom Cruise." Giggling, a little light-headed on wine and excitement, she turned a quick pirouette. "Do you believe it?"

"I have to." Gray unlocked the door. "I saw it. He seemed very taken with you."

"Oh, he just wanted to talk about Ireland. He has a fondness for it. He's charming, and madly in love with his wife. And to think they might actually come and stay at my house."

"It wouldn't surprise me to find the place lousy with celebrities after tonight." Yawning, Gray toed off his shoes. "You enchanted everyone you spoke with."

"You Yanks always fall for an Irish voice." She unclasped her necklace, running the strands through her hands before she laid them in their box. "I'm so proud of you, Gray. Everyone was saying how wonderful the movie was, and all that talk about Oscars." She beamed at him as she slipped off her earrings. "Imagine, you winning an Oscar."

"I wouldn't." He took off his jacket, tossed it carelessly aside. "I didn't write the movie."

"But . . ." She made a sound of disgust, stepping out of her shoes, lowering the zipper of her dress. "That's just not right. You should have one."

He grinned and, taking off his shirt, glanced over his shoulder at her. But the quip dried like dust on the tip of his tongue.

She stepped out of her dress and was standing there in the little strapless fancy he'd bought to go under it. Midnight blue. Silk. Lace.

Unprepared, he was hard as iron as she bent to unsnap a smoky stocking from its garters. Pretty hands with their neat, unpainted nails skimmed down over one long smooth thigh, over the knee, the calf, tidily rolling the stocking.

She was saying something, but he couldn't hear it over the buzzing in his head. Part of his brain was warning him to get a choke hold on the violent flare of desire. Another part was urging him to take, as he'd wanted to take. Hard and fast and mindlessly.

Her stockings neatly folded, she reached up to unpin her hair. His hands fisted at his sides as those fired-gold tresses spilled down over bare shoulders. He could hear his own breathing, too quick, too harsh. And could almost, almost feel that silk rip in his hands, feel the flesh beneath go hot, taste that heat as his mouth closed greedily over her.

He forced himself to turn away. He needed only a moment, he assured himself, to reclaim control. It wouldn't be right to frighten her.

"And it'll be such fun to tell everyone." Brianna set down her brush and giving into the new laugh, turned another pirouette. "I can't believe it's the middle of the night and I'm so wide awake. Just like a little child who's had too many sweets. I don't feel as though I'll ever need to sleep again." She spun toward him, wrapping her arms around his waist, pressing against his back. "Oh, I've had such a wonderful time, Gray. I don't know how to thank you for it."

"You don't have to." His voice was rough, every cell in his body on full alert.

"Oh, but you're used to this sort of thing." Innocently she planted a quick line of friendly kisses from shoulder to shoulder. He ground his teeth to hold back a moan. "I don't suppose you can really imagine what a thrill all this has been for me. But you're all knotted up." Instinctively she began to rub his back and shoulders. "You must be tired, and here I am, chattering like a magpie. Lie down, won't you? And I'll work these kinks out for you."

"Stop." The order sliced out. He whirled quickly, gripping her wrists so that she could only stand and stare. He looked furious. No, she realized. He looked dangerous.

"Grayson, what is it?"

"Don't you know what you're doing to me?" When she shook her head, he jerked her against him, his fingers biting into flesh. He could see the puzzlement in her eyes give way to dawning awareness, and to panic. And he snapped.

"Goddamn it." His mouth crushed down on hers, hungry, desperate. If she'd pushed him away, he might have pulled himself back. Instead she lifted a trembling hand to his cheek, and he was lost.

"Just once," he muttered, dragging her to the bed. "Just once."

This wasn't the patient, tenderhearted lover she'd known. He was wild, on the edge of violence, with hands that tugged and tore and possessed. Everything about him was hard, his mouth, his hands, his body. For an instant, as he used them all to batter her senses, she feared she might simply break apart, like glass.

Then the dark tide of his need swept her along, shocked, aroused, and terrified all at once.

She cried out, staggered, as those restless fingers shot her mercilessly to peak and over. Her vision hazed, but she could see him through it. In the lights they'd left blazing, his eyes were fierce.

She said his name again, sobbed it out as he pulled her up to her knees. They were torso to torso on the rumpled bed, his hands molding her, pushing her ruthlessly toward madness.

Helpless, she bowed back, shuddering when his teeth scraped down her throat, over her breast. There he suckled greedily, as if starved for her taste, while his impatient fingers drove her mercilessly higher.

He couldn't think. Each time he'd loved her he'd struggled to keep one corner of his mind cool enough to make his hands gentle, his pace easy. This time there was only heat, a kind of gleeful, glorious hell that seeped into mind as well as body and burned away the civilized. Now bombarded by his own lust, craving hers, control was beyond him.

He wanted her writhing, bucking, screaming.

And he had her.

Even the torn silk was too much of a barrier. Frantic now, he ripped it down the center, pushing her onto her back so that he could devour the newly exposed flesh. He could feel her hands drag through his hair, her nails score his shoulders as he worked his way down her, feasting.

Then her gasp, the jolt, the muffled scream when his tongue plunged into her.

She was dying. No one could live through this heat, through the pressure that kept building and exploding, building and exploding until her body was only a quivering mass of scored nerves and unspeakable needs.

The sensations pounded at her, massing too quickly to be separated. She only knew he was doing things to her, incredible, wicked, delicious things. The next climax slammed into her like a fist.

Rearing up, she grabbed at him, thrashing until they were rolling over the bed. Her mouth sprinted over him, just as greedy now, just as frenzied. Her questing hands found him, cupped him, so that her system shivered with fresh and furious pleasure when he groaned.

"Now. Now." It had to be now. He couldn't stop himself. His hands slid off her damp skin, gripped hard at her hips to lift them. He drove himself inside her deep, panting as he positioned her to take even more of him.

He rode her hard, plunging farther each time she rose to meet him. He watched her face as she plummeted over that final, vicious peak, the way her clouded eyes went dark as her muscles contracted around him.

With something perilously close to pain, he emptied himself into her.

SEVENTEEN

He'd rolled off her and was staring at the ceiling. He could curse himself, he knew, but he couldn't take back what he'd done.

All of his care, all of his caution, and in an instant, he had snapped. And ruined it.

Now she was curled up beside him, quivering. And he was afraid to touch her.

"I'm sorry," he finally said and tasted the uselessness of the apology. "I never meant to treat you that way. I lost control."

"Lost control," she murmured and wondered how it could be a body should feel limp and energized all at once. "Did you think you needed it?"

Her voice was shaky, he noted, and rough, he imagined, with shock. "I know an apology's pretty lame. Can I get you something? Some water." He squeezed his eyes shut and cursed himself again. "Talk about lame. Let me get you a nightgown. You'll want a nightgown."

"No, I don't." She managed to shift enough to look up and study his face. He didn't look at her, she noted, but only stared at the ceiling. "Grayson, you didn't hurt me."

"Of course I did. You'll have bruises to prove it."

"I'm not fragile," she said with a hint of exasperation.

"I treated you like—" He couldn't say it, not to her. "I should have been gentle."

"You have been. I like knowing it took you some effort to be gentle. And I like knowing something I did made you forget to be." Her lips curved as she brushed at the hair on his forehead. "Did you think you frightened me?"

"I know I frightened you." He shifted away, sat up. "I didn't care."

"You did frighten me." She paused. "I liked it. I love you."

He winced, squeezed the hand she'd laid over his. "Brianna," he began without a clue how to continue.

"Don't worry. I don't need the words back."

"Listen, a lot of times people get sex confused with love."

"I imagine you're right. Grayson, do you think I would be here with you, that I would ever have been with you like this if I didn't love you?"

He was good with words. Dozens of reasonable excuses and ploys ran through his mind. "No," he said at length, settling on the truth. "I don't. Which only makes it worse," he muttered, and rose to tug on his trousers. "I should never have let things go this far. I knew better. It's my fault."

"There's no fault here." She reached for his hand so that he would sit on the bed again rather than pace. "It shouldn't make you sad to know you're loved, Grayson."

But it did. It made him sad, and panicked, and for just a moment, wishful. "Brie, I can't give you back what you want or should have. There's no future with me, no house in the country and kids in the yard. It's not in the cards."

"It's a pity you think so. But I'm not asking you for that."

"It's what you want."

"It's what I want, but not what I expect." She gave him a surprisingly cool smile. "I've been rejected before. And I know very well what is it to love and not have the person love you back, at least not so much as you want, or need." She shook her head before he could speak. "As much as I might want to go on with you, Grayson, I'll survive without you."

"I don't want to hurt you, Brianna. I care about you. I care for you."

She lifted a brow. "I know that. And I know you're worried because you care more for me than you've cared for anyone before."

He opened his mouth, shut it, shook his head. "Yes, that's true. It's new ground for me. For both of us." Still uncertain of his moves, he took her hand, kissed it. "I'd give you more if I could. And I am sorry I at least didn't prepare you a little better for tonight. You're the first . . . inexperienced woman I've been with, so I've tried to take it slow."

Intrigued, she cocked her head. "You must have been as nervous as I was, the first time."

"More." He kissed her hand again. "Much more, believe me. I'm used to women who know the ropes, and the rules. Experienced or pro, and you—"

"Pro? Professional?" Her eyes went huge. "You've paid women to bed them?"

He stared back at her. He must have been even more befuddled than he'd realized to have come out with something like that. "Not in recent memory. Anyway—"

"Why would you have to do that? A man who looks like you, who has your sensibility?"

"Look, it was a long time ago. Another life. Don't look at me like that," he snapped. "When you're sixteen and alone on the streets, nothing's free. Not even sex."

"Why were you alone and on the street at sixteen?"

He stood, retreated, she thought. And there was shame in his eyes as much as anger.

"I'm not going to get into this."

"Why?"

"Christ." Shaken, he dragged both hands through his hair. "It's late. We need to get some sleep."

"Grayson, is it so hard to talk to me? There's hardly anything you don't know of me, the bad things and the good. Do you think I'd think less of you for knowing?"

He wasn't sure, and told himself he didn't care. "It's not important, Brianna. It has nothing to do with me now, with us here."

Her eyes cooled, and she rose to get the nightgown she'd said she didn't want. "It's your business, of course, if you choose to shut me out."

"That's not what I'm doing."

She tugged the cotton over her head, adjusted the sleeves. "As you say."

"Goddamn it, you're good, aren't you?" Furious with her, he jammed his hands into his pockets.

"I don't know your meaning."

"You know my meaning exactly," he tossed back. "Lay on the guilt, spread on a little frost, and you get your way."

"We've agreed it's none of my business." Moving toward the bed, she began to tuck in the sheets they'd ripped out. "If it's guilt you're feeling, it's not my doing."

"You get to me," he muttered. "You know just how to get to me." He hissed out a breath, defeated. "You want it, fine. Sit down, I'll tell you a story."

He turned his back on her, rummaging through the drawer for the pack of cigarettes he always carried and smoked only when working.

"The first thing I remember is the smell. Garbage just starting to rot, mold, stale cigarettes," he added, looking wryly at the smoke that curled toward the ceiling. "Grass. Not the kind you mow, the kind you inhale. You've probably never smelled pot in your life, have you?"

"I haven't, no." She kept her hands in her lap, and her eyes on him.

"Well, that's my first real memory. The sense of smell's the strongest, stays with you—good or bad. I remember the sounds, too. Raised voices, loud music, someone having sex in the next room. I remember being hungry, and not being able to get out of my room because she'd locked me in again. She was stoned most of the time and didn't always remember she had a kid around who needed to eat."

He looked around idly for an ashtray, then leaned back against the dresser. It wasn't so hard to speak of it after all, he discovered. It was almost like making up a scene in his mind. Almost.

"She told me once she'd left home when she was sixteen. Wanted to get away from her parents, all the rules. They were square, she'd say. Went nuts when they found out she smoked dope and had boys up in her room. She was just living her own life, doing her own thing. So she just left one day, hitched a ride and ended up in San Francisco. She could play at being a hippie there, but she ended up on the hard edge of the drug culture, experimented with a lot of shit, paid for a lot of it by begging or selling herself."

He'd just told her his mother was a prostitute, a junkie, and waited for some shocked exclamation. When she only continued to watch him with those cool, guarded eyes, he shrugged and went on.

"She was probably about eighteen when she got pregnant with me. According to her story, she'd already had two abortions and was scared of another. She could never be quite sure who the father was, but was pretty certain it was one of three guys. She moved in with one of them and decided to keep me. When I was about a year old, she got tired of him and moved in with somebody else. He pimped for her, supplied her with drugs, but he knocked her around a little too much, so she ditched him."

Gray tapped his cigarette out, paused long enough for Brianna to comment. But she said nothing, only sat as she was on the bed, her hands folded.

"Anyway, we can fast forward through the next couple of years. As far as I can tell, things stayed pretty much as they were. She moved around from man to man, got hooked on the hard stuff. In enlightened times, I guess you could say she had an addictive personality. She knocked me around a little, but she never really beat me—that would have taken a little too much effort and interest. She locked me in to keep me from wandering when she was on the street or meeting her dealer. We lived in filth, and I remember the cold. It gets fucking cold in San Francisco. That's how the fire started. Somebody in the building knocked over a portable heater. I was five, and I was alone and locked in."

"Oh, my God, Grayson." She pressed her hands to her mouth. "Oh, God."

"I woke up choking," he said in the same distant voice. "The room was filled with smoke, and I could hear the sirens and the screaming. I was screaming, and beating at the door. I couldn't breathe, and I was scared. I remember just lying down on the floor and crying. Then a fireman crashed through the door, and he picked me up. I don't remember him carrying me out. I don't remember the fire itself, just the smoke in my room. I woke up in the hospital, and a social worker was there. A pretty young thing with big blue eyes and soft hands. And there was a cop. He made me nervous because I'd been taught to distrust anyone in authority. They asked me if I knew where my mother was. I didn't. By the time I was well enough to leave the hospital ward, I'd been scooped up in the system. They put me in a children's home while they looked for her. They never found her. I never saw her again."

"She never came for you."

"No, she never came. It wasn't such a bad deal. The home was clean. They fed you regular. The big problem for me was that it was structured, and I wasn't used to structure. There were foster homes, but I made sure that didn't work. I didn't want to be anyone's fake kid, no matter how good or how bad the people were. And some of them were really good people. I was what they call intractable. I liked it that way. Being a troublemaker gave me an identity, so I made plenty of trouble. I was a real tough guy with a smart mouth and a bad attitude. I liked to pick fights, because I was strong and fast and could usually win.

"I was predictable," he said with a half laugh. "That's the worst of it. I was a product of my early environment and damned proud of it. No fucking counselor or shrink or social worker was going to get through to me. I'd been taught to hate authority, and that was one thing she'd taught me well."

"But the school, the home . . . they were good to you?"

A mocking light shimmered in his eyes. "Oh, yeah, just peachy. Three squares and a bed." He let out an impatient breath at her troubled expression. "You're a statistic, Brianna, a number. A problem. And there are plenty of other statistics and numbers and problems to be shuffled around. Sure, in hindsight, I can tell you that some of them probably really gave a damn, really tried to make a difference. But they were the enemy, with their questions and tests, their rules and disciplines. So following my mother's example, I ran off at sixteen. Lived on the streets, by my wits. I never touched drugs, never sold myself, but there wasn't much else I didn't do."

He pushed away from the dresser and began to prowl the room. "I stole, I cheated, I ran scams. And one day I had an epiphany when a guy I was running a short con on got wise and beat the living shit out of me. It occurred to me, when I came to in an alley with blood in my mouth and several busted ribs, that I could probably find a better way to make a living. I headed to New York. I sold plenty of watches along Fifth Avenue," he said with a hint of a smile. "Ran a little three-card monte, and I started to write. I'd gotten a fairly decent education in the home. And I liked to write. I couldn't admit that at sixteen, being such a tough sonofabitch. But at eighteen, in New York, it didn't seem so bad. What seemed bad, what suddenly began to seem really bad, was that I was the same as she was. I decided to be somebody else.

"I changed my name. I changed myself. I got a legit job bussing tables at a little dive in the Village. I shed that little bastard layer by layer until I was Grayson Thane. And I don't look back, because it's pointless."

"Because it hurts you," Brianna said quietly. "And makes you angry."

"Maybe. But mostly because it has nothing to do with who I am now."

She wanted to tell him it had everything to do with who he was, what he'd made himself. Instead she rose to face him. "I love who you are now." She felt a pang, knowing he was drawing back from what she wanted to give him. "Is it so distressing to you to know that, and to know I can feel sorry for the child, for the young man, and admire what evolved from them?"

"Brianna, the past doesn't matter. Not to me," he insisted. "It's different for you. Your past goes back centuries. You're steeped in it, the history, the tradition. It's formed you. and because of it, the future's just as important. You're a planner, long term. I'm not. I can't be. Damn it, I don't want to be. There's just now. The way things are right now."

Did he think she couldn't understand that, after all he'd told her? She could see him all too well, the battered little boy, terrified of the past, terrified there was no future, holding on desperately to whatever he could grab in the present.

"Well, we're together right now, aren't we?" Gently she cupped his face. "Grayson, I can't stop loving you to make you more comfortable. I can't do it to make myself more comfortable. It simply is. My heart's lost to you, and I can't take it back. I doubt I would if I could. It doesn't mean you have to take it, but you'd be foolish not to. It costs you nothing."

"I don't want to hurt you, Brianna." He linked his fingers around her wrists. "I don't want to hurt you."

"I know that." He would, of course. She wondered that he couldn't see he would hurt himself as well. "We'll take the now, and be grateful for it. But tell me one thing," she said and kissed him lightly. "What was your name?"

"Christ, you don't give up."

"No." Her smile was easy now, surprisingly confident. "It's not something I consider a failing."

"Logan," he muttered. "Michael Logan."

And she laughed, making him feel like a fool. "Irish. I should have known it. Such a gift of gab you've got, and all the charm in the world."

"Michael Logan," he said, firing up, "was a small-minded, mean-spirited, penny-ante thief who wasn't worth spit."

She sighed. "Michael Logan was a neglected, troubled child who needed love and care. And you're wrong to hate him so. But we'll leave him in peace."

Then she disarmed him by pressing against him, laying her head on his shoulder. Her hands moved up and down his back, soothing. She should have been disgusted by what he'd told her. She should have been appalled by the way he'd treated her in bed. Yet she was here, holding him and offering him a terrifying depth of love.

"I don't know what to do about you."

"There's nothing you have to do." She brushed her lips over his shoulder. "You've given me the most wonderful months of my life. And you'll remember me, Grayson, as long as you live."

He let out a long breath. He couldn't deny it. For the first time in his life, he'd be leaving a part of himself behind when he walked away.

It was he who felt awkward the next morning. They had breakfast in the parlor of the suite, with the view of the park out the window. And he waited for her to toss something he'd told her back in his face. He'd broken the law. He'd slept with prostitutes. He'd wallowed in the sewers of the streets.

Yet she sat there across from him, looking as fresh as a morning in Clare, talking happily about their upcoming trip to Worldwide before they went to the airport.

"You're not eating your breakfast, Grayson. Aren't you feeling well?"

"I'm fine." He cut into the pancakes he'd thought he'd wanted. "I guess I'm missing your cooking."

It was exactly the right thing to say. Her concerned look transformed into a delighted smile. "You'll be having it again tomorrow. I'll fix you something special."

He gave a grunt in response. He'd put off telling her about the trip to Wales. He hadn't wanted to spoil her enjoyment of New York. Now he wondered why he'd thought he could. Nothing he'd dumped on her the night before had shaken that steady composure.

"Ah, Brie, we're actually going to take a little detour on the way back to Ireland."

"Oh?" Frowning, she set her teacup down. "Do you have business somewhere?"

"Not exactly. We're stopping off in Wales."

"In Wales?"

"It's about your stock. Remember I told you I'd have my broker do some checking?"

"Yes. Did he find something unusual?"

"Brie, Triquarter Mining doesn't exist."

"But of course it exists. I have the certificate. I've got the letter."

"There is no Triquarter Mining on any stock exchange. No company by that name listed anywhere. The phone number on the letterhead is fake."

"How can that be? They offered me a thousand pounds."

"Which is why we're going to Wales. I think it would be worth the trip to do a little personal checking."

Brianna shook her head. "I'm sure your broker's very competent, Gray, but he must have overlooked something. If a company doesn't exist, they don't issue stock or offer to buy it back."

"They issue stock if it's a front," he said, stabbing at his meal as she stared at him. "A scam, Brie. I have a little experience with stock cons.

You get a post office box, a phone number, and you canvas for marks. For people who'll invest," he explained. "People looking to make a quick buck. You get a suit and a spiel, put some paperwork together, print up a prospectus and phony certificates. You take the money, and you disappear."

She was quiet for a moment, digesting it. Indeed she could see her father falling for just such a trick. He'd always flung himself heedlessly into deals. In truth, she'd expected nothing when she'd first pursued the matter.

"I understand that part, I think. And it's in keeping with my father's luck in business. But how do you explain that they answered me, and offered me money?"

"I can't." Though he had some ideas on it. "That's why we're going to Wales. Rogan's arranged for his plane to meet us in London and take us. It'll bring us back to Shannon Airport when we're ready."

"I see." Carefully she set her knife and fork aside. "You've discussed it with Rogan, him being a man, and planned it out between you."

Gray cleared his throat, ran his tongue over his teeth. "I wanted you to enjoy the trip here without worrying." When she only pinned him with those cool green eyes, he shrugged. "You're waiting for an apology, and you're not going to get one." She folded her hands, rested them on the edge of the table, and said nothing. "You're good at the big chill," he commented, "but it isn't going to wash. Fraud's out of your league. I'd have taken this trip by myself, but it's likely I'll need you since the stock's in your father's name."

"And being in my father's name makes it my business. It's kind of you to want to help."

"Fuck that."

She jolted, felt her stomach shrivel at the inevitability of the argument. "Don't use that tone on me, Grayson."

"Then don't use that irritated schoolteacher's tone on me." When she rose, his eyes flashed, narrowed. "Don't you walk away, goddamn it."

"I won't be sworn at or shouted at or made to feel inadequate because I'm only a farmer's daughter from the west counties."

"What the hell does that have to do with anything?" When she continued to walk toward the bedroom, he shoved away from the table. He snatched her arm, whirled her back. A flicker of panic crossed her face before she closed up. "I said don't walk away from me."

"I come and go as I please, just as you do. And I'm going to dress now and get ready for the trip you've so thoughtfully arranged."

"You want to take a bite out of me, go ahead. But we're going to settle this."

"I was under the impression you already had. You're hurting my arm, Grayson."

"I'm sorry." He released her, jammed his hands in his pockets. "Look, I figured you might be a little annoyed, but I didn't expect someone as reasonable as you to blow it all out of proportion."

"You've arranged things behind my back, made decisions for me, decided I wouldn't be able to cope on my own, and I'm blowing it all out of proportion? Well, that's fine, then. I'm sure I should be ashamed of myself."

"I'm trying to help you." His voice rose again, and he fought to bring it and his temper under control. "It has nothing to do with your being inadequate; it has to do with you having no experience. Someone broke into your house. Can't you put it together?"

She stared, paled. "No, why don't you put it together for me?"

"You wrote about the stock, then somebody searches your house. Fast, sloppy. Maybe desperate. Not long after that, there's somebody outside your window. How long have you lived in that house, Brianna?"

"All my life."

"Has anything like that happened before?"

"No, but . . . No."

"So it makes sense to connect the dots. I want to see what the whole picture looks like."

"You should have told me all this before." Shaken, she lowered to the arm of a chair. "You shouldn't have kept it from me."

"It's just a theory. Christ, Brie, you've had enough on your mind. Your mother, Maggie and the baby, me. The whole business about finding that woman your father was involved with. I didn't want to add to it."

"You were trying to shield me. I'm trying to understand that."

"Of course I was trying to shield you. I don't like seeing you worried. I—" He broke off, stunned. What had he almost said? He took a long step back, mentally from those tricky three words, physically from her. "You matter to me," he said carefully.

"All right." Suddenly tired, she pushed at her hair. "I'm sorry I made a scene about it. But don't keep things from me, Gray."

"I won't." He touched her cheek and his stomach trembled. "Brianna."

"Yes?"

"Nothing," he said and dropped his hand again. "Nothing. We'd better pull it together if we're going to get to Worldwide."

It was raining in Wales and too late to do more than check into the drab little hotel where Gray had booked a room. Brianna had only a fleeting impression of the city of Rhondda, of the bleak row houses in the tight groups, the sorry skies that pelted the road with rain. They shared a meal she didn't taste, then tumbled exhausted into bed.

He expected her to complain. The accommodations weren't the best and the traveling had been brutal, even for him. But she said nothing the next morning, only dressed and asked him what they would do next.

"I figured we'd check the post office, see where that gets us." He watched her pin up her hair, her movements neat, precise, though there were shadows under her eyes. "You're tired."

"A bit. All the time changing, I imagine." She glanced out the window where watery sunlight struggled through the glass. "I always thought of Wales as a wild and beautiful place."

"A lot of it is. The mountains are spectacular, and the coast. The Lleyn Peninsula—it's a little touristy, full of Brits on holiday—but really gorgeous. Or the uplands, very pastoral and traditionally Welsh. If you saw the moorlands in the afternoon sun, you'd see just how wild and beautiful the country is."

"You've been so many places. I'm surprised you can remember one from another."

"There's always something that sticks in your mind." He looked around the gloomy hotel room. "I'm sorry about this, Brie. It was the most convenient. If you want to take an extra day or two, I'll show you the scenery."

She smiled over it, the thought of her tossing responsibility aside and traveling with Gray over foreign hills and shores. "I need to get home, once we've finished what we've come for. I can't impose on Mrs. O'Malley much longer." She turned from the mirror. "And you're wanting to get back to work. It shows."

"Got me." He took her hands. "When I finish the book, I'll have a little time before I tour for the one that's coming up. We could go somewhere. Anywhere you like. Greece, or the South Pacific. The West Indies. Would you like that? Some place with palm trees and a beach, blue water, white sun."

"It sounds lovely." He, she thought, he who never made plans was making them. She felt it wiser not to point it out. "It might be difficult to get away again so soon." She gave his hands a squeeze before releasing them to pick up her purse. "I'm ready if you are."

They found the post office easily enough, but the woman in charge of the counter appeared immune to Gray's charm. It wasn't her place to give out the names of people who rented post office boxes, she told them crisply. They could have one themselves if they wanted, and she wouldn't be discussing them with strangers, either.

When Gray asked about Triquarter, he received a shrug and a frown. The name meant nothing to her.

Gray considered a bribe, took another look at the prim set of the woman's mouth, and decided against it.

"Strike one," he said as they stepped outside again.

"I don't believe you ever thought it would be so easy."

"No, but sometimes you get a hit when you least expect it. We'll try some mining companies."

"Shouldn't we just report everything we know to the local authorities?"

"We'll get to that."

He checked tirelessly, office after office, asking the same questions, getting the same answers. No one in Rhondda had heard of Triquarter. Brianna let him take control, for the simple pleasure of watching him work. It seemed to her that he could adjust, chameleonlike, to whatever personality he chose.

He could be charming, abrupt, businesslike, sly. It was, she supposed, how he researched a subject he might write about. He asked endless questions, by turns cajoling and bullying people into answering.

After four hours she knew more about coal mining and the Welsh economy than she cared to remember. And nothing about Triquarter.

"You need a sandwich," Gray decided.

"I wouldn't say no to one."

"Okay, we refuel and rethink."

"I don't want you to be disappointed we haven't learned anything."

"But we have. We know without a shadow of doubt there is no Triquarter Mining, and never has been. The post office box is a sham and in all likelihood still being rented by whoever's fronting the deal."

"Why would you think that?"

"They need it until they settle with you, and any other outstanding investors. I imagine they've cleaned most of that up. Let's try here." He nudged her into a small pub.

The scents were familiar enough to make her homesick, the voices just foreign enough to be exotic. They settled at a table where Gray immediately commandeered the thin plastic menu. "Mmm. Shepherd's Pie. It won't be as good as yours, but it'll do. Want to try it?"

"That'll be fine. And some tea."

Gray gave their order, leaned forward. "I'm thinking, Brie, that your father dying so soon after he bought the stock plays a part in it. You said you found the certificate in the attic."

"I did, yes. We didn't go through all the boxes after he'd died. My mother—well, Maggie didn't have the heart to, and I let it go because—"

"Because Maggie was hurting and your mother would have hounded you."

"I don't like scenes." She pressed her lips together and stared at the tabletop. "It's easier to step back from them, walk away from them." She glanced up, then away again. "Maggie was the light of my father's life. He loved me, I know he did, but what they had was very special. It was only between them. She was grieving so hard, and there was already a blowup about the house being left to me, instead of my mother. Mother was bitter and angry, and I let things go. I wanted to start my business, you see. So it was easy to avoid the boxes, dust around them from time to time, and tell myself I'd get to it by and by."

"And then you did."

"I don't know why I picked that day. I suppose because things were settled quite a bit. Mother in her own house, Maggie with Rogan. And I . . ."

"You weren't hurting so much over him. Enough time had passed for you to do the practical thing."

"That's true enough. I thought I could go through the things up there that he'd saved without aching so much for him, or wishing so hard things had been different. And it was part ambition." She sighed. "I was thinking I could have the attic room converted for guests."

"That's my Brie." He took her hand. "So he'd put the certificate up there for safekeeping, and years passed without anyone finding it, or acting on it. I imagine they wrote it off. Why should they take a chance of making contact? If they did any checking, they'd have learned that Tom Concannon had died, and his heirs hadn't dealt with the stock. It might have been lost, or destroyed, or tossed out by mistake. Then you wrote a letter."

"And here we are. It still doesn't explain why they've offered me money."

"Okay, we're going to suppose. It's one of my best things. Suppose when the deal was made, it was a fairly straightforward scam, the way I explained in New York. Then suppose somebody got ambitious, or lucky. Expanded on it. Triquarter was out of the picture, but the resources, the profit, the organization was still there. Maybe you run another scam, maybe you even get into something legit. Maybe you're just playing with things on the right side of the law, using them as cover. Wouldn't it be a surprise if the legal stuff started to work? Maybe even made more of a profit than the cons. Now you've got to shed that shadowy stuff, or at least cover it up."

Brianna rubbed her temple as their meal was served. "It's too confusing for me."

"Something about those loose stock certificates. Hard to say what." He helped himself to a healthy bite. "Nope, doesn't come close to yours." And swallowed. "But there's something, and they want them back, even pay to get them back. Oh, not much, not enough to make you suspicious, or interested in further investing. Just enough to make it worth your while to cash in."

"You do know how all this business works, don't you?"

"Too much. If it hadn't been for writing . . ." He trailed off, shrugged. It wasn't something to dwell on. "Well, we can consider it luck that I happen to have some experience along these lines. We'll make a few stops after we eat, then run it by the cops."

She nodded, relieved at the idea of turning the whole mess over to the authorities. The food helped pick up her spirits. By morning they'd be home. Over her tea she began to dream about her garden, greeting Con, working in her own kitchen.

"Finished?"

"Hmm?"

Gray smiled at her. "Taking a trip?"

"I was thinking of home. My roses might be blooming."

"You'll be in the garden by this time tomorrow," he promised and, after counting out bills for the tab, rose.

Outside, he draped his arm over her shoulder. "Want to try local public transportation? If we catch a bus we'll get across town a lot quicker. I could rent a car if you'd rather."

"Don't be silly. A bus is fine."

"Then let's just . . . hold it." He turned her around, nudging her back into the pub doorway. "Isn't that interesting?" he murmured, staring down the street. "Isn't that just fascinating?"

"What? You're crushing me."

"Sorry. I want you to keep back as much as you can and take a look down there, just across the street." His eyes began to gleam. "Just on the way to the post office. The man carrying the black umbrella."

She poked her head out, scanning. "Yes," she said after a moment. "There's a man with a black umbrella."

"Doesn't look familiar? Think back a couple of months. You served us salmon as I recall, and trifle."

"I don't know how it is you can remember meals so." She leaned out further, strained her eyes. "He looks ordinary enough to me. Like a lawyer, or a banker."

"Bingo. Or so he told us. Our retired banker from London."

"Mr. Smythe-White." It came to her in a flash, made her laugh. "Well, that's odd, isn't it? Why are we hiding from him?"

"Because it's odd, Brie. Because it's very, very odd that your overnight guest, the one who happened to be out sightseeing when your house was searched, is strolling down the street in Wales, just about to go into the post office. What do you want to bet he rents a box there?"

"Oh." She sagged back against the door. "Sweet Jesus. What are we going to do?"

"Wait. Then follow him."

EIGHTEEN

They didn't have long to wait. Barely five minutes after Smythe-White walked into the post office, he walked out again. After taking one quick look right, then left, he hurried up the street, his umbrella swinging like a pendulum at his side.

"Damn it, she blew it."

"What?"

"Come on, quick." Gray grabbed Brianna's hand and darted after Smythe-White. "The postmistress, or whatever she is. She told him we were asking questions."

"How do you know?"

"Suddenly he's in a hurry." Gray checked traffic, cursed, and pulled Brianna in a zigzagging pattern between a truck and a sedan. Her heart pounded in her throat as both drivers retaliated with rude blasts of their horns. Already primed, Smythe-White glanced back, spotted them, and began to run.

"Stay here," Gray ordered.

"I'll not." She sprinted after him, her long legs keeping her no more than three paces behind. Their quarry might have dodged and swerved, elbowing pedestrians aside, but it was hardly a contest with two younger, healthy pursuers on his heels.

As if he'd come to the same conclusion, he came to a stop just outside a chemist's, panting. He dragged out a snowy white handkerchief to wipe his brow, then turned, letting his eyes widen behind his sparkling lenses.

"Well, Miss Concannon, Mr. Thane, what an unexpected surprise." He had the wit, and the wherewithal, to smile pleasantly even as he pressed a hand to his speeding heart. "The world is indeed a small place. Are you in Wales on holiday?"

"No more than you," Gray tossed back. "We've got business to discuss, pal. You want to talk here, or should we hunt up the local constabulary?"

All innocence, Smythe-White blinked. In a familiar habit, he took off his glasses, polished the lenses. "Business? I'm afraid I'm at a loss. This isn't about that unfortunate incident at your inn, Miss Concannon? As I told you, I lost nothing and have no complaint at all."

"It's not surprising you'd have lost nothing, as you did the damage yourself. Did you have to dump all my dry goods on the floor?"

"Excuse me?"

"Looks like the cops, then," Gray said and took Smythe-White by the arm.

"I'm afraid I don't have time to dally just now, though it is lovely to run into you this way." He tried, and failed, to dislodge Gray's grip. "As you could probably tell, I'm in a hurry. An appointment I'd completely forgotten. I'm dreadfully late."

"Do you want the stock certificate back or not?" Gray had the pleasure of seeing the man pause, reconsider. Behind the lenses of the glasses he carefully readjusted, his eyes were suddenly sly.

"I'm afraid I don't understand."

"You understand fine, and so do we. A scam's a scam in any country, any language. Now, I'm not sure what the penalty for fraud, confidence games, and counterfeiting stocks is in the United Kingdom, but they can be pretty rough on pros where I come from. And you used the mail, Smythe-White. Which was probably a mistake. Once you put a stamp on it and hand it over to the local post, fraud becomes mail fraud. A much nastier business."

He let Smythe-White sweat that before he continued. "And then there's the idea of basing yourself in Wales and doing scams across the Irish Sea. Makes it international. You could be looking at a very long stretch."

"Now, now, I don't see any reason for threats." Smythe-White smiled again, but sweat had begun to pearl on his brow. "We're reasonable people. And it's a small matter, a very small matter we can resolve easily, and to everyone's satisfaction."

"Why don't we talk about that?"

"Yes, yes, why don't we?" He brightened instantly. "Over a drink. I'd be delighted to buy both of you a drink. There's a pub just around the corner here. A quiet one. Why don't we have a friendly pint or two while we hash all this business out?"

"Why don't we? Brie?"

"But I think we should—"

"Talk," Gray said smoothly and, keeping one hand firmly on Smythe-White's arm, took hers. "How long have you been in the game?" Gray asked conversationally.

"Oh, dear, since before either of you were born, I imagine. I'm out of it now, truly, completely. Just two years ago, my wife and I bought a little antique shop in Surrey."

"I thought your wife was dead," Brianna put in as Smythe-White led the way to the pub.

"Oh, no, indeed. Iris is hale and hearty. Minding things for me while I put this little business to rest. We do quite well," he added as they stepped into the pub. "Quite well. In addition to the antique shop, we have interests in several other enterprises. All quite legal, I assure you." Gentleman to the last, he held Brianna's chair out for her. "A tour company, First Flight, you might have heard of it."

Impressed, Gray lifted a brow. "It's become one of the top concerns in Europe."

Smythe-White preened. "I like to think that my managerial skills had something to do with that. We started it as rather a clandestine smuggling operation initially." He smiled apologetically at Brianna. "My dear, I hope you're not too shocked."

She simply shook her head. "Nothing else could shock me at this point."

"Shall we have a Harp?" he asked, playing the gracious host. "It seems appropriate." Taking their assent for granted, Smythe-White ordered for the table. "Now then, as I said, we did do a bit of smuggling. Tobacco and liquor primarily. But we didn't have much of a taste for it, and the touring end actually made more of a profit with no risk, so to speak. And as Iris and I were getting on in years, we decided to retire. In a manner of speaking. Do you know the stock game was one of our last? She's always been keen on antiques, my Iris, so we used the profits from that to buy and stock our little shop." He winced, smiled sheepishly. "I suppose it's poor taste to mention that."

"Don't let that stop you." Gray kicked back in his chair as their beer was served.

"Well, imagine our surprise, our dismay, when we received your letter. I've kept that post office box open because we have interests in Wales, but the Triquarter thing was well in the past. All but forgotten really. I'm ashamed to say your father, rest him, slipped through the cracks in our reorganization efforts. I hope you'll take it as it's meant when I say I found him a thoroughly delightful man."

Brianna merely sighed. "Thank you."

"I must say, Iris and I very nearly panicked when we heard from you. If we were connected with that old life, our reputation, the little businesses we've lovingly built in the past few years could be ruined. Not to mention the, ah . . ." He dabbed at his lip with a napkin. "Legal ramifications."

"You could have ignored the letter," Gray said.

"And we considered it. Did ignore the first. But when Brianna wrote again, we felt something had to be done. The certificate." He had the grace to flush. "It's lowering to admit it, but I actually signed my legal name to it. Arrogance, I suppose, and I wasn't using it at the time. Having it float to the surface now, come to the attention of the authorities could be rather awkward."

"It's as you said," Brianna murmured, staring at Gray. "It's almost exactly as you said."

"I'm good," he murmured and patted her hand. "So, you came to Blackthorn to check out the situation for yourself."

"I did. Iris couldn't join me as we were expecting a rather lovely shipment of Chippendale. Admittedly, I got a charge out of going under again. A bit of nostalgia, a little adventure. I was absolutely charmed by your home, and more than a little concerned when I discovered that you were related by marriage to Rogan Sweeney. After all, he is an important man, a sharp one. It worried me that he would take charge. So . . . when the opportunity presented itself, I took a quick look around for the certificate."

He put a hand over Brianna's, gave it an avuncular squeeze. "I do apologize for the mess and inconvenience. I couldn't be sure how long I'd have alone, you see. I'd hoped if I could put my hands on it, we could put a period to the whole unhappy business. But—"

"I gave the certificate to Rogan for safekeeping," Brianna told him.

"Ah. I was afraid of something like that. I find it odd he didn't follow up."

"His wife was about to have a baby, and he had the opening of the new gallery." Brianna stopped herself, realized she was very nearly apologizing for her brother-in-law. "I could handle the matter myself."

"I began to suspect that as well after only a few hours in your home. An organized soul is a dangerous one to someone in my former trade. I did come back once, thinking I might have another go, but between your dog and your hero in residence, I had to take to my heels."

Brianna's chin came up. "You were looking in my window."

"With no disrespectful intent, I promise you. My dear, I'm old enough to be your father, and quite happily married." He huffed a bit, as if insulted. "Well, I offered to buy the stock back, and the offer holds."

"A half pound a piece," Gray reminded him dryly.

"Double what Tom Concannon paid. I have the paperwork if you need proof."

"Oh, I'm sure someone with your talent could come up with any paper transaction he wanted."

Smythe-White let out a long-suffering sigh. "I'm sure you feel you have the right to accuse me of that sort of behavior."

"I think the police would be fascinated by your behavior."

Eyes on Gray, Smythe-White took a hasty sip of beer. "What purpose would that serve, really now? Two people in their golden years, taxpayers, devoted spouses, ruined and sent to prison for past indiscretions."

"You cheated people," Brianna snapped back. "You cheated my father."

"I gave your father exactly what he paid for, Brianna. A dream. He walked off from our dealing a happy man, hoping, as too many hope, to make something out of next to nothing." He smiled at her gently. "He really only wanted the hope that he could."

Because it was true, she could find nothing to say. "It doesn't make it right," she decided at length.

"But we've mended our ways. Changing a life is an effortful thing, my dear. It takes work and patience and determination."

She lifted her gaze again as his words hit home. If what he said of himself was true, there were two people at that table who had made that effort. Would she condemn Gray for what he'd done in the past? Would she want to see some old mistake spring up and drag him back?

"I don't want you or your wife to go to prison, Mr. Smythe-White."

"He knows the rules," Gray interrupted, squeezing Brianna's hand hard. "You play, you pay. Maybe we can bypass the authorities, but the courtesy is worth more than a thousand pounds."

"As I explained—" Smythe-White began.

"The stock isn't worth dick," Gray returned. "But the certificate. I'd say that would come in at ten thousand."

"Ten thousand *pounds*?" Smythe-White blustered while Brianna simply sat with her mouth hanging open. "That's blackmail. It's robbery. It's—"

"A pound a unit," Gray finished. "More than reasonable with what you've got riding on it. And with the tidy profit you made from the investors, I think Tom Concannon's dream should come true. I don't think that's blackmail. I think it's justice. And justice isn't negotiable."

Pale, Smythe-White sat back. Again, he took out his handkerchief and mopped his face. "Young man, you're squeezing my heart."

"Nope, just your bankbook. Which is fat enough to afford it. You caused Brie a lot of trouble, a lot of worry. You messed with her home. Now, while I might sympathize with your predicament, I don't think you realize just what that home means to her. You made her cry."

"Oh, well, really." Smythe-White waved the handkerchief, dabbed with it again. "I do apologize, most sincerely. This is dreadful, really dreadful. I have no idea what Iris would say."

"If she's smart," Gray drawled, "I think she'd say pay up and count your blessings."

He sighed, stuffed the damp handkerchief into his pocket. "Ten thousand pounds. You're a hard man, Mr. Thane."

"Herb, I think I can call you Herb because, at this moment, we both know I'm your best friend."

He nodded sadly. "Unfortunately true." Changing tactics, he looked hopefully at Brianna. "I really have caused you distress, and I'm terribly sorry. We'll clear the whole matter up. I wonder, perhaps we could cancel the debt in trade? A nice trip for you? Or furnishings for your inn. We have some lovely pieces at the shop."

"Money talks," Gray said before Brianna could think of a response.

"A hard man," Smythe-White repeated and let his shoulders sag. "I suppose there's very little choice in the matter. I'll write you a check."

"It's going to have to be cash."

Another sigh. "Yes, of course it is. All right then, we'll make arrangements. Naturally, I don't carry such amounts with me on business jaunts."

"Naturally," Gray agreed. "But you can get it. By tomorrow."

"Really, another day or two would be more reasonable," Smythe-White began, then seeing the gleam in Gray's eyes, surrendered. "But I can wire Iris for the money. It will be no trouble to have it here by tomorrow."

"I didn't think it would."

Smythe-White smiled wanly. "If you'd excuse me. I need the loo." Shaking his head, he rose and walked to the rear of the pub.

"I don't understand. I don't," Brianna whispered when Smythe-White was out of earshot. "I kept quiet because you kept kicking me under the table but—"

"Nudging you," Gray corrected. "I was only nudging you."

"Aye, and I'll have a limp for a week. But my point is, you're letting him go, and you're making him pay such a huge amount. It doesn't seem right."

"It's exactly right. Your father wanted his dream, and he's getting his dream. Good old Herb knows that sometimes a con goes sour and you count your losses. You don't want to send him to jail and neither do I."

"No, I don't. But to take his money—"

"He took your father, and that five hundred pounds couldn't have been easy for your family to spare."

"No, but—"

"Brianna. What would your father say?"

Beaten, she dropped her chin on her fist. "He'd think it was a grand joke."

"Exactly." Gray cast his eyes toward the men's room, narrowed them. "He's taking too long. Hang on a minute."

Brianna frowned into her glass. Then her lips began to curve. It really was a grand joke. One her father would have greatly appreciated.

She didn't expect to see the money, not such a huge amount. Not really. It was enough to know they'd settled it all, with no real harm done.

Glancing up, she saw Gray, eyes hot, storm out of the men's room and head toward the bar. He had a quick conversation with the barman before coming back to the table.

His face had cleared again as he dropped into his chair and picked up his beer.

"Well," Brianna said after the moment stretched out.

"Oh, he's gone. Right out the window. Canny old bastard."

"Gone?" Staggered by the turn of events, she shut her eyes. "Gone," she repeated. "And to think, he had me liking him, believing him."

"That's exactly what a con artist's supposed to do. But in this case, I think we got more of the truth than not."

"What do we do now? I just don't want to go to the police, Gray. I couldn't live with myself imagining that little man and his wife in jail." A sudden thought stabbed through, making her eyes pop wide. "Oh, bloody hell. Do you suppose he really has a wife at all?"

"Probably." Gray took a sip of beer, considered. "As to what we do now, now we go back to Clare, let him stew. Wait him out. It'll be easy enough to find him again if and when we want."

"How?"

"Through First Flight Tours. Then there's this." Before Brianna's astonished eyes, Gray drew out a wallet. "I picked his pocket when we were out on the street. Insurance," he explained when she continued to gape. "After all these years, I'm not even rusty." He shook his head at himself.

"I should be ashamed." Then he grinned and tapped the billfold against his palm. "Don't look so shocked, it's only a little cash and I.D."

Calmly Gray took bills from the wallet and stuck them in his own pocket. "He still owes me a hundred pounds, more or less. I'd say he keeps his real money in a clip. He's got a London address," Gray went on, tucking the lifted wallet away. "I glanced through it in the men's room. There's also a snapshot of a rather attractive, matronly looking woman. Iris, I'd think. Oh, and his name's Carstairs. John B., not Smythe-White."

Brianna pressed her fingers between her eyes. "My head's spinning."

"Don't worry, Brie, I guarantee we'll be hearing from him again. Ready to go?"

"I suppose." Still reeling from the events of the day, she rose. "He's a nerve, that one. He clipped out, too, without buying us the drinks."

"Oh, he bought them." Gray hooked an arm through hers, sending a salute to the barman on the way out. "He owns the damn pub."

"He—" She stopped, stared, then began to laugh.

NINETEEN

It was good to be home. Adventures and the glamour of traveling were all very fine, Brianna thought, but so were the simple pleasures of your own bed, your own roof, and the familiar view out your own window.

She would not mind winging off somewhere again, as long as there was home to come back to.

Content with routine, Brianna worked in her garden, staking her budding delphiniums and monkshood, while the scent of just blooming lavender honeyed the air. Bees hummed nearby busy flirting with her lupine.

From the rear of the house came the sound of children laughing, and Con's excited barks as he chased the ball her young American visitors tossed for him.

New York seemed very far away, as exotic as the pearls she'd tucked deep inside her dresser drawer. And the day she had spent in Wales was like some odd, colorful play.

She glanced up, adjusting the brim of her hat as she studied Gray's window. He was working, had been almost around the clock since they'd set down their bags. She wondered where he was now, what place, what time, what people surrounded him. And what mood would he be in when he came back to her?

Irritable if the writing went badly, she thought. Touchy as a stray dog.

If it went well, he'd be hungry—for food, and for her. She smiled to herself and gently tied the fragile stems to the stakes.

How amazing it was to be wanted the way he wanted her. Amazing for both of them, she decided. He was no more used to it than she. And it worried him a bit. Idly she brushed her fingers over a clump of bellflowers.

He'd told her things about himself she knew he'd told no one else. And that worried him as well. How foolish of him to have believed she would think less of him for what he'd been through, what he'd done to survive.

She could only imagine the fear and the pride of a young boy who had never known the love and demands, the sorrows and the comforts, of family. How alone he'd been, and how alone he'd made himself out of that pride and fear. And somehow through it, he'd fashioned himself into a caring and admirable man.

No, she didn't think less of him. She only loved him more for the knowing.

His story had made her think of her own, and study on her life. Her parents hadn't loved each other, and that was hurtful. But Brianna knew she'd had her father's love. Had always known it and taken comfort from it. She'd had a home and roots that kept body and soul anchored.

And in her own way Maeve had loved her. At least her mother had felt the duty toward the children she'd borne enough to stay with them. She could have turned her back at any time, Brianna mused. That option had never occurred to Brianna before, and she mulled it over now as she enjoyed the gardening chores.

Her mother could have walked away from the family she'd created—and resented. Gone back to the career that had meant so much to her. Even if it was only duty that had kept her, it was more than Gray had had.

Maeve was hard, embittered; she too often twisted the heart of the scriptures she so religiously read to suit her own means and uses. She could use the canons of the church like a hammer. But she had stayed.

With a little sigh Brianna shifted to stake the next plant. The time would come for forgiveness. She hoped she had forgiveness in her.

"You're supposed to look happy when you garden, not troubled."

Putting a hand on top of her hat, Brianna lifted her head to look at Gray. A good day, she decided at once. When he'd had a good day, you could all but feel the pleasure of it vibrate from him.

"I was letting my mind wander."

"So was I. I got up and looked out of the window and saw you. For the life of me I couldn't think of anything else."

"It's a lovely day for being out-of-doors. And you started working at dawn." With quick and oddly tender movements, she staked another stem. "Is it going well for you, then?"

"It's going incredibly well." He sat beside her, indulged himself with a gulp of the perfumed air. "I can barely keep up with myself. I murdered a lovely young woman today."

She snorted with laughter. "And sound very pleased with yourself."

"I was very fond of her, but she had to go. And her murder is going to spearhead the outrage that will lead to the killer's downfall."

"Was it in the ruins we went to that she died?"

"No, that was someone else. This one met her fate in the Burren, near the Druid's Altar."

"Oh." Despite herself, Brianna shivered. "I've always been fond of that spot."

"Me, too. He left her stretched over the crown stone, like an offering to a bloodthirsty god. Naked, of course."

"Of course. And I suppose some poor unfortunate tourist will find her."

"He already has. An American student on a walking tour of Europe." Gray clucked his tongue. "I don't think he'll ever be the same." Leaning over, he kissed her shoulder. "So, how was your day?"

"Not as eventful. I saw off those lovely newlyweds from Limerick this morning, and I minded the American children while their parents had a lie-in." Eagle-eyed, she spotted a tiny weed and mercilessly ripped it out of the bed. "They helped me make hot cross buns. After, the family had a day at Bunratty, the folk park, you know. Only returned shortly ago. We're expecting another family this evening, from Edinburgh, who stayed here two years past. They've two teenagers, boys, who both fell a bit in love with me last time."

"Really?" Idly he ran a fingertip down her shoulder. "I'll have to intimidate them."

"Oh, I imagine they're over it now." She glanced up, smiled curiously at his snort of laughter. "What?"

"I was just thinking you've probably ruined those boys for life. They'll never find anyone to compare with you."

"What nonsense." She reached for another stake. "I talked to Maggie earlier this afternoon. They might be in Dublin another week or two. And we'll have the baptism when they get back. Murphy and I are to be godparents."

He shifted, sat cross-legged now. "What does that mean, exactly, in Catholic?"

"Oh, not much different, I'd imagine, than it means in any church. We'll speak for the baby during the service, like sponsors, you see. And we'll promise to look after his religious upbringing, if something should happen to Maggie and Rogan."

"Kind of a heavy responsibility."

"It's an honor," she said with a smile. "Were you not baptized ever, Grayson?"

"I have no idea. Probably not." He moved his shoulders, then cocked a brow at her pensive frown. "What now? Worried I'll burn in hell because nobody sprinkled water over my head?"

"No." Uncomfortable, she looked away again. "And the water's only a symbol, of cleansing away original sin."

"How original is it?"

She looked back at him, shook her head. "You don't want me explaining catechism and such, and I'm not trying to convert you. Still, I know Maggie and Rogan would like you at the service."

"Sure, I'll go. Be interesting. How's the kid anyway?"

"She says Liam's growing like a weed." Brianna concentrated on what her hands were doing and tried not to let her heart ache too much. "I told her about Mr. Smythe-White—I mean Mr. Carstairs."

"And?"

"She laughed till I thought she'd burst. She thought Rogan might take the matter a bit less lightly, but we both agreed it was so like Da to tumble into a mess like this. It's a bit like having him back for a time. 'Brie,' he might say, 'if you don't risk something, you don't win something.' And I'm to tell you she was impressed with your cleverness in tracking Mr. Carstairs down, and would you like the job we've hired that detective for."

"No luck on that?"

"Actually, there was something." She sat back again, laid her hands on her thighs. "Someone, one of Amanda Dougherty's cousins, I think, thought she might have gone north in New York, into the mountains. It seems she'd been there before and was fond of the area. The detective, he's taking a trip there, to, oh, that place where Rip van Winkle fell asleep."

"The Catskills?"

"Aye, that's it. So, with luck, he'll find something there."

Gray picked up a garden stake himself, eyeing it down the length, wondering absently how successful a murder weapon it might be. "What'll you do if you discover you've got a half brother or sister?"

"Well, I think I would write to Miss Dougherty first." She'd already thought it through, carefully. "I don't want to hurt anyone. But from the tone of her letters to Da, I think she'd be a woman who might be glad to know that she, and her child, are welcome."

"And they would be," he mused, setting the stake aside again. "This, what, twenty-six-, twenty-seven-year-old stranger would be welcome."

"Of course." She tilted her head, surprised he would question it. "He or she would have Da's blood, wouldn't they? As Maggie and I do. He wouldn't want us to turn our back on family."

"But he—" Gray broke off, shrugged.

"You're thinking he did," Brianna said mildly. "I don't know if that's the way of it. We'll never know, I suppose, what he did when he learned of it. But turn his back, no, it wouldn't have been in him. He kept her letters, and knowing him, I think he would have grieved for the child he would never be able to see."

Her gaze wandered, followed the flitting path of a speckled butterfly. "He was a dreamer, Grayson, but he was first and always a family man. He gave up a great deal to keep this family whole. More than I'd ever guessed until I read those letters."

"I'm not criticizing him." He thought of the grave, and the flowers Brianna had planted over it. "I just hate to see you troubled."

"I'll be less troubled when we find out what we can."

"And your mother, Brianna? How do you think she's going to react if this all comes out?"

Her eyes cooled, and her chin took on a stubborn tilt. "I'll deal with that when and if I have to. She'll have to accept what is. For once in her life, she'll have to accept it."

"You're still angry with her," he observed. "About Rory."

"Rory's over and done. And has been."

He took her hands before she could reach for her stakes. And waited patiently.

"All right, I'm angry. For what she did then, for the way she spoke to you, and maybe most of all for the way she made what I feel for you seem wicked. I'm not good at being angry. It makes my stomach hurt."

"Then I hope you're not going to be angry with me," he said as he heard the sound of a car approaching.

"Why would I?"

Saying nothing, he rose, drawing her to her feet. Together they watched the car pull up, stop. Lottie leaned out with a hearty wave before she and Maeve alighted.

"I called Lottie," Gray murmured, squeezing Brianna's hand when it tensed in his. "Sort of invited them over for a visit."

"I don't want another argument with guests in the house." Brianna's voice had chilled. "You shouldn't have done this, Grayson. I'd have gone to see her tomorrow and had words in her home instead of mine."

"Brie, your garden's a picture," Lottie called out as they approached. "And what a lovely day you have for it." In her motherly way she embraced Brianna and kissed her cheek. "Did you have a fine time in New York City?"

"I did, yes."

"Living the high life," Maeve said with a snort. "And leaving decency behind."

"Oh, Maeve, leave be." Lottie gave an impatient wave. "I want to hear about New York City."

"Come in and have some tea then," Brianna invited. "I've brought you back some souveniers."

"Oh, what a sweetheart you are. Souveniers, Maeve, from America." She beamed at Gray as they walked to the house. "And your movie, Grayson? Was it grand?"

"It was." He tucked her hand through his arm, gave it a pat. "And after I had to compete with Tom Cruise for Brianna's attention."

"No! You don't say?" Lottie's voice squeaked and her eyes all but fell out in astonishment. "Did you hear that, Maeve? Brianna met Tom Cruise."

"I don't pay mind to movie actors," Maeve grumbled, desperately impressed. "It's all wild living and divorces with them."

"Hah! Never does she miss an Errol Flynn movie when it comes on the telly." Point scored, Lottie waltzed into the kitchen and went directly to the stove. "Now, I'll fix the tea, Brianna. That way you can go fetch our presents."

"I've some berry tarts to go with it." Brianna shot Gray a look as she headed for her bedroom. "Baked fresh this morning."

"Ah, that's lovely. Do you know, Grayson, my oldest son, that's Peter, he went to America. To Boston he went, to visit cousins we have there. He visited the harbor where you Yanks dumped the British tea off the boat. Gone back twice again, he has, and taken his children. His own son, Shawn, is going to move there and take a job."

She chatted on about Boston and her family while Maeve sat in sullen silence. A few moments later Brianna came back in, carrying two small boxes.

"There's so many shops there," she commented, determined to be cheerful. "Everywhere you look something else is for sale. It was hard to decide what to bring you."

"Whatever it is, it'll be lovely." Eager to see, Lottie set down a plate of tarts and reached for her box. "Oh, would you look at this?" She lifted the small, decorative bottle to the light where it gleamed rich blue.

" 'Tis for scent, if you like, or just for setting out."

"It's lovely as it can be," Lottie declared. "Look how it's got flowers carved right into it. Lilies. How sweet of you, Brianna. Oh, and Maeve, yours is red as a ruby. With poppies. Won't these look fine, setting on the dresser?"

"They're pretty enough." Maeve couldn't quite resist running her finger over the etching. If she had a weakness, it was for pretty things. She felt she'd never gotten her fair share of them. "It was kind of you to give me a passing thought while you were off staying in a grand hotel and consorting with movie stars."

"Tom Cruise," Lottie said, easily ignoring the sarcasm. "Is he as handsome a lad as he looks in the films?"

"Every bit, and charming as well. He and his wife may come here."

"Here?" Amazed at the thought, Lottie pressed a hand to her breast. "Right here to Blackthorn Cottage?"

Brianna smiled at Lottie. "So he said."

"That'll be the day," Maeve muttered. "What would so rich and high-flying a man want with staying at this place?"

"Peace," Brianna said coolly. "And a few good meals. What everyone else wants when they stay here."

"And you get plenty of both in Blackthorn," Gray put in. "I've done a great deal of traveling, Mrs. Concannon, and I've never been to a place as lovely or as comfortable as this. You must be very proud of Brianna for her success."

"Hmph. I imagine right enough you're comfortable here, in my daughter's bed."

"It would be a foolish man who wasn't," he said amiably before Brianna could comment. "You're to be commended for raising such a warm-hearted, kind-natured woman who also has the brains and the dedication to run a successful business. She amazes me."

Stumped, Maeve said nothing. The compliment was a curve she hadn't expected. She was still searching through it for the insult when Gray crossed to the counter.

"I picked up a little something for both of you myself." He'd left the bag in the kitchen before he'd gone out to Brianna. Setting the scene, he thought now, as he wanted it to play.

"Why, isn't that kind." Surprise and pleasure coursed through Lottie's voice as she accepted the box Gray offered.

"Just tokens," Gray said, smiling as Brianna simply stared at him, baffled. Lottie's little gasp of delight pleased him enormously.

"It's a little bird. Look here, Maeve, a crystal bird. See how it catches the sunlight."

"You can hang it by a wire in the window," Gray explained. "It'll make rainbows for you. You make me think of rainbows, Lottie."

"Oh, go on with you. Rainbows." She blinked back a film of moisture and rose to give Gray a hard hug. "I'll be hanging it right in our front window. Thank you, Gray, you're a darling man. Isn't he a darling man, Maeve?"

Maeve grunted, hesitated over the lid of her gift box. By rights, she knew she should toss the thing into his face rather than take a gift from a man of his kind. But Lottie's crystal bird was such a pretty thing. And the combination of basic greed and curiosity had her flipping open the lid.

Speechless, she lifted out the gilt and glass shaped like a heart. It had a lid as well, and when she opened it, music played.

"Oh, a music box." Lottie clapped her hands together. "What a beautiful thing, and how clever. What's the tune it's playing?"

" 'Stardust,' " Maeve murmured and caught herself just before she began to hum along with it. "An old tune."

"A classic," Gray added. "They didn't have anything Irish, but this seemed to suit you."

The corners of Maeve's mouth turned up as the music charmed her. She cleared her throat, shot Gray a level look. "Thank you, Mr. Thane."

"Gray," he said easily.

Thirty minutes later, Brianna placed her hands on her hips. There was only she and Gray in the kitchen now, and the plate of tarts was empty. " 'Twas like a bribe."

"No, 'twasn't like a bribe," he said, mimicking her. "It *was* a bribe. Damn good one, too. She smiled at me before she left."

Brianna huffed. "I don't know who I should be more ashamed of, you or her."

"Then just think of it as a peace offering. I don't want your mother giving you grief over me, Brianna."

"Clever you were. A music box."

"I thought so. Every time she listens to it, she'll think of me. Before too long, she'll convince herself I'm not such a bad sort after all."

She didn't want to smile. It was outrageous. "Figured her out, have you?"

"A good writer's a good observer. She's used to complaining." He opened the refrigerator, helped himself to a beer. "Trouble is, she doesn't have nearly enough to complain about these days. Must be frustrating." He popped the top off the bottle, took a swig. "And she's afraid you've closed yourself off to her. She doesn't know how to make the move that'll close the gap."

"And I'm supposed to."

"You will. It's the way you're made. She knows that, but she's worried this might be the exception." He tipped up Brianna's chin with a fingertip. "It won't. Family's too important to you, and you've already started to forgive her."

Brianna turned away to tidy the kitchen. "It's not always comfortable, having someone see into you as though you were made of glass." But she sighed, listened to her own heart. "Perhaps I have started to forgive her. I don't know how long the process will take." Meticulously she washed the teacups. "Your ploy today has undoubtedly speeded that along."

"That was the idea." From behind her he slipped his arms around her waist. "So, you're not mad."

"No, I'm not mad." Turning, she rested her head in the curve of his shoulder, where she liked it best. "I love you, Grayson."

He stroked her hair, looking out the window, saying nothing.

They had soft weather over the next few days, the kind that made working in his room like existing in endless twilight. It was easy to lose track of time, to let himself fall into the book with only the slightest awareness of the world around him.

He was closing in on the killer, on that final, violent meeting. He'd developed a respect for his villain's mind, mirroring perfectly the same emotions of his hero. The man was as clever as he was vicious. Not mad, Gray mused as another part of his mind visualized the scene he was creating.

Some would call the villain mad, unable to conceive that the cruelty, the ruthlessness of the murders could spring from a mind not twisted by insanity.

Gray knew better—and so did his hero. The killer wasn't mad, but was cold-bloodedly sane. He was simply, very simply, evil.

He already knew exactly how the final hunt would develop, almost every step and word was clear in his head. In the rain, in the dark, through the wind-swept ruins where blood had already been spilled. He knew his hero would see himself, just for one instant see the worst of himself, reflected in the man he pursued.

And that final battle would be more than right against wrong, good against evil. It would be, on that rain-soaked, wind-howling precipice, a desperate fight for redemption.

But that wouldn't be the end. And it was in search of that unknown final scene that Gray raced. He'd imagined, almost from the beginning, his hero leaving the village, leaving the woman. Both of them would have been changed irrevocably by the violence that had shattered that quiet spot. And by what had happened between them.

Then each would go on with the rest of his life, or try. Separately, because he'd created them as two dynamically opposing forces, drawn together, certainly, but never for the long haul.

Now, it wasn't so clear. He wondered where the hero was going, and why. Why the woman turned slowly, as he'd planned, moving toward the door of her cottage without looking back.

It should have been simple, true to their characters, satisfying. Yet the closer he came to reaching that moment, the more uneasy he became.

Kicking back in his chair, he looked blankly around the room. He hadn't a clue what time of day it was, or how long he'd been chained to his work. But one thing was certain, he'd run dry.

He needed a walk, he decided, rain or no rain. And he needed to stop second-guessing himself and let that final scene unfold in its own way, and its own time.

He started downstairs, marveling at the quiet before he remembered the family from Scotland had gone. It had amused him, when he'd crawled out of his cave long enough to notice, how the two young men had sniffed around Brianna's heels, competing for her attention.

It was tough to blame them.

The sound of Brianna's voice had him turning toward the kitchen.

"Well, good day to you, Kenny Feeney. Are you visiting your grandmother?"

"I am, Miss Concannon. We'll be here for two weeks."

"I'm happy to see you. You've grown so. Will you come in and have a cup of tea and some cake?"

"I wouldn't mind."

Gray watched a boy of about twelve give a crooked-toothed grin as he stepped out of the rain. He carried something large and apparently heavy wrapped in newspaper. "Gran sent you a leg of lamb, Miss Concannon. We slaughtered just this morning."

"Oh, that's kind of her." With apparent pleasure Brianna took the grisly package while Gray—writer of bloodthirsty thrillers—felt his stomach churn.

"I have a currant cake here. You'll have a piece, won't you, and take the rest back to her?"

"I will." Dutifully stepping out of his wellies, the boy stripped off his raincoat and cap. Then he spotted Gray. "Good day to you," he said politely.

"Oh, Gray, I didn't hear you come down. This is young Kenny Feeney, grandson of Alice and Peter Feeney from the farm down the road a bit. Kenny, this is Grayson Thane, a guest of mine."

"The Yank," Kenny said as he solemnly shook Gray's hand. "You write books with murders in them, my gran says."

"That's right. Do you like to read?"

"I like books about cars or sports. Maybe you could write a book about football."

"I'll keep it in mind."

"Will you have some cake, Gray?" Brianna asked as she sliced. "Or would you rather have a sandwich now?"

He cast a wary eye toward the lump under the newspaper. He imagined it baaing. "No, nothing. Not now."

"Do you live in Kansas City?" Kenny wanted to know. "My brother does. He went to the States three years ago this winter. He plays in a band."

"No, I don't live there, but I've been there. It's a nice town."

"Pat, he says it's better than anywhere. I'm saving me money so I can go over when I'm old enough."

"Will you be leaving us, then, Kenny?" Brianna ran a hand over the boy's carrotty mop.

"When I'm eighteen." He took another happy bite of cake, washed it down with tea. "You can get good work there, and good pay. Maybe I'll play for an American football team. They have one, right there in Kansas City, you know."

"I've heard rumors," Gray said and smiled.

"This is grand cake, Miss Concannon." Kenny polished off his piece.

When he left a bit later, Brianna watched him dart over the fields, the cake bundled under his arm like one of his precious footballs.

"So many of them go," she murmured. "We lose them day after day, year after year. Shaking her head, she closed the kitchen door again. "Well, I'll see to your room now that you're out of it."

"I was going to take a walk. Why don't you come with me?"

"I could take a short one. Just let me—" She smiled apologetically as the phone rang. "Good afternoon, Blackthorn Cottage. Oh, Arlene, how are you?" Brianna held out a hand for Gray's. "That's good to hear. Yes, I'm fine and well. Gray's just here, I'll . . . oh?" Her brow cocked, then she smiled again. "That would be grand. Of course, you and your husband are more than welcome. September's a lovely time of the year. I'm so pleased you're coming. Yes, I have it. September fifteenth, for five days. Indeed yes, you can make a number of day trips from right here. Shall I send you some information about it? No, it would be my pleasure. And I look forward to it as well. Yes, Gray's here as I said. Just a moment."

He took the phone, but looked at Brianna. "She's coming to Ireland in September?"

"On holiday, she and her husband. It seems I tickled her curiosity. She has news for you."

"Mmm-hmmm. Hey, gorgeous," he said into the receiver. "Going to play tourist in the west counties?" He grinned, nodded when Brianna offered him tea. "No, I think you'll love it. The weather?" He glanced out the window at the steadily falling rain. "Magnificent." He winked at Brianna, sipped his tea. "No, I didn't get your package yet. What's in it?"

Nodding, he murmured to Brianna. "Reviews. On the movie." He paused, listening. "What's the hype? Mmm. Brilliant, I like brilliant. Wait, say that one again. 'From the fertile mind of Grayson Thane,' " he repeated for Brianna's benefit. "Oscar worthy. Two thumbs straight up." He laughed at that. "And the most powerful movie of the year. Not bad, even if it's only May. No, I don't have my tongue in my cheek. It's great. Even better. Early quotes on the new book," he told Brianna.

"But you haven't finished the new book."

"Not that new book. The one that's coming out in July. That's the new book, what I'm working on is the new manuscript. No, just explaining some basic publishing to the landlady."

Pursing his lips, he listened. "Really? I like it."

With an eye on him Brianna went to the stove for her roaster. He was making noises, the occasional comment. Occasionally he'd grin or shake his head.

"It's a good thing I'm not wearing a hat. My head's getting big. Yeah, publicity sent me an endless letter about the plans for the tour. I've agreed to be at their mercy for three weeks. No, you make the decision on that sort of thing. It just takes too long for them to mail stuff. Yeah, you, too. I'll tell her. Talk to you later."

"The movie's doing well," Brianna said, trying to resist pumping him.

"Twelve million in its first week, which is nothing to sneeze at. And the critics are smiling on it. Apparently they like the upcoming book, too.

I'm at the top of my form," he said, reaching into a canister for a cookie. "I've created a story dense in atmosphere with prose as sharp as a honed dagger. With, ah, gut-wrenching twists and dark, biting humor. Not too shabby."

"You should be very proud."

"I wrote it almost a year ago." He shrugged, chewed. "Yeah, it's nice. I have an affection for it that will dim considerably after thirty-one cities in three weeks."

"The tour you were speaking of."

"Right. Talk shows, bookstores, airports, and hotel rooms." With a laugh he popped the rest of the cookie into his mouth. "What a life."

"It suits you well, I'd think."

"Right down to the ground."

She nodded, not wanting to be sad, and set the roaster on the counter. "In July, you say."

"Yeah. It's crept up on me. I've lost track. I've been here four months."

"Sometimes it seems you've been here always."

"Getting used to me." He grazed an absent hand over his chin, and she could see his mind was elsewhere. "How about that walk?"

"I really need to get dinner on."

"I'll wait." He leaned companionably against the counter. "So, what's for dinner?"

"Leg of lamb."

Gray gave a little sigh. "I thought so."

TWENTY

On a clear day in the middle of May, Brianna watched the workmen dig the foundation for her greenhouse. A small dream, she thought, flipping the braid she wore from her shoulder to her back, come true.

She smiled down at the baby who gurgled in the portable swing beside her. She'd learned to be content with small dreams, she thought, bending to kiss her nephew on his curling black hair.

"He's grown so, Maggie, in just a matter of weeks."

"I know. And I haven't." She patted her belly, grimaced a little. "I feel less of a sow every day, but I wonder if I'll ever lose all of it again."

"You look wonderful."

"That's what I tell her," Rogan added, draping an arm around Maggie's shoulders.

"And what do you know? You're besotted with me."

"True enough."

Brianna looked away as they beamed at each other. How easy it was for them now, she mused. So comfortably in love with a beautiful baby cooing beside them. She didn't care for the pang of envy, or the tug of longing.

"So where's our Yank this morning?"

Brianna glanced back, wondering uneasily if Maggie was reading her mind. "He was up and out at first light, without even his breakfast."

"To?"

"I don't know. He grunted at me. At least I think it was at me. His moods are unpredicable these days. The book's troubling him, though he says he's cleaning it up. Which means, I'm told, tinkering with it, shining it up."

"He'll be done before long, then?" Rogan asked.

"Before long." And then . . . Brianna was taking a page out of Gray's book and not thinking of *and thens*. "His publisher's on the phone quite a lot now, and sending packets by express all the time, about the book that's coming out this summer. It seems to irritate him to have to think of one when he's working on another." She glanced back at the workmen. "It's a good spot for the greenhouse, don't you think? I'll be pleased to be able to see it from my window."

"It's the spot you've been talking of for months," Maggie pointed out and refused to be turned from the topic. "Are things well between you and Gray?"

"Yes, very well. He's a bit sulky right now as I said, but his moods never last very long. I told you how he engineered a truce with Mother."

"Clever of him. A trinket from New York. She was pleasant to him at Liam's christening. I had to give birth before I could achieve close to the same."

"She's mad for Liam," Brianna said.

"He's a buffer between us. Ah, what's the trouble, darling," she murmured as Liam began to fuss. "His nappie's wet, that's all." Lifting him, Maggie patted his back and soothed.

"I'll change it."

"You're quicker to volunteer than his Da." With a shake of her head, Maggie laughed. "No, I'll do it. You watch your greenhouse. It'll only take a minute."

"She knows I wanted to talk to you." Rogan led Brianna toward the wooden chairs set near the blackthorns for which the cottage was named.

"Is something wrong?"

"No." There was an edginess about her under a forced calm that was out of character. That, Rogan decided with a slight frown, would have to be Maggie's department. "I wanted to talk with you about this Triquarter Mining business. Or the lack of it." He sat, laid his hands on his knees. "We haven't really had the chance to talk it through since I was in Dublin, then the baby's christening. Maggie's satisfied with the way things have shaken down. She's more interested in enjoying Liam and getting back to her glass than pursuing the matter."

"That's how it should be."

"For her, perhaps." He didn't say what was obvious to both of them. Neither he nor Maggie required any of the monetary compensation that might result from a suit. "I have to admit, Brianna, it doesn't sit well with me. The principle of it."

"I can understand that, you being a businessman yourself." She smiled a little. "You never met Mr. Carstairs. It's difficult to hold a grudge once you have."

"Let's separate emotion from legalities for a moment."

Her smile widened. She imagined he used just that brisk tone with any inefficient underling. "All right, Rogan."

"Carstairs committed a crime. And while you might be reluctant to see him imprisioned, it's only logical to expect a penalty. Now I'm given to understand that he's become successful in the last few years. I took it on myself to make a few discreet inquiries, and it appears that his current businesses are aboveboard as well as lucrative. He's in the position to compensate you for the dishonesty in his dealings with your father. It would be a simple matter for me to go to London personally and settle it."

"That's kind of you." Brianna folded her hands, drew a deep breath. "I'm going to disappoint you, Rogan, and I'm sorry for it. I can see your ethics have been insulted by this, and you want only to see justice served."

"I do, yes." Baffled, he shook his head. "Brie, I can understand Maggie's attitude. She's focused on the baby and her work and has always been one to brush aside anything that interfered with her concentration. But you're a practical woman."

"I am," she agreed. "I am, yes. But I'm afraid I have a bit of my father in me as well." Reaching out, she laid a hand over Rogan's. "You know, some people, for whatever reason, start out on unsteady ground. The choices they make aren't always admirable. A portion of them stays there because it's easier, or what they're used to, or even what they prefer. Another portion slides onto a stable footing, without much effort. A bit of luck, of timing. And another, a small, special portion," she said, thinking of Gray, "fights their way onto the solid. And they make something admirable of themselves."

She fell into silence, staring out over the hills. Wishing.

"I've lost you, Brie."

"Oh." She waved a hand and brought herself back. "What I mean to say is I don't know the circumstances that led Mr. Carstairs from one kind of life to another. But he's hurting no one now. Maggie has what she wants, and I what contents me. So why trouble ourselves?"

"That's what she told me you'd say." He lifted his hands in defeat. "I had to try."

"Rogan." Maggie called from the kitchen doorway, the baby bouncing against her shoulder. "The phone. It's Dublin for you."

"She won't answer the damn thing in our own house, but she answers it here."

"I've threatened not to bake for her if she doesn't."

"None of my threats work." He rose. "I've been expecting a call, so I gave the office your number if we didn't answer at home."

"That's no problem. Take all the time you need." She smiled as Maggie headed out with the baby. "Well, Margaret Mary, are you going to share him now or keep him all to yourself?"

"He was just asking for you, Auntie Brie." With a chuckle, Maggie passed Liam to her sister and settled in the chair Rogan had vacated. "Oh, it's good to sit. Liam was fussy last night. I'd swear between us Rogan and I walked all the way to Galway and back."

"Do you suppose he's teething already?" Cooing, Brianna rubbed a knuckle over Liam's gums, looking for swelling.

"It may be. He drools like a puppy." She closed her eyes, let her body sag. "Oh, Brie, who would have thought you could love so much? I spent most of my life not knowing Rogan Sweeney existed, and now I couldn't live without him."

She opened one eye to be certain Rogan was still in the house and couldn't hear her wax so sentimental. "And the baby, it's an enormous thing this grip on the heart. I thought when I was carrying him I understood what it was to love him. But holding him, from the very first time I held him, it was so much more."

She shook herself, gave a shaky laugh. "Oh, it's those hormones again. They're turning me to mush."

" 'Tisn't the hormones, Maggie." Brianna rubbed her cheek over Liam's head, caught the marvelous scent of him. "It's being happy."

"I want you to be happy, Brie. I can see you're not."

"That isn't true. Of course I'm happy."

"You're already seeing him walk away. And you're making yourself accept it before it even happens."

"If he chooses to walk away, I can't stop him. I've known that all along."

"Why can't you?" Maggie shot back. "Why? Don't you love him enough to fight for him?"

"I love him too much to fight for him. And maybe I lack the courage. I'm not as brave as you, Maggie."

"That's just an excuse. Too brave is what you've always been, Saint Brianna."

"And if it is an excuse, it's mine." She spoke mildly. She would not, she promised herself, be drawn into an argument. "He has reasons why he'll go. I may not agree with them, but I understand them. Don't slap at me, Maggie," she said quietly and averted the next explosion. "Because it does hurt. And I could see this morning when he left the house that he was already walking away."

"Then make him stop. He loves you, Brie. You can see it every time he looks at you."

"I think he does." And that only increased the pain. "That's why he's in a hurry all at once to move on. And he's afraid, too. Afraid he'll come back."

"Is that what you're counting on?"

"No." But she wanted to count on it. She wanted that very much. "Love isn't always enough, Maggie. We can see that from what happened with Da."

"That was different."

"It's all different. But he lived without his Amanda, and he made his life as best he could. I'm enough his daughter to do the same. Don't worry over me," she murmured, stroking the baby. "I know what Amanda was feeling when she wrote she was grateful for the time they had together. I wouldn't trade these past months for the world and more."

She glanced over, then fell silent, studying the set look on Rogan's face as he came across the lawn.

"We may have found something," he said, "on Amanda Dougherty."

Gray didn't come home for tea, and Brianna wondered but didn't worry as she saw that her guests had their fill of finger sandwiches and Dundee cake. Rogan's report on Amanda Dougherty was always at the back of her mind as she moved through the rest of her day.

The detective had found nothing in his initial check of the towns and villages in the Catskills. It was, to Brianna's thinking, hardly a surprise that no one remembered a pregnant Irishwoman from more than a quarter of a century in the past. But Rogan, being a thorough man, hired thorough people. Routinely, the detective made checks on vital statistics, reading through birth and death and marriage certificates for a five-year period following the date of Amanda's final letter to Tom Concannon.

And it was in a small village, deep in the mountains, where he had found her.

Amanda Dougherty, age thirty-two, had been married by a justice of the peace, to a thirty-eight-year-old man named Colin Bodine. An address was given simply as Rochester, New York. The detective was already on his way there to continue the search for Amanda Dougherty Bodine.

The date of the marriage had been five months after the final letter to her father, Brianna mused. Amanda would have been close to term, so it was most likely the man she had married had known she'd been pregnant by another.

Had he loved her? Brianna wondered. She hoped so. It seemed to her it took a strong, kind-hearted man to give another man's child his name.

She caught herself glancing at the clock again, wondering where Gray had gone off to. Annoyed with herself, she biked down to Murphy's to fill him in on the progress of the greenhouse construction.

It was time to finish dinner preparations when she returned. Murphy had promised to come by and check over the foundation himself the following day. But Brianna's underlying purpose, the hope that Gray had been visiting her neighbor as he often did, had been dashed.

And now, with more than twelve hours passed since he'd left that morning, she moved from wonder to worry.

She fretted, eating nothing herself as her guests feasted on mackerel with gooseberry sauce. She played her role as hostess, seeing there was brandy where brandy was wanted, an extra serving of steamed lemon pudding for the child who eyed it so hopefully.

She saw that the whiskey decanter in each guest room was filled, and towels were fresh for evening baths. She made parlor conversation with her guests, offered board games to the children.

By ten, when the light was gone and the house quiet, she'd moved beyond worry to resignation. He would come back when he would come, she thought, and settled down in her room, her knitting in her lap and her dog at her feet.

A full day of driving and walking and studying the countryside hadn't done a great deal to improve Gray's mood. He was irritated with himself, irritated by the fact that a light had been left burning for him in the window.

He switched it off the moment he came inside, as if to prove to himself he didn't need or want the homey signal. He started to go upstairs, a deliberate move, he knew, to prove he was his own man.

Con's soft woof stopped him. Turning on the stairs, Gray scowled at the dog. "What do you want?"

Con merely sat, thumped his tail.

"I don't have a curfew, and I don't need a stupid dog waiting up for me."

Con merely watched him, then lifted a paw as if anticipating Gray's usual greeting.

"Shit." Gray went back down the stairs, took the paw to shake, and gave the dog's head a good scratch. "There. Better now?"

Con rose and padded toward the kitchen. He stopped, looked back, then sat again, obviously waiting.

"I'm going to bed," Gray told him.

As if in agreement, Con rose again as if waiting to lead the way to his mistress.

"Fine. We'll do it your way." Gray stuffed his hands in his pockets and followed the dog down the hall, into the kitchen, and through to Brianna's room.

He knew his mood was foul, and couldn't seem to alter it. It was the book, of course, but there was more. He could admit, at least to himself, that he'd been restless since Liam's christening.

There'd been something about it, the ritual itself, that ancient, pompous, and oddly soothing rite full of words and color and movement. The costumes, the music, the lighting had all melded together, or so it had seemed to him, to tilt time.

But it had been the community of it, the belonging he'd sensed from every neighbor and friend who'd come to witness the child's baptism, that had struck him most deeply.

It had touched him, beyond the curiosity of it, the writer's interest in scene and event. It had moved him, the flow of words, the unshakable faith, and the river of continuity that ran from generation to generation in the small village church, accented by a baby's indignant wail, fractured light through stained glass, wood worn smooth by generations of bended knees.

It was family as much as shared belief, and community as much as dogma.

And his sudden, staggering wish to belong had left him restless and angry.

Irritated with himself, and her, he stopped in the doorway of Brianna's sitting room, watching her with her knitting needles clicking rhythmically. The dark green wool spilled over the lap of her white nightgown. The light beside her slanted down so that she could check her work, but she never looked at her own hands.

Across the room, the television murmured through an old black-and-white movie. Cary Grant and Ingrid Bergman in sleek evening dress embraced in a wine cellar. *Notorious*, Gray thought. A tale of love, mistrust, and redemption.

For reasons he didn't choose to grasp, her choice of entertainment annoyed him all the more.

"You shouldn't have waited up."

She glanced over at him, her needles never faltering. "I didn't." He looked tired, she thought, and moody. Whatever he'd searched for in his long day alone, he didn't appear to have found it. "Have you eaten?"

"Some pub grub this afternoon."

"You'll be hungry, then." She started to set her knitting aside in its basket. "I'll fix you a plate."

"I can fix my own if I want one," he snapped. "I don't need you to mother me."

Her body stiffened, but she only sat again and picked up her wool. "As you please."

He stepped into the room, challenging. "Well?"

"Well what?"

"Where's the interrogation? Aren't you going to ask me where I was, what I was doing? Why I didn't call?"

"As you've just pointed out, I'm not your mother. Your business is your own."

For a moment there was only the sound of her needles and the distressed commercial voice of a woman on television who'd discovered chip fat on her new blouse.

"Oh, you're a cool one," Gray muttered and strode to the set to slam the picture off.

"Are you trying to be rude?" Brianna asked him. "Or can't you help yourself?"

"I'm trying to get your attention."

"Well, you have it."

"Do you have to do that when I'm talking to you?"

Since there seemed no way to avoid the confrontation he so obviously wanted, Brianna let her knitting rest in her lap. "Is that better?"

"I needed to be alone. I don't like being crowded."

"I haven't asked for an explanation, Grayson."

"Yes, you have. Just not out loud."

Impatience began to simmer. "So, now you're reading my mind, are you?"

"It's not that difficult. We're sleeping together, essentially living together, and you feel I'm obliged to let you know what I'm doing."

"Is that what I feel?"

He began to pace. No, she thought, it was more of a prowl—as a big cat might prowl behind cage bars.

"Are you going to sit there and try to tell me you're not mad?"

"It hardly matters what I tell you when you read my unspoken thoughts." She linked her hands together, rested them on the wool. She would not fight with him, she told herself. If their time together was nearing an end, she wouldn't let the last memories of it be of arguments and bad feelings. "Grayson, I might point out to you that I have a life of my own. A business to run, personal enjoyments. I filled my day well enough."

"So you don't give a damn whether I'm here or not?" It was his out, wasn't it? Why did the idea infuriate him?

She only sighed. "You know it pleases me to have you here. What do you want me to say? That I worried? Perhaps I did, for a time, but you're a man grown and able to take care of yourself. Did I think it was unkind of you not to let me know you'd be gone so long when it's your habit to be here most evenings? You know it was, so it's hardly worth me pointing it out to you. Now, if that satisfies you, I'm going to bed. You're welcome to join me or go upstairs and sulk."

Before she could rise, he slapped both hands on either arm of her chair, caging her in. Her eyes widened, but stayed level on his.

"Why don't you shout at me?" he demanded. "Throw something? Boot me out on my ass?"

"Those things might make you feel better," she said evenly. "But it isn't my job to make you feel better."

"So that's it? Just shrug the whole thing off and come to bed? For all you know I could have been with another woman."

For one trembling moment the heat flashed into her eyes, matching the fury in his. Then she composed herself, taking the knitting from her lap and setting it in the basket. "Are you trying to make me angry?"

"Yes. Damn it, yes." He jerked back from her, spun away. "At least it would be a fair fight then. There's no way to beat that iced serenity of yours."

"Then I'd be foolish to set aside such a formidable weapon, wouldn't I?" She rose. "Grayson, I'm in love with you, and when you think I'd use that love to trap you, to change you, then you insult me. It's for that you should apologize."

Despising the creeping flow of guilt, he looked back at her. Never in the whole of his life had another woman made him feel guilt. He wondered if there was another person in existence who could, with such calm reason, cause him to feel so much the fool.

"I figured you'd find a way to get an I'm sorry out of me before it was over."

She stared at him a moment, then saying nothing, turned and walked into the adjoining bedroom.

"Christ." Gray scrubbed his hands over his face, pressed his fingers against his closed eyes, then dropped his hands. You could only wallow in your own idiocy so long, he decided.

"I'm crazy," he said, stepping into the bedroom.

She said nothing, only adjusted one of her windows to let in more of the cool, fragrant night air.

"I am sorry, Brie, for all of it. I was in a pisser of a mood this morning, and just wanted to be alone."

She gave him no answer, no encouragement, only turned down the bedspread.

"Don't freeze me out. That's the worst." He stepped behind her, laid a tentative hand on her hair. "I'm having trouble with the book. It was lousy of me to take it out on you."

"I don't expect you to adjust your moods to suit me."

"You just don't expect," he murmured. "It's not good for you."

"I know what's good for me." She started to move away, but he turned her around. Ignoring the rigid way she held herself, he wrapped his arms around her.

"You should have booted me out," he murmured.

"You're paid up through the month."

He pressed his face into her hair, chuckled. "Now you're being mean."

How was a woman supposed to keep up with his moods? When she tried to push away, he only cuddled her closer.

"I had to get away from you," he told her, and his hand roamed up and down her back, urging her spine to relax. "I had to prove I could get away from you."

"Don't you think I know that?" Drawing back as far as he would permit, she framed his face in her hands. "Grayson, I know you'll be leaving soon, and I won't pretend that doesn't leave a crack in my heart. But it'll hurt so much more, for both of us, if we spend these last days fighting over it. Or around it."

"I figured it would be easier if you were mad. If you tossed me out of your life."

"Easier for whom?"

"For me." He rested his brow on hers and said what he'd avoided saying for the last few days. "I'll be leaving at the end of the month."

She said nothing, found she could say nothing over the sudden ache in her chest.

"I want to take some time before the tour starts."

She waited, but he didn't ask, as he once had, for her to come with him to some tropical beach. She nodded. "Then let's enjoy the time we have before you go."

She turned her face so that her mouth met his. Gray laid her slowly onto the bed. And when he loved her, loved her tenderly.

TWENTY-ONE

For the first time since Brianna had opened her home to guests, she wished them all to the devil. She resented the intrusion on her privacy with Gray. Though it shamed her, she resented the time he spent closed in his room finishing the book that had brought him to her.

She fought the emotions, did everything she could to keep them from showing. As the days passed, she assured herself that the sense of panic and unhappiness would fade. Her life was so very nearly what she wanted it to be. So very nearly.

She might not have the husband and children she'd always longed for, but there was so much else to fullfill her. It helped, at least a little, to count those blessings as she went about her daily routine.

She carried linens, fresh off the line, up the stairs. Since Gray's door was open, she went inside. Here, she set the linens aside. It was hardly necessary to change his sheets since he hadn't slept in any bed but hers for days. But the room needed a good dusting, she decided, since he was out of it. His desk was an appalling mess, to be sure.

She started there, emptying his overflowing ashtray, tidying books and papers. Hoping, she knew, to find some little snatch of the story he was writing. What she found were torn envelopes, unanswered correspondence, and some scribbled notes on Irish superstitions. Amused, she read:

Beware of speaking ill of fairies on Friday, because they are present and will work some evil if offended.

For a magpie to come to the door and look at you
is a sure death sign, and nothing can avert it.

A person who passes under a hempen rope will die a violent death.

"Well, you surprise me, Brianna. Snooping."

Blushing red, she dropped the notepad, stuck her hands behind her back. Oh, wasn't it just like Grayson Thane, she thought, to come creeping up on a person.

"I was not snooping. I was dusting."

He sipped idly at the coffee he'd gone to the kitchen to brew. To his thinking, he'd never seen her quite so flummoxed. "You don't have a dust rag," he pointed out.

Feeling naked, Brianna wrapped dignity around her. "I was about to get one. Your desk is a pitiful mess, and I was just straightening up."

"You were reading my notes."

"I was putting the notebook aside. Perhaps I glanced at the writing on it. Superstitions is all it is, of evil and death."

"Evil and death's my living." Grinning, he crossed to her, picked up the pad. "I like this one. On Hallowtide—that's November first."

"I'm aware of when Hallowtide falls."

"Sure you are. Anyway, on Hallowtide, the air being filled with the presence of the dead, everything is a symbol of fate. If on that date, you call the name of a person from the outside, and repeat it three times, the result is fatal." He grinned to himself. "Wonder what the garda could charge you with."

"It's nonsense." And gave her the chills.

"It's great nonsense. I used that one." He set the notebook down, studied her. Her high color hadn't quite faded. "You know the trouble with technology?" He lifted one of his computer disks, tapping it on his palm as he studied her with laughing eyes. "No balled up papers, discarded by the frustrated writer that the curious can smooth out and read."

"As if I'd do such a thing." She flounced away to pick up her linens. "I've beds to make."

"Want to read some of it?"

She paused halfway to the door, looking back over her shoulder suspiciously. "Of your book?"

"No, of the local weather report. Of course of my book. Actually, there's a section I could use a local's spin on. To see if I got the rhythm of the dialogue down, the atmosphere, interactions."

"Oh, well, if I could help you, I'd be glad."

"Brie, you've been dying to get a look at the manuscript. You could have asked."

"I know better than that, living with Maggie." She set the linens down again. "It's worth your life to go in her shop to see a piece she's working on."

"I'm a more even-tempered sort." With a few deft moves he booted his computer, slipped in the appropriate disk. "It's a pub scene. Local color and some character intros. It's the first time McGee meets Tullia."

"Tullia. It's Gaelic."

"Right. Means peaceful. Let's see if I can find it." He began flipping screens. "You don't speak Gaelic, do you?"

"I do, yes. Both Maggie and I learned from our Gran."

He looked up, stared at her. "Son of a bitch. It never even occured to me. Do you know how much time I've spent looking up words? I just wanted a few tossed in, here and there."

"You'd only to have asked."

He grunted. "Too late now. Yeah, here it is. McGee's a burned-out cop, with Irish roots. He's come to Ireland to look into some old family history, maybe find his balance, and some answers about himself. Mostly, he just wants to be left alone to regroup. He was involved in a bust that went bad and holds himself responsible for the bystander death of a six-year-old kid."

"How sad for him."

"Yeah, he's got his problems. Tullia has plenty of her own. She's a widow, lost her husband and child in an accident that only she survived. She's getting through it, but carrying around a lot of baggage. Her husband wasn't any prize, and there were times she wished him dead."

"So she's guilty that he is, and scarred because her child was taken from her, like a punishment for her thoughts."

"More or less. Anyway, this scene's in the local pub. Only runs a few pages. Sit down. Now pay attention." He leaned over her shoulder, took her hand. "See these two buttons?"

"Yes."

"This one will page up, this one will page down. When you finished what's on the screen and want to move on, push this one. If you want to go back and look at something again, push that one. And Brianna?"

"Yes?"

"If you touch any of the other buttons, I'll have to cut all your fingers off."

"Being an even-tempered sort."

"That's right. The disks are backed up, but we wouldn't want to develop any bad habits." He kissed the top of her head. "I'm going to go back downstairs, check on the progress on your greenhouse. If you find something that jars, or just doesn't ring quite true, you can make a note on the pad there."

"All right." Already reading, she waved him off. "Go away, then."

Gray wandered downstairs, and outside. The six courses of local stone that would be the base for her greenhouse were nearly finished. It didn't surprise him to see Murphy setting stones in place himself.

"I didn't know you were a mason as well as a farmer," Gray called out.

"Oh, I do a bit of this, a bit of that. Mind you don't make that mortar so loose this time," he ordered the skinny teenager nearby. "Here's my nephew, Tim MacBride, visiting from Cork. Tim can't get enough of your country music from the States."

"Randy Travis, Wynonna, Garth Brooks?"

"All of them." Tim flashed a smile much like his uncle's.

Gray bent down, lifted a new stone for Murphy, while he discussed the merits of country music with the boy. Before long he was helping to mix the mortar and making satisfying manly noises about the work with his companions.

"You've a good pair of hands for a writer," Murphy observed.

"I worked on a construction crew one summer. Mixing mortar and hauling it in wheelbarrows while the heat fried my brain."

"It's pleasant weather today." Satisfied with the progress, Murphy paused for a cigarette. "If it holds, we may have this up for Brie by another week."

Another week, Gray mused, was almost all he had. "It's nice of you to take time from your own work to help her with this."

"That's *comhair,*" Murphy said easily. "Community. That's how we live here. No one has to get by alone if there's family and neighbors. They'll be three men or more here when it's time to put up the frame and the glass. And others'll come along if help's needed to build her benches and such. By the end of it, everyone will feel they have a piece of the place. And Brianna will be giving out cuttings and plants for everyone's garden." He blew out smoke. "It comes round, you see. That's *comhair.*"

Gray understood the concept. It was very much what he had felt, and for a moment envied, in the village church during Liam's christening. "Does it ever . . . cramp your style that by accepting a favor you're obliged to do one?"

"You Yanks." Chuckling, Murphy took a last drag, then crushed the cigarette out on the stones. Knowing Brianna, he tucked the stub into his pocket rather than flicking it aside. "You always reckon in payments.

Obliged isn't the word. 'Tis a security, if you're needing a more solid term for it. A knowing that you've only to reach out a hand, and someone will help you along if you need it. A knowing that you'd do the same."

He turned to his nephew. "Well, Tim, let's clean up our tools. We need to be getting back. You'll tell Brie not to be after fiddling with these stones, will you, Grayson? They need to set."

"Sure, I'll—Oh Christ, I forgot about her. See you later." He hurried back into the house. A glance at the kitchen clock made him wince. He'd left her for more than an hour.

And she was, he discovered, exactly where he'd left her.

"Takes you a while to read half a chapter."

However much his entrance surprised her, she didn't jolt this time. When she lifted her gaze from the screen to his face, her eyes were wet.

"That bad?" He smiled a little, surprised to find himself nervous.

"It's wonderful." She reached into her apron pocket for a tissue. "Truly. This part where Tullia's sitting alone in her garden, thinking of her child. It makes you feel her grief. It's not like she's a made-up person at all."

His second surprise was that he should experience embarrassment. As far as praise went, hers had been perfect. "Well, that's the idea."

"You've a wonderful gift, Gray, for making words into emotions. I went a bit beyond the part you wanted me to read. I'm sorry. I got caught up in it."

"I'm flattered." He noted by the screen she'd read more than a hundred pages. "You're enjoying it."

"Oh, very much. It has a different . . . something," she said, unable to pinpoint it, "than your other books. Oh, it's moody, as they always are, and rich in detail. And frightening. The first murder, the one at the ruins. I thought my heart would stop when I was reading it. And gory it was, too. Gleefully so."

"Don't stop now." He ruffled her hair, dropped down on the bed.

"Well." She linked her hands, laid them on the edge of the desk as she thought through her words. "Your humor's there as well. And your eye, it misses nothing. The scene in the pub, I've walked into that countless times in my life. I could see Tim O'Malley behind the bar, and Murphy playing a tune. He'll like that you made him so handsome."

"You think he'll recognize himself?"

"Oh, I do, yes. I don't know how he'll feel about being one of the suspects, or the murderer, if that's what you've done in the end." She waited, hopeful, but he only shook his head.

"You don't really think I'm going to tell you who done it, do you?"

"Well, no." She sighed and propped her chin on her fist. "As to Murphy, probably he'll enjoy it. And your affection for the village, for the land here and the people shows. In the little things—the family hitching a ride home from church in their Sunday best, the old man walking with his dog along the roadside in the rain, the little girl dancing with her grandda in the pub."

"It's easy to write things down when there's so much to see."

"It's more than what you see, with your eyes, I mean." She lifted her hands, let them fall again. She didn't have words, as he did, to juggle into the right meaning. "It's the heart of it. There's a deepness to the heart of it that's different from what I've read of your writings before. The way McGee fights that tug of war within himself over what he should do. The way he wishes he could do nothing and knows he can't. And Tullia, the way she bears her grief when it's near to bending her in two, and works to make her life what it needs to be again. I can't explain it."

"You're doing a pretty good job," Gray murmured.

"It touches me. I can't believe it was written right here, in my home."

"I don't think it could have been written anywhere else." He rose then, disappointing her by hitting buttons that jangled the screen. She'd hoped he let her read more.

"Oh, you've changed the name of it," she said when the title page came up. "*Final Redemption*. I like it. That's the theme of it, is it? The murders, what's happened to McGee and Tullia before, and what changes after they meet?"

"That's the way it worked out." He hit another button, bringing up the dedication page. In all the books he'd written, it was only the second time he'd dedicated one. The first, and only, had been to Arlene.

To Brianna, for gifts beyond price

"Oh, Grayson." Her voice hitched over the tears rising in the back of her throat. "I'm honored. I'll start crying again," she murmured and turned her face into his arm. "Thank you so much."

"There's a lot of me in this book, Brie." He lifted her face, hoping she'd understand. "It's something I can give you."

"I know. I'll treasure it." Afraid she'd spoil the moment with tears, she ran her hands briskly over her hair. "You'll want to get back to work, I'm sure. And I've whittled the day away." She picked up her linens, knowing she'd weep the moment she was behind the first closed door. "Shall I bring your tea up here when it's time?"

He tilted his head, narrowed his eyes as he studied her. He wondered if she'd recognized herself in Tullia. The composure, the quiet, almost unshakable grace. "I'll come down. I've nearly done all I need to do for today."

"In an hour then."

She went out, closing the door behind her. Alone, Gray sat, and stared, for a long time, at the brief dedication.

It was the laughter and the voices that drew Gray, when the hour was up, toward the parlor rather than the kitchen. Brianna's guests were gathered around the tea table, sampling or filling plates. Brianna herself stood, swaying gently from side to side to rock the baby sleeping on her shoulder.

"My nephew," she was explaining. "Liam. I'm minding him for an hour or two. Oh, Gray." She beamed when she saw him. "Look who I have here."

"So I see." Crossing over, Gray peeked at the baby's face. His eyes were open, and dreamy, until they latched onto Gray and stared owlishly. "He always looks at me as if he knows every sin I committed. It's intimidating."

Gray moved to the tea table and had nearly decided on his choices when he noted Brianna slipping from the room. He caught up with her at near the kitchen door. "Where are you going?"

"To put the baby down."

"What for?"

"Maggie said he'd be wanting a nap."

"Maggie's not here." He took Liam himself. "And we never get to play with him." To amuse himself, he made faces at the baby. "Where's Maggie?"

"She's fired up her furnace. Rogan had to run into the gallery to handle some problem, so she came dashing down here just a little bit ago." With a laugh she bent her head close to Gray's. "I thought it would never happen. Now I have you all to myself," she murmured. She straightened at the knock on the door. "Keep his head supported, mind," she said as she went to answer.

"I know how to hold a baby. Women," he said to Liam. "They don't think we can do anything. They all think you're hot stuff right now, boy-o, but just wait. In a few years they'll figure your purpose in life is to fix small electrical appliances and kill bugs."

Since no one was looking, he bent his head to press a light kiss on Liam's mouth. And watched it curve.

"That's the way. Why don't we go in the kitchen, and—"

He broke off at Brianna's startled exclamation. Shifting Liam more securely in the crook of his arm, he hurried back down the hallway.

Carstairs stood at the threshold, a tan bowler in his hands, a friendly smile on his face. "Grayson, how nice to see you again. I wasn't certain you'd still be here. And what's this?"

"It's a baby," Gray said shortly.

"Of course it is." Carstairs tickled Liam's chin and made foolish noises. "Handsome lad. I must say, he favors you a bit, Brianna. Around the mouth."

"He's my sister's child. And what might you be doing here at Blackthorn, Mr. Carstairs?"

"Just passing through, as it were. I'd told Iris so much about the cottage, and the countryside, she wanted to see it for herself. She's in the car." He gestured to the Bentley parked at the garden gate. "Actually, we'd hoped you might have a room for us, for the night."

She goggled at him. "You want to stay here?"

"I've bragged, perhaps unwisely, about your cooking." He leaned forward confidentially. "I'm afraid Iris was a bit irked at first. She's quite a cook herself, you know. She wants to see if I was exaggerating."

"Mr. Carstairs. You're a shameless man."

"That may be, my dear," he said, twinkling. "That may be."

She huffed, sighed. "Well, don't leave the poor woman sitting in the car. Bring her in for tea."

"Can't wait to meet her," Gray said, jiggling the baby.

"She says the same of you. She's quite impressed that you could lift my wallet without me having a clue. I used to be much quicker." He shook his head in regret. "But then, I used to be much younger. Shall I bring in our luggage, Brianna?"

"I have a room. It's smaller than what you had last."

"I'm sure it's charming. Absolutely charming." He strolled off to fetch his wife.

"Can you beat it?" Brianna said under her breath. "I don't know whether to laugh or hide the silver. If I had any silver."

"He likes you too much to steal from you. So," Gray mused, "This is the famous Iris."

The photograph from the pinched wallet had been a good likeness, Brianna discovered. Iris wore a flowered dress that ruffled in the breeze around excellent legs. To Brianna's eye, Iris had used the time in the car to freshen her hair and makeup and so looked fresh and remarkably pretty as she strolled up the walk beside her grinning husband.

"Oh, Miss Concannon. Brianna, I do hope I can call you Brianna. I think of you as Brianna, of course, after hearing so much about you and your charming inn."

Her voice was smooth, cultured, despite the fact that her words all but tumbled over each other to get out. Before Brianna could respond, Iris flung out both hands, gripped hers, and barrelled on.

"You're every bit as lovely as Johnny told me. How kind of you, how sweet to find room for us when we've dropped so unexpectedly on your doorstep. And your garden, my dear, I must tell you I'm dizzy with admiration. Your dahlias! I never have a bit of luck with them myself. And your roses, magnificent. You really must tell me your secret. Do you talk to them? I chatter at mine day and night, but I never get blooms like that."

"Well, I—"

"And you're Grayson." Iris simply rolled over Brianna's response and turned to him. She freed one of Brianna's hands so that she could grip Gray's. "What a clever, clever young man you are. And so handsome, too. Why, you look just like a film star. I've read all your books, every one. Frighten me to death, they do, but I can't put them down. Wherever do you come up with such thrilling ideas? I've been so anxious to meet both of you," she continued, holding on to each of them. "Badgering poor Johnny to death, you know. And now, here we are."

There was a pause while Iris beamed at both of them. "Yes." Brianna discovered she could find little else to say. "Here you are. Ah, please come in. I hope you had a pleasant trip."

"Oh, I adore traveling, don't you? And to think with all the racketing around Johnny and I did in our misspent youth, we never came to this part of the world. It's pretty as a postcard, isn't it, Johnny?"

"It is, my sweet. It certainly is."

"Oh, what a lovely home. Just charming." Iris kept her hand firmly on Brianna's as she glanced around. "I'm sure no one could be anything but comfortable here."

Brianna gave Gray a helpless look, but he only shrugged. "I hope you will be. There's tea in the parlor if you like, or I can show you your room first."

"Would you do that? We'll put our bags away, shall we, Johnny? Then perhaps we can all have a nice chat."

Iris exclaimed over the stairway as they climbed it, the upstairs hall, the room Brianna escorted them into. Wasn't the bedspread charming, the lace curtains lovely, the view from the window superb?

In short order Brianna found herself in the kitchen brewing another pot of tea while her new guests sat at the table making themselves at home. Iris happily bounced Liam on her lap.

"Hell of a team, aren't they?" Gray murmured, helping by getting out cups and plates.

"She makes me dizzy," Brianna whispered. "But it's impossible not to like her."

"Exactly. You'd never believe there was an unscrupulous thought in her head. Everyone's favorite aunt or amusing neighbor. Maybe you should hide that silver after all."

"Hush." Brianna turned away to carry plates to the table. Carstairs immediately helped himself to the bread and jam.

"I do hope you'll join us," Iris began, choosing a scone, dipping into the clotted cream. "Johnny, dear, we do want to get business over with, don't we? So distressing to have business clouding the air."

"Business?" Brianna took Liam again, settled him on her shoulder.

"Unfinished business." Carstairs dabbed his mouth with a napkin. "I say, Brianna, this bread is tasty. Have a bit, do, Iris."

"Johnny rhapsodized over your cooking. I'm afraid I got a teeny bit jealous. I'm a fair cook myself, you know."

"A brilliant cook," a loyal Carstairs corrected, snatching his wife's hand and kissing it lavishly. "A magnificent cook."

"Oh, Johnny, you do go on." She giggled girlishly before swatting him aside. Then she pursed her lips and blew him several quick kisses. The byplay had Gray wiggling his brows at Brianna. "But I can see why he was so taken with the table you set, Brianna." She nibbled delicately on her scone. "We must find time to exchange some recipes while we're here. My speciality is a chicken and oyster dish. And if I do say so myself, it's rather tasty. The trick is to use a really good wine, a dry white, you see. And a hint of tarragon. But there I go, running on again, and we haven't dealt with our business."

She reached for another scone, gesturing to the empty chairs. "Do sit down, won't you? So much cozier to talk business over tea."

Agreeably Gray sat and began to fill his plate. "Want me to take the kid?" he asked Brianna.

"No, I've got him." She sat with Liam resting comfortably in the curve of her arm.

"What an angel," Iris cooed. "And you've such an easy way with babies. Johnny and I always regretted not having any ourselves. But then, we were always off having an adventure, so our lives were full."

"Adventures," Brianna repeated. An interesting term, she thought, for bilking.

"We were a naughty pair." Iris laughed, and the gleam in her eyes said she understood Brianna's sentiments exactly. "But what fun we had. It wouldn't be quite right to say we were sorry for it, when we enjoyed it so much. But then, one does get older."

"One does," Carstairs agreed. "And one sometimes loses the edge." He sent Gray a mild look. "Ten years ago, lad, you'd never have pinched my wallet."

"Don't bet on it." Gray sipped at his tea. "I was even better ten years ago."

Carstairs tossed back his head and laughed. "Didn't I tell you he was a pistol, Iris? Oh, I wish you'd have seen him button me down in Wales, my heart. I was filled with admiration. I hope you'll consider returning the wallet to me, Grayson. At least the photographs. The identification is easily replaced, but I'm quite sentimental over the photos. And, of course, the cash."

Gray's smile was quick and wolfish. "You still owe me a hundred pounds. Johnny."

Carstairs cleared his throat. "Naturally. Unquestionably. I only took yours, you see, to make it seem like a burglary."

"Naturally," Gray agreed. "Unquestionably. I believe we discussed compensation in Wales, before you had to leave so unexpectedly."

"I do apologize. You'd pinned me down, you see, and I didn't feel comfortable coming to a firm agreement without consulting Iris first."

"We're strong advocates of full partnership," Iris put in.

"Indeed." He gave his wife's hand an affectionate pat. "I can truthfully say that all our decisions are a matter of teamwork. We feel that, combined with deep affection, is why we've had forty-three successful years together."

"And, of course, a good sex life," Iris said comfortably, smiling when Brianna choked over her tea. "Marriage would be rather dull otherwise, don't you think?"

"Yes, I'm sure you're right." This time Brianna cleared her throat. "I think I understand why you've come, and I appreciate it. It's good to clear the air over it."

"We did want to apologize in person for any distress we've caused you. And I wanted to add my sympathies over my Johnny's clumsy and completely ill-advised search of your lovely home." She cut a stern look at her husband. "It lacked all finesse, Johnny."

"It did. Indeed it did." He bowed his head. "I'm thoroughly ashamed."

Brianna wasn't entirely certain of that, but shook her head. "Well, there was no real harm done, I suppose."

"No harm!" Iris took up the gauntlet. "Brianna, my dear girl, I'm sure you were furious, and rightly so. And distressed beyond belief."

"It made her cry."

"Grayson." Embarrassed now, Brianna stared into her teacup. "It's done."

"I can only imagine how you must have felt." Iris's voice had softened. "Johnny knows how I feel about my things. Why, if I came home and found everything topsy-turvy, I'd be devastated. Simply devastated. I only hope you can forgive him for the regrettable impulse, and for thinking like a man."

"I do. I have. I understand he was under a great deal of pressure, and—" Brianna broke off, lifting her head when she realized she was defending the man who had cheated her father and invaded her home.

"What a kind heart you have." Iris streamed into the breech. "Now if we could touch on this uncomfortable business of the stock certificate one last time. First, let me say it was very broad-minded, very patient of you not to contact the authorities after Wales."

"Gray said you'd be back."

"Clever boy," Iris murmured.

"And I didn't see any point in it." With a sigh Brianna picked up a finger of bread and nibbled. "It was long ago, and the money my father lost was his to lose. Knowing the circumstances was enough to satisfy me."

"You see, Iris, it's just as I told you."

"Johnny." Her voice was suddenly commanding. The look that passed between them held until Carstairs let out a long breath and dropped his gaze.

"Yes, Iris, of course. You're quite right. Quite right." Rallying, he reached into the inside pocket of his jacket, drew out an envelope. "Iris and I have discussed this at length, and we would very much like to settle the matter to everyone's satisfaction. With our apologies, dear," he said, handing Brianna the envelope. "And our best wishes."

Uneasy, she lifted the flap. Her heart careened to her stomach and up to her throat. "It's money. Cash money."

"A check would make bookkeeping difficult," Carstairs explained. "And then there's the taxes that would be involved. A cash transaction saves us both from that inconvenience. It's ten thousand pounds. Irish pounds."

"Oh, but I couldn't—"

"Yes, you can," Gray interrupted.

"It isn't right."

She started to hand the envelope back to Carstairs. His eyes lit up briefly, his fingers reached out. And his wife swatted them away.

"Your young man is correct in the matter, Brianna. This is quite right, for everyone involved. You needn't worry that the money will make an appreciable difference in our lives. We do quite well. It would ease my mind, and my heart, if you'd accept it. And," she added, "return the certificate to us."

"Rogan has it," Brianna said.

"No, I got it back from him." Gray rose, slipped into Brianna's rooms.

"Take the money, Brianna," Iris said gently. "Put it away now, in your apron pocket. I'd consider it a great favor."

"I don't understand you."

"I don't suppose you do. Johnny and I don't regret the way we lived. We enjoyed every minute of it. But a little insurance toward redemption wouldn't hurt." She smiled, reached over to squeeze Brianna's hand. "I'd look on it as a kindness. Both of us would. Isn't that right, Johnny?"

He gave the envelope one last, longing look. "Yes, dear."

Gray walked back in, holding the certificate. "Yours, I believe."

"Yes. Yes, indeed." Eager now, Carstairs took the paper. Adjusting his glasses, he peered at it. "Iris," he said with pride as he tilted the certificate for her to study as well. "We did superior work, didn't we? Absolutely flawless."

"We did, Johnny, dear. We certainly did."

TWENTY-TWO

"I have never in the whole of my life had a finer moment of satisfaction." All but purring, Maggie stretched out in the passenger seat of Brianna's car. She sent one last glance behind at their mother's house as her sister pulled into the street.

"Gloating isn't becoming, Margaret Mary."

"Becoming or not, I'm enjoying it." She shifted, reaching out to put a rattle in Liam's waving hand as he sat snug in his safety seat in the back. "Did you see her face, Brie? Oh, did you see it?"

"I did." Her dignity slipped just a moment, and a grin snuck through. "At least you had the good sense not to rub her nose in it."

"That was the bargain. We'd tell her only that the money came from an investment Da made before he died. One that recently paid off. And I would resist, no matter how it pained me, pointing out that she didn't deserve her third of it as she never believed in him."

"The third of the money was rightfully hers, and that should be the end of it."

"I'm not going to badger you about it. I'm much too busy gloating." Savoring, Maggie hummed a little. "Tell me what are your plans for yours?"

"I've some ideas for improvements on the cottage. The attic room for one, which started the whole business."

As Liam cheerfully flung the first one aside, Maggie pulled out another rattle. "I thought we were going to Galway to shop."

"We are." Grayson had badgered her into the idea and had all but booted her out of her own front door. She smiled now, thinking of it. "I've a mind to buy me one of those professional food processors. The ones they use in restaurants and on the cookery shows."

"That would have pleased Da very much." Maggie's grin softened into a smile. "It is like a gift from him, you know."

"I'm thinking of it that way. It seems right if I do. What about you?"

"I'll shovel some into the glass house. The rest goes away for Liam. I think Da would have wanted it." Idly she ran her fingers over the dashboard. "It's a nice car you've got here, Brie."

"It is." She laughed and told herself she'd have to thank Gray for pushing her out of the house for the day. "Imagine, me driving to Galway without worrying something's going to fall off. It's so like Gray to give outrageous gifts and make it seem natural."

"That's the truth. The man hands me a diamond pin as cheerfully as if it's a clutch of posies. He has a lovely, generous heart."

"He does."

"Speaking of him, what's he up to?"

"Well, he's either working or being entertained by the Carstairs."

"What characters. Do you know Rogan tells me when they went to the gallery, they tried to charm him into selling them the antique table in the upstairs sitting room?"

"Doesn't surprise me in the least. She's nearly talked me into buying, sight unseen, a lamp she says will be perfect for my parlor. A fine discount she'll give me, too." Brianna chuckled. "I'll miss them when they leave tomorrow."

"I have a feeling they'll be back." She paused. "When does Gray go?"

"Probably next week." Brianna kept her eyes on the road and her voice even. "He's doing no more than tinkering on the book now, from what I can tell."

"And do you think he'll be back?"

"I hope he will. But I won't count on it. I can't."

"Have you asked him to stay?"

"I can't do that, either."

"No," Maggie murmured. "You couldn't. Nor could I under the same circumstances." Still, she thought, he's a bloody fool if he leaves. "Would you like to close up the cottage for a few weeks, or have Mrs. O'Malley look after it? You could come to Dublin, or use the villa."

"No, though it's sweet of you to think of it. I'll be happier at home."

That was probably true, Maggie thought, and didn't argue. "Well, if you change your mind, you've only to say." Making a determined effort to lighten the mood, she turned toward her sister. "What do you think, Brie? Let's buy something foolish when we get to Shop Street. The first thing that strikes our fancy. Something useless and expensive; one of those trinkets that we used to look at with our noses pressed up to a shop window when Da would bring us."

"Like the little dolls with the pretty costumes or the jewelry cases with the ballerinas that spun around on top."

"Oh, I think we can find something a little more suited to our ages, but yes, that's the idea."

"All right, then. We'll do it."

It was because they'd talked about their father that memories swarmed Brianna after they reached Galway. With the car parked, they joined the pedestrian traffic, the shoppers, the tourists, the children.

She saw a young girl laughing as she rode her father's shoulders.

He used to do that, she remembered. He'd give her and Maggie turns up, and sometimes he'd run so that they'd bounce, squealing with pleasure.

Or he'd keep their hands firmly tucked in his while they wandered, spinning them stories while they jostled along the crowded streets.

When our ship comes in, Brianna my love, I'll buy you pretty dresses like they have in that window there.

One day we'll travel up here to Galway City with coins leaking out of our pockets. Just you wait, darling.

And though she'd known even then they were stories, just dreaming, it hadn't diminished the pleasure of the seeing, the smelling, the listening.

Nor did the memories spoil it now. The color and movement of Shop Street made her smile as it always did. She enjoyed the voices that cut through the lilting Irish—the twangs and drawls of the Americans, the guttural German, the impatient French. She could smell a hint of Galway Bay that carried on the breeze and the sizzling grease from a nearby pub.

"There." Maggie steered the stroller closer to a shop window. "That's perfect."

Brianna maneuvered through the crowd until she could look over Maggie's shoulder. "What is?"

"That great fat cow there. Just what I want."

"You want a cow?"

"Looks like porcelain," Maggie mused, eyeing the glossy black-and-white body and foolishly grinning bovine face. "I bet it's frightfully priced. Even better. I'm having it. Let's go in."

"But what'll you do with it?"

"Give it to Rogan, of course, and see that he puts it in that stuffy Dublin office of his. Oh, I hope it weighs a ton."

It did, so they arranged to leave it with the clerk while they completed the rest of their shopping. It wasn't until they'd eaten lunch and Brianna had studied the pros and cons of half a dozen food processors that she found her own bit of foolishness.

The fairies were made of painted bronze and danced on wires hung from a copper rod. At a flick of Brianna's fingers, they twirled, their wings beating together musically.

"I'll hang it outside my bedroom window. It'll make me think of all the fairy stories Da used to tell us."

"It's perfect." Maggie slipped an arm around Brianna's waist. "No, don't look at the price," she said when Brianna started to reach for the little tag. "That's part of it all. Whatever it costs, it's the right choice. Go buy your trinket, then we'll figure out how to get mine to the car."

In the end they decided that Maggie would wait at the shop with the cow, with Liam and the rest of their bags, while Brianna drove the car around.

In a breezy mood she strolled back to the car park. She would, she thought, hang her fairy dance as soon as she got home. And then she would play with her fine new kitchen toy. She was thinking how delightful it would be to create a salmon mousse or to finely dice mushrooms with such a precision instrument.

Humming, she slipped behind the wheel, turned the ignition. Perhaps there was a dish she could try to add to the grilled fish she intended to make for dinner. What would Gray enjoy especially? she wondered as she steered toward the exit to pay her fee. Colcannon, perhaps, and a gooseberry fool for dessert—if she could find enough ripe gooseberries.

She thought of the berries' season as those first days of June. But Gray would be gone then. She clamped down on the twinge around her heart. Well, it was nearly June in any case, she told herself and started to drive out of the lot. And she wanted Gray to have her special dessert before he went away.

Brianna heard the shout as she started into her turn. Startled, she jerked her head. She only had time to suck in a breath for the scream as a car, taking the turn too sharp and on the wrong side, crashed into hers.

She heard the screech of metal rending, of glass shattering. Then she heard nothing at all.

"So Brianna's gone shopping," Iris commented as she joined Gray in the kitchen. "That's lovely for her. Nothing puts a woman in a better frame of mind than a good shopping binge."

He couldn't imagine practical Brianna binging on anything. "She went off to Galway with her sister. I told her we could manage if she didn't make it home by tea." Feeling a little proprietary about the kitchen, Gray heaped the food Brianna had prepared earlier onto platters. "It's only the three of us tonight anyway."

"We'll be cozy right here." Iris set the teapot in its cozy on the table. "You were right to convince her to take a day for herself with her sister."

"I nearly had to drag her out to the car—she's so tied to this place."

"Deep, fertile roots. It's why she blooms. Just like her flowers out there. Never in my life have I seen such gardens as hers. Why, just this morning, I was—Ah, there you are, Johnny. Just in time."

"I had the most invigorating walk." Carstairs hung his hat on a peg, then rubbed his hands together. "Do you know, my dear, they still cut their own turf?"

"You don't say so."

"I do indeed. I found the bog. And there were stacks of it, drying in the wind and sun. It was just like stepping back a century." He gave his wife a peck on the cheek before turning his attention to the table. "Ah, what have we here?"

"Wash your hands, Johnny, and we'll have a nice tea. I'll pour out, Grayson. You just sit."

Enjoying them, and their way with each other, Gray obliged her. "Iris, I hope you're not offended if I ask you something."

"Dear boy, you can ask whatever you like."

"Do you miss it?"

She didn't pretend to misunderstand as she passed him the sugar. "I do. From time to time, I do. That life on the edge sort of feeling. So invigorating." She poured her husband's cup, then her own. "Do you?" When Gray only lifted a brow, she chuckled. "One recognizes one."

"No," Gray said after a pause. "I don't miss it."

"Well, you'd have retired quite early, so you wouldn't have the same sort of emotional attachment. Or perhaps you do, and that's why you've never used any of your prior experience, so to speak, in your books."

Shrugging, he lifted his cup. "Maybe I just don't see the point in looking back."

"I've always felt you never have a really clear view of what's coming up if you don't glance over your shoulder now and again."

"I like surprises. If tomorrow's already figured out, why bother with it?"

"The surprise comes because tomorrow's never quite what you thought it would be. But you're young," she said, giving him a motherly smile. "You'll learn that for yourself. Do you use a map when you travel?"

"Sure."

"Well, that's it, you see. Past, present, future. All mapped out." With her bottom lip clamped between her teeth, she measured out a stingy quarter spoon of sugar for her own tea. "You may plan a route. Now some people stick to it no matter what. No deviations to explore some little road, no unscheduled stops to enjoy a particularly nice sunset. A pity for them," she mused. "And oh, how they complain when they're forced to detour. But most of us like a little adventure along the way, that side road. Having a clear view of the ultimate destination doesn't have to keep one from enjoying the ride. Here you are, Johnny dear, your tea's just poured."

"Bless you, Iris."

"And with just a drop of cream, the way you like it."

"I'd be lost without her," Carstairs said to Gray. "Oh, it appears we're having company."

Gray looked toward the kitchen door as Murphy opened it. Con darted in ahead, sat at Gray's feet, laid his head in Gray's lap. Even as Gray lifted a hand to stroke the dog's ears, his smile of greeting faded.

"What is it?" He found himself springing to his feet, rattling the cups on the table. Murphy's face was too set, his eyes too dark. "What's happened?"

"There's been an accident. Brianna's been hurt."

"What do you mean she's hurt?" he demanded over Iris's murmur of distress.

"Maggie called me. There was an accident when Brie was driving from the car park to the shop where Maggie and the baby were waiting." Murphy took off his cap, a matter of habit, then squeezed his fingers on the brim. "I'll take you up to Galway. She's in the hospital there."

"Hospital." Standing there Gray felt, physically felt, the blood draining out of him. "How bad? How bad is it?"

"Maggie wasn't sure. She didn't think it was too bad, but she was waiting to hear. I'll take you to Galway, Grayson. I thought we'd use your car. It'd be faster."

"I need the keys." His brain felt dull, useless. "I have to get the keys."

"Don't let him drive," Iris said when Gray streaked from the room.

"No, ma'am, I won't be letting him do that."

Murphy didn't have to argue. He simply took the keys from Gray's hand and got behind the wheel. Since Gray said nothing, Murphy concentrated on finessing all the speed the Mercedes was built for. Another time, perhaps, he would have appreciated the response the sleek car offered. For now he simply used it.

For Gray the trip was endless. The glorious scenery of the west rushed by, but they seemed to make no progress. It was like animation, he thought dimly, run over and over again, cel by cel, while he could do nothing but sit.

And wait.

She wouldn't have gone if he hadn't bullied her into it. But he'd pressured her to go out, to take a day. So she'd gone to Galway, and now she was . . . Christ, he didn't know what she was, how she was, and couldn't bear to imagine it.

"I should have gone with her."

With the car cruising near ninety, Murphy didn't bother to glance over. "You'll make yourself sick thinking that way. We're nearly there now, then we'll see."

"I bought her the fucking car."

"True enough." The man didn't need sympathy, Murphy thought, but practicality. "And you weren't driving the one who hit it. To my way of thinking, if she'd been in that rusted bucket she had before, things would be worse."

"We don't know how bad they are."

"We soon will. So hang on to yourself until we do." He slipped off an exit, slowed, and began to maneuver through denser traffic. "It's likely she's fine and will give us grief for driving all this way."

He turned into the hospital car park. They'd no more climbed out and started for the doors when they spotted Rogan walking the baby.

"Brianna." It was all Gray could say.

"She's all right. They want to keep her through the night at least, but she's all right."

The feeling went out of Gray's legs so that he took Rogan's arm as much for balance as for emphasis. "Where? Where is she?"

"They've just put her in a room on the sixth floor. Maggie's with her yet. I brought her mother and Lottie along with me. They're up there as well. She's—" He broke off, shifting to block Gray from rushing the entrance. "She's banged up, and I think she's hurting more than she's letting on. But the doctor told us she's very lucky. Some bruises from the seat belt, which kept it from being worse. Her shoulder's wrenched, and that's causing the most pain. She's a knot on her head, and some cuts. They want her kept quiet for twenty-four hours."

"I need to see her."

"I know that." Rogan stood his ground. "But she doesn't need to see how upset you are. She's one who'll take that to heart and worry over it."

"Okay." Fighting for balance, Gray pressed his fingers to his eyes. "All right. We'll keep it calm, but I have to see her for myself."

"I'll go up with you," Murphy said and led the way in. Keeping his own counsel, he said nothing as they waited for the elevator.

"Why are they all here?" Gray demanded when the elevator opened. "Why are they here, Maggie, her mother. Rogan, Lottie, if she's all right?"

"They're family." Murphy pushed the button for six. "Where else would they be? Now, about three years past I broke an arm and cracked my head playing football. I couldn't get rid of one sister, but another would be at the door. My mother stayed for two weeks, no matter what I did to boost her on her way. And to tell the truth, I was glad to have them fussing around me. Don't go off in a mad rush," Murphy warned as the elevator stopped. "Irish nurses run a tight ship. And here's Lottie."

"Gracious, you must have flown all the way." She came forward, her smile all reassurance. "She's doing fine, they're taking grand care of her. Rogan arranged for her to have a private room so she'd have quiet and privacy. She's already fretting about going home, but with the concussion, they'll want to keep an eye on her."

"Concussion?"

"A mild one, really," she soothed, leading them down the hallway. "It doesn't seem she was unconscious for more than a few moments. And she was lucid enough to tell the man at the car park where Maggie was waiting. Look here, Brianna, you've more visitors already."

All Gray could see was Brianna, white against white sheets.

"Oh, Gray, Murphy, you shouldn't have come all this way. I'll be going home shortly."

"You'll not." Maggie's voice was firm. "You're staying the night."

Brianna started to turn her head, but the throbbing made her think better of it. "I don't want to stay the night. Bumps and bruises is all it is. Oh, Gray, the car. I'm so sorry about the car. The side of it's all bent in, and the headlamp's smashed, and—"

"Shut up, will you, and let me look at you?" He took her hand, held on.

She was pale, and a bruise had bloomed along her cheekbone. Above it, on the brow side of the temple was a neat white bandage. Beneath the shapeless hospital gown he could see more bandages at her shoulder.

Because his hand began to tremble, he drew it away, jammed it in his pocket. "You're hurting. I can see it in your eyes."

"My head aches." She smiled weakly, lifting a finger to the bandage. "I feel a bit like I've been run over by an entire rugby team."

"They should give you something."

"They will, if I need it."

"She's skittish of needles," Murphy said and leaned over to kiss her lightly. His own relief at seeing her whole showed itself in a wide, cheeky grin. "I remember hearing you howl, Brianna Concannon, when I was in Dr. Hogan's waiting room and you were getting a shot."

"And I'm not ashamed of it. Horrible things, needles. I don't want them poking me more than they already have. I want to go home."

"You'll stay just where you are." Maeve spoke from a chair beneath the window. "It's little enough to have a needle or two after the fright you've given us."

"Mother, it's hardly Brianna's fault that some idiot Yank couldn't remember which side of the road to drive on." Maggie's teeth clenched at the thought of it. "And they, with barely a scratch between them."

"You mustn't be so hard on them. It was a mistake, and all but frightened them to death." The drumming in Brianna's head increased at the idea of an argument. "I'll stay if I must, but if I could just ask the doctor again."

"You'll leave the doctor be and rest as he told you." Maeve pushed herself to her feet. "And there's no rest with all these people fussing around. Margaret Mary, it's time you took your baby home."

"I don't want Brie to be alone here," Maggie began.

"I'm staying." Gray turned, met Maeve's gaze steadily. "I'm staying with her."

She jerked a shoulder. "Sure it's no business of mine what you do. We missed our tea," she said. "Lottie and I will have something downstairs while Rogan arranges to have us taken home. Do as you're told here, Brianna, and don't make a fuss."

She leaned over, a bit stiffly, and kissed Brianna's uninjured cheek. "You were never a fast healer, so I don't expect this time to be any different." Her fingers rested, for just an instant where her lips had, then she turned and hurried out, calling Lottie to follow.

"She said two rosaries on the drive here," Lottie murmured. "Rest yourself." After a parting kiss, she trailed after Meave.

"Well." Maggie let out a long breath. "I think I can trust Grayson to see that you behave yourself. I'll find Rogan and see how we'll deal with getting them both home again. I'll come back before we go, in case Grayson needs help."

"I'll go with you, Maggie." Murphy patted Brianna's sheet-draped knee. "If they come to poke you, just turn your head away and close your eyes. That's what I do."

She chuckled and, when the room emptied, looked up at Gray. "I wish you'd sit down. I know you're upset."

"I'm fine." He was afraid if he sat, he'd go one better and just slide bonelessly to the floor. "I'd like to know what happened if you're up to telling me."

"It was all so fast." Indulging the discomfort and fatigue, she closed her eyes a moment. "We'd bought too much to carry, and I was going to fetch the car and drive it around to the shop where Maggie was waiting. Just as I pulled out of the car park, I heard someone shout. It was the attendant. He'd seen the other car coming for mine. There was nothing anyone could do then. There wasn't time. It hit on the side."

She started to shift and her shoulder twanged in protest. "They were going to tow the car away. I can't remember where."

"It doesn't matter. We'll take care of it later. You hit your head." Gently he reached down but kept his fingertips a breath away from the bandage.

"I must have, for the next thing I remember, there was a crowd around, and the American woman was crying and asking me if I was all right. Her husband had already gone to call an ambulance. I was fuddled. I think I asked that somebody get my sister, and then the three of us—Maggie, the baby and me—were riding off in an ambulance."

She didn't add that there had been a great deal of blood. Enough to terrify her until the medical attendant had staunched the flow.

"I'm sorry Maggie wasn't able to tell you more when she called. If she'd waited until the doctor had finished looking me over, she'd have saved you a lot of worry."

"I'd have worried anyway. I don't—I can't—" He shut his eyes and struggled to find the words. "It's hard for me to handle the idea of you being hurt. The reality of it is even tougher."

"It's just bruises and bumps."

"And a concussion, a pulled shoulder." For both of their sakes, he yanked himself back. "Tell me, is it truth or myth about not falling asleep with a concussion because you might not wake up?"

"It's a myth." She smiled again. "But I'm thinking seriously of staying awake for a day or two, just in case."

"Then you'll want company."

"I'll love company. I think I'd go mad lying in this bed alone, with nothing to do and no one to see."

"How's this?" Careful not to jar her, he sat on the side of the bed. "The food probably sucks here. It's hospital law in every developed country. I'll go out, hunt us up some burgers and chips. We'll have dinner together."

"I'd like that."

"And if they come in and try to give you a shot, I'll beat them up."

"I wouldn't mind if you did. Would you do something else for me?"

"Name it."

"Would you call Mrs. O'Malley? I've haddock waiting to be grilled for dinner. I know Murphy will see to Con, but the Carstairs need to be served, and there's more guests coming tomorrow."

Gray lifted her hand to his lips, then rested his brow on it. "Don't worry about it. Let me take care of you."

It was the first time in his life he'd ever made the request.

TWENTY-THREE

By the time Gray got back with dinner, Brianna's hospital room resembled her garden. Sprays of roses and freesia, spears of lupine and lilies, blooms of cheerful daisies and carnations banked her window, filled the table beside the bed.

Gray shifted the enormous bouquet he held so that he could see over it and shook his head. "Looks like these are superfluous."

"Oh, no, they aren't. They're lovely. Such a fuss really for a bump on the head." She held the bouquet in her uninjured arm, much like she held a child, then buried her face in it. "I'm enjoying it. Maggie and Rogan brought those, and Murphy those. And the last ones there were sent up from the Carstairs. Wasn't that sweet of them?"

"They were really worried." He set down the large paper bag he held. "I'm to tell you they're going to stay over another night, maybe two, depending on when you get out of here."

"That's fine, of course. And I'll be out tomorrow, if I have to climb through the window." She shot a wistful look at the bag. "Did you really bring dinner?"

"I did. Managed to sneak it past the big, eagle-eyed nurse out there."

"Ah, Mrs. Mannion. Terrifying, isn't she?"

"Scares me." He pulled a chair close to the bed, then sat to dig into the bag. "Bon appétit," he said, handing her a burger. "Oh, here, let me take those." He rose again to lift the bouquet from her arm. "I guess they need water, huh? Here, you eat." He pulled out a bag of chips for her. "I'll go find a vase."

When he left again, she tried to shift to see what else was in the bag he'd set on the floor. But the shoulder made movement awkward. Settling back again, she nibbled on the burger and tried not to pout. The sound of footsteps returning had her pasting a smile on her face.

"Where do you want them?" Gray asked.

"Oh, on that little table over there. Yes, that's lovely. Your dinner'll be cold, Gray."

He only grunted, then sitting again took his own share of the meal from the bag. "Feeling any better?"

"I don't feel nearly bad enough to be pampered this way, but I'm glad you stayed to have dinner with me."

"Only the beginning, honey." He winked and with the half-eaten burger in one hand, reached into the bag.

"Oh, Gray—a nightgown. A real nightgown." It was plain, white, and cotton and all but brought tears of gratitude to her eyes. "I can't tell you how much I appreciate that. This awful thing they put on you."

"I'll help you change after dinner. There's more."

"Slippers, too. Oh, a hairbrush. Thank God."

"Actually, I can't take credit for all this. It was Maggie's idea."

"Bless her. And you."

"She said your blouse was ruined." Bloody, he remembered she'd told him and took a moment to steady himself. "We'll take care of that tomorrow, if they spring you. Now what else do we have here? Toothbrush, a little bottle of that cream you use all the time. Almost forgot the drinks." He handed her a paper cup, topped with plastic with a hole for the straw. "An excellent vintage, I'm told."

"You thought of everything."

"Absolutely. Even the entertainment."

"Oh, a book."

"A romance novel. You have several on your shelf at the cottage."

"I like them." She didn't have the heart to tell him the headache would make reading impossible. "You went to a lot of trouble."

"Just a quick shopping spree. Try to eat a little more."

Dutifully she bit into a chip. "When you get home will you thank Mrs. O'Malley for me, and tell her please, not to bother with the wash."

"I'm not going back until you go."

"But you can't stay here all night."

"Sure I can." Gray polished off the burger, balled the wrapper, and tossed it into the waste can. "I've got a plan."

"Grayson, you need to go home. Get some rest."

"Here's the plan," he said, ignoring her. "After visiting hours, I'll hide out in the bathroom until things settle down. They probably make a sweep, so I'll wait until they come in and check on you."

"That's absurd."

"No, it'll work. Then the lights go off, and you're all tucked in. That's when I come out."

"And sit in the dark for the rest of the night? Grayson, I'm not on my deathbed. I want you to go home."

"Can't do it. And we won't sit in the dark." With a smug grin, he pulled his last purchase from the bag. "See this? It's a book light, the kind you clip on so you don't disturb your bed partner if you want to read late."

Amazed, she shook her head. "You've lost your mind."

"On the contrary, I'm extremely clever. This way I won't be at the cottage worrying, you won't be here, alone and miserable. I'll read to you until you're tired."

"Read to me?" she repeated in a murmur. "You're going to read to me?"

"Sure. Can't have you trying to focus on this little print with a concussion, can we?"

"No." She knew nothing, absolutely nothing in her life had ever touched her more. "I should make you go, but I so very much want you to stay."

"That makes two of us. You know, this sounded pretty good from the back cover copy. 'A deadly alliance,' " he read. " 'Katrina—she would never be tamed. The fiery-haired beauty with the face of a goddess and the soul of a warrior would risk everything to avenge the murder of her father. Even wed and bed her fiercest enemy.' " He lifted a brow. "Hell of a gal, that Katrina. And the hero's no slouch, either. 'Ian—he would never surrender. The bold and battle-scarred highland chief known as the Dark Lord would fight friend and foe to protect his land, and his woman. Sworn enemies, sworn lovers, they form an alliance that sweeps them toward destiny and into passion.' "

He flipped the book over to the front cover, reaching idly for a chip. "Pretty good, huh? And a fine-looking couple they are, too. See, it takes place in Scotland, twelfth century. Katrina's the only child of this widowed laird. He's let her run pretty wild, so she does a lot of guy stuff. Swordplay and archery, hunting. Then there's this evil plot and he's murdered, which makes her the laird and prey for the vicious and slightly insane villain. But our Katrina's no doormat."

Brianna smiled, reached for Gray's hand. "You've read it?"

"I paged through it when I was waiting to pay for it. There's this incredibly erotic scene on page two fifty-one. Well, we'll work our way up to that. They're probably going to come in and check your blood pressure, and we don't want it elevated. Better get rid of the evidence here, too." He gathered up the wrappings from the smuggled dinner.

He'd barely hidden them in the bag when the door opened. Nurse Mannion, big as a halfback, bustled in. "Visiting hours are nearly over, Mr. Thane."

"Yes, ma'am."

"Now, Miss Concannon, how are we doing? Any dizziness, nausea, blurred vision?"

"No, not at all. I'm feeling fine, really. In fact, I was wondering if—"

"That's good, that's good." Nurse Mannion easily overroad the expected request to leave as she made notes on the chart at the foot of the bed. "You should try to sleep. We'll be checking on you through the night, every three hours." Still moving briskly, she set a tray on the table beside the bed.

Brianna only had to take one look to go pale. "What's that? I told you I feel fine. I don't need a shot. I don't want one. Grayson."

"I, ah—" One steely glance from Nurse Mannion had him fumbling in the role of hero.

"It's not a shot. We just need to draw a little blood."

"What for?" Abandoning any pretense of dignity, Brianna cringed back. "I lost plenty. Take some of that."

"No nonsense now. Give me your arm."

"Brie. Look here." Gray linked his fingers with hers. "Look at me. Did I ever tell you about the first time I went to Mexico? I hooked up with some people and went out on their boat. This was in the Gulf. It was really beautiful. Balmy air, crystal blue seas. We saw this little barracuda swimming along the port side."

Out of the corner of his eye he saw Nurse Mannion slide the needle under Brianna's skin. And his stomach turned.

"Anyway, anyway," he said, speaking quickly. "One of the guys went to get his camera. He comes back, leans over the rail, and the mama barricuda jumps right up out of the water. It was like freeze frame. She looked right at the lens of the camera and smiled with all those teeth. Like a pose. Then she plopped back into the water, got her baby, and they swam away."

"You're making it up."

"God's truth," he said, lying desperately. "He got the picture, too. I think he sold it to *National Geographic*, or maybe it was the *Enquirer*. Last I heard he was still out in the Gulf of Mexico, hoping to repeat the experience."

"That's done." The nurse patted a bandage in the crook of Brianna's elbow. "Your dinner's on its way, miss, if you have room for it after your hamburger."

"Ah, no, thank you just the same. I think I'll just rest now."

"Five minutes, Mr. Thane."

Grayson scratched his chin when the door swung shut behind her. "Guess we didn't quite pull that off."

Now Brianna did pout. "You said you'd beat them up if they came in with needles."

"She's a lot bigger than me." He leaned over, kissed her lightly. "Poor Brie."

She tapped a finger on the book that lay on the bed beside her. "Ian would never have backed down."

"Well, hell, look how he's built. He could wrestle a horse. I'll never qualify for Dark Lord."

"I'll take you just the same. Grinning barracudas," she said and laughed. "How do you think of such things?"

"Talent, sheer talent." He went to the door, peeked out. "Don't see her. I'm going to turn off the light, duck into the bathroom. We'll give it ten minutes."

He read to her for two hours, taking her through Katrina's and Ian's perilous and romantic adventures by the tiny light of the book lamp. Now and again his hand would reach out and brush over hers, lingering over the moment of contact.

She knew she would always remember the sound of his voice, the way he slipped into a Scottish burr for the dialogue to amuse her. And the way he looked, she thought, the way his face was lit by the small bulb so that his eyes were dark, his cheekbones shadowed.

Her hero, she thought. Now and always. Closing her eyes, Brianna let the words he read drift over her.

"You're mine." Ian swept her into his arms, strong arms that trembled from the need that gripped him. "By law and by right, you're mine. And I am pledged to you, Katrina, from this day, from this hour."

"And are you mine, Ian?" Fearlessly she speared her fingers into his hair, drew him closer. "Are you mine, Dark Lord?"

"No one has ever loved you more than I." He swore it. No one ever will.

Brianna fell asleep wishing the words Gray read could be his own.

Gray watched her, knowing from the slow, steady sound of her breathing that she'd drifted off. He indulged himself then and buried his face in his hands. Keep it light. He'd promised himself he'd keep it light, and the strain was catching up with him.

She wasn't badly hurt. But no matter how often he reminded himself of that, he couldn't shake the bone-deep terror that had gripped him from the moment Murphy had stepped into the kitchen.

He didn't want her in a hospital, bruised and bandaged. He never wanted to think of her hurt in any way. And now he would always remember it, he would always know that something could happen to her. That she might not be, as he wanted her always to be, humming in her kitchen or babying her flowers.

It infuriated him that he would have this picture of her to carry with all the others. And it infuriated him all the more that he'd come to care so much he knew those pictures wouldn't fade as hundreds of other memories had.

He'd remember Brianna, and that tie would make it difficult to leave. And necessary to do so quickly.

He brooded over it as he waited for the night to pass. Each time a nurse would come to check Brianna, he listened to their murmured questions, her sleepy responses. Once, when he came back out, she called for him softly.

"Go back to sleep." He brushed the hair away from her brow. "It's not morning yet.

"Grayson." Drifting again, she reached for his hand. "You're still here."

"Yeah." He looked down at her, frowned. "I'm still here."

When she awoke again, it was light. Forgetting, she started to sit up, and the dull ache in her shoulder jarred her memory. More annoyed now than distressed, she touched her fingertips to the bandage on her head and looked around for Gray.

She hoped he'd found some empty bed or waiting room couch to sleep on. She smiled at his flowers and wished she'd asked him to put them closer so that she could touch them as well.

Warily she tugged out the bodice of her nightgown, bit her lip. There was a rainbow of bruises down her breastbone and torso where the seat belt had secured her. Seeing them, she was grateful Gray had helped her change into the nightgown in the dark.

It wasn't fair, she thought. It wasn't right that she should look so battered for the last few days they had together. She wanted to be beautiful for him.

"Good morning, Miss Concannon, so you're awake." A nurse breezed in, all smiles and youth and blooming health. Brianna wanted to hate her.

"I am, yes. When will the doctor come to release me?"

"Oh, he'll be making his rounds soon, don't worry. Nurse Mannion said you passed a peaceful night." As she spoke, she strapped a blood pressure cuff on Brianna's arm, stuck a thermometor under her tongue. "No dizziness then? Good, good," she said when Brianna shook her head. She checked the blood pressure guage, nodded, slipped the thermometer back out and nodded again at the results. "Well, you're doing fine, then, aren't you?"

"I'm ready to go home."

"I'm sure you're anxious." The nurse made notes on the chart. "Your sister's called already this morning, and a Mr. Biggs. An American. He said he was the one who hit your car."

"Yes."

"We reassured them both that you're resting comfortably. The shoulder paining you?"

"A bit."

"You can have something for that now," she said, reading the chart.

"I don't want a shot."

"Oral." She smiled. "And your breakfast is coming. Oh, Nurse Mannion said you'd need two trays. One for Mr. Thane?" Obviously enjoying the joke, she glanced toward the bathroom. "I'll be leaving in just a moment, Mr. Thane, and you can come out. She says he's a most handsome man," the nurse murmured to Brianna. "With the devil's own smile."

"He is."

"Lucky you. I'll get you something for the pain."

When the door closed again, Gray stepped out of the bathroom, scowled. "What, does that woman have radar?"

"Were you really in there? Oh, Gray, I thought you'd found a place to sleep. Have you been up all night?"

"I'm used to being up all night. Hey, you look better." He came closer, his scowl fading into a look of sheer relief. "You really look better."

"I don't want to think of how I look. And you look tired."

"I don't feel tired now. Starving," he said, pressing a hand to his stomach. "But not tired. What do you think they'll feed us?"

"You are not going to carry me into the house."

"Yes, I am." Gray skirted the hood of his car and opened the passenger door. "The doctor said you could come home, *if* you took it easy, rested every afternoon, and avoided any heavy lifting."

"Well, I'm not lifting anything, am I?"

"Nope. I am." Careful of her shoulder, he slipped an arm behind her back, another behind her knees. "Women are supposed to think this kind of stuff's romantic."

"Under different circumstances. I can walk, Grayson. There's nothing wrong with my legs."

"Not a thing. They're great." He kissed her nose. "Haven't I mentioned that before?"

"I don't believe you have." She smiled, despite the fact that he'd bumped her shoulder and the bruises on her chest were aching. It was the thought, after all, that counted. "Well, since you're playing at being Dark Lord, sweep me inside, then. And I expect to be kissed. Well kissed."

"You've gotten awfully demanding since you got hit on the head." He carried her up the walk. "But I guess I have to indulge you."

Before he could reach for the door, it swung open and Maggie rushed out. "There you are. It seems we've been waiting forever. How are you?"

"I'm being pampered. And if all of you don't watch out, I'll get used to it."

"Bring her inside, Gray. Is there anything in the car she needs?"

"About an acre of flowers."

"I'll fetch them." She dashed off as the Carstairs hurried into the hall from the parlor.

"Oh, Brianna, you poor, dear thing. We've been so worried. Johnny and I barely slept a wink thinking of you lying in the hospital that way. Such depressing places, hospitals. I can't think why anyone would choose to work in one, can you? Do you want some tea, a nice cool cloth? Anything at all?"

"No, thank you, Iris," Brianna managed when she could get a word in. "I'm sorry you were worried. It was only a little thing, really."

"Nonsense. A car accident, a night in the hospital. A concussion. Oh, does your poor head ache?"

It was beginning to.

"We're glad you're home again," Carstairs put in, and patted his wife's hand to calm her.

"I hope Mrs. O'Malley made you comfortable."

"She's a treasure, I assure you."

"Where do you want these flowers, Brie?" Maggie asked from behind a forest of posies.

"Oh, well—"

"I'll put them in your room," she decided for herself. "Rogan'll be up to see you as soon as Liam wakes from his nap. Oh, and you've had calls from the whole village, and enough baked goods sent over to feed an army for a week."

"There's our girl." Drying her hands on a towel, Lottie bustled out from the kitchen.

"Lottie. I didn't realize you were here."

"Of course I am. I'm going to see you settled and cared for. Grayson, take her right on into her room. She needs rest."

"Oh, but no. Grayson, put me down."

Gray only shifted his grip. "You're outnumbered. And if you don't behave, I won't read you the rest of the book."

"This is nonsense." Over her protests Brianna found herself in her room being laid on the bed. "I might as well be back in the hospital."

"Now, don't make a fuss. I'm going to make you a nice cup of tea." Lottie began arranging pillows, smoothing sheets. "Then you'll nap. You're going to be flooded with visitors before long and you need your rest."

"At least let me have my knitting."

"We'll see about that later. Gray, you can keep her company. See that she stays put."

Brianna poked out a lip, folded her arms. "Go away," she told him. "I don't need you about if you won't stand up for me."

"Well, well, the truth comes out." Eyeing her, he leaned comfortably on the doorjamb. "You're quite a shrew, aren't you?"

"A shrew, is it? I complain at being bullied and ordered about and that makes me a shrew?"

"You're pouting and complaining about being cared for and looked after. That makes you a shrew."

She opened her mouth, closed it again. "Well, then, I am."

"You need your pills." He took the presciption bottle out of his pocket, then walked into the bathroom to fill a glass with water.

"They make me groggy," she muttered when he came back, holding out the capsule.

"Do you want me to have to pinch your nose to get you to open up and swallow."

The notion of that humiliation had her snatching the pill, then the glass. "There. Happy?"

"I'll be happy when you stop hurting."

The fight went out of her. "I'm sorry, Gray. I'm behaving so badly."

"You're in pain." He sat on the side of the bed, took her hand. "I've been battered a couple of times myself. The first day's a misery. The second's hell."

She sighed. "I thought it would be better, and I'm angry it's not. I don't mean to snap at you."

"Here's your tea now, lamb." Lottie came in and balanced the saucer in Brianna's hands. "And let's get these shoes off so you'll be comfortable."

"Lottie. Thank you for being here."

"Oh, you don't have to thank me for that. Mrs. O'Malley and I'll keep things running around here till you're feeling yourself again. Don't you fret over a thing." She spread a light blanket over Brianna's legs. "Grayson, you see that she rests now, won't you?"

"You can count on it." On impulse he rose to kiss Lottie's cheek. "You're a sweetheart, Lottie Sullivan."

"Oh, go on." Flushing with pleasure, she bustled back into the kitchen.

"So are you, Grayson Thane," Brianna murmured. "A sweetheart."

"Oh, go on," he said. He tilted his head. "Can she cook?"

She laughed as he'd hoped she would. "A fine cook is our Lottie, and it wouldn't take much to charm a cobbler from her. If you've a taste for one."

"I'll keep that in mind. Maggie brought in the book." He picked it up from where Maggie had set it on Brianna's night table. "Are you up for another chapter of blistering medieval romance?"

"I am."

"You fell asleep while I was reading last night," he said as he paged through the book. "What's the last thing you remember?"

"When he told her he loved her."

"Well, that certainly narrows it down."

"The first time." She patted the bed, wanting him to sit beside her again. "No one forgets the first time they hear it." His fingers fumbled on the pages, stilled, and he said nothing. Understanding, Brianna touched his arm. "You mustn't let it worry you, Grayson. What I feel for you isn't meant to worry you."

It did. Of course it did. But there was something else, and he thought he could give her that, at least. "It humbles me, Brianna." He lifted his gaze, those golden-brown eyes uncertain. "And it staggers me."

"One day, when you remember the first time you heard it, I hope it pleasures you." Content for now, she sipped her tea, smiled. "Tell me a story, Grayson."

TWENTY-FOUR

He didn't leave on the first of June as he'd planned. He could have. Knew he should have. But it seemed wrong, certainly cowardly, to go before he was positive Brianna was well on the mend.

The bandages came off. He'd seen for himself the bruises and had iced down the swelling of her shoulder. He'd suffered when she turned in her sleep and caused herself discomfort. He scolded when she overdid.

He didn't make love with her.

He wanted her, hourly. At first he'd been afraid even the most gentle of touches would hurt her. Then he decided it was best as it was. A kind of segue, he thought, from lover, to friend, to memory. Surely it would be easier for them both if his remaining days with her were spent in friendship and not in passion.

His book was finished, but he didn't mail it. Gray convinced himself he should take a quick detour to New York before his tour and hand it over to Arlene personally. If he thought, from time to time, how he had asked Brianna to go off with him for a little while, he told himself it was best forgotten.

For her sake, of course. He was only thinking of her.

He saw, through the window, that she was taking down the wash. Her hair was loose, blowing back from her face in the stiff western breeze. Behind her, the finished greenhouse glistened in the sunlight. Beside her, flowers she'd planted swayed and danced. He watched as she unhooked a clothespin, popped it back on the line, moved onto the next, gathering billowing sheets as she went.

She was, he thought, a postcard. Something that personified a place, a time, a way of life. Day after day, he thought, year after year, she would hang her clothes and linens to dry in the wind and the sun. And gather them up again. And with her, and those like her, the repetition wouldn't be monotony. It would be tradition—one that made her strong and self-reliant.

Oddly disturbed, he walked outside. "You're using that arm too much."

"The doctor said exercise was good for it." She glanced over her shoulder. The smile that curved her lips didn't reach her eyes, and hadn't for days. He was moving away from her so quickly, she couldn't keep up. "I barely have a twinge now. It's a glorious day, isn't it? The family staying with us drove to Ballybunion to the beach. Da used to take Maggie and me there sometimes, to swim and eat ice-cream cones."

"If you'd wanted to go to the beach, you'd only had to ask. I'd have taken you."

The tone of his voice had her spine stiffening. Her movements became more deliberate as she unpinned a pillowslip. "That's kind of you, I'm sure, Grayson. But I don't have time for a trip to the sea. I've work to do."

"All you do is work," he exploded. "You break your back over this place. If you're not cooking, you're scrubbing, if you're not scrubbing, you're washing. For Christ's sake, Brianna, it's just a house."

"No." She folded the pillowslip in half, then half again before laying it in her wicker basket. " 'Tis my home, and it pleases me to cook in it, and scrub in it, and wash in it."

"And never look past it."

"And where are you looking, Grayson Thane, that's so damned important?" She choked off the bubbling temper, reverted to ice. "And who are you to criticize me for making a home for myself."

"Is it a home—or a trap?"

She turned then, and her eyes were neither hot nor cold, but full of grief. "Is that how you think, really, in your heart? That one is the same as the other, and must be? If it is, truly, I'm sorry for you."

"I don't want sympathy," he shot back. "All I'm saying is that you work too hard, for too little."

"I don't agree, nor is that all you said. Perhaps it was all you meant to say." She bent down and picked up her basket. "And it's more than you've said to me for these past five days."

"Don't be ridiculous." He reached out to take the basket from her, but she jerked it away. "I talk to you all the time. Let me take that."

"I'll take it myself. I'm not a bloody invalid." Impatiently she set the basket at her hip. "You've talked at me and around me, Grayson, these last days. But to me, and of anything you were really thinking or feeling, no. You haven't talked to me, and you haven't touched me. Wouldn't it be more honest to just tell me you don't want me anymore?"

"Don't—" She was already stalking past him toward the house. He'd nearly grabbed at her before he stopped himself. "Where did you get an idea that like?"

"Every night." She let the door swing back and nearly caught him in the face with it. "You sleep with me, but you don't touch me. And if I turn to you, you turn away."

"You're just out of the fucking hospital."

"I've been out of the hospital for nearly two weeks. And don't swear at me. Or if you must swear, don't lie." She slapped the basket onto the kitchen table. "Anxious to be gone is what you are, and not sure how to be gracious about it. And you're tired of me." She snapped a sheet out of the basket and folded it neatly, corner to corner. "And haven't figured out how to say so."

"That's bullshit. That's just bullshit."

"It's funny how your way with words suffers when you're angry." She flipped the sheet over her arm in a practiced move, mating bottom to top. "And you're thinking, poor Brie, she'll be breaking her heart over me. Well, I won't." Another fold, and the sheet was a neat square to be laid on the scrubbed kitchen table. "I did well enough before you came along, and I'll do well enough after."

"Very cool words from someone who claims to be in love."

"I am in love with you." She took out another sheet, and calmly began the same routine. "Which makes me a fool to be sure for loving a man so cowardly he's afraid of his own feelings. Afraid of love because he didn't have it as a boy. Afraid to make a home because he never knew one."

"We're not talking about what I was," Gray said evenly.

"No, you think you can run away from that, and do every time you pack your bag and hop the next plane or train. Well, you can't. Any more than I can stay in one place and pretend I grew up happy in it. I missed my share of love, too, but I'm not afraid of it."

Calmer now, she laid the second sheet down. "I'm not afraid to love you, Grayson. I'm not afraid to let you go. But I'm afraid we'll both be sorry if we don't part honestly."

He couldn't escape that calm understanding in her eyes. "I don't know what you want, Brianna." And he was afraid, for the first time in his adult memory, that he didn't know what he wanted himself. For himself.

It was hard for her to say it, but she thought it would be harder not to. "I want you to touch me, to lie with me. And if you've no desire for me anymore, it would hurt much less if you'd tell me so."

He stared at her. He couldn't see what it was costing her. She wouldn't let him see, only stood, her back straight, her eyes level, waiting.

"Brianna, I can't breathe without wanting you."

"Then have me now, in the daylight."

Defeated, he stepped forward, cupped her face in his hands. "I wanted to make it easier for you."

"Don't. Just be with me now. For now."

He picked her up, made her smile as she pressed her lips to his throat. "Just like in the book."

"Better," he promised as he carried her into the bedroom. "This will be better than any book." He set her on her feet, combing her wind-tossed hair back from her face before reaching for the buttons of her blouse. "I've suffered lying beside you at night and not touching you."

"There was no need."

"I thought there was." Very gently he traced a fingertip over the yellowing marks on her skin. "You're still bruised."

"They're fading."

"I'll remember how they looked. And how my stomach clenched when I saw them. How I'd tighten up inside when you'd moan in your sleep." A little desperate, he lifted his gaze to hers. "I don't want to care this much about anyone, Brianna."

"I know." She leaned forward, pressed her cheek to his. "Don't worry on it now. There's only us two, and I've been missing you so." With her eyes half closed, she ran a line of kisses up his jaw while her fingers worked on the buttons of his shirt. "Come to bed, Grayson," she murmured, sliding the shirt from his shoulders. "Come with me."

A sigh of the mattress, a rustle of sheets, and they were in each other's arms. She lifted her face, and her mouth sought his. The first frisson of pleasure shuddered through her, then the next as the kiss went deep.

His fingertips were cool against her flesh, soft strokes as he stripped her. And his lips were light over the fading bruises, as if by wish alone he could vanish them.

A bird sang in the little pear tree outside, and the breeze sent the fairy dance she'd hung singing, billowed the delicate lace of her curtains. It fluttered over his bare back as he shifted over her, as he laid his cheek under her heart. The gesture made her smile, cradle his head in her hands.

It was all so simple. A moment of gold she would treasure. And when he lifted his head, and his lips sought hers again, he smiled into her eyes.

There was need, but no hurry, and longing without desperation. If either of them thought this might be their last time together, they looked for savoring rather than urgency.

She sighed out his name, breath hitching. He trembled.

Then he was inside her, the pace achingly slow. Their eyes remained open. And their hands, palm to palm, completed the link with interlacing fingers.

A shaft of light through the window, and dust motes dancing in the beam. The call of a bird, the distant bark of a dog. The smell of roses, lemon wax, honeysuckle. And the feel of her, the warm, wet feel of her yielding beneath him, rising to meet him. His senses sharpened on it all, like a microscope just focused.

Then there was only pleasure, the pure and simple joy of losing everything he was, in her.

She knew by dinnertime that he was leaving. In her heart she had known when they had lain quiet together after loving, watching the sunlight shift through her window.

She served her guests, listened to their bright talk of their day at the seaside. As always, she tidied her kitchen, washing her dishes, putting them away again in the cupboards. She scrubbed off her stove, thinking again that she should replace it soon. Perhaps over the winter. She would have to start pricing them.

Con was sniffing around the door, so she let him out for his evening run. For a time she just stood there, watching him race over the hills in the glowing sunlight of the long summer evening.

She wondered what it would be like to run with him. To just race as he was racing, forgetting all the little details of settling the house for the night. Forgetting most of all what she had to face.

But, of course, she would come back. This was where she would always come back.

She turned, closing the door behind her. She went into her room briefly before going up to Gray.

He was at his window, looking out at her front garden. The light that hung yet in the western sky gilded him and made her think, as she had so many months before, of pirates and poets.

"I was afraid you'd have finished packing." She saw his suitcase open on the bed, nearly full, and her fingers tightened on the sweater she carried.

"I was going to come down and talk to you." Braced for it, he turned to her, wishing he could read her face. But she'd found a way to close it off from him. "I thought I could make Dublin tonight."

"It's a long drive, but you'll have light for a while yet."

"Brianna—"

"I wanted to give you this," she said quickly. Please, she wanted to beg, no excuses, no apologies. "I made it for you."

He looked down at her hands. He remembered the dark green wool, how she'd been knitting with it the night he'd come into her room late and picked a fight with her. The way it had spilled over the white of her nightgown.

"You made it for me?"

"Yes. A sweater. You might find use for it in the fall and winter." She moved toward him, holding it up to measure. "I added to the length of the sleeves. You're long in the arm."

His already unsteady heart shifted as he touched it. In the whole of his life, no one had ever made him anything. "I don't know what to say."

"Whenever you gave me a gift, you'd always tell me to say thank you."

"So I did." He took it, felt the softness and warmth on the palms of his hands. "Thank you."

"You're welcome. Do you need some help with your packing?" Without waiting for an answer, she took the sweater back and folded it neatly into his suitcase. "You've more experience with it, I know, but you must find it tedious."

"Please don't." He laid a hand on her shoulder, but when she didn't look up, dropped it again. "You've every right to be upset."

"No, I don't. And I'm not. You made no promises, Grayson, so you've broken none. That's important to you, I know. Have you checked the drawers? You'd be amazed at what people forget."

"I have to go, Brianna."

"I know." To keep her hands busy, she opened the dresser drawers herself, painfully distressed to find them indeed empty.

"I can't stay here. The longer I do now, the harder it is. And I can't give you what you need. Or think you need."

"Next you'll be telling me you've the soul of a gypsy, and there's no need for that. I know it." She closed the last drawer and turned around again. "I'm sorry for saying what I did earlier. I don't want you to go remembering hard words between us, when there was so much more."

Her hands were folded again, her badge of control. "Would you like me to pack you some food for the trip, or a thermos of tea perhaps?"

"Stop being the gracious hostess. For Christ's sake, I'm leaving you. I'm walking out."

"You're going," she returned in a cool and steady voice, "as you always said you would. It might be easier on your conscience if I wept and wailed and made a scene, but it doesn't suit me."

"So that's that." He tossed some socks into the case.

"You've made your choice, and I wish you nothing but happiness. You're welcome back, of course, if you travel this way again."

His gaze cut to hers as he snapped the case closed. "I'll let you know."

"I'll help you down with your things."

She reached for his duffel, but he grabbed it first. "I carried them in. I'll carry them out."

"As you please." Then she cut out his heart by coming to him and kissing him lightly on the cheek. "Keep well, Grayson."

"Good-bye, Brie." They went down the steps together. He said nothing more until they'd reached the front door. "I won't forget you."

"I hope not."

She walked part way with him to the car, then stopped on the garden path, waiting while he loaded his bag, climbed behind the wheel. She smiled, lifted her hand in a wave, then walked back into the cottage without looking back.

An hour later she was alone in the parlor with her mending basket. She heard the laughter through the windows and closed her eyes briefly. When Maggie came in with Rogan and the baby, she was nipping a thread and smiling.

"Well, now, you're out late tonight."

"Liam was restless." Maggie sat, lifting her arms so Rogan could pass the baby to her. "We thought he'd like some company. And here's a picture, the mistress of the house in the parlor mending."

"I'm behind in it. Would you like a drink? Rogan?"

"I wouldn't turn one down." He moved toward the decanter. "Maggie?"

"Aye, a little whiskey would go down well."

"And Brie?"

"Thank you. I think I will." She threaded a needle, knotted the end. "Is your work going well, Maggie?"

"It's wonderful to be back at it. Yes, it is." She planted a noisy kiss on Liam's mouth. "I finished a piece today. It was Gray talking about those ruins he's so fond of that gave me the notion for it. Turned out well I think."

She took the glass Rogan handed her, lifted hers. "Well, here's to a restful night."

"I'll give you no argument there," her husband said with fervor and drank.

"Liam doesn't think the hours between two and five A.M. should be for sleeping." With a laugh Maggie shifted the baby onto her shoulder. "We wanted to tell you, Brie, the detective's tracking Amanda Dougherty to—where is that place, Rogan?"

"Michigan. He has a lead on her, and the man she married." He glanced at his wife. "And the child."

"She had a daughter, Brie," Maggie murmured, cuddling her own baby. "He located the birth cirtificate. Amanda named her Shannon."

"For the river," Brianna whispered and felt tears rise up in her throat. "We have a sister, Maggie."

"We have. We may find her soon, for better or worse."

"I hope so. Oh, I'm glad you came to tell me." It helped a little, took some of the sting out of her heart. "It'll be good to think of it."

"It may just be thinking for a while," Rogan warned. "The lead he's following is twenty-five years old."

"Then we'll be patient," Brianna said simply.

Far from certain of her own feelings, Maggie shifted the baby, and the topic. "I'd like to show the piece I've finished to Gray, see if he recognizes the inspiration. Where is he? Working?"

"He's gone." Brianna sent the needle neatly through a buttonhole.

"Gone where? To the pub?"

"No, to Dublin, I think, or wherever the road takes him."

"You mean he's gone? Left?" She rose then, making the baby chortle with glee at the sudden movement.

"Yes, just an hour ago."

"And you sit here sewing?"

"What should I be doing? Flogging myself?"

"Flogging him's more like. Why, that Yank bastard. To think I'd grown fond of him."

"Maggie." Rogan laid a warning hand on her arm. "Are you all right, Brianna?"

"I'm fine, thank you, Rogan. Don't take on so, Maggie. He's doing what's right for him."

"To hell with what's right for him. What about you? Take the baby, will you?" she said impatiently to Rogan, then, arms free, went to kneel in front of her sister. "I know how you feel about him, Brie, and I can't understand how he could leave this way. What did he say when you asked him to stay."

"I didn't ask him to stay."

"You didn't—Why the devil not?"

"Because it would have made us both unhappy." She jabbed the needle, swore lightly at the prick on her thumb. "And I have my pride."

"A fat lot of good that does you. You probably offered to fix him sandwiches for the trip."

"I did."

"Oh." Disgusted, Maggie rose, turned around the room. "There's no reasoning with you. Never has been."

"I'm sure you're making Brianna feel much better by having a tantrum," Rogan said dryly.

"I was just—" But catching his eye, Maggie bit her tongue. "You're right, of course. I'm sorry, Brie. If you like I can stay awhile, keep you company. Or I'll pack up some things for the baby, and we'll both stay the night."

"You both belong at home. I'll be fine, Maggie, on my own. I always am."

Gray was nearly to Dublin and the scene kept working on his mind. The ending of the book, the damn ending just wouldn't settle. That's why he was so edgy.

He should have mailed the manuscript off to Arlene and forgotten it. That last scene wouldn't be digging at him now if he had. He could already be toying with the next story.

But he couldn't think of another when he wasn't able to let go of the last.

McGee had driven away because he'd finished what he'd come to Ireland to do. He was going to pick up his life again, his work. He had to move on because . . . because he had to, Gray thought irritably.

And Tullia had stayed because her life was in the cottage, in the land around it, the people. She was happy there the way she never would be anywhere else. Brianna—Tullia, he corrected, would wither without her roots.

The ending made sense. It was perfectly plausible, fit both character and mood.

So why was it nagging at him like a bad tooth?

She hadn't asked him to stay, he thought. Hadn't shed a tear. When he realized his mind had once again shifted from Tullia to Brianna, he swore and pressed harder on the accelerator.

That's the way it was supposed to be, he reminded himself. Brianna was a sensible, levelheaded woman. It was one of the things he admired about her.

If she'd loved him so damn much, the least she could have done was said she'd miss him.

He didn't want her to miss him. He didn't want a light burning in the window, or her darning his socks or ironing his shirts. And most of all, he didn't want her preying on his mind.

He was footloose and free, as he'd always been. As he needed to be. He had places to go, a pin to stick in a map. A little vacation somewhere before the tour, and then new horizons to explore.

That was his life. He tapped his fingers impatiently on the steering wheel. He liked his life. And he was picking it up again, just like McGee.

Just like McGee, he thought with a scowl.

The lights of Dublin glowed in welcome. It relaxed him to see them, to know he'd come where he'd intended to go. He didn't mind the traffic. Of course he didn't. Or the noise. He'd just spent too long away from cities.

What he needed was to find a hotel, check in. All he wanted was a chance to stretch his legs after the long drive, to buy himself a drink or two.

Gray pulled over to a curb, let his head fall back against the seat. All he wanted was a bed, a drink, and quiet room.

The hell it was.

Brianna was up at dawn. It was foolish to lie in bed and pretend you could sleep when you couldn't. She started her bread and set it aside to rise before brewing the first pot of tea.

She took a cup for herself into the back garden, but couldn't settle. Even a tour of the greenhouse didn't please her, so she went inside again and set the table for breakfast.

It helped that her guests were leaving early. By eight, she'd fixed them a hot meal and bid them on their way.

But now she was alone. Certain she would find contentment in routine, she set the kitchen to rights. Upstairs, she stripped the unmade beds, smoothed on the sheets she'd taken fresh from the line the day before. She gathered the damp towels, replaced them.

And it couldn't be put off any longer, she told herself. Shouldn't be. She moved briskly into the room where Grayson had worked. It needed a good dusting, she thought and ran a finger gently over the edge of the desk.

Pressing her lips together, she straightened the chair.

How could she have known it would feel so empty?

She shook herself. It was only a room, after all. Waiting now for the next guest to come. And she would put the very next one into it, she promised. It would be wise to do that. It would help.

She moved into the bath, taking the towels he'd used from the bar where they'd dried.

And she could smell him.

The pain came so quickly, so fiercely, she nearly staggered under it. Blindly she stumbled back into the bedroom, sat on the bed, and burying her face in the towels, wept.

Gray could hear her crying as he came up the stairs. It was a wild sound of grieving that stunned him, made him slow his pace before he faced it.

From the doorway he saw her, rocking herself for comfort, with her face pressed into towels.

Not cool, he thought, or controlled. Not levelheaded.

He rubbed his hands over his own face, scraping away some of the travel fatigue and the guilt.

"Well," he said in an easy voice, "you sure as hell had me fooled."

Her head shot up, and he could see now the heartbreak in her eyes, the shadows under them. She started to rise, but he waved a hand.

"No, don't stop crying, keep right on. It does me good to know what a fake you are. 'Let me help you pack, Gray. Why don't I fix you some food for your trip? I'll get along just dandy without you.' "

She struggled against the tears, but couldn't win. As they poured out, she buried her face again.

"You had me going, really had me. You never even looked back. That's what was wrong with the scene. It didn't play. It never did." He crossed to her, pulled the towels away. "You're helplessly in love with me, aren't you, Brianna? All the way in love, no tricks, no traps, no trite phrases."

"Oh, go away. Why did you come back here?"

"I forgot a few things."

"There's nothing here."

"You're here." He knelt down, taking her hands to keep her from covering the tears. "Let me tell you a story. No, go on crying if you want," he said when she tried to pull away. "But listen. I thought he had to leave. McGee."

"You've come back to talk to me about your book?"

"Let me tell you a story. I figured he had to leave. So what if he'd never cared for anyone the way he cared for Tullia. So what if she loved him, had changed him, changed his whole life. Completed it. They were miles apart in every other way, weren't they?"

Patiently he watched another tear run down her cheek. She was struggling against them, he knew. And she was losing.

"He was a loner," Gray continued. "Always had been. What the hell would he be doing, planting himself in some little cottage in the west of

Ireland? And she let him go, because she was too damn stubborn, too proud, and too much in love to ask him to stay.

"I worried over that," he continued. "For weeks. It drove me crazy. And all the way to Dublin I chewed on it—figured I wouldn't think of you if I was thinking of that. And I suddenly realized that he wouldn't go, and she wouldn't let him. Oh, they'd survive without each other, because they're born survivors. But they'd never be whole. Not the way they were together. So I did a rewrite, right there in the lobby of the hotel in Dublin."

She swallowed hard against tears and humiliation. "So you've solved your problem. Good for you."

"One of them. You're not going anywhere, Brianna." He tightened his grip until she stopped dragging at her hands. "When I finished the rewrite, I thought, I'll get a drink somewhere, and go to bed. Instead, I got in the car, turned around, and came back here. Because I forgot that I spent the happiest six months of my life here. I forgot that I wanted to hear you singing in the kitchen in the morning or see you out of the bedroom window. I forgot that surviving isn't always enough. Look at me. Please."

When she did, he rubbed one of her tears away with his thumb, then linked his hands with hers again. "And most of all, Brianna, I forgot to let myself tell you that I love you."

She said nothing, couldn't as her breath continued to hitch. But her eyes widened and two new tears plopped onto their joined hands.

"It was news to me, too," he murmured. "More of a shock. I'm still not sure how to deal with it. I never wanted to feel this way about anyone, and it's been easy to avoid it until you. It means strings, and responsibilities, and it means maybe I can live without you, but I'd never be whole without you."

Gently he lifted their joined hands to his lips and tasted her tears. "I figured you'd gotten over me pretty quick with that send-off last night. That started me panicking. I was all set to beg when I came in and heard you crying. I have to say, it was music to my ears."

"You wanted me to cry."

"Maybe. Yeah." He rose then, releasing her hands. "I figured if you'd done some sobbing on my shoulder last night, if you'd asked me not to leave you, I'd have stayed. Then I could have blamed you if I screwed things up."

After a short laugh she wiped at her cheeks. "I've accommodated you, haven't I?"

"Not really." He turned back to look at her. She was so perfect, he realized, with her tidy apron, her hair slipping from its pins, and tears drying on her cheeks. "I had to come around to this on my own, so I've got no one else to blame if I mess it up. I want you to know I'm going to try hard not to mess it up."

"You want to come back." She gripped her hands tight together. It was so hard to hope.

"More or less. More, actually." The panic was still there, brewing inside him. He only hoped it didn't show. "I said I love you, Brianna."

"I know. I remember." She managed a smile as she rose. "You don't forget the first time you hear it."

"The first time I heard it was the first time I made love to you. I was hoping I'd hear it again."

"I love you, Grayson. You know I do."

"We're going to see about that." He reached into his pocket and took out a small box.

"You didn't have to buy me a gift. You only had to come home."

"I thought about that a lot, driving back from Dublin. Coming home. It's the first time I have." He handed her the box. "I'd like to make it a habit."

She opened the box and, bracing a hand on the bed behind her, sat again.

"I harassed the manager of the hotel in Dublin until he had the gift shop opened. You Irish are so sentimental, I didn't even have to bribe him." He swallowed. "I thought I'd have better luck with a traditional ring. I want you to marry me, Brianna. I want us to make a home together."

"Grayson—"

"I know I'm a bad bet," he hurried on. "I don't deserve you. But you love me anyway. I can work anywhere, and I can help you here, with the inn."

As she looked at him, her heart simply overflowed. He loved her, wanted her, and would stay. "Grayson—"

"I'll still have to travel some." He plowed over her, terrified she'd refuse him. "But it wouldn't be like before. And sometimes you could come with me. We'd always come back here, Brie. Always. This place, it means almost as much to me as it does to you."

"I know. I—"

"You can't know," he interrupted. "I didn't know myself until I'd left. It's home. You're home. Not a trap," he murmured. "A sanctuary. A chance. I want to make a family here." He dragged a hand through his hair as she stared at him. "Jesus, I want that. Children, long-term plans. A future. And knowing you're right there, every night, every morning. No one could ever love you the way I do, Brianna. I want to pledge to you." He drew an unsteady breath. "From this day, from this hour."

"Oh, Grayson." She choked out his name. Dreams, it seemed, could come true. "I've wanted—"

"I've never loved anyone before, Brianna. In my whole life there's been no one but you. So I'll treasure you. I swear it. And if you'd just—"

"Oh, be quiet, will you," she said between laughter and tears, "so I can say yes."

"Yes?" He plucked her off the bed again, stared into her eyes. "No making me suffer first?"

"The answer's yes. Just yes." She put her arms around him, laid her head on his shoulder. And smiled. "Welcome home, Grayson."

Born in Shame

Dear Reader,

I've dreamed of Ireland. Of a land where there was magic in the mists, dark, brooding mountains that held secrets and green fields that rolled into forever. And that is what I found when I went there.

I've talked with many of my friends and family who have been to Ireland. Invariably those with roots that were transplanted from that country in the past all felt a tug when they stepped onto Irish soil. I know I did. There was a recognition, a sense of knowing, even before you took the first breath, just what the air would taste like.

There's a beauty in the little village with its pub and crooked streets, in the bustle of cities like Galway, in the cliffs that tower over the ocean, and the fields sleeping under the mists. There are simple things, like the farmer leading his cows across the road, and grand ones like the ruins of a castle standing centuries old beside the winding ribbon of river.

There are stone circles dancing in a farmer's field, and fairy hills in the forests. And just as magical are the flowers blooming in the well-tended garden or the taste of fresh scones at tea time. Simple things, and grand ones. That's what I found in Ireland.

For Born in Shame, *the last book of my Born In trilogy, I wanted to bring a woman, an American, to Ireland for the first time. To give Shannon Bodine her roots, her family, and a romance that would suit the contrasts and endurance of Ireland. To give to her that magic of simple and grand things.*

And I hope to give them to you as well.

Slainte,
Nora Roberts

For all my Irish pals,
on both sides of the Atlantic

I know my love by his way of walking
and I know my love by his way of talking.

IRISH BALLAD

PROLOGUE

Amanda dreamed dreadful dreams. Colin was there, his sweet, well-loved face crushed with sorrow. *Mandy,* he said. He never called her anything but Mandy. His Mandy, my Mandy, darling Mandy. But there'd been no smile in his voice, no laugh in his eyes.

Mandy, we can't stop it. I wish we could. Mandy, my Mandy, I miss you so. But I never thought you'd have to come so soon after me. Our little girl, it's so hard for her. And it'll get harder. You have to tell her, you know.

He smiled then, but it was sad, so sad, and his body, his face, that had seemed so solid, so close that she'd reached out in sleep to touch him, began to fade and shimmer away.

You have to tell her, he repeated. *We always knew you would. She needs to know where she comes from. Who she is. But tell her, Mandy, tell her never to forget that I loved her. I loved my little girl.*

Oh, don't go, Colin. She moaned in her sleep, pining for him. Stay with me. I love you, Colin. My sweet Colin. I love you for all you are.

But she couldn't bring him back. And couldn't stop the dream.

Oh, how lovely to see Ireland again, she thought, drifting like mist over the green hills she remembered from so long ago. See the river gleam, like a ribbon all silver and bright around a gift without price.

And there was Tommy, darling Tommy, waiting for her. Turning to smile at her, to welcome her.

Why was there such grief here, when she was back and felt so young, so vibrant, so in love?

I thought I'd never see you again. Her voice was breathless, with a laugh on the edges of it. *Tommy, I've come back to you.*

He seemed to stare at her. No matter how she tried, she could get no closer than an arm span away from him. But she could hear his voice, as clear and sweet as ever.

I love you, Amanda. Always. Never has a day passed that I haven't thought of you, and remembered what we found here.

He turned in her dream to look out over the river where the banks were green and soft and the water quiet.

You named her for the river, for the memory of the days we had.

She's so beautiful, Tommy. So bright, so strong. You'd be proud.

I am proud. And how I wish . . . But it couldn't be. We knew it. You knew it. He sighed, turned back. *You did well for her, Amanda. Never forget that. But you're leaving her now. The pain of that, and what you've held inside all these years, makes it so hard. You have to tell her, give her her birthright. And let her know, somehow let her know that I loved her. And would have shown her if I could.*

I can't do it alone, she thought, struggling out of sleep as his image faded away. Oh, dear God, don't make me do it alone.

"Mom." Gently, though her hands shook, Shannon stroked her mother's sweaty face. "Mom, wake up. It's a dream. A bad dream." She understood what it was to be tortured by dreams, and knew how to fear waking—as she woke every morning now afraid her mother would be gone. There was desperation in her voice. Not now, she prayed. Not yet. "You need to wake up."

"Shannon. They're gone. They're both of them gone. Taken from me."

"Shh. Don't cry. Please, don't cry. Open your eyes now, and look at me."

Amanda's lids fluttered open. Her eyes swam with grief. "I'm sorry. So sorry. I did only what I thought right for you."

"I know. Of course you did." She wondered frantically if the delirium meant the cancer was spreading to the brain. Wasn't it enough that it had her mother's bones? She cursed the greedy disease, and cursed God, but her voice was soothing when she spoke. "It's all right now. I'm here. I'm with you."

With an effort Amanda drew a long, steadying breath. Visions swam in her head—Colin, Tommy, her darling girl. How anguished Shannon's eyes were—how shattered they had been when she'd first come back to Columbus.

"It's all right now." Amanda would have done anything to erase that dread in her daughter's eyes. "Of course you're here. I'm so glad you're here." And so sorry, darling, so sorry I have to leave you. "I've frightened you. I'm sorry I frightened you."

It was true—the fear was a metallic taste in the back of her throat, but Shannon shook her head to deny it. She was almost used to fear now; it had ridden on her back since she'd picked up the phone in her office in New York and been told her mother was dying. "Are you in pain?"

"No, no, don't worry." Amanda sighed again. Though there was pain, hideous pain, she felt stronger. Needed to, with what she was about to face. In the few short weeks Shannon had been back with her, she'd kept the secret buried, as she had all of her daughter's life. But she would have to open it now. There wasn't much time. "Could I have some water, darling?"

"Of course." Shannon picked up the insulated pitcher near the bed, filled a plastic glass, then offered the straw to her mother.

Carefully she adjusted the back of the hospital-style bed to make Amanda more comfortable. The living room in the lovely house in Columbus had been modified for hospice care. It had been Amanda's wish, and Shannon's, that she come home for the end.

There was music playing on the stereo, softly. The book Shannon had brought into the room with her to read aloud had fallen where she'd dropped it in panic. She bent to retrieve it, fighting to hold on.

When she was alone, she told herself there was improvement, that she could see it every day. But she had only to look at her mother, see the graying skin, the lines of pain, the gradual wasting, to know better.

There was nothing to do now but make her mother comfortable, to depend, bitterly, on the morphine to dull the pain that was never completely vanquished.

She needed a minute, Shannon realized as panic began to bubble in her throat. Just a minute alone to pull her weary courage together. "I'm going to get a nice cool cloth for your face."

"Thank you." And that, Amanda thought as Shannon hurried away, would give her enough time, please God, to choose the right words.

ONE

Amanda had been preparing for this moment for years, knowing it would come, wishing it wouldn't. What was fair and right to one of the men she loved was an injustice to the other, whichever way she chose.

But it was neither of them she could concern herself with now. Nor could she brood over her own shame.

There was only Shannon to think of. Shannon to hurt for.

Her beautiful, brilliant daughter who had never been anything but a joy to her. A pride to her. The pain rippled through her like a poisoned stream, but she gritted her teeth. There would be hurt now, for what would happen soon, from what had happened all those years ago in Ireland. With all her heart she wished she could find some way to dull it.

She watched her daughter come back in, the quick, graceful movements, the nervous energy beneath. Moves like her father, Amanda thought. Not Colin. Dear, sweet Colin had lumbered, clumsy as an overgrown pup.

But Tommy had been light on his feet.

Shannon had Tommy's eyes, too. The vivid moss green, clear as a lake in the sun. The rich chestnut hair that swung silkily to her chin was another legacy from Ireland. Still, Amanda liked to think that the shape of her daughter's face, the creamy skin, and the soft full mouth had been her own gifts.

But it was Colin, bless him, who had given her determination, ambition, and a steady sense of self.

She smiled as Shannon bathed her clammy face. "I haven't told you enough how proud you make me, Shannon."

"Of course you have."

"No, I let you see I was disappointed you didn't choose to paint. That was selfish of me. I know better than most that a woman's path must be her own."

"You never tried to talk me out of going to New York or moving into commercial art. And I do paint still," she added with a bolstering smile. "I've nearly finished a still life I think you'll like."

Why hadn't she brought the canvas with her? Damn it, why hadn't she thought to pack up some paints, even a sketchbook so that she could have sat with her mother and given her the pleasure of watching?

"That's one of my favorites there." Amanda gestured to the portrait on the parlor wall. "The one of your father, sleeping in the chaise in the garden."

"Gearing himself up to mow the lawn," Shannon said with a chuckle. Setting the cloth aside, she took the seat beside the bed. "And every time we said why didn't he hire a lawn boy, he'd claim that he enjoyed the exercise, and go out and fall asleep."

"He never failed to make me laugh. I miss that." She brushed a hand over Shannon's wrist. "I know you miss him, too."

"I still think he's going to come busting in the front door. 'Mandy, Shannon,' he'd say, 'get on your best dresses, I've just made my client ten thousand on the market, and we're going out to dinner.' "

"He did love to make money," Amanda mused. "It was such a game to him. Never dollars and cents, never greed or selfishness there. Just the fun of it. Like the fun he had moving from place to place every couple of years. 'Let's shake this town, Mandy. What do you say we try Colorado? Or Memphis?' "

She shook her head on a laugh. Oh, it was good to laugh, to pretend for just a little while they were only talking as they always had. "Finally when we moved here, I told him I'd played gypsy long enough. This was home. He settled down as if he'd only been waiting for the right time and place."

"He loved this house," Shannon murmured. "So did I. I never minded the moving around. He always made it an adventure. But I remember, about a week after we'd settled in, sitting up in my room and thinking that I wanted to stay this time." She smiled over at her mother. "I guess we all felt the same way."

"He'd have moved mountains for you, fought tigers." Amanda's voice trembled before she steadied it. "Do you know, Shannon, *really* know how much he loved you?"

"Yes." She lifted her mother's hand, pressed it to her cheek. "I do know."

"Remember it. Always remember it. I've things to tell you, Shannon, that may hurt you, make you angry and confused. I'm sorry for it." She drew a breath.

There'd been more in the dream than the love and the grief. There had been urgency. Amanda knew she wouldn't have even the stingy three weeks the doctor had promised her.

"Mom, I understand. But there's still hope. There's always hope."

"It's nothing to do with this," she said, lifting a hand to encompass the temporary sickroom. "It's from before, darling, long before. When I went with a friend to visit Ireland and stayed in County Clare."

"I never knew you'd been to Ireland." It struck Shannon as odd to think of it. "All the traveling we did, I always wondered why we never went there, with you and Dad both having Irish roots. And I've always felt this—connection, this odd sort of pull."

"Have you?" Amanda said softly.

"It's hard to explain," Shannon murmured. Feeling foolish, for she wasn't a woman to speak of dreams, she smiled. "I've always told myself, if I ever took time for a long vacation, that's where I'd go. But with the promotion and the new account—" She shrugged off the idea of an indulgence. "Anyway, I remember, whenever I brought up going to Ireland, you'd shake your head and say there were so many other places to see."

"I couldn't bear to go back, and your father understood." Amanda pressed her lips together, studying her daughter's face. "Will you stay here beside me and listen? And oh, please, please, try to understand?"

There was a new and fresh frisson of fear creeping up Shannon's spine. What could be worse than death? she wondered. And why was she so afraid to hear it?

But she sat, keeping her mother's hand in hers. "You're upset," she began. "You know how important it is for you to keep calm."

"And use productive imagery," Amanda said with a hint of smile.

"It can work. Mind over matter. So much of what I've been reading—"

"I know." Even the wisp of a smile was gone now. "When I was a few years older than you, I traveled with a good friend—her name was Kathleen Reilly—to Ireland. It was a grand adventure for us. We were grown women, but we had both come from strict families. So strict, so sure, that I was more than thirty before I had the gumption to make such a move."

She turned her head so that she could watch Shannon's face as she spoke. "You wouldn't understand that. You've always been sure of yourself, and brave. But when I was your age, I hadn't even begun to struggle my way out of cowardice."

"You've never been a coward."

"Oh, but I was," Amanda said softly. "I was. My parents were lace-curtain Irish, righteous as three popes. Their biggest disappointment—more for reasons of prestige than religion—was that none of their children had the calling."

"But you were an only child," Shannon interrupted.

"One of the truths I broke. I told you I had no family, let you believe there was no one. But I had two brothers and a sister, and not a word has there been between us since before you were born."

"But why—" Shannon caught herself. "I'm sorry. Go on."

"You were always a good listener. Your father taught you that." She paused a moment, thinking of Colin, praying that what she was about to do was right for all of them. "We weren't a close family, Shannon. There was a . . . a stiffness in our house, a rigidness of rules and manners. It was over fierce objections that I left home to travel to Ireland with Kate. But we went, as excited as schoolgirls on a picnic. To Dublin first. Then on, following our maps and our noses. I felt free for the first time in my life."

It was so easy to bring it all back, Amanda realized. Even after all these years that she'd suppressed those memories, they could swim back now, as clear and pure as water. Kate's giggling laugh, the cough of the tiny car they'd rented, the wrong turns and the right ones they'd made.

And her first awed look of the sweep of hills, the spear of cliffs of the west. The sense of coming home she'd never expected, and had never felt again.

"We wanted to see all we could see, and when we'd reached the west, we found a charming inn that overlooked the River Shannon. We settled there, decided we could make it a sort of base while we drove here and there on day trips. The Cliffs of Mohr, Galway, the beach at Ballybunnion, and all the little fascinating places you find off the roads where you least expect them."

She looked at her daughter then, and her eyes were sharp and bright. "Oh, I wish you would go there, see, feel for yourself the magic of the place, the sea spewing like thunder up on the cliffs, the green of the fields, the way the air feels when it's raining so soft and gentle—or when the wind blows hard from the Atlantic. And the light, it's like a pearl, just brushed with gold."

Here was love, Shannon thought, puzzled, and a longing she'd never suspected. "But you never went back."

"No." Amanda sighed. "I never went back. Do you ever wonder, darling, how it is that a person can plan things so carefully, all but see how things will be the next day, and the next, then some small something happens, some seemingly insignificant something, and the pattern shifts. It's never quite the same again."

It wasn't a question so much as a statement. So Shannon simply waited, wondering what small something had changed her mother's pattern.

The pain was trying to creep back, cunningly. Amanda closed her eyes a moment, concentrating on beating it. She would hold it off, she promised herself, until she had finished what she'd begun.

"One morning—it was late summer now and the rain came and went, fitful—Kate was feeling poorly. She decided to stay in, rest in bed for the day, read a bit and pamper herself. I was restless, a feeling in me that there were places I had to go. So I took the car, and I drove. Without planning it, I took myself to Loop Head. I could hear the waves crashing as I got out of the car and walked toward the cliffs. The wind was blowing, humming through the grass. I could smell the ocean, and the rain. There was a power there, drumming in the air even as the surf drummed on the rocks.

"I saw a man," she continued, slowly now, "standing where the land fell away to the sea. He was looking out over the water, into the rain—west toward America. There was no one else but him, hunched in his wet jacket, a dripping cap low over his eyes. He turned, as if he'd only been waiting for me, and he smiled."

Suddenly Shannon wanted to stand, to tell her mother it was time to stop, to rest, to do anything but continue. Her hands had curled themselves into fists without her being aware. There was a larger, tighter one lodged in her stomach.

"He wasn't young," Amanda said softly. "But he was handsome. There was something so sad, so lost in his eyes. He smiled and said good morning, and what a fine day it was as the rain beat on our heads and the wind slapped our faces. I laughed, for somehow it was a fine day. And though I'd grown used to the music of the brogue of western Ireland, his voice was so charming, I knew I could go on listening to it for hours. So we stood there and talked, about my travels, about America. He was a farmer, he said. A bad one, and he was sorry for that as he had two baby daughters to provide for. But there was no sadness in his face when he spoke of them. It lit. His Maggie Mae and Brie, he called them. And about his wife, he said little.

"The sun came out," Amanda said with a sigh. "It came out slow and lovely as we stood there, sort of slipping through the clouds in little streams of gold. We walked along the narrow paths, talking, as if we'd known each other all our lives. And I fell in love with him on the high, thundering cliffs. It should have frightened me." She glanced at Shannon, tentatively reached out a hand. "It did shame me, for he was a married man with children. But I thought it was only me who felt it, and how much sin can there be in the soul of an old maid dazzled by a handsome man in one morning?"

It was with relief she felt her daughter's fingers twine with hers. "But it wasn't only me who'd felt it. We saw each other again, oh, innocently enough. At a pub, back on the cliffs, and once he took both me and Kate to a little fair outside of Ennis. It couldn't stay innocent. We weren't children, either of us, and what we felt for each other was so huge, so important, and you must believe me, so right. Kate knew—anyone who looked at us could have seen it—and she talked to me as a friend would. But I loved him, and I'd never been so happy as when he was with me. Never once did he make promises. Dreams we had, but there were no promises between us. He was bound to his wife who had no love for him, and to the children he adored."

She moistened her dry lips, took another sip from the straw when Shannon wordlessly offered the glass. Amanda paused again, for it would be harder now.

"I knew what I was doing, Shannon, indeed it was more my doing than his when we became lovers. He was the first man to touch me, and when he did, at last, it was with such gentleness, such care, such love, that we wept together afterward. For we knew we'd found each other too late, and it was hopeless.

"Still we made foolish plans. He would find a way to leave his wife provided for and bring his daughters to me in America where we'd be a family. The man desperately wanted family, as I did. We'd talk together in that room overlooking the river and pretend that it was forever. We had three weeks, and every day was more wonderful than the last, and more wrenching. I had to leave him, and Ireland. He told me he would stand at Loop Head, where we'd met, and look out over the sea to New York, to me.

"His name was Thomas Concannon, a farmer who wanted to be a poet."

"Did you . . ." Shannon's voice was rusty and unsteady. "Did you ever see him again?"

"No. I wrote him for a time, and he answered." Pressing her lips together, Amanda stared into her daughter's eyes. "Soon after I returned to New York, I learned I was carrying his child."

Shannon shook her head quickly, the denial instinctive, the fear huge.

"Pregnant?" Her heart began to beat thick and fast. She shook her head again and tried to draw her hand away. For she knew, without another word being said, she knew. And refused to know. "No."

"I was thrilled." Amanda's grip tightened, though it cost her. "From the first moment I was sure, I was thrilled. I never thought I would have a child, that I would find someone who loved me enough to give me that gift. Oh, I wanted that child, loved it, thanked God for it. What sadness and grief I had came from knowing I would never be able to share with Tommy the beauty that had come from our loving each other. His letter to me after I'd written him of it was frantic. He would have left his home and come to me. He was afraid for me, and what I was facing alone. I knew he would have come, and it tempted me. But it was wrong, Shannon, as loving him was never wrong. So I wrote him a last time, lied to him for the first time, and told him I wasn't afraid, nor alone, and that I was going away."

"You're tired." Shannon was desperate to stop the words. Her world was tilting, and she had to fight to right it again. "You've talked too long. It's time for your medicine."

"He would have loved you," Amanda said fiercely. "If he'd had the chance. In my heart I know he loved you without ever laying eyes on you."

"Stop." She did rise then, pulling away, pushing back. There was a sickness rising inside her, and her skin felt so cold and thin. "I don't want to hear this. I don't need to hear this."

"You do. I'm sorry for the pain it causes you, but you need to know it all. I did leave," she went on quickly. "My family was shocked, furious when I told them I was pregnant. They wanted me to go away, give you up, quietly, discreetly, so that there would be no scandal and shame. I would have died before giving you up. You were mine, and you were Tommy's. There were horrible words in that house, threats, utimatums. They disowned me, and my father, being a clever man of business, blocked my bank account so that I had no claim on the money that had been left to me by my grandmother. Money was never a game to him, you see. It was power.

"I left that house with never a regret, with the money I had in my wallet, and a single suitcase."

Shannon felt as though she were underwater, struggling for air. But the image came clearly through it, of her mother, young, pregnant, nearly penniless, carrying a single suitcase. "There was no one to help you?"

"Kate would have, and I knew she'd suffer for it. This had been my doing. What shame there was, was mine. What joy there was, was mine. I took a train north, and I got a job waiting tables at a resort in the Catskills. And there I met Colin Bodine."

Amanda waited while Shannon turned away and walked to the dying fire. The room was quiet, with only the hiss of embers and the brisk wind at the windows to stir it. But beneath the quiet, she could feel the storm, the one swirling inside the child she loved more than her own life. Already she suffered, knowing that storm was likely to crash over both of them.

"He was vacationing with his parents. I paid him little mind. He was just one more of the rich and privileged I was serving. He had a joke for me now and again, and I smiled as was expected. My mind was on my work and my pay, and on the child growing inside me. Then one afternoon there was a thunderstorm, a brute of one. A good many of the guests chose to stay indoors, in their rooms and have their lunch brought to them. I was carrying a tray, hurrying to one of the cabins, for there would be trouble if the food got cold and the guest complained of it. And Colin comes barreling around a corner, wet as a dog, and flattens me. How clumsy he was, bless him."

Tears burned behind Shannon's eyes as she stared down into the glowing embers. "He said that was how he met you, by knocking you down."

"So he did. And we always told you what truths we felt we could. He sent me sprawling in the mud, with the tray of food scattering and ruined. He started apologizing, trying to help me up. All I could see was that food, spoiled. And my back aching from carrying those heavy trays, and my legs so tired of holding the rest of me up. I started to cry. Just sat there in the mud and cried and cried and cried. I couldn't stop. Even when he lifted me up and carried me to his room, I couldn't stop.

"He was so sweet, sat me down on a chair despite the mud, covered me with a blanket and sat there, patting my hand till the tears ran out. I was so ashamed of myself, and he was so kind. He wouldn't let me leave until I'd promised to have dinner with him."

It should have been romantic and sweet, Shannon thought while her breath began to hitch. But it wasn't. It was hideous. "He didn't know you were pregnant."

Amanda winced as much from the accusation in the words as she did from a fresh stab of pain. "No, not then. I was barely showing and careful to hide it or I would have lost my job. Times were different then, and an unmarried pregnant waitress wouldn't have lasted in a rich man's playground."

"You let him fall in love with you." Shannon's voice was cold, cold as the ice that seemed slicked over her skin. "When you were carrying another man's child."

And the child was me, she thought, wretched.

"I'd grown to a woman," Amanda said carefully, searching her daughter's face and weeping inside at what she read there. "And no one had really loved me. With Tommy it was quick, as stunning as a lightning bolt. I was still blinded by it when I met Colin. Still grieving over it, still wrapped in it. Everything I felt for Tommy was turned toward the child we'd made together. I could tell you I thought Colin was only being kind. And in truth, at first I did. But I saw, soon enough, that there was more."

"And you let him."

"Maybe I could have stopped him," Amanda said with a long, long sigh. "I don't know. Every day for the next week there were flowers in my room, and the pretty, useless things he loved to give. He found ways to be with me. If I had a ten-minute break, there he would be. Still it took me days before I understood I was being courted. I was terrified. Here was this lovely man who was being nothing but kind, and he didn't know I had another man's child in me. I told him, all of it, certain it would end there, and sorry for that because he was the first friend I'd had since I'd left Kate in New York. He listened, in that way he had, without interruption, without questions, without condemnations. When I was finished, and weeping again, he took my hand. 'You'd better marry me, Mandy,' he said. 'I'll take care of you and the baby.' "

The tears had escaped, ran down Shannon's cheeks as she turned back. They were running down her mother's cheeks as well, but she wouldn't allow herself to be swayed by them. Her world was no longer tilted; it had crashed.

"As simple as that? How could it have been so simple?"

"He loved me. It was humbling when I realized he truly loved me. I refused him, of course. What else could I do? I thought he was being foolishly gallant, or just foolish altogether. But he persisted. Even when I got angry and told him to leave me alone, he persisted." A smile began to curve her lips as she remembered it. "It was as if I were the rock and he the wave that patiently, endlessly sweeps over it until all resistance is worn away. He brought me baby things. Can you image a man courting a woman by bringing her gifts for her unborn child? One day he came to my room, told me we were going to get the license now and to get my purse. I did it. I just did it. And found myself married two days later."

She looked over sharply, anticipating the question before it was asked. "I won't lie to you and tell you I loved him then. I did care. It was impossible not to care for a man like that. And I was grateful. His parents were upset, naturally enough, but he claimed he would bring them around. Being Colin, I think he would have, but they were killed on their drive home. So it was just the two of us, and you. I promised myself I would be a good wife to him, make him a home, accept him in bed. I vowed not to think of Tommy again, but that was impossible. It took me years to understand there was no sin, no shame in remembering the first man I'd loved, no disloyalty to my husband."

"Not my father," Shannon said through lips of ice. "He was your husband, but he wasn't my father."

"Oh, but he was." For the first time there was a hint of temper in Amanda's voice. "Don't ever say different."

Bitterness edged her voice. "You've just told me different, haven't you?"

"He loved you while you were still in my womb, took both of us as his without hesitation or false pride." Amanda spoke as quickly as her pain would allow. "I tell you it shamed me, pining for a man I could never have, while one as fine as was ever made was beside me. The day you were born, and I saw him holding you in those big clumsy hands, that look of wonder and pride on his face, the love in his eyes as he cradled you against him as gently as if you were made of glass, I fell in love with him. I loved him as much as any woman ever loved any man from that day till this. And he was your father, as Tommy wanted to be and couldn't. If either of us had a regret, it was that we couldn't have more children to spread the happiness we shared in you."

"You just want me to accept this?" Clinging to anger was less agonizing than clinging to grief. Shannon stared. The woman in bed was a stranger now, just as she was a stranger to herself. "To go on as if it changes nothing."

"I want you to give yourself time to accept, and understand. And I want you to believe that we loved you, all of us."

Her world was shattered at her feet, every memory she had, every belief she'd fostered in jagged shards. "Accept? That you slept with a married man and got pregnant, then married the first man who asked you to save yourself. To accept the lies you told me all my life, the deceit."

"You've a right to your anger." Amanda bit back the pain, physical, emotional.

"Anger? Do you think what I'm feeling is as pale as anger? God, how could you do this?" She whirled away, horror and bitterness biting at her heels. "How could you have kept this from me all these years, let me believe I was someone I wasn't?"

"Who you are hasn't changed," Amanda said desperately. "Colin and I did what we thought was right for you. We were never sure how or when to tell you. We—"

"You discussed it?" Swamped by her own churning emotions, Shannon spun back to the frail woman on the bed. There was a horrible, shocking urge in her to snatch that shrunken body up, shake it. "Is today the day we tell Shannon she was a little mistake made on the west coast of Ireland? Or should it be tomorrow?"

"Not a mistake, never a mistake. A miracle. Damn it, Shannon—" She broke off, gasping as the pain lanced through her, stealing her breath, tearing like claws. Her vision grayed. She felt a hand lift her head, a pill being slipped between her lips, and heard the voice of her daughter, soothing now.

"Sip some water. A little more. That's it. Now lie back, close your eyes."

"Shannon." The hand was there to take hers when she reached out.

"I'm here, right here. The pain'll be gone in a minute. It'll be gone, and you'll sleep."

It was already ebbing, and the fatigue was rolling in like fog. Not enough time, was all Amanda could think. Why is there never enough time?

"Don't hate me," she murmured as she slipped under the fog. "Please, don't hate me."

Shannon sat, weighed down by her own grief long after her mother slept.

She didn't wake again.

TWO

An ocean away from where one of Tom Concannon's daughters dealt with the pain of death, others celebrated the joys of new life.

Brianna Concannon Thane cradled her daughter in her arms, studying the gorgeous blue eyes with their impossibly long lashes. The tiny fingers with their perfect tiny nails, the rosebud of a mouth that no one in heaven or on earth could tell her hadn't curved into a smile.

After less than an hour she'd already forgotten the strain and fatigue of labor. The sweat of it, and even the prickles of fear.

She had a child.

"She's real." Grayson Thane said it reverently, with a hesitant stroke of a fingertip down the baby's cheek. "She's ours." He swallowed. Kayla, he thought. His daughter Kayla. And she seemed so small, so fragile, so helpless. "Do you think she's going to like me?"

Peering over his shoulder, his sister-in-law chuckled. "Well, we do—

most of the time. She favors you, Brie," Maggie decided, slipping an arm around Gray's waist for support. "Her hair will be your color. It's more russet now, but I'll wager it turns to your reddish gold before long."

Delighted with the idea, Brianna beamed. She stroked the down on her daughter's head, found it soft as water. "Do you think?"

"Maybe she's got my chin," Gray said hopefully.

"Just like a man." Maggie winked at her husband as Rogan Sweeney grinned at her across the hospital bed. "A woman goes through the pregnancy, with its queasiness and swollen ankles. She waddles about like a cow for months, then suffers through the horrors of labor—"

"Don't remind me of that." Gray didn't bother to suppress a shudder. Brianna might have put that aspect of the event behind her, but he hadn't. It would live in his dreams, he was sure, for years.

Transition, he remembered with horror. As a writer, he'd always thought of it as a simple move from scene to scene. He'd never think of the word the same way again.

Unable to resist, Maggie tucked her tongue in her cheek. Her affection for Gray made her honor bound to tease whenever the opportunity arose. "How many hours was it? Let's see. Eighteen. Eighteen hours of labor for you, Brie."

Brianna couldn't quite hide a smile as Gray began to pale. "More or less. Certainly seemed like more at the time, with everyone telling me to breathe, and poor Gray nearly hyperventilating as he demonstrated how I was to go about it."

"A man thinks nothing of whining after putting in eight hours at a desk." Maggie tossed back her mop of flame-colored hair. "And still they insist on calling us the weaker sex."

"You won't hear it from me." Rogan smiled at her. Being part of Kayla's birth had reminded him of the birth of his son, and how his wife had fought like a warrior to bring Liam into the world. Still no one thinks of what a father goes through. "How's your hand doing, Grayson?"

Brows knit, Gray flexed his fingers—the ones his wife had vised down on during a particularly rough contraction. "I don't think it's broken."

"You held back a yelp, manfully," Maggie remembered. "But your eyes crossed when she got a good grip on you."

"At least she didn't curse you," Rogan added, lifting a dark, elegant brow at his wife. "The names Margaret Mary here called me when Liam was born were inventive to be sure. And unrepeatable."

"You try passing eight pounds, Sweeney, and see what names come to mind. And all he says, when he takes a look at Liam," Maggie went on, "is how the boy has *his* nose."

"And so he does."

"But you're okay now?" In sudden panic Gray looked at his wife. She was still a little pale, he noted, but her eyes were clear again. That terrifying glaze of concentration was gone. "Right?"

"I'm fine." To comfort, she lifted a hand to his face. The face she loved, with its poet's mouth and gold-flecked eyes. "And I won't hold you to your promise never to touch me again. As it was given in the heat of the moment." With a laugh she nuzzled the baby. "Did you hear him, Maggie, when he shouted at the doctor? 'We've changed our minds,' he says. 'We're not having a baby after all. Get out of my way, I'm taking my wife home.' "

"Fine for you." Gray took another chance and skimmed a fingertip over the baby's head. "You didn't have to watch it all. This childbirth stuff's rough on a guy."

"And at the sticking point, we're the least appreciated," Rogan added. When Maggie snorted, Rogan held out a hand for her. "We've calls to make, Maggie."

"That we do. We'll look back in on you shortly."

When they were alone, Brianna beamed up at him. "We have a family, Grayson."

An hour later, Grayson was anxious and suspicious when a nurse took the baby away. "I should go keep an eye on her. I don't trust the look in that nurse's eyes."

"Don't be a worrier, Da."

"Da." Grinning from ear to ear, he looked back at his wife. "Is that what she's going to call me? It's easy. She can probably just about handle it already, don't you think?"

"Oh, I'm sure." Chuckling, Brianna cupped his face in her hands as he leaned over to kiss her. "She's bright as the sun, our Kayla."

"Kayla Thane." He tried it out, grinned again. "Kayla Margaret Thane, the first female President of the United States. We've already had a woman president in Ireland," he added. "But she can choose whichever she wants. You look beautiful, Brianna."

He kissed her again, surprised all at once that it was absolutely true. Her eyes were glowing, her rose-gold hair tumbled around it. Her face was still a bit pale, but he could see that the roses in them were beginning to bloom again.

"And you must be exhausted. I should let you sleep."

"Sleep." She rolled her eyes and pulled him down for another kiss.

"You must be joking. I don't think I could sleep for days, I've so much energy now. What I am is starved half to death. I'd give anything and more for an enormous bookmaker's sandwich and a pile of chips."

"You want to eat?" He blinked at her, astonished. "What a woman. Maybe after, you'd like to go out and plow a field."

"I believe I'll skip that," she said dryly. "But I haven't had a bite in more than twenty-four hours, I'll remind you. Do you think you could see if they could bring me a little something?"

"Hospital food, no way. Not for the mother of my child." What a kick that was, he realized. He'd hardly gotten used to saying "my wife"—now he was saying "my child." My daughter. "I'm going to go get you the best bookmaker's sandwich on the west coast of Ireland."

Brianna settled back with a laugh as he darted out of the room. What a year it had been, she thought. It had been hardly more than that since she'd met him, less since she'd loved him. And now they were a family.

Despite her claims to the contrary, her eyes grew heavy and she slipped easily into sleep.

When she awakened again, drifting hazily out of dreams, she saw Gray, sitting on the edge of her bed, watching her.

"She was sleeping, too," he began. And since he'd already taken her hand in his, he brought it to his lips. "They let me hold her again when I harassed them—said a few interesting things about the Yank, but were pretty indulgent all in all. She looked at me, Brie, she looked right at me. She knew who I was, and she curled her fingers—she's got gorgeous fingers—she curled them around mine and held on—"

He broke off, a look of sheer panic replacing the dazzled joy. "You're crying. Why are you crying? Something hurts. I'll get the doctor. I'll get somebody."

"No." Sniffling, she leaned forward to press her face to his shoulder. "Nothing hurts. It's only that I love you so much. Oh, you move me, Grayson. Looking at your face when you speak of her. It touches so deep."

"I didn't know it would be like this," he murmured, stroking her hair as he cuddled. "I didn't know it would be so big, so incredibly big. I'm going to be a good father."

He said it with such fervor, and such a sweet hint of fear, that she laughed. "I know."

How could he fail, he wondered, when she believed in him so completely? "I brought you a sandwich, and some stuff."

"Thanks." She sat back, sniffling again and wiping at her eyes. When the tears cleared, she blinked again, then wept again. "Oh, Grayson, what a wonderful fool you are."

He'd crammed the room with flowers, pots and vases and baskets of them, with balloons that crowded the ceiling with vivid color and cheerful shapes. A huge purple dog stood grinning at the foot of the bed.

"The dog's for Kayla," he told her, pulling out tissues from a box and stuffing them into her hand. "So don't get any ideas. Your sandwich is probably cold, and I ate some of the chips. But there's a piece of chocolate cake in it for you if you don't give me a hard time about it."

She brushed the fresh tears away. "I want the cake first."

"You got it."

"What's this, feasting already?" Maggie strolled in, a bouquet of daffodils in her arms. Her husband came in behind her, his face hidden behind a stuffed bear.

"Hello, Mum." Rogan Sweeney bent over the bed to kiss his sister-in-law, then winked at Gray. "Da."

"She was hungry," Gray said with a grin.

"And I'm too greedy to share my cake." Brianna forked up a mouthful of chocolate.

"We've just come from having another peek." Maggie plopped down on a chair. "And I can say, without prejudice, that she's the prettiest babe in the nursery. She has your hair, Brie, all rosy gold, and Gray's pretty mouth."

"Murphy sends his love and best wishes," Rogan put in, setting the bear beside the dog. "We called him just a bit ago to pass the news. He and Liam are celebrating with the tea cakes you finished making before you went into labor."

"It's sweet of him to mind Liam while you're here."

Maggie waved off Brianna's gratitude. "Sweet had nothing to do with it. Murphy'd keep the boy from dawn to dusk if I'd let him. They're having a grand time, and before you ask, things are fine at the inn. Mrs. O'Malley's seeing to your guests. Though why you'd accept bookings when you knew you'd be having a baby, I can't say."

"The same reason you kept working with your glass until we carted you off to have Liam, I imagine," Brianna said dryly. "It's how I make my living. Have Mother and Lottie gone home then?"

"A short time ago." For Brianna's sake, Maggie kept her smile in place. Their mother had been complaining, and worrying about what germs she might pick up in the hospital. That was nothing new. "They looked in and saw you were sleeping, so Lottie said she'd drive Mother back and they'd see you and Kayla tomorrow."

Maggie paused, glanced at Rogan. His imperceptible nod left the decision to share the rest of the news up to her. Because she understood her sister, and Brianna's needs, Maggie rose, sat on the side of the bed opposite Gray, and took Brianna's hand.

"It's as well she's gone. No, don't give me that look, I mean no harm in it. There's news to tell you that it isn't time for her to hear. Rogan's man, his detective, thinks he's found Amanda. Now wait, don't get too hopeful. We've been through this before."

"But this time it could be real."

Brianna closed her eyes a moment. More than a year before she'd found three letters written to her father by Amanda Dougherty. Love letters that had shocked and dismayed. And finding in them that there had been a child had begun a long and frustrating search for the woman her father had loved, and the child he'd never known.

"It could be." Not wanting to see his wife disappointed yet again, Gray spoke carefully. "Brie, you know how many dead ends we've run into since the birth certificate was found."

"We know we have a sister," Brianna said stubbornly. "We know her name, we know that Amanda married, and that they moved from place to place. It's the moving that's been the trouble. But sooner or later we'll find them." She gave Maggie's hand a squeeze. "It could be this time."

"Perhaps." Maggie had yet to resign herself to the possibility. Nor was she entirely sure she wanted to find the woman who was her half sister. "He's on his way to a place called Columbus, Ohio. One way or the other, we'll know something soon."

"Da would have wanted us to do this," Brianna said quietly. "He would have been happy to know we tried, at least, to find them."

With a nod, Maggie rose. "Well, we've started the ball on its roll, so we won't try to stop it." She only hoped no one was damaged by the tumble. "In the meantime, you should be celebrating your new family, not worrying over one that may or may not be found."

"You'll tell me, as soon as you know something," Brianna insisted.

"One way or the other, so don't fidget about it in the meantime." A glance around the room had Maggie smiling again. "Would you like if we took some of these flowers home for you, Brie, set them around so they'd be there when you bring the baby home?"

With some effort Brianna held back the rest of the questions circling in her head. There were no answers for them yet. "I'd be grateful. Gray got carried away."

"Anything else you'd like, Brianna?" With cheerful good humor, Rogan accepted the flowers his wife piled in his arms. "More cake?"

She glanced down, flushed. "I ate every crumb, didn't I? Thanks just the same, but I think that'll do. Go home, both of you, and get some sleep."

"So we will. I'll call," Maggie promised. The worry came back into her eyes as she left the room with Rogan. "I wish she wasn't so hopeful, and so sure that this long-lost sister of ours will want to be welcomed into her open arms."

"It's the way she's made, Maggie."

"Saint Brianna," Maggie said with a sigh. "I couldn't bear it if she was hurt because of this, Rogan. You've only to look at her to see how she's building it up in her head, in her heart. No matter how wrong it might be of me, I wish to God she'd never found those letters."

"Don't fret over it." Since Maggie was busy doing just that, Rogan used his elbow to press the elevator button.

"It's not my fretting that's the problem," Maggie muttered. "She shouldn't be worrying over this now. She has the baby to think of, and Gray may be going off in a few months on his book tour."

"I thought he'd canceled that." Rogan shifted tilting blooms back to safety.

"He wants to cancel it. She's badgering him to go, wants nothing to interfere with his work." Impatient, annoyed, she scowled at the elevator doors. "So damn sure she is that she can handle an infant, the inn, all those bleeding guests, and this Amanda Dougherty Bodine business as well."

"We both know that Brianna's strong enough to handle whatever happens. Just as you are."

Prepared to argue, she looked up. Rogan's amused smile smoothed away the temper. "You may be right." She sent him a saucy look. "For once." Soothed a little, she took some of the flowers from him. "And it's too wonderful a day to be worrying about something that may never happen. We've ourselves a beautiful niece, Sweeney."

"That we do. I think she might have your chin, Margaret Mary."

"I was thinking that as well." She stepped into the elevator with him. How simple it was really, she mused, to forget the pain and remember only the joy. "And I was thinking now that Liam's beginning to toddle about, we might start working on providing him with a sister, or a brother."

With a grin Rogan managed to kiss her through the daffodils. "I was thinking that as well."

THREE

I am the Resurrection and the Light.

Shannon knew the words, all the priest's words, were supposed to comfort, to ease, perhaps inspire. She heard them, on this perfect spring day beside her mother's grave. She'd heard them in the crowded, sun-washed church during the funeral Mass. All the words, familiar from her youth. And she had knelt and stood and sat, even responded as some part of her brain followed the rite.

But she felt neither comforted nor eased nor inspired.

The scene wasn't dreamlike, but all too real. The black-garbed priest with his beautiful baritone, the dozens and dozens of mourners, the brilliant stream of sunlight that glinted off the brass handles of the coffin that was cloaked in flowers. The sound of weeping, the chirp of birds.

She was burying her mother.

Beside the fresh grave was the neatly tended mound of another, and the headstone, still brutally new, of the man she had believed all of her life to be her father.

She was supposed to cry. But she'd already wept.

She was supposed to pray. But the prayers wouldn't come.

Standing there, with the priest's voice ringing in the clear spring air, Shannon could only see herself again, walking into the parlor, the anger still hot inside her.

She'd thought her mother had been sleeping. But there had been too many questions, too many demands racing in her head to wait, and she'd decided to wake her.

Gently, she remembered. Thank God she had at least been gentle. But her mother hadn't awakened, hadn't stirred.

The rest had been panic. Not so gentle now—the shaking, the shouting, the pleading. And the few minutes of blankness, blessedly brief, that she knew now had been helpless hysteria.

There'd been the frantic call for an ambulance, the endless, terrifying ride to the hospital. And the wait, always the wait.

Now the waiting was over. Amanda had slipped into a coma, and from a coma into death.

And from death, so said the priest, into eternal life.

They told her it was a blessing. The doctor had said so, and the nurses who had been unfailingly kind. The friends and neighbors who had called had all said it was a blessing. There had been no pain, no suffering in those last forty-eight hours. She had simply slept while her body and brain had shut down.

Only the living suffered, Shannon thought now. Only they were riddled with guilt and regrets and unanswered questions.

"She's with Colin now," someone murmured.

Shannon blinked herself back, and saw that it was done. People were already turning toward her. She would have to accept their sympathies, their comforts, their own sorrows, as she had at the funeral parlor viewing.

Many would come back to the house, of course. She had prepared for that, had handled all the details. After all, she thought as she mechanically accepted and responded to those who walked to her, details were what she did best.

The funeral arrangements had been handled neatly and without fuss. Her mother would have wanted the simple, she knew, and Shannon had done her best to accommodate Amanda on this last duty. The simple coffin, the right flowers and music, the solemn Catholic ceremony.

And the food, of course. It seemed faintly awful to have such a thing catered, but she simply hadn't had the time or the energy to prepare a meal for the friends and neighbors who would come to the house from the cemetery.

Then, at last, she was alone. For a moment she simply couldn't think—what did she want? What was right? Still the tears and the prayers wouldn't come. Tentatively Shannon laid a hand on the coffin, but there was only the sensation of wood warmed by the sun, and the overly heady scent of roses.

"I'm sorry," she murmured. "It shouldn't have been like that between us at the end. But I don't know how to resolve it, or to change it. And I don't know how to say good-bye, to either of you now."

She stared down at the headstone to her left.

COLIN ALAN BODINE

BELOVED HUSBAND AND FATHER

Even those last words, she thought miserably, carved into granite were a lie. And her only wish, as she stood over the graves of two people she had loved all of her life, was that she had never learned the truth.

And that stubborn, selfish wish was the guilt she would live with.

Turning away, she walked alone toward the waiting car.

It seemed like hours before the crowd began to thin and the house grew quiet again. Amanda had been well loved, and those who had loved her had gathered together in her home. Shannon said her last good-bye, her last thanks, accepted her last sympathy, then finally, finally, closed the door and was alone.

Fatigue began to drag at Shannon as she wandered into her father's office.

Amanda had changed little here in the eleven months since her husband's sudden death. The big old desk was no longer cluttered, but she had yet to dispose of his computer, the modem, the fax and other equipment he'd used as a broker and financial adviser. His toys, he'd called them, and his wife had kept them even when she'd been able to give away his suits, his shoes, his foolish ties.

All the books remained on the shelves—tax planning, estate planning, accounting texts.

Weary, Shannon sat in the big leather chair she'd given him herself for Father's Day five years before. He'd loved it, she remembered, running a hand over the smooth burgundy leather. Big enough to hold a horse, he'd said, and had laughed and pulled her into his lap.

She wished she could convince herself that she still felt him here. But she didn't. She felt nothing. And that told her more than the requiem Mass, more than the cemetery, that she was alone. Really alone.

There hadn't been enough time for anything, Shannon thought dully. If she'd known before . . . She wasn't sure which she meant, her mother's illness or the lies. If she'd known, she thought again, training her mind on the illness. They might have tried other things, the alternative medicines, the vitamin concentrates, all the small and simple hopes she'd read of in the books on homeopathic medicine she'd collected. There hadn't been time to give them a chance to work.

There had been only a few weeks. Her mother had kept her illness from her, as she'd kept other things.

She hadn't shared them, Shannon thought as bitterness warred with grief. Not with her own daughter.

So, the very last words she had spoken to her mother had been in anger and contempt. And she could never take them back.

Fists clenched against an enemy she couldn't see, she rose, turned away from the desk. She'd needed time, damn it. She'd needed time to try to understand, or at least learn to live with it.

Now the tears came, hot and helpless. Because she knew, in her heart, that she wished her mother had died before she'd told her. And she hated herself for it.

After the tears drained out of her, she knew she had to sleep. Mechanically she climbed the stairs, washed her hot cheeks with cool water, and lay, fully clothed, on the bed.

She'd have to sell the house, she thought. And the furniture. There were papers to go through.

She hadn't told her mother she loved her.

With that weighing on her heart, she fell into an exhausted sleep.

Afternoon naps always left Shannon groggy. She took them only when ill, and she was rarely ill. The house was quiet when she climbed out of bed again. A glance at the clock told her she'd slept less than an hour, but she was stiff and muddled despite the brevity.

She would make coffee, she told herself, and then she would sit down and plan how best to handle all of her mother's things, and the house she'd loved.

The doorbell rang before she'd reached the base of the stairs. She could only pray it wasn't some well-meaning neighbor come to offer help or company. She wanted neither at the moment.

But it was a stranger at the door. The man was of medium height, with a slight pouch showing under his dark suit. His hair was graying, his eyes sharp. She had an odd and uncomfortable sensation when those eyes stayed focused on her face.

"I'm looking for Amanda Dougherty Bodine."

"This is the Bodine residence," Shannon returned, trying to peg him. Salesman? She didn't think so. "I'm her daughter. What is it you want?"

Nothing changed on his face, but Shannon sensed his attention sharpening. "A few minutes of Mrs. Bodine's time, if it's convenient. I'm John Hobbs."

"I'm sorry, Mr. Hobbs, it's not convenient. I buried my mother this morning, so if you'll excuse me—"

"I'm sorry." His hand went to the door, holding it open when Shannon would have closed it. "I've just arrived in town from New York. I hadn't heard about your mother's death." Hobbs had to rethink and regroup quickly. He'd gotten too close to simply walk away now. "Are you Shannon Bodine?"

"That's right. Just what do you want, Mr. Hobbs?"

"Your time," he said pleasantly enough, "when it's more convenient for you. I'd like to make an appointment to meet with you in a few days."

Shannon pushed back the hair tumbled from her nap. "I'll be going back to New York in a few days."

"I'll be happy to meet with you there."

Her eyes narrowed as she tried to shake off the disorientation from her nap. "Did my mother know you, Mr. Hobbs?"

"No, she didn't, Ms. Bodine."

"Then I don't think we have anything to discuss. Now please, excuse me."

"I have information which I have been authorized, by my clients, to discuss with Mrs. Amanda Dougherty Bodine." Hobbs simply kept his hand on the door, taking Shannon's measure as he held it open.

"Clients?" Despite herself, Shannon was intrigued. "Does this concern my father?"

Hobbs's hesitation was brief, but she caught it. And her heart began to drum. "It concerns your family, yes. If we could make an appointment to meet, I'll inform my clients of Mrs. Bodine's death."

"Who are your clients, Mr. Hobbs? No, don't tell me it's confidential," she snapped. "You come to my door on the day of my mother's funeral looking for her to discuss something that concerns my family. I'm my only family now, Mr. Hobbs, so your information obviously concerns me. Who are your clients?"

"I need to make a phone call—from my car. Would you mind waiting a few moments?"

"All right," she agreed, more on impulse than with a sense of patience. "I'll wait."

But she closed the door when he walked toward the dark sedan at the curb. She had a feeling she was going to need that coffee.

It didn't take him long. The bell rang again when she was taking her first sip. Carrying the mug with her, she went back to answer.

"Ms. Bodine, my client has authorized me to handle this matter at my own discretion." Reaching into his pocket, he took out a business card, offered it.

"Doubleday Investigations," she read. "New York." Shannon lifted a brow. "You're a long way from home, Mr. Hobbs."

"My business keeps me on the road quite a bit. This particular case has kept me there. I'd like to come in, Ms. Bodine. Or if you'd be more comfortable, I could meet you wherever you like."

She had an urge to close the door in his face. Not that she was afraid of him physically. The cowardice came from something deeper, and because she recognized it, she ignored it.

"Come in. I've just made coffee."

"I appreciate it." As was his habit, long ingrained, Hobbs scanned the house as he followed Shannon, took in the subtle wealth, the quiet good taste. Everything he'd learned about the Bodines in the last few months was reflected in the house. They were—had been—a nice, closely knit upper-income family without pretensions.

"This is a difficult time for you, Ms. Bodine," Hobbs began when he took the chair at the table Shannon gestured toward. "I hope I won't add to it."

"My mother died two days ago, Mr. Hobbs. I don't think you can make it more difficult than it already is. Cream, sugar?"

"Just black, thanks." He studied her as she prepared his coffee. Self-possessed, he mused. That would make his job easier. "Was your mother ill, Ms. Bodine?"

"It was cancer," she said shortly.

No sympathy wanted, he judged, and offered none. "I represent Rogan Sweeney," Hobbs began, "his wife and her family."

"Rogan Sweeney?" Cautious, Shannon joined him at the table. "I know the name, of course. Worldwide Galleries has a branch in New York. They're based in . . ." She trailed off, setting down her mug before her hands could shake. Ireland, she thought. In Ireland.

"You know, then." Hobbs read the knowledge in her eyes. That, too, would make his job easier. "My clients were concerned that the circumstances might be unknown to you."

Determined not to falter, Shannon lifted her cup again. "What does Rogan Sweeney have to do with me?"

"Mr. Sweeney is married to Margaret Mary Concannon, the oldest daughter of the late Thomas Concannon, of Clare County, Ireland."

"Concannon." Shannon closed her eyes until the need to shudder had passed. "I see." When she opened her eyes again, they were bitterly amused. "I assume they hired you to find me. I find it odd that there would be an interest after all these years."

"I was hired, initially, to find your mother, Ms. Bodine. I can tell you that my clients only learned of her, and your existence, last year. The investigation was initiated at that time. However, there was some difficulty in locating Amanda Dougherty. As you may know, she left her home in New York suddenly and without giving her family indication of her destination."

"I suppose she might not have known it, as she'd been tossed out of the house for being pregnant." Pushing her coffee aside, Shannon folded her hands. "What do your clients want?"

"The primary goal was to contact your mother, and to let her know that Mr. Concannon's surviving children had discovered letters she had written to him, and with her permission, to make contact with you."

"Surviving children. He's dead then." She rubbed a hand to her temple. "Yes, you told me that already. He's dead. So are they all. Well, you found me, Mr. Hobbs, so your job's done. You can inform your clients that I've been contacted and have no interest in anything further."

"Your sisters—"

Her eyes went cold. "I don't consider them my sisters."

Hobbs merely inclined his head. "Mrs. Sweeney and Mrs. Thane may wish to contact you personally."

"I can't stop them, can I? But you can forward the fact that I'm not interested in reunions with women I don't know. What happened between their father and my mother some twenty-eight years ago doesn't change the status quo. So—" She broke off, eyes sharpening again. "Margaret Mary Concannon, you said? The artist?"

"Yes, she is known for her glass work."

"That's an understatement," Shannon murmured. She'd been to one of M. M. Concannon's showings at Worldwide New York herself. And had been considering investing in a piece. The idea was almost laughable. "Well, that's amusing, isn't it? You can tell Margaret Mary Concannon and her sister—"

"Brianna. Brianna Concannon Thane. She runs a B-and-B in Clare. You may have heard of her husband as well. He's a successful mystery writer."

"Grayson Thane?" At Hobbs's nod, Shannon did nearly laugh. "They married well, it seems. Good for them. Tell them they can get on with their lives, as I intend to do." She rose. "If there's nothing else, Mr. Hobbs?"

"I'm to ask if you'd like to have your mother's letters, and if so, if you would object to my clients making copies for themselves."

"I don't want them. I don't want anything." She bit back on a sudden spurt of venom, letting out a sigh as it drained. "What happened is no more their fault than mine. I don't know how they feel about all of this, Mr. Hobbs, and don't care to. If it's curiosity, misplaced guilt, a sense of family obligation, you can tell them to let it go."

Hobbs rose as well. "From the time, effort, and money they've spent trying to find you, I'd say it was a combination of all three. And perhaps more. But I'll tell them." He offered a hand, surprising Shannon into taking it. "If you have second thoughts, or any questions come to mind, you can reach me at the number on the card. I'll be flying back to New York tonight."

His cool tone stung. She couldn't say why. "I have a right to my privacy."

"You do." He nodded. "I'll see myself out, Ms. Bodine. Thanks for the time, and the coffee."

Damn him, was all she could think as he walked calmly out of her kitchen. Damn him for being so dispassionate, so subtly judgmental.

And damn them. Damn Thomas Concannon's daughters for searching her out, asking her to satisfy their curiosity. Offering to satisfy her own.

She didn't want them. Didn't need them. Let them stay in Ireland with their cozy lives and brilliant husbands. She had her own life, and the pieces of it needed to be picked up quickly.

Wiping at tears she hadn't realized were falling, she stalked over and snatched up the phone book. She flipped through quickly, ran her finger down the page, then dialed.

"Yes, I have a house I need to sell. Immediately."

A week later Shannon was back in New York. She'd priced the house to sell, and hoped it would do so quickly. The money certainly didn't matter. She'd discovered she was a rich woman. Death had given her nearly a half a million dollars in the investments her father had made over the years. Added to her earlier inheritance, she would never have to worry about something as trivial as money again.

She'd only had to become an orphan to earn it.

Still, she was enough Colin Bodine's daughter to know the house had to be sold, and that it would bring in considerable equity. Some of the furnishings she hadn't had the heart to sell or give away were in storage. Surely she could wait a little longer before deciding what to do with every vase and lamp.

Shannon had boxed only a few sentimental favorites to bring back with her to New York. Among them were all of the paintings she'd done for her parents over the years.

Those, she couldn't part with.

Though her supervisor had offered her the rest of the week off, she'd come back to work the day after returning from Columbus. She'd been certain it would help, that work was the answer she needed.

The new account needed to be dealt with. She'd hardly begun to work on it when she'd been called away. She'd barely had two weeks to become used to her promotion, the new responsibilities and position.

She'd worked most of her adult life for that position, for those responsibilities. She was moving up the ladder now, at the brisk and steady pace she'd planned for herself. The corner office was hers, her week-at-a-glance was tidily filled with meetings and presentations. The CEO himself knew her name, respected her work, and, she knew, had an eye on her for bigger things.

It was everything she'd always wanted, needed, planned for.

How could she have known that nothing in her office seemed to matter. Nothing about it mattered in the least.

Not her drafting table, her tools. Not the major account she'd snagged on the very day she'd received the call from Columbus, and had been forced to turn over to an associate. It simply didn't matter. The promotion she'd broken her back to secure seemed so removed from her just then. Just as the life she'd led, with all its tidiness and careful planning, seemed to have belonged to someone else all along.

She found herself staring at the painting of her father sleeping in the garden. It was still propped against the wall rather than hung. For reasons she couldn't understand, she simply didn't want it in her office after all.

"Shannon?" The woman who poked her head in the door was attractive, dressed impeccably. Lily was her assistant, a casual friend among what Shannon was beginning to realize was a lifetime of casual friends. "I thought you might want a break."

"I haven't been doing anything I need a break from."

"Hey." Lily stepped in, crossing over to her desk to give Shannon's shoulders a brisk rub. "Give yourself a little time. You've only been back a few days."

"I shouldn't have bothered." In an irritable move she pushed back from the desk. "I'm not producing anything."

"You're going through a rough patch."

"Yeah."

"Why don't I cancel your afternoon meetings?"

"I have to get back to work sometime." She stared out the window, at the view of New York she'd dreamed would one day be hers. "But cancel the lunch with Tod. I'm not in the mood to be social."

Lily pursed her lips and made a note of it. "Trouble in paradise?"

"Let's just say I'm thinking that relationship isn't productive, either—and there's too much backlog for lunch dates."

"Your call."

"Yes, it is." Shannon turned back. "I haven't really thanked you for handling so much of my work while I was gone. I've looked some things over and wanted to tell you that you did a terrific job."

"That's what they pay me for." Lily flipped a page in her book. "The Mincko job needs some finishing touches, and nothing's satisfied the suits at Rightway. Tilghmanton thinks you can. He sent down a memo this morning asking you to look over the drafts and come up with something new—by the end of the week."

"Good." She nodded and pushed up to her desk again. "A challenge like that might be just what I need. Let's see Rightway first, Lily. You can fill me in on Mincko later."

"You got it." Lily headed for the door. "Oh, I should tell you. Rightway wants something traditional, but different, subtle, but bold, sexy but restrained."

"Of course they do. I'll get my magic wand out of my briefcase."

"Good to have you back, Shannon."

When the door closed, Shannon let out a deep breath. It was good to be back, wasn't it.

It had to be.

Rain was pelting the streets. After a miserable ten-hour day that had concluded in a showdown with a man she'd tried to convince herself she'd been in love with, Shannon watched it from the cab window on the way back to her apartment.

Maybe she'd been right to go back to work so quickly. The routine, the demands and concentration had helped shake some of the grief. At least temporarily. She needed routine, she reminded herself. She needed the outrageous schedule that had earned her her position at Ry-Tilghmanton.

Her job, the career she'd carved out, was all she had now. There wasn't even the illusion of a satisfying relationship to fill a corner of her life.

But she'd been right to break things off with Tod. They'd been no more than attractive props for each other. And life, she'd just discovered, was too short for foolish choices.

She paid off the cab at the corner, dashed toward her building with a quick smile for the doorman. Out of habit she picked up her mail, flipping through the envelopes as she rode the elevator to her floor.

The one from Ireland stopped her cold.

On an oath she shoved it to the bottom, unlocking her door, tossing all the mail on a table. Though her heart was thudding, she followed ingrained habit. She hung her coat, slipped out of her shoes, poured herself her usual glass of wine. When she was seated at the little table by the window that looked out over Madison Avenue, she settled down to read her mail.

It took only moments before she gave in and tore open the letter from Brianna Concannon Thane.

Dear Shannon,

I'm so terribly sorry about your mother's death. You'll be grieving still, and I doubt if any words I have will ease your heart. From the letters she wrote to my father, I know she was a loving and special woman, and I'm sorry I never had the chance to meet her, and tell her for myself.

You've met with Rogan's man, Mr. Hobbs. From his report I understand that you were aware of the relationship between your mother and my father. I think this might cause you some hurt, and I'm sorry for it. I also think you may not appreciate hearing from me. But I had to write to you, at least once.

Your father, your mother's husband, surely loved you very much. I don't wish to interfere with those emotions or those memories, which I'm sure are precious to you. I wish only to offer you a chance to know this other part of your family, and your heritage. My father was not a simple man, but he was a good one, and never did he forget your mother. I found her letters to him long after his death, still wrapped in the ribbon he'd tied around them.

I'd like to share him with you, or if that isn't what you want, to offer you a chance to see the Ireland where you were conceived. If you could find it in your heart, I would very much like you to come and stay with me and mine awhile. If nothing else, the countryside here is a good place for easing grief.

You owe me nothing, Shannon. And perhaps you think I owe you nothing as well. But if you loved your mother, as I did my father, you know we owe them. Perhaps by becoming friends, if not sisters, we'll have given them back something of what they gave up for us.

The invitation is open. If ever you wish to come, you'll be welcome.

Yours truly,
Brianna

Shannon read it twice. Then, when she had tossed it aside, picked it up and read it again. Was the woman really so simple, so unselfish, so willing to open heart and home?

She didn't want Brianna's heart, or her home, Shannon told herself.

And yet. And yet . . . Was she going to deny even to herself that she'd been considering just this? A trip to Ireland. A look into the past. She toyed with the idea of going over without contacting any of the Concannons.

Because she was afraid? she wondered. Yes, maybe, because she was afraid. But also because she didn't want any pressure, any questions, any demands.

The woman who had written the letter had promised none of those. And had offered a great deal more.

Maybe I'll take her up on it, Shannon thought.

And maybe I won't.

FOUR

"I don't know why you're fussing so much," Maggie complained. "You'd think you were preparing for royalty."

"I want her to be comfortable." Brianna centered the vase of tulips on the dresser, changed her mind, and took it to the flute-edged table by the window. "She's coming all this way to meet us. I want her to feel at home."

"As far as I can see, you've cleaned the place from top to bottom twice, brought in enough flowers for five weddings, and baked so many cakes and tarts it would take an army to eat them all." As she spoke, Maggie walked over, twitching the lace curtain aside and staring out over the hills. "You're setting yourself up for a disappointment, Brie."

"And you're determined to get no pleasure out of her coming."

"Her letter accepting your invitation wasn't filled with excitement and pleasure, was it now?"

Brianna stopped fluffing bed pillows she'd already fluffed and studied her sister's rigid back. "She's the odd one out, Maggie. We've always had each other, and will still when she's gone again. Added to that she lost her mother not a month ago. I wouldn't have expected some flowery response. I'm happy enough she's decided to come at all."

"She told Rogan's man she didn't want anything to do with us."

"Ah, and you've never in your life said something you reconsidered later."

That brought a smile tugging at Maggie's lips. "Not that I can recall, at the moment." When she turned back, the smile remained. "How much time do we have before we pick her up at the airport?"

"A bit. I need to nurse Kayla first, and I want to change." She blew out a breath at Maggie's expression. "I'm not going to meet the sister I've not yet set eyes on in my apron and dusty pants."

"Well, I'm not changing." Maggie shrugged her shoulders inside the oversized cotton shirt she'd tucked into old jeans.

"Suit yourself," Brianna said lightly as she started out of the room. "But you might want to comb that rat's nest on your head."

Though Maggie curled her lip, she took a glance at herself in the mirror above the dresser. An apt description, she thought with some amusement as she noted her bright red curls were snarled and tousled.

"I've been working," she called out, quickening her pace to catch up with Brianna at the bottom of the steps. "My pipes don't care if my hair's tidy or not. It's not like I have to see people day and night like you do."

"And it's grateful those people are that you don't. Fix yourself a bit of a sandwich or something, Margaret Mary," she added as she breezed into the kitchen. "You're looking peaked."

"I am not." Grumbling but hungry, Maggie headed for the bread drawer. "I'm looking pregnant."

Brianna froze in midstride. "What? Oh, Maggie."

"And it's your fault if I am," Maggie muttered, brows knitted as she sliced through the fresh brown bread.

Laughing, Brianna swung over to give her sister a hard hug. "Well, now, that's an intriguing statement, and one I'm sure medical authorities worldwide would be interested in."

Maggie tilted her head, and there was humor in her eyes. "Who just had a baby, I ask you? And who had me holding that beautiful little girl barely minutes after she was born so that I went a bit crazy in the head?"

"You're not upset, really, that you might be having another baby?" Brianna stepped back, worrying her lip. "Rogan's pleased, isn't he?"

"I haven't told him yet. I'm a ways from being sure. But I feel it." Instinctively she pressed a hand to her stomach. "And no, I'm not upset, I'm only teasing you. I'm hoping." She gave Brianna a quick pat on the cheek and went back to her sandwich building. "I was queasy this morning."

"Oh." Tears sprang to Brianna's eyes. "That's wonderful."

With a grunt Maggie went to the refrigerator. "I'm just loony enough to agree with you. Don't say anything yet, even to Gray, until I'm sure of it."

"I won't—if you'll have that sandwich sitting down and drink some tea with it."

"Not a bad deal. Go on, feed my niece, change your clothes, or we'll be late to the airport picking up the queen."

Brianna started to snap back, drew a deep breath instead, and slipped through the door that adjoined her rooms with the kitchen.

Those rooms had been expanded since her marriage the year before. The second floor of the main house, and the converted attic, were for the guests who came and went in Blackthorn Cottage. But here, off the kitchen, was for family.

The little parlor and bedroom had been enough when it had only been Brianna. Now a second bedroom, a bright, sunwashed nursery had been added on, with its wide double windows facing the hills and overlooking the young flowering almond Murphy had planted for her on the day Kayla was born.

Above the crib, catching pretty glints of sunlight, was the mobile, the glass menagerie Maggie had made, with its unicorns and winged horses and mermaids. Beneath the dance, staring up at the lights and movements, the baby stirred.

"There's my love," Brianna murmured. And the rush still came, the flood of emotions and wonder. Her child. At last, her child. "Are you watching the lights, darling? So pretty they are, and so clever is your aunt Maggie."

She gathered Kayla up, drawing in the scent, absorbing the feel of baby. "You're going to meet another aunt today. Your aunt Shannon from America. Won't that be grand?"

With the baby curled in one arm, Brianna unbuttoned her blouse as she settled in the rocker. She glanced once at the ceiling, smiling, knowing Gray was above in his studio. Writing, she thought, of murder and mayhem.

"There you are," she cooed, thrilling as Kayla's mouth rooted, then suckled at her breast. "And when you're all fed and changed, you'll be good for your da while I'm gone, just a little while. You've grown so already. It's only a month, you know. A month today."

Gray watched them from the doorway, overwhelmed and humbled. No one could have told him, no one could have explained how it would feel to see his wife, his child. To have a wife and child. Kayla's fist rested on the curve of her mother's breast, ivory against ivory. The sun played gently on their hair, nearly identical shade for shade. They watched each other, linked in a way he could only imagine.

Then Brianna glanced up, smiled. "I thought you were working."

"I heard you on the intercom." He gestured to the small monitor. He'd insisted they put them throughout the house. He crossed to them, crouched beside the rocker. "My ladies are so beautiful."

With a light laugh Brianna leaned forward. "Kiss me, Grayson."

He did, lingering over it, then shifted to brush his lips over Kayla's head. "She's hungry."

"Has her father's appetite." Which turned her thoughts to more practical matters. "I left you some cold meat, and the bread's fresh this morning. If there's time, I'll fix you something before I go."

"Don't worry about it. And if any of the guests come back from their ramblings before you do, I'll put out the scones and make tea."

"You're becoming a fine hotelier, Grayson. Still, I don't want you to interrupt your work."

"The work's going fine."

"I can tell that. You're not scowling, and I haven't heard you pacing the floor upstairs for days."

"There's a murder-suicide," he said with a wink. "Or what appears to be. It's cheered me up." Idly he traced a finger over her breast, just above his daughter's head. Since his eyes were on Brianna's he had the satisfaction of seeing the quick jolt of pleasure reflected in her eyes. "When I make love with you again, Brianna, it's going to be like the first time."

She let out an unsteady breath. "I don't think it's fair to seduce me when I'm nursing our daughter."

"It's fair to seduce you anytime." He held up his hand, letting the sunlight glint off the gold of his wedding ring. "We're married."

"Put your glands on hold, Grayson Thane," Maggie called out from the next room. "We've less than twenty minutes before we have to leave for the airport."

"Spoilsport," he muttered, but grinned as he rose. "I suppose I'll have two of your sisters hounding me now."

But Gray was the last thing on Shannon's mind. She could see Ireland below from the window of the plane, the green of its fields, the black of its cliffs. It was beautiful, awesomely so, and oddly familiar.

She was already wishing she hadn't come.

No turning back, she reminded herself. Foolish to even consider it. It might have been true that she'd made the decision to come on impulse, influenced by the drag of her own guilt and grief, and the simple understanding in Brianna's letter. But she'd followed the impulse through, taking a leave of absence from her job, closing up her apartment, and boarding a plane for a three-thousand mile journey that was minutes away from being complete.

She'd stopped asking herself what she expected to find, or what she wanted to accomplish. She didn't have the answers. All she knew was that she'd needed to come. To see, perhaps, what her mother had once seen. The doubts plagued her—worry that she was being disloyal to the only father she'd ever known, fears that she would suddenly find herself surrounded by relatives she had no desire to acknowledge.

With a shake of her head, she took her compact from her purse. She'd been clear enough in her letter, Shannon reminded herself as she tried to freshen her makeup. She'd edited and revised the text three times before she'd been satisfied enough to mail a response to Brianna. It had been polite, slightly cool, and unemotional.

And that was exactly how she intended to go on.

She tried not to wince when the wheels touched down. There was still time, she assured herself, to work on her composure. Years of traveling with her parents had made her familiar with the routine of disembarking, customs, passports. She moved through it on automatic while she calmed her mind.

Confident now, assured that she once again felt slightly aloof to the circumstances, she joined the crowd moving toward the main terminal.

She didn't expect the jolt of recognition. The absolute certainty that the two women waiting with all the others were the Concannons. She could have told herself it was the coloring, the clear creamy skin, the green eyes, the red hair. They shared some features, though the taller of the two had a softer look, and her hair was more gold while the other was pure flame.

But it wasn't the coloring, or the family resemblance that had her zeroing in on only two when there were so many people weeping and laughing and hurrying to embrace. It was a deep visceral knowledge that was surprisingly painful.

She had only an instant to sum them up, the taller, neat as a pin in a simple blue dress, the other oddly chic in a baggy shirt and tattered jeans. And she saw her recognition returned, with a glowing smile by one, a cool, measured stare by the other.

"Shannon. Shannon Bodine." Without hesitation or plan, Brianna hurried forward and kissed Shannon lightly on the cheek. "Welcome to Ireland. I'm Brianna."

"How do you do?" Shannon was grateful her hands were gripped on the luggage cart. But Brianna was already neatly brushing her aside to take the cart herself.

"This is Maggie. We're so glad you've come."

"You'll want to get out of the crowd, I imagine." Reserving judgment on the aloof woman in the expensive slacks and jacket, Maggie inclined her head. "It's a long trip across the water."

"I'm used to traveling."

"It's always exciting, isn't it?" Though her nerves were jumping, Brianna talked easily as she pushed the cart. "Maggie's done a great deal more than I have of seeing places. Every time I get on a plane I feel as though I'm someone else. Was it a pleasant trip for you?"

"It was quiet."

A little desperate now as it seemed she would never draw more than one short declarative sentence from Shannon at a time, Brianna began to talk of the weather—it was fine—and the length of the trip to the cottage—mercifully short. On either side of her Shannon and Maggie eyed each other with mutual distrust.

"We'll have a meal for you," Brianna went on as they loaded Shannon's luggage in the car. "Or you can rest a bit first if you're tired."

"I don't want to put you to any trouble," Shannon said, so definitely that Maggie snorted.

"Going to trouble is what Brie does best. You'll take the front," she added coolly. "As the guest."

Quite the bitch, Shannon decided, and jerked up her chin, much as Maggie had a habit of doing, as she slid into the passenger seat.

Brianna set her teeth. She was used, much too used to family discord. But it still hurt. "You've never been to Ireland, then, Shannon?"

"No." Because the word had been curt, and made her feel as bitchy as she'd concluded Maggie was, she deliberately relaxed her shoulders. "What I saw from the air was lovely."

"My husband's traveled everywhere, but he says this spot is the loveliest he's seen." Brianna tossed a smile at Shannon while she negotiated her way out of the airport. "But it's his home now, and he's prejudiced."

"You're married to Grayson Thane."

"Aye. For a year come the end of June. He came to Ireland, to Clare, to research a book. It'll be out soon. Of course, he's working on another now, and having a fine time murdering people right and left."

"I like his books." A safe topic, Shannon decided. A simple one. "My father was a big fan."

And that brought a moment of thick, uncomfortable silence.

"It was hard for you," Brianna said carefully. "Losing both your parents so close together. I hope your time here will help ease your heart a little."

"Thank you." Shannon turned her head and watched the scenery. And it was lovely, there was no denying it. Just as there was no denying there was something special in the way the sun slanted through the clouds and gilded the air.

"Rogan's man said you're a commercial artist," Maggie began, more from curiosity than manners.

"That's right."

"So what you do is sell things, market them."

Shannon's brow lifted. She recognized disdain when she heard it, however light it was. "In a manner of speaking." Deliberately she turned, leveled her gaze on Maggie's. "You sell . . . things. Market them."

"No." Maggie's smile was bland. "I create them. Someone else has the selling of them."

"It's interesting, don't you think," Brianna put in quickly, "that both of you are artists?"

"Odd more like," Maggie muttered, and shrugged when Brianna aimed a warning glance in the rearview mirror.

Shannon merely folded her hands. She, at least, had been raised with manners. "How close is your home to a town, Brianna? I thought I would rent a car."

"We're a bit of a way from the village. You won't find a car to let there. But you're welcome to the use of this one when you like."

"I don't want to take your car."

"It sits idle more often than not. And Gray has one as well, so . . . You'll want to do some sightseeing, I imagine. One of us will be happy to guide you about if you like. Sometimes people just like to wander on their own. This is our village," she added.

It was no more than that, Shannon mused, more than a little downcast. A tiny place with narrowing sloping streets and shops and houses nestled. Charming, certainly, and quaint. And, she thought with an inner sigh, inconvenient. No theater, no galleries, no fast food. No crowds.

A man glanced up at the sound of the car, grinned around the cigarette clinging to his bottom lip and lifted a hand in a wave as he continued to walk.

Brianna waved in return, and called out the open window. "Good day to you, Matthew Feeney."

"Don't stop, for Christ's sake, Brie," Maggie ordered even as she waved herself. "He'll talk from now till next week if you do."

"I'm not after stopping. Shannon wants a rest, not village gossip. Still, I wonder if his sister Colleen is going to marry that Brit salesman."

"Better had from what I've heard," Maggie said, scooting up to rest her hands on the back of the front seat. "For he's sold her something already she'll be paying for in nine months time."

"Colleen's carrying?"

"The Brit planted one in her belly, and now her father's got one hand around his throat and the other seeing the banns are read. I got the whole of it from Murphy a night or two ago in the pub."

Despite herself, Shannon felt her interest snagged. "Are you telling me they'll force the man to marry her?"

"Oh, *force* is a hard word," Maggie said with her tongue in her cheek. "*Encourage* is better. *Firmly encourage,* pointing out the very reasonable choices between marriage vows and a broken face."

"It's an archaic solution, don't you think? After all, the woman had as much to do with it as the man."

"And she'll be stuck with him just as he's stuck with her. And the best of it they're bound to make."

"Until they have six more children and divorce," Shannon said shortly.

"Well, we all take our chances on such matters, don't we." Maggie settled back again. "And we Irish pride ourselves on taking more of them, and bigger ones than most."

Didn't they just? Shannon thought as she lifted her chin again. With their IRA and lack of birth control, alcoholism and no-way-out marriages.

Thank God she was just a tourist.

Her heart gave a quick lurch as the road narrowed. The winding needle threaded through a thick tunnel of hedge planted so close to the edge of the road the car brushed vegetation from time to time. Occasionally there was an opening in the wall of green, where a tiny house or shed could be viewed.

Shannon tried not to think just what might happen if another car came by.

Then Brianna made a turn, and the world opened.

Without being aware of it, Shannon leaned forward, her eyes wide, her lips parted in surprised delight.

The valley was a painting. For surely it couldn't be real. Roll after green roll of hill unfolded before her, bisected here and there by rock walls, sliced by a patch of brown turned earth, a sudden colorful spread that was meadows of wildflowers.

Toy houses and barns had been placed in perfect spots, with dots of grazing cattle meandering, clothes waving cheerfully on lines.

Castle ruins, tumbling stones, and a sheer, high wall, stood in a field as if that spot were locked in a time warp.

The sun struck it all like gold, and glinted off a thin ribbon of silver river.

And all of it, every blade of grass was cupped under a sky so achingly blue it seemed to pulse.

For the first time in days she forgot grief, and guilt and worry. She could only stare with a smile blooming on her face, and the oddest feeling in her heart that she had known this, just exactly this, would be there all along.

"It is beautiful, isn't it?" Brianna murmured and slowed the car to give Shannon another moment to enjoy.

"Yes. I've never seen anything more beautiful. I can see why my mother loved it."

And that thought brought the grief stabbing back, so that she turned her gaze away again.

But the new view was no less charming. Blackthorn Cottage waited to welcome, windows glinting, stone flecked with mica that sparkled. A glory of a garden spread beyond the hedges that were waiting to burst into a bloom of their own.

A dog barked in greeting as soon as Brianna pulled up behind a spiffy Mercedes convertible.

"That'll be Concobar, my dog," she explained and laughed when Shannon's eyes widened as Con raced around the side of the house. "He's big, is Con, but he's harmless. You haven't a fear of dogs, have you?"

"Not normally."

"Sit now," Brianna ordered when she stepped out of the car. "And show your manners."

The dog obeyed instantly, his thick gray tail pounding the ground to show his pleasure and his control. He looked over at Shannon as she cautiously alighted, then he lifted a paw.

"Okay." Shannon took a deep breath and accepted the canine handshake. "Handsome, aren't you?" A little more confident, she patted his head. She glanced over and saw that Maggie and Brianna were already unloading her luggage. "I'll get those."

"It's no problem, no problem at all." With surprising ease for such a slender woman, Brianna hauled suitcases toward the door of the house. "Welcome to Blackthorn Cottage, Shannon. I hope you'll be comfortable here."

With this, she opened the front door and pandemonium.

"Come back here, you little devil! I mean it, Liam. She's going to have my scalp."

As Shannon watched, a black-haired toddler scrambled down the hall on short, but surprisingly quick legs, trailing crumbs from a handful of cookies. His gut-busting laughter echoed off the walls. Not far behind was a very harassed-looking man with a small, wailing baby tucked in one arm.

Spotting company, the boy grinned, showing an angelic face smeared with food. He tossed up his chubby arms. "Mum."

"Mum, indeed." With an expert swipe Maggie had her son scooped into one arm. "Look at you, Liam Sweeney, not a clean spot to be found on you. And eating biscuits before tea."

He grinned, blue eyes dancing. "Kiss."

"Just like your father. Kisses fix everything." But she obliged him before turning to aim a killing look at Gray. "So, what have you to say for yourself, Grayson Thane?"

"I plead insanity." He shifted the baby, patting, soothing, even as he dragged his hair out of his eyes. "It's not my fault. Rogan got called into the gallery, and Murphy's out plowing something, so I was drafted to watch that twenty-pound disaster. Then the baby was crying, and Liam got into the cookies. Ah, the kitchen, Brie, you don't want to go in there."

"Is that a fact?"

"Trust me on this. And the parlor's kind of . . . well, we were just playing around. I'll buy you a new vase."

Her eyes narrowed dangerously. "Not my Waterford."

"Ah . . ." Taking help where he could find it, Gray turned his attention to Shannon. "Hi. Sorry about this. I'm Gray."

"Nice to meet you." She jerked a little as Con rushed past her legs to take advantage of the crumbs littering the floor. Then jerked again when Liam leaned over and took a handful of her hair.

"Kiss," he ordered.

"Oh." Shannon's heart sank a little. Gingerly she pecked his pursed and smeared lips. "Chocolate chip."

"I made them yesterday." Taking pity on her husband, Brianna slipped Kayla into her arms. "And from the looks of it, there's none left but for the crumbs."

"I was just distracting the kid," Gray said in his own defense. "Kayla needed to be changed, and the phone was ringing. Jesus, Brie, how can two of them be more than twice as much work as one?"

"It's just one of those unfathomable mysteries. Redeem yourself, Grayson, and take Shannon's bags to her room, if you please?"

"No problem. It's really a quiet place," he assured her. "Usually. Ah, Brie, I'll explain about that spot on the parlor rug later."

Brows knit, Brie took a few steps forward, viewed the chaos of the room she'd left meticulously neat. "Be sure you will. Shannon, I'm sorry."

"It's all right." In fact, it was more so. The noisy welcome had done more to relax her than any smooth manners could have. "This is your baby?"

"Our daughter, Kayla." She stepped back so that Shannon could have a better look. "She's a month old today."

"She's beautiful." A little more stiffly, she turned back to Maggie. "And your son?"

"Such as he is. Liam, say good day to . . ." She trailed off, stumped. "To Miss Bodine," she decided.

"Shannon." Determined not to be awkward, Shannon offered a smile. "Good day to you, Liam."

He responded with something that would have required an interpreter, but the grin needed no translation.

"I'm going to clean him up, Brie. Let me have Kayla, and I'll tend them while you show Shannon her room."

"I'm grateful." She passed Kayla over so that Maggie headed toward the kitchen with a child in each arm.

"Chocolate," Liam demanded, quite clearly.

"Not on your life, boy-o," was his mother's response.

"Well." Brianna lifted her hand to her hair, which was slipping out of its pins. "Let's get you settled. I've put you in the loft room. It's two floors up, but it's the most private and the most special." She glanced over as they started upstairs. "If you'd rather not have so many stairs to deal with, I can change it in no time."

"I don't mind the stairs." She found herself uncomfortable again. Odd, she mused, how much easier it was to deal with Maggie's abrasive challenge than Brianna's open welcome.

"The room's only been ready for a few months. I had the attic converted, you see."

"It's a beautiful house."

"Thank you. Some of the changes to it I made after my father died and left it to me. That's when I started the B-and-B. Then when I married Grayson we needed more room still, for a studio for his writing, and a nursery. Our rooms are on the first floor, off the kitchen."

"Where's Kayla?" Gray wanted to know when he met them on the stairs on his way down.

"Maggie has her." In a move so natural and of such long habit she barely noticed, Brianna lifted a hand to his cheek. "You should go for a walk, Grayson, clear your head a bit."

"I think I will. It's nice to have you here, Shannon."

"Thank you." She lifted her brow when Gray kissed his wife. It didn't seem quite the casual kiss a husband might give before going off on a walk.

"I'll be back for tea," he promised and trooped off.

Brianna led the way to the next floor where a door was already open wide in invitation.

The room was more than anything Shannon could have expected. Wide and airy with a charming window seat set under the sloping eaves of one wall, and a big brass bed tucked beneath the other. Skylights and pretty arched windows let in the sun and the spring air. The lacy curtains billowed and matched the creamy spread.

Fresh flowers were waiting to be sniffed, and every surface gleamed.

She smiled, as she had when she'd seen the valley. "It's lovely. Really lovely, Brianna."

"I had it in mind for a kind of special place. You can see to Murphy's farm and beyond from the windows there."

"Murphy?"

"Oh, he's a friend, a neighbor. Murphy Muldoon. His land starts just beyond my garden wall. You'll be meeting him. He's around the house quite a bit." Brianna roamed the room as she spoke, fussing with lamp shades, twitching at the bedspread. "And this room's more private than the other rooms, a little bigger than most as well. The bath is just here. Grayson read some books, and he and Murphy designed it between them."

"I thought this Murphy was a farmer."

"He is, yes. But he's handy about all manner of things."

"Oh." Shannon's smile widened at the small, gleaming room with its claw-foot tub and pedestal sink and fussy fingertip towels hanging over brass rods. "It's like a dollhouse."

"It is, yes." Nervous as she would have been with no other guest, Brianna linked her hands together. "Shall I help you unpack, or would you rather have a rest first?"

"I don't need help, thank you. I might make use of that tub."

"Be at home then. There's extra towels in that little trunk, and I think you'll find everything else you'd be needing." She hesitated again. "Would you want me to bring you up a tray at teatime?"

It would have been easier to agree, Shannon thought. She could have snuggled into the room alone and blocked out everything else.

"No, I'll come down."

"Take all the time you need." Brianna laid a hand on Shannon's arm to let her know the statement didn't refer only to having tea. "I'll be just downstairs if you want anything."

"Thank you."

When the door closed behind Brianna, Shannon sat on the edge of the bed. In private she could let her shoulders droop and her eyes close.

She was in Ireland, and hadn't a clue what to do next.

FIVE

"So what's she like, this Yank sister of yours?" As at home as he would have been in his own kitchen, Murphy Muldoon helped himself to one of the cream tarts Brianna was arranging on a tray.

He was a tall man who tended toward lankiness. He'd taken off his cap when he'd come into the kitchen, as his mother had taught him, and his dark hair was tousled from the fingers he'd raked through them, and in need of a trim.

"Keep your fingers off," she ordered, swatting at them. "Wait until I'm serving."

"I might not get all I want then." He grinned at her, dark blue eyes dancing, before stuffing the tart in his mouth. "Is she as pretty as you, Brie?"

"Flattery won't get you another tart before tea." But there was a laugh at the edge of her voice. "Pretty isn't the word for her. She's beautiful. Her hair's calmer than Maggie's, more like the hide on that chestnut mare you love so. Her eyes are like Da's were—though she wouldn't like to hear that—the clearest of greens. She's about my height, slim. And . . . sleek, I suppose you'd say. Even after the traveling she hardly looked rumpled at all."

"Maggie says she's a cold one." Since Brianna was guarding the tarts like a hen with one chick, Murphy settled for tea.

"She's reserved," Brianna corrected. "It's that Maggie doesn't want to like her. And there's a sadness about her she hides with coolness." And that Brianna understood perfectly. "But she smiled, really smiled, when we came up over the road where the valley spreads out."

"It's a fair sight, that." Murphy moved his shoulders as he poured his tea. His back was aching a bit, for he'd been plowing since dawn. But it was a good ache, a solid-day's-work ache. "She wouldn't see the like of it in New York City."

"You always speak of New York as if it were another planet instead of across the sea."

"It's as far as the moon as far as I'm concerned."

With a laugh, Brianna glanced over her shoulder at him. He was more handsome than even he'd been as a boy. And the women of the village had talked of his angel face in those days. Now there was a good bit of the devil as well to add impact to those vivid blue eyes and quick, crooked smile.

The outdoor life he led suited him, and over the years his face had fined down to a kind of sculpted leanness that drew women's eyes. A fact that he didn't mind a bit. His unruly thatch of black waves defied proper combing. His body was tough, with muscled arms, broad shoulders, narrow hips. Brianna knew first hand that he was as strong as one of his beloved horses, and a great deal more gentle.

Despite the strength and ruggedness, there was something poetic about him. A dreaming in the eyes, she thought with affection.

"What are you looking at?" He wiped a hand over his chin. "Have I cream on my face?"

"No, I was thinking what a shame it is you haven't found a woman to share your pretty face with."

Though he grinned, he shifted with some embarrassment. "Why is it whenever a woman marries she thinks everyone should do the same?"

"Because she's happy." She looked down to where Kayla sat contentedly in her infant chair. "Don't you think she's looking more like Grayson?"

"She's the image of you. Aren't you, Kayla love?" He bent over to tickle the baby's chin. "What are you doing about your mother, Brie?"

"Nothing, at the moment." Wishing she didn't have to think of it, she gripped her hands together. "She'll have to be told, of course, but I want to give Shannon time to relax before that storm hits."

"It'll be a gale of some proportion. Are you sure she knows nothing about the matter? Has no idea there was another woman, or a child because of her?"

"As sure as I am of my own name." Brianna sighed and went back to setting up family tea. "You know how things were between them. If Mother had known, she'd have hounded him to death over it."

"That's true enough. Brie." Murphy skimmed his knuckles down her cheek until she looked back at him again. "Don't take it all on yourself. You're not alone in this."

"I know that. But it's worrying, Murphy. Things are still strained between Mother and me, and they've never been smooth between her and Maggie. I don't know how much worse this will make it. Yet there's nothing else we could do. Da would have wanted her to come, and have a chance to know her family."

"Then rest easy for a while." With his cup still in one hand, he cuddled her with the other and bent to touch his lips to her cheek.

Then his world turned upside down.

The vision stood in the doorway, watching through cool and glorious green eyes. Her skin was like the alabaster he'd read of, and looked as soft as fresh milk. Her hair shone as it followed the lines of her face to sweep the chin that was lifted high.

The fairy queen, was all he could think. And the spell was on him.

"Oh, Shannon." A flush heated Brianna's cheeks as she spotted her half sister. How much had she heard? Brianna wondered. And how to handle it? "Tea's nearly ready. I thought we'd have it in here. I'll serve the guests in the parlor."

"The kitchen's fine." She'd heard plenty, and would take time to decide just how to handle it herself. Just now her attention was focused on the man who was gaping at her as though he'd never seen a female before.

"Shannon Bodine, this is our good friend and neighbor Murphy Muldoon."

"How do you do?"

Coherent speech seemed to have deserted him. He nodded, only dimly aware that he probably resembled a slow-witted fool.

"Murphy, would you tell the others tea's ready?" When she received no response, Brianna glanced up at him. "Murphy?"

"What?" He blinked, cleared his throat, shuffled. "Aye, I'll tell them." He tore his eyes from the vision and stared blankly at Brianna. "Tell who what?"

With a laugh, Brianna gave him a shove toward the door. "You can't go to sleep on your feet like one of your horses. Go out and tell Grayson and Maggie and Liam we're having tea." One last push and he was out of the door with her shutting it behind him. "He's been working since sunrise, I'll wager, and tuckered. Murphy's usually a bit sharper than that."

Shannon doubted it. "He's a farmer?"

"He's a fine one, and he's breeding horses, too. He's like a brother to Maggie and me." Her eyes leveled with Shannon's again. "There's nothing I can't share with Murphy and trust it stays with him."

"I see." Shannon stayed where she was, just on the other side of the threshold. "So you felt you could tell him about this particular situation."

With a quiet sigh, Brianna brought the teapot to the table. "You don't know me, Shannon, nor Murphy, nor any of us. It isn't fair for me to ask you to trust people you've only just met. So I won't. Instead, I'll ask you to sit down and enjoy your tea."

Intrigued, Shannon tilted her head. "You can be a cool one."

"Maggie's got all the fire."

"She doesn't like me."

"Not at the moment."

Shannon had the oddest urge to laugh, and gave in to it. "That's fine. I don't like her, either. What's for tea?"

"Finger sandwiches, cheese, and a bit of pâté, sugar biscuits, scones, cream tarts, apple cake."

Shannon stepped in, surveying the spread. "You do this every afternoon?"

"I like to cook." Smiling again, Brianna wiped her hands on her apron. "And I wanted your first day to be special for you."

"You're determined, aren't you?"

"There's a stubborn streak in the family. Ah, here they come. Maggie, see the lads wash their hands, would you? I have to serve in the parlor."

"Cream tarts." Gray pounced. "Where'd you hide them?"

"You'll not eat my food with dirty fingers," Brianna said calmly as she finished loading a rolling tea tray. "Help yourself, Shannon. I'll be back as soon as I've seen to my guests."

"Sit." Maggie waved to the table as soon as she'd washed her son off in the sink. She plopped Liam down in a high chair, gave him a toast finger to munch on. "Will you have sugar in your tea?"

"No, thank you," Shannon returned, equally stiff. "Just black."

"You're in for a treat," Gray said as he piled his plate. "New York may have some of the best restaurants in the world, but you've never eaten anything like Brianna's cooking. You're with Ry-Tilghmanton?" he asked, taking it on himself to heap Shannon's plate himself.

"Yes—oh, not so much—I've been there over five years."

"They've got a good rep. Top of the line." Happily he bit into a sandwich. "Where'd you train?"

"Carnegie Mellon."

"Mmm. Can't do better. There's this bakery in Pittsburgh, maybe a half mile from the college. Little Jewish couple runs it. They make these rum cakes."

"I know the place." It made her smile to think of it, and easy to talk to another American. "I hit it every Sunday morning for four years."

Since Maggie was busy with Liam and all Murphy seemed capable of doing was staring at her, Shannon felt no qualms about ignoring them in favor of Gray. "Brianna told me you came here to research a book. Does that mean your next one's set here?"

"Yeah. It's coming out in a couple of months."

"I'll look forward to it. I enjoy your books very much."

"I'll see you get an advanced copy." When the baby began to fuss, Gray lifted her out and into the curve of his arm where she fell cozily silent again.

Shannon nibbled on her sandwich—which was good, certainly and filled the hole she hadn't realized hunger had dug. Satisfied but not overly impressed, she nipped into a tart.

Her whole system signaled pleasure of the most acute and sinful.

Gray merely grinned when her eyes drifted half closed. "Who needs heaven, right?"

"Don't interrupt," she murmured, "I'm having an epiphany."

"Yeah, there's something religious about Brie's pastries all right." Gray helped himself to another.

"Pig." Maggie wrinkled her nose at him. "Leave some for me to take home to Rogan at least."

"Why don't you learn to make your own?"

"Why should I?" Smug, Maggie licked cream from her thumb. "I've only to walk up the road to have yours."

"You live nearby?" Shannon felt her pleasure dim at the idea.

"Just down the road." Maggie's thin smile indicated she understood Shannon's sentiments completely.

"Rogan drags her off periodically," Gray put in. "To Dublin or one of their galleries. Things are more peaceful then." He snuck Liam a sugar cookie.

"But I'm here often enough to keep an eye on things, and to see that Brianna isn't overtaxed."

"Brianna can keep an eye on herself," said the woman in question as she came back into the kitchen. "Gray, leave some of those tarts for Rogan."

"See?"

Gray merely sneered at Maggie and pulled his wife down in the chair beside him. "Aren't you hungry, Murphy?"

Because that unblinking stare was beginning to annoy her, Shannon drummed her fingers on the table. "Mr. Muldoon's too busy staring at me to bother eating."

"Clod," Maggie muttered and jabbed Murphy with an elbow.

"I beg your pardon." Murphy snatched up his teacup hastily enough to have it slop over the rim. "I was woolgathering is all. I should get back." And maybe when he returned to his own fields he'd find his sanity waiting. "Thank you, Brie, for the tea. Welcome to Ireland, Miss Bodine."

He grabbed his cap, stuffed it on his head, and hurried out.

"Well, never did I think to see the day that Murphy Muldoon left his plate full." Baffled, Maggie rose to take it to the counter. "I'll just take it for Rogan."

"Yes, do," Brianna said absently. "Do you think he's coming down with something? He didn't look himself."

Shannon thought he'd looked healthy enough, and with a shrug forgot the odd Mr. Muldoon and finished her tea.

Later, when the sky was just losing its bloom of blue and edging toward gray, Shannon took a tour through Brianna's back gardens. Her hostess had wanted her, quite clearly, to vacate the kitchen after the family's evening meal. No particular fan of washing dishes, Shannon had agreed to the suggestion that she take some air and enjoy the quiet of evening.

It was certainly the place to do nothing, Shannon decided, intrigued as she strolled around the outside of a greenhouse. Though it appeared Brianna rarely took advantage of comfortable laziness.

What didn't the woman do? Shannon wondered. She cooked, ran the equivalent of a small, exclusive hotel, cared for an infant, gardened, enticed a very attractive man, and managed to look like some magazine shot of *Irish Country Times* while she was at it.

After circling the greenhouse, she spotted a picturesque sitting area on the edge of a bed of impatiens and violas. She settled into the wooden chair, found it as comfortable as it looked, and decided she wouldn't think about Brianna, or Maggie, or the household she was a temporary part of. She would, for just a little while, think of nothing at all.

The air was soft and fragrant. There was a pretty chiming from a copper hanging of fairies near a window close by. She thought she heard the low of a cow in the distance—a sound as foreign to her world as the legend of leprechauns or banshees.

Murphy's farm, she supposed. She hoped, for his sake, he was a better farmer than conversationalist.

A wave of fatigue washed over her, the jet lag her nerves had held at bay for hours. She let it come now, cocoon her and blur the edges of too many worries.

And she dreamed of a man on a white horse. His hair was black and streaming behind him, and his dark cloak whipped in the wind and was beaded with the rain that spewed like fury from an iron-gray sky.

Lightning split it like a lance, speared its flash over his face, highlighting the high Celtic bones, the cobalt eyes of the black Irish, and the warrior. There was a copper broach at the cloak's neck. An intricate twist of metal around a carving of a stallion's reared head.

As if in sympathy, his mount pawed the chaotic air, then pounded the turf. They drove straight for her, man and beast, both equally dangerous, equally magnificent. She caught the glint of a sword, the dull sheen of armor sprayed with mud.

Her heart answered the bellow of thunder, and the rain slapped icily at her face. But there wasn't fear. Her chin was thrust high as she watched them bullet toward her, and her eyes, narrowed against the rain, gleamed green.

In a spray of mud and wet the horse swerved to a halt no more than inches from her. The man astride it peered down at her with triumph and lust shining on his face.

"So," she heard herself say in a voice that wasn't quite hers. "You've come back."

Shannon jerked awake, shaken and confused by the strangeness and the utter clarity of the dream. As if she hadn't been asleep at all, she thought as she brushed the hair back from her face. But more remembering.

She barely had time to be amused at herself by the thought when her heart tripped back to double time. There was a man standing not a foot away, watching her.

"I beg your pardon." Murphy stepped forward out of the shadows that were spreading. "I didn't mean to startle you. I thought you were napping."

Miserably embarrassed, she pulled herself upright in the chair. "So you came to stare at me again, Mr. Muldoon?"

"No—that is, I . . ." He blew out a frustrated breath. Hadn't he talked to himself sternly about just this behavior? Damn if he'd find himself all thick-tongued and soft-headed a second time around her. "I didn't want to disturb you," he began again. "I thought for a minute you'd come awake and had spoken to me, but you hadn't." He tried a smile, one he'd found usually charmed the ladies. "The truth of it is, Miss Bodine, I'd come back around to apologize for gaping at you during tea. It was rude."

"Fine. Forget it." And go away, she thought irritably.

"I'm thinking it's your eyes." He knew it was more. He'd known exactly what it was the moment he'd looked over and seen her. The woman he'd waited for.

The breath she huffed out was impatient. "My eyes?"

"You've fairy eyes. Clear as water, green as moss, and full of magic."

He didn't sound slow-witted now, she realized warily. His voice had taken on a musical cadence designed to make a woman forget everything but the sound of it. "That's interesting, Mr. Muldoon—"

"Murphy, if it's the same to you. We're in the way of being neighbors."

"No, we're not. But Murphy's fine with me. Now, if you'll excuse—" Instead of rising as she'd intended, she shrank back in the chair and let out a muffled squeal. Something sleek and fast came charging out of the shadows. And it growled.

"Con." It took no more than the single quiet syllable from Murphy to have the dog skidding to a halt and flopping his tail. "He didn't mean to scare you." Murphy laid a hand on the dog's head. "He's been for his evening run, and sometimes when he comes across me, he likes to play. He wasn't growling so much as talking."

"Talking." She shut her eyes as she waited for her heart to stop thudding. "Talking dogs, that's all the evening needed." Then Con padded over and, laying his head in her lap, looked soulfully into her face. Even an iceberg would have melted. "So, now you're apologizing, I suppose, for scaring me out of my skin." She lifted her gaze to Murphy. "The two of you are quite a pair."

"I suppose we can both be clumsy at times." In a graceful move that belied the words, he drew a clutch of wildflowers from behind his back. "Welcome to the county of Clare, Shannon Bodine. May your stay be as sweet and colorful as the blooms, and last longer."

Flabbergasted, and damn it, charmed, she took the cheerful blossoms from him. "I thought you were an odd man, Murphy," she murmured. "It seems I was right." But her lips were curved as she rose. "Thank you."

"Now, that's something I'll look forward to. Your smile," he told her when she only lifted her brows. "It's worth waiting for. Good night, Shannon. Sleep well."

He walked away, turned again into a shadow. When the dog began to follow, he said something soft that had Con holding back and turning to wait by Shannon's side.

As the fragrance of the blossoms she held teased her senses, the man called Murphy melted into the night.

"So much for first impressions," Shannon said to the dog, then shook her head. "I think it's time to go in. I must be more tired than I'd thought."

SIX

Storms and white horses. Brutally handsome men and a circle of standing stones.

Pursued by dreams, Shannon had not spent a peaceful night.

And she woke freezing. That was odd, she thought, as the coals in the little fireplace across the room still glowed red, and she herself was buried to the chin under a thick, downy quilt. Yet her skin was icy to the point of making her shiver to warm it.

What was odder still was that she wasn't merely cold. Until she felt her face for herself, she would have sworn she was wet—as if she'd been standing out in the middle of a rainstorm.

She sat up in bed, dragging her hands through her hair. Never before in her life had she experienced dreams with such clarity, and wasn't sure she wanted it to become a habit.

But dreams and restless nights aside, she was awake now. From experience she knew there would be no cuddling back into the pillow and drifting off. Back in New York, that wouldn't have been so frustrating. There were always dozens of things that needed to be done, and she typically woke early to get a jump on the day.

There was always an account to work on, paperwork to deal with, or simple domestic chores to accomplish before heading to the office. Those done, she'd have checked her electronic organizer to see what appointments and duties were scheduled for the day—what social entertainments were on line for the evening. The morning show on television would provide her with a weather update, and any current news before she picked up her briefcase, and her gym bag depending on the day of the week, and set off for the brisk six-block walk to her office.

The satisfied, organized life of the young professional on the way up the corporate ladder. It had been precisely the same routine for over five years.

But here . . . With a sigh, she looked toward the window where the western sky was still dark. There were no deadlines, no appointments, no presentations to be given. She'd taken a break from the structure that was so familiar, and therefore comforting.

What did a person do in the Irish countryside at dawn? After crawling out of bed, she went over to poke at the fire, then padded over to the window seat to curl on its cushions.

She could make out the fields, the shadows of stone walls, the outline of a house and outbuildings, as the sky gradually lightened from indigo to a softer blue. With some amusement she heard the crow of a rooster.

Maybe she would take Brianna up on the offer of the use of her car and drive somewhere. Anywhere. This part of Ireland was famed for its scenery. Shannon thought she might as well get a look at it while she was here. Perhaps she'd use the location and the vacation time to paint if the mood struck her.

In the bath she pulled the circular curtain around the claw-foot tub and found, with pleasure, the water from the shower was hot and plentiful. She chose a dark turtleneck and jeans and nearly picked up her purse before she realized she'd have no need for it until she made transportation arrangements.

Deciding to take Brianna's invitation to make herself at home to heart, she started downstairs to brew coffee.

The house was so quiet she could almost believe she was alone. She knew there were guests on the second floor, but Shannon heard nothing but the quiet creak of the stair under her own feet as she walked down to the first floor.

It was the new view that stopped her, the window facing east that framed the stunning break of dawn. The roll of clouds on the horizon was thick, layered, and shot with swirling red. The bold color spread into the sky, beating back the more soothing blues and tamer pinks with licks of fire. Even as she watched, the clouds moved, sailing like a flaming ship as the sky slowly lightened.

For the first time in months she found herself actively wanting to paint. It had been habit more than desire that had had her packing some of her equipment. She was grateful now, and wondered how far she would have to drive to buy what other supplies she might need.

Pleased with the idea, and the prospect of a genuine activity, she wandered back toward the kitchen.

Finding Brianna already there and wrist deep in bread dough was more of a surprise than it should have been. "I thought I would be the first up."

"Good morning. You're an early riser." Brianna smiled as she continued to knead her dough. "So's Kayla, and she wakes hungry. There's coffee, or tea if you like. I've already brewed it for Grayson."

"He's up, too?" So much, Shannon thought, for a solitary morning.

"Oh, he got up hours ago to work. He does that sometimes when the story's worrying him. I'll fix you breakfast once I set the bread to rise."

"No, coffee's fine." After she'd poured a cup, Shannon stood awkwardly, wondering what to do next. "You bake your own bread?"

"I do, yes. It's a soothing process. You'll have toast at least. There's a hunk of yesterday's still in the drawer."

"A little later. I was thinking I might drive around a bit, see the cliffs or something."

"Oh, sure you'll want to see the sights." Competently Brianna patted the dough into a ball and turned it into a large bowl. "The keys are on that hook there. You take them whenever you've a mind to ramble. Did you have a good night?"

"Actually, I—" She broke off, surprised she'd been about to tell Brianna about her dreams. "Yes, the room's very comfortable." Restless again, she took another sip of coffee. "Is there a gym anywhere around?"

Brianna covered her dough with a cloth, then went to the sink to wash off her hands. "A Jim? Several of them. Are you looking for anyone in particular?"

Shannon opened her mouth, then closed it again on a laugh. "No, a gym—a health club. I work out three or four times a week. You know, treadmills, stair climbers, free weights."

"Oh." Brianna set a cast iron skillet on the stove as she thought it through. "No, we've none of that just here. A treadmill, that's for walking?"

"Yeah."

"We've fields for that. You can have a fine walk across the fields. And the fresh air's good for exercising. It's a lovely morning for being out, though we'll have rain this afternoon. You'll want a jacket," she continued, nodding toward a light denim jacket hanging on a peg by the back door.

"A jacket?"

"It's a bit cool out." Brianna set bacon to sizzling in the pan. "The exercise will give you an appetite. You'll have breakfast when you get back."

Frowning, Shannon studied Brianna's back. It looked as if she was going for a walk. A little bemused, she set down her cup and picked up the jacket. "I don't guess I'll be long."

"Take your time," Brianna said cheerfully.

Amused at each other, they parted company.

Shannon had never considered herself the outdoor type. She wasn't a fan of hiking. She much preferred the civilized atmosphere of a well-equipped health club—bottled water, the morning news on the television set, machines that told you your progress. She put in fifty minutes three times a week and was pleased to consider herself strong, healthy, and well toned.

But she'd never understood people who strapped on heavy boots and backpacks and hiked trails or climbed mountains.

Still, her discipline was too ingrained to allow her to forfeit all forms of exercise. And one day at Blackthorn had shown her that Brianna's cooking could be a problem.

So she'd walk. Shannon tucked her hands into the pockets of her borrowed jacket, for the air was chilly. There was a nice little bite in the morning that shook away any lingering dregs of jet lag.

She passed the garden where primroses were still drenched with dew, and the greenhouse that tempted her to cup her hands and peer in through the treated glass. What she saw had her mouth falling open. She'd visited professional nurseries with her mother that were less organized and less well stocked.

Impressed, she turned away, then stopped. It was all so big, she thought as she stared out over the roll of land. So empty. Without being aware she hunched her shoulders defensively in the jacket. She thought nothing of walking down a New York sidewalk, dodging pedestrians, guarding her own personal space. The blare of traffic, blasting horns, raised voices were familiar, not strange like this shimmering silence.

"Not exactly like jogging in Central Park," she muttered, comforted by the sound of her own voice. Because it was less daunting to go on than to return to the kitchen, she began to walk.

There were sounds, she realized. Birds, the distant hum of some machine, the echoing bark of a dog. Still, it seemed eerie to be so alone. Rather than focus on that, she quickened her pace. Strolling didn't tone the muscles.

When she came to the first stone wall, she debated her choices. She could walk along it, or climb over it into the next field. With a shrug, she climbed over.

She recognized wheat, just high enough to wave a bit in the breeze, and in the midst of it, a lone tree. Though it looked immensely old to her, its leaves were still the tender green of spring. A bird perched on one of its high, gnarled branches, singing its heart out.

She stopped to watch, to listen, wishing she'd brought her sketch pad. She'd have to come back with it. It had been too long since she'd had the opportunity to do a real landscape.

Odd, she thought as she began to walk again. She hadn't realized she wanted to. Yet anyone with even rudimentary skills would find their fingers itching here, she decided. The colors, the shapes, and the magnificent light. She turned around, walking backward for a moment to study the tree from a different angle.

Early morning would be best, she decided and climbed over the next wall with her attention still focused behind her.

Only luck kept her from turning headfirst into the cow.

"Jesus Christ." She scrambled backward, came up hard against stone. The cow simply eyed the intruder dispassionately and swished her tail. "It's so big." From her perch on top of the wall, Shannon let out an unsteady breath. "I had no idea they were so big."

Cautious, she lifted her gaze and discovered that bossie wasn't alone. The field was dotted with grazing cows, large placid-eyed ladies with black-and-white hides. Since they didn't seem particularly interested in her, she lowered slowly until she was sitting on the wall rather than standing on it.

"I guess the tour stops here. Aren't you going to moo or something?"

Rather than oblige, the nearest cow shifted her bulk and went back to grazing. Amused now, Shannon relaxed and took a longer, more comprehensive look around. What she saw had her lips bowing.

"Babies." With a laugh, she started to spring up to get a first-hand look at the spindly calves romping among their less energetic elders. Then caution had her glancing back into the eyes of her closest neighbor. She wasn't at all sure if cows tended to bite or not. "Guess I'll just watch them from right here."

Curiosity had her reaching out, warily, her eyes riveted on the cow's face. She just wanted to touch. Though she leaned out, she kept her butt planted firmly on the wall. If the cow didn't like the move, Shannon figured she could be on the other side. Any woman who worked out three times a week should be able to outrun a cow.

When her fingers brushed, she discovered the hair was stiff and tough, and that the cow didn't appear to object. More confident, Shannon inched a little closer and spread her palm over the flank.

"She doesn't mind being handled, that one," Murphy said from behind her.

Shannon's yelp had several of the cows trundling off. After some annoyed mooing, they settled down again. But Murphy was still laughing when they had, and his hand remained on Shannon's shoulder where he gripped to keep her from falling face first off the wall.

"Steady now. You're all nerves."

"I thought I was alone." She wasn't sure if she was more mortified to have screamed or to have been caught petting a farm animal.

"I was heading back from setting my horses to pasture and saw you." In a comfortable move he sat on the wall, facing the opposite way, and lighted a cigarette. "It's a fine morning."

Her opinion on that was a grunt. She hadn't thought about this being his land. And now, it seemed, she was stuck again. "You take care of all these cows yourself?"

"Oh, I have a bit of help now and then, when it's needed. You go ahead, pet her if you like. She doesn't mind it."

"I wasn't petting her." It was a little late for dignity, but Shannon made a stab at it. "I was just curious about how they felt."

"You've never touched a cow?" The very idea made him grin. "You have them in America I'm told."

"Of course we have cows. We just don't see them strolling down Fifth

Avenue very often." She slanted a look at him. He was still smiling, looking back toward the tree that had started the whole scenario. "Why haven't you cut that down? It's in the middle of your wheat."

"It's no trouble to plow and plant around it," he said easily. "And it's been here longer than me." At the moment he was more interested in her. She smelled faintly sinful—some cunning female fragrance that had a man wondering. And wasn't it fine that he'd been thinking of her as he'd come over the rise?

There she'd been, as if she'd been waiting.

"You've a fine morning for your first in Clare. There'll be rain later in the day."

Brianna had said the same, Shannon remembered, and frowned up at the pretty blue sky. "Why do you say that?"

"Didn't you see the sunrise?"

Even as she was wondering what that had to do with anything, Murphy was cupping her chin in his hand and turning her face west.

"And there," he said, gesturing. "The clouds gathering up from the sea. They'll blow in by noontime and bring us rain. A soft one, not a storm. There's no temper in the air."

The hand on her face was hard as rock, gentle as water. She discovered he carried the scents of his farm with him—the horses, the earth, the grass. It seemed wiser all around to concentrate on the sky.

"I suppose farmers have to learn how to gauge the weather."

"It's not learning so much. You just know." To please himself he let his fingers brush through her hair before dropping them onto his own knee. The gesture, the casual intimacy of it, had her turning her head toward him.

They may have been facing opposite ways, with legs dangling on each side of the wall, but they were hip to hip. And now eye to eye. And his were the color of the glass her mother had collected—the glass Shannon had packed so carefully and brought back to New York. Cobalt.

She didn't see any of the shyness or the bafflement she'd read in them the day before. These were the eyes of a confident man, one comfortable with himself, and one, she realized with some confusion of her own, who had dangerous thoughts behind them.

He was tempted to kiss her. Just lean forward and lay his lips upon hers. Once. Quietly. If she'd been another woman, he would have. Then again, he knew if she'd been another woman he wouldn't have wanted to quite so badly.

"You have a face, Shannon, that plants itself right in the front of a man's mind, and blooms there."

It was the voice, she thought, the Irish in it that made even such a foolish statement sound like poetry. In defense against it, she looked away, back toward the safety of grazing cows.

"You think in farming analogies."

"That's true enough. There's something I'd like to show you. Will you walk with me?"

"I should get back."

But he was already rising and taking her hand as though it were already a habit. " 'Tisn't far." He bent, plucked a starry blue flower that had been growing in a crack in the wall. Rather than hand it to her, as she'd expected, he tucked it behind her ear.

It was ridiculously charming. She fell into step beside him before she could stop herself. "Don't you have work? I thought farmers were always working."

"Oh, I've a moment or two to spare. There's Con." Murphy lifted a hand as they walked. "Rabbitting."

The sight of the sleek gray dog racing across the field in pursuit of a blur that was a rabbit had her laughing. Then her fingers tightened on Murphy's in distress. "He'll kill it."

"Aye, if he could catch it, likely he would. But chances of that are slim."

Hunter and hunted streaked over the rise and vanished into a thin line of trees where the faintest gleam of water caught the sun.

"He'll lose him now, as he always does. He can't help chasing any more than the rabbit can help fleeing."

"He'll come back if you call him," Shannon said urgently. "He'll come back and leave it alone."

Willing to indulge her, Murphy sent out a whistle. Moments later Con bounded back over the field, tongue lolling happily.

"Thank you."

Murphy started walking again. There was no use telling her Con would be off again at the next rabbit he scented. "Have you always lived in the city?"

"In or near. We moved around a lot, but we always settled near a major hub." She glanced up. He seemed taller when they were walking side by side. Or perhaps it was just the way he had of moving over the land. "And have you always lived around here?"

"Always. Some of this land was the Concannons', and ours ran beside it. Tom's heart was never in farming, and over the years he sold off pieces to my father, then to me. Now what's mine splits between what's left of the Concannons', leaving a piece of theirs on either side."

Her brow furrowed as she looked over the hills. She couldn't begin to estimate the acreage or figure the boundaries. "It seems like a lot of land."

"It's enough." He came to a wall, stepped easily over it, then, to Shannon's surprise, he simply put his hands at her waist and lifted her over as if she'd weighed nothing. "Here's what I wanted to show you."

She was still dealing with the shock of how strong he was when she looked over and saw the stone circle. Her first reaction wasn't surprise or awe or pleasure. It was simple acceptance.

It would occur to her later that she hadn't been surprised because she'd known it was there. She'd seen it in her dreams.

"How wonderful." The pleasure did come, and quickly now. Tilting her head over her eyes to block the angle of the sun she studied it, as an artist would, for shape and texture and tone.

It wasn't large, and several of the stones that had served as lintels had fallen. But the circle stood, majestic and somehow magically in a quiet field of green where horses grazed in the distance.

"I've never seen one, except in pictures." Hardly aware that she'd linked her fingers with Murphy and was pulling him with her, she hurried closer. "There are all sorts of legends and theories about standing stones, aren't there? Spaceships or druids, giants freezing or fairies dancing. Do you know how old it is?"

"Old as the fairies, I'd say."

That made her laugh. "I wonder if they were places of worship, or sacrifice." The idea made her shudder, pleasantly, as she reached out a hand to touch the stone.

Just as her fingers brushed, she drew them back sharply, and stared. There'd been heat there, too much heat for such a cool morning.

Murphy never took his eyes off her. "It's an odd thing, isn't it, to feel it?"

"I—for a minute it was like I touched something breathing." Feeling foolish, she laid a hand firmly on the stone. There was a jolt, she couldn't deny it, but she told herself it came from her own sudden nerves.

"There's power here. Perhaps in the stones themselves, perhaps in the spot they chose to raise them in."

"I don't believe in that sort of thing."

"You've too much Irish in you not to." Very gently he drew her through the arch of stone and into the center of the dance.

Determined to be practical, she folded her arms over her chest and moved away from him. "I'd like to paint it, if you'd let me."

"It doesn't belong to me. The land around it's mine, but it belongs to itself. You paint it if it pleases you."

"It would." Relaxing again, she wandered the inner circle. "I know people back home who'd pay for a chance to stand here. The same ones who go to Sedonna looking for vortexes and worry about their chakras."

Murphy grinned as he scratched his chin. "I've read of that. Interesting. Don't you think there are some places and some things that hold old memories in them? And the power that comes from them?"

She could, nearly could, standing there. If she let herself. "I certainly don't think hanging some pretty rock around my neck is going to improve my sex life." Amused, she looked back at him. "And I don't think a farmer believes it, either."

"Well, I don't know about wearing a necklace to make things more interesting in bed. I'd rather depend on myself for that."

"I bet you do," Shannon murmured and turned away to stroke one of the stones. "Still, they're so ancient, and they've stood here for longer than anyone really knows. That's magic in itself. I wonder—" She broke off, holding her breath and listening hard. "Did you hear that?"

He was only a pace away now, and waited, and watched. "What did you hear, Shannon?"

Her throat was dry; she cleared it. "Must have been a bird. It sounded like someone crying for a second."

Murphy laid a hand on her hair, let it run through as he had before. "I've heard her. So have some others. Your sisters. Don't stiffen up," he murmured, turning her to face him. "Blood's blood, and it's useless to ignore it. She weeps here because she lost her lover. So the story goes."

"It was a bird," Shannon insisted.

"They were doomed, you see," he continued as if she hadn't spoken. "He was only a poor farmer, and she was the daughter of the landlord. But they met here, and loved here, and conceived a child here. So it's said."

She was cold again and, fighting back a shiver, spoke lightly. "A legend, Murphy? I'd expect there'd be plenty about a spot like this."

"So there are. This one's sad, as many are. He left her here to wait for him, so they could run off together. But they caught him, and killed him. And when her father found her the next day, she was as dead as her love, with tears still on her cheeks."

"And now, of course, she haunts it."

He smiled then, not at all insulted by the cynicism. "She loved him. She can only wait." Murphy took her hands to warm them in his. "Gray thought of doing a murder here, but changed his mind. He told me it wasn't a place for blood. So instead of being in his book, it'll be on your canvas. It's more fitting."

"If I get to it." She should have tugged her hands away, but it felt so good to have his around them. "I need more supplies if I decide to do any serious painting while I'm here. I should get back. I'm keeping you from your work, and Brianna's probably holding breakfast for me."

But he only looked at her, enjoying the way her hands felt in his, the way the air blushed color in her cheeks. Enjoyed as well the unsteady pulse he felt at her wrists, and the quick confusion in her eyes.

"I'm glad I found you sitting on my wall, Shannon Bodine. It'll give me something to picture the rest of my day."

Annoyed with the way her knees were melting, she stiffened them and cocked her head. "Murphy, are you flirting with me?"

"It seems I am."

"That's flattering, but I don't really have time for it. And you've still got my hands."

"So I do." With his eyes on hers, he lifted them, pressed his lips to her knuckles. His smile was quick and disarming when he let her go. "Come walking with me again, Shannon."

She stood a moment when he turned and stepped out of the dance. Then, because she couldn't resist, she darted to one of the arches and watched him walk, with a whistle for the dog, over his field.

Not a man to underestimate, she mused. And she watched until he'd disappeared behind a rise, unconsciously rubbing her warmed knuckles against her cheek.

SEVEN

Shannon didn't know how to approach her first visit to an Irish pub. It wasn't that she didn't look forward to it. She always enjoyed new things, new places, new people. And even if she'd been resistant, Brianna's obvious pleasure at the idea of an evening out would have pushed her into going.

Yet she couldn't quite resolve herself to the idea of taking a baby to a bar.

"Oh, you're ready." Brianna glanced up when Shannon started down the stairs. "I'm sorry, I'm running behind. The baby was hungry, then needed changing." She swayed as she spoke, Kayla resting in the crook of one arm, a tray with two cups of tea balanced in the other. "Then the sisters complained about itchy throats and asked for some hot toddies."

"The sisters?"

"The Freemonts, in the blue room? Oh, you probably missed them. They just came in today. Seems they got caught in the rain and took a chill." Brianna rolled her eyes. "They're regulars, are the Freemonts, so I try not to mind their fussing. But they spend the three days a year they have here doing little else. Gray says it's because they've lived with each other all their lives and neither ever had a decent tumble with a man."

She stopped herself, flushed, then managed a weak smile when Shannon laughed.

"I shouldn't be talking that way about guests. But the point is, I'm a little behind things, so if you wouldn't mind waiting?"

"Of course not. Can I—"

"Oh, and there's the phone. Blast it, let it ring."

"Where's Gray?"

"Oh, he's investigating a crime scene, or killing someone else. He snarled when I poked into his studio, so he'll be no help at the moment."

"I see. Well, can I do something?"

"I'd be grateful if you could take the baby for a few minutes, just while I run this tray upstairs and pamper the sisters a bit." Brianna's eyes gleamed. "It won't take long; I used a free hand with the whiskey."

"Sure, I'll take her." Warily Shannon shifted Kayla into her arms. The baby felt so terrifyingly small there, and fragile. "I haven't had a lot of practice. Most of the women I know are concentrating on their career and putting off having children."

"A pity, isn't it, that it's still so much easier for men to do both. If you'd just walk her a bit. She's restless—as anxious I think to get out and have some music and company as I am."

With an enviable grace, Brianna darted up the steps with her tray and doctored tea.

"Restless, Kayla?" Shannon strolled down the hall and into the parlor. "I know the feeling." Charmed, she skimmed a finger down the baby's cheek and felt that quick jolt of pleasure when a tiny fist gripped it. "Strong, aren't you? You're no pushover. I don't think your mother's one, either."

Indulging herself, she snuck a kiss, then another, delighted when Kayla bubbled at her.

"Pretty great, isn't she?"

Still starry-eyed, Shannon looked up and smiled as Gray strode into the room. "She's just beautiful. You don't realize how tiny they are until you're holding one."

"She's grown." He bent down, grinned at his daughter. "She looked like an indignant fairy when she was born. I'll never forget it."

"She looks like her mother now. Speaking of which, Brianna's upstairs drugging the Freemont sisters."

"Good." Gray seemed to find that no surprise, and nodded. "I hope she does a good job of it; otherwise they'll keep her busting her ass for three days."

"She seems to do that pretty well on her own."

"That's Brie. Want a drink before we go, or would you rather wait for a pint at the pub?"

"I'll wait, thanks. You're going with us? I thought you were killing someone."

"Not tonight. They're already dead." Gray considered a whiskey, opted against. He was more in the mood for a Guinness. "Brie said you wanted to do some painting while you're here."

"I think I do. I brought some things with me, enough to get started anyway." Unconsciously she was mimicking Brianna's movements by swaying the baby. "She said I could use the car and try Ennis for more supplies."

"You'd do better in Galway, but you might find what you need there."

"I don't like to use her car," Shannon blurted out.

"Worried about driving on the left?"

"There is that—but it just doesn't feel right to borrow it."

Considering, Gray eased down on the arm of the sofa. "Want some advice from a fellow Yank?"

"Maybe."

"The people around here are a world unto themselves. Offering to give, to lend, to share everything, themselves included, is second nature. When Brie hands you the keys to her car, she isn't thinking—is she insured, does she have a driving record—she's just thinking someone needs the car. And that's all there is to it."

"It isn't as easy from my end. I didn't come here to be part of a big, generous family."

"Why did you come?"

"Because I don't know who I am." Furious that it had come out, that it had been there to come out, she handed him the baby. "I don't like having an identity crisis."

"Can't blame you," Gray said easily. "I've been there myself." He caught the sound of his wife's voice, patient, soothing. "Why don't you give yourself a little time, pal? Enjoy the scenery, gain a few pounds on Brianna's cooking. In my experience, the answers usually come when you least expect them."

"Professionally or personally?"

He rose, gave her a friendly pat on cheek. "Both. Hey, Brie, are we going or not?"

"I just have to get my bag." She hurried in, smoothing her hair. "Oh, Gray, are you going then?"

"Do you think I'd miss an evening out with you?" With his free hand he circled her waist and swept her into a quick waltz.

Her face was already glowing. "I thought you were going to work."

"I can always work." Even as her lips curved, he was lowering his to them.

Shannon waited a beat, then another before clearing her throat. "Maybe I should wait outside, in the car. With my eyes closed."

"Stop it, Grayson, you're embarrassing Shannon."

"No, I'm not. She's just jealous." And he winked at the woman he already considered his sister-in-law. "Come on, pal, we'll find a guy for you."

"No, thanks, I just got rid of one."

"Yeah?" Always interested, Gray handed the baby to his wife so that he could circle Shannon's waist. "Tell us all about it. We live for gossip around here."

"Leave her be," Brianna said with an exasperated laugh. "Don't tell him anything you don't want to find in a book."

"This wouldn't make very interesting reading," Shannon decided and stepped outside into the damp air. It had rained, and was raining still, just as predicted.

"I can make anything interesting." Gray opened the car door for his wife with some gallantry, then grinned. "So, why'd you dump him?"

"I didn't dump him." It was all just absurd enough to brighten her mood. Shannon slid into the backseat and shook back her hair. "We parted on mutually amenable terms."

"Yeah, yeah, she dumped him." Gray tapped his fingers on the back of the seat as he eased into the road. "Women always talk prissy when they break a guy's heart."

"Okay, I'll make it up." Shannon flashed Gray a smile in the rearview mirror. "He crawled, he begged, he pleaded. I believe he even wept. But I was unmoved and crushed his still-bleeding heart under my heel. Now he's shaved his head, given away all his worldly goods, and joined a small religious cult in Mozambique."

"Not too shabby."

"More entertaining than the truth. Which was we didn't really share any more than a taste for Thai food and office space, but you're welcome to use either version in a book."

"You're happier without him then," Brianna said complacently. "And that's what's important."

A little surprised at how simple it was, Shannon raised a brow. "Yes, you're right." Just as it was a great deal more simple than she had supposed to sit back and enjoy the evening.

O'Malley's pub. It was, Shannon decided as she stepped inside, an old black-and-white movie starring Pat O'Brien. The air faintly hazed from cigarettes, the murky colors, the smoke-smudged wood, the men hunkered at the bar over big glasses of dark beer, the laughter of women, the murmuring voices, the piping tune in the background.

There was a television hung behind the bar, the picture on some sort of sporting event, the sound off. A man wearing a white apron over his wide girth glanced up and grinned broadly as he continued to draw another brew.

"So, you've brought the little one at last." He set the pint down to let it settle. "Bring her by, Brie, let us have a look at her."

Obliging, Brianna put Kayla, carrier and all, atop the bar. "She's wearing the bonnet your missus brought by, Tim."

"That's a sweet one." He clucked Kayla under the chin with a thick finger. "The image of you she is, Brianna."

"I had something to do with it," Gray put in as people began to crowd around the baby.

"Sure and you did," Tim agreed. "But the good Lord in his wisdom overlooked that and gave the lass her mother's angel face. Will you have a pint, Gray?"

"I will, of Guinness. What'll you have, Shannon?"

She looked at the beer Tim O'Malley finished drawing. "Something smaller than that."

"A pint and a glass," Gray ordered. "And a soft drink for the new mother."

"Shannon, this is Tim O'Malley building your Guinness." Brianna laid a hand on Shannon's shoulder. "Tim, this is my . . . guest, Shannon Bodine from New York City."

"New York City." With his hands moving with the ease and automation of long experience, Tim beamed into Shannon's face. "I've cousins to spare in New York City. You don't happen to be knowing Francis O'Malley, the butcher."

"No, I'm sorry."

"Bodine." A man on the stool beside Shannon took a deep, considering drag from his cigarette, blew out smoke with a thoughtful air. "I knew a Katherine Bodine from Kilkelly some years back. Pretty as fresh milk was she. Kin to you, maybe?"

Shannon gave him an uncertain smile. "Not that I know of."

"It's Shannon's first trip to Ireland," Brianna explained. There were nods of understanding all around.

"I knew Bodines from Dublin City." A man at the end of the bar spoke in a voice cracked with age. "Four brothers who'd sooner fight than spit. The Mad Bodines we called them, and every man son of them ran off and joined the IRA. That'd be back in . . . thirty-seven."

"Thirty-five," the woman beside him corrected and winked at Shannon out of a face seamed with lines. "I went out walking a time or two with Paddy Bodine, and Johnny split his lip over it."

"A man's got to protect what's his." Old John Conroy took his wife's hand and gave it a bony squeeze. "There was no prettier lass in Dublin than Nell O'Brian. And now she's mine."

Shannon smiled into the beer Gray handed her. The couple were ninety if they were a day, she was sure, and they were holding hands and flirting with each other as if they were newlyweds.

"Let me have that baby." A woman came out of the room behind the bar, wiping her hands on her apron. "Go, get yourself a table," she said, gesturing Brianna aside. "I'm taking her back with me so I can spoil her for an hour."

Knowing any protest was useless, Brianna introduced Shannon to Tim's wife and watched the woman bundle Kayla off. "We might as well sit then. She won't let me have the baby back until we leave."

Shannon turned to follow, and saw Murphy.

He'd been sitting near the low fire all along, watching her while he eased a quiet tune out of a concertina. Looking at her had fuddled his mind again, slowed his tongue, so he was glad he'd had time to gather his wits before Gray led her to his table.

"Are you entertaining us tonight, Murphy?" Brianna asked as she sat.

"Myself mostly." He was grateful his fingers didn't fumble like his brain when Gray nudged Shannon into a chair. All he could see for a heartbeat of time were her eyes, pale and clear and wary. "Hello, Shannon."

"Murphy." There'd been no gracious way to avoid taking the chair Gray had pulled out for her—the one that put her nearly elbow to elbow with Murphy. She felt foolish that it would matter. "Where'd you learn to play?"

"Oh, I picked it up here and there."

"Murphy has a natural talent for instruments," Brianna said proudly. "He can play anything you hand him."

"Really?" His long fingers certainly seemed clever enough, and skilled enough, on the complicated buttons of the small box. Still, she thought he must know the tune well as he never glanced down at what he was doing. He only stared at her. "A musical farmer," she murmured.

"Do you like music?" he asked her.

"Sure. Who doesn't like music?"

He paused long enough to pick up his pint, sip. He supposed he'd have to get used to his throat going dry whenever she was close. "Is there a tune you'd like to hear?"

She lifted a shoulder, let it fall casually. But she was sorry he'd stopped playing. "I don't know much about Irish music."

Gray leaned forward. "Don't ask for 'Danny Boy,' " he warned in a whisper.

Murphy grinned at him. "Once a Yank," he said lightly and ordered himself to relax again. "A name like Shannon Bodine, and you don't know Irish music?"

"I've always been more into Percy Sledge, Aretha Franklin."

With his eyes on hers and a grin at the corners of his mouth he started a new tune. The grin widened when she laughed.

"It's the first time I've heard 'When a Man Loves a Woman' on a mini accordion."

" 'Tis a concertina." He glanced over at a shout. "Ah, there's my man."

Young Liam Sweeney scrambled across the room and climbed into Murphy's lap. He aimed a soulful look. "Candy."

"You want your mum to scrape the skin off me again?" But Murphy looked over, noted that Maggie had stopped at the bar. He reached into his pocket and took out a wrapped lemon drop. "Pop it in quick, before she sees us."

It was obviously an old routine. Shannon watched Liam cuddle closer to Murphy, his tongue caught between his tiny teeth as he dealt with the wrapping.

"So, it's family night out, is it?" Maggie crossed over, laid her hands on the back of Brianna's chair. "Where's the baby?"

"Diedre snatched her." Automatically Brianna scooted over so that Maggie could draw up another chair.

"Hello, Shannon." The greeting was polite and coolly formal before Maggie's gaze shifted, narrowed expertly on her son. "What have you there, Liam?"

"Nothing." He grinned over his lemon drop.

"Nothing indeed. Murphy, you're paying for his first cavity." Then her attention shifted again. Shannon saw the tall dark man come toward the table, two cups stacked in one hand, a pint glass in the other. "Shannon Bodine, my husband, Rogan Sweeney."

"It's good to meet you." After setting down the drinks, he took her hand, smiling with a great deal of charm. Whatever curiosity there was, was well hidden. "Are you enjoying your visit?"

"Yes, thank you." She inclined her head. "I suppose I have you to thank for it."

"Only indirectly." He pulled up a chair of his own, making it necessary for Shannon to slide another inch or two closer to Murphy. "Hobbs tells me you work for Ry-Tilghmanton. We've always used the Pryce Agency in America."

Shannon lifted a brow. "We're better."

Rogan smiled. "Perhaps I'll look into that."

"This isn't a business meeting," his wife complained. "Murphy, won't you play something lively?"

He slipped easily into a reel, pumping quick, complicated notes out of the small instrument. Conversation around them became muted, punctuated by a few laughs, some hand clapping as a man in a brimmed hat did a fast-stepping dance on his way to the bar.

"Do you dance?" Murphy's lips were so close to her ear, Shannon felt his breath across her skin.

"Not like that." She eased back, using her glass as a barrier. "I suppose you do. That's part of it, right?"

He tilted his head, as amused as he was curious. "Being Irish you mean?"

"Sure. You dance . . ." She gestured with her glass. "Drink, brawl, write melancholy prose and poetry. And enjoy your image as suffering, hard-fisted rebels."

He considered a minute, keeping time with the tap of a foot. "Well, rebels we are, and suffering we've done. It seems you've lost your connection."

"I never had one. My father was third- or fourth-generation, and my mother had no family I knew about."

That brought a frown to her eyes, and though he was sorry for it, Murphy wasn't ready to let it go.

"But you think you know Ireland, and the Irish." Someone else had gotten up to dance, so he picked up a new tune to keep them happy. "You've watched some Jimmy Cagney movies on the late-night telly, or listened to Pat O'Brien playing his priests." When her frown deepened, he smiled blandly. "Oh, and there'd be the Saint Patrick's parade down your Fifth Avenue."

"So?"

"So, it tells you nothing, does it? You want to know the Irish, Shannon, then you listen to the music. The tune, and the words when there are words to hear. And when you hear it, truly, you might begin to know what makes us. Music's the heart of any people, any culture, because it comes from the heart."

Intrigued despite herself, she glanced down at his busy fingers. "Then I'm to think the Irish are carefree and quick on their feet."

"One tune doesn't tell the whole tale." Though the child was dozing now in his lap, he played on, shifting to something so suddenly sad, so suddenly soft, Shannon blinked.

Something in her own heart broke a little as Brianna began to quietly sing the lyrics. Others joined in, telling the tale of a soldier brave and doomed, dying a martyr for his country, named James Connolly.

When he'd finished, Rogan took the sleeping boy into his own lap, and Murphy reached for his beer. "It's not all 'MacNamarra's Band,' is it?"

She'd been touched, deeply, and wasn't sure she wanted to be. "It's an odd culture that writes lovely songs about an execution."

"We don't forget our heros," Maggie said with a snap in her voice. "Isn't it true that in your country they have tourist attractions on fields of battle? Your Gettysburg and such?"

Shannon eyed Maggie coolly, nodded. "Touché."

"And most of us like to pretend we'd have fought for the South," Gray put in.

"For slavery." Maggie sneered. "We know more about slavery than you could begin to imagine."

"Not for slavery." Pleased a debate was in the offing, Gray shifted toward her. "For a way of life."

"That should keep them happy," Rogan murmured as his wife and brother-in-law dived into the argument. "Is there anything you'd particularly like to do or see while you're here, Shannon? We'd be pleased to arrange things for you."

His accent was different, she noted. Subtly different, smoother, with a hint of what she would have termed prep school. "I suppose I should see the usual tourist things. And I don't suppose I could go back without seeing at least one ruin."

"Gray's put one nearby in his next book," Murphy commented.

"He did, yes." Brianna glanced behind her, trying not to fret because Diedre had yet to return the baby. "He did a nasty murder there. I'm just going to go back and see how Kayla's fairing. Would you have another pint, Murphy?"

"I wouldn't mind. Thanks."

"Shannon?"

With some surprise, Shannon noted her glass was empty. "Yes, I suppose."

"I'll get the drinks." After passing Liam to his wife, Rogan rose, giving Brianna a pat on the cheek. "Go fuss with the baby."

"Do you know this one?" Murphy asked as he began to play again.

It only took her a moment. " 'Scarborough Fair.' " It meant Simon and Garfunkel to her, on the oldies station on the radio.

"Do you sing, Shannon?"

"As much as anyone who has a shower and a radio." Fascinated, she bent her head closer. "How do you know which buttons to push?"

"First you have to know what song you've a mind to play. Here."

"No, I—" But he had already slipped an arm around her and was drawing her hands under the straps beneath his.

"You have to get the feel of it first." He guided her fingers to the buttons, pressed down gently as he opened the bellows. The chord that rang out was long and pure and made her laugh.

"That's one."

"If you can do one, you can do another." To prove it he pushed the bellows in and made a different note. "It just takes the wanting, and the practice."

Experimentally she shifted some fingers around and winced at the clash of notes. "I think it might take some talent." Then she was laughing again as he played his fingers over hers and made the instrument come to life. "And quick hands. How can you see what you're playing?"

With the laugh still in her eyes, she shook back her hair and turned her face to his. The jolt around her heart was as lively as the tune, and not nearly as pleasant.

"It's a matter of feeling." Though her fingers had gone still, he moved his around them, changing the mood of the music yet again. Wistful and romantic. "What do you feel?"

"Like I'm being played every bit as cleverly as this little box." Her eyes narrowed a bit as she studied him. Somehow their positions had shifted just enough to be considered an embrace. The hands, those hard-palmed, limber hands, were unquestionably possessive over hers. "You have some very smooth moves, Murphy."

"It occurs to me you don't mean that as a compliment."

"I don't. It's an observation." It was shocking to realize the pulse in her throat was hammering. His gaze lowered to her mouth, lingered so that she could feel the heat, and his intention as a tangible thing. "No," she said very quietly, very firmly.

"As you please." His eyes came back to hers, and there was a subtle and simple power in them that challenged. "I'd rather kiss you the first time in a more private place myself. Where I could take my time about it."

She thought he would—take his time, that is. He might not have been the slow man she'd originally perceived. But she had a feeling he was thorough. "I'd say that completes the lesson." Determined to find some distance, she tugged her hands from under his.

"We'll have another, whenever you've a mind to." And indeed taking his time, he lifted his arm from around her, then set down the concertina to drink the last of his beer. "You've got music in you, Shannon. You just haven't let yourself play it yet."

"I think I'll stick to the radio, thanks." More agitated than she cared to admit, she rose. "Excuse me." She went off in search of the rest room, and time to settle down.

Murphy was smiling to himself when he set his empty glass down. His brow lifted when he caught Maggie's frowning stare.

"What are you about, Murphy?" she demanded.

"I'm about to have another beer—once Rogan gets back with it."

"Don't play games with me, boy-o." She wasn't sure herself if it was temper or worry brewing in her, but neither was comforting. "I know you've an eye for the ladies, but I've never seen that look in them before."

"Haven't you?"

"Stop hounding him, Maggie." Gray kicked back in his chair. "Murphy's entitled to test the waters. She's a looker, isn't she?"

"Close your mouth, Grayson. And no, you've no right to be testing these waters, Murphy Muldoon."

He watched her, murmuring a thanks when Rogan set fresh drinks on the table. "You've an objection to me getting to know your sister, Maggie Mae?"

Eyes bright and sharp, she leaned forward. "I've an objection to seeing you walking toward the end of a cliff that you'll surely fall off. She's not one of us, and she's not going to be interested in a west county farmer, no matter how pretty he is."

Murphy said nothing for a moment, knowing Maggie would be simmering with impatience as he took out a cigarette, contemplated it, lighted it, drew in the first drag. "It's kind of you to worry about me, Maggie. But it's my cliff, and my fall."

"If you think I'm going to sit by while you make an ass of yourself and get your heart tromped on in the bargain, you're mistaken."

"It's none of your business, Margaret Mary," Rogan said and had his wife's wrath spewing on him.

"None of mine? Damn if it isn't. I've known this soft-headed fool all of his life, and loved him, though God knows why. And this Yank wouldn't be here if it weren't for me and Brianna."

"The Yank's your sister," Gray commented. "Which means she's probably as prickly and stubborn as you."

Before Maggie could bare her teeth at that, Murphy was holding up a hand. "She's the right of it. It's your business, Maggie, as I'm your friend and she's your sister. But it's more my business."

The hint of steel under the quiet tone had her temper defusing and her worry leaping. "Murphy, she'll be going back soon where she came from."

"Not if I can persuade her otherwise."

She grabbed his hands now, as if the contact would transfer some sense into him. "You don't even know her."

"Some things you know before it's reasonable." He linked his fingers with hers, for the bond there was deep and strong. "I've waited for her, Maggie, and here she is. That's it for me."

Because she could see the unarguable certainty of it in his eyes, she closed her own. "You've lost your mind. I can't get it back for you."

"You can't, no. Not even you."

She only sighed. "All right then, when you've had your fall and lay broken at the bottom, I'll come around and nurse your wounds. I want to take Liam home now, Sweeney." She rose, bundling the sleeping boy into her arms. "I won't ask you to talk sense to him," she added to Gray. "Men don't see past a comely face."

When she turned, she saw that Shannon had come out of the rest room and been waylaid by the Conroys. She sent Shannon a hard look, was answered in kind, then strode out of the pub with her son.

"They've got more in common than either one of them realizes." Gray watched Shannon stare at the pub door before giving her attention back to the old couple.

"It's the common ground that's between them as much as under their own feet."

Gray nodded before looking back at Murphy. "Are you stuck on that comely face, Murphy?"

More out of habit than design, Murphy fiddled out a tune. "That's part of it." His lips curved, but the look in his eyes was distant and deep. "It's the face I've been waiting to see again."

She wasn't going to let Maggie get under her skin. Shannon promised herself that as she readied for bed later that night. The woman had set detectives on her, had her researched and reported, and now that she'd tried to be open-minded enough to meet with the Concannons face-to-face, Maggie treated her like an intruder.

Well, she was staying as long as she damn well pleased. A couple of weeks, Shannon mused. Three at the outside. No one was going to chase her away with cold looks and abrasive comments. Margaret Mary Concannon was going to come to realize that America bred tougher nuts to crack.

And the farmer wasn't going to spook her, either. Charm and good looks weren't weapons that worried her. She'd known plenty of charming, good-looking men.

Maybe she'd never met one with quite Murphy's style, or that odd something flowing so placidly under it all, but it didn't concern her. Not really.

She climbed into bed, tugged the covers up to her chin. The rain had made the air just a little cooler than comfortable. Still it was snug and almost childishly pleasant to be bundled into bed with the sound of the rain pattering and the steaming cup of tea Brianna had insisted she take with her cooling on the nightstand.

Tomorrow she'd explore, Shannon promised herself. She would swallow her pride and take the car. She'd find her art supplies, maybe some ruins, a few shops. She'd done enough traveling with her parents not to be concerned about knocking about a foreign country on her own.

And on her own is where she wanted to be for a day, without anyone watching her movements, or trying to dissect them.

Snuggling down lower in the bed, she let her mind drift to the people she'd become involved with.

Brianna, the homebody. A new mother, new wife. And a businesswoman, Shannon reminded herself. Efficient, talented. Warmhearted, certainly, but with something like worry behind her eyes.

Gray—her fellow Yank. Easygoing—on the surface, at any rate. Friendly, sharp-witted, dazzled by his wife and daughter. Content, apparently, to shrug off the high life he could be living in a major city with his fame.

Maggie. The scowl came automatically. Suspicious by nature, hotheaded, frank to the point of rudeness. Shannon considered it too bad that she respected those particular traits. Unquestionably a loving wife and mother, indisputably a major talent. And, Shannon thought, overly protective and fiercely loyal.

Rogan was cultured, smooth, the ingrained manners as much a part of him as his eyes. Organized, she would guess, and shrewd. Sophisticated, and sharp enough to run an organization that was respected around the world. And, she thought grimly, he had to have a sense of humor, and the patience of Job, to live with Maggie.

Then there was Murphy, the good friend and neighbor. The farmer with a talent for music and flirtation. Strikingly handsome and unpretentious—yet not nearly as simple as it appeared at first glance. She didn't think she'd ever met a man as completely in tune with himself.

He wanted to kiss her, she thought as her eyes grew heavy, some place private. Where he could take his time about it.

It might be interesting.

The man controlled the impatient horse with no visible effort. Rain continued to pelt, icily, so that it sounded like pebbles striking the ground. The white stallion snorted, sending out frosty clouds of smoke as man and woman watched each other.

"You waited."

She could feel the heavy thud of her own heart. And the need, the terrible need was as strong as her pride. "Walking in my own field has nothing to do with waiting."

He laughed, a full, reckless sound that rolled over the hills. At the crest of one of those hills stood the stone circle, watching.

"You waited." In a move as graceful as a dance, he leaned down and scooped her off her feet. With one arm he lifted her, then set her in the saddle in front of him. "Kiss me," he demanded, twining gloved fingers in her hair. "And make it count."

Her arms dragged him closer until her breasts were flattened against the traveling armor over his chest. Her mouth was as hungry, as desperate and rough as his. On an oath, he flung out a hand so that his cloak enfolded her.

"By Christ, it's worth every cold, filthy mile for a taste of you."

"Then stay, damn you." She pulled him close again, pressed her starving lips to his. "Stay."

In sleep Shannon murmured, rocked between pleasure and despair. For even in sleep, she knew he wouldn't.

EIGHT

Shannon took a day for herself, and was better for it. The morning was damp, but cleared gradually so that as she drove, the landscape surrounding her seemed washed and skillfully lit. Furze lining the road was a blur of yellow blossoms. Hedges of fuchsia hinted at droplets of blood red. Gardens were drenched with color as the flowers sunned themselves in the watery light. Hills, the vivid green of them, simply shimmered.

She took photographs, toying with the idea of using the best of them as a basis for sketches or paintings.

It was true enough that she had some trouble negotiating the Irish roads, and the left-side drive, but she didn't intend to admit it.

She shopped for postcards and trinkets for friends back home along the narrow streets of Ennis. Friends, she mused, who thought she was simply taking a long overdue vacation. It was lowering to realize there was no one back home she felt intimate enough with to have shared her connection here, or her need to explore it.

Work had always come first—with the ambition scrambling behind it. And that, she decided, was a sad commentary on her life. Work had been a huge part of who she was, or considered herself to be. Now she'd cut herself off from it, purposely, so that she felt like a solitary survivor, drifting alone in an ocean of self-doubt.

If she was not Shannon Bodine by birth, and the hot young commercial artist by design, who was she?

The illegitimate daughter of a faceless Irishman who'd bedded a lonely woman who'd been on her own personal oddessy?

That was a painful thought, but one that kept worrying at her mind. She didn't want to believe that she was so unformed, so weak-hearted that the bald fact of her birth should matter to the grown woman.

Yet it did. She stood on a lonely strand of beach with the wind whipping through her hair and knew it did. If she'd been told as a child, had somehow been guided through life with the knowledge that Colin Bodine was the father who chose her if not the father who'd conceived her, she felt she couldn't be so hurt by the truth now.

She couldn't change it—not the facts or the way she'd learned of them. The only option left was to face them. And in facing them, face herself.

"Rough seas today."

Shannon looked around, startled by the voice and the old woman who stood just behind her. She hadn't heard anyone approach, but the breakers were crashing, and her mind had been very far away.

"Yes, it is." Shannon's lips curved in the polite, distant smile reserved for strangers. "It's a beautiful spot, though."

"Some prefer the wildness." The woman clutched a hooded cloak around her, staring out to sea with eyes surprisingly bright in such a well-lined face. "Some the calm. There's enough of both in the world for everyone to have their choice." She looked at Shannon then, alert, but unsmiling. "And enough time for any to change their mind."

Puzzled, Shannon tucked her hands in her jacket. She wasn't used to having philosophical discussions with passers-by. "I guess most people like a little of each, depending on their mood. What do they call this place? Does it have a name?"

"Some that call it Moria's Strand, for the woman who drowned herself in the surf when she lost her husband and three grown sons to a fire. She didn't give herself time to change her mind, you see. Or to remember that nothing, good or ill, stays forever."

"It's a lonely name for such a beautiful spot."

"It is, yes. And it's good for the soul to stop and take a long look now and again at what really lasts." She turned to Shannon again and smiled with great kindness. "The older you are, the longer you look."

"I've taken a lot of long looks today." Shannon smiled back. "But I have to get back now."

"Aye, you've a ways to travel yet. But you'll get where you're going, lass, and not forget where you've been."

An odd woman, Shannon thought as she started the climb up the gentle slope of rocks toward the road. She supposed it was another Irish trait to make an esoteric conversation out of something as simple as a view. As she reached the road, it occurred to her that the woman had been old, and alone, and perhaps needed a ride to wherever she'd been going.

She turned back with thoughts of offering just that. And saw nothing but an empty strand.

The shiver came first, then the shrug. The woman had just gone about her business, that was all. And it was past time that she turn the car around and take it back to its owner.

She found Brianna in the kitchen, sitting alone for once and nursing a solitary cup of tea.

"Ah, you're back." With an effort, Brianna smiled, then rose to pour another cup. "Did you have a nice drive?"

"Yes, thanks." Meticulously Shannon returned the car keys to their pegs. "I was able to pick up some of the supplies I needed, too. So I'll do some sketching tomorrow. I noticed another car out front."

"Guests, just arrived this afternoon from Germany."

"Your inn's a regular U.N." Brianna's absent response had her lifting a brow. Shannon might not have known the other woman well, but she recognized worry when she saw it. "Is something wrong?"

Brianna twisted her hands together, caught herself in the habitual gesture, and let them fall. "Would you sit for a minute, Shannon? I'd hoped to give you a few days before talking of this. But . . . I'm cornered."

"All right." Shannon sat. "Let's have it."

"Do you want something with your tea? I've biscuits, or—"

"You're stalling, Brianna."

Brianna sighed and sat. "I'm a born coward. I need to speak with you about my mother."

Shannon didn't move, but she brought her shields down. It was instinctive, covering both defensive and offensive. And her voice reflected the shift. "All right. We both know I'm not here to take in the sights. What do you want to say about it?"

"You're angry, and I can't blame you for it. You'll be angrier yet before it's over." Brianna stared down into her tea for a moment. "Bad feelings are what I'm most cowardly about. But there's no putting this off. She's coming by. I've run out of excuses to stop her. I can't lie to her, Shannon, and pretend you're no more than a guest here."

"Why should you?"

"She doesn't know about this, any of this." Eyes troubled, Brianna looked up again. "Nothing about my father and your mother. Nothing about you."

Shannon's smile was cool and thin. "Do you really believe that? From what I've seen, wives generally have an instinct about straying husbands."

"Straying wasn't what happened between our parents, and yes, I believe it completely. If my mother had known, it would have been her finest weapon against him." It hurt to admit it, shamed her to speak of it, but she saw no choice now. "Never once in my life did I see any love between them. Only duty, the coldness of that. And the heat of resentment."

It wasn't something Shannon wanted to hear, and certainly nothing she chose to care about. She picked up her cup. "Then why did they stay married?"

"There's a complicated business," Brianna mused. "Church, children. Habit even. My mother's resentment for him was great—and to be fair, she had some reason. He could never hold on to his money, nor had he any skill in the making of it. Money and what it buys was—is—important to her. She had a career in singing, and an ambition when she met him. She never wanted to settle for a house and a little piece of land. But there was a flash, you could say, between them. The flash became Maggie."

"I see." It appeared she and her half sister had more in common than Shannon had realized. "He made a habit of being careless with sex."

Brianna's eyes went hot and sharp, a phenomenon that had Shannon staring in fascination. "You have no right to say that. No, even you have no right, for you didn't know him. He was a man of great kindness, and great heart. For more than twenty years he put his own dreams behind him to raise his children. He loved Maggie as much as any father could love any child. It was my mother who blamed him, and Maggie, for the life she found herself faced with. She lay with him to make me out of duty. Duty to the Church first. I can't think of a colder bed for a man to come to."

"You can't know what was between them before you were born," Shannon interrupted.

"I know very well. She told me herself. I was her penance for her sin. Her reparation. And after she knew she was carrying me, there was no need to be his wife beyond the bedroom door."

Shannon shook her head. It had to be as humiliating for Brianna to speak of such matters as it was for her to hear it. Yet Brianna didn't look humiliated, she noted. Brianna looked coldly furious. "I'm sorry. It's almost impossible for me to understand why two people would stay together under those conditions."

"This isn't America. 'Tis Ireland, and more than twenty years ago in Ireland. I'm telling you this so you'll understand there was pain in this house. Some of it Da brought on himself, there's no denying that. But there's a bitterness in my mother, and something inside her makes her cleave to it. If she had known, even suspected, that he'd found happiness and love with another, she'd have driven him into the ground with it. She couldn't have stopped herself, nor seen a reason to."

"And now she'll have to know."

"Now she'll have to know," Brianna agreed. "She'll see you as a slap. And she'll try to hurt you."

"She can't hurt me. I'm sorry if it seems callous to you, but her feelings and her way of displaying them just don't matter to me."

"That may be true." Brianna took a long breath. "She's better, more content than she used to be. We've set her up in her own house, near to Ennis. It's more what makes her happy. We found a wonderful woman to live with her. Lottie's a retired nurse—which comes in handy as Mother sees herself suffering from all manner of illnesses. The grandchildren have mellowed her a bit, too. Though she doesn't like to show it."

"And you're afraid this will blow things out of the water again."

"I'm not afraid it will. I know it will. If I could spare you from her anger and embarrassment, I would, Shannon."

"I can handle myself."

Brianna's face relaxed into a smile. "Then I'll ask a favor. Don't let whatever she says or does turn you away. We've had such little time, and I want more."

"I planned to stay two or three weeks," Shannon said evenly. "I don't see any reason to change that."

"I'm grateful. Now, if—" She broke off, distressed when she heard the sound of the front door opening, and the raised female voices. "Oh, they're here already."

"And you'd like to talk to her alone first."

"I would. If you don't mind."

"I'd just as soon not be around for the first act." Feigning a calmness she no longer felt, Shannon rose. "I'll go outside."

She told herself it was ridiculous to feel as though she were deserting a sinking ship. It was Brianna's mother, Shannon reminded herself as she started along the garden path. Brianna's problem.

There'd be a scene, she imagined. Full of Irish emotions, temper, and despair. She certainly wanted no part of that. Thank God she'd been raised in the States by two calm, reasonable people who weren't given to desperate mood swings.

Drawing a deep breath, she turned a circle. And saw Murphy crossing the closest field, coming toward the inn.

He had a wonderful way of walking, she noted. Not a strut, not a swagger, yet his stride had all the confidence of both. She had to admit it was a pleasure to watch him, the raw masculinity of movement.

An animated painting, she mused. Irish Man. Yes, that was it exactly, she decided—the long-muscled arms with the work shirt rolled up to the elbows, the jeans that had seen dozens of washings, the boots that had walked countless miles. The cap worn low to shade the eyes that couldn't dim that rich, startling blue. The almost mythically handsome face.

A capital *M* man, she reflected. No polished executive could exude such an aura of success striding down Madison Avenue in a thousand-dollar suit with a dozen Sterling roses in his manicured hand as Murphy Muldoon strolling over the land in worn boots and a spray of wildflowers.

"It's a pleasant thing to walk toward a woman who's smiling at you."

"I was thinking you looked like a documentary. Irish farmer walking his land."

That disconcerted him. "My land ends at the wall there."

"Doesn't seem to matter." Amused by his reaction, she glanced down at the flowers he held. "Isn't that what we call bringing coals to Newcastle?"

"But these *are* from my land. Since I was thinking of you, I picked them along the way."

"They're lovely. Thanks." She did what any woman would do and buried her face in them. "Is it your house I see from my window? The big stone one with all the chimneys?"

"It is, yes."

"A lot of house for one man. And all those other buildings."

"A farm needs a barn or two, and cabins and such. If you'll walk over one day, I'll show you about."

"Maybe I will." She glanced back toward the house at the first shout. Shannon doubted it would be the last one.

"Maeve's come, then," Murphy murmured. "Mrs. Concannon."

"She's here." A sudden thought had her looking back at Murphy, studying his face. "And so are you. Just happening by?"

"I wouldn't say that. Maggie called to tell me things would be brewing."

The resentment came as quickly as the unexpected protective instinct. "She should be here herself, and not leave this whole mess up to Brie."

"She's there. That's her you hear shouting." In an easy gesture, one more sheltering than it seemed, he took Shannon's hand and led her farther from the house. "Maggie and her mother will go at each other like terriers. Maggie'll see that she does, to keep Maeve from striking out too close to Brianna."

"Why should the woman fight with them?" Shannon demanded. "They had nothing to do with it."

Murphy said nothing a moment, moving off a little ways to examine the blossoms on a blackthorn. "Did your parents love you, Shannon?"

"Of course they did."

"And never did you have any cause to doubt it, or to take the love aside and examine it for flaws?"

Impatient now, for the house had grown ominously silent, she shook her head. "No. We loved each other."

"I had the same." As if time were only there to be spent, he drew her down on the grass, then leaned back on his elbows. "You didn't think about being lucky, because it just was. Every cuff or caress my mother ever gave me had love in it. One the same as the other."

Idly he picked up Shannon's hand, toyed with her fingers. "I don't know as I'd have thought about it overmuch. But there was Maggie and Brie nearby, and I could see that they didn't have the same. With Tom they did." Murphy's eyes lighted with the memory. "His girls were his greatest joy. Maeve didn't have that kind of giving in her. And I'm thinking, the more he loved them, the more she was determined not to. To punish them all, herself included."

"She sounds like a horrible woman."

"She's an unhappy one." He lifted her hand, brushing his lips over the knuckles in an absent gesture of long intimacy. "You've been unhappy, Shannon. But you're strong and smart enough to let the sadness pass into memories."

"I don't know if I am."

"I know." He rose then, holding out a hand. "I'll go in with you. It's been quiet long enough, so it's time."

She let him pull her to her feet, but no further. "This isn't my affair, Murphy. It seems to me everyone would be better off if I stayed out of it."

His eyes stayed on hers, dark and level and tough. "Stand with your sisters, Shannon. Don't disappoint me, or yourself."

"Damn it." His unblinking stare made her feel weak, and ashamed of the weakness. "Damn it, all right. I'll go in. But I don't need you with me."

"I'm with you just the same." Keeping her hand in his, he led her toward the house.

It was foolish to dread it, Shannon told herself. The woman could do or say nothing that would have any affect. But her muscles were coiled and her shoulders stiff when she stepped through the kitchen door with Murphy behind her.

Her first thought was that the woman seated at the table didn't look like anyone's victim. Her eyes were hot, her face set in the unforgiving lines of a judge who'd already passed sentence. Her hands were ringless, gripped together on the tabletop in what might have been an attitude of prayer had the knuckles not been white.

The other woman seated beside her was rounder, with a softer look offset by worried eyes. Shannon saw that the Concannon sisters were standing, shoulder to shoulder, with their husbands on either side in an unyielding and united wall.

Maeve pinned her with one furious look, and her lips curled. "You would bring her here, into this house, while I'm in it?"

"The house is mine," Brianna said in a voice that was frigidly calm. "And Shannon is welcome in it. As you are, Mother."

"As I am? You'd throw her in my face. This spawn of your father's adultery. This is how you show your respect, your loyalty to me, the woman who gave you life."

"And resented every breath of it we took thereafter," Maggie tossed out.

"I'd expect it from you." Maeve's wrath turned to roll over her eldest daughter. "You're no different than she. Born in sin."

"Oh, save your Bible thumping." Maggie waved the fury away. "You didn't love him, so you'll get no sympathy."

"I took vows with him, and vows I kept."

"The words, but not the heart of them," Brianna murmured. "What's done is done, Mother."

"Maeve." Lottie reached out a hand. "The girl's not to blame."

"Don't speak to me of blame. What kind of woman sneaks another's husband into her bed?"

"One who loved, I imagine." Shannon stepped forward, unconsciously moving closer to that united wall.

"Love makes it all right to sin? To defile the Church?" Maeve would have stood, but her legs felt shaky, and something inside her heart was burning. "I'd expect no less from the likes of you. A Yank, raised by an adulteress."

"Don't speak of my mother," Shannon warned in a low, dangerous voice. "Ever. She had more courage, more compassion, more sheer goodness in her than you can possibly imagine in your narrow little world. You curse the fact of my existence all you want, but you don't speak of my mother."

"You come all the way from America to give me orders in my house."

"I've come because I was invited to come." Shannon's anger was too blinding for her to realize that Murphy's hand was on her shoulder, Gray's on her arm. "And because it was one of the last things my mother wished me to do before she died. If it disturbs you, it can't be helped."

Maeve rose slowly. The girl had the look of him, was all she could think. What kind of penance was it that she had to look into the girl's face and see Tom Concannon's eyes?

"The sin's planted in you, girl. That's your only legacy from Tom Concannon." Like the snap of a whip, she shot her gaze to Murphy. "And you, Murphy Muldoon. Standing with her brings shame to your family. You're showing yourself as weak natured as any man, for you're thinking she'll be as free with herself as she was born in sin."

Murphy's hand tightened on Shannon's arm before she could step forward and attack. "Take care, Mrs. Concannon." His voice was mild, but Shannon could feel the strength of his temper through his tensed fingers. "You're saying things you'll need to repent. When you speak of my family, and of Shannon in such a way, the shame is yours."

Her eyes narrowed so that no one could see the tears swimming behind them. "So you'll all stand against me. Every one of you."

"We're of one mind on this, Maeve." Subtly Rogan blocked his wife. "When your mind's calmer, we'll talk again."

"There's nothing to talk of." She snatched her purse from the table. "You've chosen."

"You have a choice, too," Gray said quietly. "Holding on to the past or accepting the present. No one here wants to hurt you."

"I expect nothing but duty, and even that isn't offered by my own flesh and blood. I'll not come into this house again while she's under its roof." She turned and walked stiffly away.

"I'm sorry." Lottie gathered her own bag. "She needs time, and talking out." With an apologetic look at Shannon, she hurried after Maeve.

After one long minute of silence, Gray let out a breath. "Well, that was fun." Despite the lightness of tone, his arm had gone around his wife and he was rubbing his hand up and down her arm. "What do you say, Shannon. I'll go out and find a nice pointed stick to jab in your eye."

"I'd rather have a drink," she heard herself say, then her gaze focused on Brianna. "Don't apologize," she said in a shaky voice. "Don't you dare apologize."

"She won't." Determined to fight back the one that was looming in her own throat, Maggie gave her sister a nudge toward the table. "Sit down, all of you. We're having whiskey. Murphy, put on the kettle."

With his hand still on Shannon's shoulder, he started to turn. "I thought we were having whiskey."

"You are. I'll have tea." It was a good time, she decided. The perfect time for such news. She looked straight at Rogan, a gleam of unholy amusement in her eyes. "It's not wise to have spirits when you're carrying."

He blinked once, then the grin started, and spread. "You're pregnant."

"So the doctor said just this morning." Planting her hands on her hips, she tilted her head. "Are you just going to stand there, gawking like a fool?"

"No." The laughter burst out as he swept her off her feet and spun her around the kitchen. "By Christ, Margaret Mary, I love you. Pour the whiskey, Gray. We've something to celebrate."

"I'm pouring it." But he stopped long enough to give Maggie a kiss.

"She did that for you," Murphy murmured as Shannon stood beside him, watching the lightning shift of mood.

"What?"

"She told him here, told all of us here." He measured out tea as he spoke. "That was for her sisters, to ease the heaviness around their hearts."

"For Brianna," Shannon began, but Murphy cut her off with a look.

"Don't close yourself off from a gift when it's offered, darling. Her telling made you smile, just as she wanted it to."

Shannon stuffed her hands in her pockets. "You have a way of making me feel very small."

He tipped her chin up with a gentle finger. "Maybe I have a way of helping you look one level deeper."

"I think I enjoyed being shallow." But she turned away from him and walked to Maggie. "Congratulations." She took the glass Gray offered and stood awkwardly. "I don't know any Irish toasts."

"Try *Slainte o Dhia duit,*" Maggie suggested.

Shannon opened her mouth, closed it on a laugh. "I don't think so."

"Just *slainte*'s enough," Murphy said as he brought the teapot to the table. "She's just tormenting you."

"*Slainte,* then." Shannon lifted her glass, then remembered something from her childhood. "Oh, and may you have a dozen children, Maggie, just like you."

"A toast and a curse." Gray snickered. "Well done, pal."

"Aye." Maggie's lips curved. "She's done well enough."

NINE

The hours Murphy spent with his horses was his purest pleasure. Working the land was something he had always done, always would do. There was joy in it, and frustration, and disappointment and pride. He enjoyed the soil in his hands, under his feet, and the scent of growing things. Weather was equal parts his friend and his enemy. He knew the moods of the sky often better than he knew his own.

His life had been spent plowing the earth, planting it, reaping it. It was something he had always known, yet it was not all he knew.

The fine spring that the west was enjoying meant his work was hard and long, but without the bitter sorrow of root crops that rotted in soaked earth, or grains that suffered from the bite of frost or the plague of pests.

He planted wisely, combining the ways of his father and grandfather with the newer, and often experimental means he read of in books. Whether he rode his tractor toward the brown field with its rows of dark green potato plants, or walked into the shadowy dairy barn at dawn to start the milking, he knew his work was valuable.

But his horses were for him.

He clucked to a yearling, watching as the wide-chested bay gave a lazy swish of tail. They knew each other these two, and the game of long standing. Murphy waited patiently, enjoying the routine. A glossy mare stood farther out in the field, cropping grass patiently while her colt nursed. Others, including the mare who was mother to the yearling, and Murphy's prize, the chestnut filly, perked up their ears and watched the man.

Murphy patted his pocket, and with equine pride the yearling tossed his head and approached.

"You're a fine one, aren't you? Good lad." He chuckled, stroking the yearling's flank as the horse nuzzled at the pocket, and the others walked his way. "Not above bribery. Here, then." He took a chunk of the apples he'd quartered and let the colt eat out of his hand. "I'm thinking you're going on a fine adventure today. I'll miss you." He stroked, automatically checking the colt's knees. "Damned if I won't. But lazing in pasture all day isn't what you were born for. And all of us have to do what we were meant to do."

He greeted the other horses, sharing the bits of apple, then with his arm slung around the yearling's neck, he gazed over the land. Harebells and bluebells were springing up wild, and the madwort was beginning to bloom yellow beside the near wall. He could see his silo, and the barn, the cabins, the house beyond, looking like a picture against a sky of layered clouds.

Past noon, he judged, and considered going in for a cup of tea before his business appointment. Then he looked west, just beyond the stone dance, away by the wall that separated grazing from grain.

And there she was.

His heart stumbled in his chest. He wondered if it would always be so when he saw her. It was a stunning thing for a man who had gone more than thirty years without feeling more than a passing interest in a woman to see one, once, and know without doubt that she was his fate.

The wanting was there, a churning deep that made him long to touch and taste and take. He thought he could, with a careful and patient approach. For she wasn't indifferent to him. He'd felt her pulse leap, and seen the change that was desire slip into her eyes.

But the love was there, deeper yet than the wanting. And stranger, he thought now, as it seemed to have been there always, waiting. So it would not be enough to touch, to taste, to take. That would only be a beginning.

"But you have to begin to go on, don't you?" Murphy gave the yearling a last caress, then walked over the pasture.

Shannon saw him coming. Indeed, she'd been distracted from her work when he'd come among the horses. It had been like a play, she thought, the man and the young horse, both exceptional specimens, passing a few moments together in a green field.

She'd known, too, the exact moment when he'd seen her. The distance hadn't kept her from feeling the power of the look. What does he want from me? she asked herself as she went back to the canvas she'd started.

What do I want from him?

"Hello, Murphy." She continued to paint as he came to the wall that separated them. "Brianna said you wouldn't mind if I worked here for a while."

"You're welcome for as long as you like. Is it the dance you're painting?"

"Yes. And yes, you can take a look." She changed brushes, clamping one between her teeth as he swung over the wall.

She was catching the mystery of it, Murphy decided as he studied the canvas that was set on an easel. The entire circle was sketched in, with a skill he admired and envied. Though both back and foregrounds were blank still, she'd begun to add color and texture to the stones.

"It's grand, Shannon."

Though it pleased her, she shook her head. "It has a long way to go before it's close to being grand. And I've nearly lost the right light today." Though she knew, somehow, she could paint the standing stones in any light, from any angle. "I thought I saw you earlier, on your tractor."

"Likely." He liked the way she smelled when she worked—paint and perfume. "Have you been at it long?"

"Not long enough." Frowning, she swirled her brush in paint she'd smeared on her palette. "I should have set up at dawn to get the right shadows."

"There'll be another dawn tomorrow." He sat on the wall, tapping a finger against her sketchbook. "That shirt you're wearing, what does CM stand for?"

She set down her brush, took a step back to examine the canvas, and smeared more paint from her fingers to the sweatshirt. "Carnegie Mellon. It's the college I went to."

"You studied painting there."

"Umm." The stones weren't coming to life yet, she thought. She wanted them alive. "I concentrated on commercial art."

"Is that doing pictures for advertisements?"

"More or less."

He considered, picking up her sketchbook and leafing through. "Why would you want to draw up pictures of shoes or bottles of beer when you can do this?"

She picked up a rag, dampened it from her jar of turpentine. "I like making a living, and I make a good one." For some reason she found it imperative to remove a smudge of gray paint from the side of her hand. "I just copped a major account before I took my leave of absence. I'm likely to get a promotion."

"That's fine, isn't it?" He flipped another page, smiled over a sketch of Brianna working in her garden. "What sort of account is it?"

"Bottled water." She muttered it, because it seemed so foolish a thing out here in the wide fields and fragrant air.

"Water?" He did exactly what she'd expected. He grinned at her. "The fizzy kind? Why do you suppose people want to drink water that bubbles or comes in bottles?"

"Because it's pure. Not everyone has a well in their backyard, or a spring, or whatever the hell it is. Designer water's an enormous industry, and with pollution and urban development it's only going to get bigger."

He continued to smile. "I didn't ask to rile you. I was just wondering." He turned the sketchbook toward her. "I like this one."

She set her rag aside and shrugged. It was a drawing of him, in the pub holding his concertina, a half-finished beer on the table. "You should. I certainly flattered you."

"It was kind of you." He set the book aside. "I've someone coming by shortly to look at the yearling, so I can't ask you in for tea. Will you come tonight, for dinner instead?"

"To dinner?" When he rose, she took an automatic step in retreat.

"You could come early. Half six, so I could show you about first." A new light came into his eyes, one of dangerous amusement as he caught her hand. "Why are you walking backward?"

"I'm not." Or she wasn't now that he had hold of her. "I'm thinking. Brianna might have plans."

"Brie's a flexible woman." A light tug on the hand brought Shannon a step closer. "Come, spend the evening with me. You're not afraid of the two of us being alone?"

"Of course not." That would be ridiculous. "I don't know if you can cook."

"Come find out."

Dinner, she reminded herself. It was just dinner. In any case she was curious about him, how he lived. "All right. I'll come by."

"Good." With one hand still holding hers, he cupped the back of her head, inched her closer. Her nerves were already sizzling when she remembered to lift a protesting hand to his chest.

"Murphy—"

"I'm only going to kiss you," he murmured.

There was no *only* about it. His eyes stayed open, aware, alive on hers as his mouth lowered. They were the last thing she saw, that vivid, stunning blue, before she went deaf, dumb, and blind.

It was barely a whisper of a touch at first, a light brush of mouth to mouth. He was holding her as if they might slide into a dance at any instant. She thought she might sway, so soft and sweet was that first meeting of lips.

Then they left hers, surprising a sigh out of her as he took his mouth on a slow, luxurious journey of her face. The quiet exploration—her cheeks, her temples, her eyelids—weakened her knees. The trembling started there, and moved up so that she was breathless when his mouth covered hers a second time.

Deeper now, slowly. Her lips parted, and the welcome sounded in her throat. Her hand slid up to his shoulder, gripped, then went limp. She could smell horses and grass, and something like lightning in the air.

He'd come back, was all she could think before her head went swimming into dreams.

She was everything he'd wanted. To hold her like this, to feel her tremble with the same need that shook inside him was beyond glorious. Her mouth seemed to have been fashioned to meld with his, and the tastes he found there were dark, mysterious, and ripe.

It was enough, somehow it was enough, to hold back, to suffer the gnawing teeth of a less patient need. He could see how it would be, feel how it would be, to lie down in the warm grass with her, to pin her beneath him, body to body and flesh to flesh. How she would move under and against him, willing and eager and fluid. And at last, at long last, to bury himself inside her.

But this time her mouth was enough. He let himself linger, and savor and possess, drawing away gently, and with the promise of more.

His hands wanted to shake. To soothe them, he skimmed them over her face and into her hair. Her cheeks were flushed, making her, to his eye, even lovelier. How could he have forgotten how slim she was, like a willow, or how much truth and beauty could shine from her eyes.

His hand paused in her hair, and his brows drew together as image shifted over image.

"Your hair was longer then, and your cheeks were wet from rain."

Her head was spinning, actually spinning. She had always believed that was a ridiculous romantic cliché. But she had to put a hand to her temple to steady herself. "What?"

"Another time we met here." He smiled again. It was easy for him to accept such things as visions and magic, just as he could accept that his heart had been lost long before that first lovely taste of her. "I've wanted to kiss you for a long time."

"We haven't known each other a long time."

"We have. Shall I do it again, and remind you?"

"I don't think so." No matter how foolish it made her feel, she held up a hand to stop him. "That was a little more potent than I'd expected, and I think we'd both be better off . . . pacing ourselves."

"As long as we're after getting to the same place."

She let her hand drop. If she could be sure of anything it was that he wouldn't press, or make awkward or unwanted moves. Still, she took only an instant to study him, and less to look inside herself.

"I don't know that we are."

"It's enough that one of us knows. I've an appointment to keep." He brushed his fingers down her cheek so that he could take that last touch with him. "I'll look for you tonight." He caught the expression on her face before he swung over the wall. "You're not so faint of heart you'll make excuses not to come just because you liked kissing me."

It wasn't worth the effort to be annoyed that he'd seen she was about to do so. Instead she turned away to pack up her equipment. "I'm not faint of heart. And I've liked kissing men before."

"Sure and you have, Shannon Bodine, but you've never kissed the likes of me."

He went off whistling. She made sure he was out of earshot before she let the laughter loose.

It shouldn't have felt odd to go on a date—not when a woman had recently turned twenty-eight and had experienced her share of firsts and lasts in the game of singles.

Maybe it had been the way Brianna had fussed—bustling around like a nervous mother on prom night. Shannon could only smile to think on it.

Brianna had offered to press a dress, or lend her one, and had twice come up to the loft room with suggestions on accessories and shoes.

Shannon supposed she'd been a great disappointment to Brianna when she'd appeared downstairs in casual slacks and a plain silk shirt.

That hadn't stopped Brianna from telling her she looked lovely, to have a wonderful time, and not to worry about when she got in. If Gray hadn't come along and dragged his wife out of the hall, she might never have gotten away.

It was, Shannon supposed, sisterlike behavior, and didn't make her as uncomfortable as she'd expected.

She was grateful both Brianna and Gray had insisted she take the car. It wasn't a long trip to Murphy's, but the road would be dark after sunset, and it looked like rain.

Only minutes after pulling out of the driveway, she was pulling in to a longer one that squeezed between hedges of fuchsia that had already begun to bloom in bloodred hearts.

She'd seen the farmhouse from her window, but it was larger, and undoubtedly more impressive up close. Three stories of stone and wood that looked as old as the land itself, and equally well tended, rose up behind the hedge and before a tidy plot of mixed flowers.

There were flat arches of dressed stone above the tidy square windows of the first floor. She caught a glimpse of a side porch and imagined there were doors leading to it from the inside.

Two of the chimneys were smoking, puffing their clouds lazily into the still blue sky. A pickup truck was in the drive ahead of her, splashed with mud. Beside that was an aged compact raised onto blocks.

She couldn't claim to know much about cars, but it certainly had seen better days.

But the shutters and the front porch of the house were freshly painted in a mellow blue that blended softly with the gray stone. There was no clutter on the porch, only a pair of rockers that seemed to invite company. The invitation was completed by the door that was already open.

Still, she knocked on the jamb and called out. "Murphy."

"Come in and welcome." His voice seemed to come from up the stairs that shot off from the main hallway. "I'll be a minute. I'm washing up."

She stepped inside and closed the door behind her. To satisfy her curiosity, she walked a little farther down the hall and peeked into the first room, where again, a batten door was open in welcome.

A parlor, of course, she noted. Every bit as tidy as Brianna's, if lacking some of her feminine touches.

Old, sturdy furniture was set on a wide planked floor that gleamed. A turf fire simmered in a stone hearth, bringing its ancient and appealing scent into the room. There were candlesticks flanking the thick wood mantel, bold, sinuous twists of emerald. Certain they were Maggie's work, she went in for a closer look.

They looked too fluid, too molten to be solid. Yet the glass was cool against her fingers. There was a subtle, fascinating hint of ruby beneath, as though there were heat trapped inside waiting to flame out.

"You'd think you could poke your fingers straight into the heart of it," Murphy commented from the doorway.

Shannon nodded, tracing the coils again before she turned. "She's brilliant. Though I'd prefer you not tell her I said so." Her brow lifted when she studied him. He didn't look so very different from the man who walked his fields or played his music in pubs. He was without his cap, and his hair was thick, curled, and a bit damp from his washing. His sweater was a soft gray, his slacks shades darker.

She found it odd that she could picture him as easily on the cover of *GQ* as on *Agricultural Monthly*.

"You wash up well."

He grinned self-consciously. "You look at things, people, more as an artist does once you're used to them. I didn't mean to keep you."

"It's no problem. I like seeing where you live." Her gaze glanced off him and focused on a wall of books. "That's quite a library."

"Oh, that's just some of them."

He stayed where he was when she crossed over. Joyce, Yeats, Shaw. Those were to be expected. O'Neill, Swift, and Grayson Thane, of course. But there was a treasure trove of others. Poe, Steinbeck, Dickens, Byron. The poetry of Keats and Dickinson and Browning. Battered volumes of Shakespeare and equally well-thumbed tales by King and McCaffrey and McMurtry.

"An eclectic collection," she mused. "And there's more?"

"I keep them here and there around the house, so if you're in the mood, you don't have to go far. A book's a pleasant thing to have nearby."

"My father wasn't much on reading, unless it had to do with business. But my mother and I love—loved to. In the end, she was so ill, I read to her."

"You were a comfort to her. And a joy."

"I don't know." She shook herself and tried a bright smile. "So, am I getting a tour?"

"A child knows when she's loved," Murphy said quietly, then took her hand. "And yes, you'll have a tour. We'll go outside first, before it rains."

But she made him stop a half a dozen times before they'd traveled from the front of the house to the back. He explained the raftered ceiling, and the little room off the right where his mother still liked to sew when she came to visit.

The kitchen was as big as a barn, and as scrupulously clean as any she'd ever seen. Still, it surprised her to see colored jars of herbs and spices ranged on the counter, and the gleam of copper-bottomed pots hanging over it.

"Whatever you've got in the oven smells wonderful."

" 'Tis chicken, and needs some time yet. Here, try these."

He brought a pair of Wellingtons out of an adjoining room and had Shannon frowning. "We're not going to go tromping around in . . ."

"More than likely." He crouched down to slip the first boot over her shoe. "When you've got animals, you've got dung. You'll be happier in these."

"I thought you kept the cows out in the field."

Delighted, he grinned up at her. "You don't go milking them in the fields, darling, but in the milking parlor. That's done for the night." He led her out the back where he stepped easily into his own Wellies. "I kept you waiting as one of the cows took sick."

"Oh, is it serious?"

"No, I'm thinking it's not. Just needed some medicating."

"Do you do that yourself? Don't you have a vet?"

"Not for everyday matters."

She looked around and found herself smiling again. Another painting, she thought. Stone buildings neatly set among paddocks. Woolly sheep crowded together near a trough. Some huge and wickedly toothed machine under a lean-to, and the bleat and squawk of animals not ready to call it a day.

There was Con, sitting patiently beside the near paddock, thumping his tail.

"Brie sent him, I'd wager, to see I behaved myself with you."

"I don't know. He seems as much your dog as hers." She looked over at him as Murphy bent to greet the dog. "I'd have thought a farmer would have at least one or two hounds of his own."

"I had one, died seven years ago this winter coming." With the ease of mutual love, Murphy stroked Con's ears. "I think of getting another from time to time, but never seem to get around to it."

"You've got everything else. I didn't realize you raised sheep."

"Just a few. My father, now, he was one for sheep." He straightened, then took her hand as he walked. "I'm more a dairy man myself."

"Brianna says you prefer horses."

"The horses are a pleasure. In another year or two they may pay their way. Today I sold a yearling, a beautiful colt. The entertainment of horse trading nearly balances out the losing of him."

She glanced up as Murphy opened the barn door. "I didn't think farmers were supposed to get attached."

"A horse isn't a sheep that you butcher for Sunday dinner."

The image of that made her just queasy enough to let the subject stand. "You milk in here?"

"Aye." He led the way through a scrubbed milk parlor with glistening stainless machines and the faint scent of cow and milk drifting through the air. " 'Tisn't as romantic as doing it by hand—and I did that as a boy—but it's faster, cleaner, and more efficient."

"Every day," Shannon murmured.

"Twice daily."

"It's a lot of work for one man."

"The lad at the farm next helps with that. We have an arrangement."

As he showed her through the parlor, the barn, outside again to the silo and the other sheds, she didn't think one boy would make much difference in the expanse of labor.

But it was easy to forget all the sweat, the muscle that had to go into every hour of the day when he took her into the stables to show his horses.

"Oh, they're even more beautiful close up." Too enchanted to be wary, she lifted her hand and stroked the cheek of the chestnut filly.

"That's my Jenny. I've had her only two years, and she I'll never sell. There's a lass." It took only the sound of his voice to have the horse shifting her attention to Murphy. If Shannon had believed such things possible, she'd have sworn the filly flirted with him.

And why not? she mused. What female would resist those wide, skilled hands, the way they stroked, caressed? Or that soft voice, murmuring foolish endearments?

"Do you ride, Shannon?"

"Hmm." The lump that had abruptly lodged in her throat caused her to swallow hard. "No, I never have. In fact, I guess this is as close as I've ever been to a horse."

"But you're not afraid of them, so it'll be easier for you to learn if you've a mind to."

He took her through, letting her coo her fill and pet and play with the foals newly born that spring, and watched her laugh at the frisky colt who would have nibbled on her shoulder if Murphy hadn't blocked the muzzle with his hand.

"It would be a wonderful way to grow up," she commented as they walked back to the house. "All this room, all the animals." She laughed as she stopped at the rear door to toe off her boots. "And the work, of course. But you must have loved it, since you stayed."

"I belong to it. Come in and sit. I've some wine you'll like."

Companionably she washed her hands at the kitchen sink with him. "Didn't any of your family want to stay and work the farm?"

"I'm the oldest son, and when me father died, it fell to me. My older sisters married and moved away to start families of their own." He took a bottle from the refrigerator, a corkscrew from a drawer. "Then my mother remarried, and my younger sister Kate as well. I have a younger brother, but he wanted to go to school and learn about electrical matters."

Her eyes had widened as he poured the wine. "How many are there of you?"

"Five. There were six, but my mother lost another son when he was still nursing. My father died when I was twelve, and she didn't marry again until I was past twenty, so there were only five."

"Only." She chuckled, shook her head, and would have raised her glass, but he stayed her hand.

"May you have warm words on a cold evening, a full moon on a dark night, and the road downhill all the way to your door."

"Slainte," she said and smiled at him as she drank. "I like your farm, Murphy."

"I'm pleased you do, Shannon." He surprised her by leaning down and pressing his lips to her brow.

Rain began to patter softly as he straightened again and turned to open the oven door. The scents that streamed out had her mouth watering.

"Why is it I always thought Irish cooking was an oxymoron?"

He hefted out the roaster, set it on the stove top. "Well, it's the truth that it's more often a bit bland than not. I never noticed myself as a lad. But when Brie started experimenting, and trying out dishes on me, I began to see that my own dear mother had a certain lack in the kitchen." He glanced over his shoulder. "Which I would deny unto death if you repeated such slander."

"She'll never hear it from me." She rose, too intrigued not to take a closer look. The chicken was golden, beaded with moisture, flecked with spices, and surrounded by a browned circle of potatoes and carrots. "Now, that's wonderful."

"It's Brie's doing. She started me an herb garden years back, hounded me till I took the time to tend it."

Shannon leaned back on the counter, eyeing him. "Weren't you a little miffed when Gray came along and beat your time?"

He was well and truly baffled for a minute, then grinned as he transferred chicken from pan to platter. "She was never for me, nor I for her. We've been family too long. Tom was a father to me when mine died. And Brie and Maggie were always my sisters." He carved off a small slice at the breast. "Not that it's a brotherly feeling I have toward you, Shannon. I've waited for you long enough."

Alarmed, she shifted, but he'd moved smoothly to box her in, back to the counter. Still, all he did was lift the bite of chicken to her lips.

And his thumb grazed lightly, seductively, over her bottom lip when she accepted his offer. "It's good. Really." But her chest felt thick, and alarm increased when he skimmed a hand over her hair. She made her tingling spine straighten until they were eye to eye.

"What are you doing, Murphy?"

"Well, Shannon." He touched his lips to hers lightly, almost breezily. "I'm courting you."

TEN

Courting? Flabbergasted, Shannon gaped at him. It was ridiculous, a foolish word that had nothing to do with her, or her lifestyle.

Yet it had certainly tripped off his Irish tongue easily. She had to make him swallow it again, and fast.

"That's crazy. It's absurd."

His hands were on her face again, fingertips just skimming her jawline. "Why?"

"Well . . . because." In defense she moved back, gestured with her glass. "In the first place, you hardly know me."

"But I do know you." More amused than offended at her reaction, he turned back to carve the chicken. "I knew you the minute I saw you."

"Don't start that Celtic mysticism with me, Murphy." She strode back to the table, topped off her wine, and gulped it. "I'm an American, damn it. People don't go around courting people in New York."

"That might be part of what's wrong with it." He carried the platter to the table. "Sit down, Shannon. You'll want to eat while it's hot."

"Eat." She rolled her eyes before closing them in frustration. "Now I'm supposed to eat."

"You came to eat, didn't you?" Taking on the duties of host, he filled the plate by her chair, then his own before lighting candles. "Aren't you hungry?"

"Yes, I'm hungry." She plopped down in her chair. After flicking her napkin onto her lap, she picked up her knife and fork.

For the next few minutes she did eat, while her options circled around in her head. "I'm going to try to be reasonable with you, Murphy."

"All right." He sliced into the chicken on his plate, sampled, and was pleased he'd done a good job. "Be reasonable then."

"Number one, you've got to understand I'm only going to be here another week, two at the most."

"You'll stay longer." He said it placidly as he ate. "You haven't begun to resolve the problems and feelings that brought you here. You haven't once asked about Tom Concannon."

Her eyes went cold. "You know nothing about my feelings."

"I think I do, but we'll leave that for now since it makes you unhappy. But you'll stay, Shannon, because there are things for you to face. And to forgive. You're not a coward. There's strength in you, and heart."

She hated that he was seeing in her things she'd refused to admit to herself. She broke open one of the biscuits he'd brought to the table, watched the heat steam out. "Whether I stay a week or a year, it doesn't apply to this."

"It all applies to this," he said mildly. "Does the meal suit you?"

"It's terrific."

"Did you paint more today, after I left you?"

"Yes, I—" She swallowed another bite, jabbed her fork at him. "You're changing the subject."

"What subject?"

"You know very well what subject, and we're going to clear the air here and now. I don't want to be courted—by anyone. I don't know how things are around here, but where I come from, women are independent, equal."

"I've some thoughts on that myself." Idly he picked up his wine, considering his words as he drank. "It's true enough that in general your Irishman has a difficult time with seeing women as equals. Now, there's been some changes in the past generation, but it's a slow process." He set his wine aside and went back to his meal. "There are many I'd call mate who wouldn't agree with me in full, but it may be because I've done a lot of reading over the years and thought about what I've read. I feel a woman has rights same as a man, to what he has, what he does."

"That's big of you," Shannon muttered.

He only smiled. "It's a step of some proportion for someone raised as I was raised. Now in truth, I don't know just how I'd react to it if you wanted to court me."

"I don't."

"There you are." He lifted a hand, smiling still, as if she'd made his point for him. "And my courting you has nothing to do with rights or equality, doesn't make you less or me more. It's just that I've the initiative, so to speak. You're the most beautiful thing I've seen in my life. And I've been fortunate enough to see a great deal of beauty."

Flummoxed by the quick spurt of pleasure, she looked down at her plate. There was a way to handle this, to handle him, she was certain. She just had to find it.

"Murphy, I'm flattered. Anyone would be."

"You're more than flattered when I kiss you, Shannon. We both know what happens then."

She jabbed a piece of chicken. "All right, I'm attracted. You're an attractive man, with some charm. But if I'd been considering taking it any further, I wouldn't now."

"Wouldn't you?" Christ, but she was a pleasure to converse with, he thought. "And why would that be, when you want me as much as I want you?"

She had to rub her dampening palms on her napkin. "Because it's an obvious mistake. We're looking at this from two different angles, and they're never going to come together. I like you. You're an interesting man. But I'm simply not looking for a relationship. Damn it, I ended one only weeks ago. I was practically engaged." Inspiration struck. She leaned forward, her smile smug. "I was sleeping with him."

Murphy's brows quirked. "*Was* seems to be the key. You must have cared for him."

"Of course I cared for him. I don't jump into bed with strangers." Hearing herself, she hissed out a breath. How had he managed to turn that around on her?

"It's past tense as I see it. I've cared enough about a woman or two to lie with her. But I never loved one before you."

Panic had the color draining out of her face. "You're not in love with me."

"I loved you from the moment I set eyes on you." He said it so quietly, so simply, that she believed—for a moment completely believed. "Before that, somehow. I've waited for you, Shannon. And here you are."

"This isn't happening," she said shakily and pushed away from the table. "Now, you listen to me, you put this whole insane business out of your mind. It's not going to work. You're romanticizing the situation. Hallucinating. All you're going to accomplish is to embarrass both of us."

His eyes narrowed, but she was too busy fuming to notice the change, or the danger in it. "My loving you is an embarrassment to you."

"Don't twist my words around," she said furiously. "And don't try to make me seem small and shallow because I'm not interested in being courted. Jesus, *courted.* Even the word's ridiculous."

"There's another you'd prefer?"

"No, there's not another I'd prefer. What I prefer, and expect, is for you to drop it."

He sat quietly a moment, dealing with a slowly building anger. "Because you have no feelings for me?"

"That's right." And because it was a lie, her voice sharpened. "Do you really have some deluded idea that I'd just fall in meekly with whatever absurd plans you're cooking up? Marry you, live here? A farmer's wife, for God's sake. Do I look like a farmer's wife? I've got a career, a life."

He moved so quickly she only had time to suck in one shocked breath. His hands were on her arms, fingers dug in. His face was a study of the pale and dark of fury.

"And my life's beneath you?" he demanded. "What I have, what I've worked for, even what I am is something less? Something to be scorned?"

Her heart was beating like a rabbit's, in quick bumpy jerks. She could only shake her head. Who could have guessed he had such temper in him?

"I'll accept that you don't know you love me, won't clear your eyes to see that we're meant. But I won't have you disparage what I am and spurn everything I and my family for generations has struggled for."

"That's not what I meant—"

"You think the land just sits, pretty as a picture, and waits to be reaped?" The candlelight threw shadows over his face, making it as fascinating as it was dangerous. "There's blood spilled for it, and more sweat than can be weighed. Keeping it's hard, and keeping it's not enough. If you're too proud to accept it as yours, then you shame yourself."

Her breath was shuddering out. She had to force herself to draw it in slowly. "You're hurting me, Murphy."

He dropped his hands as if her flesh had burned them. He stepped back, his movements jerky for the first time since she'd known him. "I beg your pardon."

It was his turn for shame. He knew his hands were large, and knew their strength. It appalled him that he would have used them, even in blind fury, to put a mark on her.

The self-disgust on his face kept her from giving in to the urge to rub at the soreness on her arms. However huge her lack of understanding of him, she knew instinctively he was a gentle man who would consider hurting a woman the lowest form of sin.

"I didn't mean to offend you," she said slowly. "I was angry and upset, and trying to make the point that we're different. Who we are, what we want."

He slipped his hands into his pockets. "What do you want?"

She opened her mouth, then shut it on the shock of finding the answer wasn't there. "I've had a number of major changes in my life over the past couple of months, so I still need to think about that. But a relationship isn't one of them."

"Are you afraid of me?" His voice was carefully neutral. "I didn't mean to hurt you."

"No, I'm not afraid of you." She couldn't help herself. She stepped forward, laid a hand on his cheek. "Temper understands temper, Murphy." Almost certain the crisis had passed, she smiled. "Let's forget all of this, and be friends."

Instead he stopped her heart by taking her hand, sliding it around until his lips pressed tenderly into the palm. " 'My bounty is as boundless as the sea, my love as deep; the more I give to thee the more I have, for both are infinite.' "

Shakespeare, she thought as her body softened. He would quote Shakespeare in that gorgeous voice. "Don't say things like that to me, Murphy. It's not playing fair."

"We're past games, Shannon. We're neither of us children, or fools. Here now, I won't hurt you." His voice was soothing, as it was when he gentled a horse. For she'd gone skittish when he'd slipped his arms around her. "Tell me what you felt when I kissed you the first time."

It wasn't a difficult question to answer, as she was feeling it again. "Tempted."

He smiled, pressed his curved lips to her temple. "That's not all of it. There was more, wasn't there? A kind of remembering."

Her body was refusing her very sensible order to stay rigid and aloof. "I don't believe in those things."

"I didn't ask what you believed." His lips cruised from temple to jaw, patient. "But what you felt." Through the thin barrier of silk her skin was warming. He thought he might go mad holding himself from stripping that barrier away and finding all of her. "It wasn't just now." He indulged himself a few miserly degrees, sliding into the kiss, savoring the way her mouth yielded for his. "It was again."

"That's nonsense." But her own voice seemed to come from a long way off. "And this is crazy." Even as she spoke, her hands were fisting in his hair to hold him close, closer, until the pleasure bounded past reason. "We can't do this." The purr of delight sounded in her throat, rippled wonderfully into his mouth. "It's just chemistry."

"God bless science." Nearly as breathless as she, he dragged her to her toes and tortured himself. Only for a moment, he vowed. And plundered.

Explosions burst inside of her, one after another until her system was battered by color and light. On a wild spurt of greed, she all but clawed at him in a fight for more.

Touch me, damn you. The order erupted in her head. But his hands did no more than hold while her body ached to be possessed. She knew how his hand would feel. She knew, and could have wept from the power of the knowledge. Hard palm, gentle strokes that would build and build into brands.

With a feral instinct she hadn't known lurked inside her, she dug her teeth into his lip, baiting him, daring him. At his violent oath, she flung her head back, her face glowing with triumph.

Then she paled, degree by degree. For his eyes were warrior's eyes, dark, deadly, and terrifyingly familiar.

"God." The word burst out of her as she struggled away. Fighting for air, for balance, she pressed her hands to her breast. "Stop. God, this has to stop."

Teetering on the thin edge of control, Murphy fisted his hands at his sides. "I want you more than I want to take the next breath. It's killing me, Shannon, this wanting."

"I made a mistake." She dragged her trembling hands through her hair. "I made a mistake here. I'm sorry. I'm not going to let this go any further." She could feel herself being pulled toward him—negative to positive. Power to power. "Stay away from me, Murphy."

"I can't. You know I can't."

"We have a problem." Determined to calm down, she walked unsteadily to the table and picked up her wineglass. "We can solve it," she said to herself and sipped. "There's always a way to solve a problem. Don't talk to me," she ordered, holding up a hand like a traffic cop. "Let me think."

The oddest thing was she never considered herself a very sexual creature. There had been a few pleasant moments now and again with men she cared for, had respect for. "Pleasant" was a ridiculously pale description of what had erupted in her with Murphy.

That was sex, she thought, nodding. That was allowed, that was all right. They were both adults, both unencumbered. She certainly cared for him, and respected him, even admired him on a great many levels. What was wrong with one wild fling before she settled down and decided what to do with the rest of her life?

Nothing, she decided, except that foolish courting business. So, she sipped her wine again, set it down. They'd just have to get rid of the obstacle.

"We want to sleep together," she began.

"Well, I'd find sleeping with you a pleasant thing, but I'd prefer making love with you a few dozen times first."

"Don't play semantic games, Murphy." But she smiled, relieved that the humor was back in his eyes. "I think we can resolve this in a reasonable and mutually satisfying manner."

"You've a wonderful way of speaking sometimes." His voice was full of admiration and delight. "Even when what you say is senseless. It's so dignified, you know. And classy."

"Shut up, Murphy. Now if you'll just agree that the idea of a long-term commitment isn't feasible." When he only continued to smile at her, she huffed out a breath. "Okay, I'll put it simply. No courting."

"I knew what you meant, darling. I just like listening to you. I've no problem with the feasibility of living the rest of my life with you. And I've hardly begun courting you. I haven't even danced with you yet."

At her wit's end she rubbed her hands over her face. "Are you really that thick-headed?"

"So my mother always said. 'Murphy,' she'd say, 'once you get an idea in that brain of yours, nothing knocks it loose.' " He grinned at her. "You'll like my mother."

"I'm never going to meet your mother."

"Oh, you will. I'm working that out. But as you were saying?"

"As I was saying," she repeated, baffled. "How can I remember what I was saying when you keep throwing these curves? You do it on purpose, just to cloud things up when they should be perfectly simple."

"I love you, Shannon," he said and stopped her dead. "That's simple. I want to marry you and raise a family with you. But that's getting ahead of things."

"I'll say. I'm going to be as clear and concise about this as I can. I don't love you, Murphy, and I don't want to marry you." Her eyes went to slits. "And if you keep grinning at me, I'm going to belt you."

"You can take a swing at me, and we can wrestle a bit, but then we're likely to resolve the first part of this right here on the kitchen floor." He stepped closer, delighted when she jerked up her chin. "Because, darling, once I get me hands on you again, I can't promise to take them off till I'm finished."

"I'm through trying to be reasonable. Thanks for dinner. It was interesting."

"You'll want a jacket against the rain."

"I don't—"

"Don't be foolish." He'd already taken one of his own off a peg. "You'll just get that pretty blouse wet and chill your skin."

She snatched it from him before he could help her into it. "Fine. I'll get it back to you."

"Bring it with you, if you think of it, when you come to paint in the morning. I'll be walking by."

"I may not be there." She shoved her arms into the soft worn denim, stood with the sleeve flopping past her fingertips. "Good night."

"I'll walk you to the car." Even as she started to object, he took her arm and led her out of the kitchen and down the hall.

"You'll just get wet," she protested when they reached the front door.

"I don't mind the rain." When they reached the car, he wisely swallowed a grin. "It's the wrong side, darling, unless you're wanting me to drive you home."

She merely scowled and shifted direction so that she veered toward the right-side drive.

Measuring her mood, he opted to kiss her hand rather than her mouth when he'd opened the car door for her. "Dream within a dream," he murmured. "Poe had some lovely lines on that. You'll dream of me tonight, Shannon, and I of you."

"No, I won't." She said it firmly as she slammed the door. After shoving up the sleeves of his jacket, she backed out of the drive and headed up the rain-washed road.

The man had to have a screw loose somewhere, she decided. It was the only explanation. Her only choice was to give him absolutely no encouragement from this point on.

No more cozy dinners in the kitchen, no music and laughter in the pub, no easy conversations or staggering kisses in the fields.

Damn it, she'd miss it. All of it. She pulled up in Brianna's drive and set the brake. He'd gone and stirred up feelings and desires she hadn't known she was capable of, then left her with no other option but to squelch them.

Pinheaded idiot, she thought, slamming her door before racing toward the house.

Shannon fought off a scowl as she opened the door and found Brianna beaming smiles down the hallway.

"Oh, good, he lent you a jacket. I didn't think of it till after you'd left. Did you have a nice time then?"

Shannon opened her mouth, surprised when the usual platitudes simply weren't there. "The man is insane."

Brianna blinked. "Murphy?"

"Who else? I'm telling you, he's got something corked around in his head. There's no reasoning with him."

In a move so natural neither of them noticed, Brianna took Shannon's hand and began to lead her back toward the kitchen. "Did you have a quarrel?"

"A quarrel? No, I wouldn't say that. You can't quarrel with insanity."

"Hey, Shannon." When the kitchen door opened, Gray glanced up, pausing with a huge spoon of trifle halfway to a bowl. "How was dinner? Got any room for trifle? Brie makes the world's best."

"She's had a to-do with Murphy," Brianna informed him, urging Shannon into a chair before going for the teapot.

"No kidding." Intrigued, Gray dumped the trifle, then went for another bowl. "What about?"

"Oh, nothing much. He just wants me to marry him and have his children."

Brianna bobbled the teacup, barely saving it from shattering on the floor. "You're joking," she said and nearly managed a laugh.

"It's a joke all right, but I'm not making it." Absently she dug into the bowl Gray set in front of her. "He claims to be courting me." She snorted, took a swallow of trifle. "Can you beat that?" she demanded of Gray.

"Ah . . ." He ran his tongue around his teeth. "Nope."

Very slowly, her eyes wide, Brianna took her seat. "He said he was wanting to court you?"

"He said he was," Shannon corrected and spooned up more trifle. "He has this wild idea of love at first sight, and that we're meant, or some ridiculous thing. All this about remembering and recognition. Bull," she muttered and poured out the tea herself.

"Murphy's never courted anyone. Never wanted to."

With her eyes narrowed Shannon turned to Brianna. "I wish everyone would stop using that antiquated word. It makes me nervous."

"The word," Gray put in, "or the deed?"

"Both." She propped her chin on her fist. "As if things weren't complicated enough."

"Are you indifferent to him?" Brianna asked.

"Not indifferent." Shannon frowned. "Exactly."

"The plot thickens." Gray only grinned at the heated look Shannon shot at him. "You'd better understand the Irish are a stubborn race. I'm not sure if the Irish of the west aren't the most stubborn. If Murphy's got his eye on you, it's going to stay there."

"Don't make light of it, Gray." In automatic sympathy Brianna laid her hand over Shannon's. "She's upset, and there are hearts involved."

"No, there are not." About that, at least, Shannon could be firm. "Considering going to bed with a man and spending the rest of your life with him are two entirely different things. And as for him, he's just a romantic."

With her brows knit, she concentrated on scraping the last of the trifle from her bowl. "It's nonsense, the idea that a couple of odd dreams have anything to do with destiny."

"Murphy's had odd dreams?"

Distracted again, Shannon glanced at Brianna. "I don't know. I didn't ask."

"You have." Gray couldn't have been more delighted. He leaned forward. "Tell me—especially the sexy parts."

"Stop it, Grayson."

But Shannon found herself laughing. Odd, she thought, that here should be the big brother she'd always wished for. "It's all sexy," she told him and licked her lips.

"Yeah?" He leaned closer. "Start at the beginning, Don't leave anything out. No detail is too small."

"Don't pay him any mind, Shannon."

"It's all right." More than full, she pushed the empty bowl aside. "You both might find it interesting. I've never had a recurring dream before. Actually, it's more like vignettes, in random order. Or what seems to be."

"Now you're really driving me crazy," Gray complained. "Spill it."

"Okay. It starts off in the field, where the stone circle is? Funny, it's like I dreamed it was there before I saw it. But that's not possible. Anyway"—she waved that away—"it's raining. Cold, there's frost. It sounds like glass grinding when I walk on it. Not me," she corrected with a half laugh. "The woman in the dream. Then there's a man, dark hair, dark cloak, white horse. You can see the steam rising off them, and the mud that's splashed on his boots and his armor. He rides toward me—her—full out. And she stands there with her hair blowing. And—"

She broke off. She'd caught the quick, startled look in Brianna's eyes, and the silent exchange between her and Gray.

"What is it?" she demanded.

"Sounds like the witch and the warrior." Gray's eyes had darkened, focused intently on Shannon's face. "What happens next?"

Shannon put her hands under the table and linked them together. "You tell me."

"All right." Gray glanced at Brianna, who gestured for him to tell the tale. "Legend has it that there was a wise woman, a witch, who lived on the land here. She had the sight and, burdened with it as much as blessed, lived apart from the rest. One morning when she went to the dance to commune with her gods, she found the warrior in the circle, wounded, his horse beside him. She had the gift of healing and treated his wounds, nursing him until he was strong again. They fell in love. Became lovers."

He paused to add tea to the cups, picked up his own. "He left her, of course, for there were wars to be fought and battles he'd pledged to win. He vowed to come back, and she gave him a broach to pin to his cloak and remember her by."

"And did he"—Shannon cleared her throat—"come back?"

"It's said he did, riding to her across the field in a storm that shook the sky. He wanted to take her to wife, but he wouldn't give up his sword and shield. They fought over it bitterly. It seemed no matter how much they loved, there was no compromise in either. Next time he left, he gave her the broach, to remember him until he returned. But he never came back again. It's said he died in another field. And with her gift of sight, she knew it the moment it happened."

"It's just a story." Because they were suddenly chilled, Shannon wrapped her hands around her cup. "I don't believe in that kind of thing. You can't tell me you do."

Gray moved his shoulders. "Yes, I can. I can believe those two people existed, and that there was something strong between them that lingers. What I'm curious about is why you'd dream of them."

"I had a couple of dreams about a man on a horse," Shannon said impatiently. "Which I'm sure any number of psychiatrists would have a field day with. One has nothing to do with the other. I'm tired," she added, rising. "I'm going to bed."

"Take your tea," Brianna said kindly.

"Thanks."

When Shannon left, Brianna laid a hand on Gray's shoulder. "Don't poke at her too much, Grayson. She's so troubled."

"She'd feel better if she stopped holding so much inside." With a half laugh he turned his head to press his lips to Brianna's hand. "I ought to know."

"She needs time, as you did." She sighed, long and deep. "Murphy. Who would have thought it?"

ELEVEN

It wasn't as if Shannon was avoiding going out to the standing stones. She'd simply overslept. And if she'd had dreams, she thought as she picked at her late breakfast of coffee and muffins, it was hardly a surprise.

Trifle before bed and a legend by a master story spinner equaled a restless night.

Still, the clarity of them worried her. Alone, she could admit she'd felt the dream, not just envisioned it. She felt the rough blanket at her back, the prickle of grass, the heat and weight of the man's body on hers. In hers.

She blew out a long breath, pressing a hand to her stomach where the memory of the dream brought an answering tug of longing.

She'd dreamed of making love with the man with Murphy's face—yet not his face. They'd been in the stone circle, with the stars swimming overhead and the moon white, like a beacon. She'd heard the hoot of an owl, felt warm breath coming quickly against her cheek. Her hands knew the feel of those muscles, bunching and straining. And she'd known, even as her body had erupted in climax, that this would be the last time.

It hurt to think of it, hurt so that now, awake, aware, the tears still threatened and burned bitterly behind her eyes.

She lifted her coffee again. She was going to have to snap out of it, she warned herself, or join the ranks of her associates in the line at the therapist's office.

The commotion at the back door had her composing her face. Whoever it was, Shannon was grateful for the diversion.

But not grateful enough to be pleased when she saw it was Maggie.

"I'm letting you in, aren't I?" Maggie said to Con. "You needn't push."

The dog burst through the open door, raced under the table, then dropped down with a long-suffering sigh.

"I'm sure you're welcome." Maggie's easy smile chilled several degrees when she spotted Shannon alone in the kitchen. "Morning. I've brought some berries by for Brie."

"She had some errands. Gray's working upstairs."

"I'll leave them." At home, Maggie crossed to put the bag in the refrigerator. "Did you enjoy your meal with Murphy?"

"News certainly travels." Shannon couldn't keep the annoyance at bay. "I'm surprised you don't know what he served."

With a smile as thin as her own temper, Maggie turned back. "Oh, it would have been chicken. He has a hand at roasting, not that he makes a habit of cooking for women." She took off her cap, stuffed it in her pocket. "But he's taken with you, isn't he?"

"I'd say that was his business, and mine."

"You'd say wrong, and I'll warn you to mind your step with him."

"I'm not interested in your warnings, or your nasty attitude."

Maggie tilted her head in a gesture that had much more to do with disdain than curiosity. "Just what are you interested in, Shannon Bodine? Do you find it amusing to dangle yourself in front of a man? One you have no intention of doing more than toying with? You'd come by that naturally enough."

The red haze of fury was blinding. She was on her feet in a snap, fists bunched. "Goddamn you. You have no right to cast stones at my mother."

"You're right. Absolutely." And if she could have bitten her tongue, Maggie would have taken the words, and the unfairness behind them, back. "I apologize for that."

"Why? You sounded exactly like your own mother."

Maggie could only wince. "You couldn't have aimed that shaft better. I did sound like her, and I was as wrong as she. So I'll apologize again for that, but not for the rest."

To calm herself, or try, she turned to heat the kettle. "But I'll ask you, and you might be honest since it's only us two, if you haven't thought close to the same of my father as I just said of your mother."

The accuracy of the question had Shannon backing off. "If I did, at least I was too polite to articulate it."

"Seems to me politeness and hypocrisy run too often hand in hand." Pleased by the quick hiss that drew out of Shannon, Maggie reached for the canister of tea. "So let's have neither between us. Circumstances mean we share blood, a fact that doesn't please either of us overmuch. You're not a tender woman from what I can see. Neither am I. But Brianna is."

"So you're going to protect her from me, too?"

"If need be. If you hurt one of mine, I'll hound you for it." Face set, she turned back. "Understand me there. It's clear to see Brie's already opened her heart, and if Murphy hasn't, he will."

"And you've already closed yours, and your mind."

"Haven't you?" Maggie strode to the table, slapped her palms down. "Haven't you come with your heart and mind made up tight? You don't care what Da suffered. It's only yourself you're thinking of. It doesn't matter to you that he never had a chance to take his happiness. Never had . . ."

She trailed off as her vision grayed. Swearing, she leaned against the table, fighting for balance. Even as she swayed, Shannon was grabbing her shoulders.

"Sit down, for God's sake."

"I'm all right."

"Sure." The woman was pale as death and her eyes had nearly rolled back in her head. "We'll go another round."

But Maggie slid bonelessly into the chair, making not even a token protest when Shannon firmly pushed her head between her knees.

"Breathe. Just breathe or something. Shit." She gave Maggie's shoulder an awkward pat and wondered what to do next. "I'll get Gray, we'll phone the doctor."

"I don't need the doctor." Fighting the dizziness, Maggie groped out until she found Shannon's hand. "Don't bother him. It's just being pregnant is all. It was the same when I was carrying Liam the first few weeks."

Shaky, and disgusted with herself, Maggie sat back. She knew the routine and kept her eyes closed, drew air in slow and steady. Her eyes fluttered open in surprise when she felt the cool cloth on her head.

"Thanks."

"Drink some water." Hoping it was the right move, Shannon urged the glass she'd just filled into Maggie's hand. "You're still awfully pale."

"It passes. Just nature's way of reminding you you've a lot worse ahead in nine months."

"Cheerful thought." Shannon sat again, keeping her eyes glued to Maggie's face. "Why are you having another?"

"I like challenges. And I want more children—which was a big surprise to me as I never knew I'd want the first. It's an adventure, really, a little dizziness, getting queasy of a morning, growing fat as a prize hog."

"I'll take your word for it. Your color's coming back."

"Then you can stop staring at me as though I were going to sprout wings." She slid the cloth from her brow, set it on the table between them. "Thank you."

Relieved, Shannon leaned back in her chair. "Don't mention it."

"Since you bring it up." Maggie plucked at the damp cloth. "I'd be grateful if you wouldn't mention to Brie, or anyone, that I had a bit of a spell. She'd fuss, you see—then Rogan would start hovering."

"And you do better at protecting than being protected."

"You could say that."

Thoughtful, Shannon drummed her fingers on the table. They'd crossed some line, she thought, without either of them realizing it. Maybe she would take the next, deliberate step.

"You want me to keep quiet about it?"

"I do, yes."

"What's it worth to you?"

Taken off guard, Maggie blinked. "Worth?"

"We could call it an exchange of favors."

Brows knit, Maggie nodded. "We could. What favor are you after?"

"I want to see where you work."

"Where I work?" Suspicion slipped into her voice, and her eyes. "Inside my glass house?"

Nothing could have been sweeter, Shannon decided. "I hear you really hate when people come into your glass house, ask questions, poke around. That's what I want to do." She rose to take her cup to the sink. "Otherwise, it might just slip out about you nearly fainting in the kitchen."

"I didn't faint," Maggie muttered. "Body can't even have a little spell in peace," she continued as she pushed back from the table. "People are supposed to be tolerant of a woman with child. Come on then." Obviously displeased, she took her cap back out of her pocket and stuffed it on her head.

"I thought I'd drive."

"Just like a Yank," Maggie said in disgust. "We're walking."

"Fine." Shannon grabbed Murphy's jacket from the peg and followed. "Where's Liam?" she asked as they headed over the back lawn.

"With his da. Rogan had the idea I needed a lie-in this morning and took him off to the gallery for a few hours."

"I'd like to see it. The gallery. I've been in Worldwide in New York."

"This one's not as posh. Rogan's goal was to make it more a home for art than a display. We feature only Irish artists and craftsmen. It's been a year since it opened, and he's done what he set out to do. But then—he always does." Agile, she swung over the first wall.

"Have you been married long?"

"Two years soon. That was something else he set out to do." It made her smile to think of it, to remember how she'd fought him every step of the way. "You've no thoughts of marriage, a man waiting for you to come back?"

"No." As if on cue she heard the sound of a tractor, then saw Murphy riding in the far field. "I'm concentrating on my career."

"I know how that is." Maggie lifted her hand in a wave. "He'll be going back to his bog to cut turf. It's a fine day for it, and he prefers peat to wood or coal."

Peat fires and bogs, Shannon thought. But God, didn't he look fine riding over his land with the sun streaming down on him. "Will he do it all alone?"

"No, there'll be help. It's rare that a man cuts turf by himself. Not many do it now, it takes such time and effort. But Murphy always makes use of what he has." Maggie paused a minute to turn a slow circle. "He'll have a fine crop this year. After his father died, he put everything he is into this place. And he's made it shine like his father, and mine, never could." As they walked again, she slanted Shannon a look. "This was Concannon land once."

"Murphy mentioned that he'd bought it." They went over the next wall. They were close to the farmhouse now, and Shannon could see chickens scratching in the yard. "Was this your house, then, before?"

"Yes, but not in my memory. We grew up at Blackthorn. If you go back a few generations, the Muldoons and Concannons were related. There were brothers you see, who inherited all the land here, and split it between them. One couldn't but plant a seed that it would spring out of the earth. And the other seemed to grow nothing but rocks. But it's said he drank more than he plowed. There was jealousy and temper between them, and their wives wouldn't speak if they met face to face."

"Cozy," Shannon commented and was too intrigued to remember to put the borrowed jacket on the back stoop.

"And one fine day the second brother, the one who preferred beer to fertilizer, disappeared. Vanished. In the way of the inheritance, the first brother owned all the land now. He let his brother's wife and children stay in the cottage—which would be my house now. Some said he did so out of guilt, for it was suspected that he did away with his brother."

"Killed him?" Surprised, Shannon glanced over. "What's this? Cain and Abel?"

"A bit like, I suppose. Though the murdering brother inherited the garden rather than being banished from it. Their name was Concannon, and as time passed one of the daughters of the missing brother married a Muldoon. They were given a slice of land by her uncle and worked it well. And over the years the tide turned. Now it's Muldoon land, and the Concannons have only the edges."

"And you don't resent that?"

"Why should I? It's fair justice. And even if it weren't, even if that long ago brother fell into some bog in a drunken stupor, it's Murphy who loves the land as my own da never did. Here we are. This is what's mine."

"It's a lovely house." And it was, she mused, studying it. A bit more than a cottage, she decided, though that was certainly the heart of it. The pretty stone that was so typical of the area rose up two floors. There was an interesting jog in the line of it, what she assumed was an addition. And the artist's touch, she thought, in the trim that was painted a peacock purple.

"We added to it, so that Rogan could have office space, and there'd be a room for Liam." Maggie shook her head as she turned away. "And, of course, the man insisted we add another room or two while we were about it. Already planning a brood, though that slipped past me at the time."

"Looks like you're accommodating him."

"Oh, he's blissful at the idea of family, is Rogan. Comes from being an only child, perhaps. And I've discovered I feel much the same. I've a knack for motherhood, and a pride in it. Strange how one person can change everything."

"I don't think I realized how much you love him," Shannon said quietly. "You seem so . . . individual."

"What's one to do with the other?" Maggie let out a breath and frowned at the stone building that was her solitude, her sanctuary. Her shop. "Well, let's do this then. But the deal says nothing about you putting your hands all over things."

"The famed Irish hospitality."

"Bugger it," Maggie said with a grin and crossed over to open the door.

The heat was a shock. It explained the rumbling roar Shannon had begun to hear a full field away. The furnace was lit. Realizing it made her feel guilty for keeping Maggie from work.

"I'm sorry. I didn't realize I'd be holding you up."

"I've nothing pressing."

The guilt didn't have a chance against fascination. Benches, shelves were stacked with tools, scattered sheets of paper, works in progress. There was a large wooden chair with wide arms, slots, and dips carved and sanded into the sides. Buckets filled with water or sand.

In a corner, like lances stacked, were long metal poles.

"Are those pipes?"

"Pontils. You gather the glass on the end of them, do melts in the furnace. You use the pipe to blow the bubble." Maggie lifted one. "You neck it with the jacks."

"A bubble of glass." Engrossed, Shannon studied the twists and columns, the bowls and tapers Maggie had setting helter-skelter on shelves. "And you make whatever you want with it."

"You make what you feel. You have to do a second gather, roll and chill it to form what we call a skin. You do a lot of the work sitting down in your chair, getting up countless times to go back to the furnace. You have to keep the pontil or the pipe moving, using gravity, fighting it." Maggie tilted her head. "You want to try it?"

Too enthralled to be surprised by the invitation, Shannon grinned. "You bet I do."

"Something simple," Maggie muttered as she began to set things up. "A ball, flat on the bottom. Like a paperweight."

In moments Shannon found her hands encased in heavy gloves with a pontil in her hand. Following instructions, she dipped the tip into the melt, turned it.

"Don't be so greedy," Maggie snapped. "Takes time."

And effort, Shannon discovered. It wasn't work for a weakling. Sweat trickled down her back and went unnoticed when she saw the bubble begin to form on the end of the pipe.

"I did it!"

"No, you haven't." But Maggie guided her hands, showing her how to make the second gather, to roll it over the marble. She explained each step, neither of them fully aware they were working in tandem and enjoying it.

"Oh, it's wonderful." Giddy as a child, Shannon beamed at the glass ball. "Look at those swirls of color in it."

"No use making something ugly. You'll use this to flatten the base. Careful now, that's good. You've got smart hands." She shifted the pipe, showing Shannon how to attach the other end to a pontil. "Now strike it sharp, there."

Shannon blinked when the ball detached from the pipe, holding now to the pontil.

"Back in the furnace first," Maggie instructed, impatient now. "To heat the lip. That's it, not too much. Into the oven it goes. To anneal. Now take that file, strike it again."

When the ball landed on a thick pad of asbestos, Maggie closed the oven in a businesslike manner and set the timer.

"That was wonderful!"

"You did well enough." Maggie bent down to a small refrigerator and took out two cold drinks. "You're not ham-handed or stupid."

"Thanks," Shannon said dryly. She took a long drink. "I think the hands-on lesson overbalanced the bargain."

Maggie smiled. "Then you owe me, don't you?"

"Apparently." Casually Shannon brushed through the sketches littering a workbench. "These are excellent. I saw some of your sketches and paintings in New York."

"I'm not a painter. Rogan isn't one to let any bit of business pass by, so he takes what he likes from them, has them mounted."

"I won't argue that your glasswork is superior to your drawing."

Maggie swallowed the soft drink before she choked. "Won't you?"

"No. But Rogan has an excellent eye, and I'm sure he culls out your best."

"Oh, to be sure. You're the painter, aren't you? I'm sure it takes tremendous talent to draw advertisements."

Challenged, Shannon set down her drink. "You don't really think you're better at it than I am."

"Well, I haven't seen anything of yours, have I? Unless I flipped by in a magazine waiting to have my teeth cleaned."

Shannon set her own and snatched up one of Maggie's hunks of charcoal. It took her longer to find a sketch pad and a clean sheet. While Maggie leaned her hip idly on the edge of the bench, Shannon bent over her work.

She started with fast strokes, annoyance pushing her. Then she began to find the pleasure in it, and the desire for beauty.

"Why, 'tis Liam." Maggie's voice went soft as butter as she saw her son emerge. Shannon was drawing just the head and shoulders, concentrating on that impishness that danced in his eyes and around his mouth. The dark hair was mussed, the lips quirked on the verge of a laugh.

"He always looks as though he's just been in trouble, or looking for it," Shannon murmured as she shaded.

"He does, yes. He's a darling, my Liam. You've caught him so, Shannon."

Alarmed by the catch in Maggie's voice, Shannon glanced over. "You're not going to start crying. Please."

"Hormones." Maggie sniffled and shook her head. "Now I suppose I'll have to say you've a better hand than I at drawing."

"Acknowledgment accepted." Shannon dashed her initials at the corner of the page, then carefully tore it off. "Fair trade for a paperweight," she said, handing it to Maggie.

"No, it's not. The balance has tipped again. I owe you another boon."

Shannon picked up a rag to wipe the charcoal dust from her hands. She stared at her own fingers. "Tell me about Thomas Concannon."

She didn't know where the need had come from, and was no less surprised than Maggie that she had asked. The question hummed for several long seconds.

"Come inside." Maggie's tone was suddenly gentle, as was the hand she set on Shannon's arm. "We'll have tea and talk of it."

It was there Brianna found them when she walked into Maggie's kitchen with Kayla and a basket of soda bread.

"Oh, Shannon. I didn't know you were here." And she would never have pictured her there, sitting at Maggie's table while Maggie brewed tea. "I . . . I brought you some bread, Maggie."

"Thanks. Why don't we slice some up? I'm starving."

"I wasn't going to stay—"

"I think you should." Maggie glanced over her shoulder, met Brianna's eyes. "Kayla's gone to sleep in her carrier, Brie. Why don't you put her down for a nap here?"

"All right." All too aware of the tension in the room, Brianna set the bread down and took the baby out with her.

"She's worried we'll start spitting at each other," Maggie commented. "Brie's not one for fighting."

"She's very gentle."

"She is, yes. Unless you push the wrong spot. Then she's fierce. Always seems fiercer because it's never quite expected. It was she who found the letters your mother wrote. He'd kept them in the attic, you see. In a box where he liked to put things important to him. We didn't go through it, or some of his other things, for a long time after he'd died."

She brought the pot over, sat. "It was difficult for us, and my mother was living with Brie in the house until a couple years ago. To keep what peace could be kept, Brie didn't speak much of Da."

"Were things really so bad between your parents?"

"Worse than bad. They came to each other late in life. It was impulse, and passion. Though he told me there'd been love once, at the start of it."

"Maggie?" Brianna hesitated at the doorway.

"Come and sit. She wants to talk of Da."

Brianna came in, brushing a hand over Shannon's shoulder, perhaps in support, perhaps in gratitude, before she joined them. "I know it's hard for you, Shannon."

"It has to be dealt with. I've been avoiding it." She lifted her gaze, looked closely at each of her sisters. "I want you to understand I had a father."

"I would think it would be a lucky woman who could say she had two," Maggie put in. "Both who loved her." When Shannon shook her head, she barreled on. "He was a loving man. A generous one. Too generous at times. As a father he was kind, and patient, and full of fun. He wasn't wise, nor successful. And he had a habit of leaving a chore half done."

"He was always there if you needed cheering," Brianna murmured. "He had big dreams, outrageous ones, and schemes that were so foolish. He was always after making his fortune, but he died more rich in friends than in money. Do you remember the time, Maggie, when he decided we would raise rabbits, for the pelts?"

"And he built pens for them and bought a pair of those long-haired white ones. Oh, Mother was furious at the money it cost—and the idea of it." Maggie snickered. "Rabbits in the yard."

Brianna chuckled and poured out the tea. "And soon they were. Once they bred he didn't have the heart to sell them off to be skinned. And Maggie and I were wailing at the idea of the little bunnies being killed."

"So we went out one night," Maggie said, picking up the story, "the three of us sneaking about like thieves, and let them out, the mother and father and the babies. And we laughed like fools when they went bounding off into the fields." She sighed and picked up her tea. "He didn't have the heart, or the head, for business. He used to write poetry," she remembered. "Terrible stuff, blank verse. It was always a disappointment to him that he didn't have the words."

Brianna pressed her lips together. "He wasn't happy. He tried to be, and he worked hard as any man could to see that Maggie and I would be. But the house was full of anger, and as we found later, his own sorrow went deeper than anyone could reach. He had pride. He was so proud of you, Maggie."

"He was proud of both of us. He fought a terrible battle with Mother to see that I went to Venice to study. He wouldn't back down from that. And what he won for me cost him, and Brianna."

"It didn't—"

"It did." Maggie cut Brianna off. "All of us knew it. With me gone there was no choice but to lean on you, to depend on you to see to the house, to her, to everything."

"It was what I wanted, too."

"He'd have given you the moon if he could." Maggie laid a hand over Brianna's. "You were his rose. It was how he spoke of you the day he died."

"How did he die?" Shannon asked. It was hard to put the picture together, but she was beginning to see a man, flesh and blood, faults and virtues. "Was he ill?"

"He was, but none of us knew." It was painful for Maggie, would always be to go back to that day. "I went looking for him, in O'Malley's. I'd just sold my first piece of glass, in Ennis. We celebrated there. It was a huge day for both of us. It was cold, threatening rain, but he asked me to drive with him. We went out to Loop Head, as he often did."

"Loop Head." Shannon's heart stuttered, clutched.

"It was his favorite of all places," Maggie told her. "He liked to stand on the edge of Ireland, looking across the sea toward America."

No, Shannon thought, not toward a place. Toward a person. "My mother told me they met there. They met at Loop Head."

"Oh." Brianna folded her hands and looked down at them. "Oh, poor Da. He must have seen her every time he went there."

"It was her name he said, when he was dying." Maggie didn't mind the tears, and let them fall. "It was cold, bitter cold, and windy, with the rain just beginning to blow in. I was asking him why, why he'd stayed all these years in unhappiness. He tried to tell me, to explain that it takes two people to make a marriage good or bad. I didn't want to hear it. And I wondered if there'd ever been anyone else in his life. And he told me he'd loved someone, and that it was like an arrow in the heart. That he'd had no right to her."

After a shaky breath, she continued. "He staggered and went gray. The pain took him to his knees, and I was so scared, shouting at him to get up, and trying to pull him. He wanted a priest, but it was just the two of us alone there, in the rain. He was telling me to be strong, not to turn my back on my dreams. I couldn't keep the rain off him. He said my name. Then he said Amanda. Just Amanda. And he died."

Abruptly Maggie pushed the chair back and walked out of the room.

"It hurts her," Brianna murmured. "She had no one to help, had to get Da into the truck by herself, drive him all the way back. I need to go to her."

"No, let me. Please." Without waiting for assent, Shannon stood and walked into the front room. Maggie was there, staring out the window.

"I was alone with my mother when she went into the coma she never revived from." Leading with her heart, Shannon stepped closer, laid a hand on Maggie's shoulder. "It wasn't at the end of the earth, and the sun was shining. Technically, she was still alive. But I knew I'd lost her. There was no one there to help."

Saying nothing, Maggie lifted her hand, rested it over Shannon's.

"It was the day she told me about—myself. About her and Tom Concannon. I was angry and hurt and said things to her I can never take back. I know that she loved my father. She loved Colin Bodine. And I know she was thinking of her Tommy when she left me."

"Do we blame them?" Maggie said quietly.

"I don't know. I'm still angry, and I'm still hurt. And more than anything I don't know who I really am. I was supposed to take after my father. I thought I did." Her voice cracked, and she fought hard to even it again. "The man you and Brie described is a stranger to me, and I'm not sure if I can care."

"I know about the anger. I feel it, too. And I know, for different reasons, what it's like to not be sure who and what is really inside you."

"He wouldn't have asked for more than you could give, Shannon." Brianna stepped into the room. "He never asked that of anyone." She slipped her hand over Shannon's so that the three of them stood together, looking out. "We're family, by the blood. It's up to us to decide if we can be family by the heart."

TWELVE

She had a great deal to think about, and wanted the time to do it. Shannon knew she'd turned one very sharp corner in Maggie's kitchen.

She had sisters.

She couldn't deny the connection any longer, nor could she seem to stop the spread of emotion. She cared about them, their families, their lives. When she was back in New York, she imagined the contact would continue, with letters, calls, occasional visits. She could even see herself returning to Blackthorn Cottage for a week or two now and again through the years.

She'd have the paintings, too. Her first study of the stone dance was finished. When she'd stepped back from the completed canvas, she'd been stunned that the power and scope of it, the sheer passion of it, had come from her.

She'd never painted that vividly before, or felt such a fierce emotional attachment to any of her work.

And it had driven her to start another even as the paint was drying on the first. The sketch she'd done of Brianna in her garden was now a muted, undeniably romantic watercolor, nearly complete.

There were so many other ideas, varied subjects. How could she resist the luminescent light, the varied shades of green—the old man with the thick ash stick she'd seen herding his cows down a twisting road? All of it, every thing and every face she saw cried out to be painted.

She didn't see the harm in extending her stay another week, or two. A busman's holiday, she liked to think of it, where she could explore a side of her art that had been largely ignored throughout her career.

Her financial freedom was an excellent justification for lengthening her time in Ireland. If her record at Ry-Tilghmanton wasn't strong enough to hold for her sabbatical, then she'd simply find another—better—position when she returned to New York.

Now she walked down the road with Murphy's jacket over her arm. She'd meant to get it back to him before, but as she'd been working closer to the inn the last couple of days, there hadn't been the opportunity.

And it had seemed too cowardly to pass such a petty chore onto Brianna or Gray.

In any case, she was heading for the front of the house and imagined he would be out in the fields, or in the barn. Leaving it on his porch with a quick note of thanks pinned to it seemed an easy way out.

But, of course, he wasn't in the fields or in the barn. She supposed she should have known he wouldn't be with the way her luck ran when applied to him.

As she bypassed his garden gate for the driveway, she could see his scarred, worn-down boots poking out from under the pitiful little car.

"Fuck me!"

Her eyes widened, then danced with humor at the steady and imaginative stream of curses that flew from beneath the car.

"Bloody buggerin' hell. Stuck like the cock of a cur in a bitch." There was the ping of metal striking metal, the crash of a tool falling. "Biggest pile of shit outside of the pigsty."

With that, Murphy shoved himself from under the car. His face, smeared with grease, fired with frustration, underwent several rapid transformations when he spotted Shannon.

Consternation turned to embarrassment, and that to a delightfully sheepish grin.

"Didn't know you were there." He wiped the back of his hand over his chin, smearing grease and a trace of blood. "I'd have taken a bit more care with my language."

"I've been known to use a few of the same words," she said easily. "Though not with that nice, rolling lilt. Having problems?"

"Could be worse." He sat where he was a moment, then unfolded himself and rose in what was nearly balletic grace. "I've promised my nephew Patrick I'd get it on the road for him, but it's going to take a bit longer than I thought."

She studied the car again. "If you can get that running, you're working miracles."

"It's just the transmission. I can fix that." He gave the car one final scowl. "It's not my job to make it pretty. Thank Jesus."

"I won't keep you. I just—you're bleeding." She closed the distance between them in a leap, snagging his hand and fretting over the shallow slice in his thumb that was seeping blood.

"Tore it some on the bleeding—on one of the bolts."

"The one that was stuck like—"

"Aye." His color rose, amusing her. "On that one."

"You'd better clean it up." It was her turn to be embarrassed by the way she'd clamped on to his hand. She let it drop.

"I'll get to it." Watching her, he took a bandanna out of his back pocket to staunch the flow. "I was wondering when you'd come by. You've been avoiding me."

"No, I've been busy. I did mean to get this back to you before."

He took the jacket she handed him, tossed it onto the hood of the car. "It's no problem. I have another." With a half smile on his face he leaned against the car and took out a cigarette. "Sure and looking lovely today, Shannon Bodine. And safe you are as well, since I'm too filthy to bother you. Did you dream of me?"

"Don't start that, Murphy."

"You did." He lighted a match, cupping his hand over the tip of the cigarette. "I had dreams of you from now, and from before. They'd be comforting if you were in the bed beside me."

"Then you're going to be uncomfortable, because that's not going to happen."

He only tugged on his ear and smiled at her. "I saw you a few days ago, walking across the fields with Maggie. You looked more easy with her."

"We were just going over to her shop. I wanted to see it."

His brow shot up. "And she showed you?"

"That's right. We made a paperweight."

"We." Now his mouth fell open. "You touched her tools and your fingers aren't broken? I see how it was," he decided. "You overpowered her and tied her up first."

Feeling a bit smug, Shannon plucked at her sleeve. "It wasn't necessary to resort to violence."

"Must be those fairy eyes of yours." He angled his head. "There's not as much sorrow in them now. You're healing."

"I think about her every day. My mother. I was away from her and Dad so much the last few years."

"It's the nature of things, Shannon, for children to grow and move out on their own."

"I keep thinking I should have called more often, made more time to go out there. Especially after my father died. I knew how short life could be after that, but I still didn't make the time."

She turned away to look at the flowers that were blooming riotously in the softness of spring. "I lost them both within a year, and I thought I'd never get over the misery of that. But you do. The hurt dulls, even when you don't want it to."

"Neither of them would want you to mourn too long. Those who love us want to be remembered, but with joy."

She looked over her shoulder. "Why is it so easy to talk to you about this? It shouldn't be." Turning to face him, she shook her head. "I was going to dump that jacket off, figuring you'd be off somewhere. And I was going to stay away from you."

He dropped the cigarette on the drive, crushed it out. "I'd have come after you, when I'd reckoned you'd had time to settle."

"It's not going to work. Part of me is almost sorry, because I'm beginning to think you're one in a million. But it's not going to work."

"Why don't you come over here and kiss me, Shannon?" The invitation was light, friendly, and confident. "Then tell me that nonsense again."

"No." She said it firmly, then a laugh bubbled out. "That kind of cockiness should irritate the hell out of me." She tossed her hair back. "I'm going."

"Come inside, have a cup of tea. I'll wash up." He stepped forward, but took care not to touch her. "Then I'll kiss you."

The shout of joy had him checking. Looking around, he spotted Liam scrambling up the driveway. With an effort, Murphy put desire on hold.

"Well, here's a likely lad come to visit." Murphy crouched down for the noisy kiss. "How's it all going then, Liam? I'd haul you up, boy-o," he told Liam as the child lifted his arms. "But your mother'd have my skin for it."

"How about me?"

Liam shifted affections and climbed happily into Shannon's arms. She settled him onto her hip as Rogan turned into the drive.

"He's like a bullet out of a gun when he gets within ten yards of this place." Rogan lifted a brow as he scanned the little car. "How's this going?"

"A great deal more than slow. Shannon was just coming in for a cup of tea. Will you have a cup?"

"We wouldn't mind that, would we, Liam?"

"Tea," Liam said, grinning, and kissed Shannon dead on the mouth.

"It's the idea of the cake that might go with it that makes him affectionate," Rogan said dryly. "It's you I was coming to see, Shannon. You've saved me a bit of a walk."

"Oh." It looked as though she were stuck now. Taking it philosophically, she carried Liam into the house.

"Go on into the kitchen," Murphy told them. "I need to clean up."

While Liam chattered in earnest gibberish, Shannon settled into the kitchen with Rogan. It surprised her to see him fill the kettle, measure out tea, heat the pot. She supposed it shouldn't have, but he was so . . . smooth, she decided. His clothes might have been casual, but everything about him spoke of money, privilege, and power.

"Can I ask you a question?" she said quickly, before she could change her mind.

"Of course."

"What is a man like you doing here?"

He smiled, so quickly, so stunningly, she had to fight to keep her mouth from dropping open. That smile, she realized, was a major weapon.

"Not an office building," he began, "not a theater or a French restaurant in sight."

"Exactly. Not that it's not a beautiful spot, but I keep expecting someone to say 'cut,' then the screen will go blank and I'll realize I've been walking through a movie."

Rogan opened a tin, took out one of Murphy's biscuits to entertain Liam. "My initial reaction to this part of the world wasn't quite as romantic as that. The first time I came out here, I was cursing every muddy mile. Christ, it seemed it would never cease to rain, and a long way from Dublin is the west, in more than miles. Here, let me take him. He'll have crumbs all over you."

"I don't mind." Shannon snuggled Liam closer. "But you settled here," she prompted Rogan.

"We've a home here, and a home in Dublin. I'd wanted the new gallery, been working on the concept of it before I met Maggie. And after I had her under contract, fell in love with her, badgered her into marrying me, the concept became Worldwide Galleries Clare."

"You mean it was a business decision?"

"That was secondary. She's rooted here. If I'd torn her out, it would have broken her heart. So we have Clare, and Dublin, and it contents us."

He rose, going to the kettle that was shooting steam, to finish making the tea. "Maggie showed me the sketch you did of Liam. It takes skill to put so much into a few lines and shadings."

"Charcoal's simple, and kind of a hobby of mine."

"Ah, a hobby." Keeping his cards close to his vest, Rogan turned when Murphy came in. "Is your music a hobby, Murphy?"

"It's my heart." He stopped by the table to ruffle Liam's hair. "Stealing my biscuits. You'll have to pay for that." He snatched the boy up, tickling his ribs and sending Liam into squeals of laughter.

"Truck," Liam demanded.

"You know where it is, don't you? Go on then and get it." Murphy set Liam down, patted his butt. "Sit on the floor in there and play with it. If I hear anything I shouldn't, I'm coming after you."

As Liam toddled off, Murphy opened a cabinet for cups. "He's partial to an old wooden truck I had as a boy," he explained. "Partial enough that it can keep him quiet and out of trouble for ten or fifteen minutes at a go. Sit down, Rogan, I'll tend to the rest of this."

Rogan joined Shannon at the table, smiled at her again. "I had a look at the painting you've finished, the one of the standing stones? I hope you don't mind."

"No." But her brow creased.

"You do some, and Brie wasn't happy about my insisting on going up to look when she mentioned it to me. She said I was to tell you myself I'd invaded your privacy, and apologize for it."

"It doesn't matter, really." She looked up at Murphy as he filled cups. "Thanks."

"I'll offer you a thousand pounds for it."

She was grateful she'd yet to sip tea. Surely she'd have choked on it. "You're not serious."

"I'm always serious about art. If you've anything else finished, or in progress, I'd be interested in having first look."

She was beyond baffled. "I don't sell my paintings."

Rogan nodded, sipped contentedly at his tea. "That's fine. I'll sell them for you. Worldwide would be pleased to represent your work."

Speech was impossible, at least until her mind stopped spinning. She knew she had talent. She would never have risen so far at Ry-Tilghmanton if she'd been mediocre. But painting was for Saturday mornings, or vacations.

"We'd very much like," Rogan went on, knowing precisely how and when to press his advantage, "to feature your work in the Clare gallery."

"I'm not Irish." Because her voice wasn't strong, Shannon frowned and tried again. "Maggie said that you feature only Irish artists there, and I'm not Irish." That statement was met with respectful silence. "I'm American," she insisted, a little desperately.

His wife had told him Shannon would react in precisely this way. Rogan was, as he preferred to be, two steps ahead of his quarry. "If you agree, we could feature you as our American guest artist, of Irish extraction. I have no problem buying your work outright, on a piece by piece basis, but I believe it would be to our mutual benefit to have a more formal agreement, with precise terms."

"That's how he got Maggie," Murphy told Shannon, enjoying himself. "But I wish you wouldn't sell him that painting, Shannon, until I've seen it for myself. Might be I could outbid him."

"I don't think I want to sell it. I don't know. I've never had to think about this." Confused, she pushed at her hair. "Rogan, I'm a commercial artist."

"You're an artist," he corrected. "And you're foolish to put limitations on yourself. If you prefer to think about the standing stones—"

"It's *The Dance,*" she murmured. "I titled it just *The Dance.*"

It was then, by the tone of her voice, the look in her eyes, that Rogan knew he had her. But he wasn't one to gloat. "If you'd prefer to think about that particular work," he continued in the same mild, reasonable tone, "I wonder if you'd let me take it on loan and display it in the gallery."

"I . . . Well—" It seemed not only stupid, but ungracious to object. "Sure. If you'd like to, I don't have a problem with that."

"I'm grateful." He rose, half his mission complete. "I need to get Liam home for his nap. Maggie and I are switching shifts about this time today. She's been working this morning, and now I'm going into the gallery. Shall I go by and pick up the painting on my way?"

"I suppose. Yes, all right. It isn't framed."

"We'll take care of that. I'm going to be drafting up a contract for you to look over."

Confused, she stared at him. "A contract? But—"

"You'll take all the time you need to read it through, think it over, and naturally, we'll negotiate any changes you might want. Thanks for the tea, Murphy. I'm looking forward to the ceili."

Murphy only grinned at him, then turned the grin on Shannon when Rogan went out to collect his son. "He's slippery, isn't he?"

She was staring straight ahead, fumbling through the conversation that had just taken place. "What did I agree to?"

"Depending on how you look at it, nothing. Or everything. He's cagey, our Rogan. I was waiting for it, watching, and still I never saw him outflank you until it was done."

"I don't know how to feel about this," Shannon muttered.

"Seems to me if I was an artist, and a man who has a reputation around the world for being an expert on it, and for having an affection and understanding of the best of it, found my work of value, I'd be proud."

"But I'm not a painter."

Patient, Murphy folded his arms on the table. "Why is it, Shannon, you make such a habit of saying what you're not. You're not Irish, you're not sister to Maggie and Brie, you're not a painter. You're not in love with me."

"Because it's easier to know what you're not than what you are."

He smiled at that. "Now, that's a sensible thing you've said. Do you always want it easier?"

"I never used to think so. I was always smug about the fact that I went after the challenges." Confused and a little frightened, she closed her eyes. "Too much is changing on me. I can't get solid footing. Every time I seem to, it all shifts again."

"And it's hard to move with it when you're used to standing firm." He rose, then pulled her into his arms. "No, don't worry." His voice was quiet when she stiffened. "I'm not going to do anything but hold you. Just rest your head a minute, darling. Let some of the care out of it."

"My mother would have been thrilled."

"You can't feel her feelings." Gently he stroked her hair, hoping she'd take the caress as it was meant. In friendship. "Do you know, my mother once hoped I'd go off to town and make my living in music."

"Really?" She found her head nestled perfectly in the curve of his shoulder. "I would have thought your whole family would have expected—wanted—you to farm."

"It was a hope she had, when I showed an interest in instruments and such. She wanted her children to go beyond what she'd known, and she loved me more, you see, than the farm."

"And she was disappointed?"

"Maybe some, until she saw this was what I wanted." He smiled into her hair. "Maybe some even after. Tell me, Shannon, are you happy in your work?"

"Of course. I'm good at it, and I've got a chance to move up. In a few years I'll have the choice between top level at Ry-Tilghmanton, or starting a business of my own."

"Mmm. Sounds more like ambition than happiness."

"Why do they have to be different?"

"I wonder." He drew her away because he was tempted to kiss her again, and it wasn't what she needed just then. "Maybe you should ask yourself, and think it through, if drawing for somebody else puts the same feeling inside you that drawing what pulls you does."

He did kiss her, but lightly, on the brow. "Meanwhile, you should be smiling instead of worrying. Rogan takes only the best for his galleries. You haven't been out to Ennistymon yet, have you?"

"No." She was sorry he'd let her go. "Is that where the gallery is?"

"Near. I'll take you if you like. I can't today," he said with a wince at the wall clock. "I've got a bit to do around here yet, and I've promised to go by Feeney's and lend him a hand with the tractor."

"No, and I've kept you long enough anyway."

"You can keep me as long as you want." He took her hand, running his thumb over her knuckles. "Maybe you'd come down to the pub tonight. I'll buy you a drink to celebrate."

"I'm not sure what I'm celebrating, but I might do that." Anticipating him, she stepped back. "Murphy, I didn't come here to wrestle in the kitchen."

"I never said you did."

"You're getting that look in your eyes," she muttered. "And that's my clue to leave."

"My hands are clean now, so I wouldn't muss you up if I kissed you."

"I'm not worried about being mussed, I'm worried about being . . . never mind. Just keep your hands where I can see them. I mean it."

Obliging, he lifted them palms out, then felt his heart turn over when she rose on her toes and kissed his cheek.

"Thanks for the tea, and the shoulder."

"You're welcome to either, anytime."

She sighed and made herself back up another step. "I know. You make it hard to be sensible."

"If you've a mind to be insensible, Feeney can wait."

She had to laugh. No man had ever asked her to bed with quite such style. "Go back to work, Murphy. I think I'm in the mood to paint."

She went out the back, accustomed now to the way over the fields.

"Shannon Bodine."

"Yes." Laughing again, she turned, walking backward as she watched him come out the kitchen door.

"Will you paint something for me? Something that reminds you of me?"

"I might." She tossed up a hand in a wave, swiveled on her heel, and hurried away toward Blackthorn.

In the rear gardens of the inn Kayla napped in a folding crib near the flowering almond Murphy had planted for her. Her mother was weeding the perennial bed nearby, and her father was doing his level best to talk Brianna into indoor activities.

"The place is empty." Gray trailed his fingers down Brianna's arm. "All the guests are off sightseeing. The kid's asleep." He inched a little closer to nibble at the back of Brianna's neck, encouraged by her quick shiver of reaction. "Come to bed, Brianna."

"I've work."

"The flowers aren't going anywhere."

"Neither are the weeds." Her system went haywire as he skimmed the tip of his tongue along her skin. "Ah, look. I nearly pulled an aster. Go away now, and—"

"I love you, Brianna." He caught her hands, pressing his lips to the back of each.

Heart and body melted. "Oh, Grayson." Her eyes fluttered closed when he rubbed his lips persuasively over hers. "We can't. Shannon could be back any time."

"Uh-oh. Do you think she's guessed where Kayla came from?"

"That's not the point." But her arms were twining around his neck.

He slipped the first pin from her hair. "What is the point?"

She'd been sure she had one, a very simple, very valid point. "I love you, Grayson."

Strolling into the yard, Shannon stopped short. Her first reaction was amused embarrassment at having stumbled across a very private scene. The next, tripping over the first, was interest.

It was a lovely, romantic picture, she mused. The infant sleeping under a pale pink blanket, the flowers blooming, clothes blowing on the line in the background. And the man and woman, kneeling on the grass, wrapped in each other.

A pity, she thought, she didn't have a sketch pad.

She must have made some sound, as Brianna shifted, saw her, and blushed rosily.

"Sorry. 'Bye."

"Shannon." Even as Shannon turned away, Brianna was struggling free. "Don't be silly."

"Go ahead," Gray corrected when Shannon hesitated. "Be silly. Scram."

"Grayson!" Shocked, Brianna batted his hands away and rose. "We—I was just weeding the pansies."

Shannon stuck her tongue in her cheek. "Oh, I could see that. I'm going to take a walk."

"You've just had a walk."

"So, let her take another one." Gray got up, wrapped an arm around Brianna's waist, and sent Shannon a meaningful look. "A really long one." Ignoring his wife's half-hearted struggles, he plucked another pin from her hair. "Better yet, take my car. You can—" He let out a groan when Kayla began to whimper.

"She needs her nappie changed." Brianna slipped away to go to the crib. Amused, and feeling wonderfully wanted, she smiled over at her husband as she lifted the baby. "You might put some of that energy into weeding, Grayson. I still have pies to bake."

"Right." With obvious regret he watched his wife, and his hopes for an intimate hour, slip out of his reach. "Pies to bake."

"Sorry." Shannon lifted her shoulders when Brianna took the baby inside. "Lousy timing."

"You're telling me." He hooked an arm around her neck. "Now you have to help me weed."

"It's the least I can do." Companionably she settled on the grass beside him. "I take it none of the guests are around."

"Off to various points of interest. We heard your news. Congratulations."

"Thanks. I guess. I'm still a little shell-shocked. Rogan has a way of slipping around and through and over objections until you're just nodding and agreeing to everything he says."

"He does." Intrigued, Gray studied her profile. "You'd have objections to being associated with Worldwide?"

"No. I don't know." She moved her shoulders restlessly. "It came out of the blue. I like to be prepared for things. I already have a career." Which, she realized with a jolt, she hadn't given a thought to in weeks. "I'm used to deadlines, and a quick pace, the confusion of working in a busy organization. Paintings, this kind of painting, is solitary and motivated by mood rather than marketing."

"Being used to one way of life doesn't mean you can't change gears, if the reward's big enough." He glanced toward the kitchen window. "It depends on what you want, and how much you want it."

"That's what I haven't decided. I'm floundering, Gray. I'm not used to that. I've always known what step to take next, and was confident, maybe overconfident, about what I was made of."

Thoughtful, she brushed her fingers over the bright purple face of a pansy. "Maybe it was because it was only my parents and me—no other family—that I always felt able to stand on my own, do exactly what I wanted. I never made really close attachments as a kid because we moved around so much. It made me easy with strangers, and comfortable in new places and situations, but I never felt any real connection with anyone but my parents. By the time we settled in Columbus, I'd set my goals and focused on reaching them step by careful step. Now, within a year, I've lost my parents, learned that my life wasn't what I thought it was. Suddenly I'm swimming in family I never knew I had. I don't know how I feel about them, or myself."

She looked up again, managed a small smile. "Wow. That was a lot, wasn't it?"

"It usually helps to sound the feelings out." Gently he tugged on her hair. "Seems to me if someone's good at going step by step, she'd be able to shift and keep doing just that in another direction. You only have to be alone when you want to be alone. It took me a long time to learn that." He kissed her, made her smile. "Shannon, me darling, relax and enjoy the ride."

THIRTEEN

In the morning she chose to paint in the garden, putting the final touches on the watercolor of Brianna. From the house came the buzz of activity as a family from County Mayo gathered themselves up to leave the inn for the next leg of their trip south.

She could smell the hot-cross buns Brianna had made for breakfast and the roses that had burst into bloom in their climb up the trellis.

Nibbling on her knuckle, Shannon stepped back to examine the completed canvas.

"Well, that's lovely." With Liam in tow, Maggie stepped across the lawn behind her. "Of course, she makes an easy subject, does Brianna." She bent down and kissed Liam on the nose. "Your aunt Brie has your buns, darling. Go get them."

When he scrambled off, slamming the kitchen door behind him, Maggie frowned over the painting. "Rogan's right then," she decided. "It's rare that he's not, which is a trial to me. He took your painting of the stones into the gallery before I had a chance to see."

"And you wanted to check it out for yourself."

"Your sketch of Liam was more than good," Maggie conceded. "But one charcoal isn't enough to judge. I can tell you now he'll want this, and he'll badger you until you agree."

"He doesn't badger, he demolishes, bloodlessly."

Maggie's laugh was quick and rich. "Oh, that's the truth. Bless him.

What else have you?" Without invitation she picked up Shannon's sketchbook and flipped through.

"Help yourself," Shannon said dryly.

Maggie only made noises of approval and interest, then let out another delighted laugh. "You must do this one, Shannon. You must. It's Murphy to the ground. The man and his horses. Damn, I wish I had the hands to do portraits like this."

"I'd see him up there sometimes when I was painting the circle." Shannon tilted her head so that she could see the page herself. "It was irresistible."

"When you paint it, I'd be pleased to buy it for his mother." She frowned then. "Unless you've signed with Sweeney by then. If he's any say in it, he'll charge me half a leg and both arms. The man asks the fiercest prices for things."

"I wouldn't think that would bother you." With care, Shannon took the finished canvas from the easel and laid it on the table. "When I went to your show in New York a couple years ago, I lusted after this piece—it was like a sunburst, all these hot colors exploding out of a central core. Not my usual style, but God, I wanted it."

"Fired Dreams," Maggie murmured, deeply flattered.

"Yes, that's it. I had to weigh desire against a year's rent—at New York rates. And I needed a roof over my head."

"He sold that piece. If he hadn't, I'd have given it to you." At Shannon's stunned look, Maggie shrugged. "At the family rate."

Touched, and not sure how to respond, Shannon set a fresh canvas on her easel. "I'd say you're lucky to have a shrewd manager looking after your interests."

As disconcerted as Shannon, Maggie jammed her hands in her pockets. "So he's always telling me. He's got his mind set on doing the same for you."

"I won't have as much time for painting once I'm back in New York." Taking up a pencil, Shannon sketched lightly on the canvas.

Maggie only lifted a brow. When a woman was an artist down to the bone, she recognized another. "He's having contracts drafted up today."

"He moves fast."

"Faster than you can spit. He'll want fifty percent," she added, grinning wickedly. "But you can drive him down to forty using the family connection."

Shannon's throat was suddenly, uncomfortably dry. "I haven't agreed to anything yet."

"Ah, but you will. He'll harangue you, and he'll charm you. He'll be reasonable and businesslike. You'll say no, thank you very much, and he'll skip right over that. If reason doesn't work, he'll find some little weakness to twist or some private wish to tweak. And you'll be signing your name before you realize it. Do you always hold a pencil like that?"

Still frowning over the prediction, Shannon glanced down at her hand. "Yes. I keep the wrist loose."

"Mmm. I keep a firmer grip, but I might try it. I should give you this before you start mixing paints." From her pocket she took out a ball of padded paper.

The moment Shannon felt the weight, she knew. "Oh, it's great." Once the paper was pulled aside, she held the globe up to the light.

"You made it, for the most part, so you should have it."

Shannon turned it so that the swirls of deep blue inside changed shape and tone. "It's beautiful. Thank you."

"You're welcome." Maggie turned back to the canvas. She could see the outline of the man, the horse. "How long will it take you to finish? It's a nasty question, and I only ask as I'd love to give it to Mrs. Brennan, Murphy's mother, when she comes up for the ceili."

"If it starts to click, it'll only take a day or two." Shannon set the globe aside and took up her pencil again. "When's the ceili, and what is it?"

"It's Saturday next, and a ceili's a kind of party—with music and dancing and food." She glanced over as Brianna stepped out of the kitchen door. "I'm telling this poor, ignorant Yank what a ceili is. Where's my whirlwind?"

"Off to the village with Grayson. I'm told it's man's business." Brianna stopped, then beamed at the canvas on the table. "Oh, I'm so flattered. What lovely work you do, Shannon." She peeked at the new canvas, wary. Experience with Maggie had taught her artists had moods that flared like lightning. "It's Murphy, isn't it?"

"It will be," Shannon murmured, narrowing her eyes as she sketched. "I didn't realize you were having a party, Brie."

"A party? Oh, the ceili. No, Murphy's having it. We were surprised at first, since his family had just come a few weeks ago for Kayla's baptism. But the lot of them are coming again, so they can meet you."

Shannon dropped her pencil. Slowly she bent to retrieve it. "Excuse me?"

"They're anxious to get to know you," Brianna continued, too engrossed in the canvas to notice that Maggie was rolling her eyes and making faces. "It's lovely Murphy's mother and her husband can make the trip from Cork so soon again."

Shannon turned. "Why would they want to meet me?"

"Because . . ." The warning registered, just a beat too late. Fumbling, Brianna began to brush at her apron. "Well, it's just that . . . Maggie?"

"Don't look at me. You've already put your foot in it."

"It's a simple question, Brianna." Shannon waited until Brianna lifted her gaze again. "Why would Murphy's mother and his family come back here to meet me?"

"Well, when he told them he was courting you, they—"

"He what?" She threw the pencil down to cap the explosion. "Is he crazy or just brain-dead? How many times do I have to tell him I'm not interested before he gets it through that thick skull?"

"Several times more, I'd wager," Maggie said with a grin. "There's a pool in the village that's leaning toward a June wedding."

"Maggie!" Brianna said under her breath.

"Wedding?" Shannon made a sound between a groan and a curse. "That tops it. He's calling out his mother to inspect me, he's got people betting—"

"Fact is, it was Tim O'Malley who started the pool," Maggie put in.

"He has to be stopped."

"Oh, there's no stopping Tim once a wager's made."

Unable to find the humor, Shannon shot Maggie a searing look. "You think it's funny? People I don't even know are betting on me?"

Maggie didn't have to think it over. "Yes." Then with a laugh, she grabbed Shannon by the shoulders and shook. "Oh, cool yourself down. No one can make you do what you don't want."

"Murphy Muldoon is a dead man."

With less sympathy than amusement, Maggie patted her cheek. "Seems to me you'd not be so fired up if you were as disinterested as you claim. What do you think of the matter, Brie?"

"I think I've said more than enough." But her heart pushed the words out. "He loves you, Shannon, and I can't help but feel for him. I know what it is to tumble into love and not be able to find your way out, no matter how foolish it makes you. Don't be too hard on him."

Temper drained as quickly as it had flashed. "It would be harder, wouldn't it, for me to let this go on when it isn't leading anywhere?"

Maggie picked up the sketchbook, then held out the page where Murphy looked out. "Isn't it?" When Shannon said nothing, Maggie set the book aside again. "The ceili's more than a week away. You'll have some time to sort it out."

"Starting now." Shannon picked up the watercolor and carried it inside. On the way up to her room, she practiced exactly what she would say to Murphy when she tracked him down.

It was a shame that she would have to break off their friendship just when she'd begun to realize how much it meant to her. But she doubted he would understand anything less than total amputation.

And he'd brought it on himself, the idiot. With an effort, she controlled herself long enough to prop the canvas carefully against the wall of her room. Going to the window, she scanned the fields. After a moment she caught sight of movement near the back of the house.

Dandy. She'd beard the beast in his den.

Her headlong rush took her down the stairs and outside. She was halfway to the gate before she saw the car parked at the side of the road, and Brianna and Maggie on either side of it.

She didn't have to see to know an argument was in full swing. She could hear it in the sharp, impatient tone of Maggie's voice. It would have been easy to continue on her way—but she saw Brianna's face.

It was pale, and rigidly controlled, except for the eyes. Even from two yards away, Shannon could see the hurt in them.

She set her teeth. It seemed it was her day for dealing with emotional crises. And damn it, she was in the perfect mood.

The angry words came to an abrupt halt as she strode to the car and looked down at Maeve.

"Shannon." Brianna gripped her hands together. "I never introduced you to Lottie. Lottie Sullivan, Shannon Bodine."

The woman with the round face and beleaguered expression continued the process of climbing out from the driver's side.

"I'm pleased to meet you," she said with a quick, apologetic smile. "And welcome."

"Get in the car, Lottie," Maeve snapped. "We're not staying."

"Drive yourself off then," Maggie snapped right back. "Lottie's welcome here."

"And I'm not?"

"It's you who's made that choice." Maggie folded her arms. "Make yourself miserable if you like, but you won't do this to Brie."

"Mrs. Concannon." Shannon nudged Maggie aside. "I'd like to speak with you."

"I've nothing to say to you."

"Fine. Then you can listen." Out of the corner of her eye, Shannon caught Lottie's nod of approval and hoped to earn it. "We have a connection, you and I, whether we like it or not. Your daughters link us, and I don't want to be the cause of friction between you."

"No one's causing friction but herself," Maggie said hotly.

"Be quiet, Maggie." Shannon ignored her sister's hiss of temper and continued. "You have a right to be angry, Mrs. Concannon. And to be hurt, whether it's your pride that's suffering or your heart, it doesn't matter. Still, the fact is you can't change what happened, or the result of it any more than I can."

Though Maeve said nothing, only continued to stare fiercely straight ahead, Shannon was determined to finish.

"My part in this whole thing is rather indirect, a result rather than a cause. Whether or not you were part of the cause doesn't really matter."

That brought Maeve's head around, and the venom spewing. "You'd dare to say that I caused your mother to commit adultery with my husband."

"No. I wasn't there. My mother blamed no one, certainly not you, for her actions. And what I'm saying is it doesn't matter what part you played. Some might say that since you didn't love him, you shouldn't care that he found someone else. I don't agree with that. You have all the right in the world to care. What they did was wrong."

Maggie's next protest was cut off by a cold look from Shannon. "It was wrong," she said again, satisfied that no one interrupted. "Whether you look at it morally, religiously, or intellectually. You were his wife, and no matter how dissatisfied either of you were in the marriage, that should have been respected. Honored. It wasn't, and to find out it wasn't after all these years doesn't diminish the anger or the betrayal."

She took a quiet breath, aware that Maeve's attention was centered fully on her. "I can't go back and not be born, Mrs. Concannon. Nothing either of us can do will break the connection, so we're going to have to live with it."

She paused again. Maeve was watching her now, and intrigued, her eyes narrowed. "My mother died with my hard words between us. I can't fix that, either, and I'll regret it all my life. Don't let something you can't change ruin what you have now. I'll be gone soon. Maggie and Brie and your grandchildren are right here."

Satisfied she'd done her best, Shannon stepped back. "Now if you'll excuse me, I have to go murder a man."

She started down the road, had gotten no more than five paces when she heard the car door open.

"Girl."

Shannon stopped, turned, and met Maeve's gaze levelly. "Yes?"

"You made your point." Whatever effort it took to concede it, Maeve disguised in a brisk nod. "And you have some sense, more than the man whose blood runs through you ever did."

Shannon inclined her head in acknowledgment. "Thank you."

While Shannon continued on her way, everyone else gaped at Maeve as if she'd sprouted wings. "Well, are you going to stand around outside all the day?" she demanded. "Get a move on you, Lottie. I want to go in and see my granddaughter."

Not bad, Shannon decided and quickened her step. If she had half that much luck getting through to Murphy, she could consider it an excellent day's work.

When she reached the farm and circled to the back, she saw Murphy standing near the paddock of sheep beside a short, bandy-legged man who had his teeth clamped around a pipe.

They weren't speaking, but she would have sworn some sort of communication was going on.

Suddenly, the older man bobbed his head. "All right then, Murphy. Two pigs."

"I'd be grateful if you could hold them for me, Mr. McNee. For a day or two."

"That I can do." He shoved the pipe further into his mouth and had started toward the paddock when he spotted Shannon. "You've company, lad."

Murphy glanced over and smiled broadly. "Shannon. I'm happy to see you."

"Just don't start with me, you baboon." She strode forward to shove a finger into his chest. "You've got a lot of explaining to do."

Beside them, McNee perked up his ears. "Is this the one then, Murphy?"

Gauging his ground, Murphy rubbed his chin. "She is."

"You took your time picking one out, but you picked a fair one."

Temper bubbling, Shannon turned on McNee. "If you've bet on this idiot, you can kiss your money good-bye."

"Is there a pool?" McNee asked, offended. "Why wasn't I told of it?"

While Shannon considered the satisfaction of knocking their heads together, Murphy patted her arm. "If you'll excuse me just a minute, darling. Do you need help getting the lamb you fancy, Mr. McNee?"

"No, I can handle the job, and it looks like you've enough on your hands at the moment." With surprising agility, the old man swung into the paddock and sent bleating sheep scattering.

"We'll go inside."

"We'll stay right here," Shannon shot back, then swore at him when he took a firm grip on her arm.

"We'll go in," he repeated. "I prefer you do your shouting at me in private."

In his careful way he stopped at the stoop, pulled off his muddy Wellingtons. He opened the door for her, waited as any well-mannered man would for her to storm in before him.

"Will you sit?"

"No, damn you to hell and back, I won't sit."

He shrugged, leaned back against the counter. "We'll stand then. You've something on your mind?"

His mild tone only fanned the fires. "How dare you? How dare you call your family and tell them to come look me over, like I was one of your horses going up for auction."

His face relaxed. "You're mistaken about that. I asked if they'd come meet you. That's entirely different."

"It is not different. And you're having them come on false pretenses. You told them you were courting me."

"So I am courting you, Shannon."

"We've been through that, and I'm not going through it again."

"That's fine then. Can I offer you tea?"

She was surprised she had any teeth left, as hard as she was grinding them. "No, you can't offer me tea."

"I do have something else for you." He reached behind him on the counter and picked up a box. "I was in Ennis a day or so ago and bought this for you. I forgot to give it to you yesterday."

In a gesture she recognized as childish, she put her hands behind her back. "No, absolutely no. I'm not taking gifts from you. This isn't even remotely amusing anymore, Murphy."

He simply opened the box himself. "You like to wear pretty things. These caught my eye."

Despite her best intentions, she looked down at the open box. They were pretty—foolishly pretty earrings of exactly the type she might have chosen herself. Citrine and amethyst hearts were nestled, one atop the other.

"Murphy, those are expensive. Take them back."

"I'm not a pauper, Shannon, if it's my wallet you're worrying about."

"That's a consideration, but it's secondary." She forced herself to look away from the lovely stones. "I'm not taking gifts from you. It'll only encourage you."

He walked toward her until she found herself backed up against the refrigerator. "Don't you dare."

"You're not wearing any today," he observed. "So we'll try them on. Hold still, darling, I don't know if I've the knack of it."

She batted at his hands as he started to fasten the first earring, then yelped when he poked the post into her lobe.

"You asked for it," he muttered, giving the job his full concentration.

"I'm going to hit you," she said between her teeth.

"Wait till I'm done. This is clumsy work for a man. Why do they make these little clasp things so bloody small? There." Like a man satisfied with the completion of a pesky chore, he stepped back and studied the result. "They suit you."

"You can't reason with the unreasonable," she reminded herself. "Murphy, I want you to call your family and tell them not to come."

"I can't do that. They're looking forward to the ceili, and meeting you."

She bunched her hands into fists. "All right, then call and tell them you made a mistake, changed your mind, whatever, and that you and I are not an item."

His brow creased. "You're meaning I should tell them I'm not going to marry you?"

"That's it, exactly." She gave him a congratulatory pat on the arm. "You've finally got it."

"I hate to say no to you about anything, but I can't be lying to my family." He was quick enough on his feet to dodge the first punch, then the second. The third nearly caught him as he was doubled over with laughter, but he evaded by snagging her around the waist and swinging her in a giddy circle.

"God, you're for me, Shannon. I'm crazy in love with you."

"Crazy," she began, but the rest was muffled against his mouth.

He stole her breath. She couldn't get it back. While she gripped his shoulders, he continued to circle her, adding dizziness to breathlessness. His mouth added the heat. Even when he stopped the wild spinning, the room continued to revolve, and her heart with it.

There was a quick and stunning thought through the haze of desire, that he was giving her no choice but to love him.

"I'm not going to let this happen." On a panicked flood of strength, she shoved away.

Her hair was tousled, her eyes wide and stunned. He could see the pulse hammering at her throat, and the color the kiss had left blooming in her cheeks.

"Come to bed with me, Shannon." His voice was thick, rough, and edgy. "Christ Jesus, I need you. Every time you walk away there's a hole in me, and a terrible fear you won't come back." Desperate, he pulled her close again, buried his face in her hair. "I can't keep watching you walk away, and never having you."

"Don't do this." She squeezed her eyes tight and fought a vicious battle with what was inside her. "You won't let it be anything as simple as going to bed, and I can't let it be anything else."

"It is something else. It's everything else." He yanked her back. Remembering, he dropped his hands before his fingers could bruise. "Is it because I trip around you? I get clumsy sometimes because I can't always think in a clear way when I'm close to you."

"No, it's not you, Murphy. It's me. It's me and your idea of us. And I've handled it much more clumsily than you." She tried to take a deep breath, but found her chest was painfully tight. "So I'm going to fix that. I'm not going to see you again." Keeping her eyes on his cost her, but she refused to back down. "That'll make it easier for both of us. I'm going to start my arrangements to go back to New York."

"That's running," he said evenly. "But do you know if you're running from me or from yourself?"

"It's my life. I have to get back to it."

The fury crawling through him left no room even for fear. With his eyes burning into hers, he reached into his pocket and tossed what he had carried there onto the table.

Her nerves began to stretch even before she lowered her gaze and saw it. The circle of copper with the figure of a stallion embossed. It would have a pin on the back, she knew, sturdy and thick enough to clamp together a man's riding cloak.

Murphy watched her go as pale as glass. Her fingers reached out for it, then drew back sharply, curling into a defensive fist.

"What is it?"

"You know what it is." He swore with studied violence when she shook her head. "Don't lie to yourself. It's poor spirited."

She could see it against dark wool, both broach and cloak beaded with rain. "Where did you get it?"

"I found it, center of the dance when I was a boy. I fell asleep with it in my hand, right there. And dreamed of you the first time."

She couldn't take her eyes from it, even when her vision wavered. "That isn't possible."

"It happened, just as I told you." He picked it up and held it out to her.

"I don't want it." Panic snaked into her voice.

"I've kept it for you half my life." Calmer now, he slipped it back into his pocket. "I can keep it longer. There's no need for you to leave before you've had the time you're wanting with your sisters. I won't touch you in that way again, or pressure you to give me what you're not willing to. You've my word."

He would keep it. She knew him now well enough not to doubt it. How could she blame him for giving her a promise that made her feel small and weepy? "I care about you, Murphy. I don't want to hurt you."

She couldn't have any idea how much she had done just that. But he kept his voice neutral. "I'm a man grown, Shannon, and can tend to myself."

She'd been so sure she could walk away cold. Now she found she wanted to hold him again, and be held. "I don't want to lose your friendship. It's come to mean a lot to me in a short time."

"You couldn't lose it." He smiled, though he had to keep his hands close to his sides to keep from reaching for her. "You never have to worry over that."

She tried not to as she left and started up the road again. And she tried not to think too deeply about why she needed to weep.

FOURTEEN

Murphy put his back into mucking out the stables. Physical labor was part of his life, and he knew how to use strain and sweat to ease the mind.

It was a pity it wasn't working for him.

He drove his shovel into the soiled straw bedding, tossed the load into the growing pile in his wheelbarrow.

"You always had a good aim, you did, Murphy." Maggie strolled up behind him. She was smiling, but her eyes were searching his face for signs. And what she found tore at her heart.

"Why aren't you working?" He spoke without looking over or stopping. "I hear your furnace."

"I'm going to get to it." She came closer, resting a hand on the open stall door. "I didn't come by yesterday because I thought you might want a little breathing space. So I waited till this morning. Shannon looked miserable when she came back after seeing you yesterday."

"I did my best to put her at ease." He bit off the words before taking his shovel into the next stall.

"What about your ease, Murphy?" Maggie laid a hand on his back, leaving it lay despite his bad-tempered shrug. "I can see what you feel for her, and I hate to know you're so upset."

"Then you'd best be off, as I'm planning on staying this way. Move back, damn it, you'll have manure in your face."

Instead she snatched at the handle of the shovel and had an angry and brief wrestle for it. "Fine then." She let go and brushed her hands together. "You can go on shoveling at shit all you please, but you'll talk to me."

"I'm in no mood for company."

"And since when have I been company?"

"Damn it, Maggie, go away." He whirled on her, temper hot in his eyes. "I don't want your pity, I don't want your sympathy, and I don't want any bloody advice."

She fisted her hands, plopped them on her hips, and went toe to toe with him. "If you think you can shake me off with nasty words and nastier temper, you're mistaken, lad."

Of course he couldn't, and because it would do him no good with her, Murphy did what he could do to bury the fury. "I'm sorry, Maggie Mae. I shouldn't swipe at you. I need to be alone for a bit."

"Murphy—"

She'd break him if he didn't see her off, and quickly. "It's not that I'm not grateful you'd come by and want to help. I'm not ready for it. I need to lick my wounds on my own. Be a friend, darling, and leave me be."

Deflated, she did the only thing she knew how, and pressed her cheek to his. "Will you come talk to me when you can?"

"Sure I will. Go on now, be off. I've a lot to do today."

When she left him, Murphy drove his shovel into the straw and cursed softly, viciously, until he ran out of words.

He worked like a man possessed until the sun set, then rose again when it did to repeat the process. Even his well-toned muscles ached by the time he settled down with a cold sandwich and a bottle of beer.

He was already thinking of bed, though it was barely eight, when the back door swung open. Rogan and Gray came through it, followed happily by Con.

"We're on a mission, Murphy." Gray slapped him on the back, then turned to the cupboards.

"A mission, is it." Automatically he scratched Con's ears when the dog laid his head on his lap. "Of what nature?"

"We're ordered to draw off your black mood." Rogan set a bottle on the counter and broke the seal. "We're neither of us allowed back home until we've accomplished it."

"Brie and Maggie have had their heads together over you for two days," Gray put in.

"There's no need for that, or for this. I was going up to bed."

"You can't, as an Irishman, turn your back on two mates and a bottle of Jamison's." Gray slapped three glasses, one by one, on the table.

"So, we're to get drunk, are we?" Murphy eyed the bottle. He hadn't thought of that one.

"The women haven't been able to turn the tide." Rogan poured three hefty shots. "So they've conceded it's a man's job." He seated himself comfortably at the table, lifted his glass. *"Slainte."*

Murphy scratched his chin, blew out a breath. "What the fuck." He downed the first glass, winced before slapping it down for a refill. "Did you only bring one bottle?"

Laughing, Gray poured the next round.

When the bottle was half gone, Murphy was feeling more mellow. A temporary fix, he knew, and a fool's one. But he felt very much the fool.

"I gotta tell you." Already a little wobbly, Gray kicked back in his chair and puffed on one of the cigars Rogan had provided. "I can't get drunk."

"Yes, you can." Rogan studied the tip of his own cigar. "I've seen you."

"You couldn't see anything. You were too drunk." Finding that wonderfully funny, Gray leaned forward again and nearly upended. "But what I mean is, I can't get so plowed I can't make love with my wife tonight. Oh, thanks." He picked up the glass Murphy had refilled and gestured with it. "I'm making up for lost time." Deadly serious, he rested his elbow on the table. "Do you know how long you can't when a woman's pregnant?"

"I do." Rogan nodded sagely. "I can say I do know precisely."

"And it doesn't bother them much. They're . . ." Gray gestured grandly. "Nesting. So I'm making it up, and I'm not getting drunk."

"Too late," Murphy muttered and scowled into his glass.

"You think we don't know what's wrong with you?" In fellowship Gray punched Murphy on the shoulder. "You're horny."

With a snorting laugh, Murphy tossed back another shot. "It should be so easy."

"Yeah." On a windy sigh Gray went back to his cigar. "When they've got you, they've got you. Ain't that the truth, Sweeney?"

"Sterling truth. She's painting up a storm, you know."

Murphy eyed him owlishly. "My misery, your profit?"

Rogan only grinned. "We'll have her first show in the fall. She doesn't know it, but we'll work around that. Do you know she went head to head with Maeve Concannon?"

"What d'ya mean?" Preferring his cigarettes to Rogan's cigars, Murphy lighted one. "They have a brawl?"

"No, indeed. Shannon just marched up to the woman and said her piece. When she was done, Maeve said she was a sensible woman, then went along into the inn to see the baby and young Liam."

"Is that a fact?" Drenched in admiration and love, Murphy took another drink. "Jesus, she's something, isn't she? Shannon Bodine, hard of head and soft of heart. Maybe I'll go tell her myself right now." He pushed himself up, his constitution strong enough to keep him from swaying. "Maybe I'll just go on up there, fetch her, and bring her back where she belongs."

"Can I watch?" Gray wanted to know.

"No." Heaving a sigh, Murphy dropped back into the chair. "No, I promised her I wouldn't. I hate that." He picked up the bottle, filled his glass again until the whiskey danced to the rim. "I'm going to hate my head in the morning, that's the truth of it. But it's worth it." He drank deep. "To share my sorrow with two of the finest friends God gave a man."

"Damn right. Drink to it, Rogan."

"I'm thinking I might be wise to make up that time you were speaking of before now—as I'll be losing it in seven months."

Gray leaned conspiratorially toward Murphy. "This guy is so sharp, it's scary."

"I'd appreciate it if the two of you would stop blabbering on about bedding women. I'm suffering here."

"It's inconsiderate of us," Rogan agreed. "There's no need to talk of women at all. Did I hear your bay mare's breeding?"

"Hey." Gray held up a hand. "Mare, woman. Female."

"Damned if you aren't right." Agreeably, Rogan cast around for another topic. "We got a fine sculpture in today, from an artist in County Mayo. He used Conemarra marble, and it's lovely work. A nude."

"Shit, Rogan, there you go again." Grayson's exasperated disgust sent Murphy off into gales of laughter.

Being generous friends, they poured Murphy into bed when the bottle was finished, then parted, satisfied that they'd accomplished their mission.

Staying away from her was difficult. Even with the demands of the farm, Murphy found it hard to go day after day, and night after night, knowing she was just across the fields. And so far out of his reach. It helped to think he was doing it for her.

Nothing soothed the soul like martyrdom.

Well-meaning friends didn't help. A week after he'd watched her walk away, he came into Brianna's rear yard and saw Shannon standing at her easel. She was wearing her college sweatshirt, splattered and smeared with paint and a pair of baggy jeans that were torn at the knee.

He thought she looked like an angel.

With her eyes narrowed, and the tip of her brush tapping against her lips, she studied her work. He knew the moment she sensed him from the change in her eyes, her careful movement of lowering her brush before she turned her head.

He didn't speak. He knew his tongue would tangle. After an awkward moment, he walked closer and stared hard at her painting.

It was the inn, the rear view with its pretty stonework and open windows. Brianna's gardens were flows of color and shape. The kitchen door was open wide in welcome.

Shannon wished she hadn't set her brush aside, and picked up a rag more to keep her hands occupied than to worry off paint.

"So, what do you think?"

"It's nice." He couldn't think of the words. "It looks finished."

"It is. Just."

"Well." He shifted the cartons of eggs he carried. "It's nice."

She turned, fiddling with the tubes and brushes on the little stand Gray had rigged for her. "I guess you've been busy."

"I have, yes." She glanced up, into his face, and his brain seemed to disconnect. "Busy." Furious with himself, he scowled down at his cartons. "Eggs," he muttered. "Brianna called for eggs. Said she needed them."

"Oh." In turn, Shannon stared at the cartons. "I see."

From her perch at the inside corner of the kitchen window, Brianna rolled her eyes. "Look at them, the two of them. Acting like ninnies."

Because they seemed so pathetic, she changed her master plan of leaving them alone and hurried to the door.

"Ah, there you are, Murphy, and you've brought the eggs. Bless you. Come in and have a taste of this strudel I've made."

"I need to—" But she had already hurried back into the kitchen, leaving him staring disconcertedly at the door. Shifting the cartons again, he looked at Shannon. "I've, ah . . ." Damn his slow wits, he thought. "Why don't you take them in, and I'll be on my way."

"Murphy." This had to stop, Shannon told herself, and tested her ground by laying a hand on his arm. He stiffened, and she couldn't blame him. "You haven't come around in a week, and I know that you're used to dropping in to see Brianna and Gray often, and easily."

He looked down at her hand, then back at her face. "I thought it best to stay away."

"I'm sorry for that. I don't want you to feel that way. I thought we were friends still."

His eyes stayed on hers. "You haven't come into the fields anymore."

"No, I haven't. *I* thought it best to stay away, and I'm sorry for that, too." She wanted to tell him she'd missed him, and was afraid to. "Are you angry with me?"

"With myself more." He steadied himself. Her eyes, he thought, and the quiet plea in them, would undo any man. "Do you want some strudel?"

Her smile spread slowly. "Yeah. I do."

When they went inside, Brianna stopped holding her breath. "Thank you for the eggs, Murphy." Bustling now, she took the cartons from him and went to the refrigerator. "I need them for a dish I'll be making for the ceili. Did you see Shannon's painting? It's grand, isn't it?"

"It is." He took off his cap, hung it on a peg.

"This strudel's from a recipe a German woman gave me last week when she was here. You remember her, Shannon, Mrs. Metz? The one with the big voice."

"The Stormtrooper," Shannon said with a smile. "She lined up her three children in the morning for inspection—her husband, too."

"And neat as a pin they were, every one of them. You'll tell me if the strudel's as good as she claimed."

Brianna was dishing it up when the phone rang. Shannon reached for the receiver on the wall phone. "I'll get it. Blackthorn Cottage." She hesitated a moment, brows lifting in surprise. "Tod? Yes, it's me." She laughed. "I do not sound Irish."

Unable to keep his lip from curling, Murphy sat down at the table. "Tod," he muttered when Brianna set the strudel in front of him. "Sounds more like an insect than a name."

"Hush," Brianna ordered and patted his arm.

"It's beautiful," Shannon continued. "Very much like *Local Hero*. Remember? Burt Lancaster." She chuckled again. "Right. Well, I'm doing a lot of walking, and eating. And I'm painting."

"That bored, huh?" His voice was amused, and faintly sympathetic.

"No." Her brow creased. "Not at all."

"Doesn't sound like your kind of deal. Anyway, when are you coming back?"

She caught the curling phone cord in her fingers and began to twist. "I'm not sure. A couple of weeks, probably."

"Christ, Shan, you've been there a month already."

Her fingers worried the cord, twisting it tighter. Odd, it hadn't seemed like a month. "I had three weeks coming." She heard the defensiveness in the tone, and hated it. "The rest is on me. How are things going there?"

"You know how it is. Regular madhouse since we clinched the Gulfstream account. You're the golden girl there, Shan. Two major notches in your belt in six months between Gulfstream and Titus."

She'd forgotten Titus, and frowned now thinking of the concept and art she'd come up with to help sell tires. "Gulfstream's yours."

"Now, sure, but the brass knows who initiated it. Hey, you don't think I'd take credit for your work."

"No, of course not."

"Anyway, I thought I'd let you know the guys upstairs are happy, but our department's starting to feel the pinch with the fall and Christmas campaigns getting underway. We really need you back."

She felt the light throbbing in her temple, the warning of a tension headache brewing. "I have things to work out, Tod. Personal things."

"You had a rough patch. I know you, Shannon, you'll have your feet back under you again. And I miss you. I know things were a little strained between us when you left, and I wasn't as understanding as I should have been, as sensitive to your feelings. I think we can talk that out, and get back on line."

"Have you been watching *Oprah?*"

"Come on, Shan. You take a couple more days, then give me a call. Let me know your flight number and ETA. I'll pick you up at the airport, and we'll cozy down with a bottle of wine and work this out."

"I'll get back to you, Tod. Thanks for calling."

"Don't wait too long. The brass has a short collective memory."

"I'll keep that in mind. 'Bye."

She hung up, discovered the cord was wrapped messily around her fingers. She concentrated on meticulously straightening it again.

"That was New York," she said without turning around. "A friend of mine at work." Before she swung around, she made sure she had a bright smile on her face. "So, how's the strudel?"

"See for yourself." Brianna poured Shannon tea to go with it. Her first instinct was to comfort. She held back the urge, trusting Murphy to do the job. "I think I hear the baby," she said and hurried through the adjoining door.

Shannon's appetite had fled. She glanced listlessly at the strudel, bypassed it for her tea. "My, ah, office is swamped."

"He wants you back." When Shannon's eyes lifted to his, Murphy inclined his head. "This Tod wants you back."

"He's handling some of my accounts while I'm gone. It's a lot of extra work."

"He wants you back," Murphy said again, and Shannon began to poke her fork in the strudel.

"He mentioned it—in a noncommittal sort of way. We had a strained discussion before I left."

"A discussion," Murphy repeated. "A strained discussion. Are you meaning a fight?"

"No." She smiled a little. "Tod doesn't fight. Debates," she mused. "He debates. He's very civilized."

"And was he debating, in a civilized way, just now? Is that why you're all tangled up?"

"No, he was just catching me up on the office. And I'm not tangled up."

Murphy put his hands over her restless ones, stilling them until she looked at him again. "You asked me to be your friend. I'm trying."

"I'm confused about things, a number of things," she said slowly. "It doesn't usually take me so long to figure out what I want and how to get it. I'm good at analyzing. I'm good at angles. My father was, too. He could always zero in on the bottom line. I admired that, I learned it from him."

Impatient, she jerked her hands from under Murphy's. "I had everything mapped out, and I was making it work. The position with the right firm, the uptown apartment, the high-powered wardrobe, the small, but tasteful art collection. Membership in the right health club. An undemanding relationship with an attractive, successful man who shared my interests. Then it all fell apart, and it makes me so tired to think of putting it together again."

"Is that what you want to do? Have to do?"

"I can't keep putting it off. That call reminded me I've been letting it all drift. I have to have solid ground under me, Murphy. I don't function well otherwise." When her voice broke, she pressed her hand to her lips. "It still hurts so much. It still hurts to think of my parents. To know I'll never see them again. I never got to say good-bye. I never got to say good-bye to either of them."

He said nothing at all as he rose and went to her, but simply lifted her to her feet to cradle her in his arms. In his silence was an understanding so perfect, so elemental, it devastated. She could weep and know that her tears would fall on a shoulder that would never shrug away from her.

"I keep thinking I'm over it," she managed. "Then it sneaks up and squeezes my heart."

"You haven't let yourself cry it through. Go ahead, darling. You'll feel better for it."

It ripped at him, each shuddering sob, and knowing he could do no more than be there.

"I want them back."

"I know, darling. I know you do."

"Why do people have to leave, Murphy? Why do the people who we love and need so much have to leave?"

"They don't, not all the way. You still have them inside, and you can't lose them from there. Don't you hear your mother talking to you sometimes, or your father reminding you of something you did together?"

Tired and achy from crying, she turned her damp cheek so it could rest against his chest. Foolish, she realized. How foolish it had been to think it was stronger to hold in the tears than to let them go.

"Yes." Her lips curved in a watery smile. "I get pictures sometimes, of things we did together. Even the most ordinary things, like eating breakfast."

"So they haven't left all the way, have they?"

She closed her eyes, comforted by the steady beat of Murphy's heart under her ear. "Just before the Mass, my mother's funeral Mass, the priest sat down with me. He was very kind, compassionate, as he was only months before when we buried my father. Still, it was the standard line—everlasting life, mercy, and the eternal rewards both my parents would reap having been devout Catholics and good, caring people."

She pressed against him one last time, for herself, then drew back. "It was meant to comfort me, and perhaps it did, a little. What you just said helps a lot more."

"Faith's a kind of remembering, Shannon. You need to prize your memories instead of being hurt by them." He brushed a tear from her cheek with the side of his thumb. "Are you all right now? I'll stay if you like, or get Brie for you."

"No, I'm okay. Thanks."

He tipped her chin up, kissed her forehead. "Then sit down, drink your tea. And don't clutter your mind with New York till you're ready."

"That's good advice." When she sniffled, he took his bandanna out of his pocket.

"Blow your nose."

She laughed a little and obeyed. "I'm glad you came by, Murphy. Don't stay away again."

"I'll be around." Because he knew she needed time to herself now, he turned to take his cap from the peg. "Will you come to the fields again soon? I like seeing you painting there in the sunlight."

"Yes, I'll come to the fields. Murphy . . ." She trailed off, not sure how to put the question, or why it seemed so important she ask. "Never mind."

He paused at the doorway. "What? It's always better to say what's on your mind than to let it circle in there."

Circling was exactly what it was doing. "I was wondering. If we'd been . . . friends when my mother was ill, and I'd had to go away to take care of her. To be with her. When she died, if I'd told you I could handle all of it, even preferred to handle all of it alone, would you have respected that? Stayed away?"

"No, of course not." Puzzled, he settled his cap on his head. "That's a stupid question. A friend doesn't stay away from a friend who's grieving."

"That's what I thought," she murmured, then stared at him long enough, hard enough to have him rubbing the back of his hand over his chin searching for crumbs.

"What?"

"Nothing. I was—" She lifted her cup and laughed at both of them. "Woolgathering."

More puzzled than ever, he returned her smile. "I'll see you then. You'll, ah, come to the ceili, won't you?"

"I wouldn't miss it."

FIFTEEN

Music was pouring out of the farmhouse when Shannon arrived with Brianna and her family. They'd brought the car, as Brianna had made too much food for the three of them to handle all of it, and the baby, on a walk.

Shannon's first surprise of the evening was the number of vehicles along the road. Their wheels tipped up onto the grass verge left just enough room from another car, with a very brave or foolish driver, to squeeze through.

"From the looks of this, he'll have a houseful," Shannon commented as they began to unload Brianna's dishes and bowls.

"Oh, the cars and lorries are only for those who live too far away to walk. Most come on foot to a ceili. Gray, don't tip that pot. You'll spill the broth."

"I wouldn't tip it if I had three hands."

"He's cross," Brianna told Shannon, "because his publishing people have added another city to his tour." She couldn't quite keep the smugness out of her voice. "Time was the man couldn't wait to go roving."

"Times change, and if you'd come with me—"

"You know I can't leave the inn for three weeks in the middle of summer. Come on now." Despite the load they both held, Brianna leaned forward to kiss him. "Don't fret on it tonight. Ah, look, it's Kate."

She hurried forward, her call of greeting floating on the air.

"You could always cancel the tour," Shannon said under her breath as she and Gray followed.

"Tell that to her. 'You'll not be neglecting your responsibilities toward your work because of me, Grayson Thane. I'll be just where you left me when you get back.' "

"Well." Shannon would have patted his cheek if her hands hadn't been full. "She will. Cheer up, Gray. If I've ever seen a man who's got it all, it's you."

"Yeah." That lifted his spirits a little. "I do. But it's going to be hard to feel that way when I'm sleeping alone in Cleveland next July."

"Suffering though room service. In-room movies, and the adulation of fans."

"Shut up, Bodine." He gave her a nudge to send her through the door.

She hadn't realized there were so many people in the entire county. The house was full of them, alive with their voices, crowded with their movements. Before she was ten paces down the hall, she was introduced to a dozen, and hailed by that many more she'd already met.

Music of flutes and fiddles streamed out of the parlor where some were already dancing. Plates of food were piled high, balanced on knees while feet enthusiastically stomped the time. Glasses were lifted or being pressed into waiting hands.

Still more people crowded into the kitchen, where platters and bowls were jammed end to end along the counters and the center table. Brianna was there, already empty handed as the baby was passed around and cooed over.

"Ah, here's Shannon." Brianna beamed as she began to unload the dishes from Shannon's arms. "She's not been to a ceili before. We'd have the music in the kitchen traditionally, but there's no room for it. But we can hear it just the same. You know Diedre O'Malley."

"Yes, hello."

"Get yourself a plate, lass," Diedre ordered. "Before the horde leaves you nothing but crumbs. Let's have those, Grayson."

"I'll trade you for a beer."

"I can do that for you." She chuckled as she took platters. "There's plenty to be had out on the stoop there."

"Shannon?"

"Sure." She smiled as Gray stepped out the door to fetch bottles. "It doesn't look like there'll be much business at the pub tonight, Mrs. O'Malley."

"No, indeed. We've closed. A ceili at Murphy's empties the village. Ah, Alice, I was just talking of your boy."

With the bottle Gray had given her halfway to her lips, Shannon turned to see a slim woman with softly waved brown hair come in the kitchen. She had Murphy's eyes, and his quick smile.

"They've shoved a fiddle in his hands, so he'll not get past the parlor for a time." Her voice was mellow, with a laugh on the edge of it. "I thought I'd fix him up a plate, Dee, in case he finds a moment to eat."

She reached for one, then her smile brightened. "Brie, I didn't see you there. Where's that angel of yours?"

"Right here, Mrs. Brennan." With a cocky grin, Gray stepped forward to kiss her.

"Go on with you. Devil is more like. Where's that baby?"

"Nancy Feeney and young Mary Kate absconded with her," Deidre said, uncovering the dishes Brianna had brought. "You'll have to find them, then fight them for her."

"And so I will. Ah, listen to that lad play." Pride beamed into her eyes. "He's God's gift in his hands."

"I'm pleased you could come from Cork, Mrs. Brennan," Brianna began. "You haven't met Shannon. My . . . friend from America."

"I haven't, no." The shining pride shifted to caution and curiosity. Her voice didn't cool precisely, but took on a hint of formality. "I'm pleased to meet you, Shannon Bodine." She offered her hand.

Shannon caught herself wiping her palm on her slacks before accepting the greeting. "It's nice to meet you, Mrs. Brennan." What now? "Murphy favors you."

"Thank you. He's a handsome lad for certain. And you live in New York City and draw for a living?"

"Yes." Miserably uncomfortable, she took a swig from her beer. When Maggie came noisily through the back door, Shannon could have kissed her feet.

"We're late," Maggie announced. "And Rogan's bursting to tell everyone it was my fault, so I'll say it first. I had work to finish." She plopped a bowl on the table, then set Liam down to toddle. "I'm starving to death, too." She snatched one of Brianna's stuffed mushrooms from a plate and devoured. "Mrs. Brennan, just the woman I'm after."

All that stiff formality melted out of Alice's face as she scooted around the table to give Maggie a hard hug. "Lord, you were the same as a child, always noisy as six drums."

"You'll be sorry you said so when I give you your present. Come along, Rogan."

"A man's got a right to stop and get a beer." With one in his hand he maneuvered himself and the wrapped package he carried through the door.

The entrance brought fresh greetings and chatter. Seeing it as a perfect escape, Shannon began to edge toward the hall.

"No, you don't, coward." Amused, Gray blocked her way. He slung an arm around her in a gesture of affection as firm as shackles.

"Give me a break, Gray."

"Not a chance."

Stuck, she watched as Alice carefully removed the brown paper from the painting. As people crowded around, there were sounds of surprise and approval.

"Oh, 'tis him to life," Alice murmured. "That's just the way he holds his head, do you see? And how he stands. I've never had a finer gift, Maggie, that's the truth. I can't thank you enough for giving it to me, or for painting it."

"You can thank me for giving it. But Shannon painted it."

Every head in the room shifted direction, and measured.

"It's a fine talent you have," Alice said after a moment, and the lilt came back in her voice. "And a heart for seeing your subject clearly. I'm very proud to have this."

Before Shannon could think of a response, a small, black-haired woman burst in from the hallway. "Ma, you'll never guess who's—What's this?" Spying the painting, she elbowed her way to it. "Why, 'tis Murphy with his horses."

"Shannon Bodine painted it," Alice told her.

"Oh?" Eyes bright and curious, the woman turned to scan the room. It took her only seconds to zero in. "Well, I'm Kate, his sister, and I'm pleased to meet you. You're the first he's courted ever."

Shannon sagged a little against Gray's supporting arm. "It's not—we're not—Murphy exaggerated," she decided as several pair of eyes studied her. "We're friends."

"It's wise to be friends when you're courting," Kate agreed. "Do you think sometime you could draw my children? Maggie won't."

"I'm a glass artist," Maggie reminded her and kept filling her plate. "And you'll have to go through Rogan. He's managing her."

"I haven't signed the contract yet," Shannon said quickly. "I haven't even—"

"Maybe you can do it before you sign up with him," Kate interrupted. "I can gather them up and bring them to you whenever you say."

"Stop badgering the woman," Alice said mildly. "And what did you come bursting in here to tell me?"

"Tell you?" Kate looked blank for a moment, then her eyes cleared. "Oh, you won't guess who just walked in the door. Maeve Concannon," she said before anyone could try. "Big as life."

"Why, Maeve's not been to a ceili in twenty years!" Diedre said. "More, I think."

"Well, she's come, and Lottie with her."

Brianna and Maggie stared at each other, speechless. then moved quickly, like a unit.

"We'd best go see if she wants a plate," Brianna explained.

"We'd best go see that she doesn't storm down the house," Maggie corrected. "Why don't you come, Shannon? You had a way with her last time."

"Well, really, I don't think—"

But Maggie grabbed her arm and dragged her out of the kitchen and down the hall. "Music's still playing," she said under her breath. "She hasn't put the stops to that."

"Look, this is none of my business," Shannon protested. "She's your mother."

"I'll remind you of your own words, about connections."

"Shit, Maggie." But Shannon had no choice but to grit her teeth and be propelled into the parlor.

"Sweet Jesus," was all Brianna could say.

Maeve was sitting, Liam in her lap, tapping her foot to the rhythm of the reel. Her face might have been set, mouth grim, but that tapping foot gave her away.

"She's enjoying herself." Astonishment had Maggie's eyes round and wide.

"Well, for Christ's sake." With an ill-tempered jerk, Shannon freed herself. "Why shouldn't she?"

"She'd never come around music," Brianna murmured. "Not in all my memory." As Lottie swung by, dancing a Clare set in the arms of a neighbor, Brianna could only shake her head. "How did Lottie get her to come?"

But Shannon had forgotten Maeve. Across the room, Murphy stood, hip shot, a fiddle clamped between shoulder and chin. His eyes were half closed, so that she thought he was lost in the music his quick fingers and hands made. Then he smiled and winked.

"What are they playing?" Shannon asked. The fiddler was joined by a piper and another who played an accordion.

"That's Saint Steven's reel." Brianna smiled and felt her own feet grow restless. "Ah, look at them dance."

"Time to do more than look." Gray snatched her from behind and whirled her into the parlor.

"Why, she's wonderful," Shannon said after a moment.

"She'd have been a dancer, our Brie, if things had been different." Brows knit, Maggie shifted her gaze from her sister to her mother. "Maybe things were different then than they're beginning to be now."

After taking a long breath, Maggie stepped into the parlor. After a moment's hesitation, she made her way through the dancing and sat beside her mother.

"That's a sight I never thought to see." Alice stepped next to Shannon. "Maeve Concannon sitting with her daughter at a ceili, her grandson on her knee, her foot tapping away. And very close to smiling."

"I suppose you've known her a long time."

"Since girlhood. She made her life, and Tom's, a misery. And those girls suffered for it. It's a hard thing to fight for love. Now it seems she's found some contentment in the life she leads, and in her grandchildren. I'm glad for that."

Alice looked at Shannon with some amusement. "I should apologize for my own daughter for embarrassing you in the kitchen. She's always been one for speaking first and thinking last."

"No, it's all right. She was . . . misinformed."

Alice pursed her lips at the term. "Well, if there's no harm done. There's my daughter Eileen, and her husband Jack. Will you come meet them?"

"Sure."

She met them, and Murphy's other sisters, his brother, his nieces and nephews and cousins. Her head reeled with names, and her heart staggered from the unquestioning welcome she received each time her hand was clasped.

She was given a full plate, a fresh beer, and a seat near the music, where Kate chattered in her ear.

Time simply drifted, unimportant against the music and the warmth. Children toddled or raced, or fell to dreaming in someone's willing arms. She watched men and women flirt while they danced, and those too old to dance enjoy the ritual.

How would she paint it? Shannon wondered. In vivid and flashing colors, or in soft, misty pastels? Either would suit. There was excitement here, and energy, and there was quiet contentment and unbroken tradition.

You could hear it in the music, she thought. Murphy had been right about that. Every note, every lovely voice lifted in song, spoke of roots too deep to be broken.

It charmed her to hear old Mrs. Conroy sing a ballad of love unrequited in a reedy voice that nonetheless held true. She laughed along with others at the rollicking drinking song shouted out. In awe and amazement she saw Brianna and Kate execute a complex and lyrical step-toe that had more people crowding into the parlor.

She clapped her palms pink when the music stopped, then glanced over as Murphy passed off his fiddle.

"You're enjoying yourself?" he asked her.

"I'm loving every minute." She handed him her plate to share. "You haven't had a chance to eat anything. So do it quick." She grinned at him. "I don't want you to stop playing."

"There's always someone to fill in." But he picked up half her ham sandwich.

"What else can you play—besides the violin and concertina?"

"Oh, a little of this and that. I saw you met my family."

"There are so many of them. And they all think the sun rises in Murphy's eyes." She chuckled when he winced.

"I think we should dance."

She shook her head when he took her hand. "As I've explained to several lovely gentlemen, I'm very happy to watch. No, Murphy." She laughed again when he pulled her to her feet. "I can't do that stuff—jigs or reels or whatever."

"Sure you can." He was steadily drawing her out. "But they're going to play a waltz, like I asked them. The first time we dance should be a waltz."

It was his voice that had her hand going limp, the way it had softened over the words. "I've never waltzed in my life."

He started to laugh, then his eyes widened. "You're joking."

"No. It's not a popular dance in the clubs I go to, so I'll just sit this one out."

"I'll show you." He slipped an arm around her waist, changed his grip on her hand. "Put your other hand on my shoulder."

"I know the stance, it's the steps." It was too enchanting a night not to accommodate him. Lowering her head, she watched his feet.

"You know the count, surely." He smiled at the top of her head. "So you go one, and a quicker two and three. And if you slide the back foot a bit on the last count, you'd glide into it. Aye, that's it."

When he circled her, she looked up again, laughing. "Don't get fancy. I'm a fast study, but I like plenty of practice."

"You can have all you want. It's no hardship for me to hold you in my arms."

Something shifted inside her. "Don't look at me like that, Murphy."

"I have to, when I'm waltzing with you." He whirled her in three long circles, as fluid as wine. "The trick when you're waltzing is to look right into your partner's eyes. You won't get dizzy that way, when you're turning round."

The idea of spot focusing might have had its merits, but not, Shannon discovered, when the focus was those dark blue eyes. "You have lashes longer than your sisters," she murmured.

"It was always a bone of contention between us."

"Such wonderful eyes." Her head was spinning, around and around like the dance. On the edge of giddy, on the verge of dreams. "I see them in my sleep. I can't stop thinking about you."

The muscles of his stomach twisted like iron, then tightened. "Darling, I'm doing my best to keep a promise here."

"I know." Everything was in slow motion now, a drift, a turn, a note. All of the colors and movements and voices seemed to fade mistily into the background until it was only the two of them, and the music. "You'd never break a promise, whatever it cost you."

"I haven't before." His voice was as tense as the hand holding hers. "But you're tempting me. Are you asking me to break it?"

"I don't know. Why are you always there, Murphy, on the tip of my mind?" She closed her eyes and let her head fall to his shoulder. "I don't know what I'm doing—what I'm feeling. I have to sit down. I have to think. I can't think when you're touching me."

"You drive a man past the end of his tether, Shannon." With an effort he kept his hands gentle as he drew her away, led her back to her seat. He crouched in front of her. "Look at me." His voice was quiet, below the music and the laughter. "I won't ask you again, I swore I wouldn't. It isn't pride that holds me back, or that makes me tell you the next step, whatever it is, has to be yours."

No, Shannon thought. It was *honor.* As old-fashioned a word as *courtship.*

"Stop flirting with the lass." Tim stopped by to slap Murphy hard on the back. "Sing something for us, Murphy."

"I'm busy now, Tim."

"No." Shannon edged back, found a smile. "Go sing something, Murphy. I've never heard you."

Fighting to compose himself, he stared down at the hands he'd rested on his knees. "What would you like to hear?"

"Your favorite." In a gesture that was as much apology as request, she laid her hand over his. "The song that means the most to you."

"All right. Will you talk with me later?"

"Later." She smiled at him as he straightened, certain she would feel more like herself later.

"So, how do you find your first ceili?" Brianna sat down beside her.

"Hmm? Oh, it's great. All of it."

"We haven't had such a grand, big party since Gray and I married last year. The *Bacachs* we had on the night we got back from our honeymoon."

"The what?"

"Oh, a *Bacachs* is an old tradition, where people disguise themselves and come into the house after dark, and—Oh, Murphy's going to sing." She gave Shannon's hand a squeeze. "I wonder what he'll do."

"His favorite."

" 'Four Green Fields,' " Brianna murmured and felt her eyes sting before the first note was played.

It took only that first note for voices to hush. The room went still as Murphy lifted his to the accompaniment of a single pipe.

She hadn't known he had that inside him—that pure, clean tenor, or the heart behind it. He sang a song of sadness and hope, of loss and renewal. And all the while the house grew as quiet as a church, his eyes were on hers.

It was a love song, but the love was for Ireland, for the land, and for family.

Listening to him, she felt that something that had moved inside her during the dance shift again, harder, firmer, further. The blood began to hum under her skin, not in passion so much as acceptance. Anticipation. Every barrier she had built crumbled and fell, soundlessly, under the effortless beauty of the song.

His voice simply vanquished her.

There were tears on her cheeks, warm, freed by his voice and the heartbreaking words of the ballad. There was no applause when he had finished. The hush was acknowledgment of a beauty simple and grand.

Murphy's eyes stayed on Shannon's as he murmured something to the piper. A nod, and then a quick bright tune was played. The dancing began again.

She knew he understood before he'd taken the first step toward her. He smiled. She rose and took the hand he offered.

He couldn't get her out quickly. There were too many people who stopped him for a word. By the time he'd led her outside, he could feel her hand trembling in his.

So he turned to her. "Be sure."

"Yes. I'm sure. But, Murphy, this can't make any difference. You have to understand . . ."

He kissed her, slow and soft and deep so that the words slid back down her throat. Keeping her hand in his, he circled around the house toward the stables.

"In here?" Her eyes went wide, and she felt a quick tug-of-war between dismay and delight. "We can't. All these people."

He found he could laugh after all. "We'll save a roll in the hay for another time, Shannon love. I'm just getting blankets."

"Oh." She felt foolish, and not at all certain she wasn't disappointed. "Blankets," she repeated as he took two down from the line where they'd been airing. "Where are we going?"

He folded them, laid them over his arm, then took her hand again. "Where we started."

The dance. Her heart began to drum again. "I—can you just leave this way? All those people are in your house."

"I don't think we'll be missed." Pausing, he looked down at her. "Do you care if we are?"

"No." She shook her head once, quickly. "No, I don't care if we are."

They crossed into the fields under the streaming light of the moon.

"Do you like counting stars?" he asked her.

"I don't know." Automatically she looked up to a sky teeming with them. "I don't think I ever have."

"You can't ever finish." He brought their joined hands to his lips. "It's not the sum of them that matter. Not the number. It's the wonder of it all. That's what I see when I look at you. The wonder of it all."

With a laugh, he scooped her off her feet. When he kissed her again it was full of young, burgeoning joy.

"Can you pretend I'm carrying you up some fine curving staircase toward a big soft bed, plumped with satin pillows and pink lace?"

"I don't need to pretend anything." She pressed her face into his throat as emotion welled up and swamped her. "Tonight I need only you. And you're right here."

"Aye." He brushed his lips over her temple until she shifted her head to look at him. "I'm here." He nodded across the field. "We're here."

The circle of stones stood, waiting in the warm beam of the moon.

SIXTEEN

Under swimming stars and a moon that shone white like a beacon, he carried her to the center of the dance. She heard an owl hoot, a long call that drifted through the air and faded to humming silence.

He set her on her feet, then spread the first blanket, letting the other fall before he knelt in front of her.

"What are you doing?" Where had the nerves come from? she wondered. She hadn't been nervous even a moment ago.

"I'm taking off your shoes."

Such a simple thing, an ordinary thing. Yet the gesture was as seductive as black silk. He took off his own, setting them tidily beside hers. His hands skimmed up her body, from ankle to shoulders as he rose.

"You're trembling. Are you cold?"

"No." She didn't think she could ever be cold again with the furnace that was pulsing away inside her. "Murphy, I don't want you to think that this means . . . anything but what it means. I wouldn't be fair to . . ."

He was smiling as he cupped her face gently in his hands and kissed her. "I know what it means. 'Beauty is its own reason for being.' " Still soft, still tender, his lips skimmed over her cheekbone. "That's Emerson."

What manner of man was it, she wondered, who could quote poetry and plow fields?

"You're beautiful, Shannon. This is beautiful."

He would see to it, giving her his heart as much as his body. And taking hers. So his hands were soft, easy as he stroked her—her shoulders, her back, through her hair, while his mouth patiently persuaded hers to give more. To take more. Just a little more.

She trembled still, even as her body leaned more truly into his, as the sound of quiet pleasure sighed through her lips, then through his. A faint breeze danced up, through the grass, then swirled like music around them.

He drew back, his eyes on hers, and slipped the man's vest she wore from her shoulders, let it fall. A murmur of surprise and longing whimpered in her throat as he kissed her again, his hands on her face, his fingers tracing.

She'd thought she'd understood the rules of seduction, the moves and countermoves men and women executed in the path toward pleasure. But this was new, this quiet, patient dance, this savoring of each elemental step. As with the waltz he'd taught her, she could do no more than hold fast and enjoy.

Her breath caught, released shakily when his fingers rested on the top button of her shirt. Oh, she wished she'd worn silk, something flowing and feminine with some lacy fancy beneath to enchant him.

Slowly he opened the shirt, spread it, then laid his palm lightly against her heart.

The thrill shot through her like a molten bullet. "Murphy."

"I've thought about touching you." He took the hand she gripped at his shoulder, brought it to his lips. "How your skin would feel. And taste. And smell." Watching her, he slid the shirt from her shoulders. "I've rough hands."

"No." She could do no more than shake her head. "No."

His eyes were solemn as he traced a fingertip above the downward curve of her bra, and up again. He'd known she'd be soft. But the way her flesh quivered under his lightest touch, the way her head fell back in stunned surrender, added sweetness to desire.

So he didn't take—though he could already feel the way her breasts would cup, small and firm in his hands. Instead he bent his head and took her mouth again. Her lips were incredibly generous, opening and welcoming his. The dark, potent tastes curled through his system, hinting of more heated, and more intimate flavors.

"I want—" Her hands shook as she gripped his shirt. She steadied herself by staring into his eyes. "I want you, more than I ever imagined." Now watching him, she unbuttoned his shirt, reaching up to tug it over his shoulders. Then her gaze lowered.

"Oh." It was a sigh of delight and admiration. This was a body hardened and defined by labor and sweat rather than machines. Experimentally she spread her hands over his chest where the skin was smooth over solid strength, and his heartbeat jumped.

Then hers leaped into her throat as he loosened the waistband of her slacks. Mesmerized, she felt him take her hand, balancing her as she stepped free. But when she reached for him, he shook his head. Even the patience of love had its limits.

"Lie with me," he murmured. "Come lie with me."

He lowered her to the blanket and captured her mouth.

He touched her with a terrifying tenderness, molding her breasts, giving himself the aching pleasure of slipping beneath the cotton to test and tease. He needed the flavor that tempted him along her throat, over her shoulders. When his tongue skimmed, as his fingers had, under the material to lave her nipple, she arched like a bow.

"Now." Her breath sobbed out. "For God's sake."

He only flicked open the front clasp of her bra and took her silkily into his mouth.

Tormented, exhilarated, she pressed him closer. Beneath him her movements were frantic, shameless. He was undoing her with tongue and teeth and lips, making her beg with stumbling, breathless words. The flash came so fast, so hot, she reared up, gripping the blanket in defense. The hard, jittery climax had her shuddering, shuddering until she fell limply back.

Impossible. Fighting for breath she lifted a weighted hand to push at her hair. It wasn't possible. No one had ever made her feel so much.

On a groan of his own, Murphy pressed his lips to her flesh, letting his hand roam lower now, over the curve of her waist and hips. "Shannon, I love you. Ever and always."

"I can't—" Weak, she laid a hand on his back. It was damp, she realized dimly, the muscles tightly bunched. "I need a minute." But his mouth was skimming over her rib cage. "God, what are you doing to me?"

"Pleasuring you." And he intended to do more to her, had to do more to her. The need was building painfully inside him, all hot blood and violent lust he knew he could only chain down for so long. He tugged the skimpy panties over her hips, and nipped. "Pleasuring me."

Her body was a treasure of dark delights he intended to explore fully. But the time for leisure had passed. Greedy now, he took, reveling in her frenzied movements, her gasps and cries.

He wanted her like this, helplessly his, clawing at him as he drove her ruthlessly into flame after flame. And when she was writhing and wet and wild, it still wasn't enough.

He was tearing at his jeans as he took his mouth on a sprinting journey up her torso, over her heaving breasts and back to her trembling lips.

She arched urgently against him, then her legs scissored to clamp hard around him. He shook his head, not in denial, but to clear his hazed vision. He wanted to see her, and for her to see him.

"Look at me," he demanded, fighting to expel each word over the heart that pounded thick in his throat. "Damn it, look at me now."

She opened her eyes. Her focus wavered, then sharpened until all she could see was his face.

"I love you." He said it fiercely, his eyes lancing into hers. "Do you hear me?"

"Yes." She gripped his hair. "Yes."

Then she cried out in triumph as he drove himself hard and deep into her. The orgasm rolled through her like a wave of lava, leaving her shaken and scorched. As her eyes closed again he savaged her mouth while his body tirelessly plunged.

Mindlessly she matched his pace, leaping heedlessly into the storm they brewed between them. She thought she heard thunder roll, and lightning flare its wicked fingers across the sky. Her body exploded, shattered, then went glowingly limp.

Her hands slid bonelessly from his back. She heard him say her name, felt him coil, then shudder, then drop his weight onto her.

He let himself wallow in her hair, kept his face buried there while his system vibrated. She was trembling again, or still, little bursts he knew were the aftershocks of good sex. He'd have stroked her to soothe—if he could have moved.

"I'll get off you in a minute," he murmured.

"Don't you dare."

He smiled and rubbed his face in her hair. "At least I can keep you warm this way."

"I don't think I'll ever be cold again." On a little purr of pleasure, she curled her arms around him. "You're probably going to get all smug when I tell you this, but I don't think I can mind. No one's ever made me feel like this before."

It wasn't smugness he felt, but joy. "There's been no one before you."

She cuddled and laughed. "You're entirely too good at this, Murphy. I imagine there are a lot of women—"

"They were all just practice," he interrupted and made the effort to shift to his elbows so he could look at her. The way she was smiling made him grin. "Now, I can't say there wasn't a time or two I enjoyed the practicing."

"Remind me to punch you later." She laughed when he rolled her over, and over again until they were at the edge of the blanket with her cradled against his chest. "I'm going to have to paint you," she mused, tracing her finger from biceps to pectorals. "I haven't done a nude since art school, but—"

"Darling, when you get me naked, you'll be much too busy for your brushes."

Her grin flashed wickedly. "You're right." She pressed her lips to his, lost herself a moment in the lingering. With a sigh, she rested her head on his chest. "I've never made love outside before."

"You're joking."

She lifted her head again and aimed a bland look. "It's frowned upon in my neighborhood."

Because her skin was chilling, he reached for the spare blanket. "Then it's a night of firsts for you. Your first ceili." He tossed the blanket over her, fussing with the edges until he was satisfied she was covered. "Your first waltz."

"It was the waltz that did it. No, that's wrong." She shook her head, then shifted so that she could frame his face with her hands. "The waltz seduced me. But it was when you sang. When I listened to you I couldn't understand how, why, I'd ever said no."

"I'll have to remember to sing for you often." He lifted a hand, cupped the back of her neck. "Pretty green-eyed Shannon, love of all my lives. Come and kiss me."

He woke her from a light doze just as the eastern sky was pearling. He was sorry to, for he'd loved watching her sleep, the way her lashes lay on her cheek with the light flush beneath them. And he wished there was time for him to love her once again as dawn broke.

But there were obligations and family waiting for him.

"Shannon." Gently, he stroked her cheek, kissed it. "Darling, it's nearly morning. The stars are going out."

She stirred, whimpering, and clutched at his hand. "Why won't you stay? Why? How could you come back to me only to leave again?"

"Shh." He drew her close, pressed his lips to her brow. "I'm here. Right here. 'Tis only a dream."

"If you loved me enough, you wouldn't go again."

"I do love you. Open your eyes now. You're dreaming."

She followed the sound of his voice, opened her eyes as he'd asked. For a moment she was lost between two worlds, both of which seemed familiar and right.

Dawn, just before dawn, she thought hazily. And the smell of spring. The stones rising up, gray and cold in the waning dark and the feel of her lover's arms hard around her.

"Your horse." She looked around blankly. She should have heard the jingle of its bridle and the impatient stomp of hooves as it waited to ride.

"They're stabled yet." Firmly Murphy cupped her chin and turned her face back to his. "Where are you?"

"I . . ." She blinked and floated out of the dream. "Murphy?"

His eyes were narrowed on her face, with a hint of frustration in them. "Do you remember what happened then? What did I do to lose you?"

She shook her head. The sense of despair, and the fear, were waning. "I was dreaming, I guess. That's all."

"Tell me what I did."

But she pressed her face to his shoulder, relieved to find it warm and solid. "Just a dream," she insisted. "Is it morning?"

He started to argue, then backed off. "Nearly. I need to get you back to the inn."

"Too soon."

"I'd hold back the sun if I could." He squeezed her once more, then rose to get their clothes.

Cuddled under the blanket, Shannon watched him and felt the little tingles of desire begin to spark again. She sat up, let the blanket pool to her waist. "Murphy?" When he glanced back, she had the satisfaction of seeing his eyes go dark and cloudy. "Make love with me."

"There's nothing I'd like better, but my family's at the house, and there's no telling when one of them . . ." He trailed off when she rose, slim and beautifully naked. The clothes slipped out of his hands as she walked toward him.

"Make love with me," she said again, and twined her arms around his neck. "Fast and desperate. Like it was the last time."

There was a witch in her. He'd known it the first time he'd looked in her eyes. The power of it glowed out of them now, confident and challenging. Though her breath hissed out when he dragged her head back by her hair, the look never wavered.

"Like this, then." His voice was rough as he dragged her around. He braced her back against the king stone and, cupping her hips, lifted her off her feet.

She clamped herself around him, willing and eager. The power burst when he thrust into her, battering them both with the speed and desperation she'd demanded.

They were eye to eye, each violent stroke heating the gasping breaths they took. Her nails dug into his shoulders, her lips curved in triumph as their bodies convulsed together.

His legs went weak, and his palms had gone so damp he feared he'd lose his hold on her and drop her. He could hear his own breath panting out like a dog's.

"Jesus." He blinked stinging sweat out of his eyes. "Sweet Jesus Christ."

Slumped against his shoulder she began to laugh. It bubbled up through her, full of joy and fascination. He could only struggle to get back his breath and balance her as she threw her arms into the air.

"Oh, I feel so alive."

A grin tugged at his mouth as he managed to keep her from tumbling both of them. "You're alive all right. But you damned near killed me." He kissed her hard, then set her firmly on her feet. "Get your clothes on, woman, before you finish me off."

"I wish we could go running buck naked through the fields."

He blew out a breath and bent to pick up her bra. "Oh, my sainted mother would love that, if she happened to take a turn around the yard and look out."

Amused, Shannon slipped into her bra and plucked her panties out of the grass. "I bet your sainted mother knows just what you've been up to, since you didn't come home last night."

"Knowing and getting a first-hand look's two different matters." He gave her bottom a friendly pat when she bent over to pick up her shirt. "You look sexy in men's clothes. I meant to tell you."

"Men's look," Shannon corrected, buttoning the oversize shirt.

"What's the difference?" He sat on the grass to put on his shoes. "Would you go out with me tonight, Shannon, if I come calling for you?"

Baffled and pleased, she looked down at him. That the man could ask, so sweetly, when they'd barely finished going at each other like animals, charmed her. "Well, it may be I'd do that, Murphy Muldoon," she said, giving her best shot at a west county brogue.

His eyes danced as he tossed her one of her shoes. "You still sound like a Yank. But I like it—'tis a darling accent."

She snorted. "*I* have a darling accent. Right." She reached down to pick up the blanket, but he stayed her hand.

"Leave them . . . if you will."

Smiling, she turned her hand so that their fingers twined. "Yes. I will."

"Then I'll walk you to your door."

"You don't have to."

"I do have to." He led her through the arch of stone and into the field where the light was just beginning to pearl the dewy grass. "And want to as well."

Happy, she leaned her head against his shoulder as they walked. In the east, morning was rising gently in pinks and golds, like a painting washed by a pastel-tipped brush. She heard the crow of the rooster and the cheerful song of a lark. When Murphy stopped to pick a wildflower with creamy white petals, she turned, smiling, so that he could slip it into her hair.

"Look, there's a magpie." She lifted her hand to point as the bird darted low over the field. "That's right, isn't it? Brianna showed me."

"That's right. Look there, quick. Two more." Pleased at his luck, he swung his arm around her shoulders. "One is for sorrow," he told her. "Two is for mirth. Three for a wedding, and four for a birth."

She watched the flight and cleared her throat. "Murphy, I know you have very strong feelings, and—"

He lifted her up and set her over the next wall. "I'm in love with you," he said easily. "If that's what you're meaning."

"Yes, that's what I mean." She had to be careful, she realized, as her own emotions had gone so much deeper than she'd ever intended. "And I think I understand how you believe that should progress. Taking your personality, your culture, and your religion into account."

"You've a wonderful way of cluttering things up with words. What you mean is I want to marry you."

"Oh, Murphy."

"I'm not asking you at the moment," he pointed out. "What I'm doing is enjoying a morning walk with you and looking forward to seeing you again in the evening."

She slid him a glance, saw he was studying her. "So, we can keep it simple?"

"There's nothing simpler. Here. Let me kiss you before we're in Brie's garden."

He turned her into his arms, lowered his head, and melted her heart. "One more," she whispered and drew him back.

"I'll call for you." He made the effort and released her. "I'd take you out to dinner, but—"

"Your family's here," she finished. "I understand."

"They'll be gone tomorrow. If you wouldn't feel awkward with Brie, I'd like if you'd spend the night with me then, in my bed."

"No. I wouldn't feel awkward."

"Till later then." He kissed her fingertips and left her on the edge of the garden where the roses were still damp with dew.

Humming to herself, she crossed the lawn, let herself in the back door. Only to come up short when she saw Brianna measuring up coffee at the stove.

"Oh, hi." Unaware of the foolish grin on her face, Shannon stuck her hands in her trouser pockets. "You're up early."

Brianna only lifted a brow. She'd been up half an hour, the same time as she was up nearly every morning of her life. "Kayla wanted breakfast."

Shannon glanced at the clock in surprise. "I guess it's a little later than I thought. I was just . . . out."

"So I gathered. Didn't Murphy want to come in for coffee?"

"No, he—" She broke off, blew out a breath. "I guess we weren't very discreet."

"You could say I'm not surprised to see you coming in now when I saw the way you looked when you walked out with him last night." Since the coffee was brewing, Brianna turned around. "You look happy."

"Do I?" She laughed, then gave into impulse and rushed over to throw her arms around Brianna. "I must be. I must be idiotically happy. I just spent the night with a man in a horse pasture. Me. In a horse pasture. It's incredible."

"I'm happy for you." Brianna held tight, moved by this first free burst of affection of sister for sister. "For both of you. He's a special man, Murphy. I've hoped for a long time he'd find someone as special."

Shannon clung for another minute. "Brianna, it isn't quite like that. I care for him. I care for him very much. I couldn't have been with him if I didn't."

"I know. I understand that very well."

"But I'm not like you." Shannon stepped back, hoping to explain to Brianna what she needed to explain to herself. "I'm not like you or Maggie. I'm not looking to settle down here, get married, and raise a family. I have other ambitions."

The trouble had already come into Brianna's eyes before she lowered them. "He's very much in love with you."

"I know. And I'm not sure that I'm not in love with him." She turned away, thinking to keep her balance in movement. "But love isn't always enough to build a life on. You and I should understand that, because of our parents. I've tried to explain this to Murphy, and can only hope I have. Because the last thing I want to do is hurt him."

"And you don't think you'll hurt yourself by turning away from your heart?"

"I have my head to think about, too."

Brianna reached into a cupboard for cups and saucers. "That's true. It's all of you that has to decide what's right. And it's hard when one part of you tugs away from the other."

"You do understand." Grateful, Shannon laid a hand on her shoulder. "You really do."

"Of course. For Murphy it's easy. He has no questions about his thoughts or feelings or needs. They're all you. For you it's not so simple. So you have to take your happiness as it comes, and not question every step of it."

"That's what I'm trying to do. Not just with Murphy. I'm happy, Brianna," she said softly, "with you."

"It means more than I can say to hear you say that." With the love easing gently through her, Brianna turned and smiled. "To know you could say it. It's a fine morning."

"It's a great morning." Shannon caught Brianna's hands and squeezed. "The best morning. I'm going to go change."

"Take your coffee with you." Blinking at tears, Brianna poured a cup. "I'll fix you breakfast before church."

"No. I'll take the coffee," Shannon said and did so. "And I'll go change. Then I'll come back and help you fix breakfast."

"But—"

"I'm not a guest here anymore."

This time Brianna's eyes filled before she could stop them. "No, you're not. Well, be smart about it then," she ordered and turned briskly to pour herself tea. "Those that are will be rising soon."

Gray waited until Shannon had left the kitchen before he stepped in himself. He crossed over and gathered his quietly weeping wife into his arms.

"Go ahead, honey," he murmured and patted her back. "Have a good one. The two of you nearly had me bawling myself."

"Grayson." Rocked against him she sobbed happily into his shoulder. "She's my sister."

"That's right." He kissed the top of her head. "She's your sister."

SEVENTEEN

Shannon hadn't attended Sunday Mass often in New York. Her parents had been quietly devout Catholics, and she'd attended Catholic schools, gone through all the rites and rituals. She considered herself a Catholic, a modern, female Catholic who was dissatisfied with many of the doctrines and laws that came through the Vatican.

Sunday Mass was simply a habit she'd slipped out of once she'd established her life and pattern in New York.

But to the people in her small spot in County Clare, Sunday Mass wasn't a habit. It was fundamental.

She had to admit, she enjoyed the small church, the smell of flickering votive candles and polished pews that brought back sensory memories from her youth. The statues of Mary and Joseph, the plaques that illustrated the Stations of the Cross, the embroidered altar cloth were all symbols that were found across the world.

The little village church boasted small stained-glass windows through which softly colored light streamed. The pews were scarred with age, the kneelers worn, and the old floor creaked at each genuflection.

However simple the setting, the rite itself had a stirring pomp and grandeur here, as it would in Saint Patrick's magnificent cathedral on Fifth Avenue. She felt solid and steady sitting beside Brianna, listening to the lyrical tone of the priest, the murmured responses from the congregation, the occasional cry or whimper of a child.

Murphy's family was across the narrow aisle, taking up two pews. And hers—for she was beginning to think of them as her family—ranged together in one.

When they stood for the final blessing, Liam clambered over the pew and held up his arms to her. She hoisted him onto her hip, grinning when he pursed his lips.

"Pretty," he said in a stage whisper when she'd obliged him with a kiss. His pudgy fingers went to the citrine and amethyst stones she wore at her ears. "Mine."

"Nope. Mine." She carried him out with her as the congregation emptied the pews and spilled out into the late morning sunshine.

"Pretty," he said again, so hopefully, that she rooted through her purse to see if she could find something to please him.

"She is that, lad." Murphy snatched Liam away, tossing him high to make him laugh. "Pretty as a May morning."

Shannon felt a little thrill ripple up her spine. Only hours before they'd been naked, sweaty, and locked together. Now they were trimmed out for church and surrounded by people. It didn't stop fresh need from curling in her gut.

Pulling a small mirror out of her bag, she aimed it at Liam. "There's pretty."

Delighted, Liam clutched at it and began to make faces at himself.

"Look, Ma." Nearby Kate cradled her youngest on her shoulder. "They look like a little family together there. Did you ever think Murphy would set his sights on a Yank? And such a fancy one?"

"No." Alice watched them, her emotions mixed and muddled. "I didn't think it. Used to be I wondered if it would be one of Tom Concannon's daughters for him. But this I never expected."

Kate glanced down to where her three-year-old was contentedly plucking at grass and checking its flavor. "You don't mind?"

"I haven't decided yet." Shrugging off the mood, Alice bent and scooped up her grandson. "Kevin, grass isn't for eating unless you're a cow. Let's gather up the troops, Kate. We've Sunday dinner to cook."

Hearing his name hailed, Murphy lifted a hand. "I've got to get along.

I'll call for you later." He passed Liam back to her. "Will you let me kiss you here?"

"Kiss," Liam agreed and puckered up.

"Not you, lad." But Murphy kissed him anyway, before shifting up and letting his lips glide lightly over Shannon's. "Till later."

"Yes." She had to concentrate on not sighing like a schoolgirl when he walked off. "Later."

"Want me to take your load there, Aunt Shannon?" Seeing the way was clear, Rogan stepped forward.

"No. I've got him."

"Looks as though he has you." And it was a nice stroke of fate, Rogan thought, to have the boy run interference for him. "I was hoping for a word with you. Would you come home with Maggie and me? We'd be pleased to have you for tea. As would Liam."

"Tea." Liam lost interest in the mirror and bounced on Shannon's hip. "Cake."

"There's the bottom line," Rogan said with a chuckle. "Just like his mother." Without waiting for her answer, Rogan took Shannon's elbow and began to steer her toward his car.

"I should tell Brie—"

"I've told her. Maggie," he called out. "Your boy wants tea and cake."

"Which boy?" Maggie caught up with them just as Shannon reached for the car door. "Are you driving us, Shannon?"

"Damn. I do that nine times out of ten." With Liam in tow, she rounded to the passenger side and bundled the boy in his car seat.

"Once a Yank," Maggie commented and settled herself.

Shannon only wrinkled her nose and entertained Liam on the drive.

A short time later they were in the kitchen. It was Rogan, Shannon noted, who brewed the tea. "You enjoyed the ceili?" he asked.

"Very much."

"You left early." With a wicked gleam in her eye, Maggie set out small slices of frosted cake.

Shannon only lifted a brow and broke off a corner of a slice. "This is Brie's recipe," she said after a sample.

" 'Tis Brie's cake. Be grateful."

"Very grateful," Rogan put in. "Brianna's too humane to let Maggie poison us."

"I'm an artist, not a cook."

"Brianna's far more than a cook." Shannon prepared to bristle. "She's an artist. And it shows in every room of the inn."

"Well, well." Amused, and pleased, Maggie leaned back. "Quick to jump in front of her, aren't you?"

"Just as you do," Rogan said mildly as he brought pot to table. "Brianna inspires loyalty. The inn's very welcoming, isn't it?" Expertly he smoothed feathers while he poured the tea. "I stayed there myself when I first came here to batter at Margaret Mary's door. The weather was filthy," he remembered, "as was Maggie's temperament. And the inn was a little island of peace and grace amid it all."

"'Twas your temperament that was filthy as I remember," Maggie corrected. "He badgered me mercilessly," she told Shannon. "Came here uninvited, and unwanted. And as you can see I've yet to rid myself of him."

"Tenacity has its rewards." In an old habit he slid his hand over Maggie's. "Our first reward's falling asleep in his tea," he murmured.

Maggie glanced over to see Liam, slack-mouthed, eyes closed, head nodding, with one hand fisted in cake. "He's a prize, all right." She chuckled as she rose to lift him from his high chair. When he whined, she patted his bottom and crooned. "There, love, you just need a bit of a lie down. Let's go see if your bear's waiting for you. I think he is. He's waiting for Liam to come."

"She's a beautiful mother," Shannon said without thinking.

"That surprises you."

"Yes." She realized what she'd said an instant too late and fumbled. "I didn't mean—"

"It's not a problem. It surprises her, too. She was resistant to the idea of having a family. A great deal of that came from the fact that her childhood was difficult. Things mend in time. Even the oldest and rawest of wounds. I don't know if she'll ever be close to her mother, but they've made a bridge. So the distance is spanned."

He set down his cup and smiled at her. "I wonder if you'd come into the office for a moment or two."

"Your office?"

"Here. Just through the next room." He rose, knowing manners would have her going with him.

He'd wanted her on his own turf. He'd been in business long enough to know that home field advantage was a distinctive one. And that the atmosphere of business suited some deals better than the informality of deals with meals.

With Shannon, he'd already decided to make a cleave between business and family. Except when the nudge of family became useful.

Curious, Shannon followed him into the living room and through an adjoining door. On the threshold, she stopped and stared with a combination of surprise and admiration.

They may have been in the middle of the country, a stone's throw away from grazing cows and clucking chickens, but here was a professional work space worthy of any glossy high-rise in any major city.

It was tastefully, even elegantly decorated, from the Bokhara rug to the Tiffany lamp, to the gleaming antique mahogany desk. Maggie was in the room—a stunning fountain of sapphire glass rose halfway to the coffered ceiling; a delicate tangle of shapes and colors sat alone on a marble column and made Shannon think of Brianna's garden.

Marching practically with style were the tools of the executive—fax, computer, modem, copier, all sleek and high tech.

"Holy cow." Her grin started to spread as she moved in and skimmed her finger over the monitor of a top-grade P.C. "I would never have guessed this was here."

"That's the way Maggie wanted it. And I, too." Rogan gestured to a chair. "This is home for a good part of the year, but to keep it home, I have to work."

"I guess I thought you had an office at the gallery."

"I do." To establish the tone he wanted to set, he sat behind his desk. "But we both have demanding careers, and we both have a child. When scheduling allows, I can work here three days a week, tending to Liam in the mornings while Maggie's in her glass house."

"It can't be easy, for either of you. Juggling so much."

"You make certain you only drop balls that are replaceable. Compromise is the only way I know to have all. I thought we'd talk about the other paintings you've done."

"Oh." Her brow creased. "I've done a couple more watercolors, and another oil, but—"

"I've seen the one of Brianna," he interrupted smoothly. "You've finished the one of the inn—the back garden view."

"Yes. I went out to the cliffs and did a seascape. Pretty typical, I imagine."

"I doubt that." He smiled and made a quick note on a pad. "But we'll have a look. You'd have more in New York."

"There are several in my apartment, and, of course, the ones I brought back from Columbus."

"We'll arrange to have them shipped over."

"But—"

"My manager at the New York gallery can take care of the details—the packing and so forth, once you give me a list of inventory." She made another attempt to speak, and he rolled right over her. "We've only the one on display here in Clare, and I think we'll keep it that way, until we have a more polished strategy. In the meantime." He opened his top drawer and drew out a neat stack of legal-size papers. "You'll want to look over the contracts."

"Rogan, I never agreed to contracts."

"Of course you haven't." His smile was easy, his tone all reason. "You haven't read them. I'd be happy to go over the terms with you, or I can recommend a lawyer. I'm sure you have your own, but you'd want one locally."

She found a copy of the contracts dumped neatly in her hands. "I already have a job."

"It doesn't seem to stop you from painting. I'll want my secretary to contact you in the next week or so, for background. The sort of color and information we'll need for a biography and press releases."

"Press releases?" She put a hand to her spinning head.

"You'll see in the contract that Worldwide will take care of all publicity for you. Depending on your inventory in America, we should be ready for a showing in October, or possibly September."

"A showing." She left her supporting hand where it was and gaped at him. "You want—a showing?" she repeated, numb. "In Worldwide Galleries?"

"I'd considered having it in Dublin, as we'd had Maggie's first there. But I think I'd prefer the gallery here in Clare, because of your connection here." He tilted his head, still smiling politely. "What do you think?"

"I don't think," she mumbled. "I can't think. Rogan, I've been to shows at Worldwide. I can't even conceive of having one there."

"Surely you're not going to sit there, look me straight in the eye, and claim to doubt your talent?"

She opened her mouth. But the way he'd phrased it, the way he looked at her as he waited, had her shoulders moving back and settling firm. "It's simply that I've never thought of my painting in a practical vein."

"And why should you? That's my job. You paint, Shannon. You just paint. I'll handle the details of the rest. Ah, and as to details . . ." He tipped back, already savoring victory. "We'll need some photographs. I use an excellent man in Dublin for such things. I need to be back there for a couple of days this week. You can fly out with me and we'll get that taken care of."

She closed her eyes, but try as she might, she couldn't trace back the steps to the beginning of the exchange and pinpoint when she'd lost control. "You want me to go to Dublin."

"For a day or two. Unless you'd like to stay longer. You're welcome, of course, to stay in our house there as long as you please. I'll see that you have an appointment with a lawyer while we're there, to look over the contracts for you and advise you."

"I minored in business in college," Shannon mumbled. "I can read contracts for myself."

"As you please then." Though he had no need to, Rogan went through the motions of flipping through his desk calendar. "Would Tuesday suit you?"

"Tuesday?"

"For the trip? We can arrange for the photo shoot for Wednesday."

"Your photographer might be booked."

"I'm sure he'll fit us in." He was sure, as he'd already made the appointment. "Tuesday then?"

Shannon blew out a breath that ruffled her hair, then tossed up her hands. "Sure. Why not?"

She asked herself that question again on the walk back to the inn. Then she changed gears and asked herself why. Why was she going along with this? Why was Rogan pressuring her to go along?

Yes, she was talented. She could see that for herself in her work and had been told by numerous art teachers over the years. But art wasn't business, and business had always come first.

Agreeing to Rogan's deal meant inverting something she'd pursued most of her life—letting her art take the lead and allowing someone else to handle the details of business.

It was more than a little frightening, certainly more than uncomfortable. But she had agreed, she reminded herself; at least she hadn't refused outright.

And she could have, Shannon thought. Oh, yes, she recognized well the tactics Rogan had used, and used with bloodless skill. He would be a difficult man to outmaneuver, but she could have done so.

The fact was, she hadn't really tried.

It was foolish, she thought now. A crazy complication. How could she have a show in Ireland in the fall when she would be three thousand miles away at her desk by then?

But is that really what you want?

She heard the little voice murmuring in her ear. Resenting it, she hunched her shoulders and scowled down at the road as she walked.

"You look mad as a hornet," Alice commented. She was resting a hand on her son's front gate and smiled as Shannon's head shot up.

"Oh. I was just . . ." With an effort she relaxed her shoulders. "I was going over a conversation, and wondering why I lost the upper hand of it."

"We always find a way to keep that upper hand in the replay." Alice tapped her finger to her temple, then opened the gate. "Won't you come in?" She pushed the gate wider when Shannon hesitated. "My family's run off here and there, and I'd like a bit of company."

"You surprise me." Shannon stepped through and relatched the gate herself. "I'd think you'd be desperate for a couple minutes of peace and quiet."

"It's as my mother used to say—you have nothing but that when you're six feet under. I was having a look at Murphy's front garden. He's tending it well."

"He tends everything well." Unsure of her moves, or her position, she followed Alice back up onto the porch and settled in the rocker beside her.

"That he does. He does nothing unless he does it thoroughly and with care. There were times, when he was a lad, and it seemed he would plod forever through one chore or another I might give him. I would be set to snap at him, and he'd just look and smile at me, and tell me he was figuring the best way about it, that was all."

"Sounds like him. Where is he?"

"Oh, he and my husband are off in the back looking over some piece of machinery. My Colin loves pretending he knows something about farming and machinery, and Murphy loves letting him."

Shannon smiled a little. "My father's name was Colin."

"Was it? You lost him recently."

"Last year. Last summer."

"And your mother this spring." Instinctively Alice reached out to squeeze Shannon's hand. "It's a burden that nothing but living lightens."

She began to rock again, and so did Shannon, so that the silence was broken only by the creak of the chairs and the chatter of birds.

"You enjoyed the ceili?"

This time the question had a flush heating Shannon's cheeks. "Yes. I've never been to a party quite like it."

"I miss having them since we're in Cork. The city's no place for a ceili, a real one."

"Your husband's a doctor there."

"He is, yes. A fine doctor. And I'll tell you true, when I moved there with him I thought I'd died and gone to heaven. No more rising at dawn to see to cows, no worrying if the crops would grow, or the tractor run." She smiled, looking over the garden to the valley in the distance. "But parts of me miss it still. Even miss the worrying."

"Maybe you'll move back when he retires."

"No, he's a city man, my Colin. You'd understand the lure of the city, living in New York."

"Yes." But she, too, was looking out over the valley, the shimmer of green hills, the living rise of them. "I like the crowds, and the rush. The noise. It took me days to get used to the quiet here, and the space."

"Murphy's a man for space, and for the feel of his own land under his feet."

Shannon glanced back to see Alice studying her. "I know. I don't think I've ever met anyone as . . . rooted."

"And are you rooted, Shannon?"

"I'm comfortable in New York," she said carefully. "We moved around a great deal when I was a child, so I don't have the same kind of roots you mean."

Alice nodded. "A mother worries about her children, no matter how tall they grow. I see Murphy's in love with you."

"Mrs. Brennan." Shannon lifted her hands, let them fall. What could she say?

"You're thinking what does this woman want me to do? How does she expect me to answer what wasn't even a question?" A hint of a smile played around Alice's mouth. "You don't know me any more than I know you, so I can't tell by looking into your eyes what your feelings are for my son, or what you'll do about them. Feelings there are, that's plain. But I know Murphy. You're not the woman I would have chosen for him, but a man chooses for himself."

She glanced at Shannon and laughed. "Now I've insulted you."

"No," Shannon said stiffly, insulted. "You have a perfect right to speak your mind."

"I do." Smiling still, Alice began to rock. "And would if I did or not. But my meaning wasn't clear. I thought for a time, a short time, it would be Maggie for him. As much as I love that girl, it worried me fierce. They'd have driven each other to murder within a year."

Despite all common sense, Shannon felt a niggling tug of jealousy. "Murphy and Maggie?"

"Oh, nothing more than a passing thought and a little wondering between them. Then I thought it would be Brianna. Ah, now that, I told myself, was the wife for him. She'd make him a strong home."

"Murphy and Brie," Shannon said between her teeth. "I guess he was making the rounds."

"Oh, I imagine he made a few, but not with Brie. He loved her, as he loved Maggie. As he loves his sisters. It was me, planning in my head and wishing for him to be happy. I worried, you see, because he was twenty-five, and still showing no partiality for another of the girls hereabouts. He was working the farm, reading his books, playing his music. It was a family he needed, I'd tell myself. A woman beside him and children at his feet."

Shannon moved her shoulders, still irked by the images Alice had conjured in her head. "Twenty-five is young for a man to marry these days."

"It is," Alice agreed. "In Ireland men often wait years and years longer. As they know once the vows are said there's no unsaying them. Divorce isn't a choice for us, not by God, and not by law. But a mother wants her son fulfilled. I took him aside this one day in his twenty-fifth year, and I sat him down and talked to him from my heart. I told him how a man shouldn't live alone, shouldn't work himself so hard and have no one to come home to of an evening. I told him how the O'Malley girl had her eye on him, and didn't he think she was a pretty thing."

Alice's smile had faded when she looked back at Shannon again. "He agreed as she was. But when I began to press him about thinking more deeply, planning for the future, taking a wife to complete his present, he shook his head, and took my hands in his and looked at me that way he has.

" 'Ma,' " he said, " 'Nell O'Malley isn't for me. I know who is. I've seen who is.' " Alice's eyes grew dark with an emotion Shannon couldn't understand. "I was pleased, and I asked him who she was. He told me he hadn't yet to meet her, not in the flesh. But he knew her just the same as he'd seen her in his dreams since he was a boy. He was only waiting for her to come."

Shannon swallowed on a dry throat and managed to keep her voice level. "Murphy has a tendency toward the romantic."

"He does. But I know when my boy is having a fancy and when he means just what he says. He was speaking no more than the truth to me. And he spoke nothing more than the truth when he called me a short time ago to tell me that she'd come."

"It's not like that. It can't be like that."

"It's hard to judge what can and can't be. In the heart. You're holding his, Shannon Bodine. The only thing I'll ask of you is to take care, great care with it. If you find you can't keep it, or don't want it after all, hand it back to him gently."

"I don't want to hurt him."

"Oh, child, I know that. He'd never choose a woman with meanness in her. I'm sorry to have made you sad."

Shannon only shook her head. "You needed to say it. I'm sure I needed to hear it. I'll straighten things out."

"Darling." With something close to a chuckle, Alice leaned forward again to take Shannon's hand. "You may try, but he'll tangle them up again. You mustn't think I said all of this to put the burden on your shoulders alone. It's shared between you, equal. What happens between you, joy or sorrow, will be caused by both of you. If your mother was here, she'd be telling Murphy to take care with you."

"She might." The tension in Shannon's fingers relaxed a little. "Yes, she might. He's lucky to have you, Mrs. Brennan."

"And so I remind him, often. Come now, let's see if my daughters have finished cooking the lamb for dinner."

"I should get back."

Alice rose, drawing Shannon with her. "You'll have your Sunday meal with us, surely. Murphy'll want you. So do I."

She opened the front door, stepped back, and welcomed Shannon inside.

EIGHTEEN

As much as Murphy enjoyed seeing Shannon with his family, dangling one of his nieces on her knee, laughing over something Kate said, listening intently to his nephew explain about carburetors, he wanted her alone.

It seemed the family he loved so well was conspiring to keep him from fulfilling that one simple and vital wish.

He mentioned very casually that it was a lovely night for a drive, and he thought Shannon would enjoy it. Whatever response she might have made was drowned out by his sisters' chattering to Shannon about fashions.

A patient man, he waited a time, then tried again, suggesting a trip to the pub—where he was sure he could slip Shannon out in a wink. But his stepfather pulled him aside and began to drill him on the workings of the new combine.

When the sun set and the moon began its rise, he found himself dragooned into a game of Uncle Wiggly with some of the children while Shannon was across the room having an intent discussion with his teenage niece about American music.

He saw his first clear shot when the children were being bundled up for bed. Moving fast, he grabbed Shannon's hand. "We'll go put the kettle on for tea." Without breaking stride, he pulled her toward the kitchen, through it, and out the back door.

"The kettle—"

"The devil take the kettle," he muttered and whirled her into his arms. Beside the coop where the hens brooded, he kissed her as though his life depended on it. "I never noticed how many people there are in my family."

"Twenty-three," she murmured, sliding into the next kiss. "Twenty-four with you. I counted."

"And one of them's bound to be poking out the kitchen window any second. Come on. We're making a break for it."

He pulled her past paddock and pen and up the first rise until she was breathless and laughing. "Murphy, slow down. They're not going to set the dogs on us."

"If we had dogs, they might." But he shortened his stride a little. "I want you alone. Do you mind?"

"No. As a matter of fact, I've been waiting for a chance to talk to you."

"We'll talk all you like," he promised. "After I show you what I've been thinking about doing to you all day and half the night."

Heat balled, a solid, steaming weight in her stomach. "We should talk first. We haven't really set up the guidelines. It's important we both understand, well, where we stand, before we get any deeper into this."

"Guidelines." The word made him smile. "I think I can find my way without them."

"I'm not talking about the physical aspect." A thought intruded, and turned her voice cool and casual. "You didn't ever have a physical aspect with Maggie, did you?"

His first reaction was to roar with laughter, but a twist of mischief made him hum in consideration. "Well, now that you mention it . . ." He let the sentence trail off as he pulled Shannon into the stone circle.

She was abruptly far from cool and batted his hands away as he tugged off her jacket. "Now that I mention it?" she repeated with steel in her voice.

"We had a bit of an aspect," he said, ignoring her shoving hands as he worked at the buttons of her blouse. "I kissed her once, in a bit more than what you might be calling a brotherly fashion." He grinned into Shannon's eyes. "It was curious and it was sweet. I was fifteen if memory serves."

"Oh." The green-eyed monster was dwarfed by foolishness.

"I managed to sneak one in on Brie, too. But we ended up laughing at each other while our lips were still locked. It took the romance right out of it."

"Oh," she said again and pouted. "And that was it?"

"You needn't worry. I never . . . crossed any borders with either of your sisters. So . . ."

His tongue dried up as he slid her blouse aside. She wore silk beneath tonight, dark, dangerous silk that dipped low and provocative at the curve of her breasts, then draped down to shimmer beneath the waistband of her skirt.

"I want to see the rest," he managed and tugged down the zipper.

A breeze teased her hair as she stood in the shifting moonlight. She'd worn it for him, had chosen it from her drawer that morning with the image in her mind of his face as he saw her in it. It was a short, deliberate seduction of silk and lace that clung to curves.

Dazzled by it, he skimmed a hand up her thigh and felt the tip of her stocking give way to warm flesh. And his mouth watered.

"It's God's grace I didn't know what you had on under that little suit." His voice was thick and ragged at the edges. "I'd never have made it through Mass."

She'd wanted to talk to him. Needed to. But common sense was no defense against the hot spurt of lust. She reached out, tugged the sweater over his head.

"I knew what was under here. You can't imagine what I was thinking of during the Offertory."

His laugh was weak. "We'll both do penance for it. Later." He nudged a strap from her shoulder, then the other so that the bodice shifted, tenuously clung. "The goddess that guards the holy ground," he murmured. "And the witch who came after."

His words made her shiver, with fear and excitement. "I'm a woman, Murphy. Just a woman standing here, wanting you." More than eager, she stepped forward into his arms. "Show me. Show me what you thought about doing to me." She crushed her mouth to his, unbearably hungry. "Then do more."

He could have eaten her alive, consumed her inch by inch, then howled at the moon like a rabid wolf.

So he showed her, savaging her mouth, letting his hands roam as urgently as they pleased. The sounds in her throat grew stronger, more feral. He felt her teeth nip and tug at his lip, took his own to her throat to devour the curving length of satin skin.

She was already wet when he cupped her. If he drove her up ruthlessly, if her moan shivered into something closer to a scream, he was too far over the line to stop himself.

Her legs simply buckled. She felt herself falling, felt the cushion of his body under her own, then the weight of it as he rolled.

His mouth was everywhere, gloriously suckling through silk, then under it. His hands were uncannily quick, slicking here, gripping there. Hers were no less urgent, seeking flesh, finding, exploiting.

She tore and tugged at the button of his trousers, muttering promises and pleas while they wrestled over the blanket.

Gasping for breath, she straddled him, then in a move so lightning quick it staggered his senses, took him deep.

While the stunning, violent glory of it streamed through him, he watched her bow back. Her body was sinuous and sleek, her hair a rainfall of silk, her face a carving of sheer triumph and carnal pleasures.

Spellbound, he reached out, found her breasts, watched his hands close over them. He felt the weight, the hot press of her nipples, the wild thunder of her heart.

His, he thought dimly while his body shuddered with unbearable need. This time, for all times, his.

She began to rock, slowly at first, like a dance. Clouds shifted over and around and passed the moon so that her face was shuttered, then revealed, then shuttered again like a dream he couldn't quite capture.

The blood began to rage, in his loins, in his head so that he was sure it would explode and leave nothing but shattered bones.

He saw her arms lift, rise witchlike toward the sky. Her movements quickened, and he began to murmur to her, the words desperate and Gaelic. It seemed she answered him, with the same urgency, in the same tongue. Then his mind hazed, and his body erupted, emptying him into her.

On a long, shuddering moan, she slid down to him. Visions danced in her head, faded.

She must have slept, for she awakened with her heart beating slow and thick, and her skin shivering warm. Even as he cupped her breast, her lips curved and welcomed his.

His touch was gentle now, almost worshipful. So she sighed, and enjoyed and let her body be stroked tenderly back to arousal.

She opened for him, felt him fill her. Delighting in the two sides of him, she matched his leisurely pace until the last ember of need quieted.

Later, she lay beside him, cozy in the blanket he'd drawn over them.

"Darling." He stroked her hair. "We can't sleep here tonight."

She felt his muscles jerk when she ran her hand low over his belly. "We don't have to sleep."

"I mean we can't stay out here." He turned his head for the simple pleasure of burying his nose in her hair. "It's going to rain."

"It is?" She opened one eye and looked up at the sky. "Where did the stars go?"

"Behind the clouds, and there's rain coming soon."

"Hmm. What time is it?"

"I've lost track."

"Where's my watch?"

"You weren't wearing one."

"I wasn't?" In reflex she felt her wrist. Odd, she never took a step without her watch. Never used to.

"We don't need a watch to know it's time I got you under roof." With regret, he tossed the blanket aside. "Maybe you'd ask me in for tea so I could spend a little more time looking at you."

She pulled the chemise over her head. "We could have tea in my room."

"I'd feel as uncomfortable about that as I would taking you to mine while my family's in the house." He watched her smooth on her stockings. "Will you be after wearing something like that again?"

She tossed back her hair as she buttoned her blouse. "I assume you're not talking about the suit."

"No, darling, the under it."

"I don't have much along these lines, but I'll see what I can do." She rose to tug on her skirt. "Maybe I can pick up a couple of things in Dublin."

"Dublin? Are you going to Dublin?"

"Tuesday." She shrugged into her jacket, then took his outstretched hand. "Somehow, and I'm not entirely sure how it happened, I'm going with Rogan."

"Ah, you've settled the contact then."

"I haven't even read the contract. But apparently I have an appointment on Wednesday to have publicity photos taken. Plus I'm supposed to give him a list of my inventory, as he calls my paintings back in New York. He seems to think I'm having a show in the fall."

"That's grand." Delighted for her, he swung her off her feet to kiss her. "Why didn't you tell me before? We'd have celebrated."

"If we'd celebrated any more, I don't think we'd be alive to talk about it." When he laughed, she tucked her arm through his. His unhesitating pleasure, for her, even though she was unsure of her own reactions, touched deep. "In any case, I don't know if celebrating is called for. I haven't signed—though the way Rogan talks it's a done deal."

"You can trust him, if that's what's worrying at you."

"No, not at all. Worldwide's reputation is top notch. And beyond that, I'd trust Rogan absolutely. It's a big decision for me, and I like to make even small decisions after careful thought."

"But you're going to Dublin," he pointed out.

"That one got away from me. One minute we were talking about Maggie and Liam, and the next I had contracts in my hand and talk about shows and publicity ringing in my ears."

"He's the cleverest of fellows, is Rogan," Murphy said admiringly. "I'll miss you, Shannon. Will you be gone long?"

"I should be back Thursday or Friday, from what he said." They were nearly back at the inn when the first drops of rain fell. "I really wanted to talk to you, Murphy."

"So you said. Guidelines, was it?"

"Yes."

"They'll keep." He nodded toward the window. "Brie's in the kitchen. I'd like to come in, but we won't be alone, and I can't stay long."

"They'll keep," she agreed.

On Tuesday morning Shannon was packed and ready and wondering what she'd gotten herself into. She'd wondered that quite a bit since coming to Ireland, she realized. It seemed that every adjustment she made, or considered making in her life, required another.

Still, the idea of spending a few days in Dublin wasn't a hardship. It had been weeks since she'd been in anything remotely resembling a city.

"You've an umbrella," Brianna asked, hovering over the bag Shannon had set by the front door of the inn. "And an extra jacket in case the weather turns?"

"Yes, Mom."

Flushing a little, Brianna shifted the baby on her shoulder. "It drives Maggie mad when I check her packing. Grayson's given up and lets me do it for him."

"Believe me, I'm an expert, and it's only for a couple of days. Here's Rogan's car now."

"Have a wonderful time." Brianna would have taken the bag herself if Shannon hadn't beat her to it. "The Dublin house is lovely, you'll see. And Rogan's cook is a magician."

"He says the same of you," Rogan commented as he stepped up to take Shannon's bag. He gave Brianna and Kayla a kiss before stowing the suitcase.

"Don't forget to take your vitamins," Brianna told Maggie, then leaned into the car to kiss her and Liam good-bye.

"I didn't realize you were coming, Maggie." Nor did she know how she felt about it. Turning, she gave Brianna a quick embrace and kissed Kayla on the tip of her nose.

"Fly safe." Brianna jiggled the baby, watching the car until it was out of sight.

It was a short trip to the airport under leaden skies and drizzling rain. Shannon thought back to the day she had landed at the airport that shared her name.

She'd been all nerves and repressed anger. Most of the anger had faded, she realized. But the nerves were still there, jumping now as she considered what this short trip would change in her life.

There was little fuss on their arrival. Shannon decided Rogan was a man who tolerated none when it came to business. In short order they were seated on his private plane with Liam bouncing at the window, pointing out every truck or cart that came into view.

"He's a traveling man, is Liam." Maggie settled back, hoping they'd be airborne soon so that she could have a cup of tea. She'd been suffering a great deal more morning queasiness with this pregnancy than she had with her first. And she didn't care for it.

"It's wonderful he can have the experience," Shannon commented. "I always appreciated it."

"You did a lot of traveling with your parents." Rogan slipped a hand over Maggie's, wishing every bit as strongly as she that the morning sickness would run its course.

"My father's favorite hobby. One of my earliest memories is of arriving at the airport in Rome. The rush and the voices, and the color of it. I guess I was about five."

The plane began to taxi, and Liam hooted with delight.

"He likes this part best." Maggie kept a smile glued to her face as the takeoff roiled her stomach. Damn, damn, damn, she thought. She would not throw up the pitiful dry toast she'd choked down for breakfast.

"Me, too." Shannon leaned over, pressing her cheek to Liam's so they could share the excitement together. "There it goes, Liam. We're up with the birds."

"Birds! 'Bye. Bye-bye."

'Bye. Shannon sighed a little. Murphy was down there. They hadn't had their full night together as they'd hoped. Between the trip and the rain and a horse with a split hoof, they'd barely had an hour alone.

And time was running out. She was going to have to think of that very soon. New York wouldn't wait forever.

"Bloody hell."

As Shannon looked back, surprised, Maggie tore off her seat belt and bolted out of the cabin. The lavatory door slammed behind her.

"Bloody hell," Liam repeated, diction for once nearly perfect.

"Is she airsick?" Shannon reached for her own belt, wondering what, if anything, she should do.

"Morning sick." Rogan cast a troubled look toward the closed door. "It's plaguing her this time."

"Should I go see if I can help, or anything?"

"It only makes her madder when you try." Feeling helpless, Rogan moved his shoulders. "With Liam she had a couple days of queasiness, and that was the end of it. She's more insulted than anything else that she's not sailing so easily through this one."

"I suppose every pregnancy is different."

"So we're discovering. She'll want tea," he said and started to rise.

"I'll make it. Really." She got up quickly, touched a hand to his shoulder. "Don't worry."

"She likes it brutally strong."

"I know."

Shannon went into the narrow galley. The plane was very much like its owner, she decided. Sleek, efficient, elegant, and organized. She found several different types of tea and, considering Maggie's condition, went for the chamomile.

She stopped what she was doing to look around when the door to the lavoratory opened.

"Steadier?"

"Aye." But Maggie's voice was grim, somewhat like a warrior who'd just survived another bloody battle. "That ought to do it for today."

"Go sit down," Shannon ordered. "You're still white."

"A sight better than green." Maggie sniffed, eyed the pot. "You're making flowers."

"It's good for you. Here." She handed Maggie a box of crackers she'd found in a cabinet. "Go sit down, Margaret Mary, and nibble on these."

Too weak to argue, Maggie went back to her seat.

"I'm sorry," Rogan murmured, slipping an arm around her.

"Don't expect me to say it's not your fault." But she snuggled her head against him and smiled over at Liam, who was busy deciding whether he would draw with or eat the crayon his father had given him. "Do you know what I'm thinking, Rogan?"

"What are you thinking, Margaret Mary?"

"That I strolled through the world's easiest pregnancy with that little demon there." She aimed a steely look when Liam lifted the crayon toward his mouth. He grinned and began to attack the coloring book with it instead. "Could be this one's a bit less comfortable because we're going to have a sweet-tempered, biddable child who'll never cause mischief."

"Hmmm." He eyed his son, and managed to grab the fat crayon before Liam could draw on the wall of the plane. The boy howled in protest and shoved the coloring book to the floor. "Is that what you'd like?"

Maggie laughed as Liam's temper rolled through the cabin. "Not on your life."

Brianna had spoken no less than the truth. The Dublin house was lovely. Tucked behind graceful trees and gardens, it had a beautiful view of the green. The furnishings were old, with both the distinction and the elegance wealth could buy. Chandeliers dripped, floors gleamed, and servants moved with quick and silent efficiency.

Shannon was given a room with a welcoming four-poster bed, a muted Aubusson, and a stunning O'Keefe. She'd no more than freshened up in the bath before a maid had tidily unpacked her bag and set her toiletries on the Chippendale bureau.

She found Maggie waiting for her in the main parlor downstairs. "They'll be bringing a light meal in," Maggie told her. "I tend to be starving this time of day after my morning bout."

"I'm glad you're feeling better. God." Shannon's eyes widened as they fixed on the sculpture dominating one side of the room. Mesmerized, she walked toward it, her fingers unable to resist one long stroke of the glass.

It was magnificent, erotic, and nearly human in its sinuous limbs and melting features. She could almost see the man and woman, fused together in absolute fulfillment.

"Do you like it?" Maggie's voice might have been casual, but she couldn't prevent the quick spurt of pleasure at Shannon's dazzled reaction.

"It's incredible."

"*Surrender,* I called it."

"Yes, of course. You could make this," she murmured, in wonder, "something like this, in that little place in the country."

"Why not? A real artist doesn't need fancy digs. Ah, here's the food. Bless you, Noreen."

Maggie was already involved in a chicken sandwich when Shannon came over to join her. "Where's Liam?"

"Oh, one of the maids has a crush on him. She's whisked him off to the nursery to make him hot chocolate and spoil him. Better have one of these before I eat them all."

Taking her at word, Shannon chose one of the little sandwiches. "This is a magnificent house."

"It's lovely, to be sure, but never empty. Having servants about still makes me twitchy." She shrugged. "There's no doubt we'll need help after the new baby comes. I'll have to lock myself in the glass house for any privacy."

"Most people would be thrilled to be able to have housekeepers and cooks."

"I'm not most people." Maggie bit off more chicken. "But I'm learning to live with it. Rogan's on the phone," she added. "He's mad for phones. There's business at the Paris branch he should be seeing to in person. But he won't leave while I'm having this problem in the mornings. Doesn't even help to shout at him. When the man's dug in his heels, you can't budge him with a brick."

She moved on to the pasta curls and gave Shannon a speculative look. "His mind's set on having you."

"Well, mine's not set. Entirely."

"First I'm going to tell you that when the man came after me, I had no intention of being managed. By anyone at all. He has a way, Rogan does, of seeing right into you, finding those weaknesses and prides and secrets you'd just as soon keep to yourself. Then he uses them. With charm, with ruthlessness, with logic, and with such organized planning that he's always one step ahead."

"I've noticed. He got me here, when I had every intention of telling him thanks, but no thanks."

"It's not just a business with him. He'd be easier to resist if it was. He has a great love and affection for art, and for the artist. And what he's done in Clare . . ." The pride for him came into her voice, into her eyes. "He's made something important there, for art, for Ireland. He's done it because he's tied by his heart to both."

"He's a very special man, personally and professionally. You don't have to know him long to see that."

"No, you don't. So second . . ." Maggie dusted her fingers with a napkin. "I'm going to ask what the hell's wrong with you?"

Shannon's brows shot up. "Excuse me?"

"Why the devil are you dragging your heels on this? The man's offering you the moon and half the stars. An artist dreams about the chance of having what you've got right in your hands, and you keep bobbling it."

"Bobbling is not what I'm doing," Shannon corrected coolly. "Considering is."

"What do you have to consider at this point? You have the paintings, you'll do more."

"It's the doing more I'm considering."

Maggie gave a snort and forked up more pasta. "What nonsense. You can sit there and tell me you could stop—just set your brushes aside and leave your canvas blank?"

"When I get back to New York, I won't be free to indulge myself as I have here."

"Indulge." Maggie set her fork down with a clatter and leaned forward. "You have some warped idea in your head that your painting is an indulgence."

"My position at Ry-Tilghmanton—"

"Oh, fuck that."

"Is important to me," Shannon finished between her teeth. "And my responsibilities there leave me little time to paint for pleasure—much less to paint for someone who you'll agree is a demanding manager."

"What of your responsibilities to yourself, and your talent? Do you think you have the right to toss away what you've been given?" The very idea of it was an abomination in Maggie's mind and heart. "I've only seen your paintings of Ireland, but they show you have more than a good eye and a competent hand. You've got a heart that sees and understands. You've no right to toss that away so you can draw bottles of water."

"You've been doing your homework," Shannon said quietly. "I have a right to do what works for me, what satisfies me. And that's just what I'll do. If Rogan asked you to work on me—"

"You'll not blame him because I speak my own mind." They rose together, boxers meeting in the center of the mat. "He asked me only to come along so you'd have company when he was occupied."

"I'm sure he thought that was considerate. Now get this straight, this transaction, however it works out, isn't your concern. It's between me and Rogan."

"Transaction." On a sound of disgust Maggie dropped back into her chair again. "You even talk more like a businesswoman than an artist."

Shannon jerked up her chin and looked down her nose. "That fails to insult me. Now if you'll excuse me, I think I'll go out and get some air."

NINETEEN

She was not going to let it get to her. Shannon promised herself that Maggie's opinionated, out-of-line attitude was not going to sway her in any way, or put a shadow over her visit to Dublin.

The evening, at least, was companionable and pleasant. Thanks, in Shannon's opinion, to Rogan's flawless manners and hospitality. Not once through dinner, or the easy evening that followed, did he mention the contract or the plans he had in the making.

Which, she supposed, was why she was so off guard the following morning when he escorted her into his library directly after they'd shared a quiet breakfast. He shot straight from the hip.

"You have an eleven o'clock appointment with the photographer," he told her the moment they were seated. "They'll tend to your hair and makeup, so you needn't worry about it. I had in mind something on the elegant side, but not strictly formal. Jack, that's the photographer, will know what to do with you."

"Yes, but—"

"Now, Maggie's having a bit of a lie-in this morning, but she'd like to go with you. Liam will stay here, so you can have some time for the two of you to do some shopping, or for Maggie to show you around Dublin."

"That would be nice." Shannon drew a breath. She shouldn't have.

"I'm hoping you'll come by the gallery, have a tour. You said you'd been to our branch in New York."

"Yes, and—"

"I think you'll see we try to create different moods in different cities. In order to reflect the ambience. I'm going to be tied up a great deal of the day." He glanced briefly at his watch. "Starting almost immediately. But I'd appreciate it if you'd find a moment to come by the office. Maggie can bring you in about three. We can go over whatever changes you'd like in the contracts."

"Stop." She held up both hands, unsure if she wanted to scream or to laugh. "You're doing it again."

"I'm sorry. What's that?"

"Oh, don't apologize or look politely bemused. You know exactly what you're doing. You're the most elegant steamroller I've ever been flattened by." He flashed a grin that had her shaking her head. "And that—that quick charming smile is lethal. I can see how even someone as stubborn as Maggie crumbled."

"That she didn't. I had to batter away at her bit by bit. And you're much more like her than you might like me to point out." He smothered a fresh grin when Shannon's eyes flashed. "Yes, much more like her."

"Insulting me is not the way to win me over."

"Then let me say this." He folded his hands on the desk. "As your brother-in-law as much as the man who hopes to push forward your career. You didn't come here because I outflanked you, Shannon. That's part of it, yes, that pushed you to move when I pushed you to move. But what I've done is plant an idea in your head."

"All right, you have. It's an idea I toyed with years ago and dismissed as impractical. You're trying to convince me now that it's not."

Intrigued, he leaned back and studied her. "Is it money?"

"I have money. More, actually, than I need. My father was very good at making it." She shook her head. "No, it's not money. Though it's important to me to make my own, to have the satisfaction of that. I need security, and stability, and challenges. I suppose that sounds contradictory."

"Not at all."

Seeing he understood, she continued. "The painting I've done on my own, for myself, has always been a habit, a kind of obligation even—something I worked into my schedule like, well, like an appointment with myself."

"And you're hesitating on making it a focus."

"Yes, I am. I've done better work here than I have ever in my life. And it pulls me in a direction I never seriously considered taking." And now that she'd said it, she was more confused than ever. "But what happens when I go back to New York, Rogan, pick up the life I left behind there? If I sign a contract, I'd have given you my word. How can I do that when I can't be sure I'll be able to keep it?"

"Your integrity's warring with your impulses," he said, putting his finger straight to the pulse. "And that's a difficult thing. Why don't we oblige them both?"

"How do you propose to manage that?"

"Your contract with Worldwide will encompass the work you've done in Ireland, and what you have ready in New York—with an option," he continued, running a pen through his fingers, "for a first look at what you may produce over the next two years. Whether it's one piece or a dozen."

"That's quite a compromise," she murmured. "But you wanted a show. I don't know if I've enough for that, or if what I have will suit you."

"We're flexible on the size of a showing. And I'll let you know what doesn't suit me."

She met his eyes. "I bet you will."

Later, when he'd gone, Shannon wandered back upstairs. He'd given her a great deal to think over. Somehow he'd managed to open a door without forcing her to close another. She could accept his terms and go back to her life without missing a beat.

She found it odd, and more confusing than ever, that she wished he had pressed her into a corner where she'd be forced to make one clear-cut choice.

But there wasn't time to brood on it—not if she wanted to see anything of the city before the photo shoot.

A photo shoot, she thought, chuckling to herself. Imagine that.

She wiped the smile away and knocked briskly on Maggie's bedroom door. "Maggie? Rogan said to wake you." Hearing no response, Shannon rolled her eyes and knocked again. "It's past nine, Margaret Mary. Even pregnant women have to get out of bed sometime."

Impatient, Shannon turned the knob and eased the door open. She could see the bed was empty, and thinking Maggie might be dressing, and ignoring her, she pushed the door wider.

As she started to call out again, she heard the unmistakable sounds of wretched illness from the adjoining bath. It didn't occur to her to hesitate; she simply hurried through to where Maggie was heaving over the toilet.

"Get out, damn you." Maggie waved a limp hand and fought the next wave of nausea. "Can't a woman retch in private?"

Saying nothing, Shannon walked to the sink and dampened a thick washcloth with cool water. Maggie was too busy heaving to resist when Shannon held the back of her head and pressed the cloth to her clammy brow.

"Poor baby," Shannon murmured when Maggie sagged weakly. "Horrible way to start the morning. Just rest a minute, get your breath back."

"I'm all right. Go away. I'm all right."

"Sure you are. Can you handle some water?" Without waiting for an answer, Shannon walked over to fill a glass, then came back to crouch and ease it to Maggie's lips. "There you go, nice slow sips. It probably tastes like you swallowed a sewer."

"This child best be a saint." Because it was there, Maggie leaned against Shannon's shoulder.

"Have you seen your doctor?" To soothe, Shannon took the cloth and ran it gently over Maggie's face. "Isn't there something you can take?"

"I've seen the doctor. Bloody swine. A couple more weeks, he says, and I'll be right as rain. Couple more weeks," she repeated, shutting her eyes. "I nearly murdered him on the spot."

"No jury in the world—if they were women—would convict you. Here, come on, let's get you on your feet. The floor's cold."

Too weak to argue, Maggie let herself be helped up and guided in toward the bed. "Not the bed. I don't need the bed. I just want to sit a minute."

"All right." Shannon led her to a chair. "Want some tea?"

"Oh." Desperately relieved the spell was over, Maggie let her head fall back and closed her eyes. "I would. If you could call on the phone there down to the kitchen and ask if they'd mind sending some up, and some toast. Dry. I'd be grateful."

She sat still, while her system leveled off and the chill faded from her skin. "Well," she said when Shannon replaced the receiver. "That was pleasant for both of us."

"A lot worse for you." Not quite sure Maggie should be left alone yet, Shannon sat on the edge of the bed.

"It was kind of you to help me through it. I appreciate it."

"It didn't sound that way when you were swearing at me."

A grin twisted Maggie's mouth. "I'll apologize for that. I hate being . . ." She gestured. "Out of control of things."

"Me, too. You know, I've only been drunk once in my whole life."

"Once?" The smile turned into a sneer. "And you, Irish as the Rings of Kerry."

"Nevertheless, while it had its liberating aspects, I found, on hindsight, that it was debilitating. I couldn't quite hit the control button. And there was the added delight of being sick as a dog on the side of the road on the way home, and the wonder and glory of the morning after. So, I find it more practical to limit my intake."

"One warms the soul, two warms the brain. Da always said that."

"So he had his practical side as well."

"A narrow one. You have his eyes." She watched Shannon lower them and struggled against her own sense of loss and impatience. "I'm sorry you mind hearing it."

And so, Shannon discovered, was she. "Both my mother and father had blue eyes. I remember asking her once where she thought I'd gotten my green ones. She looked so sad, for just an instant, then she smiled and said an angel gave them to me."

"He'd have liked that. And he'd have been glad and grateful that she found a man like your father must have been, to love both of you." She looked over as the tea was brought in. "There's two cups," she said when Shannon rose to go. "If you'd like to have one with me."

"All right."

"Would it bother you to tell me how they met—your parents?"

"No." Shannon took her seat again and discovered it far from bothered her to tell the story. It warmed her. When Maggie burst into laughter at the idea of Colin knocking Amanda into the mud, Shannon joined her.

"I'd like to have met them," Maggie said at length.

"I think they would have liked meeting you." A little embarrassed by the sentiment, Shannon rose. "Listen, if you'd like to just kick back and rest, I can take a cab to the photographer."

"I'm fine now. I'd like to go with you—and see Jack torture you the way he did me when Rogan put me through this last."

"Thanks."

"My pleasure. And . . ." She set the tray aside and rose. "I think I'd enjoy spending some time with you."

"I think I'd enjoy that, too." Shannon smiled. "I'll wait for you downstairs."

She loved Dublin. She loved the waterways, the bridges, the buildings, the crowds. And oh, she loved the shops. Though she was impatient to do more, see more, Shannon held herself back and indulged Maggie in an enormous midday meal.

Unlike her volatile sister, Shannon hadn't found the photography shoot anything but a pleasant, interesting experience. When she'd pointed that out, Maggie had simply shuddered.

When they left the restaurant, Shannon calculated that they'd broken a record of being in each other's company without harsh words or snide remarks.

She was soon to discover that she shared at least one trait with Maggie. The woman was a champion shopper—zipping from store to store, measuring, considering, and buying without all the wavering and wobbling that annoyed Shannon in many of her friends.

"No." Maggie shook her head as Shannon held up a biscuit-colored sweater. "You need color, not neutrals."

"I like it." Pouting a little, Shannon turned toward a mirror, spreading the sweater up to her neck. "The material's gorgeous."

"It is, and the color makes you look like a week-old corpse."

"Damn it." With a half laugh Shannon folded the sweater again. "It does."

"You want this one." Maggie handed her one in mossy green. She stepped behind Shannon, narrowing her eyes at their reflections. "Definitely."

"You're right. I hate when you're right." She draped the sweater over her arm and fingered the sleeve of the blouse Maggie had over hers. "Are you buying that?"

"Why?"

"Because I'm having it if you're not."

"Well, I am." Smug, Maggie gathered her bags and went to pay for it.

"You'd probably have put it back if I hadn't said I wanted it," Shannon complained as they left the shop.

"No, but it certainly adds to the satisfaction of the purchase. There's a cookery shop nearby. I want to pick up some things for Brie."

"Fine." Still sulking over the blouse, Shannon fell into step. "What's that?"

"A music store," Maggie said dryly when Shannon stopped to stare at a display window.

"I know that. What's that?"

"A dulcimer. Hammer dulcimer."

"It looks more like a piece of art than an instrument."

"It's both. That's a lovely one, too. Murphy made one a few years back just as fine. A beautiful tone it had. His sister Maureen fell in love with it, and he gave it to her."

"That sounds just like him. Do you think he'd like it? One someone else made?"

Maggie lifted her brow. "You could give him wind in a paper bag and he'd treasure it."

But Shannon had already made her decision and was marching into the shop.

Delighted, Shannon watched the clerk take the dulcimer out of the window, then listened as he gave her a skillful demonstration of the music it could make.

"I can see him playing it, can't you?" Shannon asked Maggie. "With that half smile on his face."

"I can." Maggie waited until the happy clerk went in the back to find the right box for transport. "So you're in love with him."

Stalling, Shannon reached in her purse for her wallet. "A woman can buy a gift for a man without being in love with him."

"Not with that look in her eyes she can't. What are you going to do about it?"

"There's nothing I can do." Shannon caught herself, frowned, and selected her credit card. "I'm thinking it over."

"He's not a man to take love casually, or temporarily."

The words, and the knowledge that they were fact, frightened her. "Don't push me on this, Maggie." Rather than the snap she'd hoped for, there was a plea in Shannon's voice. "It's complicated, and I'm doing the best I know how to do."

Her eyes lifted in surprise when Maggie laid a hand on her cheek. "It's hard, isn't it, to fall where you've never been, and never really thought you'd be?"

"Yes. It's terribly hard."

Maggie let her hand slide down and rest on Shannon's shoulder. "Well," she said in a lighter tone, "he's going to trip over his tongue when you hand him this. Where's the bloody clerk? Rogan'll skin me if I don't have you there at three on the damn dot."

"Yeah, you look like you're terrified of him."

"Sometimes I let him think I am. It's a kiss on the ego, so to speak."

Shannon toyed with a display of harmonicas on the counter. "You haven't asked me if I'm going to sign."

"It's been pointed out that it's business not concerning me."

Shannon gave a smile and her credit card to the clerk when he returned. "Is that a kiss on my ego, Margaret Mary?"

"Be grateful it's not a boot to your ass."

"I'm signing," Shannon blurted out. "I don't know if I decided just this instant or the moment he asked, but I'm doing it." Swallowing hard, she pressed a shaky hand to her stomach. "Now I'm queasy."

"I had a similar reaction under the same circumstances. You've just put your wheel in someone else's hands." Sympathetic, she slipped an arm around Shannon's waist. "He'll do right by you."

"I know. I'm not sure if I'll do right by him." She watched the clerk box up the dulcimer. "It's a problem I seem to be having just lately with men I've come to care about."

"I tell you how we're handling this one, Shannon. We're going to Rogan's fine, upstanding office and getting the business part over and done quick. That's the worst part of it, I can tell you."

"Okay." She took the pen the clerk offered, mechanically signed her name to the credit slip.

"Then we're going back home and cracking open a bottle of Sweeney's best champagne."

"You can't drink. You're pregnant."

"You're doing the drinking. A whole bottle of French bubbly just for you. 'Cause, darling, I'm of the opinion that you're going to get drunk for the second time in your life."

Shannon blew out a breath that fluttered her bangs. "You could be right."

Maggie couldn't have been more right. A few hours later, Shannon found that all the doubts and worries and questions simply fizzed away with a bottle of Dom Perignon.

Maggie was the overindulger's friend, listening as Shannon rambled, making sympathetic noises as she complained, and laughing at the poorest of jokes.

When Rogan arrived home, Shannon was sitting dreamy-eyed in the parlor contemplating the last glass that could be squeezed from the bottle.

"What have you done to her, Margaret Mary?"

"She's well fuddled." Satisfied, Maggie lifted her mouth for his kiss.

He lifted a brow at the empty bottle. "Small wonder."

"She needed to relax," Maggie said airily. "And to celebrate, though you'd never be able to tell her so. You're feeling fine, aren't you, Shannon?"

"Fine and dandy." She smiled brilliantly. "Hello, Rogan, when did you get here? They warned me about you, y'know," she went on before he could answer.

"Did they?"

"They certainly did. Rogan Sweeney's slick as spit." She tipped the glass back again, swallowed hastily. "And you are."

"Take it as a compliment, darling," Maggie advised. "That's how it's meant."

"Oh, it is," Shannon agreed. "There's not one shark in New York who could outswim you. And you're so pretty, too." She hoisted herself up, chuckling when her head revolved. When he would have taken her arm to steady her, she simply leaned in and gave him a loud, smacking kiss. "I've got such cute brothers, don't I, Maggie? Just as cute as buttons."

"Darling men." Maggie's grin was wide and wicked. "Both of them. Would you like a little nap now, Shannon?"

"Nope." Beaming, Shannon snatched up her glass. "Look, there's more. I'll just take it with me while I make a call. I need to make a call. A private call, if you don't mind."

"And who are you after calling?" Maggie asked.

"I'm after calling Mr. Murphy Muldoon, in County Clare, Ireland."

"I'll just come along," Maggie suggested, "and dial the number for you."

"I'm perfectly capable. I have his number right in my trusty little electronic organizer. I never go anywhere without it." With the glass dangling dangerously from her hand, she looked around the room. "Where'd it go? No up-and-coming professional can survive without their organizer."

"I'm sure it's about." With a wink for Rogan, Maggie took Shannon's arm and led her away. "But it happens I have the number right in my head."

"You're so clever, Maggie. I noticed that about you right away—even when I wanted to punch you."

"That's nice. You can sit right here in Rogan's big chair and talk to Murphy all you like."

"He's got an incredible body. Murphy, I mean." Giggling, Shannon dropped into the chair behind Rogan's library desk. "Though I'm sure Rogan's is lovely, too."

"I can promise you it is. Here, you talk into this end and listen in this one."

"I know how to use a phone. I'm a professional. Murphy?"

"I haven't finished calling yet. I'm an amateur."

"That's all right. It's ringing now. There's Murphy. Hi, Murphy." She cradled the phone like a lover and didn't notice when Maggie slipped out.

"Shannon? I'm glad you called. I was thinking of you."

"I'm always thinking of you. It's the damnedest thing."

"You sound a bit strange? Are you all right?"

"I'm wonderful. I love you, Murphy."

"What?" His voice rose half an octave. "What?"

"I'm so buzzed."

"You're what? Shannon, go back two steps and start again."

"The last time I was a freshman in college and it was Homecoming and there was all this wine. Oceans of it. I got so awful sick, too. But I don't feel sick at all this time. I just feel . . ." She sent the chair spinning and nearly strangled herself with the phone cord. "Alive."

"Christ, what has Maggie done to you?" he muttered. "Are you drunk?"

"I think so." To test she held up two fingers in front of her face. "Pretty sure. I wish you were here, Murphy, right here so I could crawl in your lap and nibble you all over."

There was a moment of pained silence. "That would be memorable," he said in a voice tight with strain. "Shannon, you said you loved me."

"You know I do. It's all mixed up with white horses and copper broaches and thunderstorms and making love in the dance and cursing at the moon." She let her head fall back in the chair as the visions flowed and circled in her head. "Casting spells," she murmured. "Winning battles. I don't know what to do. I can't think about it."

"We'll talk it through when you get back. Shannon, have you called me from across the entire country, drunk on—what are you drunk on?"

"Champagne. Rogan's finest French champagne."

"Figures. Drunk on champagne," he repeated, "to tell me for the first time that you love me?"

"It seemed like a good idea at the time. You have a wonderful voice." She kept her heavy eyes closed. "I could listen to it forever. I bought you a present."

"That's nice. Tell me again."

"I bought you a present." At his frustrated snarl, she opened her eyes and laughed. "Oh, I get it. I'm not stupid. *Summa cum laude,* you know. I love you, Murphy, and it really messes things up all around, but I love you. Good night."

"Shannon—"

But she was aiming for the phone, with one eye closed. Through more luck than skill, she managed to jiggle the receiver in place. Then she leaned back, yawned once, and went to sleep.

TWENTY

"And the next morning, not a stagger, not a wince." While she sipped tea in Brianna's kitchen, Maggie shot Shannon an admiring glance. "I couldn't have been more proud."

"You have an odd sense of pride." But Shannon felt an odd flare of it herself. Through luck or God's pity, she'd escaped the punishment of a hangover after her romance with Dom Pérignon.

Twenty-four hours after the affair had ended, she was safely back in Clare and enjoying the questionable distinction of having a hard head.

"You shouldn't have let her overdo." Brianna began to swirl a rich and smooth marshmallow frosting over chocolate cake.

"She's a woman grown," Maggie objected.

"And the youngest."

"Oh, really." Shannon rolled her eyes at Brianna's back. "I hardly think that's an issue. You and I were born in the same year, so . . ." She trailed off as the full impact of what she'd said struck. Her brows knit, and she stared down at a spot on the table. Well, she thought. This is awkward.

"Busy year for Da," Maggie said after a long silence.

Shocked, Shannon looked up quickly and met Maggie's bland eyes. The sound of her own muffled snort of laughter surprised her nearly as much as Maggie's lightning grin. Brianna continued to frost her cake.

"An entire bottle, Maggie," Brianna went on in a quiet, lecturing tone. "You should have had more care."

"Well, I looked after her, didn't I? After she'd passed out in the library—"

"I didn't pass out," Shannon corrected primly. "I was resting."

"Unconscious." Maggie reached over to pick up her niece when Kayla began to fuss in her carrier. "And poor Murphy ringing back like a man possessed. Who talked him out of hopping in his lorry and driving all the way to Dublin if it wasn't me?" she asked Kayla. "And didn't I take her upstairs and see that she ate a bowl of soup before she slept the rest of it off?"

Her ears pricked up. "There's Liam awake." She passed the baby to Shannon, then went through to Brianna's bedroom, where she'd laid him down for a nap.

Brianna stepped back to judge the frosting job before she turned. "Other than last evening, did you enjoy your trip to Dublin?"

"Yes. It's a lovely city. And the gallery there—it's a religious experience."

"I've thought so myself. You've yet to see the one here in Clare. I was hoping we could all go, a kind of outing. Soon."

"I'd like that. Brianna . . ." She wasn't sure she was ready to ask. Far less sure she was ready for the consequences.

"Is something troubling you?"

"I think—I'd like to see the letters." She said it quickly before her courage evaporated. "The letters my mother wrote."

"Of course." Brianna laid a hand, support and comfort, on Shannon's shoulder. "I've kept them in my dresser. Why don't you come into the family parlor, and you can read them."

But before Shannon could rise, there was a commotion in the hall. Voices fussed and clashed causing the hand on Shannon's shoulder to tense once, briefly.

"It's Mother," she murmured. "And Lottie."

"It's all right." Not at all sure if she was disappointed or relieved, Shannon patted Brianna's hand. "I'll look at them later." She braced for whatever form the confrontation would take.

Maeve swept in first, still arguing. "I tell you I'll not ask. If you've no pride yourself, I can't stop you from it." She caught sight of Shannon holding her granddaughter and lifted her chin.

"Well, you're very much to home, I see."

"Yes, I am. Brianna makes it impossible to be otherwise. Hello, Mrs. Sullivan."

"Oh, Lottie, dear. You just call me Lottie like everyone. And how's my angel today?" She bent over Kayla, cooing. "Look here, Maeve, she's smiling."

"Why shouldn't she? She's being spoiled right and left."

"Brianna's an incredibly loving mother," Shannon shot back before she could stop herself.

Maeve merely sniffed. "The baby can't so much as whimper that someone's not snatching her up."

"Including you," Lottie put in. "Oh, Brie, what a lovely cake."

Resigned that she'd have to bake another now for her guests' dessert, Brianna took out a knife. "Sit down, won't you, and have a piece."

Liam shot out of the adjoining door, five paces ahead of his mother. "Cake!" he shouted.

"Got radar, that boy has." However gruff her voice, Maeve's eyes lit up at the sight of him. "There's a likely lad."

He beamed at her, sensing an ally, and lifted his arms. "Kiss."

"Come sit on my lap," Maeve ordered. "And you'll have both, the cake and the kiss. He's a bit flushed, Margaret Mary."

"He's just up from his nap. Are you cutting that cake then, Brie?"

"You should have more care with your diet, now that you're breeding again," Maeve told her. "The doctor says you've the morning sickness this time around."

It was a toss-up as to who was more shocked by the statement, Maeve or Maggie. Already wishing the words back, Maeve began to feed her grandson bits of cake.

"It's nothing."

"She's sick as a dog every morning," Shannon corrected, looking directly at Maeve.

"Maggie, you told me it was passing." There was accusation twined with the concern in Brianna's voice.

Furious and embarrassed, Maggie glared at Shannon. "It's nothing," she repeated.

"Never could bear a weakness."

Maeve's caustic comment had the fury leaping. Before Maggie could spew, Shannon nodded in agreement. "She snaps like a terrier when you try to help her through it. It's hard, don't you think, Mrs. Concannon, for a strong woman to need help? And one like Maggie, who's figured out how to handle a family and a demanding career, to lose her stomach and her control every morning . . . it's lowering."

"I was sick every morning for more than three months carrying her," Maeve said crisply. "A woman learns to get through such things—as a man never could."

"No, they'd just whine about it."

"Neither of my daughters were whiners, ever." Scowling again, Maeve looked over at Brianna. "Are you going to stand there holding that pot of tea all day, Brianna, or are you going to pour it out?"

"Oh." She managed to lift the jaw that had dropped and serve the tea. "Sorry."

"Thank you, darling." Delighted with the way things were going, Lottie beamed.

For more than two years she'd been nudging and tugging Maeve toward even a shaky bridge with her daughters. Now it looked as though the span was narrowing.

"You know, Maggie, Maeve and I were just looking through the snapshots from our trip to your home in France."

"No more pride than a beggar," Maeve muttered, but Lottie just smiled.

"They reminded us both what a lovely time we had there. It's the south of France," she told Shannon. "The house is like a palace and looks right out over the sea."

"And sits there empty, month after month," Maeve grumbled. "Empty but for servants."

Maggie started to snarl at the complaint, but caught Brianna's arched look. It cost her, but she buried the hot words and chose kinder ones. "Rogan and I were talking about just that not long ago. We'd hoped to take a few weeks there this summer, but both of us are too busy to go just now."

She let out a breath, telling herself she was earning points with the angels. "It's been a bit of a concern to me that no one's there to check on matters, and see that the staff is doing as it should."

Which was a big, bold lie she hoped wouldn't negate the points. "I don't suppose the two of you would consider taking a bit of time and going out there? It would be a great favor to me if you could manage it."

With an effort Lottie bit back the urge to spring up and dance. She looked at Maeve, cocked her head. "What do you think, Maeve? Could we manage it?"

As the image of the sunny villa, the servants dancing attendance, the sheer luxury of it all slid into her mind, she shrugged and brought the cup of tea to Liam's waiting lips.

"Traveling aggravates my digestion. But I suppose I could tolerate a bit of inconvenience."

This time it was Shannon's warning glance that held back Maggie's snarl. "I'd be grateful," she said between clamped teeth. "I'll have Rogan arrange to have the plane take you when it suits."

Twenty minutes later, Brianna listened to the front door close behind her mother and Lottie, then crossed the kitchen to give Maggie a hard hug.

"That was well done, Maggie."

"I feel as if I'd swallowed a toad. Her digestion be damned."

Brianna only laughed. "Don't spoil it."

"And you." Maggie spun to jerk an accusing finger at Shannon.

"And me?" she returned, all innocence.

"As if I couldn't see the wheels turning in your head. 'Sick as a dog, she is, Mrs. Concannon. Snaps like a terrier.' "

"Worked, didn't it?"

Maggie opened her mouth, then closed it on a laugh. "It did, but my pride's sorely injured." Catching movement through the window, she moved closer and peered out. "Well, look what Con's rooted out of the bush. There's three men coming this way, Brianna. You may want to make a new pot of tea." She stared out for another moment as a smile bloomed. "Christ Jesus, what a handsome lot they are. I'll take the jackeen," she murmured. "The two of you can scrabble over the others."

While Shannon tried to adjust her suddenly jittery system, Maggie went to the door and threw it open. Con bolted in first, streaking under the table to vacuum up the crumbs Liam had been considerate enough to drop.

"Cake." His senses as tuned as the hound's, Gray spotted the treat the moment he crossed the threshold. "With the marshmallow stuff. Guys, we've struck gold."

"Da." Liam bounced in his chair and held up sticky fingers. Rogan had the presence of mind to stop by the sink and dampen a cloth before he went to his son.

Murphy just stood there, his cap in his hands, his eyes on Shannon. "You're back."

"A couple of hours ago," she began, then her eyes widened as he marched to her, pulled her to her feet, and kissed her the way a wise man only kisses a woman in private.

"Welcome."

She didn't have a single breath left. She drew some in and nodded. She would have given her shaky legs the relief of sitting again, but he held firm to her arm.

"Come with me."

"Well, I . . ." Her gaze darted around the room, where everyone was suddenly intent on their own business.

"Hold on to yourself, Murphy," Maggie said lightly as she got out fresh plates. "Shannon's a present she wants to give you."

"Yes. That's right. I . . ." She trailed off.

"I'll get the box for you," Rogan offered.

"Will you have some tea, Murphy?" Brianna asked.

"No, thank you." He never took his eyes off Shannon's face. "We can't stay just now. Shannon'll have dinner with me tonight."

"And breakfast," Gray murmured in Brianna's ear.

"Thank you, Rogan." Shannon took the box he brought in and wondered what to do next.

"What is it?" Gray wanted to know. "Open it up. Ow." He winced as Brianna jabbed his ribs with her elbow.

"He'll open it at home," she said. "Take some cake with you." She already readied a slab and handed Murphy the covered plate.

"Thanks. Come with me," he said again and, taking Shannon's arm, led her outside.

"Good thing you gave him the plate," Maggie commented. "Else he'd have his hands all over her before they were out of the garden."

As it was, he had to call on all of his control. He wanted to drag her over the fields, down onto them. Instead he concentrated on keeping his stride from outdistancing hers.

"I should have brought the lorry."

"It's not far to walk," she said, breathless.

"Right now it is. Is that heavy? I'll take it."

"No." She shifted the box out of his reach. It wasn't light, but she wanted to carry it. "You might guess."

"You didn't have to buy me anything. Your coming back's present enough." He hooked an arm around her waist and lifted her easily over the wall. "I missed you every minute. I didn't know a man could think of a woman so many times in one day."

He forced himself to take three calming breaths. "Rogan told me you'd signed the contracts with him. Are you happy?"

"Part of me is, and part of me's terrified."

"The fear's only a motivator to do your best. You'll be famous, Shannon, and rich."

"I'm already rich."

His stride faltered. "You are?"

"Comparatively."

"Oh." He'd have to mull that one over, he decided. Think it through. But at the moment his mind kept getting muddled with images of peeling her out of that pretty tailored jacket.

When they reached the farm, he held open the kitchen door. He set the plate on the counter and would have grabbed her if she hadn't anticipated him and moved to the other side of the table.

"I'd like you to open your present." She set it on the table between them.

"I want you upstairs, on the stairs. Here on the floor."

Blood bubbled under her skin. "The way I'm feeling right now, you can have me upstairs, on the stairs, *and* here on the floor." She held up a hand when his eyes went hot. "But I'd really like you to see what I got you in Dublin."

He didn't give a damn if she'd brought him a solid-gold pitchfork or a jeweled plowshare. But the quiet request stopped him from simply leaping over the table. Instead, he lifted the lid from the box and pushed through the packing.

She saw the instant he realized what was under it. The stunned joy crept into his face. Suddenly he looked as young and bedazzled as any child who's found his heart's desire under the tree on Christmas morning.

Reverently he lifted the dulcimer out, ran his fingers over the wood. "I've never seen anything so fine."

"Maggie said you'd made one yourself just as fine, then given it away."

Enchanted, he only shook his head. "No, 'twasn't so beautiful as this." He looked up then, wonder and delight in his eyes. "What made you think to buy such a thing as this for me?"

"I saw it in the window, and I saw you playing it. Will you play it for me, Murphy?"

"I haven't played the dulcimer in a time." But he unwrapped the hammers, stroked them as he might the down of a newly hatched chick. "There's a tune I know."

And when he played it, she saw that she'd been right. He had that half smile on his face, the faraway look in his eyes. The melody was old and sweet, like some lovely wine just decanted. It filled the kitchen, made her eyes sting and her heart swell.

"It's the grandest gift I've ever had," he said as he set the hammers gently aside. "I'll treasure it."

The impatient beast that had clawed inside of him was calmed. He came around the table and took her hands gently in his. "I love you, Shannon."

"I know." She lifted their joined hands to her cheek. "I know you do."

"You called me yesterday and told me you loved me. Will you tell me now?"

"I shouldn't have called that way." She spoke quickly as nerves began to spark in her fingertips. "I wasn't thinking clearly, and . . ." He kissed those unsteady fingertips, watching her patiently over them. "I do love you, Murphy, but—"

He only laid his lips on hers, silencing the rest. "Ever since I heard you tell me, the first time, I've been aching for you. Will you come upstairs with me, Shannon?"

"Yes." She leaned closer, trapping their joined hands between. "I'll come upstairs with you." She smiled, swept up in the romance of it even as she was swept up in his arms.

The light was lovely, trailing through the windows, scattering over the stairs as he carried her up, flowing pale across the bed when he laid her on it.

It was so easy to sink into that light, into the gentle strength of his arms as they wrapped around her, into the warm promise of his mouth.

It occurred to her that this was the first time they'd loved each other with a roof overhead and a bed beneath them. She might have missed the stars and the smell of grass if it hadn't been for the sweetness he offered her in its place.

He'd brought flowers into the room. Imagining her here, he'd wanted there to be flowers. He caught the fragile scent of them as he dipped his head to trail his lips down her throat.

There were candles, for later, to replace the starlight. There were soft linen sheets, a substitute for woolen blankets and grass. He spread her hair over his pillow, knowing her scent would cling there.

She smiled as he began to undress her. She'd bought a few other things in Dublin and knew, when he'd uncovered the first hint of rose silk, she'd chosen well.

With quiet concentration, he peeled aside jacket, blouse, slacks, then drew a fingertip across the ivory lace that flirted between her breasts.

"Why do such things weaken a man?" he wondered.

Her smile spread. "I saw it in the window, then I saw you. Touching me."

His gaze lifted to hers. Very slowly he skimmed his fingertip down, over the curve of her breast, under it, then up again to graze her nipple. "Like this?"

"Yes." Her eyes fluttered closed. "Just like this."

Experimentally he followed the silk down to were it ended in an edge of that same lace just below the waist. Beneath that was a tiny swatch of matching silk. He laid his hand over the triangle and watched her arch.

When he replaced his hand with his mouth, she writhed.

To please himself, he explored every inch of the silks before moving on to the flesh beneath. He knew she was lost to reason when he'd finished. Even as she bucked beneath him, clawed, he held on to his own. He wanted one last gift.

"Tell me now, Shannon." The breath was searing his lungs, and his fists were bone white. "Tell me now that you love me, when you're burning for me, when you're desperate for me to come inside you, to fill you. To ride you."

She was gasping for air, frantic for him to drive her over that last thin edge. "I love you." Tears sprang to her eyes as emotion mixed, equal to need. "I love you, Murphy."

He thrust into her, making them both groan. Each plunge was a demand and a glory. "Tell me again." His voice was fierce as they both teetered on the brink. "Tell me again."

"I love you." Almost weeping, she buried her face in his throat and let him shatter her.

Later, after he'd lighted the candles, he pulled her down the hall to the bath where they played like children in water too hot in a tub too full.

Instead of dinner, they gorged on Brianna's cake, washed it down with beer in a combination Shannon knew should be disgusting. It tasted like ambrosia.

While she was licking her fingers, she caught the gleam in his eye. In a heartbeat they were lunging for each other, and made love like mindless animals on the kitchen floor.

She might have slept there, exhausted, but he pulled her to her feet. No steadier than drunks, they staggered out, down the hall. Then he pulled her into the parlor, and they had each other again on the rug.

When she managed to sit up, her hair was tangled, her eyes glazed, and her body aching. "How many rooms are there in this house?"

He laughed and nipped her shoulder. "You're going to find out."

"Murphy, we'll kill each other." When his hand snaked up the ladder of her ribs to cup her breast, she let out a shuddering sigh. "I'm willing to risk it if you are."

"That's a lass."

There were fifteen, Shannon thought when she collapsed onto the tangled sheets somewhere near dawn. Fifteen rooms in the sprawling stone farmhouse, and it wasn't through lack of wanting that they hadn't managed to christen all of them. Somewhere along the line their bodies had simply betrayed them. They'd tumbled back into bed with no thought of anything but sleep.

As she drifted toward it, under the weight of Murphy's arm, she reminded herself they would have to talk seriously and talk soon. She had to explain things to him. Make him see why the future was so much more complex then the present.

Even as she tried to formulate the words in her mind, she drifted deeper.

And she saw the man, her warrior, her lover, on the white horse. There was the glint of armor, the swirl of his cape in the wind.

But this time, he wasn't riding toward her across the fields. He was riding away.

TWENTY-ONE

Murphy figured it was love that made a man so energetic after an hour's sleep. He dealt with the milking, the feeding of stock, the pasturing, all with a song on his lips and a spring in his step that had the young Feeney boy grinning at him.

As usual, there were a dozen chores to see to before breakfast. Grateful it was his neighbor's turn to haul the milk away, Murphy gathered up the morning's eggs, eyed one of the older ladies who would need to do her turn in the pot shortly, and headed back toward the house.

He was having a change of heart about his earlier idea of letting Shannon sleep while he grabbed a quick cup of tea and a biscuit, then set out to turn his turf.

It seemed much more inviting to take her up that tea and biscuit and make love with her while she was warm from sleep and soft from dreaming.

He never expected to find her in his kitchen, standing at the stove with the apron his mother used when visiting wrapped around her waist.

"I thought you'd be sleeping."

She glanced over, smiling at the way he took off his cap when he came in the house. "I heard you outside, laughing with the boy who helps you milk."

"I didn't mean to wake you." The kitchen smelled gloriously of mornings from his childhood. "What are you doing there?"

"I found some bacon, and the sausages." She prodded the latter with a kitchen fork. "It's cholesterol city, but after last night, I thought you deserved it."

The foolish grin broke over his face. "You're cooking me breakfast."

"I figured you'd be hungry after doing whatever you do at dawn, so—Murphy!" She squealed, dropping the fork with a clatter as he grabbed her and swung her around. "Watch what you're doing."

He set her down, but couldn't do anything about the grin as she muttered at him and washed off the fork. "I didn't even know you could cook."

"Of course I can cook. I may not be the artist in the kitchen Brie is, but I'm more than adequate. What's this?" She poked into the bucket he'd set down when he'd come in. "There must be three dozen eggs in here. What do you do with so many?"

"I use what I need, trade away or sell the rest."

She wrinkled her nose. "They're filthy. How did they get so dirty?"

He stared at her a moment, then roared with laughter. "Oh, you're a darling woman, Shannon Bodine."

"I can see that was a stupid question. Well, clean them up. I'm not touching them."

He hauled the bucket to the sink, began to oblige when it suddenly dawned on her just where eggs came from. "Oh." She winced and flipped bacon. "It's enough to put you off omelettes. How do you know if they're just eggs and not going to be little chickies?"

He slid her a look, wanting to make sure she wasn't joking this time. Poking his tongue in his cheek, he washed off another shell. "If they don't peep, you're safe."

"Very funny." She decided she was better off in ignorance. She really preferred thinking of eggs as something you took out of nice cartons stacked in the market. "How do you want them cooked?"

"However you like. I'm not fussy. You made tea!" He wanted to kneel at her feet.

"I couldn't find any coffee."

"I'll get some next I'm in the village. It smells grand, Shannon."

The table was already set, he noted, for two. He poured them both tea, wishing he'd thought to pick her some of the wildflowers that grew alongside the barn. He sat when she carried a platter to the table.

"Thank you."

There was a humbleness in his voice that made her feel twin edges of guilt and pleasure. "You're welcome. I never eat sausage," she commented as she took her seat. "But this looks so good."

"It should. Mrs. Feeney made it fresh only a few days ago."

"Made it?"

"Aye." He offered her the platter first. "They butchered the hog they'd been fattening." His brow drew together in concern when she paled. "Is something wrong?"

"No." With hurried movement, she waved the platter away. "There are just certain things I don't care to visualize."

"Ah." He gave her an apologetic smile. "I wasn't thinking."

"I should be getting used to it. The other day I walked in on a discussion Brie was having with some guy about the spring lambs." She shuddered, knowing now just what happened to cute little lambs in the spring.

"It seems harsh to you, I know. But it's just the cycle of things. It was one of Tom's problems."

Deciding the toast she'd made was safe, Shannon glanced over. "Oh?"

"He couldn't stand to raise something for the table—for his own or someone else's. When he had chickens, he gathered the eggs well enough, but his hens died of old age more often than not. He was a tender-hearted man."

"He let the rabbits go," Shannon murmured.

"Ah, you heard about the rabbits." Murphy smiled at the memory. "Going to make a fortune off them, he was—until it came down to the sticking point. He was always after making a fortune."

"You really loved him."

"I did. He wasn't a substitute for my father, nor did he try to be one. It wasn't the male figure they say a boy needs in his life. He was as much my father from my fifteenth year as the one who made me was before. He was always there for me. When I was grieving, he'd pop up, take me for a ride to the cliffs, or a trip into Galway with the girls. He held my head the first time I sicked up whiskey I'd had no business drinking. And when I'd had my first woman, I—"

He broke off and developed a keen interest in his meal.

Shannon lifted a brow. "Oh, don't stop now. What happened, when you'd had your first woman?"

"What usually happens, I'd suppose. This is a fine breakfast, Shannon."

"Don't change the subject. How old were you?"

He gave her a pained look. " 'Tisn't seemly to discuss such matters with the woman you're currently sharing breakfast with."

"Coward."

"Aye," he agreed heartily and filled his flapping mouth with eggs.

"You're safe, Murphy." Her laughter faded. "I'd really like to know what he said to you."

Because it was important to her, he crawled over his embarrassment. "I was . . . I'd been . . ."

"You don't have to tell me that part." She smiled to soothe him. "Now, anyway."

"After," he said, relieved to have gotten past that first leap. "I was feeling proud—manly, guess you could say. And as confused as a monkey with three tails. Guilty, terrified I might have gotten the girl pregnant because I'd been too hot—young and stupid," he corrected, "to think of that before the matter. So I was sitting out on the wall, a part of me wondering when I might get back and do the whole thing again, and the other part waiting for God to strike me dead for doing it in the first place. Or for Ma to find out and do the job quicker and with less mercy than God ever would."

"Murphy." She forgot herself and bit into a slice of bacon. "You're so sweet."

"It's as much a moment in a man's life as it is a woman's I'd say. Anyway, I was sitting there thinking of what you might imagine, and Tom comes along. He sits next to me and says nothing for a time. Just sits and looks out over the fields. It must have been all over my face. He puts his arm around my shoulders. 'Made a man of yourself,' he says, 'and you're proud of it. But it takes more than sliding into a willing lass to make a man. Takes responsibility.' "

Murphy shook his head and picked up his tea. "Now I'm sick thinking I might have to marry her, and me barely seventeen and no more in love with her than she with me. And I say so. He just nods, not lecturing or scolding. He tells me if God and fate are looking kindly, he knows I'll remember it, and have more of a care next time out. 'There'll be a next time,' he says, 'because a man doesn't stop going down such a lovely path once he's begun it. And a woman is a glorious thing to hold and to have. The right woman, when you find her, is more than sunlight. You watch for her, Murphy, and while you're sniffing those sweet flowers along the way, treat them with care and affection, and don't bruise their petals. If you love with kindness, even when you can't love with permanence, you'll deserve the one who's waiting along that path for you.' "

It took Shannon a moment to find her voice. "Everyone says he wanted to be a poet, but didn't have the words." She pressed her lips together. "It sounds as though he did to me."

"He had them when it counted," Murphy said quietly. "He often lacked them for himself. He carried sadness in his eyes that showed when he didn't know you were looking."

Shannon looked down at her hands. They were her mother's hands, narrow, long fingered. And she had Tom Concannon's eyes. What else, she wondered, had they given her?

"Would you do something for me, Murphy?"

"I'd do anything for you."

She knew it, but just then couldn't let herself think of it. "Would you take me to Loop Head?"

He rose, took their plates from the table. "You'll need your jacket, darling. The wind's brisk there."

She wondered how often Tom Concannon had taken this drive, along the narrow, twisting roads that cut through the roll of fields. She saw little stone sheds without roofs, a tethered goat that cropped at wild grass. There was a sign painted on the side of a white building warning her it was the last stop for beer until New York. It nearly made her smile.

When he parked the truck, she saw with relief that there was no one else who had come to see the cliffs and sea that morning. They were alone, with the wailing wind and the jagged rocks and the crash of surf. And the whisper of ghosts.

She walked with him down the ribbon of dirt that cut through the high grass and toward the edge of Ireland.

The wind lashed at her, a powerful thing blown over the dark water and spewing surf. The thunder of it was wonderful. To the north she could see the Cliffs of Mohr and the still misted Aran Islands.

"They met here." She linked her fingers with Murphy's when he took her hand. "My mother told me, the day she went into the coma, she told me how they'd met here. It was raining and cold and he was alone. She fell in love with him here. She knew he was married, had children. She knew it was wrong. It was wrong, Murphy. I can't make myself feel differently."

"Don't you think they paid for it?"

"Yes, I think they paid. Over and over. But that doesn't—" She broke off, steadied her voice. "It was easier when I didn't really believe he loved her. When I didn't, couldn't think of him as a good man, as a father who would have loved me if things had been different. I had one who did," she said fiercely. "And I won't ever forget that."

"You don't have to love the one less to open your heart a bit to the other."

"It makes me feel disloyal." She shook her head before he could speak. "It doesn't matter if it's not logical to feel that way. I do. I don't want

Tom Concannon's eyes, I don't want his blood, I don't—" She pressed her hand to her mouth and let the tears come. "I lost something, Murphy, the day she told me. I lost the image, the illusion, that smooth quiet mirror that reflected my family. It's shattered, and now there are all these cracks and layers and overlapping edges when it's put back together."

"How do you see yourself in it now?"

"With different pieces scattered over the whole, and connections I can't turn away from. And I'm afraid I'll never get back what I had." Eyes desolate, she turned to him. "She lost her family because of me, faced the shame and fear of being alone. And it was because of me she married a man she didn't love." Shannon brushed at the tears with the back of her hand. "I know she did love him in time. A child knows that about her parents—you can feel it in the air, the same way you can feel an argument that adults think they're hiding from you. But she never forgot Tom Concannon, never closed him out of her heart, or forgot how she felt when she walked to these cliffs in the rain and saw him."

"And you wish she had."

"Yes, I wish she had. And I hate myself for wishing it. Because when I wish it I know I'm not thinking of her, or of my father. I'm thinking of me."

"You're so hard on yourself, Shannon. It hurts me to see it."

"No, I'm not. You have no idea the easy, the close-to-perfect life I had." She looked out to sea again, her hair streaming back from her face. "Parents who indulged me in nearly everything. Who trusted me, respected me every bit as much as they loved me. They wanted me to have the best and saw that I got it. Good homes in good neighborhoods, good schools. I never wanted for anything, emotionally or materially. They gave me a solid foundation and let me make my own choices on how to use it. Now I'm angry because there's a fault under the foundation. And the anger's like turning my back on everything they did for me."

"That's nonsense, and it's time you stopped it." Firm, he took her shoulders. "Was it anger that made you come here to where it began, knowing what it would cost you to face it? You know he died here, yet you came to face that, too, didn't you?"

"Yes. It hurts."

"I know, darling." He gathered her close. "I know it does. The heart has to break a little to make room."

"I want to understand." It was so comforting to rest her head on his shoulder. The tears didn't burn then, and the pang in her heart lessened. "It would be easier to accept when I understand why they all made the choices they made."

"I think you understand more than you know." He turned so that they faced the sea again, the crashing and endless symphony of wave against rock. "It's beautiful here. On the edge of the world." He kissed her hair. "One day you'll bring your paints and draw what you see, what you feel."

"I don't know if I could. So many ghosts."

"You drew the stones. There's no lack of ghosts there, and they're as close to you as these."

If it was a day for courage, she would stand on her own when she asked him. Shannon stepped back. "The man and white horse, the woman in the field. You see them."

"I do. Hazily when I was a boy, then clearer after I found the broach. Clearer yet since you stepped into Brianna's kitchen and looked at me with eyes I already knew."

"Tom Concannon's eyes."

"You know what I mean, Shannon. They were cool then. I'd seen them that way before. And I'd seen them hot, with anger and with lust. I'd seen them weeping and laughing. I'd seen them swimming with visions."

"I think," she said carefully, "that people can be susceptible to a place, an atmosphere. There are a number of studies—" She broke off when his eyes glinted at her. "All right, we'll toss out logic temporarily. I felt—feel—something at the dance. Something strange, and familiar. And I've had dreams—since the first night I came to Ireland."

"It unnerves you. It did me for a time."

"Yes, it unnerves me."

"There's a storm," he prompted, trying not to rush her.

"Sometimes. The lightning's cold, like a spear of ice against the sky, and the ground's hard with frost so you can hear the sound of the horse thundering across it before you see it and the rider."

"And the wind blows her hair while she waits. He sees her and his heart's beating as hard as the horse's hooves beat the ground."

Clutching her arms around her, Shannon turned away. It was easier to look at the sea. "Other times there's a fire in a small dark room. She's bathing his face with a cloth. He's delirious, burning with fever that's spread from his wounds."

"He knows he's dying," Murphy said quietly. "All he has to hold him to life is her hand, and the scent of her, the sound of her voice as she soothes him."

"But he doesn't die." Shannon took a long breath. "I've seen them making love, by the fire, in the dance. It's like watching and being taken at the same time. I'll wake up hot and shaky and aching for you." She turned to him then, and he saw a look he'd seen before in her eyes, the smoldering fury of it. "I don't want this."

"Tell me what I did, to turn your heart against me."

"It isn't against you."

But he took her arms, his eyes insistent. "Tell me what I did."

"I don't know." She shouted it, then, shocked by the bitterness, pressed against him. "I don't know. And if I do somehow I can't tell you. This isn't my world, Murphy. It's not real to me."

"But you're trembling."

"I can't talk about this. I don't want to think about it. It makes everything more insane and impossible than it already is."

"Shannon—"

"No." She took his mouth in a desperate kiss.

"This won't always be enough to soothe either of us."

"It's enough now. Take me back, Murphy. Take me back and we'll make it enough."

Demands wouldn't sway her, he knew. Not when she was clinging so close to her fears. Helpless to do otherwise, he kept her under his arm and led her back to the truck.

Gray saw the truck coming as he walked back to the inn and hailed it. The minute he stepped up to Shannon's window he could sense the tension. And he could see quite easily, though she'd done her best to mask it, that she'd been crying.

He sent Murphy an even look, exactly the kind a brother might aim at anyone who made his sister unhappy.

"I've just come back from your place. When you didn't answer the phone, Brianna started worrying."

"We went for a drive," Shannon told him. "I asked Murphy to take me to Loop Head."

"Oh." Which explained quite a bit. "Brie was hoping we could go out to the gallery. All of us."

"I'd like that." She thought the trip might dispel the lingering depression. "Could you?" she asked Murphy.

"I have some things to see to." He could see it would disappoint her if he made excuses, and that she wouldn't talk to him now in any case. "Could you hold off for an hour or two?"

"Sure. We'll take Maggie and the monster with us. Rogan's already out there. Come by when you're ready."

"I need to change," Shannon said quickly. She was already opening the door as she glanced back at Murphy. "I'll wait for you here, all right?"

"That's fine. No more than two hours." He nodded toward Gray, then drove off.

"Tough morning?" Gray murmured.

"In several ways. I can't seem to talk to him about what happens next." Or what happened before, she admitted.

"What does happen next?"

"I have to go back, Gray. I should have left a week ago." She leaned into him when he draped an arm over her shoulder, and looked out over the valley. "My job's on the line."

"The old rock and a hard place. I've been there a few times. No way to squeeze out without bruises." He led her through the gate, down the path, and to the steps. "If I were to ask you what you wanted in your life, for your life, would you be able to answer?"

"Not as easily as I could have a month ago." She sat with him, studying the foxglove and nodding columbine. "Do you believe in visions, Gray?"

"That's quite a segue."

"I guess it is, and a question I never figured I'd ask anyone." She turned to study him now. "I'm asking you because you're an American." When his grin broke out, hers followed. "I know how that sounds, but hear me out. You make your home here, in Ireland, but you're still a Yank. You make your living by creating fiction, telling stories, but you do it on modern equipment. There's a fax machine in your office."

"Yeah, that makes all the difference."

"It means you're a twentieth-century man, a forward-looking man who understands technology and uses it."

"Murphy has a top-of-the-line milk machine," Gray pointed out. "His new tractor's the best modern technology's come up with."

"And he cuts his own turf," Shannon finished, smiling. "And his blood is full of Celtic mystique. You can't tell me that part of him doesn't believe in banshees and fairies."

"Okay, I'd say Murphy's a fascinating combination of old Ireland and new. So your question to me is do I believe in visions." He waited a beat. "Absolutely."

"Oh, Grayson." Frustrated, she sprang up, strode two paces down the path, turned, and strode back. "How can you sit there, wearing Nikes and a Rolex and tell me you believe in visions?"

He looked down at his shoes. "I like Nikes, and the watch keeps pretty good time."

"You know very well what I mean. You're not going to have any trouble rolling into the twenty-first century, yet you're going to sit there and say you believe in fifteenth-century nonsense."

"I don't think it's nonsense, and I don't think it's stuck in the fifteenth century, either. I think it goes back a whole lot farther, and that it'll keep going through several more millenniums."

"And you probably believe in ghosts, too, and reincarnation, and toads that turn into princes."

"Yep." He grinned, then took her hand and pulled her down again. "You shouldn't ask a question if the answer's going to piss you off." When she only huffed, he toyed with her fingers. "You know when I came to this part of Ireland, I had no intention of staying. Six months maybe, write the book, and pack up. That's the way I worked, and lived. Obviously Brianna's the main reason I changed that. But there's more. I recognized this place."

"Oh, Gray," she said again.

"I walked across the fields one morning, and I saw the standing stones. They fascinated me, and I felt a tug, a power that didn't surprise me in the least."

Her hand tensed in his. "You mean that."

"I do. I could walk down the road there, or drive to the cliffs, through the village, wander around in ruins, cemeteries. I felt connected—and I'd never felt that connection with anything or anyone before. I didn't have visions, but I knew I'd been here before and was meant to come back."

"And that doesn't give you the creeps."

"It scared the shit out of me," he said cheerfully. "Just about as much as falling in love with Brianna did. What's scaring you more, pal?"

"I don't know. I have these dreams."

"So you said before. Are you going to tell me about them this time?"

"I have to tell somebody," she murmured. "Whenever I start to talk about it with Murphy I get . . . panicked. Like something's got a hold of me. I'm not the hysterical type, Gray, or the fanciful type. But I can't get past this."

She began slowly, telling him of the first dream, the details of it, the emotions of it. The words came easily now, without the hot ball in her throat that swelled each time she tried to discuss it with Murphy.

Still, she knew there was more, some piece, some final link that part of her was blocking out.

"He has the broach," she finished. "Murphy has the broach I saw in my dreams. He found it in the dance when he was a boy, and he says he started having the same dreams."

Fascinated, and with one part of his brain coolly filing away the facts and images for a story to be spun, he whistled. "That's pretty heavy stuff."

"Tell me about it. I feel like I've got the weight of a hundred-pound ax at the back of my neck."

He narrowed his eyes. "I said heavy, not scary. Certainly not threatening."

"Well, I am threatened. I don't like it, this having my unconscious intruded upon. And this nasty feeling that I'm supposed to fix whatever went wrong doesn't agree with me. Gray, when I see a magician vanish in a puff of smoke, I know it's a trick. I may enjoy it, be entertained if it's well done, but I'm fully aware there's a trapdoor and misdirection."

"Rock and a hard place again, pal. Logic against illogic. Reason against emotion. Have you considered relaxing and just seeing which side wins?"

"I've considered finding an analyst," she muttered. "And I'm telling myself the dreams will stop once I'm back in New York, back in the routine I'm used to."

"And you're afraid they won't."

"Yes, I'm afraid they won't. And I'm very afraid that Murphy won't understand why I have to go."

"Do you understand?" Gray asked quietly.

"Logically, yes. And still logically, I can understand my connection here. With Murphy, with all of you. I know I'll have to come back, that I'll never break the ties, or want to. And that the life I'm going back to will never be quite the same as the one I had before. But I can't fix dreams, Gray, and I can't stay and let my life drift. Not even for Murphy."

"Want advice?"

She lifted her hands, then let them fall. "Hell, I'll take what I can get."

"Think through what you're going back to and what you're leaving behind. Make a list if it helps the logical side. And after you've weighed them, one against the other, see which side of the scale dips."

"Pretty standard advice," she mused. "But not bad. Thanks."

"Wait till you get my bill."

She laughed, tilted her head onto his shoulder. "I really love you."

Flustered, and pleased, he pressed a kiss to her temple. "Same goes."

TWENTY-TWO

Shannon couldn't have been more delighted with Worldwide Gallery, Clare. Its manor-house style was both striking and dignified. The gardens, Murphy told her as she stepped from the truck to admire them, were Brianna's design.

"She didn't plant them," he went on, "as there wasn't enough time for her to come out every day with her spade and her pots. But she drew up the placement of every last dahlia and rosebush."

"Another family affair."

"It is, yes. Rogan and Maggie worked with the architect on the design of the house, scrutinized every paint chip. There were some lively arguments there," he remembered, taking Shannon's hand as Gray pulled up nearby. "It's a labor of love for all of them."

Shannon scanned the cars already parked in the lot. "It appears it's working very well."

"The president of Ireland's been here." There was wonder in his voice as well as pride. "Twice, and bought one of Maggie's pieces, others as well. It's no small thing to take a dream and make it into a reality that stands strong."

"No." She understood what was beneath his words and was grateful when Brianna and the rest joined them.

"You'll keep your hands in your pockets, Liam Sweeney," Maggie warned. "Or I'll handcuff you." Not trusting the threat, she hoisted him up. "What do you think then, Shannon?"

"I think it's beautiful, and every bit as impressive as Dublin and New York."

"Here's a home," she said simply and carried Liam toward the entrance.

Shannon smelled the flowers, the roses, the drifting fragrance of peonies, the scent of the trimmed lawn that was thick as velvet. When she stepped inside, she saw that it was, indeed, a home, furnished with care, and with the welcoming grace of elegance.

There were paintings on the wall of the main hall, clever pencil portraits that celebrated the faces and moods of the people of Ireland. In the front parlor were dreamy watercolors that suited the curved settee and quiet tones of the room. There were sculptures, Maggie's incomparable glass, as well as a bust of a young woman carved in alabaster, and canny little elves depicted in glossy wood. A hand-hooked rug in bleeding blues graced the floor, and a thick throw was draped over the back of the sofa.

There were flowers, fresh that morning, in vases of brilliant glass and fired pottery.

It gave her a jolt to see her own painting on the wall. Stunned, she walked closer, staring at her watercolor of Brianna.

"I'm so proud to have it here," Brianna said from beside her. "Maggie told me that Rogan had displayed three, but she didn't tell me this was one of them."

"Three?" There was something spreading in Shannon's chest, making her heart beat too fast for comfort.

Maggie stepped up, struggling with a wriggling Liam. "At first he was only going to use the one, *The Dance,* but he decided to put up the other two for a few days only. He wants to tease the clientele a bit. Give them a glimpse or two of what's to come in your fall showing, and start a buzz. He's had an offer on *The Dance* already."

"An offer?" Now whatever was stretching inside of Shannon was creeping into her throat. "Someone wants to buy it?"

"I think he said two thousand pounds. Or maybe it was three." She shrugged as Shannon stared at her. "Of course he wants twice that."

"Twice—" She choked, then certain she'd gotten the joke, shook her head. "You almost had me."

"He's greedy, is Rogan," Maggie said with a smile. "I'm forever telling him he asks outrageous prices, and he delights in forever proving me wrong by getting them. If he wants six thousand pounds for it, he'll get it, I promise you."

The logical part of Shannon's brain calculated the exchange into American dollars, and banked it. The artist in her was both flustered and grieving.

"All right, boy-o," Maggie said to the squirming Liam. "It's your da's turn." She marched out with him, leaving Shannon staring at the painting.

"When I sold the yearling," Murphy began in a quiet voice, "it broke my heart. He was mine, you see." He smiled a little when Shannon turned to him. "I'd been there at the foaling and watched through until the first nursing. I trained him to the lead and worried when he bruised his knee. But I had to sell him, and knew that in my head. You can't be in the horse business without doing business. Still, it broke my heart."

"I've never sold anything I've painted. I've given it away as gifts, but that's not the same." She took a long breath. "I didn't know I could feel this way. Excited, overwhelmed, and incredibly sad."

"It may help to know that Gray's already told Rogan he'll skin him if Rogan sells your *Brianna* to anyone but him."

"I'd have given it to them."

Murphy leaned close to whisper in her ear. "Say it soft, for Rogan's got good hearing."

That made her laugh, and she let him take her hand and lead her into the next room.

It took more than an hour before she could be persuaded from the first floor to the second. There was too much to see, and admire, and want. The first thing she spotted in the upstairs sitting room was a long sinuous flow of glass that hinted at the shape of a dragon. She could see the spread of wings, the iridescent sheen of them, the curve of the neck, the fierce turn of head and sweep of tail.

"I have to have it." Possessively she ran her fingers along the serpentine body. It was Maggie's work, of course. Shannon didn't have to see the carved M.M. under the base of the tail to know it.

"You'll let me buy it for you."

"No." She was firm as she turned to Murphy. "I've wanted a piece of hers for more than a year and know exactly what Rogan gets for her. I can afford it now. Barely. I mean it, Murphy."

"You took the earrings." And she was wearing them still, he saw with pleasure.

"I know, and it's sweet of you to offer. But this is important to me, to buy for myself something of my sister's."

The stubborn look that had come into his eyes faded. "Ah, so it's that way. I'm glad."

"So am I. Very glad." Her lips curved when his came to them.

"I beg your pardon," Rogan said from the doorway. "I'm interrupting."

"No." She went to him, hands extended. "I can't begin to tell you how I feel seeing my work here. It's something I never thought of. Something my mother always wanted. Thank you." She kept his hands in hers as she kissed him. "Thank you for making something she dreamed of come true."

"It's more than a pleasure. And I'm confident it will continue to be, for both of us, for years to come." He saw her hesitation and countered it.

"Brianna's gone to the kitchen. You can't keep her out of one. Will you come have some tea?"

"I've just started on this floor, and actually, I'd like a minute of your time."

"Rogan, there you are." With a smug smile on her face, Maggie strode into the room. "I've dumped Liam on Gray. I told him it would be good practice for when Kayla gains her feet and never stops running on them." She hooked an arm through Rogan's. "Brianna has the tea ready, and bless her, she brought a tin of her sugar biscuits from home."

"I'll be right down." He gave her hand an absent pat. "Should we go into my office, Shannon?"

"No, it's not necessary. I want to discuss the dragon."

He didn't need for her to gesture toward the sculpture. "Maggie's *Breath of Fire,*" he said with a nod. "Exceptional."

"Of course it is," Maggie retorted. "I worked my ass off on it. Started three different times before it came right."

"I want it." Shannon was an excellent negotiator, had bargained with the best of them in the diamond district, in the little galleries of Soho. But in this case her skills had no chance against sheer desire. "I'd like to arrange to buy it and have you ship it back to New York for me."

No one but Maggie noticed that Murphy went suddenly and absolutely still.

"I see." Considering, Rogan kept his eyes on Shannon's face. "It's one of her more unique works."

"No argument. I'll write you a check."

Maggie looked away from Murphy and squared her shoulders for battle. "Rogan, I'll not have you—"

It amused Shannon to see Maggie seethe into silence when Rogan raised a hand. "Artists tend to have an emotional attachment to their work," he said mildly while his wife glared at him. "Which is why they need a partner, someone with a head for business."

"Fathead," Maggie muttered. "Bloodsucker. Damn contracts. He makes me sign them still as if I hadn't borne him a child and didn't have another in the womb."

He only spared her a brief glance. "Finished?" he asked, then continued before she could swear at him. "As Maggie's partner, I'll speak for her and tell you that we'd like you to have it, as a gift."

Even as Shannon started to protest, Maggie was sputtering in shock. "Rogan Sweeney, never in my life did I expect to hear such a thing come out of your mouth." After a burst of delighted laughter, she grabbed his face in both her hands, then kissed him long and hard. "I love you." Still beaming, she turned back to Shannon. "Don't you dare argue," she ordered. "This is a moment of great pride and astonishment for me in the man I married. So shake hands on the deal before he comes back to his normal avaricious senses."

Trapped by kindness, Shannon did what she was told. "It's very generous. Thank you. I guess I'll have that tea now, and gloat, before I finish the tour."

"I'll take you down. Maggie, Murphy?"

"We'll be right along." Maggie sent him a quick, silent signal, then waited until their footsteps faded away. She thought it best to say nothing for the moment and simply wrapped her arms around Murphy.

"She didn't realize what she was saying," Maggie began, "about having it shipped to New York."

That was the worst of it, he thought, closing his eyes and absorbing the dull, dragging ache. "Because it's automatic to her. The leaving."

"You want her to stay. You have to fight."

His hands fisted on her back. He could fight with those if the foe was flesh and blood. But it was intangible, as elusive as ghosts. A place, a mindset, a life he couldn't grasp even with his brain.

"I haven't finished." He said it quietly, with a fire underneath that gave Maggie hope. "And neither, by Jesus, has she."

He didn't ask if she'd come back to the farm with him, but simply drove there. When they got out of the truck, he didn't lead her into the house, but around it.

"Do you have to do something with the animals?" She glanced down at his feet. He wasn't wearing his boots, but the shoes she knew he kept for church and town.

"Later."

He was distracted. She'd sensed that all along the drive back from Ennistymon. It worried her that he was still brooding about what they said to each other at Loop Head. There was a stubborn streak under all those quiet waters, just as there was a flaming wave of passion always stirring under the surface. Already the panic was creeping up at the idea he might insist they talk about the dreams again.

"Murphy, I can tell you're upset. Can't we just put all this aside?"

"I've put it aside too long already." He could see his horses grazing. He had a client for the bay colt, the one that was standing so proud just now. And he knew he'd have to give him up.

But there was some things a man never gave up.

He could feel the nerves in her hand, the tension in it that held the rest of her rigid as he drew her into the circle of stones. Then he let her go and faced her without touching.

"It had to be here. You know that."

Though there was a trembling around her heart, she kept her eyes level. "I don't know what you mean."

He didn't have a ring. He knew what he wanted for her—the claddaugh with its heart and hands and crown. But for now, he had only himself.

"I love you, Shannon, as much as a man can love. I tell you that here, on holy ground while the sun beams between the stones."

Now her heart thudded, as much with love as with nerves. She could see what was in his eyes and shook her head, already knowing nothing would stop him.

"I'm asking you to marry me. To let me share your life, to have you share mine. And I ask you that here, on holy ground, while the sun beams between the stones."

Emotion welled up until she thought she could drown in it. "Don't ask me, Murphy."

"I have asked you. But you haven't answered."

"I can't. I can't do what you're asking."

His eyes flashed, temper and pain like twin suns inside him. "You can do anything you choose to do. Say you won't, and be honest."

"All right, I won't. And I have been honest, right from the start."

"No more to me than to yourself," he shot back. He was bleeding from a hundred wounds and could do nothing to stop it.

"I have." She could only meet temper with temper, and hurt with hurt. "I told you all along there was no courtship, no future, and never pretended otherwise. I slept with you," she said, her voice rising in panic, "because I wanted you, but that doesn't mean I'll change everything for you."

"You said you loved me."

"I do love you." She said it in fury. "I've never loved anyone the way I love you. But it isn't enough."

"For me it's more than enough."

"Well, not for me. I'm not you, Murphy. I'm not Brianna, I'm not Maggie." She whirled away, fighting the urge to pound her fists on the stones until they bled. "Whatever was taken away from me when my mother told me just who I am, I'm getting it back. I'm taking it back. I have a life."

Eyes dark and churning, she spun back to him. "Do you think I don't know what you want? I saw your face when you walked in this morning and I was cooking breakfast. That's what you want, Murphy, a woman who'll tend your house, welcome you in bed, have your children, and be content year after year with gardens and a view of the valley and turf fires."

She cut to the core of what he was. "And such things are beneath the likes of you."

"They're not for me," she countered, refusing to let the bitter words hurt her. "I have a career I've put on hold long enough. I have a country, a city, a home to get back to."

"You have a home here."

"I have a family here," she said carefully. "I have people who mean a great deal to me here. But that doesn't make it home."

"What stops it?" he demanded. "What stops you? You think I want you so you can cook my meals and wash my dirty shirts? I've been doing that fine on my own for years, and can do it still. I don't give a damn if you never lift a hand. I can hire help if it comes to that. I'm not a poor man. You have a career—who's asking you not to? You could paint from dawn till dusk and I'd only be proud of you."

"You're not understanding me."

"No, I'm not. I'm not understanding how you can love me, and I you, and still you'd walk away from it, and from me. What compromises do you need? You've only to ask."

"What compromise?" she shouted, because the strength of his need was squeezing her heart. "There's no compromise here, Murphy. We're not talking about making adjustments. It's not a matter of moving to a new house, or relocating in a different city. We're talking continents here, worlds. And the span between yours and mine. This isn't shuffling around schedules to share chores. It's giving up one way for something entirely different. Nothing changes for you, and everything changes for me. It's too much to ask."

"It's meant. You're blinding yourself to that."

"I don't give a damn about dreams and ghosts and restless spirits. This is me, flesh and blood," she said, desperate to convince both of them. "This is here and now. I'll give you everything I can, and I don't want to hurt you. But when you ask for more, it's the only choice I have."

"The only choice you'll see." He drew back. His eyes were cool now, with turmoil only a hint behind the icy blue. "You're telling me you'll go, knowing what we've found together, knowing what you feel for me, you'll go to New York and live happily without it."

"I'll live as I have to live, as I know how to live."

"You're holding your heart back from me, and it's cruel of you."

"I'm cruel? You think you're not hurting me by standing here and demanding I choose between my right hand and my left?" Abruptly chilled, to the bone, she wrapped her arms around herself. "Oh, it's so easy for you, damn you, Murphy. You have nothing to risk, and nothing to lose. Damn you," she said again, and her eyes were bright and bitter and seemed not quite her own. "You won't find peace any more than I will."

With the words searing on her tongue, she whirled and ran. The buzzing in her ears was temper, she was sure of it. The dizziness outraged emotions, and the pain in her heart a violent combination of both.

But she felt as though someone were running with her, inside her, as desperately unhappy as she, as bitterly hopeless.

She fled across the fields, not stopping when she reached Brianna's garden and the dozing dog leaped up to greet her. Running still when she stumbled into the kitchen and a startled Brianna called her name.

Running until she was closed in her room alone, and there was nowhere left to run.

Brianna waited an hour before she knocked softly on the door. She expected to find Shannon weeping, or sleeping off the tears. The single glimpse Brianna had had of her face as she'd streaked in and out of the kitchen spoke of misery and temper.

But when she opened the door, she didn't find Shannon weeping. She found her painting.

"The light's going." Shannon didn't bother to look up. The sweep of her brush was passionate, frenetic. "I'll need some lamps. I've got to have light."

"Of course. I'll bring you some." She stepped forward. It wasn't the face of grief she saw, but the face of someone half wild. "Shannon—"

"I can't talk now. I have to do this, I have to get it out of my system once and for all. I have to have more light, Brie."

"All right. I'll see to it." Quietly she closed the door behind her.

She painted all night. She'd never done that before. Never needed to or cared enough. But she'd needed this. It was full morning when she stopped, her hands cramped, her eyes burning, her mind dead. She hadn't touched the tray Brianna had brought up sometime during the night, nor was she interested in food now.

Without looking at the finished canvas, she dropped her brushes in a jar of turpentine, then turned and tumbled fully dressed into bed.

It was nearly evening again before she woke, stiff, groggy. There'd been no dreams this time, or none she remembered, only the deep, exhausted sleep that left her feeling hulled out and light-headed.

Mechanically she stripped off her clothes, showered, dressed again, never once looking at the painting she'd been driven to start and finish within one desperate night. Instead, she picked up the untouched tray and carried it downstairs.

She saw Brianna in the hall, bidding good-bye to guests. Shannon passed without speaking, going into the kitchen to set aside the tray and pour the coffee that had been made for her hours before.

"I'll make fresh," Brianna offered the moment she came in.

"No, this is fine." With something close to a smile, Shannon lifted the cup. "Really. I'm sorry, I wasted the food."

"Doesn't matter. Let me fix you something, Shannon. You haven't eaten since yesterday, and you look pale."

"I guess I could use something." Because she couldn't find the energy to do anything else, she went to the table and sat.

"Did you have a fight with Murphy?"

"Yes and no. I don't want to talk about that right now."

Brianna turned the heat on under her stew before going to the refrigerator. "I won't press you then. Did you finish your painting?"

"Yes." Shannon closed her eyes. But there was more to finish. "Brie, I'd like to see the letters now. I need to see them."

"After you've eaten," Brianna said, slicing bread for a sandwich. "I'll call Maggie, if you don't mind. We should do this together."

"Yes." Shannon pushed her cup aside. "We should do this together."

TWENTY-THREE

It was a difficult thing to look at the three slim letters, bound together by a faded red ribbon. And it was a sentimental man, Shannon mused, who tied a woman's letters, so few letters, in a ribbon that time would leach of color.

She didn't ask for the brandy, but was grateful when Brianna set a snifter by her elbow. They'd gone into the family parlor, the three of them, and Gray had taken the baby down to Maggie's.

So it was quiet.

In the lamplight, for the sun was setting toward dusk, Shannon gathered her courage and opened the first envelope.

Her mother's handwriting hadn't changed. She could see that right away. It had always been neat, feminine, and somehow economical.

My dearest Tommy.

Tommy, Shannon thought, staring at the single line. She'd called him Tommy when she'd written to him. And Tommy when she'd spoken of him to her daughter for the first, and the last time.

But Shannon thought of him as Tom. Tom Concannon, who'd passed to her green eyes and chestnut hair. Tom Concannon, who hadn't been a good farmer, but a good father. A man who had turned from his vows and his wife to love another woman—and had let her go. Who had wanted to be a poet, and to make his fortune, but had died doing neither.

She read on, and had no choice but to hear her mother's voice, and the love and kindness in it. No regrets. Shannon could find no regrets in the words that spoke of love and duty and the complexity of choices. Longing, yes, and memories, but without apology.

Always, she'd ended it. *Always, Amanda.*

With great care, Shannon refolded the first letter. "She told me he'd written back to her. I never found any letters with her things."

"She'd not have kept them," Brianna murmured. "In respect for her husband. Her loyalty and her love were with him."

"Yes." Shannon wanted to believe that. When a man had given all of himself for more than twenty-five years, he deserved nothing less.

She opened the second letter. It began in the same way, ended in the same way as the first. But between there were hints of something more than memories of a brief and forbidden love.

"She knew she was pregnant," Shannon managed. "When she wrote this, she knew. She'd have been frightened, even desperate. She'd had to be. But she writes so calmly, not letting him know, or even guess."

Maggie took the letter from her when she'd folded it again. "She might have needed time to think about what she would do, what she could do. Her family—from what Rogan's man found—they wouldn't have stood with her."

"No. When she told them, they insisted that she go away, then give me up and avoid the scandal. She wouldn't."

"She wanted you," Brianna said.

"Yes, she wanted me." Shannon opened the last letter. It broke her heart to read this. How could there have been joy? she wondered. No matter how much fear and anxiety she might read between the lines, there was unmistakable joy in them. More, there was a rejection of shame—of what was expected for an unwed woman pregnant with a married man's child.

It was obvious she'd made her choice when she'd written the letter. Her family had threatened her with disinheritance, but it hadn't mattered. She'd risked that, and everything she'd known, for a chance, and the child she carried.

"She told him she wasn't alone." Shannon's voice trembled. "She lied to him. She was alone. She'd had to go north and find work because her family had cut her off from themselves and from her own money. She had nothing."

"She had you," Brianna corrected. "That's what she wanted. That's what she chose."

"But she never asked him to come to her, or to let her come back to him. She never gave him a chance, just told him that she was pregnant and that she loved him and was going away."

"She did give him a chance." Maggie laid a hand on Shannon's shoulder. "A chance to be a father to the children he already had, and to know he would have another who'd be well loved and cared for. Perhaps she took the decision out of his hands, one that would have split him in two either way he turned. I think she did it for him, and for you, and maybe even for herself."

"She never stopped loving him." Again she folded the letter. "Even loving my father as much as she did, she never stopped. He was on her mind when she died, just as she was in his. They both lost what some people never find."

"We can't say what might have been." Tenderly Brianna tied the ribbon around the letters again. "Or change what was lost or was found. But don't you think, Shannon, we've done our best for them? Being here. Making a family out of their families. Sisters out of their daughters."

"I'd like to think that she knows I'm not angry. And that I'm coming to understand." There was peace in that, Shannon realized. In understanding. "If he'd been alive when I came here, I would have tried to care for him."

"Be sure of it." Maggie gave her shoulder a squeeze.

"I am," Shannon realized. "Right now it's about the only thing I'm sure of."

Fresh weariness dragged at her when she stood. Brianna stood with her and held out the letters. "These are yours. She'd want you to have them."

"Thank you." The paper felt so thin against her hand, so fragile. And so precious. "I'll keep them, but they're ours. I need to think."

"Take your brandy." Brianna picked up the glass and held it out. "And a hot bath. They'll ease mind, body, and spirit."

It was good advice, and she intended to take it. But when she walked into her room, Shannon set the snifter aside. The painting drew her now, so she turned on the lamps before crossing to it.

She studied the man on the white horse, the woman. The glint of copper and a sword. There was the swirl of a cape, the sweep of chestnut hair lifted by the wind.

But there was more, much more. Enough to have her sit carefully on the edge of the bed while her gaze stayed riveted on the canvas. She knew it had come out of her, every brushstroke. Yet it seemed impossible that she could have done such work.

She'd made a vision reality. She'd been meant to do so all along.

On a shuddering breath, she closed her eyes and waited until she was sure, until she could see inside herself as clearly as she had seen the people she'd brought to life with paint and brush.

It was all so easy, she realized. Not complicated at all. It was logic that had complicated it. Now, even with logic, it was simple.

She had calls to make, she thought, then picked up the phone to finish what she'd started when she'd first stepped onto Ireland.

She waited until morning to go to Murphy. The warrior had left the wise woman in the morning, so it was right the circle close at the same time of day.

It never crossed her mind that he wouldn't be where she looked for him. And he was standing in the stone circle, the broach in his hand and the mist shimmering like the breath of ghosts above the grass.

His head came up when he heard her. She saw the surprise, the longing, before he pulled the shutter down—a talent she hadn't known he possessed.

"I thought you might come here." His voice wasn't cool; that he couldn't manage. "I was going to leave this for you. But since you're here now, I'll give it to you, then ask if you'll listen to what I have to say."

She took the broach, was no longer stunned or anxious when it seemed to vibrate in her palm. "I brought you something." She held out the canvas, wrapped in heavy paper, but he made no move to take it. "You asked if I'd paint something for you. Something that reminded me of you, and I have."

"As a going-away gift?" He took the canvas, but strode two paces away to tilt it, unopened, against a stone. "It won't do, Shannon."

"You might look at it."

"They'll be time for that when I've said what's on my mind."

"You're angry, Murphy. I'd like to—"

"Damn right I'm angry. At both of us. Bloody fools. Just be quiet," he ordered, "and let me say this in my own way. You were right about some things, and I was wrong about some. But I wasn't wrong that we love each other, and are meant. I've thought on it most of the past two nights, and I see I've asked you for more than I've a right to. There's another way that I didn't consider, that I turned a blind eye to because it was easier than looking straight at it."

"I'm been thinking, too." She reached out, but he stepped back sharply.

"Will you wait a damn minute and let me finish? I'm going with you."

"What?"

"I'm going with you to New York. If you need more time for courting—or whatever the bloody hell you chose to call it, I'll give it. But you'll marry me in the end, and make no mistake. I won't compromise that."

"Compromise?" Staggered, she dragged a hand through her hair. "This is a compromise?"

"You can't stay, so I'll go."

"But the farm—"

"The devil take the fucking farm. Do you think it means more to me than you? I'm good with my hands. I can get work wherever."

"It's not a matter of a job."

"It's important to me that I not live off my wife." He shot the words at her, daring her to argue. "You can call me sexist and a fool or whatever you choose, but it doesn't change the matter. I don't care whether you've a mountain of money or none at all, or if you choose to spend it on a big house or fancy cars, miser it away or toss it off on one roll of dice. What's an issue to me is not that I support you, but that I support myself."

She closed her mouth for a minute and tried to calm. "I can hardly call you a fool for making a perfectly sane statement, but I can call you one for even thinking about giving up the farm."

"Selling it. I'm not an idiot. None of my family are interested in farming, so I'll speak with Mr. McNee, and Feeney and some of the others. It's good land." His gaze swept past her and for a moment held pain as it traveled over the hills. "It's good land," he repeated. "And they'd value it."

"Oh, that's fine." Her voice rose on fresh passion. "Toss away your heritage, your home. Why don't you offer to cut out your heart while you're at it?"

"I can't live without you," he said simply. "And I won't. It's dirt and stone."

"Don't ever let me hear you say that." She fired up, flashed over. "It's everything to you. Oh, you know how to make me feel small and selfish. I won't have it." She turned, fisting her hands as she strode from stone to stone. Then she leaned heavily against one as it struck, and struck hard that this was it. From the beginning it had been spiraling toward this.

She steadied herself and turned back so that she could see his face. Odd, she thought, that she was suddenly so calm, so sure.

"You'd give it up for me, the thing that makes you what you are." She shook her head before he could answer. "This is funny, really funny. I searched my soul last night, and the night before. Part of it I ripped out to do that painting. And when I finally took a good long look, I knew I wasn't going anywhere."

She saw the light come into his eyes before he carefully controlled it again. "You're saying you'd stay, do without what you want. Is that supposed to comfort me, knowing you're here but unhappy?"

"I'm giving up a lot. Really making a sacrifice." With a half laugh she combed her fingers through her hair. "I finally figured that out, too. I'm leaving New York. You can't smell the grass there, or see horses grazing. You can't watch the light strike over the fields in a way that makes your throat hurt. I'm trading the sound of traffic for the sound of mockingbirds and larks. It's going to be real tough to live with that."

She stuffed her hands in her pockets and began to pace in a way that warned him not to touch her. "My friends—acquaintances mostly, will think of me with amusement now and again and shake their heads. Perhaps some of them will come to visit and see just what I've given up the fast lane for. I'm trading that for family, for people I've felt closer to than almost anyone I've known. That's a bad deal all right."

She stopped, looking out between the stones as the warming sun burned off the mist. "Then there's my career, that all-important ladder to climb. Five years more, and I guarantee I would have had that metaphorical key to the executive washroom. No question, Shannon Bodine's got the drive, she's got the talent, she's got the ambition, and she doesn't blink at sixty-hour weeks. I've put in plenty of those weeks, Murphy, and it occurs to me that not one of them ever gave me the joy or the simple satisfaction I've felt since the first time I picked up a paintbrush here in Ireland. So I guess it's going to be real tough for me to turn in my Armani jacket for a smock."

She turned back. "That leaves one last thing by my calculation. I'm back in New York, boosting myself up the next rung on that ladder, and I'm alone while the man who loves me is three thousand miles away." She lifted her hands. "There doesn't seem to be any contest. I'm giving up nothing, because there's nothing there. That's the bright flash I had last night. There's nothing there I want, or need, or love. It's all right here, right here with you.

"But you had to jump right in, didn't you?" she tossed out when he would have stepped forward. "Now I'll never be able to throw in your face during an argument what I've done for you. Because I'm not doing anything, and I know it. And you would have done everything."

He wasn't sure he could speak, and when he did it was only one unsteady sentence. "You're staying with me."

She circled over to where he'd balanced the painting. With impatient rips, she tore the protective paper aside. "Look at this and tell me what you see."

A man and a woman on a white horse, their faces as familiar to him as his own, in a land washed with light. The stone circle in the background with two of the cross stones that had fallen still in place. The copper brooch clipped to a swirling cape.

But what he saw most was that while the man held the horse from bolting with one hand, his other held the woman close. And she him.

"They're together."

"I didn't mean to paint them that way. He was supposed to be riding away, as he did, leaving her when she begged him to stay. When she pleaded and cast aside every iota of pride and wept."

Shannon took a careful breath and finished telling him what she had seen in her mind, and her heart, when she'd painted.

"He left her because he was a soldier, and his life was battles. I imagine wars demand to be tended, just as the land does. He wanted to marry her, but he wouldn't stay, and she needed him to stay more than she needed marriage, though she knew she was carrying his child."

Murphy's gaze shot up, arrested on her face. "His child."

"She never told him. It may have made the difference, but she never told him. She wanted him to stay for her, to put his sword aside because he loved her more than what he was. When he wouldn't, they fought, here. Right here. And said things to each other to wound because each was wounded. He gave her back the broach in anger, not in memory as the legend suggests, and rode away from her. Always believing she'd wait. She cursed him as he left her, and shouted out that he'd never have peace, any more than she, he'd never have it until he loved her enough to give up everything else."

Shannon pressed the broach into his palm, kept hers over it. "She saw, in the fire when he fell in battle, when he bled and died. And she delivered his child alone. She's been waiting, endlessly, for him to love her enough."

"I've wondered for a long time, tried to see it, and never could."

"Knowing the answers spoils the magic." She set the canvas aside so it would no longer be between them. "They're together now. I want to stay, Murphy. Not her choice. Not my mother's. Mine. I want to make a life here with you. I swear I love you enough."

He took her hand, brought it fiercely to his lips. "Will you let me court you, Shannon?"

"No." It came out on a broken laugh. "But I'll let you marry me, Murphy."

"I can settle for that." He pulled her against him, buried his face in her hair. "You're the one, Shannon. You're the only one for me."

"I know." Closing her eyes, she rested her head on his heart. It beat there, strong and steady, as he was. Love, she thought, closed every circle. "Let's go home, Murphy," she murmured. "I'll cook you breakfast."